Mia & Korum

The Complete Krinar Chronicles Trilogy

Anna Zaires

♠ Mozaika Publications ♠

Published by Mozaika Publications, an imprint of Mozaika LLC.
www.mozaikallc.com

Cover by Najla Qamber Designs.

e-ISBN: 978-1-63142-005-4
ISBN: 978-1-63142-004-7

Close Liaisons

The Krinar Chronicles: Volume 1

PROLOGUE

Five Years Earlier

"Mr. President, they're all waiting for you."

The President of the United States of America looked up wearily and shut the folder lying on his desk. He had slept poorly for the past week, his mind occupied by the deteriorating situation in the Middle East and the continued weakness in the economy. While no president had it easy, it seemed like his term had been marked by one impossible task after another, and the daily stress was beginning to affect his health. He made a mental note to get himself checked out by the doctor later this week. The country didn't need a sick and exhausted president on top of all of its other woes.

Getting up, the President exited the Oval Office and headed toward the Situation Room. He had been briefed earlier that NASA had detected something unusual. He'd hoped that it might be nothing more than a stray satellite, but that didn't appear to be the case, given the urgency with which the National Security Advisor requested his presence.

Entering the room, he greeted his advisors and sat down, waiting to hear what necessitated this meeting.

The Secretary of Defense spoke first. "Mr. President, we have discovered something in Earth's orbit that doesn't belong there. We don't know what it is, but we have reason to believe that it may be a threat." He motioned toward the images displayed on one of the six flat screens lining the walls of the room. "As you can see, the object is large, bigger than any of our satellites, but it seems to have come out of nowhere. We didn't see anything launching from any point on the globe, and we haven't detected anything approaching Earth. It's as though the object simply appeared here a few hours ago."

The screen showed several pictures of a dark blur set against a dark, starry background.

"What does NASA think it could be?" the President asked calmly, trying to analyze the possibilities. If the Chinese had come up with some new satellite technology, they would have already known about it, and the Russian space program was no longer what it used to be. The presence of the object simply didn't make any sense.

"They don't know," the National Security Advisor said. "It doesn't look like anything they've ever seen before."

"NASA couldn't even venture an educated guess?"

"They know it's not any kind of an astronomical body."

So it had to be man-made. Puzzled, the President stared at the images, refusing to even contemplate the outlandish idea that had just occurred to him. Turning to the Advisor, he asked, "Have we reached out to the Chinese? Do they know anything about this?"

The Advisor opened his mouth, about to reply, when there was a sudden flash of bright light. Momentarily blinded, the President blinked to clear his vision—and froze in shock.

In front of the screen that the President had just been looking at, there was now a man. Tall and muscular, he had black hair and dark eyes, and his olive skin contrasted with the white color of his outfit. He stood there calmly, relaxed, as though he had not just invaded the inner sanctum of the United States government.

The Secret Service agents reacted first, shouting and firing at the intruder in panic. Before the President could think, he found himself pushed against the wall, with two agents forming a human shield in front of him.

"There's no need for that," the intruder said, his voice deep and sonorous. "I don't intend to hurt your president—and if I did, there's nothing you can do about it." He spoke in perfect American English, without even a hint of an accent. Despite the gunfire that had just been directed at him, he appeared to be completely uninjured, and the President could now see the bullets lying harmlessly on the floor in front of the man.

Only years of handling one major crisis after another enabled the President to do what he did next. "Who are you?" he asked in a steady voice, ignoring the effects of terror and adrenaline rushing through his veins.

The intruder smiled. "My name is Arus. We've decided that it's time for our species to meet."

CHAPTER ONE

The air was crisp and clear as Mia walked briskly down a winding path in Central Park. Signs of spring were everywhere, from tiny buds on still-bare trees to the proliferation of nannies out to enjoy the first warm day with their rambunctious charges.

It was strange how much everything had changed in the last few years, and yet how much remained the same. If anyone had asked Mia ten years ago how she thought life might be after an alien invasion, this would have been nowhere near her imaginings. *Independence Day, The War of the Worlds*—none of these were even close to the reality of encountering a more advanced civilization. There had been no fight, no resistance of any kind on government level—because *they* had not allowed it. In hindsight, it was clear how silly those movies had been. Nuclear weapons, satellites, fighter jets—these were little more than rocks and sticks to an ancient civilization that could cross the universe faster than the speed of light.

Spotting an empty bench near the lake, Mia gratefully headed for it, her shoulders feeling the strain of the backpack filled with her chunky twelve-year-old laptop and old-fashioned paper books. At twenty-one, she sometimes felt old, out of step with the fast-paced new world of razor-slim tablets and cell phones embedded in wristwatches. The pace of technological progress had not slowed since K-Day; if anything, many of the new gadgets had been influenced by what the Krinar had. Not that the Ks had shared any of their precious technology; as far as they were concerned, their little experiment had to continue uninterrupted.

Unzipping her bag, Mia took out her old Mac. The thing was heavy and slow, but it worked—and as a starving college student, Mia could not afford anything better. Logging on, she opened a blank Word document and prepared to start the torturous process of writing her Sociology paper.

Ten minutes and exactly zero words later, she stopped. Who was she kidding? If she really wanted to write the damn thing, she would've never come to the park. As tempting as it was to pretend that she could enjoy the fresh air and be productive at the same time, those two had never been compatible in her experience. A musty old library was a much better setting for anything requiring that kind of brainpower exertion.

Mentally kicking herself for her own laziness, Mia let out a sigh and started looking around instead. People-watching in New York never failed to amuse her.

The tableau was a familiar one, with the requisite homeless person occupying a nearby bench—thank God it wasn't the closest one to her, since he looked like he might smell very ripe—and two nannies chatting with each other in Spanish as they pushed their Bugaboos at a leisurely pace. A girl jogged on a path a little further ahead, her bright pink Reeboks contrasting nicely with her blue leggings. Mia's gaze followed the jogger as she rounded the corner, envying her athleticism. Her own hectic schedule allowed her little time to exercise, and she doubted she could keep up with the girl for even a mile at this point.

To the right, she could see the Bow Bridge over the lake. A man was leaning on the railing, looking out over the water. His face was turned away from Mia, so she could only see part of his profile. Nevertheless, something about him caught her attention.

She wasn't sure what it was. He was definitely tall and seemed well-built under the expensive-looking trench coat he was wearing, but that was only part of the story. Tall, good-looking men were common in model-infested New York City. No, it was something else. Perhaps it was the way he stood—very still, with no extra movements. His hair was dark and glossy under the bright afternoon sun, just long enough in the front to move slightly in the warm spring breeze.

He also stood alone.

That's it, Mia realized. The normally popular and picturesque bridge was completely deserted, except for the man who was standing on it. Everyone appeared to be giving it a wide berth for some unknown reason. In fact, with the exception of herself and her potentially aromatic homeless neighbor, the entire row of benches in the highly desirable waterfront location was empty.

As though sensing her gaze on him, the object of her attention slowly turned his head and looked directly at Mia. Before her conscious brain could even make the connection, she felt her blood turn to ice, leaving her paralyzed in place and helpless to do anything but stare at the predator who now seemed to be examining her with interest.

* * *

Breathe, Mia, breathe. Somewhere in the back of her mind, a small rational voice kept repeating those words. That same oddly objective part of her noted his symmetrical face structure, with golden skin stretched tightly over high cheekbones and a firm jaw. Pictures and videos of Ks that she'd seen had hardly done them justice. Standing no more than thirty feet away, the creature was simply stunning.

As she continued staring at him, still frozen in place, he straightened and began walking toward her. Or rather stalking toward her, she thought stupidly, as his every movement reminded her of a jungle cat sinuously approaching a gazelle. All the while, his eyes never left hers. As he approached, she could make out individual yellow flecks in his light golden eyes and the thick long lashes surrounding them.

She watched in horrified disbelief as he sat down on her bench, less than two feet away from her, and smiled, showing white even teeth. No fangs, she noted with some functioning part of her brain. Not even a hint of them. That used to be another myth about them, like their supposed abhorrence of the sun.

"What's your name?" The creature practically purred the question at her. His voice was low and smooth, completely unaccented. His nostrils flared slightly, as though inhaling her scent.

"Um . . ." Mia swallowed nervously. "M-Mia."

"Mia," he repeated slowly, seemingly savoring her name. "Mia what?"

"Mia Stalis." Oh crap, why did he want to know her name? Why was he here, talking to her? In general, what was he doing in Central Park, so far away from any of the K Centers? *Breathe, Mia, breathe.*

"Relax, Mia Stalis." His smile got wider, exposing a dimple in his left cheek. A dimple? Ks had dimples? "Have you never encountered one of us before?"

"No, I haven't." Mia exhaled sharply, realizing that she was holding her breath. She was proud that her voice didn't sound as shaky as she felt. Should she ask? Did she want to know?

She gathered her courage. "What, um—" Another swallow. "What do you want from me?"

"For now, conversation." He looked like he was about to laugh at her, those gold eyes crinkling slightly at the corners.

Strangely, that pissed her off enough to take the edge off her fear. If there was anything Mia hated, it was being laughed at. With her short, skinny stature and a general lack of social skills that came from an awkward teenage phase involving every girl's nightmare of braces, frizzy hair, and glasses, Mia had more than enough experience being the butt of someone's joke.

She lifted her chin belligerently. "Okay, then, what is *your* name?"

"It's Korum."

"Just Korum?"

"We don't really have last names, not the way you do. My full name is much longer, but you wouldn't be able to pronounce it if I told you."

Okay, that was interesting. She now remembered reading something like that in *The New York Times*. So far, so good. Her legs had nearly stopped shaking, and her breathing was returning to normal. Maybe, just maybe, she would get out of this alive. This conversation business seemed safe enough, although the way he kept staring at her with those unblinking yellowish eyes was unnerving. She decided to keep him talking.

"What are you doing here, Korum?"

"I just told you, making conversation with you, Mia." His voice again held a hint of laughter.

Frustrated, Mia blew out her breath. "I meant, what are you doing here in Central Park? In New York City in general?"

He smiled again, cocking his head slightly to the side. "Maybe I'm hoping to meet a pretty curly-haired girl."

Okay, enough was enough. He was clearly toying with her. Now that she could think a little again, she realized that they were in the middle of Central Park, in full view of about a gazillion spectators. She surreptitiously glanced around to confirm that. Yep, sure enough, although people were obviously steering clear of her bench and its otherworldly occupant, there were a number of brave souls staring their way from further up the path. A couple were even cautiously filming them with their wristwatch cameras. If the K tried anything with her, it would be on YouTube in the blink of an eye, and he had to know it. Of course, he may or may not care about that.

Still, going on the assumption that since she'd never come across any videos of K assaults on college students in the middle of Central Park, she was relatively safe, Mia cautiously reached for her laptop and lifted it to stuff it back into her backpack.

"Let me help you with that, Mia—"

And before she could blink, she felt him take her heavy laptop from her suddenly boneless fingers, gently brushing against her knuckles in the process. A sensation similar to a mild electric shock shot through Mia at his touch, leaving her nerve endings tingling in its wake.

Reaching for her backpack, he carefully put away the laptop in a smooth, sinuous motion. "There you go, all better now."

Oh God, he had touched her. Maybe her theory about the safety of public locations was bogus. She felt her breathing speeding up again, and her heart rate was probably well into the anaerobic zone at this point.

"I have to go now . . . Bye!"

How she managed to squeeze out those words without hyperventilating, she would never know. Grabbing the strap of the backpack he'd just put down, she jumped to her feet, noting somewhere in the back of her mind that her earlier paralysis seemed to be gone.

"Bye, Mia. I will see you later." His softly mocking voice carried in the clear spring air as she took off, nearly running in her haste to get away.

CHAPTER TWO

"Holy shit! Get out of here! Seriously? Tell me what happened, and don't leave out any details!" Her roommate was nearly jumping up and down in excitement.

"I just told you . . . I met a K in the park." Mia rubbed her temples, feeling the band of tension around her head left over from her earlier adrenaline overdose. "He sat down on the bench next to me and talked to me for a couple of minutes. Then I told him that I had to go and left."

"Just like that? What did he want?"

"I don't know. I asked him that, but he just said he wanted to talk."

"Yeah, right, and pigs can fly." Jessie was as dismissive of that possibility as Mia herself had been. "No, seriously, he didn't try to drink your blood or anything?"

"No, he didn't do anything." Except briefly touch her hand. "He just asked me my name and told me his."

Jessie's eyes now resembled big brown saucers. "He told you his name? What is it?"

"Korum."

"Of course, Korum the K, makes perfect sense." Jessie's sense of humor often kicked in at the strangest times. They both snickered at the ridiculousness of that statement.

"Did you know immediately that he was a K? How did he look?" Recovering, Jessie continued with her questions.

"I did." Mia thought back to that first moment she saw him. How did she know? Was it his eyes? Or something instinctual in her that knew a predator when she saw one? "I think it maybe had to do with the way he moved. It's difficult to describe. It's definitely inhuman. He looked a lot like the Ks you'd see on TV—he was tall, good-looking in that particular way that they have, and had strange-looking eyes—they looked almost yellow."

"Wow, I can't believe it." Jessie was pacing the room in circles. "How did he talk to you? What did he sound like?"

Mia let out a sigh. "Next time I get ambushed in the park by an extraterrestrial, I will be sure to have a recording device handy."

"Oh come on, like you wouldn't be curious if you were in my shoes."

True, Jessie did have a point. Sighing again, Mia relayed the whole encounter to her roommate in full detail, leaving out only that brief moment when his hand brushed against hers. For some odd reason, that touch—and her reaction to it—seemed private.

"So you told him 'bye,' and he said he will see you later? Oh my God, do you know what that means?" Far from satisfying Jessie, the detailed story seemed to send her into excitement overdrive. She was now almost bouncing off the walls.

"No, what?" Mia felt weary and drained. It reminded her of the feeling after an interview or an exam, when all she wanted was to give her poor overworked brain a chance to unwind. Maybe she shouldn't have told Jessie about the encounter until tomorrow, when she'd had a chance to relax a bit.

"He wants to see you again!"

"What? Why?" Mia's tiredness suddenly vanished as adrenaline surged through her again. "It's just a figure of speech! I'm sure he meant nothing by that—English is not even his first language! Why would he want to see me again?"

"Well, you did say he thought you were pretty—"

"No, I said that *he* said he was there to meet 'a pretty curly-haired girl.' He was just mocking me. I'm sure that was just his way of toying with me . . . He was probably just bored standing there, so he decided to come by and talk to me. Why would a K be interested in me?" Mia cast a disparaging glance in the mirror at her two-year-old Uggs, worn jeans, and a too-big sweater she got on sale at Century 21.

"Mia, I told you, you're constantly underestimating your appeal." Jessie sounded earnest, the way she always did when trying to boost Mia's self-confidence. "You look very cute, with that big mass of curly hair. Plus, you have really pretty eyes—very unusual, to have blue eyes with hair as dark as yours—"

"Oh, please, Jessie." Mia rolled said eyes. "I'm sure *cute* doesn't cut it if you're a gorgeous K. Besides, you're my friend—you have to say nice stuff to me."

As far as Mia was concerned, Jessie was the pretty one in the room. With her curvy athletic build, long black hair, and smooth golden skin, Jessie was every guy's fantasy—particularly if they happened to like Asian girls. A former high school cheerleader, her roommate of the last three years also had the outgoing personality to match her looks. How the two of them had become such good friends will always remain a mystery to Mia, as her own social skills at the age of eighteen had been all but nonexistent.

Thinking back to that time, Mia remembered how lost and overwhelmed she'd felt arriving in the big city after spending all her life in a small town in Florida. New York University was the best school she'd been accepted to, and her financial aid package ended up being generous, making her parents very happy. However, Mia herself had been far from excited about going to a big-city school with no real campus. Getting caught up in the competitive college application process, she'd applied to most of the top fifteen schools, only to face numerous rejections and inadequate financial aid offers. NYU had seemed like the best alternative all around. Local Florida schools had not even been considered by Mia's parents at the time, as the rumor had been that the Ks might set up a Center in Florida and her parents wanted her far away from there if that happened. It hadn't happened—Arizona and New Mexico ended up being the preferred K locales in the United States. However, by then it was too late. Mia had started her second semester at NYU, met Jessie, and slowly began to fall in love with New York City and everything it had to offer.

It was funny how everything turned out. Only five years ago, most people thought they were the only intelligent beings in the universe. Sure, there had always been crackpots claiming UFO sightings, and there had even been things like SETI—serious, government-funded efforts to explore the possibility of extraterrestrial life. But people had no way of knowing whether any kind of life—even single-celled organisms—actually existed on other planets. As a result, most had believed that humans were special and unique, that homo sapiens were the pinnacle of evolutionary development. Now it all seemed so silly, like when people in the Middle Ages thought that the Earth was flat and that the moon and the stars revolved around it. When the Krinar arrived early in the second decade of the twenty-first century, they upended everything that scientists thought they knew about life and its origins.

"I'm telling you, Mia, I think he must've liked you!" Jessie's insistent voice interrupted her musings.

Sighing, Mia turned her attention back to her roommate. "I highly doubt it. Besides, what would he want from me even if he did? We're two different species. The thought of him liking me is just plain scary . . . What would he want from me, my blood?"

"Well, we don't know that for a fact. That's just a rumor. Officially, it's never been announced that the Ks drink blood." Jessie sounded hopeful for some weird reason. Maybe Mia's social life was so bad in her roommate's eyes that she was eager to have Mia date someone, anyone— same species optional.

"It's a rumor that many people believe. I'm sure there's a reason for that. They're vampires, Jessie. Perhaps not the Draculas of legend, but everyone knows they're predators. That's why they've set up their Centers in isolated areas . . . so they can do whatever they want there with none the wiser."

"All right, all right." Her excitement waning, Jessie sat down on her bed. "You're right, it would be very scary if he actually did intend to see you again. It's just fun to pretend sometimes that they're simply gorgeous humans from outer space, and not a completely different mystery species."

"I know. He was unbelievably good-looking." The two girls exchanged understanding glances. "If only he were human . . ."

"You're too picky, Mia. I've always told you that." Shaking her head in mock reproach, Jessie used her most serious tone of voice. Mia looked at her in disbelief, and they both burst out laughing.

* * *

That night, Mia slept restlessly, her mind replaying the encounter over and over. As soon as she would drift off to sleep, she would see those mocking amber eyes and feel that electrifying touch on her skin. To her embarrassment, her unconscious mind took things even further, and Mia dreamed of him touching her hand. In her dream, his touch would send shivers through her entire body, warming her from within—then he would slide his hand up her arm, cupping her shoulder, and bring her toward him, mesmerizing her with his gaze as he leaned in for the kiss. Her heart racing, Mia would close her eyes and lean toward him, feeling his soft lips touch hers, sending waves of warm sensations throughout her body.

Waking up, Mia felt her heart pounding in her chest and heat pooling slowly between her legs. It was 5 a.m. and she'd barely slept for the last five hours. Dammit, why was a brief encounter with an alien having such an effect on her? Maybe Jessie was right, and she needed to get out more, meet some more guys. Over the past three years, under Jessie's tutelage, Mia had shed a lot of her former shyness and awkwardness. For her high school graduation, her parents got her laser eye surgery, and her post-braces smile was nice and even. She now felt comfortable going to a party where she knew at least a few people, and she could even go out dancing after having a sufficient number of shots. But for some reason, the dating world still eluded her. The few dates she'd been on in recent months had been disappointing, and she couldn't remember the last time she had actually kissed a guy. Maybe it was that nice kid from biology last year? For some reason, Mia had never clicked with any of the men she'd met, and it was becoming embarrassing to admit that she was still a virgin at twenty-one years of age.

Thankfully, she and Jessie no longer shared a room, having found a flex one-bedroom that could be converted into a two-bedroom apartment for a reasonable (for NYC) rate of only $2,380. Having her own room meant a degree of freedom and privacy that was very nice in situations like this.

Turning on her bedside lamp, Mia looked around the room, making sure that the door to her bedroom was fully closed. Reaching into her bedside drawer, she took out a small package that was normally hidden all the way in the back of the drawer behind her face cream, hand lotion, and a bottle of Advil. Carefully unwrapping the bundle, she took out the tiny rabbit-ears vibrator that had been a gag gift from her older sister. Marisa had given it to her for high school graduation with the joking admonition to use it whenever she "felt the urge" and "to stay away from those horny college boys in the big city." Mia had blushed and laughed at the time, but the thing had actually proven handy. At certain times in the dark of the night, when her loneliness became more acute, Mia played with the device, gradually exploring her body and learning what a real orgasm felt like.

Pressing the small object to the sensitive nub between her legs, Mia closed her eyes and relived the sensations brought on by her dream. Gradually increasing the speed of vibration on the toy, she let her imagination soar, picturing the K's hands on her body and his lips kissing her, stroking her, touching her in sensitive and forbidden places, until the ball of tension deep within her belly got even tighter and

14

exploded, sending tingly warmth all the way to her toes.

* * *

The next morning, Mia woke up to a grey and overcast sky. Reaching for the phone to check the weather, she groaned. Ninety percent chance of rain with temperature in the mid-forties. Just what she needed when her Sociology paper awaited. Oh well, maybe she would make it to the library before the rain started.

Jumping out of bed, she pulled on her comfiest pair of sweats, a long-sleeved T-shirt, and a big hooded sweater she got on a high-school trip to Europe. It was her studying/paper-writing outfit, and it looked just as ugly today as it had the first time she'd worn it while cramming for her algebra test in tenth grade. The clothes fit her about the same now too, as she seemed to have developed a disgusting inability to gain inches either in girth or height since the age of fourteen.

Hastily brushing her teeth and washing her face, Mia stared critically in the mirror. A pale, slightly freckled face looked back at her. Her eyes were probably her best feature, an unusual shade of blue-grey that contrasted nicely with her dark hair. Her hair, on the other hand, was a whole different animal. If she spent an hour carefully blowdrying it with a diffuser, then she could maybe get her corkscrew curls to resemble something civilized. Her normal routine of going to sleep with it wet, however, was not conducive to anything but the frizzy mess she had on her head right now. Letting out a deep sigh, she ruthlessly pulled it back into a thick ponytail. Some day soon, when she had a real job, she might go to one of those expensive salons and try to get a straightening treatment. For now, since she didn't have an hour each morning to waste on her hair, Mia figured she just had to live with it.

Library time. Grabbing her backpack and her laptop, Mia pulled on her Uggs and headed out of the apartment. Five flights of stairs later, she exited her building, paying little attention to the peeling paint on the walls and the occasional cockroach that liked to live near the garbage chute. Such was student life in NYC, and Mia was one of the lucky ones to have a semi-affordable apartment so close to campus.

Real estate prices in Manhattan were as high as they'd ever been. In the first couple of years after the invasion, apartment prices in New York had cratered, just as they had in all the major cities around the world. With the hokey invasion movies still ruling the public's imagination, most people figured that cities would be unsafe and departed for rural areas if they could. Families with children—already a rare commodity in Manhattan—left the city in droves, heading for the most remote areas they could find. The Ks had encouraged the migration, as it relieved the worst of the pollution in and around urban areas. Of course, people soon realized their folly, since the Ks wanted nothing to do with the major human cities and instead chose to build their Centers in warm, sparsely populated areas around the globe. Manhattan prices skyrocketed again, with a few lucky people making fortunes on the real estate bargains they'd picked up in the crash. Now, more than five years after K-Day—as the first day of the Krinar invasion came to be called—New York City rents were again testing record highs.

Lucky me, Mia thought with mild irritation. If she had been a couple of years older, she could've rented her current apartment for less than half the price. Of course, there was something to be said for graduating next year, instead of in the depths of the Great Panic—the dark months after Earth first faced the invaders.

Stopping by the local deli, Mia ordered a lightly toasted bagel (whole-grain, of course, the only kind available) with an avocado-tomato spread. Sighing, she remembered the delicious omelets her mom used to make, with crumbled bacon, mushrooms, and cheese. Nowadays, mushroom was the only ingredient on that list that was in any way affordable for a college student. Meat, fish, eggs, and dairy were premium products, available only as an occasional treat—the way foie gras and caviar used to be. That was one of the main changes that the Krinar had implemented. Having decided that the typical developed-world diet of the early twenty-first century was harmful both to humans and their environment, they shut down the major industrial farms, forcing meat and dairy producers to switch to growing fruits and vegetables. Only small farmers were left in peace and allowed to grow a few farm animals for special occasions. Environmental and animal-rights organizations had been ecstatic, and obesity rates in America were quickly approaching Vietnam's. Of course, the fallout had been huge, with numerous companies going out of business and food shortages during the Great Panic. And later on, when the Krinar's vampiric tendencies were discovered (though still not officially proven), the Far Right activists had claimed that the real reason for the forced change in diet was that it made the human blood taste sweeter to the Ks. Be that as it may, the majority of the food that was available and affordable now was disgustingly healthy.

"Umbrella, umbrella, umbrella!" A scruffy-looking man stood on the corner, hawking his wares in a strong Middle Eastern accent. "Five-dollar umbrella!"

Sure enough, less than a minute later, a light drizzle began. For the umpteenth time, Mia wondered if the street umbrella vendors had some kind of sixth sense about rain. They always seemed to appear right before the first drop fell, even if there was no rain in the forecast. As tempting as it was to buy an umbrella to stay dry, Mia only had a few blocks left to go and the rain was too light to justify an unnecessary expenditure of five dollars. She could've brought her old umbrella from home, but carrying an extra object was never high on her list of priorities.

Walking as fast as she could while lugging her heavy bag, Mia turned the corner on West 4th Street, with the Bobst Library already in sight, when the downpour began. Crap, she should've bought that umbrella! Mentally kicking herself, Mia broke into a run—or rather a jog, given the backpack weighing her down—as raindrops pelted her face with the force of water bullets. Her hair somehow managed to escape from the ponytail, and was in her face, blocking her vision. A bunch of people rushed past her, hurrying to get out of the rain, and Mia was pushed a few times by pedestrians blinded by the combination of heavy rain and umbrellas held by more fortunate souls. At times like this, being 5'3" and barely a hundred pounds was a severe disadvantage. A big man brushed past her, his elbow bumping into her shoulder, and Mia stumbled, her foot catching on a crack in the sidewalk. Pitching forward, she managed to catch herself with her hands on wet pavement, sliding a few inches on the rough surface.

All of a sudden, strong hands lifted her from the ground, as though she weighed nothing, standing her upright under a large umbrella that the man held over both of their heads.

Feeling like a dirty, drowned rat, Mia tried to brush her sodden hair off her face with the back of one scraped hand, while blinking the remnants of rain out of her eyes. Her nose decided to add to her humiliation, choosing that particular moment to let loose with an uncontrollable sneeze all over her rescuer.

"Oh my God, I'm so sorry!" Mia frantically apologized in utter mortification. Her vision still blurry from the water running down her face, she desperately tried to wipe her nose with a wet sleeve to prevent another sneeze. "So sorry, I didn't mean to sneeze on you like that!"

"No apologies necessary, Mia. Obviously, you got cold and wet. And injured. Let me see your hands."

This could not be happening. Her discomfort forgotten, all Mia could do was stare in disbelief as Korum carefully lifted her wrists palms-up and examined her scrapes. His large hands were unbelievably gentle on her skin, even as they held her in an inescapable grip. Although she was soaked to the skin in chilly mid-April weather, Mia felt like she was about to burst into flames, his touch sending a wave of heat rushing through her body.

"You should get those injuries treated immediately. They could scar if you're not careful. Here, come with me, and we'll get them taken care of." Releasing her wrists, Korum put a proprietary arm around her waist and began shepherding her back toward Broadway.

"Wait, what—" Mia tried to recover her wits. "What are you doing here? Where are you leading me?" The full danger of the situation was just now beginning to hit home, and she began to shiver from a combination of cold and fear.

"You're obviously freezing. I'm getting you out of this rain, and then we'll talk." His tone brooked no disagreement.

Desperately looking around, all Mia saw were people rushing to get out of the pouring rain, not paying any attention to their surroundings. In weather like this, a murder in the middle of the street was likely to go unnoticed, much less the struggles of one small girl. Korum's arm was like a steel band around her waist, completely unmovable, and Mia found herself helplessly going along in whichever direction he was leading her.

"Wait, please, I really can't go with you," Mia protested shakily. Grasping at straws, she blurted out, "I have a paper to write!"

"Oh really? And you're going to write it in this condition?" His tone dripping with sarcasm, Korum gave her a disparaging once-over, lingering on her dripping hair and scraped hands. "You're hurt, and you're probably going to catch pneumonia—with that puny immune system you've got."

As before, he somehow managed to get a rise out of her. How dare he call her puny! Mia saw red. "Excuse me, my immune system is just fine! Nobody catches pneumonia from getting stuck in the rain these days! Besides, what concern is it of yours? What are you doing here, stalking me?"

"That's right." His reply was smooth and completely nonchalant.

Her temper immediately cooling, Mia felt tendrils of fear snaking through her again. Swallowing to moisten her suddenly dry throat, she could only croak out one word. "W-Why?"

"Ah, here we are." A black limo was sitting at the intersection of West 4th and Broadway. At their approach, the automatic doors slid open, revealing a plush cream-colored interior. Mia's heart jumped into her throat. No way was she getting into a strange car with a K who admitted to stalking her.

She dug in her heels and prepared to scream.

"Mia. Get. In. The. Car." His words lashed at her like a whip. He looked angry, his eyes getting more yellow by the second. His normally sensuous-looking mouth appeared cruel all of a sudden, set in an uncompromising line. "Do NOT make me repeat myself."

Shaking like a leaf, Mia obeyed. Oh God, she just wanted to survive this, whatever the K had in store for her. Every horror story she'd ever heard about the invaders was suddenly fresh in her mind, every image from the gruesome fights during the Great Panic. She stifled a sob, watching as Korum got in the limo and closed the umbrella. The car doors slid shut.

Korum pressed the intercom button. "Roger, please take us to my place." He looked much calmer now, eyes back to the original golden brown.

"Yes, sir." The driver's reply came from behind the partition that fully blocked him from view.

Roger? That was a human name, Mia thought in desperation. Maybe he could help her, call the police on her behalf or something. Then again, what could the police do? It's not like they could arrest a K. As far as Mia knew, they were above the reach of human law. He could pretty much do anything he wanted with her, and there was no one to stop him. Mia felt tears running down her rain-wet face as she thought about her parents' grief when they found out that their daughter was missing.

"What? Are you crying?" Korum's voice held a note of incredulity. "What are you, five?" He reached for her, his fingers locking around her upper arms, and pulled her closer to stare into her face. At his touch, Mia started shaking even harder, gasping sobs breaking out of her throat.

"Hush, now. There's no need for that. Shhh . . ." Mia suddenly found herself cradled fully on his lap, her face pressed against a broad chest. Still sobbing, she vaguely registered a pleasant scent of freshly laundered clothing and warm male skin, as his hand moved in soothing circles on her back. He really was treating her like a five-year-old crying over a boo-boo, she thought semi-hysterically. Strangely enough, the treatment was working. Mia felt her fear ebbing as he held her gently in those powerful arms, only to be replaced by a growing sense of awareness and a warm sensation somewhere deep inside. Adrenaline amplified attraction, she realized with a peculiar detachment, remembering a study on the subject from one of her psychology classes.

Still ensconced on his lap, she managed to pull away enough to look up at his face. Up close, his appearance was even more striking. His skin, a warm golden hue that was a couple of shades darker than her roommate's, was flawless and seemed to glow with perfect health. Thick black lashes surrounded those incredible light-colored eyes—which were framed by the straight dark slashes of his eyebrows.

"Are you going to hurt me?" The question escaped her before she could think any better of it.

Her kidnapper let out a surprisingly human-like sigh, sounding exasperated. "Mia, listen to me, I mean you no harm . . . Okay?" He looked straight into her eyes, and Mia couldn't look away, mesmerized by the yellow flecks in his irises. "All I wanted was to get you out of the rain and to treat your injuries. I'm taking you to my place because it's nearby, and I can provide you with both medical assistance and a change of clothes there. I really didn't mean to scare you, much less get you into this kind of state."

"But you said . . . you said you were stalking me!" Mia stared at him in confusion.

"Yes. Because I found you interesting at the park and wanted to see you again. Not because I want to hurt you." He was now rubbing her upper arms with a gentle up-and-down motion, as though soothing a skittish horse.

At his admission, a wave of heat surged through her body. Did that mean he was attracted to her? Her heart rate picked up again, this time for a different reason.

There was something else she needed to understand. "You forced me to get into the car . . ."

"Only because you were being stubborn and refusing to listen to common sense. You were wet and cold. I didn't want to waste time arguing in the rain when a warm car was standing right there." Put like that, his actions sounded downright humanitarian.

"Here." Pulling a tissue from somewhere, he carefully blotted the remaining tears on her face and gave her another tissue to wipe her nose, watching with some amusement as she tried to blow into it as delicately as possible. "Feeling better now?"

Strangely enough, she was. He could be lying to her, but what would be the point? He could do anything he wanted with her anyway, so why waste time trying to soothe her fears? Her earlier terror gone, Mia suddenly felt exhausted from her emotional roller coaster. As though sensing her state, Korum gathered her closer to him, pressing her face

20

gently against his chest again. Mia did not object. Somehow, sitting there on his lap, inhaling his warm scent and feeling the heat of his body surrounding her, Mia felt better than she had in a long time.

CHAPTER THREE

"Here we are. Welcome to my humble abode."

Mia stared around in amazement, her gaze lingering on floor-to-ceiling windows looking out over the Hudson, gleaming wooden floors, and luxurious cream-colored furnishings. A few pieces of modern art on the walls and luscious-looking plants near the windows provided tasteful touches of color. It was the most beautiful apartment she had ever seen. And it looked completely human.

"You live here?" she asked in astonishment.

"Only when I come to New York."

Korum was hanging his trench coat in the closet by the door. It was such a simple, mundane action, but somehow his movements were just too fluid to be fully human. He was now clad only in a blue T-shirt and a pair of jeans. The clothes hugged his lean, powerful body to perfection. Mia swallowed, realizing that her incredible surroundings paled next to the gorgeous creature who was apparently occupying them.

How could he afford this place? Were all the Ks rich? When the limo had pulled into the parking garage at the newest luxury high-rise in TriBeCa, Mia had been shocked to find herself escorted to a private elevator that took them directly to the penthouse floor. The apartment looked huge, particularly by Manhattan standards. Did it occupy the entire top floor of the building?

"Yes, the apartment is the whole floor."

Mia blushed, just realizing that she had asked the question out loud. "Umm . . . it's a beautiful place you've got here."

"Thank you. Here, sit down." He led her to a plush leather couch—

cream-colored, of course. "Let me see your hands."

Mia hesitantly extended her palms, wondering what he intended to do. Use his blood to heal them, the way vampires from popular fiction used to do?

Instead of cutting his palm or doing anything vampiric, Korum brought a thin silvery object toward her right palm. The size and thickness of an old-fashioned plastic credit card, the thing looked completely innocuous. That is, until it began to emit a soft red light directly over her hand. There was no pain, just a pleasant, warm sensation where the light touched her damaged skin. As Mia watched, her scrapes began to fade and disappear, like pencil marks getting erased. Within a span of two minutes, her palm was completely healed, as though there had been nothing there to begin with. Mia tentatively touched the area with her fingers. No pain whatsoever.

"Wow. That is amazing." Mia exhaled sharply, releasing a breath she hadn't even realized she was holding. Of course, she had known that the Ks were far more technologically advanced, but seeing what amounted to a miracle with her own eyes was still shocking.

Korum repeated the process on her other hand. Both of her palms were now completely healed, with no trace of an injury.

"Uh . . . thank you for that." Mia didn't really know what to say. Was this a K version of offering a Band-Aid, or did he just perform some kind of a complicated medical procedure on her? Should she offer to pay him? And if he said yes, would he accept student health insurance? *Snap out of it, Mia! You're being ridiculous!*

"You're welcome," he said softly, still lightly holding her left hand. "Now let's get you changed out of your wet clothes."

Mia's head jerked up in horrified disbelief. Surely he couldn't mean to—

Before she even had a chance to say anything, Korum blew out an exasperated breath. "Mia, when I said that I don't intend to harm you, I meant it. My definition of harm includes rape, in case you think we have some cultural differences there. So you can relax, and stop jumping at every word I say."

"I'm sorry, I didn't mean to imply . . ." Mia wished the ground would open up and simply swallow her. Of course, he wouldn't rape her. He probably wasn't even interested in her that way. Why would he want some skinny, pale little human when he could have any of the gorgeous K females she'd seen on TV? He'd never said he was attracted to her—just that he found her "interesting." For all she knew, he could be a K scientist studying the New York breed of humans—and he had just found a curly-haired lab rat.

Letting out another sigh, Korum rose gracefully from the couch, his every move imbued with inhuman athleticism. "Here, come with me."

Still feeling embarrassed, Mia barely paid attention to her surroundings as he led her down the hall. However, she couldn't help but gasp at the first sight of the enormous bathroom that lay before her.

The glass shower enclosure was bigger than her entire bathroom back home, and a large elevated jacuzzi occupied the center of the room. The entire bathroom was done in shades of ivory and grey, an unusual combination that nonetheless paired well in this luxurious environment. Two of the walls were floor-to-ceiling mirrors, further adding to the spacious feel. There were plants here too, she noticed with bemusement. Two exotic-looking plants with dark red leaves seemed to be thriving in the corners, apparently getting enough sunlight from the large skylight in the ceiling.

"This is for you." Korum slid open part of the glass wall and took out a large ivory towel and a soft-looking thick grey robe. "You can take a hot shower and change into this, and then I will throw your clothes in the dryer."

With a nod and a murmured thank-you, Mia accepted the two items, watching as Korum exited the room and closed the door behind him.

A sense of unreality gripped her as she stared at the cutting-edge luxury all around her. This could not be happening to her. Could this be a really vivid dream? Surely Mia Stalis, from Ormond Beach, Florida, was not standing here in a bathroom fit for a king, having been told to take a hot shower by a K who had practically kidnapped her in order to heal her insignificant scratches with an alien magic device. Maybe if she blinked a few times, she would wake up back in her cramped room at the apartment she shared with Jessie.

To test that theory, Mia shut her eyes tightly and opened them again. Nope, she was still standing there, feeling the plush towel and robe heavy in her arms. If this was a dream, then it was the most realistic dream she'd ever had. She might as well take that shower—now that the excitement was starting to wear off a bit, she felt the chill from her damp clothes sinking deep into her bones.

Putting down her burden on the edge of the tall jacuzzi tub, Mia walked to the door and locked it. Of course, if Korum really wanted to get in, it was doubtful that the flimsy lock would keep him out. The incredible strength of the Krinar was discovered in the first few weeks after the invasion, when some guerrilla fighters in the Middle East ambushed a small group of Ks in violation of the recently signed Coexistence Treaty. Video footage of the event, recorded by some bystander on his iPhone, showed scenes straight out of a horror science fiction movie. The band of thirty-plus Saudis, armed with grenades and automatic assault rifles, had stood no chance against the six unarmed Ks. Even wounded, the aliens moved at a speed exceeding that of all known living creatures on Earth, literally tearing apart their attackers with bare hands. One particularly dramatic scene showed a K throwing two screaming men—each with one hand—high up into the air. The exact height of the throw was later determined to be about sixty feet. Needless to say, the men had not survived their descent. The sheer savagery of that fight—and some subsequent encounters during the days of the Great Panic—stunned the human population, lending credence to the rumors of vampirism that emerged some months later. For all their advances in technology and seeming eco-consciousness, the Ks could be as brutal and violent as any vampire of legend.

And here she was stuck with one. Who wanted to heal her negligible scratches and have her take a hot shower in his fancy penthouse. And put her clothes in his dryer.

A hysterical giggle escaped Mia at the thought.

Of course, he might like his snacks clean and sweet-smelling, but somehow Mia believed him when he said he didn't want to hurt her. Besides, there was very little she could do about her current situation— she might as well stop freaking out and take advantage of the most luxurious shower of her life.

Peeling off her wet clothes, Mia caught sight of herself in the mirror. Why was he interested in her? Sure, she was skinny, which was still in vogue, but he probably had the most beautiful women of both species fawning over him. Standing there naked, Mia tried to look at herself objectively and not through the eyes of a self-conscious teenager. The mirror reflected a thin young woman, with small, but nicely rounded breasts, slim hips, and a narrow waist. Her butt was reasonably curvy, considering the rest of her frame. Naked, she didn't look like the shapeless stick figure she always felt like in her baggy clothes. If she were taller, she might even think she had a nice figure. However, her skin was way too pale and the dark mess of curls framing her face was much too frizzy for her to ever be considered more than moderately cute or passably pretty.

Sighing, Mia stepped into the shower. After a brief battle with the touchscreen controls, she figured out how to work them and was soon enjoying warm water coming at her from five different directions. She even used his soap, which had a very faint but pleasing scent of something tropical.

Ten minutes later, Mia regretfully turned off the water and stepped out onto a thick ivory bath rug. She dried herself with the towel Korum had so graciously provided, wrapped it around her wet hair, and put on the robe—which was, to her surprise, only a little big on her. It had to be a woman's robe, she realized with an unpleasant pang of something that felt oddly like jealousy. *Don't be silly, Mia, of course he has female guests!* A creature that gorgeous would hardly be celibate. He might even have a girlfriend or a wife.

Mia swallowed to get rid of an obstruction in her throat that seemed to rise up at that thought. *Stop it, Mia!* She had no idea what he wanted from her, and she had absolutely no reason to feel like this about an alien from outer space who may or may not drink human blood.

Padding to the door in her bare feet, Mia picked up her discarded clothes from the floor. They felt wet and yucky in her hands, and she was glad she was no longer wearing them. Carefully opening the door, she peeked out into the hallway, spotting a soft-looking pair of grey house slippers that Korum apparently left for her.

No sign of Korum himself.

Putting on the slippers, Mia left the bathroom and headed to the left, hoping that she was going back toward the living room. The last thing she wanted was to stumble into his bedroom, even though that thought made her feel warm and flushed all over.

He was sitting on the couch, looking at something in his palm. Sensing her presence, he lifted his head, and a luminous smile slowly lit his face at the sight of her standing there in the too-big robe and turban-like towel on her head.

"You look adorable in that." His voice was low and somehow intimate, even from across the room, making her insides clench in a strangely sexual way. Oh God, what did he mean by that? Was he actually interested in her? Mia was sure she had just turned beet-red as her heart rate suddenly picked up.

"Ah, thanks," she mumbled, unable to think of a better response. Was it her imagination, or did his eyes turn an even deeper shade of gold?

"Here, let me have those." Before she had a chance to recover her composure, he was next to her, taking her wet clothes from her slightly shaky arms. "Have a seat, and I'll drop these in the dryer."

With that, he disappeared down the hall. Mia stared after him, wondering if she should be worried. He said he wasn't going to hurt her, but would he take no for an answer if he really was interested in her sexually? More importantly, would she be able to say no, given her response to him thus far?

She'd heard of humans having sex with Ks, so their species were definitely compatible in that way. In fact, there were even websites where people who wanted to have sex with Ks posted ads designed to attract them. Some of the ads must have garnered responses, since the websites stayed in business. Mia always used to think that these xenos—short for xenophiles, a derogatory term for K addicts—were crazy. Sure, most of the invaders tended to be very good-looking, but they were so far from being human that one might as well have sex with a gorilla; there were fewer differences between gorilla and human DNA than between human and Krinar.

Yet here she was, apparently very attracted to one particular K.

A minute later, Korum returned empty-handed, interrupting Mia's chain of thought. "The clothes are drying," he announced. "Are you hungry? I can make us something to eat in the meanwhile."

Ks could cook? Mia suddenly realized that she was, in fact, famished. With all the excitement of the past hour, her bagel breakfast seemed like a very long time ago. Cooking and eating also seemed like a very innocuous way to pass the time.

"Sure, that sounds great. Thank you."

"Okay, come with me to the kitchen, and I'll make something."

With that promise, he walked over to a door she hadn't noticed before and slid it open, revealing a large kitchen. Like the rest of the penthouse, it was striking. Gleaming stainless steel appliances, black and ivory marble floors, and black enameled lava countertops populated the space, for an almost futuristic look. Some kind of big-leafed plants in silvery pots hung from the ceiling near the windows, seeming very much at home in an otherwise sterile-looking environment.

"How do you feel about a salad and a roasted veggie sandwich?" Korum was already opening the refrigerator, which looked like the latest version of the iZero—a smart fridge jointly created by Apple and Sub-Zero a couple of years ago.

"That sounds great, thanks," Mia answered absentmindedly, still studying her surroundings. Something was nagging at her, some obvious question that begged an answer.

Suddenly, it hit her.

"Your home only has our technology in it," Mia blurted out. "Well, except for the little healing tool you used on me. All of these appliances, all of our technology—it must seem so primitive to you. Why do you use it instead of whatever you guys have instead?"

Korum grinned, revealing the dimple in his left cheek again, and walked over to the sink to rinse the lettuce. "I enjoy experiencing different things. A lot of your technology is really so ingenious, considering your limitations. And, to use one of your sayings, when in Rome . . ."

"So you're basically slumming," Mia concluded. "Living with the primitives, using their basic tools—"

"If you want to think of it that way."

He started chopping the veggies, his hands moving faster than any professional chef's. Mia stared at him in fascination, struck by the incongruity of a creature from outer space making a salad. All of his movements were fluid and elegant—and somehow very inhuman.

"What do you normally eat on Krina?" she asked, suddenly very curious. "Is your diet very different from ours?"

He looked up from the chopping and smiled at her. "It's different in some ways, but very similar in other ways. We're omnivorous like you, but lean even more toward plant foods in our diet. There's a huge variety of edible plants on Krina—more so than here on Earth. Some of our plants are very dense in calories and rich in flavor, so we never quite developed the taste for meat that humans seem to have acquired recently."

Mia blinked, surprised. There was something predatory in the way he moved—the way all Ks moved. Their speed and strength, as well as the violent streak they'd displayed, did not make sense for a primarily herbivorous species. So there must be something to the vampire rumors after all. If they didn't hunt animals for their meat, then how had they evolved all these hunter-like traits?

She wanted to ask him that, but had a feeling that she might not want to know the answer. If his species really did view humans as prey, it was probably best not to remind him about it when she was alone with him in his lair.

Mia decided to stick with something safer instead. "So is that why you guys emphasize plant foods so much for us? Because you like it yourselves?"

He shook his head, continuing to chop. "Not really. Our main concern was the abuse of your planet's resources. Your unhealthy addiction to animal products was destroying the environment at a much faster rate than anything else you were doing, and that was not something we wanted to see."

Mia shrugged, not being particularly environmentally conscious herself. Since he was being so accommodating, though, she decided to resume her earlier line of questioning. "Is that why you're here in New York, to experience something different?"

"Among other reasons." He turned on the oven and placed sliced zucchini, eggplant, peppers, and tomatoes on a tray inside.

How frustrating. He was being evasive, and Mia didn't like it one bit. She decided to change her approach. "What brings you to Earth in general? Are you one of the soldiers, or the scientists, or do you do something else . . ." Her voice trailed off suggestively.

"Why, Mia, are you asking me about my occupation?" He sounded like he was again laughing at her.

Predictably, Mia felt her hackles rising. "Why, yes, I am. Is that classified information?"

He threw back his head and burst out laughing. "Only for curious little girls." Mia stared back at him with a stony expression on her face. Still chuckling, he revealed, "I'm an engineer by profession. My company designed the ships that brought us here."

"The ships that brought you here? But I thought the Krinar had been visiting Earth for thousands of years before you formally came here?" That had been one of the most striking revelations about the invaders— the fact that they'd been observing humans and living among them long before K-Day.

He nodded, still smiling. "That's true. We've been able to visit you for a long time. However, traveling to Earth had always been a dangerous task—as was space travel in general—so only a few intrepid individuals would attempt it at any given time. It's only in the past few hundred years that we fully perfected the technology for faster-than-light travel, and my company succeeded in building ships that could safely transport thousands of civilians to this part of the universe."

That was interesting. She'd never heard this before. Was he telling her something that wasn't public knowledge? Encouraged and unbearably curious, Mia continued with her questions. "So have *you* been to Earth before K-Day?" she asked, staring at him in wide-eyed fascination.

He shrugged—a human gesture that was apparently used by the Ks as well. "A couple of times."

"Is it true that all our UFO sightings are based on actual interactions with the Krinar?"

He grinned. "No, that was mostly weather balloons and your own governments testing classified aircraft. Less than one percent of those sightings could actually be attributed to us."

"And the Greek and Roman myths?" Mia had read recent speculation that the Krinar may have been worshipped as deities in antiquity, giving rise to the Greek and Roman polytheistic religions. Of course, even today, some religious groups had embraced the Ks as the true creators of humankind, spawning an entirely new movement dedicated to venerating and emulating the invaders. The Krinarians, as these K-worshippers were known, sought every opportunity to interact with the beings they viewed as real-life gods, believing it increased their odds of reincarnating as a K. The Big Three—Christianity, Islam, and Judaism—had reacted very differently, refusing to accept that Ks were in any way responsible for the origin of life on Earth. Some more extreme religious factions had even declared the Krinar to be demons and claimed that their arrival was part of the end-of-days prophecy. Most people, however, had accepted the aliens for what they were—an ancient, highly advanced species that had sent DNA from Krina to Earth, thus starting life on this planet.

"Those *were* based on the Krinar," confirmed Korum. "A few thousand years ago, a small group of our scientists, sent here to study and observe, became overly involved in human affairs—to the point that they overstayed their mission by a few hundred years. They ultimately had to be forcibly returned to Krina when it became obvious that they were purposefully preying on human ignorance."

Before Mia had a chance to digest that information, the oven let out a little beep signifying the food's readiness.

"Ah, here we go." He took out the roasted veggies and dropped them into a marinade he'd managed to whip up during their conversation. Placing a large salad in the middle of the table, he picked up a sizable portion and deposited it on Mia's plate. "We can start with this while the veggies are marinating."

Mia dug into her salad, holding back an inappropriate giggle at the thought that she was literally eating food of the gods —or at least food that had been prepared by someone who would've been worshipped as a god a couple of thousand years ago. The salad was delicious—crispy lettuce, creamy avocado, crunchy peppers, and sweet tomatoes were combined with some type of tangy lemony dressing that was mildly spicy. She was either super-hungry, or it was the best salad she'd had in a long time. In the past few years, she'd learned to tolerate salad out of necessity, but this kind of salad she could actually grow to like.

"Thank you, this is delicious," she mumbled around a mouthful of salad.

"You're welcome." He was digging in as well, with obvious enjoyment. For a little while, there was only the sound of them munching on the salad in companionable silence. After finishing his portion—he even ate faster than normal, Mia noticed—Korum got up to make the sandwiches.

Two minutes later, a beautifully made sandwich was sitting in front of Mia. The dark crusty bread appeared to be freshly baked, and the veggies looked tender and were seasoned with some kind of orange spices. Mia picked up her portion and bit into it, nearly stifling a moan of enjoyment. It tasted even better than it looked.

"This is great. Where did you learn to cook like this?" Mia inquired with curiosity after swallowing her fifth bite.

He shrugged, finishing up his own larger sandwich. "I enjoy making things. Cooking is just one manifestation of that. I also like to eat, so it's helpful to know how to make good food."

That made sense to her. Mia ate the last bite of her sandwich and licked her finger to get the remainder of the delicious marinade. Lifting her head, she suddenly froze at the look on Korum's face.

He was staring at her mouth with what looked like raw hunger, his eyes turning more golden by the second.

"Do that again," he ordered softly, his voice a dark purr from across the table.

Mia's heart skipped a beat.

The atmosphere had suddenly turned heavy and intensely sexual, and she had no idea how to deal with it. The full vulnerability of her situation dawned on her. She was completely naked underneath the thick robe. All he had to do was pull on the flimsy belt holding the robe together, and her body would be fully revealed to him. Not that clothes would provide any protection against a K—or a human male for that matter, given her size—but wearing only a robe made her feel much more exposed.

Slowly getting up, she took a step away from the table. Her heartbeat thundering in her ears, Mia nervously blurted out, "Thank you for the meal, but I should really get going now. Do you think my clothes might be dry?"

For a second, Korum did not respond, continuing to look at her with that disconcertingly hungry expression. Then, as if coming to some internal decision, he slowly smiled and got up himself. "They should be ready by now. Why don't you put the dishes in the dishwasher while I go check?"

Mia nodded in agreement, afraid that her voice would tremble if she spoke out loud. Her legs felt like cooked noodles, but she started gathering the dishes. Korum smiled approvingly and exited the room, leaving Mia alone to recover her composure.

By the time he came back, his arms loaded with her dry clothes, Mia had managed to convince herself that she had overreacted to a potentially harmless remark. Most likely, her imagination was working in overdrive, adding sexual overtones to where there were none. Given his apparent fascination with human technology and lifestyle, it wasn't all that surprising that he would find an actual human interesting as well— maybe even cute in something they did—the same way Mia felt about animals in the zoo.

Feeling slightly bad about her earlier awkwardness, Mia tentatively smiled at Korum as he handed her the clothes. "Thanks for drying these—I really appreciate it."

"No problem. It was my pleasure." He smiled back, but there was a hint of something mildly disturbing in the look he gave her.

"If you don't mind, I'll just go change." Still feeling inexplicably nervous, Mia turned toward the kitchen exit.

"Sure. Do you remember the way to the bathroom? You can go change there." He pointed down the hall, watching with a half-smile as she gratefully escaped.

Locking the bathroom door, Mia hurriedly changed into her comfortably ugly—and pleasantly warm from the dryer—clothes. He had somehow managed to dry her Uggs as well, Mia noticed with pleasure as she pulled them on. Feeling much more like herself, she unwrapped the towel from her hair, which was only slightly damp at this point, and left the curly mess down to finish drying. Then, thinking that she was as ready as she would ever be, Mia left the relative safety of the bathroom and ventured back out into the living room to face Korum and his confusing behavior.

He was again sitting on the couch, analyzing something in his palm. He seemed very absorbed in it, so Mia cautiously cleared her throat to notify him of her presence.

At the sound, he looked up with a mysterious smile. "There you are, all nice and dry."

"Ah, yeah, thanks for that." Mia self-consciously shifted from one foot to another. "And thanks again for your hospitality. I really should get going now, try to write that paper and finish up some other homework . . ."

"Sure, I'll take you wherever you want to go." He got up in one smooth motion, heading to the coat closet.

"Oh no, you don't have to do that," protested Mia. "Really, I have no problem taking the subway. The rain has stopped, so I'll be totally fine."

He just gave her an incredulous look. "I said I will take you there." His tone left no room for negotiation.

Mia decided not to argue. It's not as if she rode in a limo every day. Since Korum was so determined to give her a lift, she might as well enjoy the experience. So Mia kept quiet and meekly followed him as he entered a posh-looking elevator and pressed the button for the ground floor.

Roger and his limo were already waiting in front of the building. The doors slid open at their approach, and Korum courteously waited until Mia climbed inside before getting in himself. Mia wondered where he had learned all of these polite human gestures. Somehow she doubted that "ladies first" was a universal custom.

"Where would you like to go?" he inquired, sitting down next to her.

Mia thought about it for a second. As much as she'd love to run home and blab about the entire unbelievable encounter to Jessie, the deadline for her paper was looming. She needed to go to the library. She only hoped that she could put the day's events out of her mind for a few hours, or however long it took her to write the damn paper. "The Bobst Library, please, if it's not too much trouble," she requested tentatively.

"It's no trouble at all," he reassured her, pressing the intercom button and conveying the instructions to Roger.

Sitting in the closed quarters of the limo, Mia became increasingly aware of his large, warm body less than a foot away from her. Her body reacted to his nearness without reservations.

He really was an incredibly beautiful male specimen by anyone's standards, Mia thought with an almost analytical detachment. She guessed his height to be somewhere just over six feet, and he appeared to be quite muscular, judging by the way his T-shirt fit him earlier. With his striking coloring, he was easily the most handsome man she'd ever seen, in real life or on video. It was no wonder he was having such an effect on her, she told herself—any normal woman would feel the same. Understanding the rationale behind her attraction to him, however, did not lessen its power one bit.

"So, Mia, tell me about yourself." His softly spoken directive interrupted her thoughts.

"Um, okay." For some reason, the question flustered her. "What do you want to know?"

He shrugged and smiled. "Everything."

"Well, I'm a junior at NYU, majoring in psychology," Mia began, hoping she wasn't babbling. "I'm originally from a small town in Florida, and I came to New York to go to school."

He stopped her with a shake of his head. "I know all that. Tell me something more than basic facts."

Mia stared at him in shock, suddenly feeling like a hunted rabbit. With surprising calm, she asked, "How do you know all this?"

"The same way I knew where to find you today. It's very easy to find information on humans, especially those with nothing to hide." He smiled, as though he hadn't just shattered all of her illusions about privacy.

"But why?" Mia could no longer hold back a question that had been tormenting her for the last two days. "Why are you so interested in me? Why go to all these lengths?" She waved her hand, indicating the limo and everything he had done so far.

He looked at her steadily, his gaze nearly hypnotizing in its intensity. "Because I want to fuck you, Mia. Is that what you're afraid of hearing, why you've been acting so scared of me all along?" Without giving her a chance to catch her breath, he continued in the same gently mocking tone. "Well, it's true. I do. For some reason, you caught my attention yesterday, sitting there on that bench with your curly hair and big blue eyes, so frightened when I looked your way. You're not my type at all. I don't typically go for scared little girls, particularly of the human variety, but you—" he reached across with his right hand and slowly stroked her cheek, "—you made me want to strip you down right there in the middle of that park, and see what's hidden underneath these ugly clothes of yours. It took all my willpower to let you go then, and, when you licked your little finger so enticingly in my kitchen, I could barely stop myself from spreading open your robe and burying myself between your thighs right there on the kitchen table."

His touch felt like it was leaving burning streaks in its aftermath as he tucked a strand of hair behind her ear and gently brushed his knuckles across her lips. "But I'm not a rapist. And that's what it would be right now—rape—because you're so frightened of me, and of your own sexuality." Leaning closer, he murmured softly, "I know you want me,

34

Mia. I can see the flush of arousal on your pretty cheeks, and I can smell it in your underwear. I know your little nipples are hard right now, and that you're getting wet even as we speak, your body lubricating itself for my penetration. If I were to take you right now, you would enjoy it once you got past the fear and the pain of losing your virginity—yes, I know about that too—but I will wait for you to get used to the idea of being mine. Just don't take too long—I only have so much patience left for you."

CHAPTER FOUR

Mia hardly remembered the remainder of the ride.

At some point in the next few minutes, the limo had pulled up to the Bobst Library, and Korum had courteously opened the door for her again and handed her the backpack. He then proceeded to gently brush his lips against her cheek, as though parting ways with his sister, and left her standing on the curb in front of the imposing library building.

Moving on autopilot, Mia somehow found herself inside, sitting in one of the plush armchairs that were her favorite place to study. Going through the motions, she took out her Mac and placed it on the side table, noting with some interest that her hand was shaking and her fingernails had a slight bluish tint to them. She also felt cold deep inside.

Shock, Mia realized. She had to be in a state of mild shock.

For some reason, that pissed her off. Yes, she felt like he had stripped her naked with his words in the car, leaving her feeling raw and vulnerable. Yes, if she thought too deeply about the meaning of his last words, she would probably start running and screaming. But she was hardly a Victorian maiden—her lack of experience notwithstanding—and she refused to let a few explicit phrases send her into vapors.

Resolutely getting up, Mia left her bag in the chair as a placeholder—nobody would steal a computer that old—and headed to the coffee shop to get something hot to drink. On the way there, she stopped by the bathroom. Splashing warm water on her face in an attempt to regain her equilibrium, Mia inadvertently caught a glimpse of herself in the mirror. The usual pale face staring back at her looked subtly different—somehow softer and prettier. Her lips appeared fuller, as though slightly swollen where he had touched them. Her eyes looked brighter, and there was a hint of color on her cheeks.

He was right, Mia thought. She had been extremely turned on in the car, his words alone bringing her nearly to the edge of orgasm—despite her shock and fear. What that said about her was not something she cared to analyze too deeply. Even now, she could feel the residual dampness in her underwear and a slight pulsing sensation deep within her sex whenever she thought back to that limo ride.

Taking a deep breath, Mia squared her shoulders and exited the restroom. Her sex life in all its extraterrestrial manifestations would have to wait until the paper was done and submitted.

Her priorities were two-fold right now—an extra-large coffee and a few hours of uninterrupted quality time with the Mac.

* * *

The ringing of the doorbell and an excited squeal by her roommate woke up Mia twelve minutes before her alarm.

Groaning, she rolled over and put her pillow over her head, hoping that the source of the noise would go away and let her get the remaining few minutes of precious sleep.

She had gotten home at three in the morning, after finally finishing the evil paper. Unfortunately, she had a 9 a.m. class on Mondays, which meant that she would get less than five hours of sleep that night. Even so, her overtired brain had refused to let go of the day's events, with dark, erotic dreams interrupting her sleep—dreams in which she would see his face, feel his touch burning her skin, hear his voice promising both pain and ecstasy.

And now she couldn't even enjoy a few moments of peaceful rest, as Jessie apparently couldn't contain her excitement over whatever it was that came to the door.

"Mia! Mia! Guess what?" Jessie was practically singing as she knocked on Mia's bedroom door.

"I'm sleeping!" Mia growled, wanting to smack Jessie for the first time in her life.

"Oh come on, I know your alarm is about to go off. Rise and shine, Sleeping Beauty, and see what you got from Prince Charming!"

Mia bolted upright in her bed, all trace of sleepiness forgotten. "What are you talking about?" Jumping out of bed, she flung open the door, confronting her disgustingly cheerful and bright-eyed roommate.

"This!" With a huge excited grin, Jessie gestured toward a large vase of exotic pink and white flowers that occupied the center of their kitchen table. "The delivery guy just came and brought this. Look, there's even a card and everything! Do you know who sent it? Is there some secret admirer that you haven't told me about?"

Mia felt a sudden inner chill even as her pulse speeded up. Approaching the table, she reached for the card and opened it with trepidation. The content of the note—written in neat, but clearly masculine handwriting—was simple:

Tonight, 7pm. I will pick you up. Wear something nice.

Her hand shaking slightly, Mia put down the note. For some reason, she hadn't thought he would want to see her again so soon, much less come to her apartment.

"Well? Don't keep me in suspense!" Unable to wait any longer, Jessie grabbed the note and read it herself. "Ooh, what's this? You have a date?"

Mia felt the beginnings of a throbbing headache. "Not exactly," she said wearily. "Let me get dressed for class, and we can talk on the way."

Ten minutes later, Mia grabbed a breakfast bar and headed out the door with Jessie, who was nearly bursting with curiosity at this point. Sighing, Mia relayed a shortened version of the story, leaving out a few details that she felt were too private to share—such as his exact words and her reaction to him.

"Oh my God." Jessie's face reflected horrified disbelief. "And now he wants to see you again? Mia—this is bad, really bad."

"I know."

"I can't believe he just openly told you he intends to have sex with you." Jessie was wringing her hands in distress. "What if you don't show up tonight—go to the library instead or something?"

"I'm pretty sure he'll be able to find me there. He's done that before. And I don't know what he'll do if he gets mad."

Jessie's eyes widened. "Do you think he would hurt you?" she asked in a hushed tone.

Mia thought about it for a few seconds. All his actions toward her thus far had been . . . solicitous, for lack of a better word. It could all be an act, of course, but somehow she doubted that he would physically abuse her.

"I don't think so," she said slowly. "But I don't know what else he might be capable of."

"Like what?"

"Well, that's the thing—I just don't know." Mia nervously tugged at one long curl. "He's definitely not playing by any kind of normal dating rules. I mean, he practically kidnapped me off the street yesterday . . ."

"What if you go home to Florida?" Jessie was obviously desperate to find a solution.

"That seems like an overreaction. Besides, it's the middle of the semester. I can't go anywhere until this summer."

"Crap." Jessie sounded stumped for a second. "Well, then just tell him no when he shows up tonight. Do you think he would force you to go with him anyway?"

"I have no idea," Mia said wryly, pausing in front of the building that was her destination. "I'm going to have to think about this some more. Maybe if I look particularly ugly tonight, he'll lose interest."

"That's a great idea!" Jessie clapped her hands in excitement. "He wants you to wear something nice tonight? Well, you show him! Put on your ugliest clothes, eat some fresh garlic and onion, put some oil in your hair so it looks all greasy, and maybe do something that makes you sweaty—like a run—and don't shower or use deodorant afterwards!"

Mia stared at her roommate in fascination. "You're scary. How did you come up with all of this? It's not like you try to un-attract guys on a regular basis."

"Oh, it's easy. Just think of all the things you'd do to get ready for a date—and do just the opposite." Jessie breezily waved one hand with such a know-it-all expression that Mia couldn't help but burst out laughing.

* * *

At six o'clock, Mia began implementing Jessie's plan. Her roommate had been dying to see her first K and lend Mia moral support for the confrontation, but she had a biology lab that couldn't be missed. Mia was glad about that. The last thing she wanted was to put Jessie in harm's way.

She started out by doing jumping jacks, lunges, squats, and sit-ups. Within fifteen minutes, her leg and stomach muscles—unused to so much exertion—were burning, and Mia was covered with a fine layer of sweat. Without bothering to shower, she put on her oldest, rattiest underwear, thick brown tights that her sister absolutely despised, and a long-sleeved black dress that Jessie had once claimed made her look completely washed out and shapeless. A pair of old black Mary-Janes with medium-height heels, worn out and scuffed, completed the look. No makeup, except for a slight dusting of dark blue shadow directly under her eyes—to imitate under-eye circles. Her hair already looked like a frizzy mess, but Mia brushed it for good measure and added hair conditioner only to the roots, leaving the ends to poof out in every direction. And for the grand finale, she cut up an entire clove of garlic, mixed it with green onion, and thoroughly chewed it, making sure that the smelly mixture got into every nook and corner of her mouth before she spit it out. Satisfied, she took one last look in the mirror. As expected, she looked ghastly—like somebody's crazy spinster aunt—and probably smelled even worse. If Korum remained interested in her after tonight, she would be very surprised.

When the doorbell rang promptly at seven, Mia put on her scruffy wool peacoat and opened the door with a mixture of trepidation and barely contained glee.

The sight that greeted her was breathtaking.

Somehow, in the short span of a day, Mia had managed to forget just how beautiful he was. Dressed in a pair of dark designer jeans and a light grey button-down shirt that fit his tall, muscular body to perfection, he fairly gleamed with health and vitality, his bronzed skin and glossy black hair providing a stark contrast for those incredible amber-colored eyes. Mia suddenly felt irrationally embarrassed about her own grungy appearance.

At the sight of her, his lips parted in a slow smile. "Ah, Mia. Somehow I suspected that you would be difficult."

"I don't know what you're talking about," Mia said defiantly, lifting her chin.

"I'm glad you decided to play this game." He reached out and stroked her cheek, sending an unwanted shiver of pleasure down her spine. "It will make your eventual surrender that much sweeter."

Still smiling, he politely offered her his arm. "Ready to go?"

Fuming, Mia ignored his offer, stomping down the stairs on her own. *Idiot!* She should've realized he would see her deliberately ugly appearance as a challenge. With his looks and apparent wealth, he probably had women fawning all over him. It must be refreshing to meet someone who didn't immediately fall into his bed. Maybe she should just sleep with him and get it over with. If the pursuit was what he enjoyed, then he would lose interest very quickly if he got what he wanted.

The limo was waiting as they exited the building. "Where are we going?" Mia asked, wondering about it for the first time.

"Percival," Korum answered, opening the door for her. The place he named was a popular restaurant in the Meatpacking District that was notoriously difficult to get into, even on a Monday night.

Mia mentally kicked herself again. It was one thing to look repellent for Korum—a wasted effort, as it turned out—but it was a whole different level of embarrassing to show up in the fanciest, trendiest district of New York City looking and smelling like a homeless person. Still, she'd rather die of embarrassment than give Korum the satisfaction of knowing how discomfited she felt.

He climbed into the car and sat down next to her. Reaching out, he took one of her hands and brought it to his lap, studying her palm and fingers with some apparent fascination. Her hand looked tiny in his large grasp, his golden skin appearing much darker next to her own whiteness, creating a surprisingly erotic contrast. Mia attempted to yank her hand away, trying to ignore the sensations his touch was provoking in her nether regions. He held her hand just long enough to let her feel the futility of her struggles, and then let go with a small smile.

It was strange, Mia thought, somewhere along the way she had stopped being so afraid of him. For some reason, knowing his intentions toward her—as crude and base as they were—gave her a peace of mind. The scared girl who sat in this car yesterday would not have dared to oppose him in any way for fear of unknown retaliation. Mia no longer had such qualms, and it was oddly liberating.

A minute later, the limo pulled up to the door of the restaurant. Korum exited first and Mia followed, noticing with mortification the double-takes they got from the well-dressed men and women on the street. A gorgeous K in his limo was bound to attract attention, and Mia was sure they wondered about his dowdy companion.

A tall, rail-thin hostess greeted them at the door. Without even asking for their reservations, she led them to a private booth in the back of the restaurant. "Welcome back to Percival," she purred, leaning suggestively over Korum while handing them the menus. "Should I start you off with sparkling or flat?"

"Sparkling would be fine, Ashley, thanks," he said absentmindedly, studying the menu.

Mia felt a sudden, shocking urge to tear out every straight blond hair from Ashley's model-like head. A strange nausea-like sensation roiled her stomach as she pictured the two of them together in bed, his muscular body wrapped around the blonde's. *Stop it, Mia! Of course, he slept with other women!* Undoubtedly, the creature left a trail of Ashleys anywhere he went.

"Have you decided what you'd like?" he inquired, looking up from his menu, seemingly oblivious to the murderous expression on Mia's face.

"No, not yet." Taking a deep breath, she forced herself to concentrate on the menu. This was undoubtedly the nicest restaurant she'd ever been to, and the menu—which lacked prices for some reason—listed some dishes and ingredients that she'd never heard of. Her eyes widened as she noticed goat cheese and caviar in the appetizer section and eggs in one of the noodle dishes. Her mouth watered. "I think I'll get the roasted beets and goat cheese salad, followed by the pesto-artichoke Pad Thai."

Korum smiled at her indulgently. "Of course." He motioned to the waiter and relayed her order. "And I will have the watercress jicama salad and the shiitake parsnip ravioli in cashew cream. We'll also get a bottle of Dom Perignon."

Mia looked at him in fascination. She hadn't known that Ks consumed alcohol. In fact, there was so much that she—and the public in general—didn't know about the invaders who now lived alongside them. It dawned on Mia that she had the perfect opportunity to learn sitting across her at the table.

Feeling slightly reckless, she decided to start with the question that had been bothering her ever since their first meeting. "Is it true that you drink human blood?"

Korum's eyebrows shot up on his forehead, and he nearly choked on his drink. "You don't pull any punches, do you?" A big grin breaking out on his face, he asked, "Are you asking if we have to drink human blood, or if we do it anyway?"

Mia swallowed. She was suddenly far from sure this was the best line of questioning. "I guess both."

"Well, let me set your mind at ease . . . We no longer require blood for survival."

"But you did before?" Mia's eyes widened in shock.

"Originally, when we first evolved into our current form, we needed to consume significant amounts of blood from a group of primates that had certain genetic similarities to us. It was a deficiency in our DNA that made us vulnerable and tied our existence to another species. We have since corrected this defect."

"So it's true? There were humans on your planet?" Mia was staring at him open-mouthed.

"They weren't exactly human. Their blood, however, had the same hemoglobin characteristics as yours."

"What happened to them? Are they still around?"

"No, they are now extinct."

"I don't understand," Mia said slowly, trying to make sense of what she'd learned thus far. "If you needed them to survive, how and when did they go extinct? Was that before or after you ... um ... fixed your defect?"

"It happened long before then. We succeeded in developing a synthetic substance before the last of their kind disappeared, and it enabled us to survive their demise. They were an endangered species for millions of years. It was partially our fault for hunting them, but a lot of it had to do with their own low birth rate and short lifespan. Just like you, they had a weak immune system, and a plague nearly wiped them out. That's when we began to work on alternative routes of survival for our species—synthetic hemoglobin substitutes, experimentation with our own DNA, and attempting to develop a comparable species both on Krina and on other planets."

A lightbulb went off in Mia's brain. "Is that why you planted life here on Earth? Is that how humans came to be—you needed a comparable species?"

"More or less. It was a shot in the dark, with minuscule odds of success. We disseminated our DNA as far as our then-primitive technology could reach. We didn't know which planets and where would be hospitable to life, much less bear any similarities to Krina, so we blindly sent billions of drones to planets that are located in what you now call the Goldilocks Zones."

"Goldilocks Zones?"

"Yes, these are also called the habitable zones—regions in the universe around various stars that potentially have the right atmospheric pressure to maintain liquid water on the surface. Based on our knowledge, those are the only places where life similar to Krina's could arise."

Mia nodded, now remembering learning about that in high school.

Satisfied that she was following along, he continued his explanation. "One of the drones reached Earth, and the first simple organisms succeeded in surviving here. Of course, we didn't know that at the time. It wasn't until some six hundred million years ago that we reached this part of the galaxy and found Earth."

"Right before the Cambrian explosion began?" asked Mia, goosebumps breaking out on her arms. It was public knowledge now that the Ks had influenced evolution on Earth to a fairly significant degree, the timing of their initial arrival coinciding with the previously puzzling appearance of many new and complex life forms during the early Cambrian period. But their motives for planting life on Earth and later manipulating it had remained a mystery, and it was incredible to hear him speak about it so nonchalantly, revealing so much to her over dinner.

"Exactly. We have occasionally stepped in to guide your evolution, particularly when it threatened to drastically diverge from ours—such as when the dinosaurs had become a dominant life form—"

"But I thought the dinosaurs had been killed by an asteroid?"

"They were. But we could have easily deflected that strike. Instead, we simply ensured that the necessary life forms, such as the early versions of mammals, survived."

Mia stared at him open-mouthed as he continued the story.

"When the first primate appeared here, it was a tremendous achievement for us because its blood carried the hemoglobin. However, we no longer needed it by then because we'd recently had the breakthrough that allowed us to manipulate our own DNA without adverse consequences."

He paused when the salads were served, and continued speaking between bites of his watercress. "At that point, Earth and its primate species had become the grandest scientific experiment in the history of the known universe. The challenge for us became to see whether we could nudge along evolution just enough to see another intelligent species emerge."

Mia felt chills going down her spine as she listened to the story of human origins told by an alien from the gazillion-year-old civilization that had essentially played God. An alien who was munching on his salad at the same time, as though discussing nothing more important than the weather.

"You see," he continued, "the primates on Krina were of the same intelligence level as your chimpanzees, and few of us thought that a species as short-lived as yours could develop a truly sophisticated intellect. But we persisted, occasionally stepping in with genetic modifications to make you look more like us, and the result has surpassed all our expectations. While you share a lot of the characteristics of the Krinian primates—presence of the hemoglobin, a relatively weak immune system, and a short lifespan—you have a much higher birth rate and an intelligence that's nearly comparable to ours. Your evolution rate is also much faster than ours—mostly due to that higher birth rate. The transition from primitive primates to intelligent beings took you only a couple of million years, while it took us nearly a billion."

Dozens of questions were running through Mia's mind. She latched onto the first one. "Why did you care if we looked like you? Is that somehow a requirement for intelligence?"

"No, not really. It just made the most sense to the scientists who were overseeing the project at the time. They wanted to create a sister species, intelligent beings that looked like us, so that it would be easier for us to relate to them, easier to communicate with them. Of course," he said with a wicked smile, twirling his empty fork, "there was an unexpected side benefit."

Mia looked at him warily. "What benefit?"

"Well, you see, when the first Earth primates appeared, some of the Krinar tried drinking their blood out of curiosity. And they quickly discovered that, in the absence of the biological need for the hemoglobin, drinking blood gave them a very pleasurable high—an almost sexual buzz. It was better than any drug, although synthetic versions of your blood have since become quite popular in our bars and nightclubs."

Mia nearly choked on her salad. Coughing, she drank some water to clear the obstruction in her throat while he watched with an amused look on his face.

"But the best thing of all was our more recent discovery." He leaned closer to her, his eyes turning a now-familiar shade of deeper gold. "You see, it turns out that there's nothing quite as pleasurable as drinking blood from a living source during sex. The experience is simply indescribable."

Mia reflexively swallowed, feeling horrified and oddly aroused at the same time. "So you want to drink my blood while . . . fucking?"

The corners of his mouth turned upward in a sensuous smile. "That would be the ultimate goal, yes."

She had to know, even if the answer made her sick to her stomach. "Would I die?"

He laughed. "Die? No, taking a few sips of your blood won't kill you any more than giving blood at a doctor's office. In fact, our saliva contains a chemical that makes the whole process quite pleasurable for humans. It was originally intended for our prey, to make them drugged and docile when we fed on them—but now it merely serves the purpose of enhancing your experience."

Mia's head felt like it was exploding with everything she'd just learned, but there was something else she needed to find out. "How exactly do you do it?" she asked cautiously. "Drink blood, I mean? Do you have fangs?"

He shook his head. "No, that's an invention of your literary fiction. We don't need fangs—the edges of our top teeth are sharp enough that they can penetrate the skin with relative ease, usually by just slicing through the top layer."

Their main course arrived, giving Mia a few precious moments to regain her composure.

It was too much, all of it.

Her thoughts spun around, all jumbled and chaotic. Somehow, in the past twenty-four hours, she'd gotten used to the idea that an extraterrestrial wanted to have sex with her, for whatever reason. But now he also wanted her to serve as a blood donor during sex. His species had basically created her kind, and they now used human blood as some sort of an aphrodisiac. The idea was disturbing and sickening on many levels, and all Mia wanted to do was crawl into her bed, pulling covers over her head, and pretend that none of this was happening.

Something of her inner turmoil must have shown on her face because Korum reached out, gently covering her hand with his, and said softly, "Mia, I know this is all a huge shock to you. I know that you need time to understand and get to know me better. Why don't you relax and enjoy your meal, and we can discuss something else in the meantime?" He added with a teasing smile, "I promise not to bite."

Mia nodded and obediently dug into her food as soon as he released her hand. It was either that or run out of the restaurant screaming, and she wasn't sure how he would react to that. After everything she'd learned today, the last thing she wanted was to provoke whatever predatory instincts his species still possessed.

The Pad Thai was delicious, she realized, tasting the rich flavors complemented by bits of real egg. For some reason, despite her delicate build, nothing ever interfered with her appetite. Her family often joked that Mia must really be a lumberjack in disguise, given the large quantities of food she liked to consume on a regular basis. "How is your ravioli?" she asked between bites of her noodles, searching for the most innocuous subject.

"It's great," he answered, enjoying his dish with similar gusto. "I often come to this restaurant because they have one of the best chefs in New York."

"I don't know," Mia teased, trying to keep the conversation light.

"The salad and sandwich you made yesterday was pretty tasty."

He grinned at her, exposing the dimple that made him seem so much more approachable. It was only on his left cheek, not the right—a slight imperfection in his otherwise flawless features that only added to his appeal. "Why, thank you. That's the best compliment I got all year."

"Do you cook a lot for yourself or mostly go out to restaurants?" Food seemed like a nice safe topic.

"I do both quite a bit. I like to eat, as you apparently do too—" he motioned to her rapidly disappearing portion with a smile, "—so that necessitates a lot of both. What about you? I imagine it's tough to go out too much in New York on a student's budget."

"That would be an understatement," Mia agreed. "But there are some really nice cheap places near NYU and in Chinatown, if I want to venture out that far."

"What made you decide to come to New York for school? Your home state has a number of good universities, and the weather is so much better there." He seemed genuinely perplexed.

Mia laughed as the irony of her school choice only now occurred to her. "When I was applying to colleges, my parents were afraid that you— the Krinar, I mean—might establish a Center in Florida, so they wanted me to go to an out-of-state school."

Korum smiled in response. "We did actually think about settling there, but it was too densely populated for our taste." He took a sip of his champagne. "So I'm guessing they wouldn't be particularly happy that you're here with me today?"

"God, no." Mia shuddered. "My mom would probably be hysterical, and my dad would get one of his stress migraines."

"And your sister?"

"Um, she wouldn't be particularly happy either." For a moment, she had almost forgotten how much he knew about her.

"She's older than you, right?"

"By nearly eight years. She got married last year."

"I wonder what it would be like to have a sibling," he mused. "It's not a very common occurrence for us, having more than one child."

Mia shrugged. "I'm not sure if my experience was particularly authentic, given our age difference. By the time I was old enough to be anything more than a brat, she had already left for college." Her curiosity kicking in again, she asked, "So you don't have any siblings? What about your parents?"

"I'm an only child. My parents are back on Krina, so I haven't seen them in a while. We do communicate remotely, though, on a regular basis."

Their waiter returned to clear the table and give them their dessert menus. Mia chose tiramisu—made with real cheese and eggs—and Korum went with the apple pecan tart. Somehow, in the course of their conversation, she'd managed to down two glasses of champagne, and was beginning to feel buzzed. The evening took on a slightly surreal tint in her mind, from the restaurant filled with Manhattan's most beautiful people to the gorgeous predator who sat across the table from her, blithely chatting about their families.

Mia wondered how old he was. She knew the Ks were very long-lived, so there was really no way to tell his age from appearance. Had he been human, she would have guessed late twenties. Her curiosity got the best of her again, and she blurted out, "How old are you?"

"About two thousand of your Earth years."

Mia stared at him in shock. That would put him somewhere in the very ancient category by human standards. Two thousand years ago, the Roman Empire still ruled the Western world, and the Christian religion was just getting its start. And he had been alive since that time?

She drank some more champagne to help with the dryness in her throat. "Does that make you old or young in your society?"

He shrugged his broad shoulders. "I guess on the younger side. My parents are much older. It doesn't matter, though. Once we reach full maturity, age literally becomes just a number."

"We must all seem like infants to you then, huh?" Mia took a big gulp from her glass and felt the room tilt slightly. She hoped she wasn't slurring her words. She probably should stop with the champagne. He could easily take advantage of her if she got drunk. But, then again, he could easily take advantage of her sober too. She was completely at the mercy of an alien who wanted to fuck her and drink her blood, so she might as well enjoy this undoubtedly excellent vintage.

"Not infants. Just naive in certain ways. More like teenagers, if anything."

Mia rubbed an itchy spot on her nose with the back of her hand, wondering if she wanted to know the answer to her next question. She decided to go for it. "So are you immortal, like the vampires of our legends?"

"We don't think of it that way. Everybody can die. Our species has always enjoyed negligible senescence, but we can still be killed or die in a bad accident."

"Negligible senescence?"

"Basically, we don't have the symptoms of aging. Before we were sufficiently advanced with our science and medicine, we could still die from a variety of natural causes, but we've now succeeded in achieving a very low—almost negligible—mortality rate."

"How is this possible?" asked Mia. "How can a living creature not age? Is that something peculiar to Krina?"

"Not really. There are actually a number of species right here on Earth that have that same characteristic. For instance, have you ever heard of the four-hundred-year-old clam?"

"What? No!" He had to be making fun of her ignorance; surely such a thing didn't exist.

He nodded. "It's true—look it up if you don't believe me. There are a number of creatures that don't lose their reproductive or functional capabilities with age—some species of mussels and clams, lobsters, sea anemones, giant tortoises, hydras ... In fact, hydras are pretty much biologically immortal; they die from injury or disease, but not from old age."

Trying to process this incredible information, Mia rubbed her nose again. That's it, she realized, no more alcohol for her. For some reason, her nose had a tendency to get itchy after a few drinks, and Mia had learned to respect it as a sign of when to stop. The few times she'd ignored this warning, the consequences hadn't been pretty.

Seeing her weaving slightly in her seat, Korum motioned the waiter for the check. Mia hazily wondered if she should offer to split it, the way she always did when she went out with college guys. Nah, she decided. He had practically forced her to come out today, so she might as well get a free meal out of it. Besides, she wasn't sure she could afford this place, given the priceless menu. So instead, she just observed when Korum waived his wristwatch phone-wallet over the waiter's tiny digital receptor, and added what seemed to be a generous tip, judging by the grateful expression on the waiter's face.

"Ready to go?" He helped her put on her coat and again offered her his arm. Mia accepted this time, as she felt somewhat woozy and didn't have a high degree of confidence in her own ability to make it out of the restaurant without tripping at some point.

"Are you drunk?" he asked with amusement, observing her slightly unsteady gait as they exited onto the street. "I only saw you drink a couple of glasses."

Mia raised her chin and lied, "I'm perfectly fine." She hated it when people pointed out what a lightweight she was.

"If you say so." He looked like he was about to laugh, and Mia wanted to smack him.

Roger and the limo were waiting at the curb, of course. Mia hesitated, her heart rate accelerating at the realization that she would be alone with an extraterrestrial predator who wanted her blood.

She turned to him. "You know, I really feel like getting some fresh air. I can just walk from here—my apartment is only about a dozen blocks away, and the weather is really quite nice and refreshing." The last bit was a lie. It was actually quite chilly, and Mia was already shivering in her thin coat.

His expression darkened. "Mia. Get in. I will take you home." It was his scary tone of voice, and it worked just as well on her the second time around. Shaking slightly from a combination of nerves and the cold air, she climbed into the car.

The ride to her apartment was oddly uneventful, taking only a few minutes in the absence of traffic. He again held her hand, gently rubbing her palm in a soothing manner. Despite her initial nervousness, Mia closed her eyes, leaned back against the comfortable seat, and was just starting to drift off when they arrived at their destination.

He walked her up the five flights of stairs to her apartment, holding her arm as an apparent precaution against any alcohol-induced unsteadiness. She felt tired and sleepy, wanting nothing more than to collapse into her bed at home. At one point, she managed to stumble and nearly fall anyway, missing a step with her high-heeled shoe. Korum sighed and lifted her into his arms, carrying her up the remaining two flights despite her mumbled protestations.

Upon reaching her apartment, he carefully set her back on her feet, briefly keeping her pressed against his hard body before letting her pull away. His hands remained on her waist, holding her at a short distance. Mia stared at him, mesmerized. Her breathing picked up, and warm moisture pooled between her legs as she realized what the large bulge she'd felt in his jeans meant. His breathing was a little fast too, and she doubted that it had anything to do with carrying a hundred-pound human girl up two flights of stairs. He leaned toward her, eyes nearly yellow at this point, and Mia froze as he cupped the back of her head and pressed his lips to hers.

He kissed her leisurely, his tongue exploring her mouth with exquisite gentleness, even as he held her against him in an unbreakable grip. Mia moaned, a wave of heat surging through her body and leaving an oddly pleasurable sense of lethargy in its wake. Somewhere in the back of her mind, a warning bell was going off, but all she could concentrate on was his mouth and the sensations spreading throughout her body. He brought her closer, pressing his groin against her belly, and she felt his hardness again, her sex clenching in response. He lightly sucked on her lower lip, pulling it into his mouth, and his hand slid down her back to cup her buttocks, lifting her off the ground so he could grind his erection directly against her clitoris through their layers of clothing.

The pressure building inside her was different and stronger than anything she'd ever experienced, and Mia groaned with frustration, wanting more. Her hands somehow found their way to his shoulders, kneading the heavy muscles through his shirt, and it was not enough. She wanted, needed the feel of his naked skin against her own, the slide of his heavy cock into her sex, quenching the empty pulsing sensation she felt there. She wrapped her legs around his waist, grinding against him, and the sensations built to a fever pitch. She hovered on the edge for a few delicious seconds, and then went over, climaxing with a muffled scream against lips. He groaned as well, his other hand reaching under her skirt and tearing at her tights as he let go of her mouth to press burning kisses on her neck and collarbone.

"Mia? Is that you?" A familiar voice reached through her daze, and Mia realized with mortification that Jessie had opened the apartment door and was staring at them in shock. "Are you okay? Do you want me to call the police?" Her roommate clearly wasn't sure how to interpret what she was seeing.

Still wrapped around Korum, Mia felt a shudder go through his body as he visibly fought to regain control. Suddenly fearing for Jessie, Mia barked at her, "Yes, I'm fine! Go back inside and leave us alone!" A hurt look appeared on her roommate's face, and she vanished inside the apartment, slamming the door behind her.

Mia pushed at Korum, trying to put some distance between them. "Please let me go," she said quietly, wanting nothing more than to curl up into a little ball in her room and cry. He hesitated for a second, and then lowered her to her feet, still keeping her pressed against his body. His golden skin appeared flushed from within, and his eyes still had a strong yellow undertone. The bulge against her stomach showed no signs of abating, and Mia shivered, realizing that he was holding onto his self-control by a hair. "Please," she repeated, knowing that there was nothing she could do to make him release her until he was ready.

"You want me to let you go? After all that?" His voice was harsh and guttural, and the arms locked around her back tightened until she could barely breathe.

Mia nodded, trembling, the white-hot desire she'd felt earlier giving way to a confusing jumble of fear and acute embarrassment. He looked at her, his expression dark and unreadable, and then very deliberately removed his arms from around her waist and stepped away.

"All right," he said softly. "Have it your way. Go to your little room, and tell your roommate all about it. Have yourself a good cry about what a little slut you are, coming like that from a kiss right out in the hallway." His eyes glittered at the stricken expression on her face. "And then you better get used to the idea that you'll come a lot more, from everything I do to you—and I will literally do everything."

With that promise, he turned away and walked toward the stairs. Pausing before entering the stairwell, he looked back and said, "I will pick you up after class tomorrow. No more games, Mia."

CHAPTER FIVE

Her legs shaking, Mia made her way into the apartment with as much dignity as she could muster considering that her underwear was soaking wet and her tights were hanging in shreds around her knees. Jessie sat on the couch in the living room, waiting for her to come in. She didn't look mad anymore, just extremely concerned.

"Oh my God, Mia," she said slowly. "What the hell was that out in the hallway?"

Mia shook her head, barely holding back tears. "Jessie, I'm sorry. I really can't talk now," she said, going directly to her room and closing the door.

Collapsing on the bed, she wrapped the coverlet around herself and pulled her knees up to her chest. Her body seemed like it didn't belong to her, with her sex still pulsating in the aftermath of her orgasm. Her lips were swollen from his kisses, and her nipples felt so sensitive that the bra was too abrasive against her skin. She also felt raw and devastated inside, exposed in a way that she'd never before experienced in her life.

She didn't want this—any of this. The complete loss of control over her own body was overwhelming, and the fact that Korum was the one to solicit such a powerful response made her feel even more vulnerable.

He frightened her.

She was completely out of her league with him, and she knew it. As scary as it was to think about what the sexual act with an extraterrestrial vampire was likely to entail, the thing that Mia dreaded most was the effect he had on her emotions. He would take everything from her—her body and her soul—and when he was done, he would move on, leaving her broken and scarred for life, unable to ever forget her dark alien lover.

This was not how her life was supposed to turn out. Coming from a family of second-generation Polish immigrants, Mia had always followed the right path. She studied hard in school, both to please her parents and out of her own desire for achievement. Once she finished grad school, she intended to use her degree to counsel high school or college students on their own career path. She was close to her parents and sister, and she hoped to be a good mother to her own children one day. At some point, she was supposed to fall in love with a nice man from a good family and have a long happy marriage, the way her own parents did. While other girls dreamed of adventures and chased after bad boys, Mia just wanted a regular life, done the right way.

She had always known that she was a sexual creature. Despite her lack of experience, she had no doubt that she would enjoy sex once she found the right person. She loved reading racy novels and watching R-rated movies, and she considered herself far from a prude. In fact, she liked the idea of trying out new things and having several relationships before ultimately settling down. When she went out clubbing with Jessie, Mia frequently found herself turned on from dancing with some attractive guy, particularly after having a couple of shots. For some reason, it had never gone beyond a few kisses, perhaps because Mia was too cautious and rational to pick up a guy at a club for a one-night stand. Still, she had looked forward to her first time, preferably with a special someone that she cared about and who cared about her. An alien predator who wanted to fuck her and drink her blood was as far removed from that ideal as anything that Mia could imagine.

She wanted a shower.

Slowly getting up, Mia took off her clothes. The tights were beyond salvation, so she threw them in the trash. Her black dress was also slightly ripped in the front—Mia could not even remember when that happened—and she discarded it also. Feeling reckless, she chucked the Mary-Janes and her underwear into the bin as well, wanting nothing to remind her of this night. Wrapping herself in her robe, Mia left the safety of her room and headed into the shower, hoping that Jessie had gone to sleep.

* * *

The next morning, Mia woke up with a headache.

As soon as she opened her eyes, the events of the last evening rushed back into her mind, accompanied by a scalding feeling of humiliation. He had mockingly called her a slut, and she very much felt like one, particularly given what Jessie had been privy to. She also remembered what he'd said about picking her up today, and she suddenly felt nauseous from a combination of fear and some kind of sick excitement.

She only had one class today, and it didn't start until eleven. It was just as well, since she didn't even know if she wanted to get out of bed at all.

There was a timid knock on her door.

"Yes, come in," Mia said in resignation, knowing that Jessie must've been anxiously waiting for her to wake up and listening for any movements in her room.

Her roommate entered sheepishly and sat down on Mia's bed. "So I guess my patented guy-repellent strategy was a total fail, huh?"

Mia rubbed her eyes and gave Jessie a bitter smile. "It's pretty fair to say, yes." Taking a deep breath, she said, "Look, I'm sorry about yesterday. I didn't mean to yell at you—I just really didn't want you out there, seeing what I guess you saw."

Jessie nodded, clearly having figured it out on her own. "No worries. I would've done the same. I was just worried that he was forcing you or something. So, are you, like, really into him now?"

Mia groaned and buried her head in her pillow. "I don't know. Every sane part of me says to run as far away as I can, but every time he touches me, I just can't help myself. It's like I don't have any control over this thing. I hate it."

Jessie's eyes widened. "Oh, wow. That's *so* hot. It's like the kind of thing you read about in romance novels—he kisses her and she swoons!"

An elusive something kept nagging at Mia this morning, and Jessie's words suddenly put the puzzle pieces together.

Of course! He did kiss her, and he had explicitly told her that K saliva contained some chemical that kept their prey docile and drugged. It all made sense now—the pleasant lethargy that had spread through her veins and the way her brain had simply turned off the second his lips touched hers, leaving her to operate on pure animal instinct. The chemical was probably even more potent directly in the bloodstream, but she had undoubtedly gotten a nice dose of it last night.

No wonder she had acted like such a slut—not only was she drunk from champagne, but she was also literally high from his kiss.

A burning fury slowly built in her stomach, replacing the sense of humiliation she'd felt earlier. The bastard. He had basically drugged her and very nearly took advantage, and then he had the nerve to accuse *her* of playing games. Well, screw him! If he thought she would meekly go with him today after class, he had another thing coming.

Her brain whirled, searching for alternatives.

"Jessie," she said slowly. "Didn't you once tell me that a cousin of yours had some kind of connections in the Resistance?"

"Uh—" Jessie was clearly surprised. "Are you talking about that thing I once told you about Jason? That was a long time ago, when we were still freshmen. I'm pretty sure he doesn't have anything to do with that anymore, not that I've kept in touch with him." She stared at Mia with a concerned look on her face. "Why are you even asking? What, you want to join the freedom fighters now?"

Mia shrugged, not sure where she was going with this. All she knew was that she refused to meekly become Korum's sex toy, to be used and discarded at whim.

She had never believed in the anti-K movement and thought that the Resistance fighters were crazy. The Krinar were here to stay. Human weapons and technology were hopelessly primitive in comparison to theirs, and Mia had always thought that trying to fight them was the equivalent of banging your head against the wall—futile and likely dangerous. Besides, it didn't seem all that bad, once the days of the Great Panic were over. The Ks had mostly left them alone, choosing to live in their own settlements, and life went on with a few minor differences— cleaner air, a healthier diet, and a lot of shattered illusions about humanity's place in the universe. However, now that she'd had some personal interactions with one particular K, she felt a bit more sympathetic to the fighters' cause—not that it made the Resistance movement any less futile.

She sighed. "Never mind, it was just a stupid idea. I think I just need to clear my head." Hopping out of bed, Mia pulled on her jeans, an old T-shirt, and a comfy sweater.

"Wait, Mia. What's going on?" Jessie was confused by her actions. "Are you upset about what happened last night?"

Mia pulled on her socks and a pair of sneakers. "I guess," she muttered. Telling her roommate the whole story would just make her worry, and a worried Jessie sometimes did drastic things—such as calling the police once to report Mia missing, when she had simply fallen asleep in the library with a dead phone battery. Not that Jessie could do anything in this case, but she still preferred not to cause her unnecessary distress. "Look, I'm fine," Mia lied. "I just really need to take a walk and get some air. You know I haven't exactly had a lot of experience with this type of thing, and this is a little like being thrown in the deep end of the pool. I just want to try to figure out how I feel about all this before I can even begin to talk about it."

Jessie looked at her with a faintly hurt expression. "Okay, well, sure. Whatever you need to do." Then she brightened. "Are you going to be home for dinner tonight? I was thinking of cooking some pasta, and we could just have a girls' night in, watch some old movies . . ."

Mia shook her head with regret. "That sounds amazing, but I really don't know. I think I'll be seeing him again today."

Seeing the worried look on Jessie's face, she quickly added with a sly smile, "And it might be quite fun." Before Jessie had a chance to reply, Mia grabbed her backpack and ran out the door with a quick "see you later."

She walked briskly down the street with no particular destination in mind. Stopping by a deli, she bought a pack of chewing gum—since she hadn't even brushed her teeth this morning—and a wrap loaded with hummus, avocado, and fresh veggies. Her brain seemed to have gone into hibernation, and she simply walked without thinking about anything in particular, enjoying the feel of her feet striking the pavement and the mid-morning sun warming her face. She must've walked like that for a long time because, by the time she started paying attention to street signs, she was already in TriBeCa, a block away from the luxury high-rise that she'd been in less than forty-eight hours ago.

And just like that, she knew what she was going to do—what her subconscious must've known even earlier because it had brought her here.

It was really quite simple.

Running was futile. He could track her down anywhere she went, and he had already proven that he could manipulate her body into responding to his with the aid of various chemical substances. No, running wasn't the answer. He was a hunter. The chase was what he loved, and there was really only one thing she could do to thwart him. She could deny him the chase, take away the enjoyment of pursuing a reluctant prey.

She could come to him herself.

* * *

Having reached the decision, Mia lost no time in putting it into action.

Entering the lobby of his building, she calmly told the concierge that she was there to see Korum. The man's eyes widened a little—he clearly knew what the occupant of the top floor was—and he notified the unit of her presence. Ten seconds later, he motioned toward the elevator that was positioned a little to the left of the main one. "Please go ahead, miss. Just enter in 1159 when prompted for a code, and it will take you to the penthouse floor."

Korum was waiting when the elevator doors opened.

Despite her intention to remain unmoved, her breath caught in her throat and her pulse jacked up at the sight. He wore a soft-looking pair of grey pajama pants and nothing else. His upper body was completely bare, with bronze skin covering chiseled muscle and a light smattering of dark hair visible around small, masculine nipples. Broad shoulders, thick with ropy muscles, tapered down to a slim waist, and an actual six pack covered his flat abdomen. There wasn't an ounce of fat anywhere on his powerful body.

Mia swallowed to help the dryness in her throat, suddenly far less sure of the wisdom of her plan.

"Mia," he purred, leaning on the doorway and looking for all the world like a big jungle cat about to pounce. "To what do I owe this pleasure? I was not expecting to see you so early." Something in her expression must've betrayed her because he let out a short laugh. "Ah, I see. It was *because* I wasn't expecting you. Well, come on in."

Padding to the kitchen in his bare feet, he asked, "Have you had breakfast?"

Mia nodded, feeling like a mute but afraid that her voice might betray her nervousness. This was definitely not the best plan. Why had she thought that bearding the lion in his den was somehow better than trying to avoid him altogether?

But there was no turning back now.

"Okay, then, perhaps I might interest you in some coffee or tea?" His tone was overly courteous, making a mockery of the normally polite question.

Her chin went up at the realization that he found the whole situation amusing. "No, thanks," she said coolly, taking pride in the level tone of her voice. "You know why I'm here. Why don't *you* stop playing games, so we can just get on with it?"

He stopped and looked at her. There was no trace of laughter on his face. "All right, Mia," he said slowly. "If that's how you wish it."

"One more thing," she said, wanting to needle him and no longer caring about the consequences. "No drugs of any kind. No alcohol and no saliva anywhere in my body. If you want my blood, you can just cut my vein and drink it that way. And no mouth-to-mouth kissing. I don't want to be drunk *or* high today."

His face darkened, and his eyes seemed to turn into pools of liquid gold. "You think you were high yesterday? Is that what you're telling yourself to explain what happened? That a couple of glasses of champagne and my magic kisses turned you into a nymphomaniac?" He laughed sardonically. "Well, sorry to disappoint you, darling, but the chemical in our saliva only works if it gets directly into your blood. Maybe if I kissed you all day long, after a few hours you might feel a tiny buzz—if you're lucky. Of course, if I kissed you all day long, you would probably come dozens of times and be long past noticing any kind of saliva-induced effects." Still smiling, he said pleasantly, "But have it your way. No kissing and no biting. All else is fair game."

Coming up to her, he took her hand and led her down the hall. Her heart pounding, Mia went without protest, knowing that the time for changing her mind was long past. She didn't know whether to believe him and, more importantly, she didn't want to believe him. If he was telling the truth, then she had made a huge mistake in coming here today. Some foolish part of her had thought that she could do this—let him have sex with her unwilling, unresponsive body, reduce him to being the rapist he'd claimed he was not—and walk away with her emotions untouched, maintaining some kind of moral high ground. If he wasn't lying, then she was, quite literally, screwed.

He led her into what had to be his bedroom. Like the rest of his penthouse, the room was both modern and opulent at the same time. A large circular bed dominated the center of the room. It was unmade and had obviously been recently slept in. The sheets were a soft ivory color, and the thick blankets and pillows strewn around the bed were a pale shade of blue. Mia's heart climbed into her throat as she fully realized what she'd just agreed to do.

He released her hand and stepped back, leaving her standing in the middle of the room. "All right," he said softly, "now take off your clothes."

Mia stood there frozen, a hot wave of embarrassment rolling through her. He wanted her to remove her clothes, right there in the middle of the sunlit room?

"You heard me," he repeated, his voice cold despite the yellow heat in his eyes. "Take them off." Seeing her hesitation, he added, "I can guarantee your clothes will not survive it if I lay my hands on them."

Mia's hands shook as she slowly raised them to pull the sweater over her head. He merely watched her, his face inscrutable despite the hunger in his eyes. She took off her sneakers, and her jeans were next, leaving her clad in pink boy-short panties and a T-shirt. She had forgotten to wear a bra and now acutely felt that lack, with her nipples hard and visible against the thin fabric of the T-shirt.

"Now take off your shirt," he instructed, seeing her pause. The front of his pants was tented, she noticed, and somehow that was oddly reassuring—to know that she had that kind of effect on him, that he wasn't turned off by her awkwardness or her skinny body. Trembling slightly, she pulled the shirt over her head, revealing her breasts to male eyes for the first time. It took all her willpower not to cross her arms over her chest in a silly virginal gesture; instead, she stood there with her hands fisted at her sides, letting him look his fill.

He came toward her then and touched her, slowly stroking one palm down her back while another hand cupped her left breast, gently kneading it as though to test its weight and texture. "You're very pretty," he murmured, looking down at her as his hands deliberately explored her body, every stroke sending ripples of heat down to her nether regions. Standing there in her bare feet, Mia was acutely aware of how much larger his body was compared to hers, with her head barely reaching his shoulder and each of his arms thicker than half of her torso. His hands appeared dark against her pale skin, and she shivered when he moved his palm down to her belly, the width of his open hand nearly spanning the distance between her hip bones. His erection prodded her side, the thin material of his pajama pants doing little to conceal its heat and hardness.

Without the blurring effect from the alcohol or the shield of darkness, there was no retreat from his brutally intimate actions, no merciful escape into a sensual fog. Instead, Mia stood there in broad daylight, exposed and vulnerable, intensely aware of each stroke of his large hands over her body and the warm moisture lubricating her sex in response.

Hooking his thumbs into her underwear, he pushed her panties down her legs, removing her last defense. "Step out of them," he hoarsely ordered, and Mia obeyed, standing completely naked in his arms. The fact that he was still wearing his pants somehow made the whole thing worse, adding to her sense of complete powerlessness.

He touched her buttocks, his hands curving around the small pale globes of her ass and lightly squeezing them. "Very nice," he whispered, and Mia blushed for some inexplicable reason. The dark curls between her legs attracted his attention next, and Mia flinched when his fingers slowly stroked her pussy hair, looking for the tender flesh underneath. Feeling her wetness, he smiled with purely masculine satisfaction, and Mia's embarrassment grew tenfold. This was the worst part—knowing that her own body betrayed her, that a creature who was not even human could provoke this kind of response from her under the circumstances.

"No mouth-to-mouth, right?" he murmured, picking her up and carrying her over to the bed. Mia nodded, squeezing her eyes shut in the hopes that it would be over with quickly. Instead, he placed her in the middle of the circular bed, like some virginal sacrifice, and crawled down her body until his head was above the juncture of her legs. Mia tried to rear up then, realizing his intentions, but he had no intention of letting her go. Instead, he easily held down her flailing legs with his elbows while his fingers leisurely parted her folds, exposing her most sensitive place to his burning gaze. Lowering his head, he gently pressed his tongue, soft and flat, against her clitoris—just holding it there and letting her struggle until she could bear it no longer, her entire body arching with the most powerful climax of her life.

While she lay there, still shuddering with little aftershocks, he rose up on his knees, deftly stripping off the pants to reveal a large jutting penis. Mia's eyes widened as she realized that her first time would likely involve more than a minor discomfort, given the size of the cock in front of her.

Seeing her fear, he paused. "Mia," he said quietly, "we don't have to do this if you're not ready. I can wait—"

She shook her head, unable to think past the fog of desire clouding her brain. It had taken all her courage to get this far, to allow him so much intimacy. To retreat now seemed cowardly, and Mia felt a sudden, irrational dread that this was it—that if she gave up a chance to experience such passion now, she would never feel it again.

He didn't need much encouragement. Before her logical side could reassert itself, he was already over her, parting her legs with one powerfully muscled thigh and settling in between them. Looking steadily into her eyes, he began to push his cock into her opening, slowly working it in inch by slow inch.

Regretting her decision almost immediately, Mia writhed under him, feeling like a heated baseball bat was attempting to enter her channel. Despite the wetness from her orgasm, her inner muscles did not want to let him in, desperately clenching to repel the invasion. "Shhh," he whispered soothingly as tears rolled down her face at the burning discomfort that threatened to morph into pain. Beads of sweat appeared on his own face at the obvious strain of holding back, his arms flexing as he held himself steady, trying to let the delicate muscles stretch around his shaft before proceeding. But Mia could not hold still, every instinct leading her to fight the penetration, little cries escaping from her throat as he pressed further, pausing briefly at the internal barrier. "I'm sorry," he said hoarsely, and Mia screamed as he pushed forward in one smooth motion, tearing through the membrane that was blocking his entrance and sheathing his cock to the hilt, his pubic hair pressing against her own.

Mia's vision went dark for a second, and hot nausea boiled up her throat as a knife-like pain tore through her insides. She had never expected to feel such agony, and she dug her nails into his shoulders, raw, guttural cries breaking out from her throat, desperately wanting to escape the object tearing her body apart. All earlier pleasure forgotten, she writhed under him like a fish on a hook, barely registering the soothing platitudes he was murmuring in her ear and the gentle kisses he was raining on her cheeks and forehead.

At some point, the agonizing pain began to abate, and she realized that he wasn't moving, just holding himself deep inside her, his muscles quivering from the effort it took to stay still. "I'm sorry," he was saying, apparently repeating it for the umpteenth time, "it will get better, I promise. Just let yourself relax, and it won't hurt like that anymore, I promise you . . . Shhh, my darling, just relax . . . there's a good girl . . . It will get better soon, I promise . . ."

Liar, Mia thought bitterly. How could it get better when he was still inside her, the organ that had caused her so much pain lodged deeply within? She felt violated and betrayed, pinned under his much larger body with no hope of escape until he was done. "Just finish it," she told him harshly, willing to tolerate anything to have this be over.

A small smile curved his lips despite the strain on his face. "Ah Mia, my sweet brave girl, your wish is my command." He pulled out slowly, and Mia squeezed her eyes shut, unable to hold back tears as the motion brought more pain at first. He kept moving, however, slowly retreating from her body and penetrating her again, and the ancient rhythm somehow ignited a small spark inside her again. Sensing it, he gradually picked up the pace and changed his angle slightly, so that the broad head of his shaft nudged some sensitive spot deep inside. His arm reached between them, knowing fingers unerringly finding her clitoris, and he pressed lightly, keeping the pressure steady and letting his strokes move her against his hand. Mia's body tensed again, this time for a different reason, and liquid heat began to gather in her core. She found herself starting to pant, echoing his heavy breathing, and the tension inside her became nearly unbearable, every thrust of his cock bringing her closer and closer to the edge without sending her over. The pain didn't go away—it was still there—but somehow it didn't matter as every nerve in Mia's body focused on her desperate need for the release. He groaned, his hips now hammering at her, and she screamed in frustration, small fists beating uselessly against his chest, her body vibrating like a guitar string from the intolerable tension deep inside. And suddenly it was too much. She felt him swell up even more, and then he was coming with one final deep thrust that sent her over the edge, his pelvis grinding against her sex as her entire body seemed to explode with an orgasm so powerful that she literally saw stars, her brain almost short-circuiting from the intensity of the climax.

She lay there afterwards, feeling his cock still twitching inside her even as it became softer and smaller. His shoulders and back were slick with sweat, and his breathing sounded like he had just run a marathon, his body lying heavily on top of hers. Her own limbs were shaking slightly, she noticed with a curiously detached interest, and her heart was pounding as though from a physical exertion.

He pulled out then, and Mia felt the loss of heat from his body, a strange inner coldness taking its place. He left the room, and she brought her knees up to her chest in a slow, painful motion, her body feeling foreign as she curled into a fetal position on her side, her mind oddly blank. There were streaks of blood on her thighs, much more blood than the spotting she'd always thought was the norm.

He came back a minute later, a small white tube in his hands. Squeezing out some clear substance, he coated his finger in it and reached between her legs, entering her sore opening despite her faint protest. Almost immediately, Mia felt the burning pain beginning to abate as the mystery gel worked its magic.

"It's an analgesic, and it will speed your recovery," he explained, wiping his hand on the sheets to get rid of the excess. "Unfortunately, I can't heal you completely because the last thing I want is for your membrane to regrow itself."

Mia responded by curling up into an even smaller ball. More than anything, she wanted to shrink and disappear, to pretend that none of this was real. He didn't let her though, gathering her closer to him in a spooning position, his large warm body curling around her own. "I hate you," she told him, wanting to lash out and hurt him somehow. She felt his sigh against her back. "I know," he said, gently stroking her tangled curls.

They must have lain like that for a few minutes. The sheets smelled like sex, Mia noticed, and like him. There was also a metallic odor that Mia realized had to be the remnants of her virginity.

"You never drank my blood," she said, finding it easier to communicate like that, with her back turned toward him.

"No, I didn't," he agreed, adding, "I think you've had enough new experiences for one day."

How considerate of him, Mia thought bitterly. Such a gentleman, sparing the poor virgin additional trauma. Never mind that he was the cause of that trauma in the first place.

As though sensing the direction of her thoughts, he said, continuing to stroke her hair, "I'm sorry it was so painful for you. I know you won't believe me right now, but I never wanted to hurt you like that and I never will again. Had I known how narrow you were inside and how thick your membrane would be, I would have made sure to remove it before we got anywhere near this bedroom. Once I was inside you, it was too late—I just couldn't stop. It won't be like this next time, I promise."

Mia listened to his little speech with a growing dread in her stomach. "Just to be clear," she said slowly, "I don't ever want to do this with you again. Ever. If you touch me again, it will be rape in the very real sense of the word."

Korum didn't answer, and Mia realized with a sinking feeling that he very much intended for there to be a next time. "You're a monster," she told him, trying to pull away. He let her go, getting up himself. Before she realized what he wanted, he bent over the bed and lifted her in his arms, carrying her naked out of the room.

He brought her to the same bathroom Mia had showered in before. At some point, he must have filled the jacuzzi because it was ready for them. He carefully set her on her feet in the wonderfully hot water that came up to her waist. Her legs still felt shaky, so Mia lowered herself into the bubbles, finding a step on which she could sit. Powerful jets pleasantly massaged her tired muscles, washing off dried blood and semen on her thighs, and Mia leaned back against the edge and closed her eyes, trying to ignore Korum's naked presence.

A scary thought suddenly entered her mind, causing her eyes to pop open. "You didn't use any protection," she hissed at him, horrified at the realization. "Am I going to catch some kind of a weird STD or worse— get pregnant?"

He laughed, throwing his head back. "No, my sweet—both would be an impossibility. You're far safer having sex with me than with any human male, regardless of how many condoms he wears."

Mia exhaled in relief. The gel he'd used earlier and the hot water were doing wonders for her physical state, and she felt nearly back to her old self. She was also hungry, she realized.

"I should get going," she said, looking around the bathroom for a towel or a robe to wrap herself in. She still didn't feel comfortable being naked in front of him.

"Why?" he asked lazily, moving his muscular back to take better advantage of the jets. "You already missed your class and you don't have anything on Wednesdays."

Apparently, he knew her class schedule by heart.

Mia shrugged, no longer surprised by anything. "I'm hungry, and I want to go home," she said, telling the truth.

He grinned at her, looking happy for some reason. "I'll make you something to eat. Why don't you relax here some more, and I'll come get you when the food is ready."

She nodded, deciding not to argue at the memory of the delicious meal he'd made before.

Still smiling, Korum rose and stepped out of the tub, water streaming down his golden skin and well-defined muscles. Despite everything that happened, Mia felt a spark of arousal at the sight of him fully naked. His back was broad and muscular, and his hips were narrow. His ass was the best she'd ever seen on a man, tight with muscle, and his legs looked powerful. She wondered if Ks needed to work out to maintain their looks and resolved to ask him at some point later.

"Like what you see?" he asked with a sly smile, obviously noticing her scrutiny.

Mia blushed a little and then told herself not to be a ninny. "Sure," she said with a straight face. "You're very pretty, like a male Barbie doll."

Far from offended, he laughed with genuine amusement. "Not like Ken, I hope. Isn't he missing the requisite equipment?"

Mia just shrugged in response, not wanting to get into this kind of banter with him right now. Grinning, he exited the room, leaving her alone to enjoy the jacuzzi for the next twenty minutes.

By the time he came back, Mia was already showered and wrapped in the familiar robe she'd discovered in the bathroom closet. She even found the slippers she'd worn before and gladly put them on. Showering here was becoming a habit.

She accompanied Korum to the kitchen, her mouth watering at the delicious smells emanating from there. He had made another one of his signature salads and a dish of roasted buckwheat with stir-fried carrots and mushrooms. Feeling like she was starving, Mia attacked her food with appreciation, and so did he. For a while, the kitchen was silent, except for chewing noises and the clattering of their silverware. Finally feeling replete, Mia leaned back in her chair. He was done with his portion, as usual, and was observing her with a half-smile.

"What?" asked Mia self-consciously, wondering if she had a bit of lettuce stuck between her teeth.

"Nothing," he said, and his smile got wider. "I just love watching you eat. You do it with such enthusiasm—it's very endearing."

Mia flushed a little. He obviously thought she was a glutton. Shrugging her shoulders, she said, "Yeah, what can I say? I really like food."

He grinned. "I know. I really like that about you. Very unexpected in a girl your size."

Mia smiled back tentatively and got up from her chair. Now was as good a time as any. "Okay, well, thank you for the meal. I'll just change and get out of your hair."

The smile left his face. He clearly didn't like hearing that. "Why don't you stay?" he suggested softly. "I promise not to touch you again today, if that's what worries you."

Mia swallowed, suddenly feeling on edge. "I really have to get going," she said, hoping that she was misreading his body language—that he didn't really have the intention of keeping her there against her will.

He looked directly into her eyes. Whatever he had seen there seemed to make up his mind. "Okay," he said slowly. "You can go home." Mia's breath escaped in relief—prematurely, as it turned out. Because he added next, "But I want you to come back here tonight. Gather whatever you need for the next day or two—or I can buy you new things if you prefer—and come back here by 7 p.m. I'll make us dinner."

Mia stared at him. "And if I don't?" she asked defiantly.

"Then I will come and get you," he answered, the look in his eyes leaving no doubt of his seriousness.

"But why?" Mia burst out in frustration. "Why do you want to be with someone who doesn't want you? Who hates you, in fact? Surely, there can't be a shortage of willing women for you. You've already gotten what you wanted from me. Can't you move on to another victim?"

His eyes narrowed in anger. "Well, Mia, you're right. There is no shortage of women who would love to be in your shoes, and I could easily get myself another 'victim,' as you so nicely put it." He took a step toward her. "The reason why I want you—as unwilling as you pretend to be—is because chemistry like ours is very rare. You're very young, even for a human, so you don't realize what we have. Do you honestly think that sex would be like that for you with another man? Or that just any woman could have that kind of effect on me?" He paused and continued in a softer tone, "This kind of attraction happens once in a blue moon, and I know better than to give up on it even if you're running scared right now." Staring into her shocked face, he added with a familiar golden gleam in his eyes, "I know this is all very new to you, and that you probably felt more pain than enjoyment today. It won't be like that again. The next time you're in my bed, I promise that your only screams will be those of pleasure."

CHAPTER SIX

Mia left his apartment and walked home, her thoughts whirling in chaos. She was no longer a virgin, and she had the residual soreness between her thighs to prove it. His gel thingy had helped with the majority of the pain, but she could still feel echoes of his fullness inside her. Her sex clenched slightly at the memory of the orgasms he'd given her, and she shivered with the intensity of her recollection. And he wanted to see her again, tonight. In fact, it sounded like he had no intention of dropping his pursuit—in complete disregard of her wishes.

At that thought, Mia got angry again. He had no right to do this to her. His species may have guided human evolution, but that didn't mean he owned her. Whatever special chemistry he thought they had did not excuse his behavior, and Mia hated the idea that he thought he could have her whenever he wanted. She wished there was something she could do to thwart him, but her own response to him had made a mockery of any resistance.

It was a long walk back to her apartment, but Mia wanted to stretch her legs and clear her head before potentially seeing her roommate. By the time she got to her building, she was sufficiently tired that going up five flights of stairs seemed like a chore. She was looking forward to plopping down on the couch and doing something totally brainless—like watching a show on her laptop.

This was not her day, however. Jessie had guests, Mia realized as she opened the door and heard masculine voices in the living room. Walking in, she was surprised to see two men she'd never met before.

One of them—an Asian guy—looked to be somewhere in his mid-twenties, while the other had to be at least thirty. The older guy caught her attention immediately. There was something about the way he sat on the couch that gave her the impression of a coiled spring. His hair was blond, and his ice-blue eyes were extraordinarily watchful. He looked to be of medium height and lean, maybe even a bit on the skinny side.

At Mia's entrance, they both got up. Jessie remained sitting, looking pale and strangely guilty. "Hi, Mia," she said with some hesitation. "This is my cousin Jason and his friend John."

Mia's eyebrows rose. "The Jason we mentioned this morning?" she asked in confusion.

The Asian guy nodded. "The one and only."

"Oh, hi . . . nice to meet you," Mia said politely, trying to connect the dots.

"They're here to talk to you," Jessie said, and Mia realized why she looked so guilty.

"Are you guys, like, the Resistance or something?" she asked incredulously. At their non-response, she drew her own conclusion. "Look, I don't know what Jessie told you, but we really don't have anything to talk about—"

"On the contrary, Miss Stalis," John said, speaking for the first time in a slightly raspy voice, "we have a lot to discuss. Jason—why don't you catch up with your cousin while Miss Stalis and I conclude our discussion?"

Seeing Mia's response in the stormy expression gathering on her face, Jessie gave her a pleading look. "Please, Mia, I know you're mad at me, but I really think they can help you. Just hear them out, okay? Jason said they can give you some good tips on how to handle this situation—that's why they're here."

Mia sighed heavily and bit out, "Fine." Apparently, her relaxing afternoon at home was not to be.

"When does he want to see you again?" John asked quietly.

Mia blinked in surprise. "Uh—tonight at seven."

"Okay," he said, "that gives us enough time to bring you up to speed. Tell me—have you been shined?"

"Shined?"

"Did he use any kind of alien device on you that shined a reddish light on any part of your body where the skin was broken?"

Mia stared at him in shock. "How do you know about that?"

Taking that as an affirmative, he said, "You can't leave the apartment then. Jason—why don't you take your cousin to see a movie while Miss

Stalis and I talk here?"

Jason nodded and left with Jessie in tow, although Mia could see that her roommate was just dying with curiosity.

When they were alone, Mia asked angrily, "What do you mean, I can't leave the apartment?"

"You have been shined. He basically branded you—you now have little nano machines embedded in whatever part of your body has been shined on. They transmit your location to him at all times. If you were to do something he doesn't expect, such as leaving your apartment when he thinks you should be home, he would know immediately—and it could make him suspicious."

Mia looked at her palms in horror. "You mean, when he healed my scrapes, he was really putting a tracking device inside me? Why would he do this?" She raised her head with suspicion. "And how do you know all this?"

"Miss Stalis—" he said wearily.

"Please call me Mia," she interrupted.

"—okay, Mia," he agreeably repeated, "we have been fighting the Krinar for a very long time. Don't you think we would've learned a lot about our enemy in the process?"

"Okay," Mia said slowly, "let's say I believe you. Why would he do this? Brand me like that?"

"To know your whereabouts at all times, of course. It's standard operating procedure for them."

Mia stared at him with shock. "Well then, what can you do to help me?"

"We can't help you, Mia," John said bluntly. "But you can help us."

Mia inhaled sharply. She was afraid it might be something like this. "I think you've been misinformed. I don't want to get involved with your cause in any way, shape, or form. You can't win, and the last thing we need is to return to the days of the Great Panic. I just want to be left alone—by Korum, by you, and by everyone else—and if you can't help me with that, then you should just get out." She pointed at the door.

"You are already involved, Mia, whether you like it or not. Do you know who your K lover is?"

"He's not my lover!" Mia said sharply.

"You haven't slept with him?" Seeing the color flooding her face, he said, "That's what I thought. I'm sure he wasted no time taking exactly what he wanted from you, just like they took our planet."

Mia fought her embarrassment. "What do you mean, do I know who he is?"

"Did he tell you anything about himself? Do you know why he's here, in New York? How the Ks ended up coming to Earth in general?"

Mia nodded slowly. "He said that he's an engineer, that the company he works for made the ships that brought them here to Earth."

"An engineer? That's rich." John let out a humorless chuckle. "He's one of the most powerful Ks on this planet, Mia. He owns the ships that brought them here—his company, in fact, has been the driving force behind them settling on Earth."

Seeing the look of sheer disbelief on her face, he added, "He's part of their ruling council—some even say he runs the council. His company provides everything for their Centers. Without him, there would be no K Centers and no Krinar on Earth."

"I don't understand," Mia said in confusion. "If he's all that, then why is he here? And what does he want with me?"

"He's here because, for the first time since K-Day, we actually stand a chance against them." John's eyes glittered with excitement. "Because he knows that we're very close to being able to give them a fair fight. Because he wants to stamp out the Resistance before we go any further."

He took a deep breath. "As to what he wants with you, it's pretty obvious. Do you know what a charl is?"

Mia shook her head, feeling overwhelmed.

"The literal translation of charl is *one who pleases*. It's the term they use for the human slaves they keep in their settlements. The purpose of the charl is to provide Ks with pleasure. As you may or may not know yet, they enjoy drinking blood during sex. So they keep us as captives, locked up in their high-tech cages, and use us whichever way they want."

Mia felt hot bile rising in her throat. "You're lying. Why would they do this? We're intelligent beings."

"They don't necessarily think of us that way. Most of them regard us as pets that they bred explicitly for this purpose—little better than the primates they'd hunted into extinction on their planet."

"So what are you saying? That Korum wants to keep me as a slave?" Mia asked incredulously. "That's bullshit. If he wanted to keep me locked up, I wouldn't be here, now would I?"

He sighed. "Mia, I don't know exactly what game he's playing with you. Maybe he finds it fun to give you the illusion of freedom for now. It's not real—you understand that, right? If you tried to leave New York instead of staying here and going to him whenever he wants, I don't know what he would do, whether your family would ever see you again.

You're a smart girl. You sensed that, right? That's why you haven't been exactly avoiding him. That's why your roommate was so scared for you, why she came running to Jason even though they haven't spoken in three years—because she said you were in way over your head."

Mia wanted to throw up. If John was telling the truth, then her situation was far worse than she'd imagined. He was right; her subconscious must have realized the danger of running from Korum because she had never seriously contemplated leaving town. Her brain buzzed with a million questions, even as a hopeless pit of despair grew in her stomach.

"So what do you want from me?" she asked bitterly. "Did you come all the way here to tell me that I'm screwed? That I'm going to end up as an alien's pet, locked up somewhere and used for sex? Is that what you're here to say?"

"Yes, Mia," John answered calmly, his expression oddly flat. "There are no good options for you. If he gets tired of you, then you might be able to resume your life—particularly if you're still in New York at that time. Of course, you might also catch the attention of some other K and never be seen again. That's what happened to my sister—that's why I'm doing what I'm doing, so that other innocent young women can have a normal life."

Mia looked at him in horror. "Your sister? What happened to her?"

His mouth twisted bitterly. "What happened is I gave her a trip to Mexico as a college graduation present. She went with her girlfriends and met a handsome stranger on the beach. Turns out, he wasn't exactly human . . . The night before they were supposed to return home, Dana disappeared from her room. For the longest time, we had no idea what happened—just suspicions that the K was somehow involved. That's why I started fighting the Ks, to avenge my sister. It wasn't until a year ago that I learned she's still alive and is being held as a charl in the Costa Rican K Center."

Mia's eyes welled up with tears as she pictured his family's suffering. "Oh my God, I'm so sorry," she said. "Is there any way you can get her back?"

"No." He shook his head with angry regret. "Even if we succeeded in rescuing her from there—an impossibility in and of itself—she's been shined, like all charl. They will always know her exact whereabouts—there's no way we can reverse that procedure."

"Shined," Mia said. "Like all charl—like me."

"Like you," John agreed.

She wanted to scream and cry and throw things. She settled for asking, "So why did you come here today?"

"Because, Mia, although we can't really help you, you are actually in a position to help us. If we succeed, not only will you get your life back, but you will also have saved countless other young women—and men—from my sister's fate."

"I don't understand . . . What are you asking me?" Mia said slowly, her pulse picking up.

"We want you to work with us. To notify us of Korum's whereabouts, what he likes to eat, how he sleeps, any weaknesses that he might have. And if you happen to come across any information that might be even remotely useful—any passwords, security measures, anything at all—to convey that information to us."

"You're asking me to spy for you?" Mia's voice rose incredulously.

"I'm asking you to make the best of your admittedly unfortunate situation. To help yourself and all of humanity. All you have to do is keep your eyes and ears open when you're with him and occasionally report your findings to us."

"And you think I will be able to pull this off? With no training of any kind and no acting skills? Somehow fool one of the most powerful Ks on this planet? What makes you think he's not already aware that you're here, particularly if his goal is to crush your movement?"

"This apartment is not bugged—we checked. He would have no reason to spy on you here if you don't do anything suspicious and continue to play along. He doesn't know that we're here—if he did, we'd already be dead. Look, we're not asking you to be James Bond or some kind of femme fatale. You don't need to try to get close to him or seduce him or anything like that—just continue your relationship with him, such as it is, and occasionally give us information."

"How? And what would that accomplish anyway? What makes you think you have a chance in hell when all the governments in the world with their nuclear weapons were completely helpless in the invasion?" The whole thing was insane, and Mia had no intention of becoming a martyr in the name of some hopeless cause.

"The how—leave that up to us. If he still gives you a similar degree of freedom, it will definitely be much easier. If not, then it gets more complicated, but we have our ways." He paused for a second, apparently debating the wisdom of his next words. "As to why we think we can win, let's just say that not all Ks are the same. They don't all share the same beliefs about human inferiority. I can't tell you more without putting you in danger, but rest assured—we have some powerful allies."

Human allies among the Ks? The implications of that were mind-boggling.

"I don't know," Mia said, trying to think it through. "What if he catches on? What will happen to me then?"

He said truthfully, "I don't know. He may choose to have you killed or punished in some other way. I honestly don't know."

Mia let out a short bitter laugh. "And you don't care, right?"

John sighed. "I do, Mia. More than anything, I wish that things were different. That I wasn't asking you to do this, that the only thing you had to worry about were your midterms. But we don't live in that kind of world anymore. If we are to regain our freedom, we have to risk everything. You are our best chance to get close to Korum. You can really make a difference, Mia."

Mia walked over to the table and sat down, closing her eyes for a minute so she could think. She had no reason to trust John, and she had no idea if anything he had told her was the truth. Still, she was somehow inclined to believe him. There was too much pain in his voice when he talked about his sister; he was either the best actor in the world, or the Ks really were abducting and enslaving humans who caught their eye. The way she had inadvertently caught Korum's.

Another question occurred to her. Opening her eyes, she asked, "What if Korum knows that Jason is Jessie's cousin, and he is already suspicious of me?"

John shrugged. "It's a possibility, of course. But Jason is Jessie's third cousin, so the connection is very distant. Also, he's a nobody in our operation—he has barely been involved in the last two years. He only came to me today because Jessie had called him about you. We can't completely rule out this possibility, but the odds are in our favor. Also, don't forget—Korum is the one who has been pursuing you, not the other way around, so he really has no reason to suspect anything."

"All right," said Mia, "let's pretend for a second that I do decide to spy for you. How do you expect me to go to him tonight, knowing everything you've just told me, and act like nothing has changed? He's thousands of years old—he can read me like an open book. I don't stand a chance."

"I don't know, Mia. At this point, you know him far better than we do. I know you've never been tested like this, but I believe in you. Your biggest advantage may simply be the fact that he likely underestimates your intelligence. As long as you're just his charl, he may not see you as a threat."

Mia had finally had enough. She stood up, a feeling of exhaustion washing over her.

"John," she said wearily, "I understand what you're trying to do, and I do sympathize with your cause. I can't promise you anything. I will not put my life in danger to report to you on Korum's whereabouts and what he had for dinner. But if I do happen to come across any information that could be material, I will do my best to get it to you."

He nodded. "That's fair, Mia. If you need to get in touch with us, just talk to Jessie—or if that's not possible, send her an email with 'Hi' in the subject line—we'll be monitoring her account. That way, if he decides to keep tabs on your email—which he probably will—he won't get suspicious. You'll just be saying hi to your roommate."

Mia nodded in agreement, wanting nothing more than to be alone. Her head was pounding with a brutal headache, and she gladly locked the door behind John as soon as he left.

Making her way to her room, she collapsed on the bed.

She felt sick, her stomach churning from John's revelations. It just couldn't be true—she didn't want to believe it. Yes, Korum did seem to ride roughshod over her objections, and he really hadn't given her much choice in their relationship thus far. But to actually keep her as a very real sex slave? To take away all her freedom and keep her locked up somewhere within a K Center? If the existence of the charl was anything more than a figment of John's imagination—and Korum intended to make her one—then he was definitely the monster that she'd accused him of being.

Mia felt nauseous at the thought that she would see him tonight and feel his touch on her body. And probably respond to it, as though he were really her lover. That last part made her want to throw up again. How could her body want him when he didn't even regard her as a person with basic human—or rather, intelligent being's—rights?

She was also terrified about spying on him. If she got caught, she was sure that she would probably be killed—perhaps even tortured first, for information. Anyone who kept slaves likely wouldn't blink at torture.

She shuddered.

In fact, if he found out about her conversation with John today, she might be doomed.

She tried to imagine him intentionally inflicting pain on her. For some reason, it was difficult. For the most part, he had been very gentle with her. Even her loss of virginity this morning—as traumatic as that had been—could have been much worse if he hadn't tried to control himself. In fact, some of his actions were almost caring—feeding her, making sure she was warm and dry, healing her (well, maybe not that one, given what she'd just learned)—and that hardly jived with the villainous image John had painted for her. Then again, she wouldn't want to hurt a kitten either, but would have no problem keeping said kitten locked up in her house. If that was truly how he saw her—as a cute pet that he just happened to want to fuck—then his behavior made perfect sense.

Mia tried not to think about the implications of it all, but it was impossible. Her future had always seemed so bright, and she had enjoyed thinking about it, planning out the next few years of her life. And now she had no idea what the next few weeks would hold—whether she would even be alive, much less still attending NYU.

The thought that she might end up as Korum's charl in an alien settlement was devastating, especially if she started thinking of her family's reaction to her disappearance. Would he at least let her tell them that she was alive, or would she vanish without a trace?

A wave of self-pity washing over her, Mia felt the hot prickle of tears behind her eyelids. Unable to contain her battered emotions any longer, she buried her face in her pillow and sobbed at the bitter unfairness of it all—until her eyes were red and swollen and she couldn't squeeze out another tear.

Then she got up, washed her face, and began to pack her things for tonight as per Korum's suggestion.

* * *

At 6:45 p.m. she took the subway down to TriBeCa and entered Korum's building at 6:59. Mentally patting herself on the back, Mia thought that she made quite a punctual spy.

He greeted her with a slow sensuous smile, looking as gorgeous as ever in a pair of light blue jeans and a plain white T-shirt. Even after John's revelations, Mia's heart skipped a beat at the sight. Her inner muscles clenched, and she felt herself starting to get wet. His smile got wider, exposing that damnable dimple. He could obviously sense her arousal.

Mia cursed her body. It had gotten conditioned to respond to him, despite everything. Then again, if she was literally sleeping with the enemy, she figured she might as well enjoy it. Now that she knew the truth about his kind and his probable intentions toward her, she was fairly certain that she could keep her emotions in check, no matter how many screaming orgasms he gave her.

The dinner that he prepared was outstanding as usual. Tender roasted potatoes with wild mushrooms, dill, and caramelized onions were the main course, preceded by an appetizer of spinach salad with poached pears. The dessert was a platter of fresh fruit, cut in various unique shapes, with a sweet walnut dip. The entire meal was served by candlelight. If she didn't know better, she would have thought he was wooing her with a romantic dinner. The more likely explanation was that he simply enjoyed great food in a beautiful setting, and she was the beneficiary of that.

Still, this hardly fit with the evil overlord image John had painted.

Despite Mia's initial concern, she found it easy to act naturally with him—perhaps because she didn't have to pretend to like him or be calm in his presence. He knew her feelings toward him perfectly well from this morning, and he wouldn't expect her to be anything but nervous, snarky, and reluctantly turned on—all of which Mia genuinely was.

Dinner flew by, dominated by light banter—she learned that he really enjoyed American movies from the early twenty-first century—and delicious food. As the meal drew to a close, Mia's anxiety levels began to rise at the thought of what awaited her later in the evening. Despite the gel he'd used on her, she still felt a slight discomfort deep inside and was not looking forward to experiencing sex again any time soon—even if, theoretically, it would hurt less the second time. She doubted that it could ever be completely pain-free, given the size of his cock and her own supposedly unusual narrowness. Still, her body did not appear to care as warm moisture gathered between her legs in anticipation.

After dinner was over, Mia helped Korum clean up, stacking the dishes in the dishwasher and wiping the table. It was a disconcertingly domestic task—something that she might have done with a boyfriend or husband in the future—and it made her even more aware of the strange turn her life had taken. It was difficult to believe that just four days ago, she was dreading her Sociology paper and worrying that her dating life was in the dumps. And now she was trying not to get caught spying on a two-thousand-year-old extraterrestrial who likely wanted to keep her as a sex slave.

Once the clean-up was done, Korum led her to the bedroom.

At this point, Mia felt like a nervous wreck, fear and desire fighting with each other in her stomach. Noticing her obvious apprehension, he said, "No intercourse tonight, I promise. I know you're still sore."

Mia's anxiety ratcheted up another notch. What exactly did he intend to do if intercourse was out of the question?

They entered the bedroom, and he led her to the familiar circular bed, now covered with a fresh set of blue and ivory sheets. The room was lit with a soft yellow light, and some kind of sensuous music was playing in the background. Sitting down on the bed, he pulled her closer to him until she stood between his open legs. In this position, Mia was nearly at his eye level. Trembling slightly, she stood still and tried not to look at him as he pulled her shirt over her head, revealing a plain white bra that she had remembered to wear this time. "You're so beautiful," he murmured, holding her gently by her sides while studying the body revealed to him thus far. Inexplicably, Mia blushed, her insecure inner teenager absurdly pleased at the compliment.

Bending toward her, he pressed a warm kiss to the sensitive spot where her neck met her shoulder. Mia shivered from the sensation, goosebumps appearing all over her body. Apparently pleased with the reaction, he did it again, and then lightly blew cool air on the damp spot his mouth left behind. Mia gasped, her nipples hardening from the pleasurable chill. He smiled, eyes gleaming with gold. "Still no mouth-to-mouth?" he asked softly, and Mia shrugged, remembering what happened the last time she set that condition.

Interpreting that as consent, he brought her toward him, burying one hand in her hair and keeping the other on the small of her back. Putting her own hands on his clothed shoulders, Mia closed her eyes and felt him press small butterfly-light kisses on her cheeks, forehead, and closed lids. By the time his soft lips reached her mouth, she was nearly squirming with anticipation.

At first, he kissed her very lightly, just brushing her mouth with his. Then he began gently nibbling on her lips, carefully teasing the rim with his tongue. She moaned, her body pressing closer to his, and he pushed his tongue into her mouth, penetrating it in an obvious imitation of the sexual act. A rush of moisture inundated her already wet sex as he alternated fucking her mouth with his tongue and lightly sucking on her swollen and sensitive lips.

Lost in the sensations, Mia only vaguely registered his unfastening of her bra. Tearing his mouth away from hers, he kissed her ear, sucking carefully on her earlobe. She arched with pleasure, knees buckling and head falling back, and he took advantage, licking and sucking his way down the delicate column of her throat and the collarbone region until his hot mouth reached the small white globes of her breasts. "So pretty," he whispered, before pulling one pink nipple into his mouth and scraping it softly with his teeth. Mia cried out, her clit throbbing on the verge of orgasm, and he gave her other breast the same treatment, holding her tightly as she writhed in his arms, maddeningly close to finding relief. He held her like that, pausing for a few seconds until the sensation waned a bit, and then lifted her astride one of his bent legs, grinding her jean-clad pussy firmly against his knee and swallowing her scream with his mouth as the long-awaited climax rushed powerfully through her body.

Collapsing bonelessly against him, Mia felt her inner muscles pulsing with little aftershocks. Without waiting for her to recover, Korum got up, lifting her in his arms, and lowered her onto the bed. Stripping off his own clothes with a speed that made her blink, he climbed over her, unzipped her jeans, and pulled them off together with her panties.

Lying there completely naked, Mia was unpleasantly reminded of the pain that followed the last time she was in this position. However, despite the large cock jutting aggressively at her, all he did was gently kiss his way down her body, starting with the sensitive spot near her shoulder and ending near her lower belly. She tensed in anticipation, and he did not disappoint. Pulling open her legs with strong hands, he bent his head and gently licked her folds, avoiding direct contact with the clitoris. Mia was surprised to feel herself getting turned on again, just minutes after her last orgasm. One long finger slowly entered her opening, pressing carefully on some sensitive spot deep inside, while his tongue flicked over her nub in an accelerating rhythm. There was no slow build-up this time; instead, her body simply spasmed around his finger, releasing the tension that had managed to coil inside her in a matter of seconds.

Stunned, Mia lay there. At some point, she must have grabbed his head because her fingers were buried in his short glossy strands. Feeling irrationally embarrassed, she let go, pulling her hands away. He slowly took his finger out, making her sex clench with a residual tremor, and licked it while looking up at her. Mia nearly moaned again.

He sat up, still maintaining eye contact with her. Mia realized that he was still extremely hard, not having come yet. She licked her lips nervously, wondering what he intended. His eyes hungrily followed her tongue, and she suddenly knew what he wanted her to do.

Sitting up herself, Mia cautiously extended her hand and gently brushed against his shaft with her fingers, feeling its smooth hardness. To her surprise, it jumped in her hand, as though alive. Mia's eyes flew up to

Korum's face, and what she saw there was reassuring. He looked like he was in pain, eyes tightly shut and sweat beading up near his temples. Feeling her pause, he opened his eyes and hoarsely whispered, "Go ahead."

Emboldened, Mia wrapped her fingers around his cock and slowly stroked it in an up-and-down motion, the way she'd seen it done in porn. Her hand looked white and small wrapped around his thickness, and she wondered how it had ever fit inside her. He groaned at her action, his whole body tensing, and Mia suddenly felt very empowered. To know that she had this effect on him, that this formidable creature was at the mercy of her touch—somehow that went a long way toward restoring the balance of power in a relationship that had been very one-sided thus far.

Deciding to take things further, she got on her knees and bent over him. Her dark curls brushing against his thighs, she tentatively licked the engorged head. He hissed, thrusting his hips toward her, and she smiled, reveling in her ability to control him like this. Holding his shaft with one hand, she cupped his heavy balls with the other hand and squeezed gently, exploring the unfamiliar part with curiosity. "Mia..." he groaned, and she smiled, pleased. She wanted to wring an even stronger response from his body, the way he had from hers. Still holding his balls, she carefully wrapped her lips around the tip of his cock and swirled her tongue around it inside her mouth while moving her other hand on his shaft in a rhythmic motion. He let out a hoarse cry, his hips bucking, and she felt a warm, slightly salty liquid spurting out into her mouth. Surprised and delighted, Mia let him go, watching as the rest of the thick cream-colored fluid landed on his bronzed stomach. There was a strange taste in her mouth—not unpleasant—and she wondered briefly if there were differences between K and human semen. His cock was still twitching slightly before her eyes, even as it began to diminish in size.

Looking up, Mia found him staring at her with a smile. "Have you ever done this before?" he asked, motioning toward his sex.

Mia shook her head in response. For some weird reason, she had never wanted to go past a few kisses with any of the guys she'd dated in the past.

"Well, then, you're a natural," he said, his smile getting even wider. Reaching somewhere under the bed, he pulled out a box of tissues and used one to wipe his stomach. Mia blinked, wondering what else he kept under there. After cleaning himself, he got up and walked to the door completely naked. "Shower?" he asked, and Mia gladly agreed, following him to the bathroom.

They got into the giant shower stall together, and Korum set the water controls to have warm water raining at them from all directions. Pouring shampoo into his hand, he massaged it into her hair, washing it with experienced movements. Eyes closed, Mia just stood there, enjoying the feel of his fingers on her scalp and the water pouring over her sensitized skin. Afterwards, he washed her entire body, making her blush with his thoroughness. Feeling slightly shy, Mia tentatively reciprocated, rubbing soap all over his golden skin and powerful muscles. He unashamedly took pleasure in her touch, arching into it like a big cat getting stroked.

When they were done, he dried her body with a thick towel and then toweled off himself. Relaxed from the warm water and the two orgasms, Mia felt a wave of drowsiness washing over her. Noticing her barely stifled yawn, Korum picked her up and carried her back to bed. Putting her in the middle, he pulled a soft blanket toward them and lay down next to her, hugging her from the back. Feeling oddly comforted by the feel of his large body curving around her own, Mia closed her eyes and fell asleep easily for the first time since her world got turned upside down by the extraterrestrial lying next to her.

CHAPTER SEVEN

Streaming sunlight woke up Mia the next morning.

Keeping her eyes closed against the brightness, Mia thought with a minor annoyance that she must've forgotten to close the blinds last night. It didn't matter, though; she felt well-rested and extremely comfortable. *Perhaps too comfortable?* At the sudden realization that the bed she was lying on was much too soft to be her own IKEA mattress, Mia jackknifed to a sitting position and stared in shock at her surroundings. Memories of yesterday rushed into her brain, and she recognized where she was.

She was also completely naked and alone.

Pulling the blanket up to her chest, Mia warily surveyed the room. She was sitting in the middle of the giant round bed—she guesstimated it had to be at least fifteen feet in diameter—in Korum's beautifully decorated bedroom. A few potted plants were thriving near the large window that looked out over the Hudson River.

Noticing the robe and slippers that Korum must have left for her, she put them on and went in search of the restroom. Surprisingly, there wasn't one connected to the bedroom. Peeking out into the hallway, Mia spotted the bathroom door. She made a quick beeline for it, not wanting Korum to know that she was awake yet.

After taking care of business, Mia gratefully brushed her teeth with the toothbrush that he left for her and washed her face. Staring into the bedroom mirror, she was surprised to see that she actually looked quite well. Her pale skin was almost radiant, and her eyes looked unusually bright. Even her hair—the bane of her existence—seemed silkier, with dark brown curls glossy and nicely defined. Whatever shampoo he had used on her yesterday clearly worked miracles. As did orgasms, apparently.

Mia wondered where her clothes were. Her tummy rumbled, reminding her that the dinner last night was already in the distant past. Still wearing the robe, she decided to go in search of food.

Entering the living room, Mia heard voices coming from somewhere to her left.

Thinking that Korum might be watching TV, she headed in that direction. The voices got louder, and she realized that they were speaking in a foreign language she'd never heard before. Slightly guttural, it nonetheless flowed smoothly, unlike anything she was familiar with.

Mia's breath caught.

She had to be listening to the Krinar language—which meant that Korum likely had visitors, and there were other Ks in the house. This might be her chance to learn something useful, she realized even as her heart skipped a beat.

Quietly approaching the room, she was startled when the heavy doors abruptly slid open in front of her, revealing its occupants and exposing her to their eyes.

Korum and two other Ks stood around a large table that had some kind of a three-dimensional image displayed on it. At the sight of her, Korum waved his hand and the image vanished, leaving only a smooth wooden surface.

Mia froze as three pairs of alien eyes examined her.

The expression on Korum's face was cold and distant, unlike anything she'd seen before. The other male K, about Korum's height, had brown hair and hazel eyes, with a similarly golden skin tone. The female was a bit lighter-skinned, closer to Jessie's color, and the silky hair streaming down to her waist was an unusual shade of dark red. Her eyes were nearly black and looked enormous in her strikingly beautiful face. She was also tall, probably close to 5'9", and wore a dress that looked like it had been poured on her curves. She could have easily stepped off the pages of an old Victoria's Secret catalogue—if they had first air-brushed the image, of course.

Standing there in her bath robe, Mia felt like a naughty child getting caught stealing from a cookie jar.

There was no help for it. She cleared her throat, heart pounding in her chest. "Um, hi. I was just looking for the kitchen—"

A small smile appeared on Korum's face, warming up his features, and his distant look vanished. "Of course," he said, "you must be hungry."

He turned toward his visitors. "Mia, these are my . . . colleagues," he said, seeming to hesitate slightly at the last word, "Leeta and Rezav."

"It's nice to meet you," Mia said politely, eyeing them with caution.

She had a strong impression that those two were not happy to see her. Leeta stared back, her beautiful mouth pinched with dislike. Rezav was a bit friendlier, curving his lips in a half-smile and inclining his head graciously toward her. Speaking to Korum, he asked him something in their language, to which Korum absently nodded in response.

"Okay, well, I didn't mean to intrude," Mia apologized, her pulse roaring in her ears. "I'll leave you to your work."

Korum gestured toward the kitchen. "Feel free to grab some fruit or whatever you wish. I'll join you soon."

With a muttered thanks, Mia escaped as fast as her shaking legs could carry her.

Entering the kitchen, she sank down on one of the chairs, hugging herself protectively. Her head spun in a sickening manner, and her stomach churned with nausea.

Because in Rezav's question, spoken entirely in Krinar, Mia had caught one familiar word: *charl.*

* * *

By the time Korum came to the kitchen, Mia had managed to compose herself.

At his entrance, she gave him a small smile and continued eating her blueberries as though she had not a care in the world—as though she had not just heard him confirm her worst fears.

He came toward her and bent down, thoroughly kissing her mouth. For the first time, Mia simply endured his touch, the bile in her stomach too strong to allow her normal sexual response.

She didn't know why she'd needed this confirmation. For the most part, she had believed John when he'd told her about the Ks and their atavistic approach to human rights. Yet some small part of her must have been clinging to the hope that John was mistaken—that Korum would feel differently about her, that she was somehow special in his eyes.

To hear him admit that she was his glorified sex slave—his human pet—was like being punched repeatedly in the stomach.

If he had treated her with cruelty from the very beginning, it would have been easy to hate him. Instead, his arrogance toward her was often tempered with tenderness—and that made the whole thing so much worse. Despite her better judgment and common sense, he had succeeded in getting under her skin, and today's revelation felt like the cruelest of betrayals.

Sensing her lack of response, he pulled away and frowned slightly. "What's the matter?" he asked, perplexed. "Are you feeling all right?"

Mia's brain worked quickly. It would be dangerous for her—and for the Resistance—if he knew she had understood Rezav's question. However, she couldn't hide the fact that she was upset—Korum was too astute for that. Suddenly, a risky but brilliant idea came to her.

"I'm fine," she said with quiet dignity, obviously lying.

"Uh-huh," Korum said sarcastically, "sure you are."

Sitting down next to her, he lifted her chin toward him so he could look into her eyes. "Now tell me again what's going on."

Mia felt a furious tear escape. "Nothing," she told him angrily.

"Mia," he said her name in that special tone he reserved for intimidating her. "Stop lying to me."

Staring directly into his beautiful eyes, Mia channeled all of her frustrated fury and irrational feelings of betrayal into her next words. "How often do you fuck her?" she threw at him, summoning up remembered feelings of jealousy at his familiarity with Ashley the hostess. "In general, how many women do you go through in any given day? Two, three, a dozen?"

At the surprised look on his face, she continued, injecting as much bitterness into her tone as possible, "Why are you even forcing me to be here if you have her? And Ashley, and God knows how many others?"

Still holding her chin with his fingers, Korum said slowly, "Are you talking about Leeta? You think we're somehow involved?"

Mia allowed another tear to slide down her face. "Aren't you?"

He shook his head. "No. In fact, we're actually distant cousins, so that would be an impossibility."

"Oh," Mia said, pretending to be embarrassed about her outburst. She tried to pull away, and he let her go, watching as she got up and walked over to the window, carelessly wiping her face with the robe sleeve.

Mia stood there, looking out over the Hudson. Some stupidly romantic part of her was foolishly glad to hear about Leeta, even though her little jealousy act had been designed to throw him off track. She didn't say anything when he came up to her, embracing her from behind. He didn't make any promises or offer any other clarifications, Mia noticed. Of course, why should he try to reassure her, to convince her that she meant something special to him when she clearly didn't? She wouldn't have been particularly concerned about her dog's feelings either.

"I'm thinking of going for a walk in the park," he murmured, still holding her close. "Would you like to come with me?"

She was to be given a choice? What would happen if she said no? "I don't know," she said. "I have some studying that needs to get done, and I wanted to catch up with my parents. Wednesday is usually our day to Skype . . ."

She couldn't see his expression, and she was glad about that. Now he would show his true colors, she thought.

"Okay," he said, "that sounds good."

Mia blinked, surprised. Then he continued, "For tonight, I made us a reservation at Le Bernardin at 7 p.m. I'll pick you up at 6:30. Since you don't seem to have any nice clothes, I'll have something appropriate sent to your apartment."

Now that was the dictator she knew—and now truly hated.

"I don't need any clothes," Mia protested. "I have better dresses. I just didn't wear them that time."

Turning her around in his arms, he looked down and smiled. "Mia, no offense, but I haven't seen you wear a single piece of clothing that was in any way flattering. You're a very pretty girl, but your clothes make you look like a ten-year-old boy most of the time. I think it's safe to say that dressing nicely is not one of your strengths."

Mia flushed with anger and embarrassment, but decided to hold her tongue. If he wanted to dress her up like a doll, then let him. It was hardly the worst thing he would likely do to her, anyway.

At the mutinous expression on her face, his smile got wider and his eyes gleamed with gold. Lifting her by the waist, he brought her up toward him and kissed her again. His lips were softly searching on hers, and his tongue stroked the recesses of her mouth with such expertise that Mia felt a spark of desire kindling again. Relieved that she no longer had to act, she looped her arms around his neck, let her mind go blank, and focused on the sensations. Her body, already so used to his touch, reacted with animal instinct, and she kissed him back with all the passion she could muster.

At her response, he groaned and pressed her closer to him, grinding his hips against her and letting her feel the hard bulge that had developed in his pants. Mia's insides clenched, and she found herself rubbing against his body like a cat in heat. All of a sudden, he was no longer satisfied with just kissing. Mia felt the shift of gravity as he lay her down on the table, her butt near the edge and legs hanging over the side. Stepping between her open legs, Korum pulled apart her robe with impatient hands. Before she even realized his intentions, he already had his jeans unzipped and was pushing into her opening.

Mia was wet, but not enough, and he could only get the tip inside her before she cried out in pain. Pulling out, he lowered himself to a squatting position, his head between her spread thighs, and licked her folds with his tongue, spreading moisture around her entrance. She arched, blindsided by the sudden intensity, and he pushed his finger inside her, rubbing the sensitive spot until her inner muscles spasmed uncontrollably. Before the pulsations even stopped, he was already over her, pressing his thick cock to her opening and pushing it inside in a slow, agonizing slide.

Mia writhed beneath him, little cries escaping from her throat as her interior channel tried to expand around his width. Despite the orgasm, his penetration was far from easy, and she could see the strain on his face from the effort it took him to go slowly.

There was no pain this time—just an uncomfortable feeling of invasion and extreme fullness. He felt too big, his shaft like a heated pipe entering her body. Yet there was a promise of something more behind the discomfort. He continued his inexorable advance, and Mia gasped as her inner muscles gave way, allowing him to bury his full length inside her. He paused, letting her adjust to the unfamiliar sensation, and then pulled out slowly and pushed back in. A wave of heat rushed through her veins as his cock rubbed that same sensitive spot, and she cried out from the intense pleasure, digging her nails into his shoulders.

At the feel of her sharp nails on his skin, the last shred of his restraint seemed to dissolve. With a low growl, he began thrusting in a deep, driving rhythm, each stroke of his cock pushing her back and forth on the slick table. Somewhere in the distance, a woman's cries seemed to echo his thrusts, and Mia vaguely realized that she was that woman. Every cell in her body screamed for completion, for relief from the terrible tension that was gripping her every muscle and tendon, and then it was suddenly there—a climax so powerful that it seemed to tear her asunder, leaving her bucking uncontrollably in his arms even as he reached his own peak with a guttural roar.

CHAPTER EIGHT

Mia walked back to her apartment, desperately needing some alone time before she faced Jessie and her questions.

She felt raw and emotional, filled with self-loathing. Rationally, she knew that responding to him that way made her task easier and more tolerable. It would have been infinitely worse if she had found him repulsive or had to pretend to feel passion where there was none. However, the romantic teenager buried deep inside her was weeping at the perversion of her love story. There was no hero in her romance, and the villain made her feel things that she had never imagined she could experience.

After he had finished fucking her on the kitchen table, he carried her back to the bathroom and gently cleaned her off. He then allowed her to get dressed and go home, with a parting kiss and an admonition to be dressed and ready by 6:30 p.m. Mia had meekly agreed, wanting nothing more than to get away, her body still throbbing in the aftermath of the episode.

She debated how much to tell Jessie. The last thing she wanted was to drag her into this whole mess. Then again, Jessie was already involved through Jason, and one could argue that she'd made things worse for Mia by unintentionally bringing her into the anti-K movement.

Entering the apartment, she was surprised and relieved to find that no one was there. Jessie had to be out studying or running errands.

Sighing, Mia decided to use the quiet time to catch up with her family. The last time she'd spoken to them was last Saturday, which now seemed like a lifetime ago. Her parents likely thought that she was swamped with schoolwork, so they hadn't bothered her beyond sending a couple of text messages to which Mia had managed to respond with a generic "things r good - luv u."

She powered on her old computer and saw that her mom was already waiting for her on Skype. Her dad was in the back of the room, reading something. Seeing Mia log in, a big smile broke out on her mom's face.

"Sweetie! How are you? We haven't heard from you all week!"

If there was one thing that Mia was grateful to the Ks for, it was the impact they'd had on her parents and other middle-aged Americans across the nation. The new K-mandated diet had done wonders for her parents' health, reversing her father's diabetes and drastically lowering her mom's abnormally high cholesterol levels. Now in their mid-fifties, her parents were thinner, more energetic, and younger-looking than she remembered them ever being in the past.

Mia grinned at the camera with pleasure. The worst thing about being in New York was seeing her parents so infrequently. Although she went back home every chance she got—flying to Florida for spring break was hardly a chore—she still missed them. One day, she hoped to move closer to them, perhaps once she'd finished grad school.

"I'm good, mom. How are things with you guys?"

"Oh, you know, same old—all the news are with you youngsters these days. Have you spoken to your sister yet?"

"Not yet," said Mia, "why?'

Her mom's smile got really big. "Oh, I don't know if I should tell you. Just call her, okay?"

Mia nodded, dying of curiosity.

"How are things in school? Did you finish your paper?" her mom asked.

Mia barely remembered the paper at this point. "The paper? Oh, yeah, the Sociology paper. I finished it on Sunday."

"You've had more papers since then?" Her mom asked disapprovingly. Without waiting for a response, she continued, "Mia, honey, you study way too hard. You're twenty-one—you should be going out and having fun in the big city, not sitting holed up in that library. When is the last time you had a date?"

Mia flushed a little. This was an old argument that came up more and more frequently these days. For some reason, unlike every other parent out there who would love to have a studious and responsible daughter, her mom fretted about Mia's lack of a social life.

Mia tried to imagine her parents' reaction if she told them just how active her dating life had been in the past week. "Mom," she said with exasperation, "I go on dates. I just don't necessarily tell you all about it."

"Yeah, right," her mom said disbelievingly. "I remember perfectly well the last date you went on. It was with that boy from biology, right? What was his name? Ethan?"

Mia smiled ruefully in response. Her mom knew her too well. Or at least she knew the Mia she'd been prior to last Saturday, when her world had gone topsy-turvy.

"By the way," her mom said, "you look really nice. Did you do something to your hair?" Turning behind her, she said to Mia's dad, "Dan, come here and take a look at your daughter! Doesn't Mia look great these days?"

Her father approached the camera and smiled. "She always looks great. How are you doing, hon? You meet any nice boys yet?"

"Dad," Mia groaned, "not you too."

"Mia, I'm telling you, all the good ones get taken early." Once her mom got on this topic, it was difficult to get her to stop. "One more year for you, and you're going to be done with college, and then where are you going to meet a good boy?"

"In grad school, on the street, online, at a party, in a club, in a bar, or at work," Mia responded by listing the obvious. "Look, mom, just because Marisa met Connor in college does not mean that it's the only way to meet someone." One could also meet an alien in the park—she was proof of that.

Her mom shook her head in reproach, but wisely moved on to another topic. They chatted about some other inconsequential things, and Mia learned that her parents were contemplating going on vacation to Europe for their thirtieth wedding anniversary and that her mom's job search was going well. It was a wonderfully normal conversation, and Mia reveled in it, wanting to remember every moment in case this was the last time she would speak to her parents this way. Finally, she reluctantly said goodbye, promising to call Marisa right away.

Her acting skills must have drastically improved in the last few days, Mia thought. Despite her inner turmoil, her parents hadn't suspected a thing.

Trying to reach Marisa on Skype was always a little challenging, so she called her cell instead.

"Mia! Hey there, baby sis, how are you? Did you see any of my postings on Facebook?" Her sister sounded incredibly excited.

"Um, no," Mia said slowly. "Did something happen?"

"Oh my God, you're such a study-wort! I can't believe you never go on Facebook anymore! Well, something did happen. You're going to have a niece or nephew!"

"Oh my God!" Mia jumped up, nearly screaming in excitement. "You're pregnant?"

"I sure am! Oh, I know you're going to think I'm too young, and we just got married, and blah, blah, blah, but I'm really excited."

"No, I think it's great! I'm very happy for you," Mia said earnestly. "I can't believe my favorite sis is having a baby!"

At twenty-nine, Marisa had exactly the kind of life Mia had always hoped to have. She was happily married to a wonderful guy who adored her, lived an hour's drive away from their parents in Florida, and worked as an elementary school music teacher. And now she had a baby on the way. Her life could not have been more perfect, and Mia was truly glad for her. And if she felt a twinge—okay, more than a twinge—of envy, she would never let it intrude on Marisa's happiness. It was not her sister's fault that Mia's own life had become such a screw-up in the last week.

They caught up some more, with Mia learning all about the first-trimester nausea and cravings, and then Marisa had to run since her lunch break was over. Mia let her go, already missing her cheerful voice, and then decided to use the remaining time for studying.

An hour later, Mia had gone through the requisite Statistics exercises and had just started reviewing her Child Psychology textbook when Jessie showed up.

"Mia!" she exclaimed with relief, spotting her curled up on the couch. "Oh, thank God! I was so worried when you didn't come home last night! I called Jason, but he said that you were probably fine and that I shouldn't worry. What happened? Did John tell you anything useful?"

Mia stared at her roommate, once more debating how much to share with the girl who had been her best friend for the last three years. "He did," she said slowly, trying to come up with something that would put Jessie at ease.

"Well, what did he say? And where were you last night? Was it with that K?"

Mia sighed, deciding on a plausible storyline. "Well, John basically said that the Ks occasionally get interested in humans this way. It's usually a passing fancy, and they get tired of the relationship and move on fairly quickly. It's nothing to worry about, and I should just play along and enjoy it for as long as it lasts."

"Enjoy what? Sleeping with the K?" Jessie's eyes widened in shock.

"Pretty much," Mia confirmed. "It's really not that bad. He also takes me out to nice places. We're going to Le Bernardin tonight."

"Wait, Mia, you're sleeping with him now?" Jessie's voice rose incredulously. "But you've never been with anyone before! Are you telling me you lost your virginity to him already?"

Mia blushed, feeling embarrassed. At this point, she was about as far from being a virgin as one could get. Seeing her answer in the color washing into Mia's face, Jessie softly said, "Oh my God. How was it? You weren't hurt, were you?"

Mia's blush deepened. "Jessie," she said desperately, "I really don't feel like discussing this in detail. We had sex, and it was good. Now can we please change the topic?"

Jessie hesitated and then reluctantly agreed. Mia could see that her roommate was dying with curiosity, but Mia knew she could not keep up her brave act for long. More than anything, Mia wanted to tell Jessie the whole messy story, to reveal the sickening fear she felt at the prospect of ending up as a sex slave or getting caught spying for the Resistance. But doing so would likely put Jessie in danger as well, and that was the last thing Mia wanted.

Lying was a small price to pay for keeping her loved ones safe.

Before Mia had a chance to do much more studying, she was interrupted by the ringing of the doorbell. Opening the door, she was surprised to see a sharply dressed middle-aged woman and a young flamboyantly trendy man standing at her doorstep. The man was holding a zippered clothing bag that was nearly as tall as he was. "Yes?" she said warily, fully expecting to hear them say that they've got the wrong apartment.

"Mia Stalis?" the woman asked with a faint British accent.

"Uh, yeah," Mia said, "that would be me."

"Great," the woman said. "I'm Bridget, and this is Claude. We're personal shoppers from Saks Fifth Avenue, and we're here to remake your wardrobe."

Light dawned.

Trying to hold on to her temper, Mia asked, "Did Korum sent you? I thought he was just getting me a dress for tonight."

"He did. This is your dress right here. We're going to make sure it fits you properly, and then we'll take some additional measurements." Bridget sounded snooty, or maybe that was just the British accent.

Mia took a deep breath. "All right," she acquiesced, "come on in." By now, Jessie had come out of her room and was observing the proceedings with great interest, and Mia didn't want to throw a scene over something so inconsequential.

They came in, and Claude unzipped the bag with a flourish. "Wow," Jessie said in a reverent tone, "I think I've seen that dress on the runway . . ."

The dress was truly beautiful, made of a shimmery blue fabric that seemed to flow with every move. It had three-quarter-length sleeves—perfect for a chilly restaurant—and looked like it might end just above the knees. It also seemed tiny, and Mia doubted that even she would be able to fit in it.

Nonetheless, she went to her room and tried it on. Twirling in front of her mirror, she was shocked to see that it actually fit her like a glove. The dress was very modest in the front, but had a deep plunge in the back, so she couldn't wear a bra. However, it was so cleverly made, with the cups already sewn in, that no bra was necessary for someone of Mia's size. The young woman reflected in the mirror was more than merely pretty; she actually looked hot, with all her small curves highlighted and shown to their best advantage.

Feeling shy, Mia walked out of her bedroom and modeled the dress to her audience. Claude and Bridget made admiring noises, and Jessie wolf-whistled at the sight. "Wow, Mia, you look amazing!" she exclaimed, walking around Mia to look at her from all angles.

"Here," Bridget said, her tone less snooty now, "you can wear these tights and shoes with it." She was holding up a pair of silky black pantyhose and simple black pumps with red soles.

Trying on the shoes and tights, Mia discovered that they were a great fit as well. She wondered how Korum knew her size so precisely. If she had been the one choosing the clothes, she would have never gone for the dress, sure that it was too small to fit her. Still caught up in the beauty of the dress, Mia graciously allowed Bridget to take her full measurements.

Checking on the time, Mia was surprised to see that it was already six o'clock. She only had a half-hour to get ready—not that she needed all that time given that she was already dressed. Her hair was still magically behaving, so she only needed to worry about makeup. Two minutes later, she was done, having brushed on two coats of mascara, a light sprinkling of powder to hide the freckles, and a tinted lip balm. Satisfied, she settled on the couch to finish studying and wait for Korum to pick her up.

* * *

Greeting Korum at the door, she was pleased to see his eyes turn a brighter amber at the sight of her in the dress.

"Mia," he said quietly, "I always knew you were beautiful, but you look simply incredible tonight."

Mia blushed at the compliment and mumbled a thank-you.

The dinner was the most amazing affair of Mia's life. Le Bernardin was utterly posh, with the waiters anticipating their every wish with almost uncanny attentiveness and the food somewhere between heavenly and out-of-this-world. They got a special tasting menu, and Mia tried everything from the warm lobster carpaccio to the stuffed zucchini flower. The wine paired with their courses was delicious as well, although Korum kept a strict eye on her alcohol consumption this time, stopping the waiter when he tried to refill her glass too often.

Keeping the conversation neutral was surprisingly easy. Korum was a good listener, and he seemed genuinely interested in her life, as simple and boring as it must have seemed to him. Since he knew everything about her anyway and she wasn't trying to get him to like her, Mia found herself opening up to him in a way that she'd never had with her dates before. She told him about the first boy she'd ever kissed—an eight-year-old she'd had a crush on when she was six—and how jealous she'd felt of her perfect older sister when she was a young child. She spoke of her parents' high expectations and of her own desire to positively influence young lives by serving as a guidance counselor.

She also learned that he normally lived in Costa Rica. Supposedly, the climate there best mimicked the area of Krina where he was from. "Our Center in Guanacaste is the closest thing we have to a capital here on Earth. We call it Lenkarda," he explained. She remembered then that Costa Rica was where John had said his sister was being held. She wondered if Korum had ever seen her there. It was feasible—he'd said there were only about five thousand Ks living in each of their Centers.

As the dinner went on, she found herself straying more and more from the safe topics. Unable to contain her curiosity, she asked him about life on Krina and what the planet was like, in general.

"Krina is a beautiful place," Korum told her. "It's like a very lush green Earth. We have many more species of plants and animals, given our longer evolutionary history. We've also succeeded in preserving the majority of our biodiversity there, avoiding the mass extinctions that took place here in recent centuries." For which humans were responsible—that part he didn't have to say out loud.

"The majority, with the exception of your human-like primates, right?" Mia asked caustically, slightly chafing at his holier-than-thou attitude.

"With the exception of them, yes," Korum agreed. "And a few other species that were particularly ill-equipped to survive."

Mia sighed and decided to move on to something less controversial. "So what are your cities like? Since you're so long-lived, your planet must be very densely populated by now."

He shook his head. "It's actually not. We're not as fertile as your species, and few couples these days are interested in having more than one or two children. As a result, our birth rate in modern times has been very low, barely above replenishment levels, and our population hasn't grown significantly in millions of years." Pausing to take a sip of his drink, he continued, "Our cities are actually very different from yours. We don't enjoy living right on top of each other. We tend to be very territorial, so we like to have a lot of space to call our own. Our cities are more like your suburbs, where the Krinar live spread out on the edges and commute into the denser center, which is only for commercial activities. And everywhere you go, the air is clean and unpolluted. We like to have trees and plants all around us, so even the densest areas of our cities are nearly as green as your parks."

Mia listened with fascination. This explained the flora all over his penthouse. "It sounds really nice," she said. Then an obvious question occurred to her. "Why would you leave all that and come to Earth, with all of our pollution and overpopulation? It must be really unpleasant for you to be in New York, for instance."

He smiled and reached for her hand, stroking her palm. "Well, I've recently discovered some definite perks to this city."

"No, but seriously, why come to Earth?" she persisted. "I can't believe you'd give up your home planet just to come here and drink our blood." Which he still hadn't done with her for some reason, she realized.

He sighed and looked at her, apparently coming to some decision. "Well, Mia, it's like this. As beautiful as our planet is, it's not immortal. Our sun, which is a much older star than yours, will begin to die in another hundred million years. If we're still on Krina at that time, our entire race will perish. So we have no choice but to seek out some other alternatives."

"In a hundred million years?" That seemed like a very long time to Mia. "But that's so far away. Why come here now? Why not enjoy your beautiful planet for, say, another ninety million years?"

"Because, my darling, if we had left Earth to humans for another ninety million years, there might not have been a habitable planet for us to come to." He leaned forward, his expression cooling. "Your kind has turned out to be incredibly destructive, with your technology evolving much faster than your morals and common sense. When your Industrial Revolution began, we knew that we would have to intervene at some point because you were using up your planet's resources at an unprecedented pace. So we began preparations to come here because we saw the writing on the wall." He paused, taking a deep breath. "And we were right. Each generation has been more and more greedy, each successive advance in your technology doing more and more damage to your environment. As short-lived as you are, you think in decades—not even hundreds of years—and that leads you not to care about the future. You're like a child who takes a toy apart for the fun and pleasure of it, not caring that tomorrow he won't have that toy to play with anymore."

Mia sat there, feeling like said child getting castigated by the teacher. The tips of her ears burned with anger and shame. Maybe what he was saying was the truth, but he had no right to sit in judgment of her entire species, particularly in light of what she knew about his kind. Humans may be primitive and short-sighted compared to the Krinar, but at least they had the wisdom—and morals—to stop enslaving intelligent beings.

"So you came to our planet to take it over for your own use?" she asked resentfully. "All under the guise of saving it from our environmentally unfriendly ways?"

"No, Mia," he said patiently, as though explaining the obvious to a small child. "We came to share your planet. If we had wanted to take it over, believe me, we would have. We've been more than generous with your species. Other than banning a few of your particularly stupid practices, we've generally left you alone, to live as you wish. That's far better than the way you have treated your own kind."

Seeing the stubborn look on her face, he added, "When the Europeans came to the Americas, did they let the natives live in peace? Did they respect their traditions and ways of life enough to let them continue, or did they try to impose their own religion, values, and mores on them? Did they treat them as fellow human beings or as savage animals?"

Mia shook her head in denial. "That was a long time ago. We've changed, and we've learned our lessons. We would never do something like that again."

"Maybe not," he conceded. "But you still have no problem exterminating other species through negligence and willful ignorance. As recently as a few years ago, you treated the animals you raised for food as though they were not living creatures. And don't even get me started on the Holocaust and the other atrocities you've perpetuated against other humans during the last century. You're not as enlightened as you'd like to think you are."

He was right, and Mia hated him for it. As much as she would have liked to throw their own use of human slaves in his face, she was not supposed to know about that. So she asked instead, "If we're so awful, then why do you even want me? I certainly wouldn't want to be with someone of whom I had such a low opinion."

Korum sighed with exasperation. "Mia, I never said you're awful. Especially not you, specifically. Your species is still immature and in need of guidance, that's all."

"Plus, I'm just your fuck toy, right?" Mia said bitterly, not sure why she was even bothering to go there. "I guess it doesn't matter what you think of humans as a whole in that case."

He just stared at her impassively. "If that's how you want to think about it, fine. I certainly enjoy fucking you quite a bit." His eyes turned a deeper shade of gold, and he leaned toward her. "And you love getting fucked. So why don't you stop trying to slap labels on everything and just enjoy the way things are?"

Sitting back, he motioned to the waiter for the check. Mia's cheeks burned with embarrassment, even as her body involuntarily responded to his words with swift arousal.

He paid the bill, and they left, heading back to his penthouse.

As soon as they got into the limo, Korum pulled her onto his lap and thoroughly kissed her until all she could think about was getting to the bedroom. His hands found their way under the skirt of her dress, pressing rhythmically between her legs until she was moaning softly and squirming in his arms. Before she could reach her peak, they had arrived at their destination.

He carried her swiftly through the lobby of his building, and Mia hid her face against his chest, pretending not to see the shocked stares from the concierge and the few residents passing by. As soon as they were alone in the elevator, he kissed her again, his tongue leisurely exploring her mouth until she was nearly ready to come again. Without pausing to take off their clothes, he brought her inside the bedroom and threw her onto the bed.

At their entrance, the background music and soft lighting came on, creating a romantic ambiance. Mia hardly noticed, her arousal nearly at fever pitch. She watched hungrily as he stripped off his own clothes with inhuman speed, revealing the powerfully muscled body underneath. It was no wonder she was so addicted to him, she thought with some coolly rational part of her mind. He was probably the most gorgeous male she would ever be with in her life.

He came over her then and pulled off the dress, barely taking the time to unzip it. She was left lying there in her black pantyhose and high-heeled pumps, with her upper body completely exposed to his starving gaze. "You look so hot," he told her, his voice rough with lust. The thick, swollen cock pointing in her direction corroborated his words. Bending toward her breasts, he closed his mouth over her left nipple and sucked hard, making her arch off the bed with the intensity of the sensation. Doing the same thing to her other nipple, he simultaneously pressed at the throbbing place between her thighs, and Mia screamed as she came, her entire body shuddering from the force of her orgasm.

Before she could recover, he started kissing her again with an oddly intent look on his face. Starting at her lips, his warm mouth moved down her face and neck, lingering over the sensitive juncture of her neck and shoulder and making her shiver with pleasure.

Suddenly, there was a brief slicing pain, and Mia realized that he must have bitten her. She gasped in shock, but before she could feel anything more than a twinge of fear, hot ecstasy seemed to rush through her veins. Every muscle in her body simultaneously tightened and immediately turned to mush, and her skin felt like it had been set on fire from within. Her last rational thought was that it had to be the chemical in his saliva, and then she could no longer think at all, her entire being tuned only to the pull of his mouth at her neck and the feel of his body entering her own with one powerful thrust.

The rest of the night passed in a blur of sensations and images. She was vaguely aware that she climaxed repeatedly, her senses heightened to a nearly unbearable degree. All the colors seemed brighter, and she felt like she was floating in a warm sea, with the currents caressing her skin and lapping at her insides, making them clench and release in ecstasy. He was relentless in his passion, his cock driving into her in a savage, unending rhythm until she was nothing more than pure sensation, her essence reduced down to its very basics, her very personhood burned away in the all-consuming rapture.

Hours may have passed, or days. Mia didn't know and didn't care. At some point, her voice gave out from her constant screams, and she couldn't come anymore, her body wrung dry from the ceaseless orgasms. He came hard too, shuddering over her several times throughout the night, and then penetrating her again a few moments later. Finally exhausted, Mia literally passed out, falling into a deep and dreamless sleep that ended the most unbelievable sexual experience of her life.

CHAPTER NINE

Over the next couple of weeks, Mia settled into a routine—if sleeping with an extraterrestrial while trying to spy on him could be called anything that mundane.

He insisted on seeing her every evening, for dinner and beyond. She spent every night at his penthouse, no longer sleeping in her own apartment. During the day, he allowed her to attend class, go home to study, or spend time Skyping with her family. Her social life—never particularly active—now revolved around her relationship with him, and Jessie was horrified by that.

"I'm telling you, Mia," she earnestly tried to convince her, "I know you said it's only temporary, but I'm really worried about you. All you do is go to him—it's like you don't have a life anymore. It's not healthy, the way he just completely took over all your free time. I barely see you anymore—and we share an apartment. Can't you just spend one night away from him, just to hang out with the girls or go to a house party? You're in college, for Christ's sake!"

Mia shrugged, not wanting to get into an argument with Jessie. Let her think that she was simply obsessed with her first lover. It was better than explaining the reality of her precarious situation.

John contacted her on Thursday, wondering if she had any useful information. Mia had nothing. Leeta and Rezav had come by Korum's place a few times, but they had gone into that room and Mia had been too scared to try spying on them again. Walking in Central Park, Korum and Mia had once been approached by a group of three Ks that she'd never seen before. Their attitude toward Korum had been somewhat deferential, giving Mia a glimpse of the power he supposedly wielded over the Krinar on this planet. However, they'd spoken in their own language, and Mia had no clue what they said. She was surprised to see them, however; she hadn't known that Manhattan was such a popular place for the Ks to hang out.

On Fridays and Saturdays, he took her out to see Broadway shows and new movie releases. Mia greatly enjoyed herself. For some reason, despite living in New York City, she rarely got a chance to go to the shows—and it was fun pretending to be a tourist for a night. He also took her out to expensive restaurants or made gourmet meals at home on the days that they stayed in. For an outsider looking in, her life was the stuff of every girl's fantasy—complete with a handsome, wealthy lover who drove her around in a limo and generally treated her like a princess.

Her wardrobe had undergone a complete change as well. The personal shoppers from Saks had gone all out, replacing every piece of Mia's clothing with something nicer, more flattering, and infinitely more expensive. Stylish new coats and fluffy parkas kept her warm and cozy in the unpredictable spring weather. All of her underwear was now mostly silk and lace, with a few cotton pieces mixed in for everyday comfort and exercise. Her bulky old sweaters and baggy sweatpants were exchanged for comfortable, but formfitting yoga pants and soft fleecy tops. Even her jeans were deemed to be too old and poorly fitting, and designer brands now proudly resided on her shelves. And, of course, the beautiful dresses that now hung in her closet were in a category of their own. Her shoes had not escaped either, with brand-new high-end boots, sneakers, flats, and heels taking place of her old Uggs and worn-out All Stars from high school.

Mia's strident objections at Korum's extravagant expenditures on her behalf were completely ignored.

"Are you under the impression that this is something more than pocket change for me?" he asked her arrogantly, arching one black eyebrow at her protests. "I like to see you dressed well, and I want you to wear these."

And that was the end of that topic.

The sex between them was explosive—literally and figuratively out-of-this-world. Korum was a very mercurial lover. One day, he could be playful and tender, spending hours massaging Mia with scented oils until she purred with pleasure; other times, he was merciless, driving into her with unrelenting force until she screamed in ecstasy. On days when he took her blood—not every day, because it could be addictive for them both, he'd explained—she thought she could easily lose her mind from the intensity of the experience. Although Mia had never tried the hard-core drugs herself, she knew about the effects of various substances on the brain through her Psychology of Addiction class, and she imagined that the sex-blood combo with Korum was probably like doing heroin at the same time as ecstasy.

She often felt bitter about that, knowing that she could never feel the same way with a regular human man. Even if she was able to return to her normal life some day, she knew that she would never be the same, that he was too deeply imprinted on her mind and body. With each day that passed, she grew to crave his touch more, every cell in her body aching for him when he was not around. All he had to do was smile or look at her with those amber eyes and she was ready, her body softening and melting in preparation for his.

The calm, rational Mia Stalis of the past twenty-plus years was replaced with an insecure, emotional wreck. When she was with Korum, feeling his touch and basking in his presence, Mia felt like she was floating on air. As soon as she stepped away, however, she was filled with self-loathing and gut-wrenching fear—fear of being caught spying, of being unable to carry out her mission before he tired of her, and, most of all, of losing him.

It was inevitable, she knew. Even if he hadn't been the enemy, even if his kind had not been enslaving her own, there was no future for them. They were different species, and, if that hadn't been enough of an obstacle, her life span was like that of a fruit fly compared to his. In another few years—a dozen years at most—she would begin the inevitable aging process, and his attraction to her would fade, assuming that it lasted that long in the first place.

In her darkest moments, a small insidious voice inside her head wondered if it would truly be that awful—being his charl in Costa Rica. Would he treat her any differently from the way he did today? If not, then what did it matter what label was placed on their relationship as long as she could continue to be with him? And then she would be disgusted with herself, sickened that she could even contemplate the idea.

Despite her best attempts to remain upbeat for them, her family had begun to notice that something was amiss. Her mom ascribed it to stress from the proximity of finals, but her dad was more observant. "Did you meet someone, honey?" he asked one day out of the blue, startling Mia. She had vehemently denied it, of course, but she could see that he still had some doubts. Out of her entire family, her father was the only one who could read the subtleties of Mia's moods, and she was sure that her artificially bright smile did little to conceal the turmoil within from his sharp gaze.

The only time she felt like her old self was when she would bury herself in the library, absorbed in her studies. The end of the semester was approaching quickly, and Mia's workload tripled, with papers and finals looming in the near future. Under normal circumstances, Mia would have been tense and snappy from the stress. These days, however, studying brought a welcome relief from the drama of the rest of her life, and she gladly pored over textbooks and practiced linear regression every chance she got.

The first days of May brought unseasonably warm weather to New York, and the entire city came alive, with residents quickly donning their new summer clothes and tourists arriving in droves.

As much as Mia would've liked to join the other students lounging on the lawn with their books, she needed four walls around her in order to concentrate. Korum was becoming increasingly reluctant to have her go to the library, given her tendency to forget about the time while there, so she tried to study more in his penthouse. He set up a desk and a comfortable lounge chair for her in a small sunny room next to his own office—the place where he had met with Leeta and Rezav—and she began spending hours there instead.

She was also starting to think about the summer. After finals, Mia was supposed to fly home to Florida to see her parents. She had been fortunate to get an internship at a camp for troubled kids in Orlando, where she would be one of the counselors. Since Orlando was only about ninety minutes away from Ormond Beach, she could easily visit her parents on the weekends or whenever she had days off. Although dealing with troubled children would not be the easiest gig, the experience was considered valuable for someone in her field and would greatly aid her on grad school applications.

She had no idea how Korum would react to her essentially leaving for the next couple of months. It was possible that in another couple of weeks he would be tired of her, and then the issue would never arise. Thus far, he had not prevented her from carrying on with her schoolwork, and she hoped they might be able to come up with a workable solution for the summer as well—if their relationship lasted that far. For now, she decided to keep quiet and not rock the boat.

Two days before her Statistics exam, with Mia beginning to think and dream in correlations, Korum got called away for some unknown emergency. Sitting in her study room, she heard raised voices speaking in Krinar across the wall. Minutes later, he came into her room and told her tersely that he would be away for the rest of the day.

"If you need to go home to study or you want to hang out with your roommate tonight, feel free," he added as an afterthought. "I may not be home tonight."

Surprised, Mia nodded in agreement and watched him depart swiftly, with only a quick peck on her cheek.

Her heart jumped into her throat as she realized that this may be the chance she had been waiting for.

She sat for a few minutes, making sure that he was truly gone. For good measure, she leisurely strolled to the bathroom and splashed cold water on her cheeks, trying to convince herself that there was nothing to worry about . . . that she was completely alone in the house. Her hands were shaking a bit, she noticed as she raised them to her face, and her eyes stood out against her unusually pale face. *You can do this, Mia. All you have to do is just take a look around.*

She casually walked toward his office, ready to run into her own study at the first sign of his return. The penthouse was eerily quiet, with only her footsteps breaking the uneasy silence. Her heartbeat thundering in her ears, Mia tiptoed toward the office door.

As before, the doors slid open automatically at her approach. Even though Mia had been expecting it, she still jumped at the quiet "whoosh." Stepping in, she quickly surveyed her surroundings.

The room was completely empty.

A large polished table stood in the center, dominating the space. There were a few chairs positioned around the table, with the whole setup reminiscent of a corporate conference room. Mia was not sure what she'd hoped to see—perhaps a few papers left lying around or a computer carelessly turned on. But there was nothing.

Of course, she realized, he would not be using anything as primitive as paper or a tablet computer. Whatever the K equivalent of a computer was, she likely wouldn't even recognize it as such given the state of their technology.

Not for the first time, Mia cursed her own technological ineptitude. Someone who had problems keeping up with all the latest human gadgets was particularly ill-equipped to spy on an alien from a much more advanced civilization.

Walking into the room, she carefully approached the table. It looked like a regular table surface, but Mia remembered the three-dimensional image she'd seen on it that one time. She tried to remember what it was that Korum did to make it disappear. Was it a wave of his hand?

Trying to imitate the gesture, she motioned with her right arm. Nothing. She waved her left arm. Still nothing. Frustrated, she stomped her foot. Unsurprisingly, that didn't do anything either.

Mia circled around the table, studying every nook and cranny. Getting down on her knees, she crawled underneath and tried to look at the underside in the crazy hope that there might be a recognizable button somewhere there. There wasn't one, of course. The surface above her was completely innocuous, made of nothing more mysterious than plain wood.

Trying to crawl out, Mia bumped against one of the chairs. Exactly like a corporate office chair, it had wheels and swiveled in the middle. A fleecy sweater Korum occasionally wore around the house was carelessly hanging on the back of it. She crawled around the chair, not wanting to disturb the arrangement in case Korum had a good memory for furniture placement.

Sitting on the cold floor next to the chair, Mia stared despondently around the room. It was hopeless . . . John had been crazy to think that Mia could help somehow. If they were truly relying on her, then they were doomed. She was, quite simply, the worst spy in the world.

Her butt was getting cold from sitting, and the whole thing was utterly pointless anyway.

Trying to get up, Mia inadvertently brushed against the chair and lost her balance for a second. Grabbing onto the chair for support, she accidentally pulled off Korum's sweater.

Great. She wasn't just a useless spy—she was also a clumsy one. Lifting the sweater, she brought it closer to her nose and inhaled the familiar scent. Clean and masculine, it made her warm deep inside. *You have it bad, Mia. Stop mooning over the enemy you're spying on.*

She tried to arrange the sweater back in its original position, and her fingers felt something unusual. A small protrusion on the edge of the sleeve that didn't seem to belong on a soft sweater like that.

Her pulse jumping in excitement, Mia lifted the sleeve to take a closer look.

On the bottom of the sleeve, a tiny chip was embedded in the fabric. It was the size of a small button, and it was sheer luck that Mia's fingers had landed on it—otherwise, she would not have noticed it in a million years.

A light went on in her head. Korum had been wearing this sweater when he waved his arm and made the image disappear, Mia remembered with chills going down her spine. He had literally had a trick up his sleeve!

Nearly jumping in excitement, Mia examined the little computer—or at least, that's what she presumed it was—with careful attention. The thing was tiny and had no obvious on or off button.

"On," Mia ordered, wondering if it would respond to voice commands.

Nothing.

Mia tried again. "Turn on!"

There was no response this time either.

This was frustrating. Either the chip did not respond to voice commands, or it did not understand English. Then again, it could be programmed to respond only to Korum's voice or his touch.

Maybe if she massaged it herself?

She tried it. Nothing.

Blowing in frustration at a curl that had fallen over her eye, Mia considered her options. If the thing responded to Korum's touch, then it probably knew his DNA signature or something like that. In which case, she had no chance of getting it to work.

Discouraged, Mia sat down on the floor again. It seemed to help the last time she was stumped. If only there was some way she could test her theory—like a chunk of his hair or something . . .

Suddenly hopeful, Mia jumped up and ran to the bedroom to see if she could find any stray hairs. To her huge disappointment, the room was utterly hair-free, except for a couple of long curly strands that could only be her own. Korum was either a clean freak, or he simply didn't shed his hair the way humans did.

Furiously thinking it through, Mia ran to the bathroom and grabbed his electric toothbrush. Maybe it had some traces of his saliva or gum tissue . . . She held up the toothbrush to the little device with bated breath.

The device blinked, powering up for a second, and then fizzled out again.

Mia nearly screamed in excitement.

She held the toothbrush even closer, nearly brushing the sweater with it, but the chip remained silent and dark.

Mia's teeth snapped together in frustration. She was on the right path, but she needed a bigger chunk of his DNA. His clothes might have some, his shoes, the sheets on the bed ... But those would likely be trace amounts, like those on the toothbrush.

The sheets on the bed! A big grin slowly appeared on Mia's face. She knew exactly where to get that big chunk.

Going into the laundry room, she dug through the pile of towels and dirty linens that had piled up in the recent week. Korum tended to do his own laundry for some weird reason, and he usually did it on Mondays. Given that today was a Saturday, the room was chock-full of DNA tidbits, courtesy of their active sex life.

Mia pulled out a particularly stained pillowcase, blushing a little when she remembered how it got that way. Bringing it into the office, she held it up to the little device and waited, hardly daring to hope.

Without any sound, the chip blinked and turned on. A giant three-dimensional image appeared on the table surface. Her heart in her throat, Mia slowly hung the sweater back on the chair—which did not affect the image at all—and walked around the table, trying to make sense of what she was seeing.

CHAPTER TEN

Spread out before her was a giant three-dimensional map of Manhattan and the surrounding boroughs. It was like a much fancier, much more realistic version of Google Earth.

Slowly pacing around the table, Mia stared at the familiar landscape laid out in front of her. There was Central Park, right in the middle of the tall narrow island that was still the cultural and financial center of the United States of America. Much lower, all the way on the west side, Mia could see Korum's luxury high-rise, outlined in perfect detail.

Fascinated, she stretched her hand toward the small building image, wondering if it had any substance to it. Her fingers passed right through it, but she felt a small electric pulse run through her palm. All of a sudden, reality shifted and adjusted . . . and Mia cried out in panic as she found herself standing on the street and looking directly at the building itself—not its image, but the real thing.

Gasping, she stumbled backwards, falling and catching herself with her hands.

There was no pain at the contact with rough surface of the sidewalk; in fact, the sidewalk felt like nothing at all. Everything seemed strangely muted and silent. There were no cars passing on the street and no pedestrians leisurely strolling by.

It had to be a dream, Mia realized with a shiver, or a really vivid hallucination. Maybe she was really dying from the contact with the alien technology, and this was her brain's last hurrah. It didn't feel like that, though—it just felt weird, like she had fallen into a reflective pool of something and the reflections turned out to be real.

Virtual reality.

Mia knew it with sudden certainty. Even today's human technology could give a weak imitation of it through all the three-dimensional movies and video games. The Ks could obviously do much better, making her feel like she was actually in the image herself. This had to be the K version of Google Maps, where, instead of placing the little orange figure on the digital map to look around via pictures, the map simply placed the viewer into the three-dimensional reality.

The question now was how to get out.

Maybe if she closed her eyes and reopened them, she would find herself back in the office. Squeezing her lids shut, Mia tried counting to five. Halfway through, she lost her patience and peeked. Nope, she was still definitely in front of the building.

Her next initiative was to pinch herself . . . hard.

Ouch.

She definitely felt that pain, but her view didn't budge. She stomped her foot. Her leg communicated that sensation to her brain as well, but Mia was still in that mysterious world.

Crap. She was starting to panic. What if she could never leave this place, or worse, what if she was still in it when Korum got home? He would know immediately that she had been snooping. There was no way to spin this in a positive light, or to pass it off as random curiosity. She had clearly gone to extraordinary lengths to access his files.

Think, Mia, think. If she had entered this world so easily, there had to be an equally easy way to get out. Something had to be real in this surreal place, even if everything seemed fake.

Raising her arms at her sides, Mia slowly turned in a circle. Initially, her outstretched hands encountered nothing but air. She took a step to the right and repeated the process. Then another step and another. On her fifth attempt, her fingers brushed against something soft and familiar. The sweater! She couldn't see it, but she could definitely feel it.

Grabbing it with a desperate grip, Mia attempted to locate the device. And there it was, a tiny nub near the edge of the sleeve. As soon as Mia touched it, the familiar electric pulse ran through her hand. For a second, she experienced that feeling of disorientation, and then she was standing on solid ground—on the floor of Korum's office inside the building she had just been looking at.

Nearly shaking in relief, she stared at the map still spread out before her. She'd done it! She—Mia Stalis, who had to be taught how to operate the latest iPads—had actually entered an alien virtual reality world and come out unscathed.

Of course, she still hadn't learned anything useful. As much as she wanted to stop and go back to memorizing the standard deviation formula, she had to explore this opportunity further.

This time around, Mia knew what she had to do to avoid getting lost in that strange world. She put on Korum's sweater herself. It was huge on her, nearly reaching down to her knees. His deliciously familiar scent surrounded her, almost as if she was standing in his arms. For some reason, she found it very comforting, even though she knew that he might kill her if he saw her in this moment.

Walking around the table, she examined the map in detail. The image seemed to pulse slightly, and there were areas that shimmered more than others. One particular building in Brooklyn almost had a glow around it.

A glow? Mia had to investigate it further.

Extending her hand toward the tiny image, she closed her eyes and braced for the reality shift. When she opened them, she was on the street, looking at a quiet tree-lined residential block populated by a row of red-brick townhouses.

To her surprise, the scene was far from empty. Stifling a startled gasp, she watched a man hurry into one of the houses. He walked right past Mia on the street, without even a cursory glance to acknowledge her presence. Of course, Mia realized, she wasn't really there from his perspective. She was either watching a live video feed—a very realistic one—or, more likely, a pre-recorded video.

A saying she'd once heard nibbled on the edge of her mind. Something about advanced technology being indistinguishable from magic. That's exactly what it was like with the Ks, thought Mia. She felt a little like Harry Potter in his invisibility cloak—though her adversary was admittedly much better-looking than Voldemort.

Gathering her courage, she followed the man up the steps and into the house. *This is not real, Mia. They can't see you. You can get out any time you like.* She opened the door—which was unlocked for some reason—and stepped inside.

There was no one in the hallway, but she could hear people in the living room. Her heart pounding in her throat, Mia slowly approached the gathering. The big sweater wrapped around her felt like a security blanket, giving her the nerve to continue.

Tiptoeing into the room, Mia hovered in the doorway, waiting for someone to yell out, "Intruder!" But the occupants of the room were unaware of her presence. Feeling much calmer, Mia began to observe the proceedings.

There were about fifteen people gathered there, of various ages and nationalities. Only three of them were women, including a middle-aged lady who looked like a professor. The other two women were young, probably around Mia's age, although the stressed look on their faces aged them somehow. A lean blond man was sitting with his back turned to Mia, but there was something about him that looked familiar.

"John," said the middle-aged woman, addressing the blond man, "we really need to work out these details. We can't just blindly trust them—"

He turned his head to respond, and Mia realized with a sinking feeling in her stomach that she knew this John—that she had spoken to him twice in the last few weeks. And that meant only one thing: what she was observing had to be a meeting of the Resistance— and if she was observing it through Korum's virtual reality video, then he was obviously onto them.

Oh dear God. They thought they were safe, that they weren't being tracked. Why else would they all be gathered here like this? John had said that Korum was specifically in New York to stamp out the Resistance movement . . . because they were getting close to some breakthrough. But clearly, Korum was even closer to his goal of hunting down the freedom fighters.

She had to warn them. They were sitting ducks in that Brooklyn house. Korum could ambush them at any moment.

Suddenly, Mia felt every hair on the back of her neck rising. The puzzle pieces snapped into place, and she gasped in horrified realization.

It may already be too late for John and his friends.

Why else would Korum leave so abruptly today? He knew exactly where they were. There was no reason for him to wait any longer. The ambush—if it hadn't occurred yet—was about to take place.

Without waiting a second longer, Mia touched the little device on her sleeve and was immediately transported back to Korum's office. Waving her hand as she had seen Korum do, she nearly collapsed with relief when the action actually worked and the map winked out of existence. Quickly taking off the sweater, she hung it on the back of the chair, making sure that no stray hairs from her head remained anywhere on the fleecy fabric. Then she positioned the chairs back to how she remembered them being and ran out of the room. Last minute, she remembered the pillowcase and grabbed that too, dropping it back in the laundry pile on her way out of the apartment. Two minutes later, she had her purse and shoes and was getting into the elevator.

She needed to contact John, right away.

Pulling out her old-fashioned pocket cell phone, Mia shot an email to Jessie, writing 'Hi' in the subject line. In the body of the text, she mentioned that she would be home tonight and asked if Jessie wanted to have a girls' night in. That should put John on alert, she thought, if he was indeed monitoring Jessie's account. Now all she could do was hope and pray that she was not too late.

Wanting to get home as quickly as possible, Mia hailed a cab. It was a wasteful extravagance, but if there was ever a good reason to hurry—this was it. Climbing in, she gave the driver her home address and leaned back against the seat, closing her eyes.

Thoughts and ideas zoomed around her brain, jumping from one topic to another. How did Korum know where they were meeting? He had to have bugged the fighters' house without their knowledge . . . But John had reassured her that he could tell if a room was bugged or not. Either John had lied to her or Korum was ten steps ahead of whatever knowledge John's crew thought they possessed. That last part made sense to her. Humans could never hope to win against the K technology. If Korum wanted to watch the Resistance, he could obviously do so without their knowledge.

The full danger of the game she was playing dawned on Mia. Depending on how long Korum had been spying on them, he could know all of their plans by now . . . and he could know about Mia's involvement, limited though it had been up until today. At that thought, Mia's stomach turned over and she felt a sickening cold spread down to her toes. She had never seen Korum truly angry, but she had no doubt it would not be a pleasant sight.

Arriving at her destination, Mia paid the driver with cold, clammy fingers and walked up the five flights of stairs to her apartment. Jessie wasn't home, and Mia enviously thought that she was probably out enjoying the beautiful day with her friends. Either that or studying for finals—and both options sounded amazing to Mia right about now.

She settled in to wait.

About a half hour had passed, and Mia had nearly worn a hole in the carpet pacing up and down the living room. Finally, just as she was about to go out of her mind with frustration, the doorbell rang.

John and one of the young women from the meeting were at her door. The girl's hair was a sandy shade of brown and cut short, almost like a man's. She also looked very athletic. If it hadn't been for her elfin features, she could have easily passed for a teenage boy.

"Mia, this is Leslie," said John. "Leslie—this is Mia, the girl I was telling you about."

Mia nodded in greeting and let them into the apartment.

"John," she said without a preamble, "I just learned that you're in danger."

"No shit," Leslie said sarcastically. "We had no idea."

Mia was taken aback. This girl had no reason to dislike her, yet her tone was almost contemptuous. She felt her own hackles rising. "That's right," she said coolly. "You obviously had no idea . . . else you wouldn't have had that meeting where Korum could get a nice video of you all—including you, Leslie."

John's eyes widened in shock. "What are you talking about? What video?"

"I'm not even sure if video is the right word for it. It's really more of a virtual reality show—"

She relayed to them exactly what she'd seen today. By the time she finished, John looked pale and Leslie's arrogant smirk had been wiped from her face.

"I don't understand," he said slowly. "How did he know where to find us? All of our regular meeting places get swept for bugs and tracking devices daily. We all get regular scans too—"

"It's obviously not enough," said Leslie. "Either that, or we were betrayed."

They looked at each other in dismay.

"How are you even doing this?" asked Mia. "How do you even know what to look for when you do your scans? They can hide their tracking devices in anything. You even told me I have them in me . . ."

"That's true," John nodded, "but we can still find them—"

"Usually," said Leslie.

"Right, usually, because we're not just relying on our own modern technology—"

"John," said Leslie warningly.

"Leslie, Mia should know. She clearly risked a lot finding this information for us tonight—"

"But how can you trust her? She sleeps with him every day!"

"She has no choice in the matter! And how else would she have come across this today? You should be kissing her feet that she risked her life like that—"

"Excuse me," interrupted Mia, flushed with anger and embarrassment, "what is it you think I should know?"

Leslie just stared angrily, looking like she wanted to hit John. He ignored her and said, "Look, Mia . . . I don't want you to think that we're just a bunch of idiots bumbling around, in over our heads. Maybe that's what the movement was in the early stages, when we had no clue what they were or what they were capable of. It's different now. We know our adversary well. And we have help—"

"Help from the Ks?" interrupted Mia, her heart beating faster at the thought.

"From the Ks," confirmed John. "As I told you before, they're not all the same. Some of them believe it's wrong, the way the Ks have come to this planet to steal it from us . . . to enslave our population. They want to help us—to share their technology with us, to help us advance until we become their equals—"

"They're like the PETA version of the Ks," said Leslie, giving in to the inevitable, but with a frown still on her face. "We call them KETHs—Ks for the Ethical Treatment of Humans."

"KETHs, or Keiths, to make it easier to pronounce," clarified John.

Mia stared at them in amazement. He'd hinted at their powerful allies before, but this clearly went beyond just one or two rogue K individuals.

"What kind of pull do the Keiths have within their society?" she asked, trying to put it all into perspective.

"Not a ton," admitted John.

"They're kind of a fringe group, from what we understand," added Leslie. "But they do have access to K technology, and they supply us with what we need to stay ahead—the scanning tools we use, the shielding technology . . ."

"But to what end?" asked Mia, still not comprehending. "So you run around unseen—or not, as we learned today—but what can a fringe group do to really make a difference? You still can't fight them, even if you have a few bug scanning devices. Unless—"

She gasped in realization.

"Unless they were supplying us with more than a few scanning devices, that's right," John said helpfully.

"That's enough, John," Leslie said in a harsh tone. "Now she knows as much as most members of our group. If you tell her anything else and she gets caught—"

John sighed. "Leslie's right. Your lover already knows everything we've told you so far. I can't tell you anything else without putting you in danger. In even greater danger, I mean . . ."

Mia nodded in understanding. There was no reason for her to know the particulars of the Resistance plans. The last thing she needed was to be tortured for information. Of course, she had no idea if she could withstand even the threat of torture. Just the thought of Korum being angry with her was frightening in and of itself.

"Okay, then," she said. "I have to ask you one thing . . . Since your security is not as good as you thought it was, is there a chance that Korum could know about me? Did you talk about me at any time in that place in Brooklyn? Because if you did—"

"No, Mia, you're safe." John understood immediately where she was leading. "There's always a chance that he could know . . . but I really doubt it. You're our secret weapon. I've never spoken about you with anyone. Except for Jason—and Leslie, who happened to be with me today when I saw your email—no one knows that you're working for us."

Seeing the surprised look on Mia's face, he explained, "I didn't want to put you in any unnecessary danger. If we were to get caught and interrogated, your name would not come up."

He paused, apparently thinking about his next words. "And, frankly, I wasn't sure you would be able to come across anything useful. What you just told us today is so far above my expectations . . . I can't even begin to tell you how grateful we are. You see, tonight we were supposed to have a final brainstorming session—more than thirty of our top fighters were scheduled to attend. Korum must know about this . . . We talked about it in the last meeting—the one that you partially saw. If he had ambushed us tonight, he could have dealt a serious blow to the movement. You probably saved many lives today, Mia."

Mia looked at him, her cheeks flaming with mixed emotions. She was glad she could help the Resistance and hugely relieved that her secret was safe for now. But she was also a little offended at his low opinion of her capabilities. Then again, it was sheer luck that she'd stumbled upon this information today. Prior to this, she really had been useless to the movement, so she could hardly blame him for thinking that.

"All right," she said. "I hope that you can reschedule whatever you've got planned for tonight. Korum said he may not be home at all this evening, so whatever he's doing is probably big."

CHAPTER ELEVEN

"Hey stranger, welcome back!"

Jessie had apparently gotten her email and came home, bubbling with enthusiasm.

Mia grinned back and gave her roommate a big hug, genuinely happy to see her cheerful face. Her meeting with the Resistance fighters had left her unsettled, and Jessie was exactly the distraction she needed.

"So tell me," Jessie joked, "how did the big bad K let you come out for a night? I was sure he was keeping you under lock and key there."

Mia flushed. It was a little too close to the truth for comfort. Shrugging, she said, "I think he has to work this evening or something. He wasn't sure if he'd be home at all, so he suggested we hang out."

"Wow, how nice of him," Jessie said, comically widening her eyes. "Do you know what this means?"

"No, what?" Mia said, laughing at the dramatic expression on Jessie's face.

"It means we're going out! It's a Saturday night, and we're going to party!"

Mia wrinkled her nose a little. "Really? Right before finals?"

"Damn right! Oh, don't give me that look. I know you've been cramming for weeks already. One evening out won't make or break your grade. But since your K overlord decided to let you out only for tonight, we're going to have ourselves a blast!"

Mia grinned. Jessie's enthusiasm was catching, and suddenly the idea of getting utterly wasted while dancing all night sounded just about perfect.

Two hours later, the girls began preparations for the night out. Showering and shaving every inch of her body, Mia washed her hair and thoroughly conditioned it. The regular use of Korum's shampoo had turned it soft and silky, infinitely more manageable, and blowdrying resulted in a soft mass of well-defined dark curls cascading halfway down her back.

Makeup was next, and Mia went for the dramatic smoky-eye look, keeping the rest of her face neutral. Her wardrobe, however, presented a dilemma, for which she needed expert advice. "Jessie!" she yelled for the expert.

Her roommate came in, dressed to the nines herself. In her short red dress and sky-high heels, she looked like a million bucks. "Let me guess. You still don't know what to wear?" she asked with a big grin.

"I need your help." Mia gave her a helpless look, motioning toward the closet.

"Okay, let's see, what have we got here . . . Prada, Gucci, Badgley Mischka—oh poor you, you really have nothing to wear!" Jessie shook her head in mock reproach. "This is unbelievable, Mia—he totally spoils you. No wonder you never come home anymore."

Digging through Mia's closet, Jessie pulled out a risqué Dolce & Gabbana dress and thrust it at Mia. "Here, try this one on."

Mia eyed it doubtfully. "Won't I be cold?" There wasn't much to the dress. It looked like two scraps of purple fabric held together by a few hooks and zippers.

"Dancing in a hot, crowded club? Oh please." Jessie snorted dismissively. "And if you wear this, I can guarantee you we won't have to stand in line outside."

Mia decided to listen to the expert. Shimmying into the dress, she walked out of the room to show it to Jessie.

"Wow." Jessie was almost speechless. "I don't know what he's been feeding you, but you look amazing. I mean, you always looked cute—but this is a whole other level."

Mia blushed a little. The dress was definitely sexy, showing off her legs and exposing her back and shoulders. It was a bit too provocative for Mia's taste, with the flimsy ties around her neck being the only things holding the top in place. She couldn't wear a bra with it, given the low cut in the back, and she felt like her nipples were visible under the clingy fabric. To complete the look, she slipped on a sexy pair of heels and grabbed a tiny sparkly purse.

She was ready to party.

* * *

For the club, they chose the trendiest place in the Meatpacking District. It was a popular destination for celebrities, models, model wannabes, and any other beautiful people who liked to party. Pre-Korum Mia would have never gone to such place, sure that she wouldn't make it through the door without waiting for two hours in the cold. However, her newly confident well-dressed self had no such qualms.

Strolling right up to the bouncer, Mia and Jessie gave him big sexy smiles. He eyed them with a purely masculine appreciation and lifted the rope, letting them through without a word.

"Nicely done," Jessie whispered as they walked down the steps toward the deafening music.

Even at 11 p.m. the club was packed and happening. The music was excellent, a mix of old hip-hop favorites and some of the latest dance-hop. The dance floor was not particularly large, and every inch of it was filled with gorgeous girls grinding against each other and the few lucky guys who'd managed to get past the bouncer thus far. Sometimes it was really nice to be a girl, Mia thought. The only way most men could get into a place like this was by spending a ridiculous amount of money, whereas the girls were let in for free—as bait, of course.

Going up to the bar, the two girls quickly found a pair of stools and ordered four vodka shots. A couple of guys immediately offered to buy them drinks, and Jessie declined with a giggle. "Too early for that," she told Mia. "We want to dance, not hang out with these bozos all night."

Mia laughingly agreed, and they did their first shot, biting into a lemon afterward.

The evening got even brighter, taking on that special sparkle that only the first glass of alcohol and anticipation of a fun night could bring. Mia felt young and pretty—and, for the moment, utterly carefree. Tomorrow she could worry again, but tonight—tonight she was going to party.

"Cheers!"

The second shot went down even smoother, and things acquired a pleasant fuzzy glow in Mia's mind. The dance floor beckoned, the pulsating rhythm of the music reverberating in her bones. Grabbing Jessie's hand, she pulled her toward the gyrating crowd.

For the next hour, they danced nonstop. One good song after another came on, driving the dance floor into a frenzy. Mia danced with Jessie, with two other girls who had danced up to them, with a group of Wall Street types who kept trying to touch her naked back, and with Jessie again. She danced until she was hot and sweaty and breathless, her leg muscles quivering from all the squatting motions that a proper grinding dance entailed. She danced until she could no longer remember why she'd felt so crappy earlier today and what tomorrow could bring.

"Need water!" Jessie yelled out, trying to be heard above the music. Laughing, Mia accompanied her back to the bar. They each got a glass of tap water and another round of vodka. This time, Jessie was too buzzed to refuse when a handsome guy who looked vaguely familiar—a reality TV star, perhaps—offered to pay for their shots.

Edgar—who turned out to be an actor in a recently canceled drama—hit it off with Jessie right away. Her roommate, flattered by attention from a celebrity, flirted and giggled for all she was worth. Feeling slightly left out, Mia went to the bathroom by herself.

When she came back, a couple of Edgar's friends had joined them at the bar. They were both cute in that slightly boyish way that was popular now, and looked to be in great shape. They introduced themselves, and Mia learned that they were from the show as well. Peter was a stunt double, while Sean was a member of the supporting cast. "What is this, *Entourage*?" Mia joked, and they laughed, agreeing that their lives had much in common with the old show.

Apparently realizing they were horning in on a girls' night out, the guys ordered another round of drinks for everyone. It was tequila this time, and Mia nearly gagged at the strong taste that remained in her mouth even after biting into her lime. Her alcohol-barometer nose was long past its itching point, and she knew she would probably regret this tomorrow. But at this particular moment, with vodka and tequila surging through her system, she couldn't bring herself to care.

Mia wasn't planning on chatting up any guys, but Peter turned out to be a surprisingly good conversationalist. His voice was deep enough that it carried above the loud music, and she learned that they had Polish ancestry in common. His parents had actually come to this country fairly recently, even though he was an American citizen and had no accent. He had recently graduated from NYU himself—the Tisch School of the Arts—and wanted to be a film producer longer term. Since he had always been athletic, stunt-doubling was the best way for him to break into the field and start getting to know people, and he had been lucky enough to land a spot on the recently cancelled show.

He also seemed genuinely interested in Mia, his blue eyes sparkling whenever he looked at her. With his wavy blond hair, he looked like a mischievous angel, and Mia couldn't help laughing at some of the over-the-top compliments he directed her way. Under normal circumstances, a fun, outgoing guy like that would never have been interested in someone as shy and studious as Mia—and she couldn't help but be flattered by his attention. So when Peter asked for her number, she gave it to him without thinking, the alcohol in her veins slowing her thinking just enough to remove all caution.

They went on the dance floor again—Edgar and Peter joining her and Jessie. Sean, probably feeling like a fifth wheel, left to join another group of girls. They danced as a group at first, and then Peter starting dancing closer to Mia, his movements graceful and athletic. She smiled, closing her eyes and swaying to the pulsing rhythm, and it didn't occur to her to move away when he put his hands on her waist.

It felt good to just dance with a regular guy she liked, whose intentions she had no need to second-guess. Nothing could come of this, of course, but some silly drunk part of her hoped that maybe—if she survived all this and was still in New York when Korum inevitably tired of her—she could look up Peter on Facebook one day. Out of all the guys she'd met in recent years, she liked him the most, and she could easily envision herself becoming friends with him . . . and maybe something more.

A new song came on, with even more explicit lyrics. The crowd let out a whoop, and the movement on the dance floor picked up. Peter stepped closer to her, his hips rubbing suggestively against her own. He was of average height, and Mia's high heels put the top of her head nearly at his temple. He smiled at her, eyes twinkling, and Mia smiled back, experiencing a pleasantly mild attraction—nothing like the maddening, all-consuming heat Korum made her feel. And even though her stupid body was wishing that it was Korum who was holding her like this, she still enjoyed the sexy dance with a cute guy . . . who, under different circumstances, could have been her date.

"You're really pretty," said Peter, practically yelling it over the music.

Mia grinned, moving to the rhythm. It was always nice to get compliments. "Thanks," she yelled back, "so are you!"

Her head was spinning from the drinks, and the whole night started to seem a little surreal—right down to the angelically handsome guy dancing with her. Still dancing, she closed her eyes for a second while holding on to Peter's waist to combat a slight dizziness. Mistaking her actions, he leaned toward her, and his mouth brushed against her lips for a brief second.

Startled, Mia pushed Peter away, taking a step back. Embarrassed, she looked to the side and suddenly froze, paralyzed with dread.

Looking directly at her from the edge of the dance floor was a familiar pair of amber-colored eyes. And the icy rage reflected in them was the most terrifying thing she had ever seen in her life.

CHAPTER TWELVE

He knew.

In the suffocating panic engulfing her, Mia had only one clear thought: Korum knew. Somehow, he had found out about today—about what she'd done for the Resistance fighters—and he had come here to find her.

Her survival instinct kicked in, and a surge of adrenaline cleared the alcohol-induced fog from her mind. She fought a desperate urge to run, knowing that he would hunt her down in a matter of seconds. Instead, she just stood there, watching as he stalked toward her through the dance floor crowd, his eyes nearly yellow with fury.

Through the pulsing music and the terrified pounding of her own heart, she heard her name.

"Mia! Mia!" It was Peter, and he was talking to her. "Hey Mia, listen, I didn't mean to be so pushy—"

He broke off in the middle of his apology and followed her gaze. "What the hell . . . is that your boyfriend or something?"

"Or something," Mia said dully, staring at Korum easily pushing his way through the normally impassable mob. Her stomach churned with nausea and fear. Would he kill her on the spot or bring her elsewhere to interrogate first?

And then he was there, standing right in front of her.

"Hey man, listen, I think there's been a misunderstanding—" Peter bravely stepped up, not realizing in the darkness what he was dealing with. In a blink of an eye, Korum's hand was wrapped around Peter's throat.

"No!" screamed Mia as Peter was lifted off the floor, feet kicking in the air and hands clawing helplessly at the iron grip around his throat. "No, please, let him go—"

"You want me to let him go?" Korum asked calmly, as though he was not killing a grown man with one hand in a crowded club.

"Please! He had nothing to do with it," begged Mia, horrified tears running down her face.

"Oh really?" said Korum, his voice dripping with sarcasm. "So my eyes deceived me then. He wasn't the one just pawing you . . . It was someone else?"

Pawing her? Korum was upset that she had danced with Peter? Her brain could barely process the implications.

"Korum, please," she tried again, "you're mad at *me*. He didn't do anything—"

"He touched what's mine." The words sounded like a verdict.

"Korum, please, he didn't know! It was all me—"

The dancers around them realized that something unusual was going on, and a ring of spectators was starting to form around them.

"Please, don't kill him!" she begged, grabbing at Korum's arm in desperation. "Please, I will do anything—"

"Oh, you will," he said softly, "you will do anything I want regardless."

Peter's face was turning purple, and the frantic clawing of his fingers was slowing. There were panicked cries from the crowd, but no one dared to intervene.

"PLEASE!" screamed Mia hysterically, tugging uselessly at his arm. He didn't even look at her.

And then he suddenly released Peter, letting his body drop to the floor with a thump.

The crowd gasped as Peter drew in air for the first time, choking and gagging.

Sobbing, Mia nearly collapsed in relief. Her hands were still holding Korum's forearm, and she let go, taking a step back.

He didn't allow her to get far. His hand shot out, steely fingers wrapping around her upper arm.

"Let's go," he said quietly, his tone leaving no room for arguments.

And Mia went with him, ignoring shocked stares from the people around her.

She was certain now that she would not survive this night.

There was no limo waiting for them. Instead, he hailed a cab and tersely gave the address of his building to the driver.

The ride was mercifully short. He didn't speak to her at all, the silence in the cab interrupted only by the sound of her quiet weeping.

She'd always known that Ks had great capacity for violence, but she had never witnessed it in person. Korum had always been so careful, so gentle with her . . . It had been difficult for Mia to imagine him tearing apart a human being—like those Ks had done with the Saudis. But now she knew that he was no different, that he could snuff out a human life as casually as swatting a fly.

She didn't want to die. She felt like she had barely started living. Thoughts tumbled around in her mind, frantically searching for a way out and finding none. Would he interrogate her first? She didn't know anything of significance, but he might not believe her. She shuddered at the thought of torture. She'd never experienced real pain, and she didn't know if she could withstand it. The last thing she wanted was to die like this, sniveling and begging for her life. If only she were braver—

They arrived at the building, and he dragged her out of the cab, still holding her arm. Her legs were weak with fear, and she stumbled on the stairs. He caught her and lifted her in his arms, carrying her through the lobby and into the penthouse elevator. The warmth of his body felt wonderful against her frozen skin, reminding her of the other night he'd carried her like this—under vastly different circumstances.

Once inside the apartment, he set her down on the couch and went to the closet to hang up his jacket. Of course, Mia thought resentfully, he wanted to be as comfortable as possible for the upcoming torture and mutilation.

To her utter mortification, she felt a strong urge to pee, her bladder nearly bursting from all the earlier drinks. She desperately wanted to hold on to her last shreds of dignity—dying while peeing her pants seemed like the ultimate humiliation.

"Please," she whispered, her voice trembling, "can I go to the bathroom?"

He nodded, a small mocking smile appearing on his lips.

Mia went as quickly as her shaking legs could carry her. Once inside, she quickly relieved herself and washed her hands. Her fingernails had a faint bluish tinge, she noticed, and the warm water felt almost scalding on her icy hands.

Finishing, she stared at the closed door and the flimsy lock on it. It was useless, she knew. But she didn't want to go out there. For some strange reason, the thought of her blood spilling all over the cream-colored furniture was too disturbing. She would wait here, she decided. He would undoubtedly come get her in another few minutes. But when these might be the last moments of her life, every second counted.

She sat down on the edge of the jacuzzi and waited. It felt like an eternity had passed. Her reflection in the mirrored wall looked nothing like her normal self, from the provocative purple dress to the raccoon-like circles around her eyes from the smeared mascara. It was oddly fitting that she would die looking like this—not at all like the Mia Stalis from Florida that her family knew and loved. At the thought of their grief, a sharp pain sliced through her chest, and Mia nearly doubled over from the force of it. She couldn't think about this now. If she did, she would break down and plead for her life, and it was strangely important to retain at least a semblance of pride—

There was a knock on the door.

Mia stifled a hysterical giggle. He was being polite before he killed her.

"Mia? What are you doing? Open the door and come out." He sounded annoyed.

Mia didn't respond, her eyes trained on the entrance.

"Mia. Open the fucking door."

She waited.

"Mia, if you make me open this door myself, you will regret it."

She believed him, but she refused to go meekly, like a lamb to the slaughter. At the very least, she wanted him to have to deal with some house repairs afterwards.

The door flew off the hinges, crashing onto the floor. Even though she expected it, Mia still jumped from the suddenness of the violent action.

Korum stood in the doorway, looking magnificent and angry. His high cheekbones were flushed with color, and his eyes were almost pure gold.

"Are you seriously hiding from me in my own bathroom?" he asked, his tone dangerously quiet.

Mia nodded, afraid that her voice would tremble if she spoke. Despite her best intentions, fat tears kept sliding down her cheeks.

He came toward her then, and Mia shut her eyes, hoping that it will be over quickly. Instead, she felt his hands on her naked shoulders, lightly stroking her skin.

Her eyes flew open, and she stared up at him.

"Get in the shower," he said. "You have his stink all over your body."

In the shower? He wanted her clean. Mia's stomach churned with nausea at the realization that he intended to have sex with her—maybe for the last time—before he killed her.

She shook her head in refusal.

His expression darkened. Before Mia could further contemplate the wisdom of her actions, the little dress lay in shreds on the floor and he was carrying her—naked and squirming—to the shower stall. A surge of adrenaline kicked in, and she arched in mindless panic, furiously kicking and scratching anything she could reach. Suddenly, she was standing on her feet inside the stall, and he was looming over her with an incredulous look on his face.

"Are you insane?" he asked her softly. "Did all that alcohol fuck with your brain?"

Panting from exertion and fear, she stared up at him defiantly through the tears blurring her vision. "If you're going to kill me, just get it over with! I don't want to be fucked first!"

His eyebrows rose, and he looked genuinely taken aback. "You think I'm going to kill you?" he asked slowly, as though not believing his ears.

"You're not?" It was Mia's turn to be surprised. Her heart pounded as if she'd run a marathon, and she could barely think.

He took a step back. He was still wearing his clothes, she noticed now. The expression on his face was strange. If she hadn't known better, she would have thought she'd wounded him somehow.

"Mia," he said wearily, "just because I'm angry with you doesn't mean that I'm going to hurt you in any way, much less kill you."

"You're not?"

She had difficulty processing this. Ever since she'd laid eyes on him at the club, she'd been so certain that she would not survive the discovery.

"Of course not," he said, still looking at her with that strange expression. "You betrayed my trust tonight, but you were drunk and stupid—"

Mia blinked. Something didn't add up.

"—and I should have known better than to let you out like that on a Saturday night."

She stared at him in confusion, hardly daring to hope. "You're upset that I went out clubbing?"

"Upset is a very mild term for what I feel right now," he said quietly. "You let that pretty worm put his hands all over you, and you kissed him right in front of my eyes. No, Mia, upset doesn't even begin to approximate it."

He didn't know.

Her knees almost buckled in relief, and she grabbed the shower wall for support. As unbelievable as it seemed, his anger tonight was due to misplaced jealousy and had nothing to do with the Resistance movement.

It was a mind-boggling realization, and Mia desperately wished that she could think past the fog that seemed to permeate her every thought. She shook her head in an attempt to clear it. "I'm sorry," she said cautiously. "I didn't think you'd care if I went out tonight. I just wanted to have fun with Jessie and . . . I didn't think you'd care either way. I wasn't going to do anything but dance, I swear . . ."

He just continued looking at her, as though trying to decipher her thoughts.

"All right, Mia," he said slowly, "just take that shower now, okay? We'll talk when you're done."

And then he left, walking around the broken door lying on the floor.

CHAPTER THIRTEEN

She was going to live. He said he wasn't going to hurt her, despite his anger.

Korum didn't know about her real betrayal. She had gotten incredibly lucky.

Her head spun, and every muscle in her body trembled in the adrenaline rush aftermath. As she stood there, she felt her stomach twist with sudden nausea. Scrambling for the toilet, Mia barely made it before the contents of her stomach came up, the toxic brew of alcohol and residual terror proving too much for her system to handle.

Mortified, she kneeled naked in front of the toilet, shaking uncontrollably. Flushing the disgusting mess, she used her remaining strength to crawl back into the shower stall and turn on the water, shuddering in relief as the warm stream poured over her frozen body.

The hot shower worked miracles. After a few minutes, Mia felt well enough to get up off the floor. She washed and shampooed every inch of her body, rinsing away all traces of the horrible night. When done, she toweled herself off, put on a big fluffy robe, and brushed her teeth twice to remove the unpleasant taste in her mouth. She was now ready to face Korum again, even though all she wanted to do was pass out and sleep for the next ten hours.

He was waiting in the living room, again looking at something on his palm. At her tentative entrance, he looked up and motioned to have her come closer. Mia cautiously approached, still feeling wary.

"Here, drink this."

He had picked up a glass filled with a pinkish liquid from the table next to him and was holding it out to her.

"What is it?" asked Mia with visible nervousness.

"Not poison, so you can relax." At her continued reluctance, he added, "Just something to reduce the strain on your liver from all the crap you drank tonight."

Mia flushed with embarrassment. He had clearly heard her vomiting earlier. Without further arguments, she took the glass and tried the liquid. It tasted like slightly sweet water and was wonderfully refreshing. She gulped down the rest of the glass.

"Good," said Korum. "Now sit down and let's talk about expectations in our relationship . . . specifically, my expectations for your behavior."

Mia swallowed nervously and sat down next to him. The liquid was already working its way through her system, and she felt the cobwebs clearing from her mind.

He turned toward her and took one of her hands in his, lightly stroking her palm. His eyes were nearly back to their normal shade of amber, with only a few traces of the dangerous yellow flecks.

"You're mine, Mia," he told her, his thumb caressing the inside of her wrist. "You've been mine from the moment I saw you in the park that day. I don't share what's mine. Ever. If you so much as look at another male—human or Krinar—you will regret it. And whoever lays a hand on you will be signing his own death warrant. Do I make myself clear?"

Mia nodded, unable to speak past the volatile mixture of emotions brewing in her chest.

"Good. The pretty boy you were dancing with tonight is very lucky he walked away. If there's ever a next time, I won't be so merciful."

Her free hand curled into a fist on the couch.

"You acted foolishly tonight. Two pretty girls going out dressed like that—any number of bad things could have happened to you. And drinking until you throw up—you might as well schedule a liver transplant for yourself in the near future. Your human body is already fragile, and I won't allow you to abuse it like this."

Mia's nails dug into her palm in frustrated anger. To be lectured like this, as though she was a stupid teenager, was beyond humiliating.

"If you want to go out dancing, I will take you. And no more nights out with your roommate—the two of you clearly cannot be trusted."

Mia just stared at him with a mutinous look on her face.

"And now," he said softly, "we should discuss your little misconception earlier . . . the fact that you actually believed that I would kill you for kissing a boy in a club."

"You nearly killed Peter," said Mia, frantically searching for an explanation for her earlier panic. "Why are you so surprised that I was scared?"

"*Peter* deserved exactly what he got for touching what's mine." He leaned toward her. "*You*, on the other hand, have nothing to fear from me. When have I ever hurt you—aside from the loss of your virginity?"

It was true. He had never caused her physical pain—at least not of the unpleasant kind. He was always very careful not to hurt her with his much greater strength. Of course, he didn't know she was helping the Resistance.

"Mia, I know we literally come from different worlds, but some things are universal across both species. I sleep with you every night, I kiss and caress your body, I take great pleasure in having sex with you—and you think that I could just snuff out your life like that, with no regrets?"

He still might, if he discovered her true betrayal.

Taking her silence for the affirmative, he shook his head in disappointment. "Mia, I'm really not the monster you've made me out to be in your mind. I would not hurt you—ever, under any circumstances. Do you understand me?"

"Yes," she whispered, suppressing a slight yawn. She felt completely drained, exhaustion creeping up on her during their conversation. Even after the restorative potion he'd fed her, she was more than ready to go to sleep. Tomorrow she would gladly analyze all the ins and outs of his words, but for tonight—she was completely done.

"All right," he said, "I can see that you're tired. Let's go to bed. You'll feel much better after some rest."

Mia nodded gratefully, and he picked her up, carrying her to the bedroom.

Entering the room, he placed her gently on the bed.

Too tired to move, Mia just lay there, watching as he stripped off his clothes. His body was truly beautiful—all muscle, covered with that smooth golden skin. All of his movements were inhumanly graceful and carefully controlled. For the first time, Mia realized that he probably exerted a lot of effort to reign in the enormous strength she'd witnessed today.

He came toward her, his cock already stiff, and opened her robe. "You're so lovely," he murmured, studying her body with obvious appreciation. Despite her exhaustion, she felt her inner muscles clenching in anticipation.

Climbing over her, he bent down and kissed the sensitive part of her neck. Mia held her breath, waiting for the familiar rush of bite-induced ecstasy, but he just continued nibbling his way down the rest of her body, with only his lips and tongue touching her. She moaned softly, wanting more, but he was ruthlessly slow, branding every inch of her skin with his mouth.

He reached her feet, and Mia giggled, feeling his lips closing over one of her toes. And then his warm hands touched her foot, massaging with a light yet firm pressure, and Mia arched in unexpected pleasure as his thumb found a spot that sent sensations directly to her nether regions. All of a sudden, she didn't feel like giggling anymore as tension started building in her sex. He gave her other foot the same treatment, and she cried out, feeling as if he was touching her clit instead.

He flipped her over then and removed the robe completely. Grabbing a pillow, he placed it under her hips, elevating her butt. For some reason, Mia felt very vulnerable, lying there face down, with her back exposed to the predator she was sleeping with.

Leaning over her, Korum lifted the dark mass of curly hair off her shoulders, revealing the tender spot of her nape. Bending down, he kissed it lightly, his mouth feeling hot on her sensitive skin. She shivered from the sensation, and he moved lower, kissing his way down each vertebra of her spine until he reached her tailbone. His hands touched her butt, lightly squeezing the pale globes, and she felt his mouth leisurely making its way down to the opening of her sex, teasing the crevice between her cheeks on the way with his tongue. She jumped, startled by the unfamiliar sensation, and he laughed softly at her reaction. "Don't worry," he whispered, "we'll leave that for another time."

And then playtime was over.

He settled over her, his legs pushing between her own, opening her wider. Mia gasped as she felt the heavy force of his cock pushing into her. Despite her wetness, he felt impossibly big in this position, and she whimpered slightly, her muscles quivering, trying to adjust to the intrusion. Sensing her difficulty, he paused for a second and reached under her hips, applying steady pressure to her clitoris even as he moved his pelvis in a series of small, shallow thrusts, working himself deeper into her. With his much larger body over her like that, she felt completely dominated, unable to move an inch, and she groaned in frustration, hovering on the verge of relief yet not climaxing. He moved deeper still, touching her cervix, and she froze as every nerve ending stood on edge, waiting for something—pleasure, pain, she didn't care which as long as she could reach the elusive peak.

He withdrew halfway then and slowly worked himself back in. The tension was becoming unbearable, and Mia resorted to begging, pleading him to do something, to make her come. "Not yet," he told her, moving in that maddeningly slow rhythm that kept her at an agonizing intensity level. Whenever he sensed her orgasm approaching, he would slow down further, and then thrust faster when the sensation receded a bit. It was literally torture, and Mia realized that this was to be her punishment for tonight.

"Korum, please," she begged, but he was intractable. The slow drag and thrust of his cock was driving her insane. In any other position, she would have been able to do something, to move her hips in a way that speeded up the climax. But lying there like that, with his heavy body pressing her down, she could only scream in frustration.

"You're mine, do you understand it now?" he said hoarsely, still keeping up that mercilessly slow pace. "Only I can give you this—what your body craves. No one else . . . Do you understand that?"

"YES! Please, just let me—"

"Let you what?" he panted, the torture exerting a toll on him as well.

"Just let me come! Please!"

And he did. His thrusts gradually picked up speed, winding her up even tighter, and her screams got even louder . . . and then she went over the cliff, her entire body pulsing and spasming in a release so powerful that every muscle in her body trembled in its aftermath. Her orgasm sent him over the edge as well, and he came deep inside her with a hoarse groan, his seed spurting in warm bursts inside her belly.

Mia lay there afterwards, feeling his weight pressing her down. She couldn't breathe easily, but she didn't care. She felt utterly boneless, unable to move in any case. And then Korum rolled away, freeing her. She shivered slightly at the feel of cool air on her naked sweaty back. He picked her up and took her into the shower again, for a quick rinse this time. And then they finally slept, with him cradling her possessively even in his sleep.

CHAPTER FOURTEEN

Mia woke up the next morning feeling surprisingly well. Dry mouth, a pounding headache, and the generally shitty overall state that came with the morning after clubbing—none of these were present today, likely due to Korum's magic potion.

As usual, she was alone in the bedroom. She had learned that Ks needed significantly less sleep than humans—some as little as a couple of hours a night—so Korum was a very early riser. It was just as well. She wasn't sure she was eager to face him this morning.

For some reason, she had never expected him to be jealous. With his looks and skills in bed, she couldn't imagine that any female would prefer another man over him. Her light flirtation with Peter last night had been just that—harmless fun that would've never led anywhere.

Most of the time, she had trouble deciphering his emotions. He usually seemed so calm and controlled, with that slightly mocking expression on his beautiful face. She knew she frequently amused him, and he often liked to tease her just to see her temper flare up. She imagined she was something like a kitten to him, a little creature that he liked to pet and play with on occasion. His reaction last night did not jive with that casual attitude, however. The extreme possessiveness he'd displayed didn't make sense in light of what their relationship really was. He definitely liked having sex with her, but she could not imagine that she meant anything more to him than that.

Then again—although she might have misinterpreted his expression last night—it seemed like he'd been genuinely hurt that she'd thought him capable of killing her. Could it be? Did he actually care for her as a person—as something more than his human toy? At this thought, an odd ache started in her chest. It couldn't be, of course, but if he really did care for her . . .

And then she remembered a little tidbit about life on Krina. They were territorial, he'd said, and didn't like to live right on top of each other.

And she wanted to cry.

It was all clear now. Of course he had been mad at Peter last night: the poor guy had inadvertently infringed on Korum's territory. As far as Korum was concerned, she belonged to him now, for as long as he wanted to keep her.

She was another one of his possessions. And he didn't like to share.

As much as she wanted to laze in bed all day, there were things to be done. Her Stat final was tomorrow, and she still didn't feel fully ready. The last thing she needed was the distraction of her screwed-up love life.

Getting up, Mia brushed her teeth and got breakfast. Korum wasn't home at all, and she wondered where he went.

Before she settled down to study, she decided to check her phone to make sure that Jessie got home safely last night. Sure enough, there were about a dozen missed calls from her roommate and an equal number of texts and emails—each getting progressively more worried. Mia groaned. She should've texted Jessie last night before falling asleep, but it had been the last thing on her mind at the time.

There was no help for it. Studying would have to wait. She called Jessie instead.

Her roommate picked up at the first ring. "Oh my God, Mia, are you all right?!? What the fuck happened last night? If that alien bastard hurt you in any way—"

"No, Jessie, he didn't! Look, I'm totally fine—"

"Totally fine? Everybody was talking about it last night—how he dragged you off after nearly killing Peter! I came back from the bathroom, and you were gone, and the poor guy was still choking on the floor—"

"Is he all right now?" interrupted Mia, suddenly overcome by guilt.

"He was taken to the hospital, but it was mostly swelling and bruises, they said. He's probably going to have difficulty speaking for a few days, and I'm sure he was scared out of his mind . . ."

"Oh my God, I am so sorry about that," Mia groaned. "I should have never put him in danger like that—"

"Him? What about yourself? Mia, this K of yours is insane! He was about to kill a person for dancing with you—"

"Kissing me actually . . ."

"Whatever! It's not like you slept with the poor guy, but even if you had . . . that's just crazy!"

Mia sighed. "I know. I learned too late that they're apparently very territorial and possessive. If I'd known before, I obviously would've never gone to the club in the first place—"

"Territorial and possessive? More like homicidal! Mia . . . you really need to leave him. I'm scared for you . . ."

"Jessie," said Mia softly, wondering how to best phrase it, "I'm not sure that I can leave him yet."

"What do you mean? Like he would force you to stay somehow?"

"I don't really know, but I don't think it's the best idea to break up right now—"

"Oh my God, I knew it! You *are* afraid of him! Did he threaten you in any way?"

"No, Jessie, it's not like that . . . He said he would never hurt me. I just think it's best to let the relationship play out naturally. I'm sure he'll get bored soon and move on—"

"And you're okay with that? Just waiting around until he tires of you? Wait, what about the summer, when you go home to Florida?"

"Um, I'm not really sure how that's going to play out yet . . . I haven't really talked to him about that—"

"Well, you better, because it's coming up! Finals are next week, and then you're gone. What is he going to do then? Not let you go home?"

Jessie had a valid point. Mia had no idea what would happen at the end of next week. For some reason, she had thought that Korum might get bored of her before Florida became an issue. His actions last night, however, were not those of someone who was getting bored with his new toy; in fact, he seemed very determined to hold on to said toy. Mia was starting to worry, but Jessie didn't need to know that.

"No, I'm sure we'll figure something out. Look, Jessie, I know it sounds bad, but he's really not mistreating me or anything. If I just act more considerately, everything will be totally fine. He'll go back to his K Center soon, and I will have lots of interesting stories to tell my grandchildren . . ."

"I don't know, Mia. This is starting to sound like he's almost holding you captive—"

"Don't be silly! Of course he's not!"

"Uh-huh," said Jessie skeptically, "sure he's not. You can just go anywhere you want, do anything you want—"

"Well, no," admitted Mia, "not exactly—"

"Not at all! He's keeping you prisoner there—"

"No, he's not," protested Mia. Taking a deep breath, she added, "But even if he was, there's nothing anyone can do about it. You saw it last night—they can nearly kill someone in public and nobody will say boo. Whether we like it or not, they are not subject to our laws. Jessie—please, just let it go . . . I know how to handle my relationship with him. Obviously, it's not like dating another NYU student, but it's not all bad—"

"Not all bad? You mean the sex is good?"

Mia blushed, glad that Jessie couldn't see her. "Well, definitely that— it's actually pretty amazing . . . but also just spending time with him. He can be really fun . . . and romantic, and he's a great cook—"

"Oh, don't tell me . . . are you falling in love with him?"

"No! Of course not!" Mia sincerely hoped she wasn't lying. "He's not even human—"

"That's right! He's not human! Mia, he's dangerous. Please be careful, okay? If you feel like you can't break up with him yet, then don't . . . but just don't fall for him, okay? I don't want to see you get hurt . . ."

"Of course, Jessie. Please don't worry so much—I'm totally fine. But enough about me," Mia said with false brightness. "What's the deal with that hot actor you were flirting with all night?"

"Oh, he was a total sweetheart. I gave him my number, and he said he will call today—"

And Jessie told her all about the cute guy and how he was in town for at least a few more months, and how they both enjoyed Chinese food and had the same taste for nineties music . . . It was all so uncomplicated, and Mia envied her roommate for being able to fret over something as ordinary as whether Edgar would call today as promised.

They wrapped up the conversation, and Mia promised to see Jessie the next morning after the Stat exam. And then she settled in to study for the rest of the day.

CHAPTER FIFTEEN

On Monday morning, Mia walked out of her Stat exam feeling like she had conquered the world. She'd known the answer to every question and finished the test in half the time. Now she only had to turn in three papers, and the school year would be officially over.

Elated, she texted Jesse to let her know that she was done. Her roommate was probably still taking her BioChem final, so Mia decided to chill in the park for a bit and wait for Jessie to finish up.

Parking herself on a bench, she pulled out her phone to call her parents and let them know that the test had gone well. But before she could even press a button, a man sat down right next to her, and Mia found herself looking into a familiar pair of blue eyes.

"John! What are you doing here?" Mia asked in surprise. She had always seen him inside her apartment, and it was a bit of a shock to see him out in the open like this.

"I wanted to talk to you about something important, and I wasn't sure when you would be home next," he said. "But first, let me ask you . . . are you all right?"

"Uh, yeah." Mia flushed a little. "Why, did Jessie talk to Jason again?"

"No, but we heard about what happened. Your Saturday night adventure made the local papers."

Mia shuddered. That was embarrassing. A scary thought occurred to her. "Was my name in the paper? If my parents find out—"

"No, there was only a description. I doubt your family will make the connection."

Mia exhaled in relief. "Yeah, well, as you can see—I'm totally fine."

"Why did he attack that guy like that?

Mia shrugged. "He's just possessive, I guess. I was really scared, actually, because I thought he'd found out I was helping you. Turns out I was wrong, but there was a very unpleasant hour when I was certain he would kill me."

John regarded her with a calm, level gaze. "It's a risk that we all run, unfortunately," he said.

Mia shivered slightly. She didn't want to think about the nearly paralyzing terror that had gripped her that night. Instead, she asked him brightly, "So how did things work out for you guys this weekend? You moved your meeting, right?"

"We did. That's why I'm here to talk to you today. There's been a change of plans."

"What kind of change? But, wait, first—did you figure out how he was videotaping you?"

"Do you remember the Keiths that we mentioned the last time?

Mia nodded.

"They were able to find the devices. They were embedded in the curtains and the couch fabric—even the tree branches outside. It was a new and different technology—something that they must've developed recently. We are lucky that one of the Keiths has a design background and was able to figure out what the things were based on their new nano-signature."

Mia listened in fascination. "So what now?"

"We got very lucky that you came across that information. The Keiths thought so too—"

"They know about me now?" Mia wasn't sure if she should worry about that.

"Yes. We had to explain how we learned about being recorded in the first place."

The expression on her face must've seemed concerned because he added, "Look, I promise you they're not all the same. The Keiths really believe in our cause—they won't do anything to put you in danger."

"I don't understand something," said Mia. "Are these Keiths openly walking around their communities talking about their views and the fact that they're helping you guys?"

"No, of course not! If Korum knew who they were, he would quickly neutralize them. They have a lot to lose if their identities are discovered before we put our plan into action."

"Okay," said Mia, "so what's the plan? And should I really know about it, given my proximity to you-know-who?"

"Unfortunately, you do have to know . . . because you're a big part of this plan now."

Mia felt her heart skip a beat. "Okay," she said slowly, "I'm all ears."

"Do you remember when I told you that Korum is one of the key reasons they came here? That his company essentially runs the K Centers?"

Mia nodded.

"Well, the reason why he has all this power is because his company developed a lot of proprietary, classified technology that's not available to the general Krinar population. We don't know much about their science, but we think they probably have mature nanotechnology—"

"What does that mean, mature nanotechnology?" asked Mia.

"Basically, we believe they can manipulate matter on an atomic level. As the Keiths have explained to us, they can create almost anything using technology that's right in their homes—as long as they have simple input materials and the design for it. Their designers—which are a bit like our software engineers—create the nano blueprints for all the things they use in daily life, as well as for their weapons, ships, houses, et cetera . . . Do you understand what I'm saying?"

Mia didn't fully understand, but she nodded anyway.

"Korum is one of their most brilliant designers. A lot of the blueprints that he and his company have created are not available to the general public. That includes the design of their ships—that's highly classified information—and many of their security details, including shields and weapons for the K Centers. If you're a regular run-of-the-mill K, you can easily go on the Krinar version of the Internet and get yourself a design for their standard weapons and technologies. That's how the Keiths have been helping us until now—by providing us with the basic tools we need to evade capture and some simple weapons. Ultimately, the goal was to use their own weapons to attack their Centers and kick them off our planet.

"But, like I said, the K Centers are protected by technology that only Korum and his trusted lieutenants have access to. One of the Keiths has spent months trying to hack into their files . . . but with no success. We thought we were close to being able to penetrate their defenses, but we learned this weekend that we're as far away as we've ever been. Korum continues to develop newer and more complicated designs—the devices he used to spy on us are particularly ingenious—"

"Can't the Keiths reverse-engineer these designs?" interrupted Mia.

Not that she knew anything about technology, but that seemed logical.

"Most of Korum's designs contain a self-destruct feature that gets triggered when you try to take apart the device on the molecular level—which is what you'd have to do to figure out the structure of it. That's how he has a monopoly on this stuff—the patent or copyright protection is built into the design itself."

"Okay, so let me see if I understand this . . . The Keiths are willing to help you attack their own Centers, but they can't break the code on the technology that protects the settlements? Am I getting that right?"

"Exactly. There are fifty thousand Ks and billions of us. They may be stronger and faster, but we could easily overtake them if they didn't have their technology. If we could somehow disable their shields and get our hands on some of their weapons, we could take our planet back."

Mia rubbed her temples. "But why would the Keiths help you so much against their own kind? I mean, I understand that they think it's wrong the way humans have been treated . . . But to endanger the lives of fifty thousand other Ks for the sake of helping us? That doesn't fully make sense to me—"

"We promised to minimize the Krinar casualties as much as possible and to grant them safe passage back to Krina. We also promised that the Keiths—and whoever else they think can be trusted—can stay here on Earth and live among humans, as long as they obey our laws.

"You see, Mia, they would be our teachers, our guides . . . bringing us into the new technological era and greatly accelerating our natural progress. They would be heroes to all of humankind, their names revered for ages. They would help us cure cancer and other diseases, and give us ways of extending our lifespan." His face was glowing with fervor. "Mia . . . they would be like gods here on Earth, after all the other Ks leave. Why wouldn't they want that instead of leading the regular lives they've already led for thousands of years?"

Mia was reaching her own conclusion. "So they're bored and looking to do something epic?"

"If you want to think about it that way. I believe they're genuine in their desire to help our species evolve to a higher level."

"Okay, so let's go back for a second. If they can't hack into the files, then what are you going to do? Sounds to me like Korum is winning the war before you even got a chance at a single battle."

"Not quite," said John, his eyes burning with excitement. "We can't hack into the files—but we can steal the information anyway."

Mia didn't like where this was going. "Steal it how?" she asked slowly.

"Well, the rumor is that Korum keeps many of his particularly sensitive designs on him at all times. For instance, have you ever seen him doing anything like looking into his palm or at his forearm?"

"I've seen him looking into his palm," said Mia reluctantly, starting to get a really bad feeling about this.

"Then that's where he has one of their computers embedded. I use the term computer loosely, of course. It has as little in common with human computers as our computers do with the original abacus. Still, he has information stored there—literally in the palm of his hand. We could never hope to get to it because even if we captured and immobilized him—which is a nearly impossible task—he would probably be able to wipe the data in a matter of seconds."

"So what can you do then?" asked Mia in confusion.

"*We* can't do anything . . . but *you* can. You're the only one who gets close enough to him to be able to gain access to that information—"

"What? Are you insane? It's in his palm—how would I get to it? It's not like he's just going to hand it over!"

"No, of course not," sighed John. "But we do have this . . ."

He was holding a small silver ring.

"What is it?" asked Mia warily.

"It's a device that scans data. The Keiths deliberately made it look like jewelry, so you could wear it without raising suspicions. If you could somehow hold it to Korum's palm for about a minute, it should be able to access his files and get us the blueprints."

"Hold it for a full minute against his palm? What, like he wouldn't find it suspicious?"

"Not if he was otherwise distracted . . ." His voice trailed off suggestively.

"Oh my God, are you serious? You want me to steal data from him during sex?" Mia's stomach turned over at that thought.

"Look, the when is up to you. He could be sleeping—"

"He only sleeps for a few hours, and I'm usually passed out during that time."

"Okay, then, do you ever go anywhere with him when he just holds your hand?"

Mia thought about it. When they walked somewhere together, she would usually put her arm through the crook of his elbow. Or sometimes he would put his hand on the small of her back. If he ever held her hand, it was usually for a brief period of time only. "Not really."

"Well then, it has to be when it wouldn't be strange for you to be touching him . . ."

"So you do mean during sex?"

"If that's the only time, then yes."

Mia stared at John in shock, unable to believe he was asking her to do this. "John," she said slowly, "I'm not some femme fatale who can just do stuff like this. The last time, when I thought that Korum had caught me, I was completely freaking out. I'm not cut out to be a spy, not even close. And Korum knows me by now—if I suddenly start acting weirdly, he'll catch on right away—"

"Look, I understand that it's not going to be easy. You're right—you're not a seasoned agent. But you're literally our last hope. The Keiths believe that Korum is getting closer to figuring out who they are. He knows that we're getting help from the inside, and the Keiths think that their ruling council will not look kindly on those who pose a threat to the Centers here. At best, they're looking at forced deportation to Krina and some serious punishment there. At worst, well . . ."

"John," said Mia wearily, feeling the beginnings of a headache, "I just can't—"

"Mia, please, just wear the ring. That's all I will ask you to do. If you get an opportunity, great. If not, well, at least we will have tried."

"And if I get caught wearing this device? If Korum is as brilliant as you say, won't he recognize their technology from a mile away?"

"He has no reason to suspect you. You're just his charl. He won't be expecting a threat from you. And here, see, the ring is truly nice-looking. You could claim that it's a gift from your sister if he asks."

Mia stared at the device. The little silver circle was thin and stylish, and it probably wouldn't look out of place on her finger. To confirm that theory, she extended her hand. "All right, let me try it on—see if it's even my size."

John gave her the ring with a relieved smile. Mia slid it on the middle finger of her right hand. It fit perfectly. If she hadn't known its purpose, she would have never thought it was anything other than a simple piece of jewelry. She hoped that Korum would be fooled as easily.

With his mission accomplished, John rose to his feet. "Mia," he said, "I hope you realize that if this works, if you succeed, then our species will enter into an entirely new era. We will have our planet back, and our freedom. And we will have a lot more knowledge—science and technology that we wouldn't have had for hundreds or maybe thousands more years. You will be a hero, your name written in the history books for generations to come—"

Mia felt chills going down her spine.

"—and you will have nothing to fear from him again, ever. And girls like my sister will finally be reunited with their families, and they would be able to lead normal lives again—as will you."

He painted a compelling picture, but Mia couldn't imagine how she could possibly bring something like this pass. "John," she said, "I'll try. That's all I can promise you."

"That's all I want." He put his hand on her shoulder and gave it a reassuring squeeze. "Good luck."

And then he walked away, leaving Mia with the alien device that was supposed to determine the future of humankind sitting innocuously on her finger.

CHAPTER SIXTEEN

Jessie joined Mia in the park a few minutes later. "Ugh," she said, "I hate BioChem. So glad that torture is over."

Mia smiled at her. "No one said it's easy being a pre-med."

"Yes, well, not all of us chose the easy route with a psych major—"

"Easy, please! I have to write three papers by Thursday, and I'm only done with one so far!"

"My heart bleeds for you . . . it really does—"

"Oh shut up," said Mia, and they both grinned at each other.

"So what are you doing now? Going to the library?" asked Jessie, wrinkling her nose.

"Nah, I think I'll head back to Korum's place. All my books and stuff are there now—"

Jessie's expression immediately darkened. "Of course. I should've known."

"Jessie," said Mia tiredly, "please don't give me a hard time over this. One way or another, I'm sure this relationship will be over soon—"

"Mia, is there something you're not telling me?" Jessie was looking at her suspiciously.

"No! I just meant that I will be going home to Florida—and he may not want to continue seeing me when I return, that's all."

"You've talked to him about this already?"

Mia shook her head. "I'll do it tonight."

"Okay, good luck with that. Let me know how that goes." She paused and then added, "Oh, and by the way, Edgar said that Peter's been asking about you."

"What? Why?"

Jessie shrugged. "I guess he's suicidal. That, or he really likes you. It's hard to tell, you know?"

"Is he feeling better now?"

Jessie nodded. "He seems to be fine, just some residual bruising."

"Well, I'm glad. Listen, tell Edgar that Peter should just forget about my existence. If it's ever safe, when this thing with Korum is over, I'll contact him myself."

Jessie promised to do so, and they chatted some more about Edgar. Jessie was supposed to see him tonight, and Mia again envied the ease and simplicity of her roommate's life.

Mia was now literally wearing the fate of her species on her finger, and the burden felt far heavier than the light silver circle could ever be on its own.

* * *

That night, Korum made dinner for them again. After agonizing over the best way to approach summer plans, Mia decided to just tell him straight out. First, though, she wanted to make sure that he would be in a good mood and receptive to the idea.

The dinner was delicious, as usual. Mia gladly consumed another creatively made salad—she had definitely developed a taste for them— and a bean crepe wrapped in seaweed with a spicy mushroom sauce.

If she succeeded in her mission, there would be no more dinners like this. Korum would be forced to go back to Krina—if he even survived the attack on their settlements.

At that thought, Mia felt a strange squeezing sensation in her chest. She didn't want him killed. He might be the enemy, but she didn't want to see him get hurt in any way.

Furiously thinking about this, she resolved to ask John to grant Korum safe passage—if she did get her hands on the data. Of course, even the thought of him simply leaving the planet was oddly agonizing. *You silly twit, he did manage to get under your skin.*

"A penny for your thoughts," teased Korum, apparently noticing the introspective look on Mia's face.

"Um, I'm just thinking about all the stuff I still have to do before the end of the week—turn in all those papers and then start packing . . ." Mia let her voice trail off. It seemed like a good segue into what she wanted to discuss today.

"Packing?" A slight frown appeared on his smooth forehead.

"Yes, well, you know the semester will be over soon," Mia said cautiously, her heart rate beginning to increase. "After finals, I have to go home, to Florida, to see my parents, and then I have an internship in Orlando—"

His expression visibly darkened. "And when were you going to tell me about this?" His voice was deceptively calm.

Mia slowly chewed the last bite of her food and swallowed it. "I thought you knew everything about me already, including my summer plans." The evenness of her tone matched his, despite the pounding of her heart.

"The background check I did on you a month ago was not sufficiently comprehensive, I guess," he said, still dangerously calm.

Mia shrugged. "I guess not." She was proud of how bravely she was handling this discussion. Maybe she would make a decent spy yet.

"I don't want you to go," he said quietly. His eyes were taking on that golden tint that she now associated with all kinds of strong emotions.

"Korum, I have to." Mia tried to think of ways to convince him. "I have to see my parents and sister—she's pregnant, actually—and then I have a really good internship lined up at a local camp, where I would be a counselor for children who are going through a difficult time . . ."

He just looked at her, his lack of expression scaring her more than any outward anger.

"All right," he said. "I will take you to see your family this summer . . . just not next week. I can't leave New York quite yet. And if you want, I will find you an internship here as well, something within your field that you would enjoy."

Mia felt a cold sensation radiating from her core all the way down to her toes. Up until now, even though she knew he regarded her as his pleasure toy, their relationship had a semblance of normality. He might have considered her his human pet, but she could still pretend he was her boyfriend—an arrogant and domineering one, for sure . . . but still just a boyfriend. Now that illusion was broken. If he really did go so far as to disregard her summer plans made months in advance, then he had absolutely no respect for her rights as a person—and probably no qualms about keeping her as his charl indefinitely, until he got bored with her.

Her fists were tightly clenched on the table, she noticed, and she forced herself to relax her fingers before proceeding. "And when you're done with your business in New York," she asked quietly, "what happens then?"

He regarded her with a level gaze. "Why don't we cross that bridge when we come to it?" he suggested gently. "That might not be for a while."

"No," said Mia, past the point of caring. "I want to cross that bridge now. If your business gets done next week, what would happen then?"

He didn't answer.

Mia could feel herself getting even colder inside. Slowly getting up from the table, she searched for something to say. There was really nothing. She wanted to yell and scream and throw something at him, but that would not accomplish anything. The clueless Mia that she was supposed to be would not read anything particularly sinister into his silence. It was only Mia the spy who knew what could happen to a girl that a K regarded as his charl.

So she acted the way he would expect any normal girl to act when her boyfriend was being unreasonable. "Korum," she told him with a stubborn expression on her face, "I'm going to Florida this summer—and that's that. I have a life that doesn't just revolve around you. I made these plans months before I knew you, and I can't change things around just because you want me to—"

"Mia," he said softly, "you *can* change things around and you will. If you try to leave at the end of the week, I will stop you. Do you understand me?"

She did. She understood him perfectly. But the Mia she was pretending to be wouldn't.

"What, you're going to prevent me from getting on the airplane? That's ridiculous," she said, even as her stomach twisted with fear.

"Of course," he said. "All I have to do is make one phone call, and your name will be on a no-fly list at all your human airports."

She stared at him in shock. Somehow, she hadn't expected him to go to such lengths to detain her. She figured he might lock her in the apartment or something. But it made perfect sense... Why do something as crude as physically restraining her when he could simply exercise his power with the U.S. government?

She felt tears welling up in her eyes, and she held them back with great effort. "I hate you," she told him, barely able to speak past the constriction in her chest. And she really did in that moment. If she'd had any doubts about helping the Resistance, they dissolved as she stared at his uncompromising expression. He had no right to do this to her, to take over her life like that—and his kind deserved exactly what they got. If Mia could really make a difference in the fight against the Ks, then she had an obligation to do so—even if it meant losing her life in the process.

He got up then and came toward her. "You don't hate me," he said in a silky tone. "You may wish you did, but you don't . . ." He grasped her chin, forcing her to meet his gaze. His eyes were nearly yellow at this point. "You're mine," he said quietly, "and you're not going anywhere without me. The sooner you come to terms with it, my darling, the easier it will be for you."

And so the gloves had come off then. He was not going to hide his true colors any longer.

Mia's fists clenched with impotent rage.

"I'm not coming to terms with anything," she hissed at him. "I'm a human being. I have rights. You can't order me around like this—"

"That's right, Mia," he said in that same dangerously smooth tone. "You're a human being—the creation of my kind. We made you. If it weren't for the Krinar, your species would not exist at all. Your people came up with all kinds of imaginary deities to worship, to explain how you came to be on this Earth. The things you have done in the name of your so-called gods are simply preposterous. But *we* are your true creators—*we* made you in our image. The only reason you have the rights you think you have is because we choose to let you have them. And we've been extremely lenient with your species, interfering as little as possible since we came to your planet." He leaned closer to her. "So if I want to keep one little human girl with me, and I have to order her around because she's too inexperienced to realize that what we have is very special—well, then, that's the way it's going to be."

Mia could barely think past the fury clouding her brain. Staring up at his beautiful face, she felt a surge of hatred so strong that she would have gladly stabbed him in that moment if she'd had a knife nearby. "Screw you," she told him bitterly, taking a step back to avoid his touch. "You and your kind should just go back to whatever hell you came from and leave us the fuck alone."

He smiled sardonically in response, letting her go for the moment. "That's not going to happen, Mia. We're here and we're staying—you might as well get used to it."

No, they weren't. Mia would make sure of that.

But he couldn't know that yet, so she said nothing, just looking up at him in defiance.

"And Mia," he added gently, "I can be very nice . . . or not—it's really up to you."

"Fuck you," she told him furiously, and watched his eyes flare even brighter.

"Oh, you will—and gladly." He smiled in anticipation.

Mia wanted to hit him. If he thought she would melt into a puddle at his touch, he had another thing coming. Unless . . .

"Fine," she said slowly, "but I call the shots tonight." And she smiled back at him, ignoring the rapid beating of her heart.

His eyes glittered with sudden interest. "Oh really? And why is that?"

"Because that's the only way I'm having sex with you tonight . . . willingly, I mean." Her smile took on a taunting edge. "You can always force me, of course—maybe even make me enjoy it. But I will always hate you for it . . . and you will ultimately regret it."

"Okay," he said softly, the bulge in his pants growing before her eyes, "let's pretend you're calling the shots . . . What would you like to do?"

Mia moistened her suddenly dry lips with the tip of her tongue and watched his eyes follow the motion with a hungry look. "Let's go into the bedroom," she said huskily, and walked past him, making the safe assumption that he would follow her there.

CHAPTER SEVENTEEN

They entered the room.

Mia walked over to the bed and sat down on it, fully dressed. He was about to do the same, but she stopped him with a shake of her head. "Not yet," she murmured, and watched him pause in response.

"I want you to take off your clothes," she said quietly, and waited to see what would happen.

To her surprise and growing excitement, he did as she asked, removing his T-shirt with one smoothly controlled motion. She inhaled sharply, the sight of his muscular half-naked body making her inner muscles clench with desire. Watching her with an amused half-smile, he unzipped his jeans and lowered them to the floor, stepping out of them gracefully. His erection was now covered only by a pair of briefs, and Mia could feel herself getting even wetter inside.

"Okay," he said softly, "now what?"

Mia's heart was galloping in her chest. "Lie down on the bed," she said, hoping she didn't sound as nervous as she felt.

He smiled and obeyed, sprawling out on his back, his hands behind his head.

Mia got up and started taking off her own clothes, watching the bulge in his briefs growing even larger as she shimmied out of her jeans and unbuttoned her shirt. Still wearing her bra and underwear, she climbed on top of him, straddling his hips. All of a sudden, he no longer looked amused, his entire body tensing up as her sex pressed against his erection, with only the two layers of underwear standing in the way of his cock.

Mia smiled triumphantly and put her hands on his chest, feeling the powerful muscles bunching under her fingers. The game she was playing was incredibly dangerous, yet she couldn't help but be aroused by the control she was exerting over her normally dominant lover. Running her hands over his chest, she leaned forward and touched the flat masculine nipple with her tongue, loving the way his cock jumped beneath her at the simple action.

"Give me your hands," she whispered, her hair brushing against his naked chest. He reached for her, but she intercepted him, grabbing his wrists. His eyebrows rose in surprise, but he let her stop him, observing her actions with a heavy-lidded amber gaze.

She twined her fingers with his and pressed his hands into the pillow above his head, as though her small human hands could contain his Krinar strength for even a second. His eyes burned brighter with lust, but he did not resist, letting her hold him captive for now. She leaned closer to him and kissed his neck, and he arched beneath her with a sharp hiss. Reveling in his response, she lightly scraped the area with her teeth and was rewarded with a low growl. Rising up a bit, she repeated the action on the other side of his neck. By now, his body was nearly vibrating with tension, and she wondered hazily how much longer he would allow her to tease him like that. Still holding his hands, she kissed him on the lips, her tongue tentatively entering his mouth. He kissed her back with barely controlled aggression, and she sucked lightly on his tongue, causing him to buck underneath her. Leaving his mouth, she nibbled his neck again, focusing on the tightly corded muscle connecting it to his shoulder, and he groaned as though in pain.

Loving her newfound power, Mia licked the side of his neck and tongued his ear, softly biting the earlobe. His hips thrust at her in response, but the underwear was in the way of his penetration. She moaned, her panties getting soaked with her juices as his erection rubbed against her clit.

"Keep your arms raised," she whispered, finally letting go of his palms.

He did, and Mia could see the effort it took him not to touch her in the sweat beading up on his forehead. She moved down his body then, licking and kissing every inch of skin along the way until her mouth reached his flat stomach. His abdominal muscles quivered in anticipation, and she smiled with excitement, gently squeezing his balls through the briefs as her lips followed the dark trail of hair down from his navel to where it disappeared into his underwear. He groaned her name, and she hooked her fingers into his briefs, slowly pulling them down. As he lifted his hips to help her, his cock sprang up at her, the bulbous shaft stiff and the tip glistening with pre-ejaculate.

Mia swallowed with nervousness and excitement, wondering what would happen if he lost control—if she drove him as crazy as he could make her.

Grasping his shaft with one hand, she lowered her head and slowly licked the underside of his balls, which were tightly drawn against his body with extreme arousal. He hissed at her action, torso arching and cock jumping in her hand, and Mia let go of it, using her hands to cup his balls instead. Simultaneously, she closed her lips around the tip of his cock and moved to take him further into her mouth, stopping only when he reached the back of her throat. She could taste the saltiness of his pre-cum, and her sex contracted in excitement. His body vibrating from the tension, he growled low in his throat, hips thrusting at her in a wordless demand to take him deeper, but Mia resisted, moving her lips up and down his shaft in a torturously slow and shallow rhythm.

And then he snapped.

Before she even realized what happened, he had her on her back, her panties ripped to shreds and his cock pushing into her in one heavy stroke. She cried out in shock, her nails digging into his upper arms as he penetrated her all the way without giving her any time to adjust to his fullness. She was dripping wet, but it didn't matter, and her inner muscles trembled in the desperate attempt to accommodate the invasion. There was pain, but there was pleasure too, as his hips hammered at her in a merciless, driving rhythm. She screamed—in agony, in ecstasy, she didn't know which—and felt him swell even more, becoming impossibly harder and thicker, and then he was coming, his head thrown back with a roar and his pelvis grinding into her sex. Mia cried out in frustration, her own release only a few elusive seconds away, and then his teeth sank into her shoulder, and her entire world exploded from the sudden rush of heated ecstasy through her veins.

It was not enough for him, of course, with the taste of her blood driving him into a frenzy, and his cock stiffened again inside her before her pulsations even ended. And Mia could no longer think at all, the drug-like high from his saliva turning her body into a pure instrument of pleasure, her skin unbearably sensitized to his touch and her insides burning with liquid desire. He drove into her relentlessly, and she screamed from the excruciating tension until she climaxed, over and over, in a never-ending cascade of orgasmic peaks and valleys, the night turning into a nonstop marathon of sex and blood.

Finally passing out toward the morning, Mia slept, her body still joined with his and her mind void of any thoughts.

* * *

Mia woke up the next day to the feel of someone's hand gently playing with her hair.

Surprised, she opened her eyes just a bit and saw Korum sitting by the edge of the bed, looking oddly concerned.

"Wh-what are you doing here?" she muttered sleepily, blinking in an attempt to focus.

"How are you feeling?" he asked quietly, brushing back a stray curl that fell over her eye.

"Um . . ." Mia tried to think. Moving a little, she became aware of various aches and pains, as well as an extreme soreness between her thighs.

Obviously not satisfied with her response, Korum pulled off the blanket, uncovering her naked body to his eyes. Her mind still feeling fuzzy, Mia followed his gaze as it lingered on the faint bruises covering her breasts and torso, many in the shape of finger marks.

His face darkened with guilt, and he groaned. "Mia, I'm so sorry about this . . . I should've never let you play that game with me last night. I can usually control myself with you because I know how small and fragile you are, but I completely lost it last night . . . I never meant to hurt you like this—please believe me . . ."

Mia nodded, still trying to understand what happened. All she could recall was the mind-blowing sex, mixed with the ecstatic rush from his bite.

He gently stroked her shoulder, caressing the soft skin. "I am really sorry about this," he murmured. "You're so delicate . . . I should've never lost control like that. I'll make you feel better, I promise—"

The events of last night were slowly coming back to Mia. Her hand clenched into a fist as she remembered what had led her to tease him like that, and the feel of the ring on her finger was utterly reassuring.

She might be sore this morning, but she was also hopeful that the little device had worked as promised. There was no guarantee, of course, but her finger's proximity to Korum's palm last night should've been sufficient to get access to the necessary blueprints. Now she just had to get the ring over to John and, for that, she needed Korum to leave her alone.

"It's all right," she mumbled, trying to think of something appropriate to say. He was obviously feeling guilty about leaving a few bruises on her body. It struck her as hypocritical, this extreme concern for her physical well-being, since he obviously had no problem causing her emotional pain by upending her entire life. Then again, her being sore could interfere with their sex life, and he probably didn't want that.

"I'll bring something, okay?" he said, and disappeared from the room with inhuman speed.

Mia buried her head in the pillow while waiting for his return, desperately thinking of ways to get the information over to John quickly. She still needed to write her papers, so maybe she could tell Korum she had to get some books from the library.

He was back a minute later, carrying the familiar device that had "shined" her and something else that she'd never seen before. The second object looked most like a lipstick tube, but was made of some strange material.

"Um, I'm all right—really, there's no need for this," said Mia quickly, not wanting him to plant any additional tracking devices on her. For all she knew, the next batch of nanotechnology in her body might broadcast her every thought to him, and that was the last thing she wanted.

"There's every need," he said, obviously surprised at her reluctance. "You're hurt, and I can fix it. Why not?"

Why not indeed. She didn't have a good answer for that, and protesting further would make him suspicious. Getting caught so close to the end of her mission would be stupid, and it's not like she didn't already have the tracking devices embedded in her palms. What's a few more?

So she just shrugged her shoulders in response, letting him do as he wanted.

He activated the "shining" device and ran the warm red light over her bruises. Seeing it work the second time was still incredible, with the marks on her skin disappearing as though they were never there. He was very thorough, inspecting every inch of her skin, and Mia blushed slightly at having so much attention paid to her naked body in broad daylight. Once he was done, he took the tube-like device in his hand and brought it toward her thighs.

"What are you going to do with that?" she asked suspiciously, eyeing it with distrust. There was only one place remaining on her body that still hadn't been healed, and the red light from the device could not reach there. She hoped the little tube wasn't really going where it looked like it could go.

Korum sighed and said, "It's something we use for deep internal damage, when you have to heal various organs before you can mend the outer layer of the skin. I know it's overkill for what you've got, but it's the only thing I have in this apartment that can reach inside you to help you with the soreness."

So it was going there. Mia's blush got worse. The thing was about the size of a tampon, and the thought of having something medical like that inserted in broad daylight was embarrassing.

"Seriously?" he asked with incredulity. "After last night, you're going to blush at this?"

Mia refused to look at him. "Just do it already," she mumbled, plopping down and hiding her face in the pillow.

He laughed softly and did as she requested, sliding the little device inside her sore and swollen opening. It went in easily, and Mia didn't feel anything for a few seconds until the tingling began.

"It feels funny," she complained, still shielded by the pillow.

"It's supposed to—that means it's working."

The tingling went on for a couple of minutes and then it stopped. She didn't feel sore anymore, which was nice, although the feel of the foreign object inside her was disconcerting.

"It should be done by now," said Korum, reaching inside her with his long fingers and pulling out the tube. "That's it—all finished. You can stop hiding now."

"Okay, thanks," muttered Mia, still refusing to meet his eyes. "I think I'm going to shower now."

He laughed and kissed her exposed shoulder. "Go for it. I have some things to take care of, so I'll be out the rest of the day. The dinner will probably be a late one, so be sure to grab a good lunch."

And then he walked out of the room, finally leaving Mia alone to carry out the rest of the plan.

CHAPTER EIGHTEEN

As soon as Korum left, Mia sprang into action, her heart pounding at the magnitude of what she was about to do.

Before hopping into the shower, she sent a quick 'Hi' email to Jessie, letting her know that she would be stopping by the apartment today and asking how Jessie's Anatomy final had gone. Hopefully, John would see the email and contact Mia quickly. It was already early afternoon; due to her complete exhaustion, Mia had slept far later than planned, and there was a lot to get done before this evening.

Korum had thoughtfully left her a sandwich for lunch, and Mia gratefully gobbled it down before heading out the door. When he did things like that—considerate little gestures—she could almost believe that he genuinely cared about her, and she would feel an unwelcome pang of guilt at betraying his trust. Even today, after everything that happened last evening, the thought of him coming to any harm made her feel sick. It was ridiculous, of course; he would most likely be fine—and even if he wasn't, it was his own fault for invading Earth and trying to enslave her species. Still, she would much rather see him safely deported back to Krina, so she could resume her normal life knowing that he was thousands of light years away and would never bother her again.

Or so she told herself.

Deep inside, some silly romantic part of her wanted to cry at the thought of never seeing Korum again—never feeling his touch or hearing his laughter, never glimpsing the dimple that so incongruously graced his left cheek. He was her enemy, but he was also her lover, and she had gotten attached to him despite everything. The pleasure that he gave her went beyond the sexual; just being with him made her feel excited and alive, and—if she ever let herself forget the exact nature of their relationship—oddly happy.

She could not imagine having sex with someone else after experiencing Korum's lovemaking. It would be like eating sawdust for the rest of her life after first tasting ambrosia. It made perfect sense that he would be a good lover, of course; aside from whatever special chemistry he said they had together, Korum was also thousands of years old—and had had plenty of time to learn exactly how to please a woman. How could a human man compare to that? And she didn't even want to think about how he made her feel when he took her blood. She wasn't sure that it was healthy, to feel a pleasure so intense, but the thought of never experiencing it again was nearly more than she could bear.

For the first time, she wondered about the xenos she'd heard about before. The motives of these people—who supposedly advertised online with the goal of entering into sexual relations with the Krinar—had always been a mystery to her. But she wondered now if they were perhaps truly addicted... if they'd had a taste of paradise and knew that everything else would pale in comparison. Korum had warned that addiction was a possibility for both of them if he took her blood too frequently. Mia shuddered at the thought. That was the last thing she needed—to actually develop a physical need for him. It was enough that she would probably miss him with every fiber of her being when he was finally gone from her life; the last thing she needed was to crave some elusive high that she could only achieve with him.

There was no other alternative for her; she had to complete the mission. Their relationship was bound to end—it was just a matter of time. Even if she were willing to put up with his autocratic nature—or if she even went so far as to accept being his charl—he would tire of her in a few short years and then she would be alone anyway, completely heartbroken and devastated at his desertion.

No, she had to do this. There was no other way. She couldn't have lived with herself knowing that she'd had a chance to make a real difference in the course of human history and failed to do so because of her weakness for one particular K—for someone who regarded her as nothing more than his plaything.

Arriving at her apartment, Mia was surprised to see that John was already there. So were Jessie and Edgar, the actor her roommate had apparently started seeing.

As soon as she walked through the door, John asked if they could speak in private. Mia nodded and led him into her room, closing the door behind her. Before the door was fully shut, Mia heard Edgar ask Jessie if her roommate was seeing John as well, but Jessie's reply was already inaudible.

"I think I have it," said Mia without any preamble.

John's entire face lit up. "You do? That's great! How did you manage it so quickly?" Seeing the color flooding her face, he added hastily, "Never mind, that's not important."

Mia shrugged and pulled the ring off her finger. There was a little indentation left behind on her skin. She sincerely hoped that Korum was not particularly observant when it came to women's jewelry; otherwise, he might wonder why she'd worn that ring once and never again.

"I need you to promise me something," Mia said slowly, still holding on to the ring.

"What?"

"Promise me that Korum will not be harmed in whatever you're planning to do."

John hesitated, and Mia's eyes narrowed. "Promise me, John. You owe me that much."

"Why? He doesn't deserve it—"

"It doesn't matter what he does or does not deserve. This is my condition for helping you. Korum gets safe passage home."

John looked at her and then sighed heavily. "All right, Mia, if that's what you truly want. We'll make sure that he gets safely deported."

Mia nodded and handed him the ring. "So what now?" she asked. "How long do you think it will take your Keiths to do something with this information?"

He grinned at her, looking like a kid at Christmas. "They'll have to look at it and make sure that it's not more complicated than they think, but if they're right . . . we could be looking at a potential attack within days."

Days? That was much faster than Mia had ever thought possible.

"Won't it take them time to make . . . well, whatever it is that those blueprints are for?" she asked hesitantly.

He shook his head. "No, not that much time at all. Remember what I told you about how they manufacture everything using nanotechnology—and can make things almost instantly if they have the design for it?"

Mia vaguely recalled something like that, so she nodded.

"Well, they will now have the blueprints, and they already have the technology to create those designs. They just need to get that technology to a safe location outside of their settlements, and then they can manufacture the necessary weapons to penetrate the K Center shields. Once the shields are gone, the human forces will be ready."

Forces?

"Is the government in on this?" asked Mia with surprise.

John hesitated. "Not exactly. But there are those within the government who believe that it was wrong to sign the Coexistence Treaty, to allow them to build the settlements. These individuals are sympathetic to our cause and they have the ability to bring us reinforcements. Some of these are highly placed people in the Army and the Navy, as well as within the CIA and other equivalent agencies worldwide."

Mia looked at him in shock. She hadn't realized the full scope of the anti-K movement. For some reason, she'd envisioned it as being a few hundred suicidal individuals within the Resistance—or those like John, who had a personal vendetta against the Ks—helped by a few human-sympathizing aliens. But it made sense, of course, that the freedom fighters couldn't have come as far as they did—and gained the assistance of the Keiths—if they hadn't had at least a decent chance of success.

"Wow," she said softly, "so it's really happening then? We're kicking them off our planet?"

John nodded with barely contained glee. "It's happening, Mia. If the information on this ring is as good as we hope it is, we're looking at Earth's liberation within a week—a couple of weeks at the most."

That was crazy. Mia tried to imagine what would happen when the Ks learned that they were being attacked. She remembered the days of the Great Panic and shuddered.

"John," she said slowly, "would they really go without a big fight? You know what happened before . . . how much damage they could do even with bare hands—"

"That's true," agreed John, "they could definitely fight back—and it could get very bloody for both sides. That's why the information you got for us is so crucial. You see, if the Keiths are right, these blueprints also contain the design for one of their most advanced weapons. Once the shields are down and we let the Ks know that we have this weapon, they would be suicidal to do anything but surrender. Because if they fight, we *will* use it—and every K in their colonies would be turned to dust."

"Turned to dust? What kind of weapon can do that?" asked Mia in horrified shock.

"It's weaponized nanotechnology on a massive scale. It can be programmed with very specific constraints, so we could set it to only destroy Ks within a certain radius and to spare whatever humans may be in the area at the time."

Mia's eyes widened, and John continued, "Of course, we still expect some Ks to try to escape from the colonies when they learn of the attack, so we'll have our fighters stationed all around to capture and contain those—and that could get bloody. We might still end up suffering heavy casualties, but we stand a very real chance of winning here."

Mia swallowed, feeling nauseous at the thought of any bloodshed. Knowing that something she did led to "heavy casualties" or extermination of thousands of intelligent beings—she didn't know how she would handle that kind of responsibility.

But there was no choice now, not that there had ever been any for her. Ever since she'd laid eyes on Korum at the park, her fate had been decided. Her only choice had been to meekly accept being his charl or to fight back—and she had chosen to fight. And now that decision might result in the loss of many lives, both human and Krinar.

Mia bitterly wished she'd never gone to the park that day, had never learned about what goes on in the K Centers. If she could somehow turn back the clock and go back to her regular life, knowing next to nothing about the Ks, she would gladly do so—and leave the liberation of Earth to someone better equipped to deal with it. But she knew, and that burden felt unbearably heavy right now as she looked into John's glowing face and imagined the upcoming bloody battle.

"Mia," said John, apparently sensing her distress, "please don't forget: *they* came to our planet, *they* imposed their rules on us—and killed thousands of people in the process, until we had no choice but to give in. Do you remember how it was during the Great Panic?"

Mia nodded, thinking of the terrifying chaos and bloody street fights of those dark months.

Satisfied, John continued, "I know that your only exposure to them has been through Korum, and he has probably treated you nicely so far . . . because he thinks of you as his current favorite pet. But they're not nice at all. They're predators by nature. They evolved as parasites, as vampires, sustaining themselves by consuming the blood of other species. In fact, they developed humans for that purpose—to satisfy their own perverse urges with us—"

That wasn't exactly what Korum had told her, but she didn't feel like arguing that point right now.

"—and they have no regard for our rights. Most of them view us as inferior, and they would not hesitate to enslave us completely if it suited their purposes."

"I know," said Mia, rubbing her temples to get rid of the tension. "I know all of that—that's why I'm helping you, John. I just really wish there was another way ... some way we could just make them go away without spilling any blood."

"I wish there was too," said John, sighing heavily. "But there isn't. They invaded our planet with force—and now we take it back from them in the same way. And if some lives have to be lost in the process—well, we just have to hope that not too many of them are on our side. It's war, Mia—the real *War of the Worlds.*"

John left, and Mia sat down on her bed to digest everything.

How had she—a regular college student—managed to get involved in a war? Spying was something she'd always associated with glamorous secret agents, men and women who've had extensive training in everything from martial arts to defusing a bomb. A psychology major from NYU just didn't fit the bill. Yet here she was, supposedly aiding the Resistance in their most important fight against the Ks.

A terrifying thought occurred to her. Once Korum knew what was happening—that their settlements were being attacked—would he realize that she was the one responsible? Would he make the connection between his carefully guarded blueprints being stolen and the human girl he slept with every night? Because if he did—and he was still in New York at the time—then her days were likely numbered as well.

A tentative knock on her door interrupted her dark musings.

"Yes, come in!" she called out, relieved to have a distraction from that line of thinking.

To her surprise and dismay, it was not Jessie. Instead, Peter stood in her bedroom doorway, his wavy blond hair and blue eyes looking even more angelic in the bright light of the day. There were still black and blue marks on his throat.

"Peter!" she exclaimed. "What are you doing here?"

"I came to see you," he said. "Your roommate told Edgar that you would be home today, and I just wanted to make sure you were all right after what happened that night—"

"Oh gosh, Peter, that's really nice of you," said Mia, desperately trying to think of the quickest way to get rid of him. She couldn't imagine that Korum would be pleased to know that Peter was anywhere near her right now, much less in her bedroom. He probably wouldn't find out, but she didn't want to chance it. It was enough that she had almost gotten him killed in that club.

Peter was looking at her with a concerned expression. "What happened that night, Mia? Did that monster hurt you in any way?"

"No, of course not," she tried to reassure him. "He just got jealous—I never expected him to react like that, believe me. I'm really sorry about everything that happened. I should've never danced with you that night. You got hurt because of me—"

He waved his hand dismissively. "It's not a big deal. I was once beaten up in high school because the head quarterback thought I was flirting with his girlfriend. Believe me, this was nothing in comparison." And he grinned at her, his smile utterly infectious.

Mia smiled back a little. It was good to hear that he didn't hold a grudge against her. But he still needed to go away for his own safety.

"Listen, Peter, thanks for checking up on me," she said. "That was really sweet of you. But we now know that my boyfriend is not too keen on our friendship—and it's really for the best if he doesn't find out you were here—"

"Mia," said Peter seriously, his smile completely gone, "are you really dating that creature? I just never pictured you as a xeno—"

"I'm not!"

"You're not a Krinarian, are you?"

"Of course not! I'm not religious at all!"

"Then why are you seeing him?"

Mia sighed. "Look, Peter, that's not really any of your business. He's my boyfriend—that's all you need to know. I'm sorry I didn't tell you that when we first met. I was just having a fun time at a girls' night out. I really didn't mean to mislead you in any way—"

"That's bullshit," said Peter vehemently. "A boyfriend—that's a human guy, not some vicious alien who drags you out of the club like that." He paused for a second and asked quietly, "Mia, is he forcing you to be with him?"

"What? Why would you think that?" Mia stared at him, wondering what would make him ask something like that.

He looked back at her, his brows furrowed in a frown. "You just don't seem like the type to seek out one of these monsters."

"What type is that?" wondered Mia, genuinely curious to hear the answer.

He tugged at his ear in frustration. "Well, a lot of people in the entertainment industry actually . . . models, actresses, singers—they get bored and look for something to spice up their lives . . . They're shallow, and many of them are stupid—all they see are the pretty faces and not the evil underneath—"

"Evil underneath?" asked Mia, surprised that he felt so strongly about the Krinar. Prior to her own close encounters with Korum, she'd had zero exposure to the invaders and no real opinion about them. Maybe Peter was religious himself and believed the claim that the Ks were demons?

He grimaced. "I've seen people disappear, Mia, when they get involved with these creatures. That, or end up really messed up at the end. It's not natural for us—to be with their kind. It never ends well . . ."

Mia took a deep breath and said firmly, "Peter, look, I appreciate the concern, but there's really no need in this case. I know what I'm doing. I'm neither shallow nor stupid—"

"I never said you were," protested Peter.

"—and I don't really appreciate you implying anything about my relationship. I'm with Korum because I want to be, and that's all there's to it."

She sincerely hoped that was enough to get Peter to go away. The last thing she needed was a bumbling white knight trying to save her from the evil monster—a white knight who would definitely end up getting slain in the process. Maybe later, if she survived the next couple of weeks, she would apologize to Peter for being so harsh. She liked him, and it would be nice to become friends with him, particularly if her life ever got back to normal.

He looked slightly hurt. "Of course, I'm sorry, I didn't mean to imply anything. Obviously, you can be with whomever you choose. I just wanted to make sure you were all right, that's all."

Mia nodded and gave him a faint smile. "I understand. Thanks again for stopping by." Reaching into her bag, she pulled out the laptop and a couple of books.

Peter immediately got the hint. "Sure. I'll see you around, okay?" he said, and walked out of the room. Mia heard him talking to Jessie and Edgar for a minute, and then he was gone, the front door closing decisively behind him.

Mia plopped down on her bed with relief. How had it happened that a cute guy—with whom she actually had a decent connection—had come along at such a wrong time in her life? Had she met him two months ago, she had no doubt that she would have been ecstatic to have him pay attention to her like that—but it was too late now.

Like those people he knew, she would likely end up messed up in the end—either that or dead at the hands of her alien lover.

CHAPTER NINETEEN

Shortly after Peter left, Edgar departed as well. Mia heard them kissing and giggling by the door, and then there was silence. Almost immediately afterwards, Jessie came into her room.

"So," said Mia, smiling at her roommate, "I take it things are going well with Edgar?"

Jessie gave her a huge grin. "They are going *very* well. He's just so nice, and so fun, and so cute . . ."

Mia laughed and said, "I'm glad for you. You deserve a good guy like that."

"That I do," said Jessie without any false modesty, still grinning. And then her expression abruptly became serious. "And so do you, Mia—"

Uh-oh, thought Mia. Here comes the lecture.

"—and you're clearly not getting it."

"Jessie, please, let's not beat a dead horse—"

"A dead horse? I'd like to beat up a certain K!" Jessie took a deep breath, clearly riled on Mia's behalf. "Peter is such a nice guy, and he seems to really like you—to come all the way here like this after everything that happened . . . and you're stuck with that monster!"

Mia rubbed the back of her neck to get rid of some tension there. "Jessie, please stop worrying about my relationship . . . everything will get resolved in its own time

"Speaking of getting things resolved, did you talk to him about the summer?"

Mia bit her lip. She hated lying to Jessie, and she so badly wanted to talk to someone about the whole maddening mess. If John was right about the Keiths' timing, her trip to Florida would be merely delayed—and not even by all that much. Of course, that assumed she would still be alive at the time. Mia decided on a slightly edited version of the truth.

"I have," she said slowly.

"And?"

"And we agreed that I'll go later in the summer, and do an internship here in New York instead."

Jessie stared at her in shock. "What internship?"

"I'm not sure yet. Korum promised to find me something in my field."

"Oh my God, he's not letting you go, is he?" Jessie looked completely horrified.

"Not exactly," admitted Mia. "He did say, though, that we'll go to Florida together once his business in New York is done."

"Together? What, he's going to meet your family?" The expression on Jessie's face was utterly incredulous.

"I have no idea," said Mia, and she really didn't. She hadn't had a chance to think about it, with everything that had gone on—but she couldn't imagine her normal down-to-earth family interacting calmly with her alien lover. "We didn't get as far as discussing the particulars—"

"That bastard! I can't believe he's doing it to you! No wonder you're helping the Resistance—you probably hate his guts."

Mia couldn't believe her ears. "What? What did you just say?"

"Oh come on, Mia," said Jessie calmly. "I'm not an idiot. I can put two and two together. John was waiting for you here in the apartment even before you showed up. Clearly, he knew you were coming. You're communicating with them, aren't you?"

Damn it. Sometimes Mia forgot just how astute her pretty, bubbly roommate could be. Denying it any longer would be pointless, but Jessie could not know the extent of Mia's involvement—it would be much too dangerous for both of them.

Mia gave her a piercing look. "Jessie, listen to me, don't ever say something like that—and don't ever talk about it with anyone, not even Edgar. Do you promise me?"

Jessie nodded, her eyes narrowed. "I would never say anything. When Edgar asked me if you and John were dating, I just said that he was an old friend of your family's."

"That's good," said Mia with relief. Then she added, "Look, I am not doing anything too crazy, I promise. John just asked me to keep an eye on Korum's activities and report to him occasionally. That's all I was doing today. Korum met a couple of other Ks recently, and I just wanted to tell John about it. Turns out he already knew, so it really wasn't a big deal." Mia had no idea where she had learned to lie so smoothly.

"Not a big deal? Mia... you're dealing with an extraterrestrial who has no regard for human life. You saw what he did to Peter—and that was just for dancing with you! If he catches you spying, he would kill you for sure! Of course, it's a big deal!" Jessie blew out a frustrated breath.

There was nothing Mia could really say to that, so she just shrugged.

"And it's all my fault for blabbing about you to Jason! I can't believe those bastards decided to use you like that."

Mia rubbed her neck again. "They just saw an opportunity and decided to use it. It doesn't really change my situation. I'm still with Korum, whether or not I'm spying on him. So I might as well try to help out, you know?"

Jessie gave her a frustrated look. "I can't believe all this shit is happening to you. You're the most by-the-book person I know... and you end up sleeping with a K and spying on him."

Mia sighed heavily. "I know. I'm so screwed, Jessie—and not just in a good way."

A small smile broke out on Jessie's face, and she shook her head in reproach. "Mia..."

Mia grinned at her. "I know, I know, that was pretty bad."

"Not James Bond caliber, that's for sure." And Jessie grinned back.

* * *

That evening, Korum got home around eight o'clock. Mia was already back at his place and frantically working on her paper.

He entered her study room and came up to kiss her. "Hey there, looks like somebody is hard at work," he teased, brushing his lips briefly against her cheek.

Mia gave him a little frown. "Yeah, I have to finish this paper tonight. I have this and my Child Psychology paper due Thursday, and I'm not done with even one of them."

"Sounds terrible," Korum said, the slight curve of his lips giving away his amusement.

"It is!" said Mia, her frown getting worse. Couldn't he see she was stressed? He didn't have to laugh at her just because her worries seemed minor to him.

"Do you want some help with it?" he asked, causing Mia to give him an incredulous look.

"Help with my papers?" Was he serious?

"Isn't that what you're stressing about?" He didn't look like he was joking.

"Uh . . ." Mia was speechless. Finally finding her tongue, she mumbled, "That's okay, thanks . . . I should be able to handle it."

Stifling a grin, she imagined turning in a paper on the effects of environmental factors in early childhood development—written from the perspective of a two-thousand-year-old extraterrestrial. The look on Professor Dunkin's face would be priceless.

"I can write in English, you know," said Korum, apparently offended by her reluctance.

Mia smiled with some condescension. "Of course you can." This was the strangest conversation ever. "But there's more to writing an academic paper than just knowing the language. You have to have read all these books and attended the lectures . . ." She gestured toward the big pile of paper books sitting at the corner of her desk.

"So," said Korum, shrugging nonchalantly, "I can read the books right now."

Mia gave him a dumbfounded look. "There's about ten of them . . ." She swallowed to get rid of the sudden dryness in her throat. "H-How fast do you read?"

"Pretty fast," he said. "I also have what you would call a photographic memory, so I don't need to read the material more than once."

Mia stared at him in shock. "So you can read all these books in a matter of hours?"

He nodded. "I would probably need about two hours to finish them all."

That was incredible. "Is that normal for your kind?" Mia asked, still digesting that shocking tidbit.

"Some of us have that ability naturally, while others choose to enhance it with technology to keep up. I was born this way."

Mia could feel her heart rate picking up. She'd known that he was very smart, of course, and John had told her that Korum was one of the best designers among the K. She just hadn't expected him to have what amounted to superhuman intelligence.

"I probably seem really stupid to you then," Mia said quietly, "given how long it takes me to do all this—"

He sighed. "No, Mia, of course not. Just because you're lacking certain abilities doesn't mean you're not smart."

Yeah, right. "What else can you do?" asked Mia, realizing how little she still knew about her alien lover.

He shrugged. "I can probably do some math in my head that you would need a calculator for."

This was fascinating and scary at the same time. "What's 10,456 times 6,345?" she asked, simultaneously reaching for her phone to check the answer.

"66,343,320."

That was exactly right. And he'd given her the answer before she even had time to input the numbers into the calculator on her phone. Mia swallowed again.

"So do you want my help with the paper or not?" Korum was beginning to look impatient.

Mia shook her head. "Uh, no—that's all right, thanks. I'm sure you could write a great paper—probably better than me—but I still have to do this myself."

"Okay, sure, whatever you want," he said, shaking his head at her stubbornness. "Are you hungry? Do you want me to make something?"

Mia had snacked throughout the day, so she wasn't starving. "I don't know," she said tentatively. "I don't think I have time for a sit-down meal today." She looked up at him, hoping that he would understand.

"Of course," he said, "I'll bring you something to eat here." Giving her a quick smile, he left the room.

Mia stared at the door in frustration. Why did he have to be so nice to her today? It would be so much easier if he treated her with cruelty or indifference. The guilt burning her up inside made no sense; she knew she was doing the right thing by helping the Resistance. The Ks had invaded their planet, not the other way around; liberating her species should not make her feel like this—like she was betraying someone she cared about.

Taking a deep breath, she tried to focus back on the paper. It was an impossible task. Her thoughts kept wandering, jumping from one unpleasant topic to another. Had she set in motion something that would result in the loss of thousands of lives? And would Korum be one of the casualties? It still didn't seem entirely real to her, the potential impact of her actions.

Korum came back a few minutes later. He had made some kind of sushi-like rolls with crunchy lettuce and peppers and an apple-walnut dish for dessert.

Mia thanked him and gladly dug in, finding that she was quite hungry after all.

He smiled at her and bent down to kiss her forehead. "Enjoy. I'll be next door if you need me."

And then he left, letting her work on her papers—and battle her own dark thoughts.

CHAPTER TWENTY

That night, he was incredibly tender with her.

His fingers unerringly finding every knot and tense muscle, he massaged every inch of her body until she lay there in a boneless puddle of contentment. Once he was satisfied that she was fully relaxed, he flipped her over onto her back and began kissing her, starting with the tips of her fingers. His lips were soft and felt warm on the skin of her hand, and when he sucked her index finger into his mouth and swirled his tongue around it, Mia moaned from the unexpectedly erotic sensation.

Leaving her fingers alone, his mouth traveled up her palm, licking the sensitive spot on the inside of her wrist, and then further, up her arm, until he reached the arched column of her throat. Mia held her breath, waiting for the familiar biting pain, but he merely placed a series of light kisses there, sending goosebumps down her leg and arm, and nibbled softly on her earlobe. Mia moaned again, overcome by the pleasure of his touch, and buried her fingers in his hair, pulling his face down for a deep French kiss.

He kissed her back, passionately and intensely, and Mia felt the strength of his desire in the rigid erection brushing against her thigh. His hand found her breasts, gently squeezing and massaging the small globes, and his thumb flicked across her left nipple, causing it to stiffen further.

Lifting himself up on his elbows, he looked down at her with a warm golden gaze. "You're so beautiful," he murmured, staring into her eyes, and the tender expression on his face made her want to cry. Why was he doing this to her today of all days? This might be one of the last few times she was having sex with him, and she didn't want to remember it like this—like the lovemaking that it could never be.

He kissed her again, and she sucked on his tongue, hoping to make him lose control, so she could forget everything in the mind-bending ecstasy and finally turn off her brain. He groaned in response, and she felt his cock jump against her leg, but his touch on her body remained exceedingly gentle, with none of the raw lust from last night.

Frustrated, Mia pushed at his shoulders. "I want to get on top," she told him huskily. He was clearly doing penance for his roughness yesterday, but that wasn't what Mia wanted tonight.

His eyes widened a little in surprise, but he rolled off her onto his back. Mia climbed over him and grabbed his head with both hands, bringing his face to hers for a deep tongue-filled kiss while simultaneously rubbing her sex on his without allowing actual penetration. He wrapped his arms around her in response, so tightly that she could barely breathe, and kissed her back with the intensity she was seeking. She could see a fine layer of sweat on his forehead as his body strained with the effort of holding himself back. Mia moved her hips suggestively then, grinding against his cock, and his hips lifted off the bed, trying to get more. His embrace loosened slightly, and Mia worked her right hand in between their bodies and wrapped her fingers around his shaft. He hissed, his body tensing up, and she carefully guided his cock to her opening, starting to lower herself onto him in a maddeningly slow motion.

He growled low in his throat and his hips thrust up, penetrating her in one powerful stroke. Mia cried out, feeling her muscles quivering, adjusting to the extreme fullness. He grasped her hips, his thumb finding her clit through the closed folds and pressing on it, his touch torturously light, bringing her closer to the desired peak without sending her over. Mia moaned, her sex clenching around his cock. She wanted more— more of the madness, of the mindless bliss that only he could make her feel. "Bite me," she told him, and watched his eyes turn even more yellow even as he shook his head in denial. "You don't know what you're asking," he muttered roughly, and rolled over so that he was over her again, their bodies still joined.

Before she could say anything else, he twisted his hips slightly, and the head of his cock nudged the sensitive spot deep inside. Mia moaned, arching toward him, and he repeated the action, again and again, until the monstrous tension coiling inside her became unbearable, and she screamed, raking her nails down his back as the long-awaited climax finally rushed through her, obliterating all rational thought in its wake.

But he wasn't done with her yet. He still hadn't come, despite the rhythmic squeezing of her inner muscles, and his shaft was lodged inside her, as hard and thick as ever. Burying his hand in her hair, he kissed her deeply and began thrusting, alternating a shallow stroke with a deeper one, until the tension started building again and every cell in her body was crying out for the release. She tried to move her hips, to force him into that constant pace she needed to reach her climax, but he wouldn't let her, his large, powerful body holding her down. His kiss was relentless, his tongue ravishing her mouth, and Mia felt like she would explode from the intensity of the sensations. And then suddenly she was there, her entire body convulsing in his arms, and he was coming as well, his pelvis grinding into her own as his cock pulsed inside her, releasing his semen in short, warm bursts.

Afterwards, he rolled off her and gathered her to him, leaving her lying partially on top, her head on his chest and her left leg draped over his hips. They were both slick with sweat, and Mia could hear the rapid beating of his heart gradually beginning to slow as his breathing returned to its normal pace.

She didn't really know what to say, so she didn't say anything. The sex had been incredible, and she hated the fact that he could make her feel like this—even without any chemical enhancers.

Why did it have to be him, she thought bitterly, looking at his flat bronzed stomach moving up and down with every breath. Why couldn't she have fallen for a normal human guy instead of an alien genius whose kind was taking over her planet?

She felt the hot prickling of tears behind her eyelids and squeezed them tightly, not letting the moisture escape. Her body felt languid and tired in the aftermath of the sex session, but her mind kept buzzing, working overtime, looking for a solution where none could be found. Even if he cared for her in his own way, those feelings would turn to hatred once he learned the depths of her betrayal—and the hands that held her so gently now would likely end up wrapped around her throat.

She must have tensed at the thought because he pulled away to look at her face and asked curiously, "What's the matter?"

When she hesitated, a worried frown appeared on his face. "Mia? What's the matter? I didn't hurt you, did I?"

Mia shook her head, trying not to look him directly in the eyes. "No, of course not," she said huskily, "it was wonderful . . . you know that—"

"Then what?" he prodded, reaching out to grasp her chin and force her to meet his gaze.

Mia tried to control herself, but the stupid tears wouldn't leave her alone, welling up in her eyes.

"It's nothing," Mia lied, silently cursing the fact that her voice was shaking, "I just . . . g-get this way when I'm stressed—"

His frown got deeper. "Why are you so stressed? Is it your papers?" he asked, studying her with a perplexed look in his eyes.

Mia nodded slightly, squeezing her eyes shut and trying to calm herself. He might become suspicious if her tears didn't have a good explanation. Unless . . .

Opening her eyes, she looked at him, no longer caring if he saw the glimmer there. "I really miss my family," she confessed, and it was the truth. In this moment, she desperately wanted to be a child again, safe and sound in her parents' house, with her mom making chicken soup with matzah balls and her dad reading a newspaper on the couch. She wanted to turn back the clock and go back to the last decade, to a time before people knew that there was life on other planets—and that their own planet would not belong to them much longer. To a time before she met the alien who was staring at her now with his beautiful amber eyes— the lover whom she had no choice but to betray.

Korum seemed to accept her explanation. "Mia," he said quietly, letting go of her chin, "you'll see them soon, I promise. I'm getting closer to completing my business here, and then I will take you there—"

"I haven't even told them yet that I'm not coming," said Mia, her voice thick with tears. "They're expecting me this Saturday, and my plane ticket is nonrefundable—"

He looked exasperated. "Are you worrying about money now? I will refund you the cost of the ticket—"

"My parents are the ones who bought it."

"Okay, then I will refund the cost to your parents." Taking a deep breath, he added, "Mia, you don't ever have to worry about these logistics when you're with me. I'll always take care of you and your family—you don't need to stress about money ever again. I know your parents' finances are tight, and I would be more than happy to assist them financially—or in whichever way they need."

Mia swallowed a sob, feeling like an iron fist was squeezing her heart. As arrogant and high-handed as that statement was, she had no doubt that he was genuine in his offer. "Th-thank you," she whispered, her voice breaking, "that's very . . . generous of you—"

"Mia," he said softly, "I care about you, okay? I want you to be happy with me, and I will do whatever I can to make that happen."

His every word felt like he was cutting her with a knife, and she could no longer hold back. Burying her face in the pillow, she turned away from him and broke down crying, her entire body shaking from the force of her sobs.

"Mia?" His voice sounded uncertain for the first time since she'd met him. "What . . . Why are you crying?"

She cried even harder. She couldn't tell him the truth, and the guilt was like acid in her chest, eating her up inside.

Tentatively touching her back, he stroked it in a soothing manner, murmuring little endearments. When that didn't seem to help, he pulled her into his arms, letting her bury her face in the crook of his neck and cry while he stroked her hair.

So Mia cried. She cried for herself, and for him, and for the relationship that could never be . . . not even if he weren't the enemy that she'd been spying on.

After a few minutes, when her sobs began to quiet down, he reached somewhere and handed her a tissue, letting her wipe her face and blow her nose before asking softly again, "Why?"

Mia looked at him, her vision still blurry with tears. The full truth was out of the question, of course, but she could tell him something that had been tormenting her for a while. "This is not right," she whispered, her voice rough with residual tears. "You, me—it's not right, it's not natural . . . And it can never last—"

"Why not?" he said softly. "It can last for as long as we want it to last."

"You're not human," she said, looking at him in disbelief. "How could it ever work for us?"

He hesitated for a second and then said, gently brushing her hair off her face, "It can—just trust me on that, darling. I can't really say more right now, but we will talk about it later . . . when the time comes."

Mia blinked in surprise, staring at him. This was something she hadn't expected. Did he mean that there was some way for them to be together . . . as an actual couple? The implications of that were too big to contemplate right now, with her head pounding and her mind barely functioning in the aftermath of her emotional storm.

He pulled away then and got off the bed. "I'll bring you something to make you feel better," he said, and left the room.

Mia looked at the door, stifling a hysterical giggle at the thought that this was becoming a nightly occurrence. She just hoped he didn't bring back the little tube.

He brought back a glass filled with some kind of milky liquid and handed it to her.

"What is it?" she asked, sniffing it with suspicion. It didn't smell like anything.

He grinned at her, showing the dimple. "Not poison, I promise. It's just a little something to help you sleep better and take away your headache."

How did he know that her head was hurting? Mia blinked at him again.

As though reading her mind, he said, "I know how humans feel after crying. This drink is meant more for helping with a cold or a flu, but it doesn't have any harmful side effects, so you might as well drink it now and feel better."

Mia nodded in agreement and tasted the liquid. It didn't have any flavor either; if not for the color, she would have thought she was drinking water. She felt dehydrated, so she gladly drank the entire glass. Almost immediately, the painful pressure around her temples eased, and the congested feeling in her nose disappeared. Another K wonder drug, apparently.

"Why do you have all these medicines for humans?" she asked, the thought only now occurring to her. "Do you also use these for yourself?"

He shook his head, smiling. "No, they're human-specific. We have other ways to heal ourselves."

"So why have it then?" Mia persisted.

He shrugged. "I knew that I would be living among humans and interacting with them. It only made sense to have a few basics handy in case of various emergencies."

Interacting with humans at his apartment? Mia suddenly felt an unwelcome pang of jealousy at the thought of other women being here, in this very bed. It wasn't surprising, of course; he was a healthy, attractive male with a strong sex drive—it was perfectly normal for him to have had other sex partners before her, both human and K.

Or so she told herself. The green-eyed monster inside refused to listen to reason.

Something of her thoughts must have shown on her face because he said softly, "And no, none of those interactions have been human women in recent months—definitely none since I met you."

"What about K women?" she blurted out, and then mentally kicked herself. She had no right to be jealous after what she'd done. He was her enemy, and she had treated him as such. It was absurd to feel so relieved that she was the only woman in his life right now. Their days together were numbered, and it shouldn't matter whether Korum had been faithful to her or if he had fucked a hundred women in the past month. Yet somehow it mattered to her—and it mattered a lot.

"None since we've met," he said, smiling. He seemed pleased by her jealousy, and Mia nearly broke down crying again. Taking a deep breath, she controlled herself with great effort. A second crying fit would be even more difficult to explain.

"Let's go to sleep, shall we?" he suggested softly. "You still seem stressed, and you'll probably feel better in the morning."

Mia nodded in agreement and lay down, covering herself with the blanket. Korum followed her example, pulling her toward him until they lay in his favorite spooning position.

Against all odds, Mia drifted off to sleep as soon as she closed her eyes, feeling comforted by the heat of his body wrapped around her own.

CHAPTER TWENTY-ONE

Mia woke up on Wednesday morning with a sense of dread in her stomach.

Today she had to tell her parents that she wasn't coming to see them on Saturday. She still hadn't come up with a good reason to explain the delay, especially since she was supposed to start her internship at the camp on Monday.

And if Korum discovered her involvement in what was about to befall the K colonies, then it might be the last time she was speaking to her family in general. That made it even more imperative that she present an upbeat and positive image today, so as not to make her parents worry prematurely. It would be better if she left only good memories behind when she disappeared from their lives.

At that thought, stupid tears threatened again, and Mia took a deep breath to control herself. She didn't have time for this right now; she still had to write the last paper. Although it made no sense to care about something so trivial in her precarious situation, not writing the paper would be like giving up—and some small part of Mia was still hopeful that there might be light at the end of this tunnel, that some semblance of a normal life was still possible if she made it through the next couple of weeks unscathed.

Clinging to that thought, Mia dragged herself out of bed and into the shower. Korum was nowhere to be found in the apartment, and she guessed he was off doing whatever he normally did during the day. It probably had something to do with tracking the Resistance fighters, but she had no way of knowing that for sure. Grabbing a quick breakfast, she headed to the library in the hopes that she might be better able to concentrate there.

The day was beautiful and sunny—a perfect foil for her gloomy mood. Under normal circumstances, Mia would have taken a nice lengthy walk to the library, but time was of essence and she took a cab instead. Staying at Korum's place and eating nearly all her meals with him, Mia was flush with cash for the first time in her college career. The student grants that helped pay for tuition and books also provided a minimal allowance for food and other living expenses, but it was usually just enough for her to survive on. Eating out in restaurants or taking cabs were indulgences that Mia could not normally afford, and it was nice to be able to splurge now that she didn't worry so much about the cost of food.

The library was a zoo. Just about every NYU student was there, frantically cramming for exams and writing papers. Of course, Mia realized, it was finals week. She should've just stayed in the comfortable study room Korum had set up for her, but she'd wanted to be some place where nothing reminded her of the mess that her life had become.

After wandering around for a good fifteen minutes, she finally located a soft chair that had just been vacated by a pimply red-headed boy who looked like he was all of twelve years old. Quickly occupying it before anyone else saw her prize, Mia smiled to herself. Not that she was all that old, but some of the freshmen looked ridiculously young to her these days.

Five hours later, Mia triumphantly finished the last sentence and saved her work. She still had to proofread the damn thing, but the bulk of the job was done. Gathering her things, she left the library and went to her own apartment, hoping to see Jessie and have a chance to talk to her parents.

Jessie wasn't home when she got there, so that left only the parents. Taking a deep breath, Mia turned on her computer and prepared to be as bright and bubbly as any college student who was almost done with finals week.

"Mia! Sweetheart, how are you?" Her mom was in fine form today, her blue eyes sparkling with excitement and a huge smile on her face.

Mia grinned back at her. "I'm almost done! Just have to proofread the last paper, and then the school year is officially over for me," said Mia, keeping her voice purposefully upbeat.

"Oh, that's great!" her mom exclaimed. "We can't wait to see you this weekend! Marisa and Connor are coming over on Sunday, and we'll have a big dinner. I'll make all your favorites. I already bought some eggs and even a bit of goat cheese—"

"Mom," interrupted Mia, feeling like she was dying a little inside, "there's something I need to tell you . . ."

Her mom paused for a second, looking puzzled. "What is it, honey?"

Mia took a deep breath. This was not going to be easy. "One of my professors asked me for a big favor this week," she said slowly, having come up with a semi-plausible story in the last few minutes. "There's a program here at NYU where psychology students go and spend some time with disadvantaged high school kids from some of the worst neighborhoods . . ."

"Uh-huh," said her mom, a small frown appearing on her face.

"It's a great program," lied Mia. "These kids don't really have anyone to help them figure out the next steps, whether they should go to college or not, how they should apply if they decide to go . . . And you know, that's exactly what I want to do—provide that type of counseling . . ."

Her mom's frown got a little deeper.

Mia hurried with her explanation. "Well, I didn't know about this program before, but I was chatting with my professor this week and mentioned my interest in counseling to him. And that's when he told me about this program, and that he was actually desperately looking for a volunteer to help out for a week or two this summer—"

"But you're flying home on Saturday," her mom said, looking increasingly unhappy. "When would you be able to do this?"

"Well, that's the thing," said Mia, hating herself for lying like this, "I don't think I can come home this weekend, not if I do this program—"

"What! What do you mean, you can't come home this weekend?" Her mom appeared livid now. "You already have a ticket and everything! And what about your camp internship? Aren't you supposed to start that on Monday?"

"I already spoke with the camp director," lied Mia again. "He's fine with pushing back my start date by two weeks. I explained the whole situation, and he was very understanding. And my professor said he'll reimburse me for the cost of the ticket and even buy me another one to make up for this—"

"Well, that's the least he could do! What about the money you were going to earn during those two weeks of your internship?" her mom said angrily. "And what about the fact that we haven't seen you since March?

How could he ask you to do something like that, so last-minute?"

"Mom," said Mia in a pleading tone, "it's a great opportunity for me. This is exactly what I want to do career-wise, and it'll really boost my chances of getting into a good grad school. Plus, the professor said he'll write me a glowing recommendation if I do this—and you know how important those are for grad school applications . . ."

Her mom was blinking rapidly, and there was a suspicious glimmer in her eyes. "Of course," she said, a wealth of disappointment in her voice, "I know that stuff is important . . . We were just so looking forward to seeing you this Saturday, and now this—"

Every word her mom said was like a knife scraping at Mia's insides. "I know, mom, I'm really sorry about this," she said, blinking to hold back her own tears. "I'll see you in a couple of weeks, okay? It won't be so bad, you'll see . . ."

Her mom sniffed a little. "So no family dinner this Sunday, I guess."

Mia shook her head with regret. "No . . . but we'll have one in two weeks, okay? I'll cook and everything—"

"Oh, please, Mia, you couldn't cook to save your life!" her mom said irately, but a tiny smile appeared on her face. "I've never met anyone who couldn't manage to boil water—"

"I can boil water now," said Mia defensively. "I've been living on my own for the last three years, you know, and I can even make rice—"

The tiny smile became a full-blown grin. "Wow, rice? That *is* progress," her mom said with barely contained laughter. "I honestly don't know what you're going to do when you meet someone . . ."

"Oh, mom, not this again," groaned Mia.

"It's true, you know. Men still like it when a woman can make a good meal, and keep the house—"

"And do laundry, and be a general domestic slave, and yadda yadda yadda," finished Mia, rolling her eyes. Her mom could be amazingly old-fashioned sometimes.

"Exactly. Mark my words, unless you find some guy who likes to cook, you'll be stuck eating takeout for the rest of your life," her mom said ominously.

Mia shrugged, biting the inside of her cheek to avoid bursting into semi-hysterical laughter. The irony of it was that she had actually found such a guy—except he wasn't human. She wondered what her mom would say if she told her about Korum. *He's great: he loves to cook and even does laundry for us both. Just one tiny issue—he's a blood-drinking alien.* No, that probably wouldn't go over well at all.

"Mom, don't worry about me, okay? Everything will be fine." At least Mia sincerely hoped that was the case. "We'll see each other soon, and maybe I'll really try to learn how to cook this summer. How about that?" Mia gave her mom a big smile, trying to prevent any more lectures.

Her mom shook her head in reproach and sighed. "Sure. I'll tell your dad what happened. He'll be so disappointed . . ."

Mia felt terrible again. "Where is he?" she asked, wanting to speak to her father as well.

"He's out getting the car fixed. The damn thing broke again. We should really get a new one . . . but maybe next year."

Mia nodded sympathetically. She knew her parents' financial situation was not the best these days. Her mom was currently between jobs. As an elementary school teacher, she was usually in demand. However, the private school where she had taught for the past eight years had closed recently, resulting in a number of teachers losing their positions and all applying for the same few openings in the local public schools. Her dad—a political science professor at the local community college—was now supporting the family on his one salary, and they had to be careful with bigger expenses, such as a new car. In general, her family, like many other middle-class Americans with 401(k) retirement plans, had suffered in the K Crash—the huge stock market crash that took place when the Krinar had arrived. At one point, the Dow had lost almost ninety percent of its value, and it was only about a year ago that the markets had recovered fully.

"All right," said Mia, "I'll try to log back in later, see if I can reach dad."

"Call Marisa too," her mom said. "I know she was really looking forward to seeing you on Sunday."

Mia nodded. "I will, definitely."

Her mom sighed again. "Well, I guess we'll talk to you soon then."

"I love you, mom," said Mia, feeling like her chest was getting squeezed in a vise. "I hope you know that. You and dad are the best parents ever."

"Of course," her mom said, looking a bit puzzled. "We love you too. Come home soon, okay?"

"I will," said Mia, blowing an air kiss toward the computer screen, and ended the conversation.

Her sister was next. For once, she was actually reachable on Skype.

"Hey there, baby sis! What's this text I just got from mom about you not coming home?"

Mia hadn't seen her sister since she got pregnant, and she was surprised to see Marisa looking pale and thin, instead of having that pregnancy glow she'd always heard about.

"Marisa!" she exclaimed. "What's going on with you? You don't look well. Are you sick?"

Her sister made a face. "If you can call having a baby sickness, then yes. I'm throwing up constantly," she complained. "I just can't keep anything down. I've actually lost five pounds since I got pregnant—"

Mia gasped in shock. Five pounds was a lot for someone her sister's size. While a little taller and curvier than Mia, Marisa was also small-boned, with her normal weight hovering somewhere around 110-115 pounds. Now she looked too thin, her cheekbones overly prominent in her usually pretty face.

"—and my doctor is not happy about that."

"Of course, he's not happy! Did he say what you should do?"

Marisa sighed. "He said to get more rest and try not to stress. So I am working from home today, preparing my lessons for next week, and they got someone to substitute for me for a few days."

"Oh my God, you poor thing," said Mia sympathetically. "That sucks. Can you eat anything, like maybe crackers or some broth?"

"That's what I'm subsisting on these days. Well, that and pickles." Marisa gave her a wan smile. "For some reason, I can't stop eating those Israeli pickles—you know, the little crunchy ones?"

Mia nodded, stifling a grin. Her sister had always been a pickles fan, so it really wasn't surprising she was going pickle-crazy during her pregnancy.

"So anyway, enough about my stomach issues . . . What's going on with you? Why aren't you coming this Saturday? We were all ready and excited to come over, see you and the parents—"

Mia took a deep breath and repeated the whole story to Marisa. She was getting so good at lying that she could almost believe herself. Maybe she should think about starting such a program at NYU next year—if she was still alive and attending school at that time, of course.

Her sister listened to everything with a vaguely disbelieving expression. And then, being Marisa, she asked, "Is the professor cute?"

To her horror, Mia felt her cheeks turning pink. "What? No! He's old and has kids and stuff!"

"Uh-huh," said Marisa. "So I'm supposed to believe you would be

ANNA ZAIRES

willing to do something like this at the request of an ugly professor? Just to pad your resume a little?" She shook her head slightly. "Nope, I just don't see it." A sly smile appearing on her face, she asked, "Just how old is old?"

Mia cursed her poor acting skills. Now Marisa would probably go blabbing to their parents that Mia had a crush on her professor. She tried to imagine liking Professor Dunkin that way and shuddered. Between his receding hairline and the yellowish spittle that frequently appeared in the corners of his mouth when he spoke, he was probably one of the least attractive individuals she'd ever met.

"Old," Mia said firmly. "And unattractive."

Marisa grinned, undeterred. "Okay, then, who is he?" she persisted. "I know you, baby sis . . . and you're hiding something. If it's not the old and unattractive professor you're staying in New York for, then who is it?"

"No one," said Mia. "There's no man in my life . . . you know that." And she wasn't lying. There wasn't a human man—just an extraterrestrial of the male variety. Who was also old—a lot older than her sister could imagine.

"Oh, please, then why are you acting so weird? You've been kinda strange for the past month, in fact," said Marisa, looking at her intently. "Mia . . . is something wrong?"

Mia shook her head in denial and silently cursed Marisa's sisterly intuition. It had been so much easier to fool her mom. "No, everything's fine. It's just been stressful, you know, with finals and all . . ."

"Uh-huh," said Marisa, "you've had finals for the past three years, and it's never been like this. I can see you're not yourself, Mia. Now fess up . . . what's happening?"

Mia shook her head again, and tried putting on a bright smile. "Nothing! I don't know what you're talking about—there's absolutely nothing wrong. I just got a great opportunity to get some valuable work experience, and I am taking advantage of it. I'll see you soon, just in a couple of weeks. There's nothing to worry about—"

"Have you already bought tickets?" interrupted Marisa. "Do you have a set date when you're flying in?"

"Not yet," Mia admitted. "I'll do that soon. The professor said he'll buy me a new plane ticket, so there's nothing to worry about about—"

"Nothing to worry about? Mia, I know when you're lying," said Marisa, giving her a strict look. "You're terrible at it. You've been such a good girl your whole life, you've had absolutely no practice deceiving

184

your parents—or me. You've never even snuck out to a party in high school . . ."

Mia bit her lip. How did Marisa get to be so observant? This was a big problem. Maybe if she told her a partial truth . . .

"Okay," said Mia, choosing her words carefully. "Let's say that there's something to what you're saying . . . If I tell you, do you promise not to tell the parents? They'll worry, and it's really not necessary—"

Marisa looked at her, her blue eyes narrowed in consideration. "Okay," she said slowly, "you can always talk to me, baby sis, you know that. I'll keep your secret . . . but only if it's nothing life-threatening that parents must know about."

It actually *was* something life-threatening, but parents definitely didn't need to know about that. Mia sighed. Since she started going down this path, she might as well tell her sister something, or else her entire family will be calling in panic within a half-hour.

Taking a deep breath, Mia said, "You're right. I did meet someone—"

"I knew it!" yelled Marisa triumphantly.

"—and he's not exactly someone you'd be happy to see me with."

Marisa stared at her in surprise. "Why? Who is he? Another student?"

Mia shook her head. "No, that's the problem. He's older, and he's not exactly first-boyfriend material."

"Are we talking about the professor now?" asked Marisa in confusion.

"No, the professor is just the professor. It's someone else. He's actually a senior executive in a tech company," fibbed Mia, trying to stick as close as possible to the truth. "I met him in the park one day, and we've been sleeping together—"

"What?" Her sister was gaping at her in disbelief. "Is he married? Does he have any children?"

"No, and no. But I know it's just a temporary fling for him, so I really didn't want to go into any details with you and the parents . . ."

As Mia was speaking, a big smile slowly appeared on Marisa's face. "A fling? Wow. When my baby sis decides to finally lose her virginity, she does it with style! A senior executive no less . . ."

Mia shrugged, trying to be nonchalant about the whole thing.

"What's his name?"

"Uh, I'd rather not say," mumbled Mia. "He'll be leaving in a couple of weeks, and there's no point in discussing the whole thing—"

"Leaving to go where?"

"Um . . . Dubai." Mia had no idea why she'd chosen that particular location, but it seemed to fit the story.

"Dubai? Is he from there originally?" Her sister's curiosity knew no bounds.

Mia sighed. "Marisa, listen, there's really no point in discussing it. He'll leave, and that's that."

Her sister cocked her head to the side, studying Mia's face. "And you're okay with that, baby sis?" she asked quietly. "Your first lover leaving just like that?"

Mia looked away, trying to hide the moisture in her eyes. "He has to leave, Marisa. There's no choice. It doesn't matter if I'm okay with it or not."

"Of course, it matters," said Marisa. "Do you think he cares for you at all? Or are you just a pretty college girl he's sleeping with while in New York?"

Mia shrugged. "I don't know. I think he might care about me a little."

"But not enough to stay?"

"No, he can't stay," said Mia. "And it doesn't matter. We're not right for each other, anyway. The relationship was doomed from the start."

"Why did you start it then?" asked Marisa, eyeing her with bewilderment. "Is he really good-looking? Did he sweep you off your feet or something?"

Mia nodded. "He's gorgeous, and he's smart, and he knows a lot about everything . . ." Those were all true statements. "And he took me out to all kinds of fancy restaurants and Broadway shows—"

"Wow, Mia," said Marisa, looking envious for the first time in Mia's memory, "that sounds like a dream guy."

Mia smiled. "And he's also a great cook, and does laundry—"

"Oh my God, where did you find this paragon?"

"I know, right? Mom would have a cow if she heard about this."

And the sisters grinned at each other in perfect understanding.

Then Marisa got serious again. "So why can't it work out for the two of you? He sounds perfect. Does he have some major character flaw that you can't stand?"

"Well, he's very bossy and autocratic," admitted Mia, "so I definitely have a problem with that. And where he comes from, they don't necessarily view, um, women . . . as equals, if you know what I mean?" That was as close to the truth as she could get.

Marisa's eyes widened in understanding. "Ohhh, is he one of those Middle Eastern types? With a harem and all . . . who require their women to be veiled from head to toe?"

Mia shrugged. "Something like that. So it could never really go anywhere. We come from very different worlds." Mia meant that in the literal sense, but Marisa didn't need to know that.

"Wow, baby sis." Marisa was looking at her with newfound respect. "I have to say, you've surprised me. No boring college boys for you . . . oh, no—you've gone straight for the big leagues. A sheikh from Dubai, huh?"

Mia flushed. "He's not a sheikh, just an executive."

"Wow." Her sister was still looking impressed. "So did he give you any fancy gifts or jewelry?"

Mia smiled. Her sister was so predictable sometimes. Even though she lived a simple life for the most part, Marisa definitely appreciated the finer things in life—nice hotels, designer clothes, beautiful accessories.

"He bought me a whole new wardrobe from Saks Fifth Avenue," admitted Mia. "He really didn't like my old clothes—"

"OH MY GOD, FROM SAKS?" Marisa's shriek was ear-piercing. "Are you serious? You've gotta let me borrow something when you come!"

Mia laughed. "Of course! Whatever you want, it's yours."

"Oh crap, never mind," said Marisa, "I just realized that soon I won't be able to borrow anything from anyone—especially from my tiny baby sister. In a couple of months, I'll be a total cow."

"Oh please," said Mia, laughing at the image of her svelte sister looking even remotely cow-like, "you'll look like one of those actresses in Hollywood—all normal, just with a cute little baby bump."

Marisa shuddered. "I certainly hope so. But I have to say, so far, pregnancy is nothing like what I'd imagined."

Mia looked at her sympathetically. "That sucks. Hang in there, okay? It's just a few more months, and then you'll have a beautiful child . . ."

Marisa beamed at her. "That's true. And you too, baby sis, hang in there, okay? Call me if you ever want to talk about Mr. Gorgeous again. And I promise I won't say anything to the parents. You're right—they would worry unnecessarily. This type of stuff is best left for talks with your sister."

Mia smiled and said, "That's what I thought. I love you. Say hello to Connor for me, okay?"

"Will do," said Marisa, and disconnected with one final wave.

Relieved, Mia stared at the blank computer screen. She had lied to her family, but at least she'd managed to prevent them from freaking out completely. In a way, the conversation with Marisa had been therapeutic. Although she couldn't tell her sister the whole truth, she'd been able to share enough details to make herself feel much better about the situation. Marisa's nonjudgmental, sympathetic ear had been exactly what she'd needed at this point.

Now she had to finish editing the paper—and then she will have completed everything she'd set out to do for the day.

CHAPTER TWENTY-TWO

Now that she was done with studying, Mia had no idea what to do with herself. Waking up on Thursday morning, she submitted her papers online and decided to go for a walk in Central Park. Korum again left early in the morning, before she had woken up, so she was on her own for the day. She texted Jessie, but her roommate had her Calculus exam in the afternoon and was frantically cramming. Mia wished there was someone else she could hang out with, just to avoid being alone with her thoughts, but most other students were too busy packing for the summer or still in the middle of finals.

The middle of May was usually a 'hit-or-miss' weather in New York. This year, it seemed like summer had started early, and the temperature that day was a balmy seventy-five degrees. Mia gladly put on one of her new spring dresses, a simple blue cotton sheath, and a pair of cream-colored sandals that managed to be both comfortable and stylish. And then she headed out to join the hordes of New Yorkers and tourists that came out to enjoy Central Park.

It was hard to believe that only a month ago Mia had been walking here by herself, with no real knowledge of the Ks, thinking about nothing more than her Sociology paper. She hadn't met Korum yet, and had no idea what a drastic turn her life would take in the next few minutes. What would have happened if she hadn't sat down on that bench that day? Would she even now be packing to go home on Saturday?

As though her feet had a mind of their own, Mia found herself heading toward Bow Bridge, the place of her first close encounter. Unlike the last time, the little bridge was teeming with people today, all seeking to take photos of the picturesque view. Mia found herself a spot on a bench next to a young couple and settled in to read the latest bestselling thriller—something she only had time to do when school wasn't in session.

After a half hour, the couple left, and Mia got the entire bench to herself. Before she could enjoy it for long, however, she heard her name being called. Startled, she looked up and saw a young woman, dressed in a pair of ripped jeans and a white sleeveless shirt, approaching the bench. Her short sandy hair was tousled, like a boy's, and her arms were sleekly muscled. It was Leslie, the girl she'd met that one time with John—one of the Resistance fighters.

"Hey Mia," she said, "do you mind if I join you for a minute?" Without waiting for a response, she sat down on Mia's bench.

"Sure, be my guest," said Mia, somewhat rudely. Leslie was not her favorite person, and she really didn't feel like being tasked with something else right now. As far as Mia was concerned, she had carried out her mission, and all she wanted was to be left alone.

"Look," said Leslie, her tone far friendlier than before, "I know we got off on the wrong foot. I just wanted to say thanks for what you did, and to give you something from John." She held out a small oval object that looked vaguely like a garage opener or an automatic car key.

"What is it?" asked Mia warily, not taking it from her.

"It's a weapon," said Leslie, "a weapon that you can use to protect yourself in case Korum figures out what happened before we have a chance to neutralize him."

"Neutralize him?"

Leslie sighed. "As per your request, we'll try to capture him alive, so he can be deported back to Krina. It's not going to be easy, but we'll do our best."

Mia swallowed. "What . . . um, when are you going to do it?"

"We can't do it before the shields are down, and the attack on the K Centers is underway. He might be able to warn them, or get reinforcements, if we try to take him now, so we can't risk it. It'll have to be almost simultaneous. He's not the only one. There are other Ks who are outside their Centers right now. As soon as they learn of the attack on their colonies—and they'll learn it almost immediately—they will join in the fight. But they're not in some remote areas—they are in our cities, near our government centers. If they realize that we've broken the treaty, they will attack us—and many civilian lives will be lost before we would be able to stop them. So we need to plan everything very carefully, or else it's going to turn into a bloodbath."

This was bad, thought Mia. Really bad. She hadn't thought of that aspect—other Ks who, like Korum, were living among humans for whatever reason. Strong, fast, and armed with K technology, even one individual could inflict a tremendous amount of damage on the human population. She tried to imagine Korum fighting to protect his kind, and shuddered at the thought. Just that one brief glimpse of his rage in the club had been frightening. She had no doubt that he could be truly brutal if the occasion called for it.

Turning her attention back to the little object, Mia asked, "So what is this weapon supposed to do?"

"It dissolves molecular bonds, breaking down everything in its path," said Leslie. "Essentially, it'll turn whatever you want into dust. It's a simple miniature version of the big weapon we intend to use to make the Ks surrender."

Aghast, Mia stared at the small, harmless-looking device in Leslie's palm. "So it could turn a person to dust?"

Leslie nodded. "It'll work on whatever is in its path. The nanomachines it releases work for a period of only about thirty seconds before they become inactive, but that time is usually enough to completely dissolve a person. You don't even need to worry about shooting him in the chest or whatever—if the nanos get on any part of his body, he's toast."

Mia nearly gagged at the thought. "What? No! I could never do something like this!" she exclaimed in horror. "I can't use it on him—"

"You can, and you will," said Leslie, "if your life is at stake. I have no idea if he'll make the connection between what's happening in the K Centers and you—but he's supposed to be some kind of a genius, so I wouldn't be surprised if he did." Running her hand through her short hair in a frustrated motion, Leslie added, "And it's best if you do it quickly, before he has a chance to react. Just point and shoot, no thinking . . . do you understand me? They're fast, Mia, really fast."

Mia shook her head. "I won't do it. I can't—"

Leslie shrugged. "That's your call. If you'd rather die, then so be it—it's none of my business. John asked me to give it to you, and here it is. You can take it and not use it, if that's what you want. But at least you won't be completely helpless when all this shit goes down." She put the device on Mia's lap. "If you want to use it, just feel for the little indentation on the side—if you press firmly there, it's going to go off. Just be sure to point the rounded end toward him—"

Mia shook her head again. "I won't use it," she said with firm conviction.

Leslie looked at her with something resembling pity. "You idiot," she said softly, "you've fallen for the monster, haven't you?"

Mia looked away. "That's none of your business," she said quietly, examining her fingernails. "I did what needed to be done. He'll leave, and that's all there is to it."

"You stupid girl," said Leslie in a contemptuous tone, "you're nothing to him—less than nothing. He'll crush you like a bug if you're anywhere in the vicinity when we attack. Just because he likes to fuck you doesn't mean he'll have mercy on you if he learns what you've done. He's slept with hundreds of women just like you—thousands, probably—and you're nothing special—"

"You don't know anything!" interrupted Mia, feeling each word like a stab in the heart. "You've never even met him—"

Leslie's eyes narrowed. "I don't need to meet him to know exactly what he's like—what all of them are like, Mia. They have no regard for us, for human life. We're just an experiment to them, something they've created. As far as they're concerned, we're their creatures—theirs to do with as they please. And if it pleases them, they will get rid of us and take over our planet for their own use. And you're a fool if you think he's somehow different. He's as bad as they come—he's the one who led them here . . ."

Leslie was right. Mia knew all of that with the rational part of her mind, but her stupid heart refused to get with the program. The knowledge that he would be gone from her life in a few short days was strangely painful, and the thought that he might be harmed in the process made her stomach twist with fear. And yet Leslie was right—he probably would not hesitate to kill her if he learned that her actions had threatened the Ks' agenda here on Earth.

She didn't want to die, but she didn't think she could kill him, not even in self-defense.

Taking a deep breath, Mia asked, "When is it happening? How long until the attack takes place?"

Leslie hesitated, apparently wondering if Mia was still trustworthy.

"Leslie," Mia said wearily, "I know what would happen if he found out I was helping you. I won't warn him. I can't, not without losing my life in the process. I have no regrets about what I've done. Just because I can't kill someone I've been intimate with for the past month doesn't mean I would betray our cause. I just want to know how much longer I have—"

"Until tomorrow," said Leslie. "You have until tomorrow. My advice is to disappear in the morning—get away as far as you can. Don't pack, don't do anything to raise his suspicions. Just leave. One way or another, everything will be over by this weekend."

* * *

That evening, Korum came home late, closer to nine o'clock.

Mia found herself pacing back and forth in the living room starting at five o'clock, unable to sit still or relax in anticipation of what was to come. If Leslie had told her the truth, this would be her last night together with Korum . . . and maybe the last night she was alive. To maximize her chances of survival, she decided to follow Leslie's advice about leaving first thing in the morning. Korum would likely be gone from the apartment by then, and she would have a chance to escape—maybe taking the subway to one of the boroughs. The dissolver, as she'd decided to call it, was sitting in her purse, safe and sound. She had no intention of using it on Korum, but it was still good to know that she had something she could defend herself with, in case all hell did break loose on Friday.

Just to keep herself busy, she went through her closet and tried on a few of her new dresses. Her wardrobe was so large now that many of her clothes still had tags on them, and she had no idea what she owned. Everything fit her perfectly, of course; the shoppers from Saks had done their job. After an hour of trying on one outfit after another, Mia settled on a simple grey sleeveless dress, made of some cotton-silk blend, that hugged her upper body and flared gently from the waist down to her knees. Despite the conservative color and cut, it looked stylish and sexy—as did most of what Mia wore now. To go with the dress, Mia decided to apply some makeup, putting on one coat of mascara and a light dusting of powder. She had no idea why it was suddenly so important to look good tonight, since she didn't normally obsess over such things, but she wanted to appear particularly attractive to Korum this evening. Finishing the outfit with a pair of strappy black heels, Mia resumed her impatient pacing.

He had given her a phone number where he could be reached in case she needed him, but Mia had never used it before. As eight o'clock rolled by, however, she seriously contemplated calling him to find out his whereabouts. But that would be so far out of character for her that he might wonder—and she didn't want to chance his getting suspicious.

Finally, the door opened at a quarter to nine. He came in, dressed in a simple pair of blue jeans and a black T-shirt. It didn't matter what he wore, of course; he would have looked stunning in rags. At the sight of her standing there, a wide dimpled smile appeared on his beautiful face, lighting his features and making those amber eyes crinkle at the corners. And then a familiar golden glow lit his gaze.

Before she had a chance to say anything, he was next to her, lifting her up effortlessly for a deep, thorough kiss. His tongue stabbed into her mouth, and Mia wound her arms around him and kissed him back, passionately and a little desperately. Her legs found their way around his hips, and they stayed like that, locked in each others' arms, until Mia was gasping for breath and writhing against him, her breasts rubbing against his chest and her sex grinding on his pelvis. He groaned low in his throat, and she could feel his erection grow even bigger, pressing into her nether regions through the material that separated them. Holding her up with one arm, he found the lacy scrap of material that covered her pussy and tore it off, his fingers petting and exploring her moist folds. Mia moaned, driven nearly mindless with desire, and heard the sound of a zipper sliding down. And then he was inside her, his cock thrusting up into her even as he still held her like that, lifted up against him while he was standing in the middle of the living room.

Shocked at the suddenness of his penetration, Mia cried out, her inner tissues struggling to accommodate the intrusion, and he paused for a second, letting her get used to the feel of him in the unfamiliar position. And then he started moving, raising her up and down with one hand while his other hand buried itself in her hair, bringing her mouth back toward him. There was no slow and gentle build-up this time, as everything inside Mia tensed simultaneously, and then she was hurling into the climax, her muscles clamping down on his shaft, and he was coming too, so deeply inside her that she felt his contractions in her belly.

Panting, Mia collapsed against him, unable to believe that this happened just now, in the span of all of two minutes. His breathing was heavy as well, and she could feel his powerful chest moving up and down as she hung in his grasp, his cock still inside her. Once the pulsations of his orgasm ended, he lifted her up and placed her carefully on the ground, his hands still wrapped around her waist. Mia's legs were shaking, and she clung to him, grateful for the support.

Staring up at him, Mia noticed that his eyes were returning back to their regular amber color. His lips curling into a small, wry smile, he said huskily, "I guess I have to apologize again—clearly I don't have any control where you're concerned. I really didn't mean to jump you like that first thing. You're probably hungry too . . ."

Mia actually was, but it didn't matter. Blushing a little at the feel of his semen sliding down her leg, she mumbled quietly, "No, no need for apologies . . . you know that I really enjoyed it too . . ."

His smile now held purely masculine satisfaction. "I'm glad," he murmured. "Now how about some dinner?"

Mia nodded in agreement, and blushed even more when he disappeared for a second and came back with a paper towel that he handed to her. Embarrassed, Mia looked away as she cleaned off the remnants of their passion.

He laughed softly. "You're still such a prude," he teased gently. "We'll have to cure you of that at some point. It's all natural, you know."

Mia shrugged, purposefully not meeting his eyes. For some reason, she still had these occasional bouts of shyness around him, despite all the hot and raunchy sex they've had in the past month.

Korum laughed some more, and then asked, "Since you're dressed so nicely, how do you feel about going out for some French cuisine?"

Mia felt great about that, and she told him so.

"Okay, then, let me take a quick rinse and change, and we'll go," he said, stripping off the T-shirt on the way to the bathroom. The sight of his lean, muscled back made her insides clench with desire again. Why him, she wondered again in desperation, why did he have to be the one to make her feel this way? And how would she be able to bear it when he was gone for good?

The dinner was at a little French place Mia had never heard of. Nonetheless, the meal was outstanding, from the ratatouille Mia had gotten for her main course to the super-light pastry they ended up sharing for dessert.

"So are you now officially done with school for this year?" Korum asked, taking a sip of his red wine. He seemed to like wine and champagne, Mia had noticed, although she had never seen it have any effect on him. Then again, she'd never seen him have more than a couple of glasses.

"That's it," she replied, spearing a piece of zucchini with her fork. "The school year is officially over for me. I turned in all the papers today, and now I can be a total bum."

He grinned. "Somehow I can't quite envision you bumming around all day. Ever since I've known you, you've been busy studying or doing something for school." Reaching for her, he lightly stroked her cheek, his expression becoming more serious. "It'll be nice to have you relax a little. You've been working way too hard in these past couple of weeks. I don't think all that stress is good for your health."

Mia gave him a surprised look. "I'm fine," she protested. "I feel great—it's really not a problem at all."

Korum regarded her intently, a concerned expression on his face. "I don't know," he said, shaking his head. "Your immune system is so delicate, so fragile—it's really not good for you to overload yourself like that."

Mia shrugged, wondering what got him started on that topic. "My immune system is fine," she said. "It's as strong as that of any other human. You really don't need to worry about me—I don't get sick often or anything like that."

"As strong as any human is not all that strong," he said, a slight furrow between his dark brows. He looked at her speculatively, and Mia had no idea what he was thinking. Whatever it was, he apparently came to some conclusion, because his forehead smoothed out. Changing the topic, he asked about her day, and the conversation again flowed casually and easily.

As the dinner went on, Mia couldn't help but stare at him, drinking in the sight of his face, the animated gestures he used when he spoke about something he found exciting, the way his tall, muscular body moved in his chair—even the smallest of motions endowed with that athletic, inhuman grace. Her flesh craved him sexually, but it now went beyond that. Every cell in her body yearned to be with him, and the thought of tomorrow filled her with a cold, sick horror. She couldn't tell him, couldn't warn him of what was to come, but she could try to remember every moment of this evening, to commit to her memory the curve of his mouth, the bold slashes of his eyebrows, the way his laugh sounded when she said something amusing.

An agonizing realization tore through her then: she loved him. Despite everything she knew about him, despite everything he'd done to her, despite the fact that he was her enemy and she'd betrayed him—despite all that, she loved him with every fiber of her being.

And tomorrow, she would lose him forever.

CHAPTER TWENTY-THREE

A faint but steady sound of rain woke up Mia the next morning. Still half-asleep, she stretched, reluctant to face the day for some reason—and then her brain connected the dots and she sat up, gasping at the realization of what was to take place this morning.

Jumping out of bed, she forced herself to walk to the restroom and brush her teeth, following her usual morning routine in case Korum was still in the house. Once done, she pulled on a pair of jeans and a comfy long-sleeved shirt and carefully ventured out into the living room to check on the situation.

The living room and the kitchen areas were empty, and Mia almost shuddered with relief. Korum must have followed his usual routine, leaving for the day to do whatever it was that he did. And after the wave of relief came disappointment. Rationally, she knew that she should be glad she would have a chance to get away, that fate was being kind by enabling her to avoid one last—potentially deadly—encounter with her alien lover, but that didn't help the gaping wound in her heart that had opened at the recognition that she would never see him again.

Last night had been incredible, the sex between them as close to lovemaking as Mia had ever experienced. He had treated her like a princess, worshipping her with his body, and Mia had cried again in the aftermath, unable to stem the flood at the knowledge of what tomorrow would bring. He had tried to soothe her, to find out what was causing her distress this time, but Mia had been incoherent. And finally, he had simply taken her again, his body driving into hers in a savage, relentless rhythm until she could not think about anything at all, her worries burning up in the heat of passion—until she screamed in ecstasy as he brought her to peak, over and over again. And then she had simply passed out, too exhausted to remember why she had been crying in the first place.

But she couldn't think about that now. Not if she wanted to get out alive.

Grabbing her purse, Mia laced up her sneakers and prepared to leave Korum's apartment. With one last look at the cream-colored furniture and leafy plants, she walked toward the door, each step feeling heavier than the rest.

She wasn't sure what made her turn back, to go toward his office, leaving her purse sitting on the couch in the living room. Was her subconscious still clinging to the hope that he was here? That she might be able to see him one final time? She didn't think so, but her feet appeared to have a mind of her own, bringing her toward the sliding doors that parted at her approach.

There was no one in the room, but a giant three-dimensional map shimmered before her, looking like nothing she had ever seen before.

Her heart hammering in her chest, Mia stepped into the room, as though drawn in by an invisible string.

This was not New York spread out before her; she would have recognized that at a glance. In fact, it was not like a city at all. Vegetation was everywhere. Lush green plants seemed to dominate the landscape, ranging from the familiar to the exotic. Pale-colored oblong structures could be seen peeking through the trees, looking a bit like strange mushroom caps. If it hadn't been for the structures, Mia would've thought she was looking at a park or a forest in some tropical country. The place was beautiful . . . and alien. Every little hair on her nape stood up as Mia realized exactly what she was looking at.

It had to be a K Center . . . perhaps even their main one in Costa Rica. Lenkarda, Korum had called it once.

Her heart racing, Mia assessed the situation. She needed to leave, and she needed to do so now. Why would Korum be looking at a map of one of the K Centers? Was he suspecting something? And why would he be so careless as to leave it visible like that? Did he suspect her after all? Was this a trap?

At the last thought, Mia felt a cold wave of terror rushing through her veins. She had to leave right now.

Yet she couldn't tear her eyes away from the incredible picture in front of her. How many humans had seen such an amazing sight? The K Centers were closely guarded, with a no-fly zone established over them. Even human satellites could not view them; the Krinar shields had rendered the settlements all but invisible to human electronics. And here was a chance for her to look at an alien colony, to see where Korum had lived.

A terrible curiosity drove Mia now. Ignoring all reason and common sense, she stepped further into the room, slowly circling around the table and studying the tableau laid out in front of her.

The buildings—if that's what they were—were spaced widely apart and blended harmoniously into their surroundings. There were no paved roads or sidewalks as far as Mia could see; instead, each structure stood alone, right in the middle of all the greenery. And there were no windows or doors, Mia realized—at least none visible to her eyes. Each building was light in color; ivory, cream, and soft beige were the most prevalent, although light grey and pale peach shades could also be seen.

Toward the center of the map, there were several larger structures, including one big circular dome. They were purely white in color. Mia surmised that those were probably common gathering areas. There were no sidewalks or roads leading to them either, and no visible entrances or exits.

On the outer edges of the settlement, some smaller circular buildings were spaced evenly apart, surrounding the entire perimeter. They were green and brown and blended into the scenery so well that Mia had to look carefully to discern their presence. It was like camouflage, she realized. If it hadn't been for a slight shimmer that the buildings seemed to emit, she wouldn't have known they were there. Mia wondered if these were some kind of guard posts. The Ks were in hostile territory after all, far outnumbered by the natives; it only made sense that the security in their colonies would be strong.

Beyond the green-brown buildings lay more greenery, the plant life dominating everything in sight. And to the west, Mia saw a large body of water—perhaps an ocean of some kind. If this was Costa Rica, then it was likely the Pacific; although the country had two coasts, the Guanacaste region that Korum had mentioned was located on the Pacific side.

As Mia stared in wonder at the three-dimensional images, she noticed a familiar glow surrounding one of the areas near the ocean. Peering closer at it, she saw a small wooden structure that looked human in origin—like a hut of sorts. Hardly daring to breathe, Mia extended her hand toward it, and then jerked back, remembering what had happened the last time she entered this virtual reality world without a way to get back. Casting a desperate glance around the room, she saw Korum's sweater hanging on the back of one of the chairs. Ah-hah!

Quickly putting on the sweater, Mia touched the glowing image with her hand, bracing for the reality shift she'd experienced before.

And then she was there, standing on the beach, breathing in the salt-scented breeze, feeling the warm sun on her face, and hearing the roar of the ocean. A dragonfly whizzed by, followed by a bee. She could see a little crab-like creature scuttling across the sand a few feet away from her. It all seemed so real, yet she knew she was probably in a recording of some kind.

Squinting against the brightness, Mia stared at her surroundings. There was a little path leading from the beach toward the hut-like building she saw nestled among the trees. Feeling a bit like Alice in Wonderland, she headed toward it, unbearably curious to see what was inside.

The hut looked old and decrepit, even more so on closer inspection. It had to be human-made; judging by the condition of the wood, it definitely predated the Ks' arrival. It also had a door, which meant that Mia could go inside and explore. Holding her breath in anticipation, she pushed open the door, wincing at the squeaky sound of the rusted hinges.

The interior of the hut was immaculately clean, free of cobwebs and other unpleasant things one might expect to find in an abandoned building. The furniture was old and plain, but still serviceable, with a small table and a few chairs arranged around it. There was also a pallet on the floor, apparently for sleeping. And the place was completely empty. Disappointed, Mia looked around. Why did Korum have this recording? Clearly, nothing was happening.

And then the door opened, and a male K came in. He looked very typical of their kind, tall and good-looking, with black hair and darkly bronzed skin. He wore a pair of grey shorts made of some unusual material, a loosely fitting sleeveless top, and some type of thin sandals on his feet. Hardly daring to breathe, Mia stared at him, but he was obviously unaware of her presence. He did seem nervous, however. Casting a brief, furtive look around, he walked toward the table. Just in case, Mia scooted out of his way, climbing onto the pallet, uncertain what would happen if she physically touched someone in this strange virtual world.

The K moved the table to the side and squatted, looking at something on the floor. Then he pressed on one of the floorboards, and it seemed to give under his fingers. Loosening it further, he pulled on something, and the entire section of the floor opened up. Without any hesitation, he jumped down, and the opening slowly began to close behind him.

Mia's heart raced as she observed his actions. Here was her chance, but did she dare follow him? How far down was his destination, and what would happen if she jumped after him? Would she be hurt, injured? This wasn't real; she was just watching a very realistic movie. But certain sensations were still there—heat, smell, touch. Yet falling down on the sidewalk the last time hadn't hurt at all. And the opening in the floor was closing more with each second. To hell with it, Mia decided. She was already risking her life by being here—what's a potential injury in a virtual world?

Taking one deep breath, she jumped.

At first, there was only darkness and the stomach-churning sensation of falling, and then the hard floor was beneath her feet, and Mia landed on it easily, like a cat. Gasping for air, hardly daring to believe that she had made it, Mia felt her legs and knees with her hands. Everything seemed to be fine, and Mia's breathing began to return to normal. She had survived the jump in one piece, and now she just needed to figure out where she was.

The room where she had landed was small and nondescript, but there was a door. The K had to have gone through there. Carefully opening it, Mia peeked inside.

Beyond the door lay a large room, occupied by several Ks, including the one Mia had been following. Her heart skipped a beat. She had never seen so many aliens gathered in one place, and it was a striking sight.

There were five males and two females, all tall and beautiful in their own way. Their clothes were clearly intended for hot weather, with the males wearing shorts and various styles of sleeveless shirts and the females dressed in light, floaty dresses that only covered their breasts and hips, leaving most of their golden skin exposed. Despite their attire, Mia doubted they were there to enjoy the ocean breeze. They looked tense and worried, their gestures sharp and almost violent as they argued about something in the Krinar language. In general, they reminded Mia of a pride of lions, prowling around the room with that animalistic grace peculiar to their species.

Finally, one of them looked at his wrist, where a little device seemed to be attached. Barking out what sounded like a command, he pressed some button and a holographic image appeared in the middle of the room. The rest of the Ks gathered around, and Mia moved closer, trying to see what they were looking at. To her surprise, it was a human man, possibly someone in the military, judging by the uniform he wore.

"We're all safe," said the black-haired K in a perfectly accented American English. "All of us left the Center at various points this morning and last night. Are you ready on your end, General?"

General? Mia felt icy terror spreading through her veins. These had to be the Keiths—and they were working with the human forces that John had mentioned. And since she was observing them this way, their identities were no longer secret. Korum knew exactly who they were and what they were up to. Nearly hyperventilating in panic, Mia stared in horror at the scene that she knew could not possibly end well.

The general nodded. "We're ready. Our people are stationed at the agreed-upon points outside the Centers. The operation will commence upon your signal."

One of the female Ks, a brown-haired hazel-eyed beauty, approached the image. "And the ones outside? Do you have someone ready to take each of them out?"

"We do," said the general slowly, "but there's one small problem. One of them is missing."

The female's eyes narrowed. "What do you mean, missing? Who?"

"Korum. We haven't been able to locate him this morning."

The Ks hissed in anger, breaking into angry speech in their own language. The female who spoke gesticulated wildly, trying to convince the black-haired male of something, but he merely shook his head, repeating some phrase over and over. Mia desperately wished she understood what they were saying, but all she could catch was the occasional mention of Korum's name.

Apparently deciding on something, the black-haired K turned to the image again. "General, this is a major problem. Why weren't we notified of this earlier?" His voice was harsh with anger.

"We had the situation under control up until thirty minutes ago. Our two best fighters were on him, tracking him as he left his apartment. And then he walked inside a Starbucks and just disappeared. We never saw him come out, and we searched the entire place top to bottom. I was notified of this development a few minutes ago myself."

"You idiots," the female spat at him. "How many times have we told you how dangerous he is? Why would he disappear like that? Did he spot your fighters?"

The general stared at her with an impassive gaze. "Do you want us to call off the operation?"

The Ks looked at each other, discussing it some more in their language. After about a minute, they seemed to reach a conclusion of some kind. "No," the female said in English, shaking her head, "it's too late for that. If something made him suspicious, then the worst thing to do would be to retreat at this point. We'll have to deal with him later, and hope that not too many lives will be lost in the process."

"Do we have your go-ahead to proceed then?"

"You do," said the black-haired male, and the female nodded.

"Very well," said the general. "Operation Liberty will commence at nine hundred hours, Eastern time."

Mia frantically looked around the room, trying to figure out the time now. An old rusted clock hung on one of the walls. It showed 6:55. If that was correct and she was indeed in Costa Rica, then the attack would take place in less than five minutes, since the Central American country was two hours behind New York.

The image of the general disappeared, and another picture took its place. This one was of a forest, with the familiar greenish-brown circular structures in the background. It was the edge of the colony, Mia realized. The Keiths were going to observe the attack from this underground bunker, where they thought they were safe.

Mia felt her hands beginning to shake. Oh dear God, if only she could warn them ... But it was too late now. When Mia had walked into Korum's office, it was already well after ten in New York. Had an attack taken place, Mia would have heard about it, would have gotten worried texts from Jessie or an urgent alert from some news source on her phone.

No, the Resistance must have failed. All she could do now was watch helplessly as the disaster unfolded right in front of her eyes.

The Keiths paced around the room, occasionally trading brief comments, but keeping silent for the most part. The holograph showed a calm and peaceful border, with only the occasional flying insect providing some entertainment. Time seemed to have slowed, each second passing by more leisurely than the next. Mia found herself biting her nails, something she hadn't done since high school, and watching the Ks as they grew more and more anxious.

The clock hit seven, and all hell broke loose.

Something shimmered at the edge of the forest, and there was a flash of blue light. The Keiths yelled in triumph, and Mia realized that something had gone their way—perhaps a shield had been breached.

And then there was a blinding light, and the circular structure disappeared, dissolving before her eyes. Another flash of light and another structure was gone. Oh God, realized Mia, the attack was real; it was actually happening. They were taking out the guard posts, breaking through the Center's defenses.

Suddenly, the human forces appeared, rushing toward the border. Dressed in army fatigues, they all seemed to be trained soldiers, and there were many of them—dozens, no, hundreds... They ran toward the border, everything in their path disappearing in those flashes of bright light.

The holographic image shifted then, zooming out, and Mia could see the magnitude of what was taking place.

Thousands of human troops had massed at the border, most of them armed with human weapons. As the guard posts dissolved, that seemed to serve as a signal of some kind, and the attack began in earnest, the massive wave of human soldiers rolling toward the Center and then spreading out to encircle the perimeter.

She could hear the Resistance broadcasting their demand for the Ks' surrender, announcing that they had the nano-weapon ready to be used.

And in the blink of an eye, everything changed.

As the first wave of soldiers approached the border, there was another flash of blue light and the shimmer was back. The Keiths shouted something, and Mia watched in horror as the people in the front were thrown back by some invisible force, their bodies burned to a crisp.

Her mouth opened in a wordless scream of terror, and then it was suddenly over. A huge wave of red light blasted through the battlefield, and the remaining human troops fell to the ground in unison and didn't move again. Thousands of human soldiers were now nothing more than bodies lying limply on the grass. It was as if a bomb had gone off, but instead of blowing them to bits, it had simply killed them with that bright red light.

Mia couldn't breathe, couldn't tear her eyes away from the destruction taking place. Her chest felt like it would explode from the force of her heart hammering against her ribcage, and hot bile rushed into her throat. It was all her fault; if she hadn't done what she'd done, none of this would be happening. There wouldn't be an attack, and all these people would be home with their families, going about their day instead of dying before her eyes. Thousands of human deaths were now on her conscience.

The Keiths were panicking now, and the room was filled with their shouts and arguments. They were deciding whether to run or to stay here, Mia realized with a sick feeling in her stomach. They had risked everything and lost—and now there would be consequences for their actions. And then the ceiling about their heads shattered, and the Keiths screamed in terror as the bright morning light streamed down, the hut above them apparently destroyed. Mia screamed too, diving for cover even as her brain told her that this wasn't real—that she was not the one in danger. Petrified, she huddled in the corner, hugging her knees against her chest and watching helplessly as other Ks jumped down into the room, dressed in the simple dark grey outfits that she recognized as their military uniforms.

The black-haired male sprang at one of the soldiers, his attack fast and sudden, his motions almost a blur to Mia's eyes—and he was thrown back just as fast, his body jerking uncontrollably as he collapsed on the floor. Another soldier—their leader, Mia guessed—barked out a command, and the jerking motions stopped. The black-haired Keith was now unconscious. The other Keiths stood still, unwilling to share his fate, their expressions ranging from rage to bitter defeat. Whatever invisible weapons the soldiers possessed were clearly enough to dissuade the Keiths from fighting any further.

It was all over, Mia thought dully. Tears streamed down her face as she watched the soldiers place silvery circles around the Keiths' necks. The K version of handcuffs, perhaps . . . The circles locked into place with a faint click, and there was a sense of finality within that sound—the sound of defeat. The Resistance had lost, their forces utterly decimated and their alien allies captured. Operation Liberty had failed, and thousands of human lives had been lost. There would be no liberation of Earth, not today . . . and probably not ever.

Another K jumped down into the room then, his movements gracefully controlled. Unlike the others, he was dressed in human clothes, a pair of blue jeans and a beige T-shirt. And Mia recognized the familiar slash of dark eyebrows above piercing golden eyes, the sensuous mouth that now looked cruel, set in an uncompromising line in his strikingly beautiful face.

It was Korum. Her enemy, her lover . . . whose kind had just killed thousands of people before her very own eyes.

CHAPTER TWENTY-FOUR

Mia couldn't think, her entire body shaking from shock and fear as she watched Korum prowl toward the Keiths. The expression on his face was unlike anything she had ever seen before, a blend of icy fury and extreme contempt. He spoke to the brown-haired female in Krinar, his voice low and cold, and she flinched, as though he had physically slapped her. The other female interrupted, her tone pleading, and Korum turned his attention to her and said something that silenced her right away. The male Keiths just stared, their looks ranging from fear to defiance. Then Korum turned to the leader of the soldiers and asked him a question. Whatever answer he received made him nod, apparently satisfied.

"I asked him if all the other Centers were secured as well . . . in case you were curious about the translation."

Mia froze, her blood turning to ice. Slowly turning her head to the side, she looked into the gold-flecked eyes of the alien she had just been observing on the other side of the room.

This Korum was wearing the same clothes as his virtual alter ego, but the mocking half-smile on his face was different. So was the fact that he was looking straight at her and speaking in English. Out of the corner of her eye, she could see the drama continuing to unfold in the room, but it no longer mattered. Instead, all she could do was stare at the real-life version of her lover . . . who now undoubtedly knew about her betrayal.

"Fortunately, they were," he continued, his voice deceptively calm. "With the exception of the traitors you see before you, none of the Krinar were harmed. Only a few of our shield posts were destroyed, and they will be easily replaced within the next hour."

Mia could barely hear him above the roar of her heartbeat, his words not registering in the panicked whirl of her thoughts. *He knew.* He knew what she had done, and nothing she said or did would change the outcome. All she could hope for now was to delay the inevitable.

"H-how?" she croaked, her bloodless lips barely moving. Her throat felt strangely dry, and she could taste the saltiness of her own tears gathering in the corners of her mouth.

"How did I know?" Korum asked, approaching her corner and crouching down next to her. Raising his hand, he gently tucked the stray curl behind her ear and brushed his knuckles down the side of her face, his touch burning her frozen skin.

Mia nodded, trembling at his proximity.

"How could I not know, Mia?" he said softly. "Did you honestly think that I wouldn't realize what was taking place under my own roof? That I wouldn't know that the woman I slept with every night was working with my enemies?"

"Wh-what are you saying?" she whispered, her brain working agonizingly slowly. "Y-you knew all along?"

He smiled bitterly. "Of course. From the moment they approached you and you agreed to spy for them, I knew."

"I don't . . . I don't understand. You knew and you let me do it anyway?"

"It was your choice, Mia. You could've said no. You could've refused them. And even after you agreed—at any point, you could've told me the truth, warned me. Even last night—you could've still told me. But you chose to lie to me, to the very end." His voice was oddly calm and remote, and that bitter expression still twisted his lips.

"But . . . but you knew—" Mia couldn't process that part, couldn't understand what he was telling her.

"I did," he said, reaching out to pick up a lock of her hair. "I knew, and I let things unfold as they will. It wasn't part of my original plan; it wasn't why I was in New York. I wanted to find and capture one of their leaders, to extract the identities of the traitors you saw today. But when you chose to betray me, I knew that a rare opportunity had presented itself—that we could strike a blow to the Resistance from which they would never recover . . . and I could catch the traitors in the process."

He paused, playing with her hair, twisting and untwisting the strand around his fingers. Mia stared at him, hypnotized, feeling like a rabbit caught by a snake.

"And so I played along. I gave you every chance to succeed in your treacherous mission—and you did. You turned out to be resourceful and clever, quite inventive really." His eyes took on a familiar golden gleam. "That night when you stole my designs was . . . memorable, to say the least. I very much enjoyed it."

Mia swallowed, beginning to realize where he was leading. "Y-you planted fake designs," she whispered, a searing agony spreading through her chest.

He nodded, a small triumphant smile curving his lips. "I did. I gave them just enough rope so they could hang themselves with it. They learned how to disable the shields, but not how to keep them disabled. The weapon they were relying on wouldn't have functioned properly; I had designed it to work under testing conditions but not when it was really deployed. And I let them have a few minor weapons, so they could do some damage and get caught red-handed trying to escape . . . like the cowards that they really are. I knew that they would trust you when you brought them the designs—because you had already given them enough real information by that point."

"So you used me," said Mia quietly, feeling like she was suffocating. The pain was indescribable, even though logically she knew she had no right to feel this way.

"It hurts, doesn't it?" he said astutely, a savage smile on his face. "It hurts to be the one used, the one betrayed . . . doesn't it?"

"Was any of it real?" asked Mia bitterly. "Or was the whole thing a lie? Did you set it all up, right down to our meeting in the park?"

"Oh, it was real, all right," he said softly, now stroking the edge of her ear. "From the moment I saw you, I knew that I wanted you—more than anyone I've wanted in a very long time. And I grew to care about you, even though I knew it was foolish. With time, I hoped that you would feel the same way about me, that if I showed you how good it could be between us, you would realize what you were doing, the mistake that you were making. And you were close, I know . . . Yet you still betrayed me in the end, not caring what happened, whether I would live or die—"

"No!" interrupted Mia, her eyes burning with a fresh set of tears. "That's not true! They promised me . . . they promised you'd be all right, that they would give you safe passage back home—"

"Back to Krina?" he asked, his voice dangerously low. "Where I would be out of your life forever? And how would they have ensured that I stayed there?"

Mia could only stare at him. Somehow that thought had never crossed her mind. In the background, virtual Korum left the room, and so did the soldiers with their prisoners in tow.

He gave a short, harsh laugh. "I see. That never occurred to you, did it? That deportation was a temporary solution at best? No, the traitors would've never deported me . . . I am too dangerous in their eyes because I have both the desire and the means to return to Earth with reinforcements—and that's the last thing they would want."

Mia felt like she'd been punched in the stomach. She hadn't known . . . They'd lied to her. She couldn't have gone through with it, couldn't have done it knowing that he would be killed in the process. She had to convince him of that. "Korum," she said desperately, "I didn't know, I swear—"

He shook his head. "It doesn't matter," he said. "Even if you didn't mean for me to get killed, you still had every intention of exiling me from your life forever, you still betrayed me . . . and that's not something I can forgive easily."

"So what now?" asked Mia wearily. She was beginning to feel numb, and she welcomed the sensation, as it took the edge off her terror and pain. "Are you going to kill me?"

He stared at her, his gaze turning a colder yellow. "Kill you? Did you listen to anything I said in the last ten minutes?"

He wasn't going to kill her? The numbness spread, and she could only look at him, unable to feel anything more than a vague sense of relief.

At her lack of reply, he said slowly, "No, Mia. I'm not going to kill you. I've already told you that before. I'm not the unfeeling monster you persist in thinking me to be."

Getting up in one lithe motion, Korum waved his hand, and Mia shut her eyes, seeing the virtual world dissolving around her. When she opened them again, she was sitting on the floor of Korum's office, against the wall, still hugging her knees to her chest.

Bending down, he offered her his hand. Her fingers trembling, Mia placed her hand in his, allowing him to help her up. To her embarrassment, her legs were shaking, and she swayed slightly. Letting out a sigh, he caught her, swinging her up into his arms and carrying her out of the office.

"Where are you taking me?" asked Mia in confusion, disoriented after the recent reality shift. Oh God, surely he wasn't thinking of having sex right now; she didn't think she could bear that kind of intimacy after everything that happened.

"To the kitchen," Korum replied, walking swiftly. Before she could ask him why, they were there, and he was setting her down on one of the chairs. Mia blinked up at him, too drained to attempt to understand his inexplicable behavior.

"When was the last time you had something to eat?" he asked, looking at her with a slight frown on his face.

"Um . . . last night." Mia couldn't fathom where he was going with this.

He nodded, as though she had confirmed something for him. "No wonder you're so shaky," he said reprovingly. "You didn't eat breakfast, and your blood sugar is low." Walking to the refrigerator, he filled a glass with some clear liquid and brought it to her. "Drink this, while I make you something to eat," he ordered, ignoring the incredulous look on Mia's face.

He wanted to feed her right now? Was he serious? Cautiously sniffing the glass, Mia discerned a faintly sweet coconut scent. What the hell, she decided, if he wanted her dead, she sincerely doubted he would use poison to kill her. Taking a sip, she realized that her nose hadn't lied; Korum had indeed given her fresh coconut water to drink. It was exactly what her body was craving right now, a perfect blend of carbohydrates and electrolytes. The frozen numbness that had been encasing her like armor began to crack, and tears welled up in Mia's eyes again. Why was he acting like this now, after everything that she had done to him?

Finishing her drink, she watched him move about the kitchen, making her an avocado-tomato sandwich. Now that the main adrenaline rush was over, she was starting to think again, her brain beginning to function at some fraction of its normal ability. The truth about their relationship had been revealed. This entire time she'd thought that she was spying on him for the benefit of all humanity, but he had really been using her to crush the Resistance once and for all. All those lives today had been lost because of her . . . No, she couldn't focus on that now, or she would shatter into a million pieces.

She concentrated on the puzzle of Korum's intentions instead. He wasn't going to kill her, he'd said. But would he punish her in some other way? She couldn't imagine that he would want her around after the way she had betrayed him. Their farce of a relationship was over. He had won: Earth would remain firmly under Krinar control. And Mia had outlived her usefulness. He didn't need an unwitting double agent anymore—

"Here, eat this," the object of her musings said, placing the sandwich in front of her and sitting down across the table. "And then we'll talk."

"Thank you," Mia said politely and obediently bit into the sandwich. Her stomach growled, and she was suddenly starving, her lumberjack appetite making its appearance despite the trauma of this morning's events. In less than a minute, she had devoured the sandwich and looked up, slightly embarrassed by her greediness. The smile on his face was a genuine one this time, and she remembered that he liked that about her—the healthy appetite she possessed despite her small size.

"So what now?" Mia repeated her earlier question, and Korum's smile faded. He regarded her with an inscrutable gaze, and Mia shifted in her seat, growing increasingly nervous.

"So now," Korum said quietly, "you will come with me while I help clean up this mess."

Mia felt all blood drain from her face. "Come with you where?" Surely he couldn't mean—

A small smile appeared on his lips. "To the same place you went while snooping this morning: Lenkarda, our settlement in Costa Rica."

All of a sudden, there wasn't enough air in the room for Mia to breathe properly, and the sandwich felt like a rock inside her stomach. What was he saying? He couldn't still want her, not after everything . . .

"Why?" she managed to squeeze out, staring at him in horrified disbelief.

"Because, Mia, I want you with me, and I can't stay in New York any longer," he said calmly, with an unreadable expression on his face. "I've been away far too long. There are things that require my attention—not the least of which is what to do with the traitors."

Mia shook her head, trying to get rid of the mental fog that seemed to be slowing her thinking. "B-but why do you want me with you?" she stammered. "You were just using me—"

"I was using *you* because you chose to betray *me*—don't ever forget that, darling," he said in a dangerously silky tone. "I've wanted you from the very beginning, and nothing you've done changes that fact. You're mine, and you'll remain with me for as long as I want you. Do you understand that?"

There was a dull roaring in her ears. "No," she whispered, her words barely audible. "No. I'm not going anywhere. I won't be a slave . . . I refuse, do you hear me?" Her voice had risen in volume with each sentence until she was almost yelling at him, the red mist of fury taking over her vision and getting rid of any remnants of caution.

"A slave?" he asked with a puzzled frown on his face. And then his forehead smoothed out as he apparently realized what she was talking about. "Ah, yes, I almost forgot that you've been laboring under a misconception this whole time. You're referring to being my charl, aren't you?"

"I will not be your charl!" Mia snarled, her hands clenching into fists under the table.

"You will be anything I wish you to be, my darling," he said softly, a mocking smile curving his lips. "However, your friends in the Resistance have misinformed you—either inadvertently or on purpose—about the real meaning of charl."

Her temper cooling slightly, Mia stared at him. "What do you mean? Are you telling me that you *don't* keep humans in your Centers as your . . . pleasure slaves?" She spit out the last words with disgust.

He shook his head, with that same sardonic look on his face. "No, Mia. A charl is a human companion—a human mate, if you will. It's a unique term that we use to describe a special bond between a human and a Krinar. Being a charl is a privilege, an honor—not whatever it is that you've been imagining."

"A privilege to be with you against my will?" asked Mia bitterly. "To be forced to go where I don't want to go—unable to see my family, my friends?"

"Don't lie to me, Mia," he said quietly. "Or to yourself. Being with me is hardly a chore for you. Do you think I don't know why you've been crying this week? You need me . . . just as much as I need you. What we have together is rare and special—even though you've done your best to tear us apart. If I were young and foolish, I would let my hurt and anger get the best of me . . . and leave you, full of bitterness at your betrayal. But I've been around long enough to understand that when you find a good thing, you hold on to it; you don't throw it away on a whim."

"Really? You hold on to it even if the other person doesn't want you?" said Mia sarcastically, infuriated by his arrogant assumption that he knew all about her feelings. Maybe she *had* fallen for him; maybe she'd even thought she loved him—but that was before she knew how he'd used her, before she witnessed the deaths of thousands of human soldiers as a result of what he'd done. He might be able to get over his hurt and anger, but Mia couldn't be so magnanimous right now.

"Oh, you want me," Korum said softly. "That much I know for a fact. Would you like me to prove it?"

And before she could come up with a retort, he was next to her, swinging her up into his arms and bringing her toward him for a deep kiss, his tongue pushing into the recesses of her mouth. Infuriated, Mia tried to remain impassive, to temper her response, but her body didn't know, didn't care that he was about to ruin her life. It only knew the pleasure of his touch, and Mia found herself melting against him, her hands clinging to his shoulders instead of pushing him away. A familiar wave of heat swept through her, and she felt a surge of moisture between her legs, her body eagerly preparing itself for his possession.

Still holding her in his arms, he walked somewhere, and Mia was too far gone to care where. They ended up in the living room, and he lowered her onto the couch, still kissing her with those deep, penetrating kisses that never failed to make her crazy. She heard the zipper of her jeans getting unfastened, and then he was tugging them off her legs along with her sneakers, leaving her lower body clad only in a pair of white lacy panties. His thumb found the sensitive nub between her legs, and he pressed on it through the underwear, circling it in a way that made her insides tighten, and Mia moaned helplessly, arching toward him, wanting more of the magic that she had only experienced in his arms.

He let go of her then, taking a step back to remove his own clothes, stripping off the T-shirt with one smooth motion and then swiftly taking off his jeans and underwear, leaving himself fully naked. Mia stared at him with unabashed lust, taking in the powerful muscles covered with that beautiful bronzed skin, the smattering of dark hair on his chest, and the hairy trail on his lower abdomen leading down to a large, fully aroused cock, with the heavy balls swinging underneath.

He didn't let her enjoy the view for long, grasping her shirt to pull it over her head and unclasping her bra. A second later, her panties were pulled off her legs and joined the heap of clothes lying on the floor. He paused for a second, raking her naked body with a burning gaze, and then he bent over her, his hot mouth closing over her left breast, sucking on it. Mia moaned, feeling the pull of his mouth deep within her belly, and he sucked on the other breast, his tongue flicking over her nipple in a way that made her desperately wish his head was two feet lower. As though reading her mind, he touched her wet folds with his hand, one finger pushing into her opening, pressing on the ultra-sensitive spot inside her pussy, and Mia gasped from the intensity of the sensation, her body throbbing on the verge of release. Without removing his finger, he brought his mouth down toward her sex, his tongue finding its way inside her folds to tease the area directly around her clit. At the same time, his finger moved slightly within her, starting to find a rhythm, and Mia's entire body tensed as the tingles of pre-orgasmic sensation began to radiate from her lower regions outward. His tongue flicked at her nub, first lightly and then with increasing pressure, and Mia screamed under the almost cruel lash of pleasure, her inner muscles clamping down on his finger and then pulsating with the aftershocks of the release.

Withdrawing his finger, he flipped her over, pulling her toward the edge of the couch. Lifting her briefly, he placed her so that she was bent over the plush couch arm, face down and her feet on the floor. Covering her with his body, he began to push inside her, his cock penetrating her inch by slow inch. Mia was soft and wet from the orgasm, and her body accepted his gradual entrance, the tender inner tissues stretching and expanding to accommodate the intrusion. As he pushed forward, he kissed the side of her neck, and she shivered, the tension starting to build again. Her sex spasmed around his cock, and he groaned in response, sheathing himself fully within her. Mia inhaled sharply from the feel of his shaft buried to the hilt; he was impossibly hard and thick, and she felt like she was burning from the heat of him inside her, over her, all around her.

And then he began to move, his thrusts pressing her deeper into the arm of the couch. Every muscle in her body tensed, and she cried out, each stroke intensifying the agonizing pleasure, until her world narrowed to nothing more than the cock moving back and forth within her body and she existed purely for the sensations, stripped down to the raw and elemental parts of her animal nature. She could hear the rhythmic cries in the distance and knew that they had to be her own, and then the massive climax swept through her, her inner muscles rippling around him and her entire body trembling from the shock of the orgasmic wave. And, with a hoarse shout, he was coming too, his hips grinding into her as his cock pulsed inside her with his own contractions.

When it was all over, he withdrew from her, leaving her lying there naked, still bent over the sofa arm. Without his large body covering her, Mia suddenly felt cold—and the realization of what had just happened added to the icy knot growing inside her. Standing up on quivering legs, Mia bent down to pick up her clothes, refusing to look at him and trying to ignore the wetness sliding down her leg. With the heat of passion over, her anger returned, magnified by the shame of her unwanted response to him.

"Mia," he said softly, and out of the corner of her eye, she saw him standing there, completely unconcerned about his nakedness. She turned away, putting on her bra, and using her shirt to wipe off the traces of the sex session before putting on her underwear. Pulling on her jeans, she felt slightly better, but the cold fury inside remained. Without even thinking about it, she walked over to the little purse she'd left sitting on the couch earlier this morning. Reaching inside, she pulled out the little device Leslie had given her and pointed it in his direction.

"I'm leaving," she said with icy calm. A stranger seemed to have taken over her body, and the normal Mia couldn't help but marvel at her daring, even though she knew that her odds of success were nil.

At the sight of the weapon, the golden glow in Korum's eyes cooled.

"That's a dangerous toy you have there," he said quietly, staring at her with an unreadable expression on his face.

Mia nodded coolly. "Don't force me to use it."

"So you walk out of here, and then what?" he asked with mild curiosity. "There's nowhere you can go where I won't find you."

Mia hadn't thought that far; in fact, there'd been no thinking involved in her actions at all. It was too late now, though, so she just shrugged and said bravely, "I'll cross that bridge when I get there."

"Are you going to go on the run? Change your identity?" he continued, an amused note appearing in his voice. "None of that would work, you know."

"Because of the tracking stuff you put in me without my knowledge or consent?" she asked bitterly.

Korum just looked at her, neither admitting nor denying it. "There's only one way you could be free of me," he said slowly.

Mia stared at him in frustration, not understanding where he was leading. Now that the initial wave of fury had passed, the full stupidity of her actions dawned on her. He was right; even if she managed to walk out of his penthouse—a big if, given the laser-quick reflexes she was up against—he would catch her before she could go more than a few blocks. By pointing that weapon at him, she had only succeeded in angering him, and she felt a tendril of fear at the thought.

"And what way is that?" she asked, deciding to stall for time.

"You could shoot me," he said seriously. "And then all your problems would be solved."

Horrified, Mia gaped at him. The idea of actually pressing the button and watching him dissolve before her eyes, like those shield posts at the colony, was unthinkable. She'd never had any intention of actually using the weapon. All she'd wanted was to regain some measure of control, to feel like she was in charge of her own life. She'd wanted to threaten him, to make him bow to her will, to make him feel the way she felt when he took away her freedom of choice. She'd never wanted to hurt him, much less kill him.

"Go ahead, Mia," he said softly. His powerful naked body was relaxed, as though they were having a regular conversation—as though he didn't have a deadly weapon pointed at him. "Go ahead and shoot."

Her fingers trembled, her palms slick with sweat, and she felt her eyes burning with stupid, unwelcome tears. "Please," she said, not caring anymore that she sounded like she was begging. "Please don't make me do it. I just want to leave . . . to go home. Please just let me walk out of here—"

"Just press the button, Mia. And then you can go wherever you want."

Mia felt hot and cold, her stomach twisting with nausea. The tiny device in her hand was suddenly unbearably heavy, and her arm shook with the effort of holding it pointed at him. The tears spilled over, running down her cheeks, and she lowered the weapon, sinking down to the floor, her trembling legs unable to hold her any longer. Burying her face in her hands, she cried, bitter at her own cowardice, her own idiocy. She couldn't hurt him, couldn't kill him; she would have sooner cut off her own limb. How could she feel this way about him even now? What was wrong with her that she had fallen in love with someone who wasn't even human . . . an alien whose kind had just murdered thousands of people?

In the depths of her despair, she felt him wrap his arms around her, lifting her from the floor and onto his lap on the couch. "Hush, my darling," he whispered, "everything will be all right, I promise. I wouldn't have been able to press that button either—and I'm glad you couldn't." He stroked her hair gently while she cried into his naked shoulder. After a few minutes, her sobs began to quiet. Feeling embarrassed about her outburst, Mia tried to pull away, but he didn't let her, lifting her chin instead to look her in the eye.

"Mia," he said softly, "I'm not taking you with me to be cruel. After everything that happened, the Resistance—or whatever is left of it—will be looking for you. They don't know the full story, and they'll think you set them up. They'll spare no effort in trying to kill you, and if they figure out how much you mean to me, they'll try to capture you alive to use you against me. I'm sorry, but I have no choice. It's simply not safe for you to be anywhere but in Lenkarda right now."

Mia stared at him, her vision still blurred by tears. She hadn't thought about that, but it was true. As far as the Resistance was concerned, she was a traitor to all of humankind. They would definitely blame her for the huge loss of life she'd just witnessed. A terrifying thought occurred to her. "What about my family?" she asked, everything inside her turning to ice at the possibility that the freedom fighters might try to hurt those she loved.

"Your family had nothing to do with it, and I doubt the fighters would be vengeful enough to needlessly harm fellow humans. But your kind can be very unpredictable, so I will make sure that several of our best guardians are stationed near your family, to keep an eye out for them."

Mia opened her mouth to ask, but he forestalled her. "And no, that wouldn't be enough to ensure *your* safety. There are still a few key Resistance leaders unaccounted for, and they're armed with some Krinar weapons. I expect them to go into hiding and leave your family alone, but they may be willing to risk everything to get to *you*. So until they're apprehended, you will be safest in Lenkarda. And if you have to venture out, it will be with me by your side."

How convenient for him, Mia thought bitterly, he could now keep her prisoner with good justification. Of course, the Resistance would want to kill her—and they would be right to do so. She was responsible for all those deaths today . . .

"How many people were killed this morning?" asked Mia, feeling like she wanted to die herself.

Korum shrugged slightly. "I don't know if the medics got to the ones who were burned fast enough to save them. Some of them might have died from their encounter with the shield."

"What about all the other ones, the ones who were hit with that red light?" asked Mia, her heart beginning to pound in wild hope.

"They were knocked unconscious—and so were the ones who attacked our other Centers. They deserved to die, of course, but we decided to let your governments deal with them. It'll be interesting to see what their punishment will be for violating the Coexistence Treaty and endangering your entire species in the process."

The relief that Mia felt was indescribable. The painful grip in her chest seemed to ease, letting her breathe freely for the first time since she'd witnessed the attack.

And then Korum added, "Of course, we're not going to leave it to chance. All those fighters now have surveillance devices embedded in their bodies, so we'll know everything they do and everywhere they go. They've been effectively neutralized as a threat to us, and we can now use them to catch the rest—those that were not near our Centers today."

So he had succeeded in his mission of squashing the Resistance movement. Given the number of fighters lying on the field, Ks would now have thousands of walking, talking surveillance mechanisms all over the globe. It was quite clever really; why bother killing a human when you could use him instead? Pure Korum deviousness at work.

She must've looked upset because he said, "Mia, stop worrying about this. The Resistance is over. It was a foolish movement to begin with. Just think about it. So they don't like us being here and changing a few things. Is that really a good reason to risk so many lives? You have to admit, we're nothing like the alien invaders of your movies. We have no desire to enslave humans, or to take away your planet. If that had been our agenda, we would've already done it. We settled here as peacefully as possible, living in our Centers with minimal interference in human affairs. That's far better than what your Europeans had done to the American natives."

Still sitting on his lap, Mia looked away. If Korum was telling her the truth and John had lied about the meaning of charl, then the entire Resistance movement was misguided at best—and criminally irresponsible at worst.

"And do you honestly think it would've been a good thing for you to have those seven traitors as your rulers? Because, believe me, that's what they would've been. They wanted power, and they didn't care who got hurt as a result of their actions. Do you really think they would've been content to live quietly among humans, obeying your every law and selflessly sharing Krinar knowledge?"

Now that Korum put it that way, Mia could see the implausibility of what John had originally told her. Maybe the Resistance leaders had thought they could somehow control the Keiths once the other Ks had left—but that could've easily been a dangerous assumption to make. Mia mentally kicked herself. Why hadn't she probed further into the Keiths' motivations? But no, she'd blindly gone with what John was telling her, too caught up in her own personal drama to fully think about anything else.

Korum sighed, and she felt the movement of his chest. "Look, it won't be so bad being in Lenkarda, believe me. Aren't you the least bit curious to see how we live?"

Mia looked up at him again, feeling completely drained. "Korum, I just can't . . . I can't simply leave everything and everyone—"

"What if I take you to see your family in a couple of weeks as we originally discussed?" he asked softly. "Would that make you feel better?"

"We'd go to Florida?" asked Mia in surprise.

He nodded. "You could spend a few days with them before we have to go back."

She smiled, the pressure in her chest easing further. "That would be wonderful," she said quietly.

He smiled back and gently brushed a curl off her face. "And hopefully, by the end of the summer, we'll catch the rest of the Resistance fighters—so if you still want to come back to New York then, we'll return here and you can finish your last year of school."

Mia blinked at him, hardly daring to believe her ears. "You'll bring me back here?"

"I will . . . if you still want to return by then." Getting up, he placed her gently on her feet. "Now put on a shirt and some shoes while I get dressed. It's time to go."

* * *

Korum allowed her to take her purse with its entire contents, the weapon excluded, and nothing else. When she protested that she needed her computer and her clothes, he laughed. "I promise you, there's plenty of everything where we're going," he explained with a smile.

"What about my passport?" she asked, and then realized that it was a stupid question. She might be heading to a foreign country, but she sincerely doubted she would be going through airport security. Somehow, Korum had managed to travel there this morning and then come back to New York—all within a span of a couple of hours. No, thought Mia, they likely wouldn't be traveling by airplane.

Her suppositions turned out to be correct.

He led her into his office, holding her hand as if afraid she would bolt. Walking toward the back of the room, he held his other hand in front of the wall and it slid open, revealing stairs that likely led to the rooftop.

"Come," Korum said, and she followed him with hesitation, her pulse racing at the thought of where she was going. It was too late to turn back now—not that he would have let her—and Mia felt a heady mixture of excitement and fear rushing through her veins as she walked up the stairs.

They exited onto the rooftop, and Mia looked around. She wasn't sure what she was expecting to see—perhaps some alien aircraft sitting there. But there was nothing. The roof was empty, with the exception of some evergreen shrubs growing in neat rows around the perimeter. The rain had mostly stopped, but it was still wet and humid outside, and Mia could practically feel her curls frizzing up from the moisture in the air.

"What are we doing here?" she asked in surprise. "Is someone coming to get us?"

Korum shook his head and smiled. "No, we're going by ourselves."

"How?" asked Mia, burning with curiosity.

"You'll see in a second. Don't be afraid, okay?" He squeezed her palm reassuringly.

Mia nodded, and Korum let go of her hand, taking a step forward. Extending his arm, he made a gesture, as though pointing at the empty space in front of him. All of a sudden, Mia could hear a low humming. The sound was unlike anything Mia had heard before—too quiet and even to be the buzzing of insects.

"What is that?" she asked warily, wondering if Korum intended to teleport them somewhere. Mia had no idea what the limitations of K technology were, but she did know that Krinar physics had to have gone far beyond Einstein's theories; otherwise, the Ks wouldn't have been able to travel faster than the speed of light. Who knew what else they could do?

Korum turned toward her, his eyes glittering with some unknown emotion. "It's the sound of the nanomachines that I just released. They're building us our ride." And Mia realized that he was excited, pleased to be going home.

Something began to shimmer in front of them. Goosebumps appeared on Mia's arms as she stared in fascination at the strange sight. The shimmering intensified, as if a bucket of glitter had been thrown in front of them—and then the walls of the aircraft began to form in front of her eyes.

Barely holding back a gasp, Mia watched as the structure assembled itself, seemingly out of nothingness. The walls slowly solidified, thickening layer by layer, and then a small pod-like aircraft stood in front of them. It appeared to be made out of some unusual ivory material, with no visible windows or doors, and was smaller than a helicopter.

Mia exhaled sharply, releasing a breath she had been holding for the last thirty seconds.

"It's called advanced rapid fabrication technology," Korum said, smiling at the look of utter astonishment on her face. "It's one of our most useful inventions. Come with me." And taking her hand again, he led her toward the newly assembled structure.

As they approached, the wall of the pod simply disintegrated, creating an entrance for them. Mia blinked in shock, but followed Korum inside the aircraft. Once they were in, the wall re-solidified, and the entrance disappeared again.

The inside of the pod did not look like any aircraft she could have ever imagined. The walls, the floor, and the ceiling were transparent—she could see the ivory color of her surroundings, but she could also see the world outside. It was as though they were inside a giant glass bubble, even though Mia knew that the structure was not see-through from the outside. There were no buttons or controls of any kind, nothing to suggest that the pod had any kind of complex electronics. And instead of seats, there were two white oval planks floating in the air.

"Have a seat," Korum said, gesturing toward one of the planks.

"On that?" Mia had known that Krinar technology was far more advanced, of course, and she had expected to encounter some unbelievable things. But this . . . this was like stepping into some fairy realm where the normal laws of physics didn't seem to apply—and she hadn't even left New York yet.

He laughed, apparently amused by her distrust. "On that. You won't fall, I promise."

Warily, still clutching his hand, Mia perched gingerly on the plank. It moved beneath her, and she gasped as it conformed to the shape of her butt, suddenly turning into the most comfortable chair she had ever occupied. There was a back now too, and Mia found herself leaning into it, her tense muscles relaxing, soothed by the strangely cozy sensation.

Grinning, Korum sat down on a similar plank next to her, and Mia stared in amazement as the white material shifted around his body, fitting itself to his shape. She was still holding his hand with a death grip, Mia realized with some embarrassment, and she let go, trying to act as nonchalantly as possible when confronted with technology that seemed exactly like magic.

Korum nodded approvingly and waved his hand slightly.

Softly, without making a sound, the pod lifted off the ground, rising swiftly into the air. With a sinking sensation in her stomach, Mia looked down at the see-through floor, watching New York City shrinking rapidly beneath them as they gained altitude. Surprisingly, she didn't feel nauseated or pushed into her seat as one might expect during such a swift ascent; it was as though she was sitting in a chair at home, instead of rocketing straight up.

"Why don't I feel like we're flying at all?" she asked curiously, looking up from the floor where she could now see only clouds.

"The ship is equipped with a mild anti-gravitational field," Korum explained. "It's designed to make us comfortable by keeping the gravitational force at the same level as you'd experience normally on this planet; otherwise, accelerating like that would be very unpleasant for me—and probably deadly for you."

And then she could see clouds whizzing underneath them as the pod traveled at an incredible speed, taking her to a place that few humans could even imagine, much less visit in person. Never in a million years could Mia have thought that a simple walk in the park could lead to this, that she would be sitting in an alien ship headed for the main Krinar colony . . . that she would feel like this about the beautiful extraterrestrial who was sitting beside her.

A couple of minutes later, they seemed to have reached their destination, and the ship began its descent.

"Welcome home, darling," Korum said softly as the green landscape of Lenkarda appeared beneath their feet, and the ship landed as quietly as it had taken off.

Mia's new life had begun.

Close Obsession

The Krinar Chronicles: Volume 2

PROLOGUE

The Krinar stared at the image in front of him, his hands clenching into fists.

The three-dimensional hologram showed Korum and the guardians approaching the hut on the beach. One of the guardians raised his arm, and the hut blew into pieces, fragments of wood flying everywhere. The fragile human-built structure was clearly no match for the basic nano-blast weapon all guardians carried with them.

The K raised his hand and the image shifted, the flying recording device approaching the wreckage to take a closer look. He didn't worry that the device would be spotted; it was smaller than a mosquito and had been designed by Korum himself.

No, the device was perfect for this task.

As it hovered over the hut, the K could see the drama playing out in the basement, which had been exposed by the blast. The guardians jumped down there, while Korum appeared to be carefully studying the remnants of the hut above ground.

Of course, the K thought, his nemesis would be thorough. Korum would want to make sure nothing and no one escaped from the scene.

The Keiths—the K had started calling them by that name in his mind as well—were panicking, and Rafor stupidly attacked one of the guardians. A foolish move on his part, the K thought dispassionately, watching as the invisible protective shield surrounding the guardians repelled the attack. Now the black-haired Krinar male was jerking uncontrollably on the floor, his nervous system fried from contact with the deadly shield. Had he been human, he would've died instantly.

The guardians didn't let him suffer for long. At the command from their leader, one of the guardians swiftly knocked Rafor unconscious with the stun weapon embedded in his fingers.

The other Keiths were smart enough to avoid Rafor's fate and simply stood there as the silvery crime-collars were locked into place around their necks. They looked angry and defiant, but there was nothing they could do. They were now prisoners, and they would be judged by the Council for their crime.

After a couple of minutes, Korum jumped down into the basement as well, and the K could see that his enemy was furious. He'd known he would be. The Keiths were as good as gone; Korum would show them no mercy.

Sighing, the K switched off the image. He would watch it in greater detail later. For now, he had to figure out some other way to neutralize Korum and implement his plan.

The future of Earth depended on it.

CHAPTER ONE

"Welcome home, darling," Korum said softly as the green landscape of Lenkarda appeared beneath their feet, and the ship landed as quietly as it had taken off.

Her heart hammering in her chest, Mia slowly got up off the seat that had cradled her body so comfortably. Korum was already up, and he extended his hand to her. She hesitated for a second, and then accepted it, clutching his palm with a death grip. The lover she'd thought of as the enemy for the past month was now her only source of comfort in this strange land.

They exited the aircraft and walked a few steps before Korum stopped. Turning back toward the ship, he made a small gesture with his free hand. All of a sudden, the air around the pod began to shimmer, and Mia again heard the low humming sound that signified nanomachines at work.

"You're building something else?" she asked him, surprised.

He shook his head with a smile. "No, I'm un-building."

And as Mia watched, layers of ivory material appeared to peel off the surface of the ship, dissolving in front of her eyes. Within a minute, the ship was gone in its entirety, all of its components turning back into the individual atoms from which they'd been made back in New York.

Despite her stress and exhaustion, Mia couldn't help but marvel at the miracle she'd just witnessed. The ship that had just brought them thousands of miles in a matter of minutes had completely disintegrated, as though it had never existed in the first place.

"Why did you do that?" she asked Korum. "Why un-build it?"

"Because there's no need for it to exist and take up space right now," he explained. "I can create it again whenever we need to use it."

It was true, he could. Mia had witnessed it herself only a few minutes ago on the rooftop of his Manhattan apartment. And now he had un-created it. The pod that had transported them here no longer existed.

As the full implications of that hit her, her heart rate spiked again, and she suddenly found it hard to breathe.

A wave of panic washed over her.

She was now stranded in Costa Rica, in the main K colony—completely dependent on Korum for everything. He had made the ship that had brought them there, and he had just unmade it. If there was another way out of Lenkarda, Mia didn't know about it.

What if he had lied to her earlier? What if she would never see her family again?

She must've looked as terrified as she felt because Korum squeezed her hand gently. The feel of his large, warm hand was oddly reassuring. "Don't worry," he said softly. "It will be all right, I promise."

Mia focused on taking deep breaths, trying to beat back the panic. She had no choice but to trust him now. Even back in New York, he could do anything he wanted with her. There was no reason for him to make her promises that he didn't intend to keep.

Still, the irrational fear gnawed at her insides, adding to the unsavory brew of emotions boiling in her. The knowledge that Korum had been manipulating her all along, using her to crush the Resistance, was like acid in her stomach, burning her from the inside. Everything he'd done, everything he'd said—it had all been a part of his plan. While she had been agonizing over spying on him, he had probably been secretly laughing at her pathetic attempts to outwit him, to help the cause he'd known was doomed to failure from the very beginning.

She felt like such an idiot now for going along with everything the Resistance had told her. It had seemed to make so much sense at the time; she'd felt so noble helping her kind fight against the invaders who had taken over her planet. And instead, she'd unwittingly participated in a power grab by a small group of Ks.

Why hadn't she stopped to think, to fully analyze the situation?

Korum had told her that the entire Resistance movement had been wrong, completely misguided in their mission. And despite herself, Mia had believed him.

The Ks hadn't killed the freedom fighters who had attacked their Centers—and that simple fact told her a lot about the Krinar and their views on humans. If the Ks had truly been the monsters the Resistance portrayed them to be, none of the fighters would have survived.

At the same time, she didn't fully trust Korum's explanation of what a charl was. When John had spoken about his kidnapped sister, there had been too much pain in his voice for it all to be a lie. And Korum's own actions toward her fit much better with John's explanation than with his own. Her lover had denied that the Ks kept humans as their pleasure slaves, yet he'd given her very little choice about anything in their relationship thus far. He had wanted her, and, just like that, her life was no longer her own. She'd been swept off her feet and into his TriBeCa penthouse—and now here she was, in the K Center in Costa Rica, following him toward some unknown destination.

As much as she dreaded the answer to her question, she had to know. "Is Dana here?" Mia asked carefully, not wanting to provoke his temper. "John's sister? John said she's a charl in Lenkarda . . ."

"No," Korum said, shooting her an unreadable look. "John was misinformed—I'm guessing, deliberately—by the Keiths."

"She's not a charl?"

"No, Mia, she was never a charl in the true sense of the word. She was what you would call a xeno—a human obsessed with all things Krinar. Her family never knew that. When she met Lotmir in Mexico, she begged to go with him, and he agreed to take her for some period of time. The last I heard, she got someone else to take her to Krina. I imagine she's quite happy there, given her preferences. As to why she left without a word to her family, I think it probably has something to do with her father."

"Her father?"

"Dana and John haven't had a very happy childhood," Korum said, and she could feel his hand tightening on hers. "Their father is someone who should've been exterminated long ago. Based on the intelligence we've gathered about your Resistance contact, John's father has a particular fetish that involves very young children—"

"He's a pedophile?" Mia asked quietly, bile rising in her throat at the thought.

Korum nodded. "Indeed. I believe his own children were the primary recipients of his affections."

Sickened and filled with intense pity for John and Dana, Mia looked away. If this was true, then she couldn't blame Dana for wanting to get away, to leave everything connected with her old life behind. Although Mia's own family was normal and loving, she'd had some interactions with victims of domestic and child abuse as part of her internship last summer. She knew about the scars it left on the child's psyche. When they got older, some of these children turned to drugs or alcohol to dull their pain. Dana had apparently turned to sex with Ks.

Of course, this was assuming that Korum wasn't lying to her about the whole thing.

Thinking about it, Mia decided that he probably wasn't. Why would he need to? It's not like she could break up with him even if she found out that Dana was held here against her will.

"And what about John?" she asked. "Is he all right? And Leslie?"

"I assume so," he said, and his voice was noticeably cooler. "Neither one has been captured yet."

Relieved, Mia decided to leave it at that. She had a suspicion that talking to Korum about the Resistance was not the smartest course of action for her right now. Instead, she refocused on their surroundings.

"Where are we going?" she asked, looking around. They were walking through what seemed like an untouched forest. Twigs and branches crunched under her feet, and she could hear nature sounds everywhere—birds, some kind of buzzing insects, rustling leaves. She had no idea what he had in mind for the rest of the day, but she just wanted to bury her head under a blanket and hide for several hours. This morning's events and the resulting emotional upheaval had left her completely drained, and she badly needed some quiet time to come to terms with everything that happened.

"To my house," Korum replied, turning his head toward her. There was a small smile on his face again. "It's only a short walk from here. You'll be able to relax and get some rest once we're there."

Mia shot him a suspicious look. His answer was uncannily close to what she had just been thinking. "Can you read my mind?" she asked, horrified at the possibility.

He grinned, showing the dimple on his left cheek. "That would be nice—but no. I just know you well enough by now to see when you're exhausted."

Relieved, Mia nodded and focused on putting one foot in front of another as they walked through the forest. Despite everything, that dazzling smile of his sent a warm sensation all throughout her body.

You're an idiot, Mia.

How could she still feel like this after what he had put her through, after he had manipulated her like that? What kind of a person was she, to fall in love with an alien who had completely taken over her life?

She felt disgusted with herself, yet she couldn't help it. When he smiled like that, she could almost forget everything that happened in the sheer joy of simply being with him. Underneath all the bitterness, she was fiercely glad that the Resistance had failed—that he was still in her life.

Her thoughts kept turning to what he'd said earlier . . . to his admission that he'd grown to care for her. He hadn't intended for it to happen, he'd said, and Mia realized that she'd been right to fear and resist him in the beginning—that he had indeed regarded her as a plaything at first, as a little human toy he could use and discard at his leisure. Of course, "caring" was far from a declaration of love, but it was more than she'd ever expected to hear from him. Like a balm applied to a festering wound, his words made her feel just a tiny bit better, giving her hope that maybe it would be all right after all, that maybe he would keep his promises and she would see her family again—

A squishy sensation under her foot jerked her out of that thought. Startled, Mia looked down and saw that she had stepped on a large, crunchy bug. "Eww!"

"What's the matter?" Korum asked, surprised.

"I just stepped on something," Mia explained in disgust, trying to wipe her sneaker on the nearest patch of grass.

He looked amused. "Don't tell me . . . Are you afraid of insects?"

"I wouldn't say afraid, necessarily," Mia said cautiously. "It's more that I find them really gross."

He laughed. "Why? They're just another set of living creatures, just like you and me."

Mia shrugged and decided against explaining it to him. She wasn't sure she fully understood it herself. Instead, she resolved to pay closer attention to her surroundings. Despite growing up in Florida, she wasn't really comfortable with tropical nature in its raw form. She much preferred neatly paved paths in beautifully landscaped parks, where she could sit on a bench and enjoy the fresh air with minimal bug encounters.

"You don't have any roads or sidewalks?" she asked Korum with consternation, jumping over what looked like an ant hill.

He smiled at her indulgently. "No. We like our environment to be as close to its original state as possible."

Mia wrinkled her nose, not liking that at all. Her sneakers were already covered with dirt, and she was thankful that the wet season in Costa Rica had not officially begun yet. Otherwise, she imagined they would be trekking through swampland. Given the highly advanced state of Krinar technology, she found it strange that they chose to live in such primitive conditions.

A minute later, they entered another clearing, a much larger one this time. An unusual cream-colored structure stood in the middle. Shaped like an elongated cube with rounded corners, it had no windows or doors—or any visible openings at all.

"This is your house?"

Mia had seen structures like this one on the three-dimensional map in Korum's office earlier today. They'd looked very strange and alien to her from a distance, and that impression was even stronger now that she was standing next to one. It just looked so incredibly *foreign*, so different from anything she'd ever seen in her life.

Korum nodded, leading her toward the building. "Yes, this is my home—and now it's yours too."

Mia swallowed nervously, her anxiety growing at the last part of his statement. Why did he keep saying that? Did he really intend for her to live here permanently? He'd promised to bring her back to New York to finish her senior year of college, and Mia desperately clung to that thought as she stared at the pale walls of the house looming in front of her.

As they approached, a part of the wall suddenly disintegrated in front of them, creating an opening large enough for them to walk through.

Mia gasped in surprise, and Korum smiled at her reaction. "Don't worry," he said. "This is an intelligent building. It anticipates our needs and creates doorways as needed. It's nothing to be afraid of."

"Will it do that for anyone or just you?" Mia asked, stopping before the opening. She knew it was illogical, her reluctance to go in. If Korum intended to keep her prisoner, there was nothing she could do about it—she was already in an alien colony with no way to escape. Still, she couldn't bring herself to voluntarily enter her new "home" unless she was sure she could leave it on her own.

Apparently intuiting the source of her concern, Korum gave her a reassuring look. "It will do it for you as well. You'll be able to go in and out whenever you want, although it might be best if you stayed close to me for the first few weeks . . . at least until you get used to our way of life and I have a chance to introduce you to others."

Exhaling in relief, Mia looked up at him. "Thanks," she said quietly, some of her panic fading.

Maybe being here wouldn't be so bad after all. If he really did bring her back to New York at the end of summer, then her sojourn in Lenkarda might prove to be exactly that—a couple of months spent at an incredible place that few humans could even imagine, with the extraordinary creature she'd fallen in love with.

Feeling slightly better about the situation, Mia stepped through the opening, entering a Krinar dwelling for the first time.

The sight that greeted her inside was utterly unexpected.

Mia had been bracing for something alien and high-tech—maybe floating chairs similar to the ones in the ship that had transported them here. Instead, the room looked just like Korum's penthouse back in New York, right down to the plush cream-colored couch. Mia flushed at the memory of what had taken place on that couch just a little while ago. Only the walls were different; they seemed to be made of the same transparent material as the ship, and she could see the greenery outside instead of the Hudson River.

"You have the same furniture here?" she asked in surprise, letting go of his hand and taking a step forward to gape at the strange sight. She couldn't imagine that furniture stores made deliveries to K Centers—but then he could probably just conjure up whatever he wanted using their nanotechnology.

"Not exactly," Korum said, smiling at her. "I set this up ahead of your arrival. I thought it might be easier for you to acclimate if you could relax in familiar surroundings for the first couple of weeks. After you feel more comfortable here, I can show you how I usually live."

Mia blinked at him. "You set it up just for me? When?"

Even with rapid fabrication—or whatever Korum had called the technology that let him make things out of nothing—he probably still needed a little time to do all this. When would he have had a chance to even think about this, given the events of this morning? She tried to picture him making a couch while capturing the Keiths and almost snickered out loud.

"A little while ago," Korum said ambiguously, shrugging a little.

Mia frowned at him. "So . . . not today?" For some reason, the timing of this gesture seemed important.

"No, not today."

Mia stared at him. "You were planning this for a while? Me being here, I mean?"

"Of course," he said casually. "I plan everything."

Mia took a deep breath. "And if I hadn't been in danger from the Resistance? Would you have still brought me here?"

He looked at her, his expression indecipherable. "Does it really matter?" he asked softly.

It mattered to Mia, but she wasn't up to having that discussion right now. So she just shrugged and looked away, studying the room. It *was* somewhat comforting to be someplace that at least looked familiar, and she had to admit that it was a thoughtful thing to do—creating a human-like environment for her in his house.

"Are you hungry?" Korum asked, regarding her with a smile.

Making food for her seemed to be one of his favorite activities; he had even fed her this morning when she'd been afraid he would kill her for helping the Resistance. It was one of the things that had always made her feel so conflicted about him, about their relationship in general. Despite his arrogance, he could be incredibly caring and considerate. It drove Mia nuts, the fact that he'd never truly acted like the villain she'd thought him to be.

She shook her head. "No, thanks. Still full from the sandwich earlier." And she was. All she wanted to do was lie down and try to give her brain a rest.

"Okay then," Korum said. "You can relax here for a bit. I have to go out for an hour or so. Do you think you'll be all right by yourself?"

Mia nodded. "Do you have a bed somewhere?" she asked.

"Of course. Here, come with me."

Mia followed Korum as he walked down a familiar hallway to the bedroom that was identical to the one he had in TriBeCa. She noted the location of the bathroom as well.

"So everything here is stuff I know how to use?" she asked.

"Yes, pretty much," he said, reaching out to briefly stroke her cheek. His fingers felt hot against her skin. "The bed is probably more comfortable than you're used to because it utilizes the same intelligent technology as the chair in the ship and the walls of this house. I figured you wouldn't mind that. Don't be scared if it adjusts to your body, okay?"

Despite the tension squeezing her temples, Mia smiled, remembering how comfortable the seat in the aircraft had been. "Okay, that sounds good. I'm looking forward to trying it."

"I'm sure you'll enjoy it." His eyes gleamed with some unknown emotion. "Take a nap if you want, and I'll be back soon."

Bending down, he gave her a chaste kiss on the forehead and walked out, leaving her alone in an intelligent dwelling inside the alien settlement.

* * *

Less than a mile away, the Krinar watched as his nemesis arrived with his charl.'

The gentle way Korum held her hand as he led her toward his house was so out of character that the K almost chuckled to himself. This was an interesting development, the involvement of a human girl. Would it change anything? Somehow, he doubted it.

His enemy would not be swayed from his course, certainly not by some little human.

No, there was only one way to save the human race.

And he was the only one who could do it.

CHAPTER TWO

Mia woke up in total darkness.

She lay there for a moment, trying to figure out the time. She felt incredibly well-rested, every muscle in her body relaxed and her mind completely clear. Right away, she knew she was in Korum's house in Lenkarda, lying on his "intelligent" bed. Stretching with a yawn, she wondered how Korum had managed to sleep on a regular human mattress back in New York. She couldn't imagine wanting to sleep anywhere other than this bed for the rest of her life.

The sheets were wrapped around her body, caressing her bare skin with a light, sensuous touch. She was neither cold nor hot, and the pillow cradled her head and neck in exactly the right way. Whatever tension she'd felt earlier was completely gone.

She had not intended to fall asleep, but the rest had definitely done wonders for her state of mind. After Korum had left, she'd showered and climbed into bed with the goal of resting for a few minutes. As soon as she'd gotten in, the sheets had moved around her, wrapping her in a gentle cocoon, and she'd felt subtle vibrations under the most tense parts of her body. It was as though soft fingers were massaging away the knots in her back and neck. She remembered loving the sensation, and then she must've fallen asleep because she couldn't recall anything else.

Apparently sensing that she was awake, the room gradually got lighter, even though there was no obvious source of artificial light.

It was a clever idea, Mia thought, to have the light turn on so slowly. Bright light after complete darkness was often painful to the eyes, yet that's how most human light fixtures worked, simply on and off—

disregarding the fact that light-dark transitions in nature were far more subtle.

Reluctant to leave the comfort of the bed, Mia lay there and tried to figure out what to do next. The sick, panicky feeling of earlier was gone, and she could think more clearly.

It was true that Korum had used and manipulated her.

But, to be fair, he'd done it to protect his own kind—just as she'd thought she was helping all of humanity by spying on him. The sense of betrayal she'd felt yesterday had been irrational, out of place considering the nature of their relationship and her own actions toward him. The fact that he hadn't really done anything to punish her for *her* betrayal spoke volumes about his intentions.

She'd been wrong to paint him with such a dark brush before. If he hadn't hurt her for what she'd done thus far, he probably never would.

However, he clearly had no problem disregarding her wishes. Case in point: she was here in Lenkarda. Yet, if he'd spoken the truth, she would still be able to go visit her parents soon, and even come back to New York to finish college.

All in all, her situation was much better than she'd feared this morning, when she'd thought he might kill her for helping the Resistance.

Still, the circumstances she found herself in were unsettling. She was in a K Center, where she didn't speak the language, didn't know anyone except Korum, and had no idea how to use even the most basic Krinar technology. As a human, she was the ultimate outsider here. Would the Ks think she was dumb because of what she was? Because she couldn't understand the Krinar language or read ten books in a couple of hours, the way Korum could? Would they make fun of her ignorance and her technological illiteracy? She wasn't exactly tech-savvy even by human standards. In general, was Korum's arrogance simply a part of his personality, or was it typical of his species and their overall attitude toward humans?

Of course, agonizing about all this didn't change the facts. Whether she liked it or not, she was in Lenkarda for at least the next couple of months, and she had to make the best of it. And in the meantime, there was so much she could learn here—

The bedroom door opened quietly, and Korum walked in, interrupting her thoughts. "Hey there, sleepyhead, how are you feeling?"

Mia couldn't help smiling at him, forgetting her concerns for the moment. For the first time since she'd known him, Korum was dressed in Krinar clothing: a sleeveless shirt made of some soft-looking white material and a pair of loose grey shorts that ended just above his knees. It was a simple outfit, but it did wonders for his physique, accentuating his powerfully muscled build. He looked mouthwateringly gorgeous, his smooth bronze skin glowing with health and those amber eyes shining as he looked at her lying on his bed.

"The bed is awesome," Mia confided. "I don't know how you slept on anything else."

He grinned, sitting down next to her and picking up a strand of her hair to play with. "I know. It was a real sacrifice—but your presence made it quite tolerable."

Mia laughed and rolled over onto her stomach, feeling absurdly happy. "So what now? Do I get to meet other intelligent objects? I have to say, your technology is very cool."

"Oh, you have no idea just how cool our technology is," Korum said, looking at her with a mysterious smile. "But you'll learn soon."

Bending down, he kissed her exposed shoulder and then lightly nibbled on her neck, his mouth warm and soft on her skin. Closing her eyes, Mia shivered from the pleasant sensation. Her body immediately responded to his touch, and she moaned softly, feeling a surge of warm moisture between her legs.

He stopped and sat up straight.

Surprised, Mia opened her eyes and looked at him. "You don't want me?" she asked quietly, trying to keep the hurt note out of her voice.

"What? No, my darling, I very much want you." And it was true; she could see the warm golden flecks in his expressive eyes, and the soft material of his shorts did little to hide his erection.

"Then why did you stop?" asked Mia, trying very hard not to sound like a child deprived of candy.

He sighed, looking frustrated. "A friend of mine is coming over to meet you. He'll be here in a few minutes."

Mia looked at him in surprise. "Your friend wants to meet me? Why?"

Korum smiled. "Because he's heard a lot about you from me. And also because he's one of our top mind experts and can help you with the adjustment process."

Mia frowned slightly. "A mind expert? You want me to see a shrink?"

Korum shook his head, grinning. "No, he's not a shrink. In our society, a mind expert is someone who deals with all aspects of the brain. He's like a neurosurgeon, psychiatrist, and therapist combined—literally an expert on all matters having to do with the mind."

That was interesting, but didn't really answer her question. "So why does he want to see me?"

"Because I think there's something he can do to make you feel more at home here," Korum said, his fingers trailing down her arm, rubbing it softly.

He liked to do that, Mia had noticed, to just randomly touch her during their conversations, as though craving constant physical contact. Mia didn't mind. It was that chemistry he had talked about before; their bodies gravitated toward each other like two objects in space.

She forced her attention back to the conversation. "Like what?" she asked, feeling slightly wary.

"Well, for instance, would you like to be able to understand and speak our language?"

Mia's eyes widened, and she nodded eagerly. "Of course!"

"Have you ever wondered how I'm able to speak English so well? And every other human language? How all of us speak like this?"

"I didn't know you spoke other languages besides English," Mia confessed, staring at him in amazement. She had briefly wondered how he knew such perfect American English, but she'd always assumed the Ks had simply studied everything before coming to Earth. Korum was incredibly smart, so she'd never really questioned the fact that he knew her language and was able to speak it without any accent. And now he was telling her that he spoke a bunch of other languages as well?

"So you speak French?" she asked. At his nod, she continued, "Spanish? Russian? Polish? Mandarin?" He made an affirmative gesture each time.

"Okay . . . What about Swahili?" asked Mia, sure that she had caught him this time.

"That too," he said, smiling at her astounded expression.

"Okay," said Mia slowly. "I gather you're about to tell me that it's not just pure smarts on your part."

He grinned. "Exactly. I could've learned the languages on my own given enough time, but there's a more efficient way—and that's what Saret can do for you."

Mia stared at him. "He can teach me how to speak Krinar?"

"Better than that. He can give you the same abilities that I have—instant comprehension and knowledge of any language, be it human or Krinar."

Mia gasped in shock, her heart beating faster from excitement. "How?"

"By giving you a tiny implant that will influence a specific region of your brain and act as a highly advanced translation device."

"A brain implant?" Her excitement immediately turned to dread as everything inside Mia violently rejected the idea. He had already embedded tracking devices in her palms; the last thing she needed was alien technology influencing her brain. The ability he had described was incredible, and she desperately wanted it—but not at that price.

"The device is not really what you're picturing," Korum said. "It's going to be tiny, the size of a cell, and you will not feel discomfort at any point—either during insertion or afterwards."

"And if I say no, that I don't want it?" Mia asked quietly, alarmed at the idea that Korum already had the mind expert on the way here.

"Why not?" He looked at her with a small frown.

"Do you really need to ask?" she said incredulously. "You *shined* me—you put tracking devices in me under the pretext of healing my palms. Did you really think I would be okay with you putting something in my brain?"

Korum's frown deepened. "This doesn't have any extra functionality, Mia." He didn't seem the least bit repentant about shining her in the first place.

"Really?" she asked him acerbically. "It doesn't do anything extra? Doesn't influence my thoughts or feelings in any way?"

"No, my darling, it doesn't." He looked vaguely amused at the thought.

"I don't want a brain implant," Mia said firmly, looking at him with a mutinous expression on her face.

He stared back at her. "Mia," he said softly, "if I had truly wanted to put something nefarious in your brain, I could've done it in a million different ways. I can implant anything in your body at any time, and you wouldn't have a clue. The only reason why I'm offering you this ability is because I want you to be comfortable here, to be able to communicate with everyone on your own. If you don't want this, then that's your choice. I won't force it on you. But very few humans get this opportunity, so I would advise you to think really hard before you turn it down."

Mia looked away, struck by the realization that he was right. He didn't need to inform her or get her consent for anything he wanted to do to her. The panic that she thought she had under control threatened to bubble up again, and she squelched it with effort.

Something didn't quite make sense to her. Taking a deep breath, Mia turned her gaze to his face again, studying his inscrutable expression. It bothered her that she still understood him so little, that the person who had so much power over her was still such a big unknown.

"Korum . . ." She wasn't sure if she should bring this up, but she couldn't resist. The question had tormented her for weeks. "Why did you shine me? I hadn't even met the Resistance at that point, so it's not like you needed to keep tabs on me for your big plan . . ."

"Because I wanted to make sure I can always find you," he said, and there was a possessive note in his voice that frightened her. "I held you in my arms that day, and I knew I wanted more. I wanted everything, Mia. You were mine from that moment on, and I had no intention of losing you, not even for a moment."

Not even for a moment? Did he realize how crazy that sounded? He had seen a girl he wanted, and he'd made sure her location would always be known to him.

The fact that he thought he had the right to do this was terrifying. How could she deal with someone like that? He had no concept of boundaries when it came to her, no respect for her freedom of will. He had just casually admitted to a horrible and high-handed act, and she had no idea what she could say to him now.

At her silence, Korum took a deep breath and got up. "You should get dressed," he said quietly. "Saret will be here in a minute."

Mia nodded and sat up, holding the sheets to her chest. Now was not the time to analyze the complexities of their relationship. Taking a deep breath of her own, she pushed aside her fear. There was no way she could change her situation right now, and focusing on the negative would only make things worse. She needed to find a way to get along with her lover and figure out how to better manage his domineering nature.

"What should I wear?" Mia asked. "I didn't bring any clothes . . ."

"Do you want your usual jeans and T-shirts, or do you want to dress like everyone else here?" Korum asked, a smile appearing on his face. Some of the tension in the room dissipated.

"Um, like everyone else, I guess." She didn't want to stick out like a sore thumb.

"Okay, then." Korum made a small gesture with his hand and handed her a light-colored piece of material that hadn't been there only a second ago.

Wide-eyed, Mia stared at the piece of clothing he just gave her. "More instant fabrication?" she asked, trying to act like it wasn't still a huge shock to her to see things materializing out of nothing.

He grinned. "That's right. If you don't like this, I can get you something else. Go ahead, try it on."

Mia let go of the sheet and climbed out of bed, feeling comfortable with her nakedness. For all his faults, Korum had done wonders for her body image and self-confidence. Because he repeatedly told her how beautiful he found her to be, she no longer worried about being too skinny or having frizzy hair and pale skin. He would've been a boon during her insecure teenage years.

No, scratch that thought. No teenager should be subjected to someone so overwhelming.

Taking the dress, she put it on, making sure that the low-cut portion was in the back. "What do you think?" she asked, doing a small twirl.

He smiled with a warm glow in his eyes. "It looks perfect on you."

His shorts now had a bulge in them, and Mia smiled to herself in satisfaction. Despite everything, it was nice to know that she had that kind of effect on him, that his need was as strong as hers. At least in this, they were equals.

Curious to see how the dress looked, she walked over to the mirror on the other side of the bedroom.

Korum was right; the outfit was very pretty. Similar in style to the ones she'd seen the female Keiths wear, it was a beautiful shade of ivory with peach undertones, and draped over her body in exactly the right way. Her back and shoulders were mostly exposed, while her front was modestly covered, with strategic pleats around her chest area concealing her nipples. The length was exactly right for her too, with the floaty skirt stopping a couple of inches above her knees.

When she turned around, he handed her a pair of flat ivory sandals, made of some unusually soft material. Mia tried them on. They fit her feet perfectly and were surprisingly comfortable.

"Nice, thanks," she said. Then, remembering one last crucial item, she asked, "What about underwear?"

"We don't really wear it," Korum said. "I can make it for you if you insist, but you might want to try wearing just our clothes."

No underwear? "What if the dress rides up or something?"

"It won't. The material is intelligent as well. It's designed to adhere to your body in exactly the right way. If you move or bend in a certain direction, it will move with you so that you will always be covered."

That was handy. Mia thought of the countless wardrobe malfunctions in Hollywood that could've been prevented with K clothing. "Okay, then I'm ready, I guess," she said. "I have to use the restroom, and then I'm good to go."

"Excellent," Korum said, smiling. "I'll see you in the living room."

And with a quick kiss on her forehead, he exited the room.

* * *

"I like what you've done with the place. Very twenty-first-century American."

Korum's friend had just walked in and was looking around with a smile. An inch or two shorter than Korum, he was just as powerfully built, and had the darker coloring typical of the Ks. His face was rounder, however, and his cheekbones sharper, reminding her a bit of someone with Asian ancestry.

"What can I say? You know I have good taste," said Korum, getting up from the couch where he had been sitting with Mia to greet the newcomer. Approaching him, Korum lightly touched his shoulder with his palm, and the other K reciprocated his gesture.

Mia wondered if that was the K version of a handshake.

Turning toward her, Korum said, "Mia, this is my friend Saret. Saret, this is Mia, my charl."

Saret smiled, his brown eyes twinkling. He seemed genuinely pleased to see her. "Hello, Mia. Welcome to our Center. I hope you've been finding it to your liking so far?"

Mia got up and smiled in return. It was strange to be meeting another K. With the exception of a couple of brief encounters with Korum's colleagues, her lover was the only Krinar she'd interacted with thus far.

"It's been very nice, thank you."

Should she offer to shake his hand? Or do that shoulder thing Korum had just done? As soon as the thought occurred to her, she decided against it. She had no idea what the K rules on physical contact were, and she didn't want to accidentally cause offense.

"Have you had a chance to go anywhere in Lenkarda so far? Korum told me you arrived only this morning."

Mia shook her head regretfully. "No, I haven't. I'm afraid I spent most of the day sleeping." What time was it, anyway? Through the transparent walls of the house, she could see that it was dark outside. It had to be late in the evening, or maybe even the middle of the night.

"Mia was jet-lagged and exhausted from what happened earlier," Korum explained, walking back toward her and placing a proprietary hand around her back. He pulled her down on the couch next to him, and Saret sat down on one of the plush armchairs across from them.

"Of course," Saret said, "I completely understand. It had to be very traumatic for you, learning the truth that way."

Mia stared at him in surprise. How much did he know? Had Korum told him everything, including her role in the Resistance attack on their Centers? She had no idea how her actions would be viewed by the Krinar. Would she be punished somehow for aiding the Resistance earlier?

"Well, the good thing is that it's over," Korum said, taking one of Mia's hands into his and softly rubbing her palm with his thumb. Turning toward her, he promised, "You don't have to worry about any of this again."

"Actually," Saret said with a regretful look on his handsome face, "I'm afraid there might be one more thing that Mia has to do."

Korum's face darkened. "I already told them no. She's been through enough."

Saret sighed. "There was a formal request from the United Nations—"

"Fuck the Unites Nations. They don't get to request anything after this fiasco. They're damn lucky we didn't retaliate—"

"Be that as it may, the majority of the Council believes it's important to extend this gesture of goodwill to them."

Mia listened to them arguing with a cold feeling in the pit of her stomach. The United Nations? The Council? What did any of this have to do with her?

"The Council can go fuck itself too," Korum said in an uncompromising tone. "There's absolutely no need for this, and they know it. She's my charl, and they don't get to tell me what to do."

"She's not just your charl, Korum, and you know it. She's one of the witnesses in what will be the biggest trial of the last ten thousand years, not to mention the human proceedings—"

Mia wanted to throw up as she began to understand where the conversation was leading. "Excuse me," she said quietly, "what exactly is needed from me?"

"It doesn't matter," Korum said flatly. "They can't make you do anything without my permission."

Saret sighed again. "Look, the Council wants her testimony as well. It really would be for the best if you just let her do it—"

Staring at them, Mia began to feel angry. They were talking about her like she was a child or a pet of some sort. Whatever it was they wanted from her, it should be her decision, not Korum's.

"She doesn't need this right now," Korum said firmly. "They have plenty of evidence, and I'm not putting her through any additional stress—"

"Excuse me," Mia said coldly. "I want to know what the fuck you're talking about."

Clearly startled, Saret laughed, and Korum gave her a disapproving look.

"I think your charl is gutsier than you give her credit for," Saret said to Korum, still chuckling. Turning toward Mia, he explained, "You see, Mia, the traitors that you helped us catch—the Keiths, as your Resistance friends called them—will be tried according to our laws. While our judicial process is fairly different from what you're used to, we do require all available evidence to be presented—and testimony from all the witnesses. Since you were involved throughout, your testimony could play a role in whether they get convicted and how serious their punishment will be."

"You want me to testify in a Krinar trial?" Mia asked incredulously.

"Yes, exactly, and we've also received a formal request for your presence from the United Nations Ambassador—"

"She's not doing it, Saret. Forget it. You can go back to Arus and tell him it's not happening."

"Look, Korum, are you sure you want to do this? We're so close to getting the approval . . . You know this is not going to be viewed favorably—"

"I know," Korum said. "I'm willing to take that chance. It won't be the first time they were pissed at me."

Saret looked frustrated. "Okay, but I think you're making a big mistake. All she has to do is get up there and talk—"

"You know as well as I do that if she gets up there, the Protector will try to take her apart. I will not put her through that. And I don't want her anywhere near the United Nations right now—that's far too dangerous. Besides, human media might sniff out the story, and Mia doesn't need the whole world watching her testimony at the UN. Her family doesn't even know anything yet."

Her anger forgotten, Mia squeezed Korum's hand in gratitude. She couldn't help but be touched by his protectiveness. It was hard to say what appealed to her less—the idea of appearing in front of the Krinar Council or at the United Nations with the whole world watching.

"Arus said they can make other arrangements for her. The UN hearing can take place behind closed doors, with nothing leaked to the media. And the Council has agreed to accept her recorded testimony for the trial."

"Tell Arus that he can talk to me himself if he's so determined to make this happen," Korum said quietly, his eyes narrowed with anger. "She's my charl. If he wants her to do something, he needs to ask me very, very nicely. And then, if Mia says she's okay with it, I will maybe consider it."

Saret smiled ruefully. "Sure. You know I hate to be in the middle like this. You and Arus can talk it out. I was asked to deliver a message, and that's where my responsibility ends."

Korum nodded. "Understood."

The expression on his face was still harsh, and Mia shifted in her seat, feeling uncomfortable about the role she had inadvertently played in this disagreement. She needed to learn more about this trial and what it all meant, but she didn't want to ask more questions in front of Saret. Instead, wanting to lighten the tension in the room, she asked cautiously, "So how do you two know each other?"

Saret smiled at her, understanding what she was doing. "Oh, we go way back. We've known each other since we were children."

Mia's eyes widened. If they had been children together, then she was in the presence of two aliens who measured their age in thousands of years. "Were you classmates or something?" she asked in fascination.

Korum shook his head, his lips curving slightly. "Not exactly. We were playmates. Our children are educated very differently than humans—we don't have schools like you do."

"No? Then how do your children learn?"

Saret grinned at her, apparently pleased by her curiosity. "A lot of it is play-based. We let them develop most of the key skills they need through socialization and interaction with others, be it children or adults. Later on, they do apprenticeships in various fields with the goal of honing their problem-solving and critical-thinking abilities."

Mia looked at him in fascination. "But how do they learn things like math and history and writing?"

Saret waved his hand dismissively. "Oh, those are easy. I don't know if Korum has talked to you about this before—"

"I haven't yet," Korum said. "You got here as soon as Mia woke up. All I had time to do was mention the language implant."

"Oh, good." Saret sounded excited. "Would you like to get that done tonight, Mia?"

Mia hesitated. If Korum wasn't lying to her, then she would be an idiot to pass on this opportunity. "Can you please explain to me again what exactly this implant is and what it does?" she asked, looking at Saret.

Korum sighed, looking exasperated. "Yes, Saret, please tell Mia exactly what the implant is. She doesn't seem to trust my explanation."

"Can you blame me?" she asked Korum, trying to keep the bitterness out of her tone.

Saret's eyebrows rose, and he grinned again. "Still some unresolved issues, I see."

Korum shot him a warning look, and Saret's grin promptly disappeared. "Never mind," he said hastily. "I don't know what Korum told you, Mia, but the language implant is a very simple, very straightforward device that many Krinar get upon maturity—once our brain is fully developed. It's a microscopic computer made of special biological material that essentially acts as a highly advanced translator. Its function is to convert data from one form into another—thought pattern to language and vice versa. It acts on one area of the brain only and has absolutely no harmful side effects."

"Does it ever malfunction?" asked Mia. "Or can it do something else to me?"

"Like what?" Saret looked perplexed. "And no, this technology has been in existence for over ten thousand years, so it's been fully perfected. It doesn't malfunction, ever."

"Can it make me think something that I don't want? Or broadcast my thoughts?" Now that she'd said it out loud, Mia could hear how ridiculous that sounded.

Saret shook his head with a smile. "No, nothing like that. It's a very basic device. What you're talking about is far more advanced science. Mind control and thought reading are still in theoretical stages of development."

"But it is theoretically possible?" Mia asked in amazement, the psych major in her suddenly salivating at the prospect of learning even a tiny sliver of what the Krinar knew about the brain. Now that she wasn't so nervous, it occurred to Mia that the K sitting across from her was probably a veritable treasure trove of knowledge about her field of study.

Saret nodded. "Theoretically, yes. Practically, not yet."

Mia opened her mouth to ask another question, and Korum interrupted, looking amused at her unabashed interest, "So does this make you feel more comfortable about getting the implant?"

Mia considered it for a second. How much should she trust them? Korum had already proven himself to be a master manipulator, and she had no idea what Saret was like. But then again, like Korum said, they didn't really need her permission to do this. The fact that they were giving her a choice is what ultimately convinced her.

"I think so," she said slowly.

"Okay then, Saret, can you please do the honors?"

"Um, wait," Mia said, her heart starting to beat faster, "you mean I can get it right now? Is there an anesthetic or anything?"

Saret smiled. "No, nothing like that. It's very easy—you won't even feel it."

"Okay . . ."

Korum got up, still holding Mia's hand. Saret stood up also and approached them. "May I?" he asked Korum, reaching for Mia.

Korum nodded, and Saret extended his right hand, brushing Mia's hair back behind her left ear. She shuddered a little at the unfamiliar touch. Her nails dug into Korum's hand, and she fought the urge to flinch. Even though they'd told her it wouldn't hurt, she couldn't help her primal reaction.

"That's it." Saret stepped back.

"What?" Mia blinked at him in shock.

"It's done. You have the implant. We'll give it about a minute to sync with your neural pathways, and then we'll test it out."

"But how? Where did it go in?"

"It went in through the skin," Korum explained, smiling at her. "You didn't feel it, right?"

"No, I didn't feel anything." Were they playing a joke on her?

Saret laughed, enjoying her reaction. "Good, you weren't supposed to. The device itself has analgesic properties, so you shouldn't have felt the tiny cut it made in the thin skin behind your ear."

Mia raised her left hand, feeling for the wound, but there was nothing.

"So tell me, Mia, do you feel any different? Are you thinking any thoughts you shouldn't be thinking?" Korum asked her with a mocking gleam in his eyes.

Mia shook her head, frowning at him slightly. She didn't appreciate his making fun of her ignorance.

And then her breath caught in her throat.

Korum had just spoken to her in Krinar—and she had understood his every word.

"Wait a second," she said, and the words that came out of her mouth were strange and unfamiliar. Yet she knew exactly what they meant, and her facial muscles seemed to have no problem forming the sounds. "You just spoke in Krinar!"

Korum smiled. "And so did you. How does it feel?"

Mia blinked at him. It felt strange, yet effortless. "It seems to be okay," she said again in Krinar. "I just don't understand how it works. What if I want to say something in English?"

"If you want to say something in English, you just have to think English, and you'll switch languages," Saret explained. "Right now, your brain's natural response is to speak in Krinar because that's the language in which we're addressing you. You have to actively think that you want to speak in English in order to do so when confronted with Krinar speech. However, later on, when you get used to the implant, switching back and forth will be automatic and won't require any extra thought on your part. This is really not all that different from being multilingual. I'm sure you know people who speak several languages fluently—and now you have that same ability, just taken to a different level."

Mia listened to his explanation, the reality of it seeping in. "Wow," she breathed softly, "so I can really, truly speak any known language now? Just like that?"

She wanted to jump up and run around the room, screaming with glee, and she controlled herself with effort, not wanting to appear like a silly kid in front of Korum's friend. It was just so unbelievably amazing. She had always been good with languages in school, studying Spanish and French throughout high school, but she'd never managed to become fluent. And now she could speak whatever language she wanted? Her earlier reluctance forgotten, Mia could now only think of the mind-blowing possibilities.

"Just like that," Korum confirmed, looking down at her with a smile, and Saret nodded as well.

Struggling to appear dignified, Mia fought back the huge grin that threatened to split her face. "Thank you," she told Saret. "I really appreciate it."

"You're welcome, Mia. I hope to see you soon." And with that, he touched Korum's shoulder again and left, the wall to their right disintegrating to grant him passage.

CHAPTER THREE

Once Saret was gone, Mia couldn't contain her elation any longer. She felt like she would choke from the sheer delight that filled her from within, and she knew that she was grinning now, probably looking like an idiot. But she couldn't bring herself to care anymore, her excitement too strong to be restrained.

She was now a polyglot!

She tried to picture herself speaking Cantonese, and the words suddenly came to her. Opening her mouth, she heard the harsh tonal sounds coming out as she told Korum, "I can't believe this is real." Promptly switching to Russian, she continued, "I can't believe I can do this!" And then again in German, nearly jumping from excitement, "Oh my God, I can speak them all!"

He grinned at her, his face glowing with pleasure. Letting go of her hand, he brought his palm up to her face, curving it around her cheek. Looking down at her, he said in English, "I'm glad you're excited. There's so much I want to show you, darling . . ."

Mia stared up at him, her excitement over her newfound ability suddenly transforming into something else. He was so beautiful, and the warm expression on his face as he gazed down at her made her heart squeeze. "Korum," she said softly, "I . . ."

She didn't know what she could say, how she could express what she was feeling. There was still so much unresolved between them, but in this moment, she couldn't bring herself to care about the way their relationship had started, about all the mutual lies and betrayals. In this moment, she knew only that she loved him, that every part of her longed to be with him.

Reaching up, she wrapped her hand around the back of his neck and tentatively brought his face down toward her. Rising up on her toes, she kissed him on the mouth, her lips soft and uncertain on his. She rarely made the first move—he was usually the one to initiate sex in their relationship—and she could feel the sudden tension gripping his body at her touch.

He kissed her back, his mouth hot and eager, and she found herself lifted up into his arms and carried somewhere. The destination turned out to be the bedroom, and they ended up on the bed, his powerful body covering her own, pressing her into the mattress with its weight. Mia's hands frantically tore at his shirt, trying to find a way to get it off him, to feel his nakedness against her own. She felt like she was burning, her skin too sensitive, and the barrier of clothing between them was simply unbearable. Wanting more, she kissed him harder, catching his lower lip between her teeth and biting on it lightly.

Korum sucked in his breath, and she felt him abruptly pull away. Before she could do more than blink, he reared up on the bed and swiftly pulled off his shirt and shorts, revealing his large erection. Mia's mouth watered at the sight of his naked body, all toned muscle covered with that smooth golden skin, his chest lightly dusted with dark hair—and then he was on her, tearing off her dress and leaving her lying there, spread out and exposed before his eyes.

Crawling on top of her, he kissed her again, more aggressively this time, and his hand found its way down her body and toward the junction between her legs. Mia moaned into his mouth, arching her hips toward his hand, and his fingers stroked her folds softly before one finger found its way inside her opening and pressed deep, causing her inner muscles to tighten with the sudden rush of pleasure. "I love how wet you are," he murmured, penetrating her first with one finger and then two, stretching her, preparing her for his possession. Mia cried out, her head falling back, and felt the moist heat of his mouth on her neck, licking and nibbling the sensitive area.

There was something else too, a strange but pleasant sensation that registered somewhere in the back of her brain, a warm vibration that felt like massaging fingers sliding over the back of her body, stroking and caressing her shoulders, the curve of her spine, gently squeezing her buttocks and the backs of her thighs.

The bed, she realized dimly, it had to be the intelligent bed, and then she forgot about it, too immersed in what Korum was doing to pay attention to anything else. His fingers had found a rhythm, two thrusts shallow, one thrust deep, and his thumb was now circling her clitoris in a way that drove her insane. Her nails dug into his back, her entire body shaking with need, and then his thumb pressed on her clit directly and she came apart, convulsing in his arms, waves of pleasure radiating all the way down to her toes.

After the last aftershock was over, Mia opened her eyes and looked at him. He was staring at her with such burning hunger on his face that her breath caught in her throat and her stomach clenched again with answering desire. His fingers were still inside her, and he took them out slowly, causing her to shiver with pleasure.

Bringing his hand up to his face, Korum licked the fingers slowly, clearly savoring her taste. Mia stared at him, mesmerized, unable to look away even as she felt his knee parting her thighs and the hardness of his cock pressing against her vulnerable folds.

He began to enter her, still looking into her eyes, and Mia gasped from the sensation. Even though they'd had sex only a few hours earlier and he had prepared her with his fingers, her body still needed a moment to accommodate him, to stretch around the organ penetrating her so relentlessly. There was something incredibly intimate about being with him like that, feeling his bare skin against her breasts and his shaft inside her, while meeting his gaze with her own. It was as if he wanted to possess more than just her body, Mia thought vaguely, as if he wanted something more than just the sex.

Still looking at her, he began to move his hips, slowly at first and then at a faster pace, each stroke adding to the tension that had again begun to coil inside her. Giving in to the sensations, Mia moaned and closed her eyes, feeling each thrust deep within her belly. He lowered his head, and she felt the warmth of his breath against her ear as he tongued it lightly, making her shiver again. And then his pace picked up again, his hips now driving into her with such force that she was pushed into the mattress, barely able to catch her breath between each powerful stroke.

Her entire body tightened, and Mia screamed as another orgasm hit, her inner muscles squeezing him tightly. As her pulsations eased, she could feel his cock swelling up inside her, and then he came with a hoarse yell, grinding against her until his contractions were fully over.

Breathing hard in the aftermath, Mia lay there, his body feeling heavy on top of her. Apparently realizing it, he rolled off her and pulled her against him, hugging her from the back. His hand found its way to her breast, and he just held her like that, pressed up against his body. As her galloping heartbeat slowed, she felt languid, relaxed . . . and incredibly contented.

"Are you sleepy?" Korum whispered into her hair, stroking her nipple lightly with his thumb, causing it to peak against his palm.

"No," she whispered back. She felt like every muscle in her body had turned to mush, but she wasn't sleepy. Her lengthy nap earlier had taken care of that. "What time is it, anyway?"

"It's about eleven in the evening."

"I slept the entire day?" No wonder she felt so refreshed.

"You must've been exhausted," he murmured, raising his hand to move her hair to the side. The curls were probably tickling his face, Mia realized with some amusement.

"So Saret makes house calls this late?" she asked, her thoughts returning to her new and amazing ability. A huge grin appeared on her face as she imagined demonstrating her skills to her family and friends. They would be so envious . . .

"It's not that late for us," Korum explained, turning her around in his arms so that she was facing him. "You know we don't sleep as much as humans. Any time before one in the morning and after 5 a.m. are considered regular working and visiting hours."

Mia blinked at him, her grin fading. It made sense, of course, but this was yet another way she would be an outsider here. If she tried to keep their "regular" hours, she would quickly find herself sleep-deprived.

"You must've been bored in New York," she said quietly, "with me sleeping all the time, and few places open in the wee hours of the night."

He smiled and shook his head. "No, not at all. That's when I would usually get my work done, when you slept so sweetly in my bed."

"What kind of work? The designs?" Mia inquired with curiosity. There was still so much she didn't know about him, about how he spent his days—and nights—when he wasn't with her. It had been enlightening, observing his interactions with Saret today. She had caught a small glimpse of who Korum was outside of their relationship, and she was hungry to know more.

"Yes, I often work on the designs—that's my passion, that's what I really love to do," he answered readily, regarding her with a warm look in his eyes. "I also have to run my company, which takes up a big chunk of my time. I have a number of talented designers working for me, both here and on Krina, and there's always something that requires my attention—"

"You have people working for you on Krina?" Mia asked in surprise.

"How do you communicate with them or oversee them?"

"We have faster-than-light communication," Korum explained, "so it's not that much more difficult to communicate with Krina than with, say, China from here. Of course, I can't see them easily in person, but we do have what you would call 'virtual reality,' where we can have meetings that very closely simulate the real thing. You experienced it a little bit with the virtual map—"

Mia nodded, staring at him attentively. She suspected very few humans knew what he was telling her right now.

"Well, the map is a very basic version of that technology. What we use to conduct cross-planetary meetings is far more advanced."

"Is that also your design? The virtual reality, I mean?" Mia asked, wondering how far his technological reach extended.

"Some of the latest versions, yes. The basic technology has been around for a very long time; it far predates both me and my company."

Mia's stomach suddenly growled. She flushed, feeling embarrassed, and he grinned in response, handing her a tissue for clean-up.

"Of course, you must be hungry after sleeping all day. Why don't we eat and continue our conversation over dinner?"

"That sounds good," Mia said, realizing that she was starving.

He got up, pulling her out of bed as well. Before she could even ask for it, he handed her a brand-new outfit that he'd managed to create in a matter of seconds. It was another dress, similar in style to the one that was now lying torn on the bed. This one was pale yellow in color, and Mia gladly put it on, loving the feel of the soft material against her skin. Korum pulled on his shorts and shirt from earlier, which had somehow survived their sex session.

"Ready?" he asked, and Mia nodded. Taking her hand, he led her toward the kitchen.

Like the living room and bedroom, the kitchen was similar in appearance to the one in his TriBeCa apartment. Further evidence of Korum's attempt to make her feel comfortable here, thought Mia. Walking over to one of the chairs, she sat down and looked at Korum eagerly. He was an amazing cook—part of his passion for making things—and even his most basic creations were more delicious than anything Mia could come up with herself.

"What would you like?" he asked her, walking toward the refrigerator.

Mia shrugged, uncertain how to answer that. "I don't know. What do you have?"

He smiled. "Pretty much everything. Do you want to try some foods native to Krina or would you rather stick with familiar tastes for now?"

Her eyes widened. "You have foods from Krina here?"

"Well, they're not imported from Krina—they're grown right here, in Lenkarda and our other Centers—but we did bring the seeds from our planet."

"I'd love to try them," Mia said earnestly. She was an adventurous eater and loved to taste new things. Thanks to her Polish heritage, Mia had grown up eating foods that were not normally part of the standard American diet, and she now had an open mind when it came to enjoying different cuisines.

Korum grinned, looking pleased by her enthusiasm. Taking a few things out of the refrigerator, he quickly chopped up some strange-looking plants and roots and put everything in a pot to cook.

"How do you usually cook here?" she asked him, watching his actions with fascination. "I can't imagine you use all these appliances normally . . ."

"You're right, we don't. In fact, we usually don't cook," Korum said, taking out some red leafy plants that vaguely resembled lettuce. "Remember when I told you that our homes are intelligent?"

Mia nodded.

"Well, one of their functions is to always keep us supplied with food and to prepare it in whichever way we like it."

Mia gasped, unable to contain her excitement. "Seriously? Your house makes food for you whenever you want?"

He smiled, amused at her reaction. "I can see how that would be appealing to you." Mia's cooking abilities were nonexistent—a fact that her mom frequently lamented—but she loved to eat.

"Appealing? It's amazing!" Why would anyone bother cooking when they could just have their house make food for them?

"It's all right," he said with a slight shrug. "It's convenient and it definitely saves a lot of time, but sometimes I get the urge to make something on my own, to see if I can improve on the recipes the house has in its database."

"Is that how you learned to cook so well? By tinkering with those recipes?"

Korum nodded, his hands now massaging the red leafy vegetables in a way that made an orange substance emerge from the leaves. "More or less. Cooking is a fairly recent hobby of mine—I've only gotten into it since coming to Earth. And it's really only in the last few months that I've learned to use the human appliances instead of just programming the house to tweak the recipes it uses."

Mia stared at her lover in disbelief. He had an intelligent house that could make whatever food he wanted, and he was wasting time learning how to use the oven? Chopping vegetables using knives instead of utilizing their fancy technology? That was something she would never understand, Mia thought to herself. Not that she minded, of course; it was only because he had this strange hobby that she'd enjoyed so many delicious dishes back in New York.

He finished squeezing the orange liquid out of the red leaves, washed his hands, and took out a long yellow plant that looked a little like a zucchini with a shiny skin. Quickly cutting it up, he added it to the bowl where the red leaves were now swimming in the orange liquid, and then sprinkled some greenish powder over the entire dish. Placing the bowl in the middle of the table, he put a few spoonfuls of the bright-colored salad on Mia's plate and a larger helping on his. The utensils that he used were unusual, resembling some type of tongs with one flat side and one curved side.

"Try it," he invited, watching her expectantly.

A smaller version of the same utensils were lying next to Mia's bowl. Mimicking his earlier actions, Mia grabbed some of the leaves with her tongs and took a bite. The flavor exploded on her tongue, a perfect combination of sweetness, saltiness, and a tangy bite of spiciness underneath. "Oh my God, this is so good. What is it?" she managed to say once she'd swallowed. Her mouth was almost tingling from the overabundance of sensations.

He smiled. "It's a traditional dish from Rolert—the region of Krina where my family is from. It's very easy to make, as you saw, but the trick is to squeeze the *shari* well—that's the red plant—so it releases all the flavors and nutrients."

Mia listened to his explanation while gobbling down the rest of her portion. As soon as she finished, she immediately reached for a second helping. He grinned and polished off the salad on his own plate.

"That was amazing. Thank you," Mia said when the salad was completely gone.

"I'm glad you liked it," Korum said, carrying away the dishes. Instead of putting them in the dishwasher, he simply held them near a wall. An opening appeared, and he placed them there. And just like that, the dirty dishes were gone.

Seeing the surprised look on Mia's face, Korum explained, "I don't like to clean up, so I *am* using some of our technology to take care of that part."

"So the dishwasher is strictly decorative?"

"More or less. You can use it if you like, but you saw what I just did, right?"

Mia nodded.

"You can do the same thing if you're here on your own. Or just leave the dishes on the table, and the house will take care of them after a few minutes." Walking back to the table, he sat down across from her and smiled. "The main dish will be ready in a couple of minutes."

"I can't wait to try it," Mia told him, smiling back in anticipation.

So far, being in Lenkarda was proving to be a fantastic experience in every way, and she felt an intense wave of happiness washing over her as she stared at Korum's beautiful face. It was hard to believe that only this morning she thought he would be deported to Krina, and now she was sitting in his house in Costa Rica, conversing with him in Krinar language, and enjoying the food he'd prepared for her again.

As her mind drifted to the earlier events, her smile slowly faded. She could've lost him today, she realized again. If Korum was right about the Keiths' intentions, then he could've been killed if the Resistance had succeeded. A sickening cold spread through her veins at the thought.

It hadn't happened, she told herself, trying to focus on the present, but her mind kept wandering. Even though the rebels had failed, the fact was that she'd participated in the attack on the K colonies. And now they wanted her to testify, she remembered with a chill going down her spine, to go in front of their Council and the United Nations and talk about her involvement. Korum seemed to think that he had the power to protect her from the Council, but she didn't understand how something like that worked.

"What's the matter?" Korum asked, apparently puzzled by the suddenly serious expression on her face.

Mia took a deep breath. "Can we talk about what happened this morning?" she asked cautiously. "And about what happens now?"

His expression cooled slightly, the smile leaving his face. "Why?" he asked. "It's over. I want us to move past it, Mia."

She stared at him. "But—"

"But what?" he asked softly, his eyes narrowing. "Do you really want to talk again about how you betrayed me? How you nearly sent me to my death? I'm willing to let it go because I know you were scared and confused . . . but it's really not in your best interests to keep bringing this up, my sweet."

Mia inhaled sharply, trying to hold on to her temper. "I only did what I thought was best," she said evenly. "And you knew everything all along—and you *used* me. And now it seems like your Council wants to use me too, so excuse me if I'm not quite ready to 'move past it'."

"The Council doesn't have any say where you're concerned, Mia," Korum said, looking at her with an inscrutable amber gaze. "They can't tell you what to do."

"And why is that?" Mia asked, her heart beginning to beat faster. "Because I'm your charl?"

"Exactly."

She stared at him in frustration. "And what does that mean? That I'm your charl?"

He regarded her levelly. "It means that you belong to me and they don't have any jurisdiction over you."

Before Mia could say anything else, he got up and walked over to the pot on the stove. Lifting the lid, he stirred the contents slightly, and an unusual but pleasant aroma filled the kitchen. "It's almost ready," he said, coming back to the table.

The two-second pause helped Mia gather her composure. "Korum," she said softly, "I need to understand. You, me—I feel like I'm part of some game where I don't know the rules. What exactly is a charl in your society?"

He sighed. "I told you, it's our term for the humans that we're in a relationship with."

"So why doesn't your Council have jurisdiction over charl? It's like your government, right?"

"Yes, exactly," Korum said, answering the second part of her question. "The Council is our governing body."

"And you're part of it?" Mia remembered John telling her something along those lines once.

"When I choose to be. I'm not a big fan of politics, but it's unavoidable sometimes."

"How can you choose something like that?" Mia asked, staring at him in astonishment. "Are you an elected official or does it work differently on Krina?"

"It's very different for us." Korum got up and walked over to the stove again. "We don't have democracy the way you do. Who gets to be on the Council is determined based on our overall standing in society."

Mia's eyebrows rose. "What do you mean? Like you're born into the upper class or something?"

He shook his head. "No, not born. Our standing is earned over time. It's based largely on our achievements and how much we contribute to society. Our government is almost like an oligarchy of sorts—but based on meritocracy."

This was fascinating and somewhat intimidating. Korum must've contributed to the K society quite a bit, to have as much influence as he did.

"So how many of you are on the Council?" Mia asked, watching him ladle the stew-like dish into bowls for both of them. It didn't look as exotic as the shari salad, although she could see something purple among the reddish-brown vegetables.

"Currently, there are fifteen Council members. The number fluctuates over time—it's been as high as twenty-three and as low as seven. About a third of us are here on Earth, and the others are still on Krina."

Bringing the bowls back to the table, he sat down and moved one bowl toward her. "Go ahead," he said, "I'm curious if you'll like this also."

Temporarily shelving her questions, Mia tried a spoonful of the stew. To her surprise, it tasted rich and savory, as though it contained some kind of meat products. "This is all plant-based?" she asked, and Korum nodded, observing her reaction with a smile. His expression was warm again.

Mia tried another bite. The texture was soft and a little mushy, almost as if she were eating potatoes, but the flavor was completely different. It reminded her a bit of Japanese food with its subtle seaweed-like undertones, just much more nuanced. After the second bite, Mia suddenly felt ravenous, her tastebuds craving more of the rich flavor, and she quickly downed the rest of the food on her plate. "This is really good," she mumbled between the bites, and Korum nodded, finishing his own portion.

After they were finished, he repeated the process with the dishes, bringing them toward the wall and letting the house take care of cleaning them. Mia observed him carefully, taking note of his exact actions. It didn't seem difficult, the technology even more intuitive than some of the newer iPads, and she hoped she remembered how to do it if she ever needed to clean the dishes herself.

"Thank you—that was delicious," she said when Korum was done.

"You're welcome," he replied casually, sitting back down at the table.

The look on his face was amused and slightly mocking, as if he suspected exactly what she was going to say next.

Mia's temper began to simmer again, and she decided not to disappoint him. "So why are charl not within the Council's jurisdiction?" she asked stubbornly.

"Because that's the way it's always been, Mia," he replied softly. "Because humans are only accepted in Krinar society on those terms—as belonging to one of us. The only exception are those like Dana, who choose to leave their former life behind in order to become pleasure givers on Krina. So you see, my sweet, the Council cannot go to you directly. They have to go through me because, under Krinar law, you're mine."

Mia sucked in her breath, feeling like there was insufficient air in the room. "So I was right," she said quietly. "The Resistance didn't lie to me—you did."

He leaned toward her, his eyes turning a deeper shade of gold. "They did lie to you. A charl is not a pleasure slave, or whatever it was they told you. It's very rare for us to have a charl, and when we do—these are genuine and caring relationships."

"How can a genuine and caring relationship exist when the two people are not considered equals in your society?" she asked bitterly.

He laughed, looking genuinely amused. "Those types of relationships exist all the time, Mia. Just look at your human society. Are you going to tell me that you don't care for your children, your teenagers, or even your pets? Not to mention that your so-called developed nations have only recently accepted the idea of women's rights, while many regions of Earth still don't—"

"Is that what I am to you? A pet?" Her stomach churned as she waited for his answer.

He shook his head, looking at her intently. "No, Mia, you're not a pet. You're a twenty-one-year-old human girl who still has quite a bit of growing up to do. I wish I could leave you alone, so you could meet someone like that pretty boy from the club—"

He was talking about Peter, Mia realized, surprised.

"—but I can't."

Getting up, he walked around the table and sat down on a chair next to her. Raising his hand, he gently stroked her cheek while Mia stared at him, unable to look away from the golden heat in his eyes. "You've gotten under my skin," he said softly, "and now I want you, in ways that I never thought were possible. I know you still have a lot to learn about me, about your new home here, and I will do my best to make things easier for you, to help you with your adjustment. But you need to stop worrying so much and fighting me at every turn. It can be very good between us, Mia . . . especially if you give it a chance."

CHAPTER FOUR

That night—her first night in Lenkarda—Mia had strange and disturbing dreams. She was flying somewhere again, only this time Korum held her on his lap for the duration of the trip. Her body felt unusually heavy and languid, and she couldn't move—could only lie helplessly in his arms as he carried her somewhere after they landed. In her dream, he brought her into a strange white building where everything seemed to float and walls dissolved on a regular basis. Suddenly, she was lying on one of these floating objects, and it felt incredibly comfortable, as though it had been made for her body and her body alone. There was a mellow light illuminating everything, and a beautiful woman spoke to her softly, gently touching her face with elegant hands. Mia dreamed that she spoke to the woman too, told her how beautiful she was, and the woman laughed, telling Korum that his charl was charming.

And then there was only darkness and Mia slept deeply for the rest of the night, the dream fading from her memory.

As soon as she woke up the next morning, her mind immediately began replaying the conversation from yesterday and she groaned, burying her face in the pillow. Right away, the bed began a soft massage regimen designed to relax her suddenly tense muscles.

Sighing with pleasure, Mia let it do its thing while she lay there, trying to make sense of Korum and their relationship.

After his little speech last night, he had carried her to the bedroom and spent the next few hours showing her exactly how good it could be between them. Her sex still throbbed delicately when she thought of everything he'd done to her, the many ways he'd made her scream in mindless ecstasy.

She still didn't understand what Korum really wanted from her. Did he truly think she could just calmly go along with everything? From what she'd learned thus far, being a charl in Krinar society was not all that different from being a slave. As far as their law was concerned, she was Korum's possession—something that belonged to him. How could a genuine and caring relationship arise from that? He held all the power; he could do anything he wanted with her, and nobody would interfere.

And even if she were willing to accept that kind of dynamic, there were so many other issues to overcome. As he'd said, she was a twenty-one-year-old human girl—immature and inexperienced compared to a K who'd lived for two thousand years. How could he ever regard her as anything but naive and ignorant? Not only did his species have far more advanced science and technology, but Korum himself must've also gathered tremendous knowledge over his centuries of existence. How could a human ever come close to that over a mere eighty- or ninety-year lifespan? Not that he would even want her when she got older; however strong their attraction was now, he would definitely lose interest in her when she started getting wrinkles and grey hair—if not much sooner.

Closing her eyes at that painful thought, Mia tried to think about something else, to distract herself from such depressing reflections.

On the plus side, physically, she felt amazing. Despite the dreams she vaguely recalled, she must've gotten great sleep because she was filled with energy, and her body was completely free of the soreness that usually accompanied their long sex sessions. Korum must've used some healing thingy on her again, she decided.

It was difficult to believe it was only Saturday. Was it only last week that she was frantically writing her papers? It now seemed like a lifetime ago, with everything that had happened in the last couple of days.

On Monday, she was supposed to start her internship in Orlando, working as a counselor at a camp for troubled children, and instead . . . Well, Mia had no idea what she would be doing instead—or what the future held for her, in general. Her life had taken such an unexpected turn that any kind of planning was impossible.

She was also supposed to be packed and out of her room on Monday, she suddenly remembered with a sinking feeling in her stomach. Mia had made the arrangements to sublet her room out for the summer several months ago, and the subletter—a very nice girl named Rita—was supposed to move in at the beginning of next week. However, given Mia's sudden departure from New York, all of her stuff was still there.

Jumping out of bed, Mia ran to the small table where her purse was sitting. She'd brought it with her from New York, and it contained something extremely valuable: her cell phone. She needed to call Jessie as soon as possible. Her roommate was probably already getting worried since she hadn't heard from Mia yesterday, and she would definitely freak out if all of Mia's belongings were still in her room when Rita moved in. Jessie would never believe her to be so irresponsible as to forget about the sublet.

Pulling out her cell phone, Mia held her breath, praying that she had reception. But, of course, her hopes were in vain—there were zero bars. Not only was she in a foreign country, Mia realized, but the Ks' shielding technology likely blocked all cell tower signals.

Sighing, she put on a robe and went to brush her teeth before looking for Korum. If she didn't contact Jessie this weekend, her roommate could easily have the police at Korum's TriBeCa apartment by Monday.

Entering the living room, Mia saw Korum sitting on the couch with his eyes closed. Surprised, she stopped and stared at him. Was he sleeping? Hesitant to disturb him, she just stood there, using this rare opportunity to study her alien lover with his guard down.

With his eyes closed, the bronzed perfection of his face was even more striking. High cheekbones blended synergistically with a strong nose and a firm jaw, forming a face that was as masculine as it was beautiful. His eyebrows were dark and thick, slanting straight above his eyes, and his eyelashes looked incredibly long, spread out like dark fans above his cheeks. His hair had grown in the month that she'd known him—he'd probably been too busy chasing after the Keiths to get a haircut, Mia thought wryly—and it was starting to brush against his ears.

As though sensing her gaze on him, he opened his eyes and smiled when he saw her standing there. "Come here," he murmured, patting the couch next to him. "How are you feeling?"

Mia blushed slightly. "I'm fine," she told him.

He just continued looking at her with a mysterious expression on his face, almost as if studying her for some reason. Feeling a little uncertain about where they stood after yesterday's conversation, Mia cautiously approached him. Even though she'd spent most of last night writhing in pleasure in his arms, there was still so much unresolved between them. Pausing a couple of feet away, she asked, "Were you sleeping just now? I'm sorry to interrupt if you were . . ."

"Sleeping? No." He looked surprised by her assumption. "I was just taking care of some business."

"Virtually?" Mia guessed, and Korum nodded, patting the couch again.

Mia came closer, and he reached out with his hand, pulling her onto his lap. Burying his hand in the dark mass of curls, he tilted her head toward him and kissed her, his mouth hot and demanding, his tongue stroking hers until she forgot everything but the incredible sensations he was provoking in her. Barely able to breathe, Mia moaned, melting helplessly against him, her core filling with liquid heat despite the fact that she should be wrung out after the excesses of last night.

Apparently satisfied with her response, Korum raised his head and looked down at her with a half-smile, releasing her hair but still holding her tightly in his arms. "You see, Mia," he said softly, "it really doesn't matter what labels are placed on our relationship. It doesn't change anything between us."

Mia licked her lips. They felt soft and swollen after his kiss. "No, you're right. It doesn't change anything," she agreed quietly. Learning more about her role in K society didn't lessen her attraction to him one bit. Her body didn't care that, as a charl, she had no say in her own life.

Korum smiled and got up, placing her on her feet. "I have to leave in about thirty minutes for the trial. Would you like to watch it from here?"

Mia's eyes widened. "Like on TV?"

"Through virtual reality," he told her. "I don't want you there in person in case the Council tries to pressure you to testify."

"What would happen if I did? Testify, I mean?" Mia was suddenly curious why Korum was so determined to protect her from that. She wasn't exactly eager to go in front of the Krinar Council, but he did seem unduly worried about it.

"The traitors will have a Protector," Korum explained. "It's a bit like your lawyer, but different. The Protector is someone who genuinely believes in the innocence of the accused—it could be their family member or a friend. When you act as a Protector, you stake everything on the line—your reputation, your standing in society. If you don't succeed in proving the innocence of those you're protecting, then you lose almost as much as they do."

"And do the accused always have this Protector?" Mia asked, trying to wrap her mind around such a strange system.

Korum shook his head. "No. But these traitors do, unfortunately. One of them, Rafor, is the son of Loris—one of the oldest Council members—and Loris took it upon himself to be the Protector in this case. He's one of the most ruthless individuals I know, and he would stop at nothing to protect his son. He also hates me. If I let you go up there as a witness, he's going to do everything he can to make your testimony seem like it's coming from an irrational, hysterical human that I've manipulated for my own purposes. He's going to publicly humiliate you, make you break down in front of everyone, and I won't let that happen."

Mia swallowed, beginning to understand a little. "You don't have some kind of rules about the types of questions that can be asked of the witnesses?"

"No," Korum said. "With so much on the line, all is fair game. The only thing the Protector is not allowed to do is physically hurt you. But there wouldn't be anything to prevent him from verbally destroying you—and believe me, Loris is really good at that."

"I see," Mia said slowly, her stomach tying into knots at the thought of going up against a ruthless Krinar Council member determined to protect his son.

"But don't worry," Korum reassured her. "It's not going to happen. At best, they will get a recorded testimony from you—and that's only if Arus really begs for it."

"Who's Arus?" Mia remembered that name mentioned earlier, during Saret's visit.

"He's another Council member and, among other things, he's our ambassador to the human leaders."

"You don't like him either?" Mia guessed.

Korum's lips curved into a grim, humorless smile. "Let's just say we've had our share of political differences." The look in his eyes was cold and distant, and Mia shivered slightly, glad that it wasn't directed at her.

"I see," she said again. She didn't really, but she didn't think it would be wise to pursue this topic further. Taking a deep breath, she remembered the original reason why she'd wanted to talk to him. "Um, Korum, I wanted to ask you something . . ."

His expression softened a little. "Sure, what is it?"

Mia looked at him imploringly. "I have to call Jessie. My cell phone doesn't seem to have reception here . . ."

His eyebrows rose. "Call your roommate? Why?"

"Because she's going to be worried if she doesn't hear from me for a couple of days," Mia explained, "and because I have to ask her for a big favor. All my stuff is still in my room, and the girl who's subletting it will be moving in on Monday. I should've been packed and out of there yesterday, but . . ."

"But you ended up here instead," Korum said, immediately understanding. "All right, you can contact Jessie and let her know where you are. Maybe she can pack your things for you. If she does, I'll have my driver pick them up and bring them to my New York apartment."

"That would be great, thanks," Mia said, smiling in relief. "And if I could do a quick call to my parents too, that would be really awesome."

He smiled at her. "Sure. I just wouldn't tell *them* where you are."

"No, definitely not," Mia readily agreed. She tried to imagine her parents' reaction to the news that she was in an alien colony in Costa Rica, and it wasn't a pleasant picture. Thinking ahead, she asked, "What about when I go to Florida? What am I going to tell them then?"

Korum shrugged. "The truth, I imagine. I'll be with you, so they can ask me whatever questions they want to reassure themselves of your safety."

Mia's jaw dropped. "You're going to meet my parents?"

"Of course, why not?"

"Um . . ." Mia could think of a dozen reasons why not. She settled on the first one. "Well, I'm not sure how they would react to, you know, what you are . . ."

He looked amused. "A Krinar? They'll have to get used to the idea if they want to keep seeing you."

Mia stared at him. "What do you mean, if they want to keep seeing me?"

"I mean, Mia," he said softly, "that you're with me now, and your family will need to come to terms with it." At the anxious look on her face, he added, "And don't worry, I'll be patient with them. I know they care about you, and I'll do my best to set their mind at ease."

* * *

A few minutes later, with Mia still in shock at the thought of her parents meeting her alien lover, Korum gave her a thin, silvery bracelet that resembled a wristwatch.

"This is something I just created for you," he explained, placing it around her left wrist. "This will be your personal computing device while you're in Lenkarda. I made it so that it's capable of connecting with human cell phones and computers, and you can use it to call or video-chat with your family. I programmed it with all your connections—"

Surprised, Mia studied the pretty object on her arm. It looked very much like a stylish piece of jewelry, and she vaguely remembered seeing some Ks on TV wearing something similar. "How does it work?" she asked, not seeing any obvious buttons on it.

"It will respond to your verbal commands—that will be the easiest way for you to operate our technology right now."

"So it will understand me if I just say the instructions in natural speech?"

Korum nodded. "It will understand you perfectly in any language because I designed it specifically for you."

Mia blinked. She wasn't sure, but she suspected that Korum was one of the very few Ks who could do something like that—create a unique piece of technology solely for the use of his charl. "Thank you," she said gratefully. "I'll call Jessie right now."

Seeking a little privacy, Mia went into the bedroom. Sitting down on the bed, she lifted her left wrist closer to her mouth and spoke to the bracelet. "Call Jessie, please." Two seconds later, she heard what sounded like dial tones signifying that the call was connecting.

"Hello?" It was Jessie's voice, and it emanated from the little device on Mia's wrist. Unlike with the speakerphones that Mia was familiar with, she could hear Jessie with crystal-clear precision, as though she was in the room with her.

Hoping that Jessie could hear her just as well, Mia said, "Hey Jessie, how's it going? It's Mia."

"Mia? Where are you calling from?" Jessie sounded surprised. "It shows up as an unknown number."

"Uh, yeah, about that . . . I'm actually out of town right now—"

"What? Where?"

"Um . . . in Costa Rica."

"WHAT?" Jessie's shriek was earsplitting.

Mia rubbed her ears. "Yeah, it was kind of an unplanned trip, but everything's fine. I'm with Korum and—"

"Oh my God, what the fuck are you doing in Costa Rica? Did that bastard make you go there? Because if he did—"

"No, Jessie, everything's fine! Look, I just wanted to call you and let you know where I was—"

"Mia, what are you doing in Costa Rica?" Jessie sounded marginally calmer, though Mia could still hear the panicked undertone in her roommate's voice. "And where exactly in Costa Rica are you?"

Mia paused for a second, trying to think how to best explain everything. "Well, I'm actually in Lenkarda—that's the Costa Rican K Center—"

"Oh my God, Mia, he brought you there? Did he find out?" There was sheer terror in Jessie's voice now. "Does he know about . . . you know?"

Mia sighed. "Yeah. He knew all along actually. Don't worry—it's all cool now . . ."

"What do you mean, he knew all along?"

"Look, Jessie, I don't want to go into the whole story right now, but just believe me when I tell you that I'm not in any kind of danger, okay?" Mia spoke quickly, knowing that she probably only had minutes before Jessie did something drastic—like contacting the Resistance again. "We've talked about everything, and there was a misunderstanding on my part—and now everything's fine. I'm just here for the summer. We're going to go to Florida in a couple of weeks to visit my parents, and then I'll be back in New York for the next school year. It's really nothing to worry about, I promise you . . ."

There was silence for a few seconds, and then Jessie said quietly, "Mia, I just don't understand. You're telling me that the alien you've been spying on brought you to a K Center, and you expect me to believe that everything's okay?"

Mia took a deep breath. "Everything *is* okay. Honestly. I made a mistake becoming involved with the Resistance. Korum explained everything, and I just didn't understand the situation before—"

"And now you do? How do you know you can believe anything he says?"

"Look, I have to trust him, Jessie. He has no reason to lie to me now." At least, Mia hoped so.

"And he's letting you call me?"

Mia smiled. "Yes, of course, so you see—it's really not what you think." She could almost hear the wheels turning in Jessie's head.

"So you're honestly telling me that you're in a K Center and you're totally fine? You're going to come back for school and everything?"

"Absolutely," Mia said, relieved that Jessie was coming around. "It just turned out that instead of going to Florida for the summer, I went to Costa Rica, that's all."

"What about your internship in Orlando?"

"That I haven't quite figured out yet," Mia reluctantly admitted. "I'll have to call them and explain that I won't be able to do it anymore."

"So you're not going to do an internship the summer before your senior year? That's a really bad career move, Mia . . ."

"Yes, I know," said Mia, not needing her roommate to remind her of that. "Maybe I'll be able to get something during the school year with the career placement office . . . I'll figure something out. But I'll be going to Florida for a few days soon, so that'll be nice."

"Going with him?"

"Yep." Mia grinned, imagining her roommate's reaction to what she was about to tell her next. "He wants to meet my parents."

"WHAT? Are you kidding me?"

Mia laughed. "I know, right?"

"What, does he want to marry you or something?" Jessie sounded as incredulous as Mia still felt.

"No, of course not," Mia said, her mind boggling at the thought. "I think he's just being nice. Maybe. I have no idea if meeting parents is a significant thing in K culture or not. Besides, he's way older than my parents, so it's not like he's going to be intimidated by them . . ."

"Wow, Mia," Jessie said slowly. "I don't even know what to tell you—"

"You don't have to say anything, Jessie. I know the whole thing is crazy, but I'm totally fine. Look, I actually wanted to ask you for a humongous favor . . ."

"Let me guess," Jessie said dryly. "Rita is moving in on Monday, and all your wonderful new clothes are everywhere."

"Yes, precisely." Mia injected a pleading note into her voice. "Jessie, if you do this for me, I'll be so grateful . . ."

She could hear Jessie sighing. "Of course. I'll do it for you. But where should I put everything? In storage?"

"No, Korum's driver in New York can pick it up and bring it to his place."

"Oh . . . I see," Jessie said, sounding oddly hesitant. "So does this mean you're officially moving in with him?"

"No, of course not! It's just for the summer, instead of storage, you know."

"I don't know, Mia." Jessie sounded upset again. "Somehow, I don't see you living here again . . ."

"Jessie. . ." Mia didn't really know what to say. She couldn't promise anything because so much was still uncertain. Would Korum want her to live with him in TriBeCa when they came back to New York? And would it be a bad thing if he did? She'd only known him for a month at this point, and it was difficult for Mia to imagine what their relationship would be like in another two months.

"It's okay, you don't have to say anything," Jessie said, sounding falsely upbeat. "We couldn't stay as roommates forever, you know. This was bound to happen. Granted, it happened under some pretty strange circumstances, but I'm sure his penthouse is much nicer than our roach-infested building."

"Jessie, please . . . It's too soon to talk about that—"

"I don't know," Jessie said, a teasing note entering her voice. "You guys seem to be moving along pretty fast—already meeting parents and everything . . ."

Mia laughed, shaking her head in reproach even though her roommate couldn't see it. "Oh, please, now you're just being silly."

They chatted some more, with Jessie asking about Mia's experience thus far in Lenkarda. Mia gladly told her about the food and bragged about the intelligent technology she'd encountered, describing the bed in minute detail. As expected, Jessie agreed that there were some definite perks to having an affair with a K. She was also blown away by Mia's newly acquired language abilities.

"Do you really understand me?" Jessie asked in Mandarin, a language she'd picked up from her immigrant parents.

"Yes, Jessie, I really do understand you. Isn't that amazing?" Mia answered in the same language, and rubbed her ears again when Jessie shrieked with excitement.

Finally, promising to call Jessie again in a few days, Mia told the little device to hang up and disconnected.

Her parents were next on the list.

Her mom was happy to hear from her, even though she seemed concerned that Mia was not calling from her usual phone.

"Don't worry, mom," Mia explained. "My cell is malfunctioning, and I just got this temporary phone to use and haven't figured out all the settings yet." That was mostly true. Her cell phone was indeed malfunctioning in the K Center, and she hadn't yet explored all the capabilities of Korum's device.

"All right, honey," her mom said. "Just don't forget to call or text us, please."

"I won't," Mia promised. "I'll be busy for the next few days with the volunteering project, but I'll definitely call you on Wednesday."

"How is that going, by the way?" her mom asked, sounding a little irritated. Mia had told her parents she was staying in New York for an extra couple of weeks to help out her professor with a special program for disadvantaged high school kids. Naturally, her mom hadn't been pleased with the delay in seeing their youngest daughter.

"It's great," Mia lied. "I'm learning a lot, and it'll be phenomenal for my resume." She mentally cringed at having to lie to her parents like this, but she couldn't tell them the truth, not yet. Korum was right: it would be best if they learned about him in person and had a chance to talk to him to alleviate their concerns. If Mia told them where she was right now, her parents would be beside themselves.

Trying to redirect the conversation, she asked, "How is dad doing? Has he had any headaches recently?"

"Yeah, he had one a few days ago," her mom said, sighing. "It was not one of his worst ones, thankfully."

"Tell dad to stop stressing and take it easy with the computer. And take regular walks, okay?"

"Of course, honey, we're trying."

"Take care of yourselves, all right?"

Her mom promised to do so, they chatted some more, and then Mia said goodbye and went to find Korum before he left for the trial.

He'd offered her the opportunity to observe the proceedings, and Mia intended to take him up on that offer.

CHAPTER FIVE

Mia entered the tall white dome without hesitation, a chunk of the wall disintegrating to grant her passage. Korum had assured her that nobody could see, hear, or feel her in this particular version of his virtual world, and she could get the full experience of attending the trial without any stress or unpleasant encounters with the Protector. There were interactive versions of virtual reality too, he'd explained, but those were not appropriate for this situation. He himself would attend in person; it was his responsibility as a Council member and one of the chief accusers in this case.

Stepping inside the dome, Mia gasped in amazement. The place was teeming with Krinar, both male and female, all dressed in the light-colored clothes that their race seemed to favor. It was an incredible sight, with thousands of tall, gorgeous, golden-skinned aliens occupying the giant building from floor to ceiling. The spectators—at least that's what Mia assumed they were—were literally stacked one on top of another, each occupying the floating seats that Mia was beginning to learn were a staple here in Lenkarda. The seats were arranged in circles around the center of the dome, with each circle floating directly on top of the next. It was a neat arrangement, Mia realized, like an arena of sorts, but with floating seats.

At the center, there were about a dozen podium-like places, with roughly a third of them occupied by Krinar. The rest were empty.

Carefully making her way toward the center, Mia tried to avoid bumping into anyone, but it was unavoidable. The place was simply too tightly packed. The attendees couldn't feel *her*, but Mia could definitely feel *them* when she would get rammed by someone's elbow or have her foot stepped on. How this virtual reality business worked, she had no idea, but it was annoying and rather painful to be the invisible girl in a crowd. Finally, she succeeded in getting through to the center, where a large circular area was completely empty.

Standing safely in that area, Mia looked around with awe.

From the inside, the walls of the dome were transparent, and bright sunlight poured in from all directions, reflecting off the white color of the seats and the light-colored clothing of the Krinar. Unlike the loose, floaty outfits she'd seen them wear before, their clothes today seemed less casual, with more structured lines and fitted shapes for both males and females. Most of the Ks seemed to have dark hair and eyes, although here and there she could see a few with lighter brown and chestnut-colored hair. Korum was of average height here, Mia realized, observing the tall aliens all around her. Someone like her—5'3" tall and weighing a hundred pounds—would probably be considered a midget.

Turning her attention to the podium-like structures, Mia saw Korum sitting behind one of them. Grinning at the thought of observing him while he couldn't see her, Mia walked over to him. He seemed occupied with something in his palm—probably the computer he had embedded there—and paid no attention to her virtual presence. Smiling wickedly, Mia approached him from behind and touched him, running her hands over his broad back. There was no reaction from him, of course, and Mia laughed out loud, imagining the possibilities. She could do anything she wanted to him, and he wouldn't have a clue.

Testing out a theory, she licked the back of his neck. No reaction from him again, but *she* could taste the faint saltiness of his skin, smell the familiar warm scent of his body. Predictably, Mia could feel herself getting turned on, and she pressed against him, rubbing her breasts on the soft material of his ivory shirt. They were surrounded by thousands of spectators, and it didn't matter because no one—not even Korum himself—knew what she was doing.

Grinning hugely, Mia lightly bit his neck and reached for his crotch, stroking the area through his clothes. She felt incredibly naughty, like she was doing something forbidden, even though she knew the entire thing was more or less taking place inside her head. Before she could continue further, however, the noise from the crowd suddenly dropped in volume, and Mia pulled away, realizing that the trial was beginning.

The time for games was over.

The podium-like table in front of which Korum was sitting was low enough that Mia could climb on top of it, and she did so, making herself comfortable. It seemed like a good spot from which to observe the upcoming drama.

Carefully examining her surroundings, she came to the conclusion that the other podium areas were occupied by the other Council members. A third of them were there in person, while the other seats— the empty ones—were now filled with holographic images of both male and female Krinar. She assumed the holographs were for those who couldn't be there in person—perhaps because they were on Krina. She spotted Saret sitting across from them, but she had no idea who the other Krinar were. Mia counted fifteen podiums standing all around the empty circle, but only fourteen were occupied. It was probably the Protector's seat, Mia thought; it made sense that he wouldn't be judging the trial, given his son's role as one of the accused.

A chime-like sound echoed through the dome, and the crowd went completely silent. All of a sudden, the floor in the center of the circle dissolved, and seven large silvery cylinders floated out.

The floor solidified again, and the cylinders landed on it. As Mia watched with bated breath, the walls of the cylinders disintegrated, leaving only the circular tops and bottoms intact. And inside each one, Mia saw the Keiths—the seven Ks who had risked all to help humanity achieve a brighter future.

Or, according to Korum, to try to rule the Earth themselves.

* * *

The Keiths stood there, each within his or her own circle, their expressions bitter and defiant. Silvery collars encircled their necks—the same collars Mia had seen the guards put on them when they were captured. She guessed they were the K version of handcuffs. There were five males and two females, all tall and beautiful as befitting of their species.

Curious to see Korum's reaction, Mia glanced behind her and nearly recoiled at the icy contempt on his face as he looked at the traitors. She could see the dangerous yellow flecks in his eyes, and his mouth was drawn into a flat, cruel line.

He truly hated and despised the Keiths for what they'd done, Mia realized with a shiver, and she wondered again how he'd managed to forgive *her* for her actions.

The arena was still deathly silent. There were no jeers or boos, as one might have expected from such a large crowd. It was the biggest trial of the last ten thousand years, Saret had said, and Mia could see that reflected in the grave mood of the spectators.

A portion of the floor dissolved again, and another Krinar male came up. He was sitting on a broad floating seat, and he got up as soon as the floor solidified again. Unlike every other Krinar there, he was wearing clothes that were black in color. Probably the Protector, Mia thought.

Another chime echoed through the building, and all the Council members got up from behind their podiums. One of them stepped forward and approached the new arrival. Touching his shoulder, the Council member said, "Welcome, Loris."

The Protector smiled and reciprocated the shoulder-touching gesture. "Thank you, Arus." Then, turning his attention to the rest of the Council, he acknowledged their presence with a few curt nods.

So these were Korum's opponents, Mia thought, observing them with a great deal of interest. Loris's hair was jet-black, and his eyes were the color of onyx. He reminded her of a hawk, with his sharply handsome features and a faintly predatory expression on his face. In contrast, Arus seemed much more approachable. With olive skin, black hair, and dark brown eyes, he was very typical of his kind, and there was a certain genuineness in his smile that made Mia think he might not be all that bad as a person.

After the greeting was complete, Arus returned to his podium, leaving Loris standing there.

Hearing movement behind her, Mia turned around and saw that Korum had risen to his feet. He walked around the podium toward the center of the arena, his movements slow and deliberate. Smiling coldly at Loris, he asked, "Is the Protector ready for the presentation?"

Loris nodded, a look of barely contained anger on his face. It seemed that Korum hadn't exaggerated when he said that Loris hated him.

With a flick of his wrist, Korum brought up a three-dimensional image that hovered in mid-air, easily available for everyone to see.

"My fellow Earth inhabitants and all who are watching us on Krina right now," Korum said, his voice echoing throughout the dome, "I would like to show you proof of a crime so heinous that the likes of it haven't been seen in Krinar history for over a hundred thousand years. A crime in which a handful of traitors unhappy with their standing tried to send fifty thousand fellow citizens to their death in a pathetic grab for power. These traitors—the seven individuals you see before you right now—had no desire to advance us as a species, as a society. No, they simply wanted power, and they didn't care what they had to do to achieve it. They lied, they betrayed our people, they manipulated humans susceptible to their empty promises . . . and they would have killed each and every single one of you in their quest to rule this particular planet, to be worshipped by the gullible humans as their saviors—"

"That's a lie," interrupted Loris, speaking through clenched teeth. Red spots of color appeared underneath his swarthy skin, and Mia could almost feel the effort it took him to control himself. "You set them up—"

"It's not your turn to speak right now, Protector," Korum told him, his lips curving in a contemptuous smile. "It's my turn to present the evidence." And with that, he made a small gesture with his hand, and the three-dimensional recording came to life.

The scene was a familiar one for Mia—she had been there in a virtual setting only yesterday. As the recording played, she again saw the old hut where the traitors had taken shelter during the Resistance attack and heard their communication with the mysterious human general. She witnessed the Resistance forces' attempt to storm Lenkarda with their K weapons and relived their crushing defeat. And even though she was seeing this for the second time and knew that most of the human fighters had survived, Mia still felt sick to her stomach by the time the film was over.

Another movement of Korum's hand, and the next recording began to play—this one of a phone conversation between one of the Keiths and some Resistance leaders. They were clearly coordinating their actions prior to the attack. And there were more: three-dimensional videos of the Resistance meetings where they had talked about the Keiths, interactions between human government officials discussing the potential for Earth's liberation, and even a video of John telling Mia about their change in plans and how she had to steal Korum's designs.

Watching all this, Mia again realized just how thoroughly Korum had manipulated her. While she'd thought she was spying on him, he had been tracking her every move; there had never been an opportunity for her to help the Resistance—she had always been his pawn. Her stomach twisted unpleasantly at the thought.

By the time all the recordings had been shown, at least four hours had passed. Mia was hungry and thirsty, and she had a pounding headache, but she couldn't bring herself to leave her spot on top of Korum's podium, morbidly fascinated by the proceedings.

Finally, Korum's presentations appeared to be over.

In the deathly silence that gripped the arena, Korum said in a ringing tone, "And that, fellow Krinar citizens and Earth inhabitants, is why I propose the ultimate punishment for these traitors: complete rehabilitation."

A murmur ran through the crowd, and Mia could almost feel the shock emanating from some of the spectators. Whatever complete rehabilitation meant, it was clearly not something that was commonly used.

The Keiths looked shocked as well, and Mia could see the fear on some of their faces. Whatever punishment they'd been expecting was obviously different from what Korum had just proposed.

The Protector stepped forward. Like Korum, he had been standing in the center for the entire time that the recordings had been playing. His black eyes were filled with fury. "That's unthinkable, and you know it," he gritted out. "Even if they were guilty, what you're proposing is out of the question."

"Are you admitting their guilt then?" Korum asked, his tone dangerously soft.

Loris's brows snapped together. "Far from it. You know they haven't done anything wrong—"

"We'll let the Council and the Elders decide that, won't we?" Korum replied, staring at the other Krinar with a mocking look on his face. "Your turn to present is tomorrow, and I, for once, am very eager to hear how these traitors could possibly be innocent."

"Oh, you will see," Loris said, giving him a look of sheer hatred. "And so will everyone else."

And on that note, a chime sounded again. The trial proceedings were over for the day.

* * *

The Krinar drew in a deep breath, glad that the first day of the trial was over. It had gone exactly as he'd expected.

Korum had demanded the ultimate punishment for the ones he regarded as traitors. If the K hadn't taken precautions, he could have easily been the eighth figure standing there, being judged by the Council.

He had distanced himself from the Keiths just in time. Now nobody would suspect his involvement in the attack on the Centers.

He had made sure of that.

CHAPTER SIX

Starving and mentally exhausted, Mia exited the virtual reality setting by telling her wristwatch-bracelet device to bring her back home. Her breakfast this morning had been light, just a mango-avocado smoothie, and she felt almost faint with hunger at this point. Opening her eyes, she got up from the couch where she had been sitting and went in search of food.

Approaching the refrigerator, she opened it decisively and stared at the various plant foods that occupied it. Some were familiar—she saw a couple of tomatoes and sweet peppers—but others were completely foreign. Mia wished that Korum were here, so he could make one of his delicious and filling concoctions. However, since he'd been at the trial in person, she figured he might be delayed for at least a while longer.

Suddenly, she got an idea. Korum had mentioned that one of the house's functions was to prepare foods. Would it do it for her as well?

"Hey, house," Mia said tentatively, feeling like an idiot, "can you please prepare me something to eat?"

For a second, nothing happened, and then a melodious female voice asked, "What would you like, Mia?"

Mia nearly jumped in excitement. "Oh my God, you talk! That's great! Um . . . I'd like the same thing Korum made yesterday, especially if it can be prepared quickly."

"Yes, Mia," the female voice responded softly. "The shari salad will be ready in two minutes, and the kalfani stew will be done six minutes later."

Grinning in amazement, Mia walked over to the sink to wash her hands. By the time she finished and sat down at the table, a part of the wall had opened and a bowl of salad emerged, floating calmly toward the table.

Mia watched in open-mouthed shock as the salad landed neatly in front of her. It was the perfect portion size for her, and the tong-like utensil was already inside the bowl. The dish was completely ready for her consumption.

"Um, thank you," she said, trying to look around to see where the voice had been coming from. Was there a computer embedded somewhere in the ceiling?

"You're welcome, Mia," the female voice said again. "Please enjoy, and I will have the next dish ready for you within minutes."

Grinning again, Mia dug into the food. So far, she was loving Krinar technology. It was everything that people had been fantasizing about in science fiction, yet it was entirely real—and had an almost magical twist to it that Mia found very appealing. She particularly appreciated how easy it was to operate everything. Natural language voice commands, simple hand gestures—it all seemed so intuitive.

By the time she finished the salad, the stew-like dish from yesterday had floated to the table as well. Mia greedily consumed it, feeling much of the earlier tiredness leaving her as her blood sugar levels stabilized. The food was as delicious as it had been yesterday, and Mia wondered again why Korum bothered learning how to cook when he had access to such remarkable technology in his house.

Finally replete, she cleaned up by bringing the dishes toward the wall—which opened up to accept them, just as it had for Korum—and went into the living room.

It seemed like as good a time as any to call the camp director in Orlando and let him know that she wouldn't be starting on Monday.

* * *

By the time Korum arrived home an hour later, Mia had managed to get bored.

She'd spoken with the camp director and explained that unforeseen circumstances were preventing her from coming to Florida this summer. He had been disappointed, but surprisingly nice about the whole thing, which was a tremendous relief for Mia. Afterwards, she explored the house a bit and even tried talking to it, but the melodious female voice didn't seem all that interested in carrying on a conversation. It did ask whether Mia was warm and comfortable (which she was) and if she desired anything to eat or drink (which she didn't), but that was the extent of their interaction. There didn't seem to be any books around or anything else for her to amuse herself with, either.

Sighing, Mia plopped down on the couch in the living room and stared at the greenery outside. She wished she were brave enough to venture out, but the thought of getting lost in a Costa Rican forest didn't appeal to her. Studying the bracelet-like device on her wrist, Mia wondered if it would work like an actual computer, enabling her to get on the internet. She thought about trying it, but decided to wait for Korum to demonstrate more of its capabilities to her.

Finally, Korum walked in. He looked tense and a little tired, and Mia guessed that more politics had gone on behind the scenes after the trial had formally adjourned. Nevertheless, he smiled when he saw her sitting there.

"Hi," she said, ridiculously glad to see him. Despite everything that had happened between them, despite the fact that she had just seen him treat his opponents almost cruelly, she couldn't help the warm sensation that spread through her in his presence.

His smile widened. Walking over to join her on the couch, he kissed her softly and pulled her closer to him for a hug. Mia hugged him back, surprised, and mumbled into his shirt, "Is everything okay? Did anything happen?"

He shook his head and simply held her, burying his face in her hair and inhaling her scent. "No," he murmured, "everything is good now."

After a few more seconds, he pulled back and looked at her. "I hope you got something to eat? I programmed the house to respond to your verbal commands, to make sure you wouldn't have any difficulties here."

Mia smiled. "Yeah, I figured it out. Thanks for that."

"Good," he said softly, "I want you to feel comfortable here."

Mia nodded slowly. "I'm starting to, a bit. But I actually wanted to ask you something . . ."

"Of course, what is it?"

"I'm bored," Mia told him bluntly. "I don't really have anything to do when you're not here. At home, I have school, work, friends, books, TV—"

"Ah, I see," Korum said, smiling. "I haven't shown you everything that your little computer can do. Tell it that you would like to read something."

"Okay," Mia said dubiously, looking at her bracelet, "I would like to read something . . ."

Almost immediately, one of the walls parted, revealing a section hidden inside—a shelf of some kind. And as Mia watched, an object that looked like a thick sheet of paper floated out toward her.

"How does all this stuff float?" Mia asked in amazement, plucking the object out of thin air. "Plates, chairs, now this . . ."

"The premise is similar to the shields we use to protect our settlements," Korum explained. "It's a type of force-field technology, just applied on a much smaller scale."

"Oh, I see," Mia said, as if that told her anything. A technology whizz she definitely wasn't. Studying the sheet in her hands, she saw that it was actually made of some plastic-like material.

"This is something you can entertain yourself with," he said, sitting down next to her. "It's a little like your computer tablets. You can read any book—human or Krinar—that's ever been written, and you can watch any kind of film you want. This will also work with verbal commands, so you can just tell it what you want to see or read."

"Can I use it to learn more about the Krinar? To read some history books or something?" asked Mia, staring at the object with excitement.

"Sure. You can use it for whatever purpose you want."

Mia grinned. "That's great, thanks!"

He smiled back at her. "Of course. I don't want you to be bored here."

Something suddenly occurred to Mia. "Wait, you said it works by verbal commands, but I've never seen or heard you using verbal commands on anything. How do *you* control all your technology?"

"I have a very powerful computer that essentially allows me to control everything through a specific type of thinking," Korum explained, holding up his palm. "It's a type of highly advanced brain-computer interface. I use some gestures too, but that's just out of habit."

Mia stared at him. "So you control electronics with your mind?"

"Krinar electronics, yes. Human technology is not designed for that."

"What about the others? Is that how they do it too?"

Korum nodded. "Many of them, yes. Some still prefer the old-fashioned way, which is voice commands and gestures, but most have switched over. The majority of our technology is designed to accommodate both ways of doing things because our children and young ones only use the first method."

"Why?" Mia asked, looking at him in fascination.

"Because their brains aren't fully formed and developed, and because there's a learning curve involved with using brain-computer interfaces.

That's why I'm setting up everything with voice capabilities for you for now—it's much easier for a beginner to master. Later on, when you understand our technology and society better, I can set you up with the new interface."

Mia's eyes widened. He would give her the ability to control Krinar technology with her mind? The possibilities were simply unimaginable. "That sounds . . ."

"Like a little too much right now?" Korum guessed, and Mia nodded.

"Hence the voice commands for now," he said. "Your society has advanced far enough that you can easily understand that type of interface, and it's very intuitive."

"So for now, I'll be like one of your children?" Mia asked wryly.

His lips curved into a smile. "If you were Krinar, you would actually be considered an adolescent, age-wise."

"I see." Mia gave him a small frown. "And at what age do you become adults?"

"Well, physically, we attain our adult characteristics right around the same age as humans, somewhere in the late teens or early twenties. However, it's only around a couple of hundred years of age that a Krinar is considered mature enough to be a fully functioning member of our society—although it could be sooner if they make some type of extraordinary contribution."

For some reason, that upset her. Mia didn't know why it mattered to her that she would not be considered a fully functioning member of Krinar society at any point within her lifetime. It's not like they would ever view a human as such anyway. And besides, she had no idea how long her relationship with Korum would last. Still, it rankled her somewhat, the fact that Ks would always consider her little more than a child.

Not wanting to dwell on that topic, she asked, "So did the trial today go as you expected?"

Korum shrugged. "Just about. Loris will try to twist everything, to make it seem like I made the whole thing up. But there's too much evidence of their betrayal, and I don't think anything can save them at this point."

"What does complete rehabilitation mean?" Mia asked, unbearably curious. "Everyone seemed shocked when you suggested it."

"It's our most extreme form of punishment for criminals," Korum said, his eyes narrowing slightly. "It's used in cases when an individual poses a severe danger to society—as these traitors clearly do."

"Okay . . . but what is it?"

"Saret can do a better job of explaining it to you," Korum said. "The exact mechanics of it fall within his area of expertise. But essentially, whatever it was that made them act that way—that personality trait will be thoroughly eradicated."

Mia's eyes widened. "How?"

Korum sighed. "Like I said, it's not my area of expertise. But from what I know as a layman, it involves wiping out a lot of their memories and creating a new personality for them. It's only done when there's no other choice because it's very invasive for the mind. The rehabilitated are never the same afterwards—which is exactly the point in this case."

"So they wouldn't remember who they are?" That did seem pretty horrible to Mia.

"They might remember bits and pieces, so they wouldn't be completely blank slates, but the essence of their personality—and that part that made them commit the crime—would be gone."

Mia swallowed. "That does seem harsh . . ."

His eyes narrowed again. "It's better than what your kind does to criminals. At least we don't have capital punishment."

"You don't?" Mia wasn't sure why she was so surprised to hear that. Perhaps it had to do with the popular image of the Ks as a violent species, arising primarily from the bloody fights during the Great Panic.

"No, Mia, we don't," Korum told her sardonically. "We're really not the monsters you've imagined us to be."

"I never said your people were," Mia protested, and he laughed.

"No, just me, right?"

Mia lowered her eyes, unable to bear the mockery in his gaze. "I don't think you're a monster," she told him quietly. "But I do think it's wrong for you to treat me like a possession just because I'm human. I'm a person with feelings and desires, and I did have a life before you came into it—"

"And now you don't?" Korum asked, tilting her chin up until she had no choice but to look him in the eyes. Noticing the deeper gold surrounding his irises, Mia nervously moistened her suddenly dry lips. "You think that I mistreat you? That I keep you from the fascinating life you enjoyed before?"

"I liked the life I had before," Mia told him defiantly. "It was exactly what I wanted. It might've seemed boring to you, but I was happy with it—"

"Happy with what?" he asked her softly. "Studying day and night?

Hiding behind baggy clothes because you were too scared to actually try living? Being a virgin at the age of twenty-one?"

Mia flushed with anger and embarrassment. "That's right," she told him bitterly. "Happy with my family and my friends, happy living in New York and going to school there, happy with the internship I had planned for this summer—"

His expression darkened. "I already promised that you will see your family soon," he said, his tone dangerously flat. "And I told you that I will bring you back to New York for the school year. You don't trust me to keep my word?"

Mia took a deep breath, trying to control herself. It probably wasn't the wisest move on her part, arguing with him like that in her circumstances, but she couldn't help it. Some reckless demon inside her had awoken and wouldn't be denied. "You've lied to me before," she said, unable to hide the resentment in her voice.

"Oh really?" he said, his words practically dripping with sarcasm. "*I* lied to you?"

Mia swallowed again. "You manipulated me into doing exactly what you wanted," she said stubbornly. "I didn't want any part of it—all I wanted was to be left alone . . ."

He regarded her with an inscrutable expression on his face. "And do you still?" he asked softly. "Want to be left alone?"

Mia stared at him, caught completely by surprise. Her mouth opened, but no words came out.

"And don't lie to me, Mia," he added quietly. "I always know when you're lying."

Mia blinked furiously, trying to hold back a sudden rush of tears. With that one simple question, he had stripped her bare, laid out all of her vulnerabilities for him to exploit. She didn't want him to know the depth of her feelings for him, didn't want her emotions exposed for him to toy with. What kind of an idiot was she, to want to be with someone like him? To hate and love him so intensely at the same time?

His lips curved into a half-smile. "I see." Leaning toward her, he kissed her on the mouth softly, his lips strangely gentle on hers.

"I'll see what I can do about getting you an internship," he said, pulling away from her and getting up. "And I'll introduce you to some other human girls in this Center—maybe you'll meet some new friends."

And as Mia looked at him in shock, he smiled at her again and went into his office, leaving her to digest everything that had just happened.

CHAPTER SEVEN

Three hours later, Mia was lying on the bed, completely absorbed in the story of the early evolution of the Krinar, when Korum walked into the bedroom.

"We're going to dinner in twenty minutes," he told her, "so you might want to get ready."

Startled, Mia looked up at him. "To dinner where?"

"Arman is an acquaintance of mine," Korum explained, sitting down on the bed next to her and placing his hand on her leg. "He invited us over to his house when I told him about you. He also has a charl, a Costa Rican girl who's been with him for a couple of years now. She's very eager to meet you."

Mia grinned, suddenly very excited. "Oh, I'd love to meet her as well!" She couldn't wait to talk to another girl in her situation and learn about Ks from the perspective of a human who also knew them intimately—and much longer.

Korum smiled back. "I figured you would. How's your reading going so far?"

"It's fascinating," she told him earnestly. "I had no idea you had also evolved from an ape-like species."

He nodded. "We did. There were many parallels in our evolution and yours, except there ultimately ended up being two different species on Krina: us and the *lonar*—that's the primates I told you about before. We were bigger, stronger, faster, longer-lived, and much more intelligent than the lonar, but we were tied to them because we needed their blood to survive."

Mia stared at him. She'd just learned all that as well, and she couldn't get the images of the early Krinar out of her head. The book had gone into some very vivid descriptions of how the ancient Ks had hunted their prey, with each male Krinar staking out his territory around a small group of the lonar and fighting off the other Ks to preserve the blood supply for himself and his mate. Once inside a K's "territory," the lonar had very little chance of survival, as they would be constantly weakened by material blood loss and traumatized by the experience of being preyed upon. Ultimately, their numbers had dwindled, and the Krinar were forced to adapt, to learn new strategies of feeding.

At that point, the Krinar were still a primitive species, little more than hunters-gatherers. However, the rapid reduction in the lonar population meant that the Ks had to evolve beyond their territorial roots, to learn to collaborate with one another in order to preserve what remained of their critical blood supply. The next hundred thousand years were a time of rapid progress for the Krinar, marking the birth of science, technology, medicine, culture, and the arts. Instead of hunting the lonar, the Ks began to farm them, creating favorable conditions for them to live and reproduce and doing their best to feed only on those who were deemed to be past their prime reproductive age.

These efforts managed to temporarily arrest the decline in the lonar population, and the Krinar society began to prosper. Even with the low birth rate, their numbers began to grow as fewer Ks perished in violent fights to defend their territories. Innovation began to be highly valued, and the Ks invented space travel shortly thereafter. It was the first Golden Age in Krinar history, a time of tremendous scientific achievement and relatively peaceful coexistence among the different Krinar tribes and regions.

"I just got to the point where the plague began," Mia told him. It was apparently the event that ended the first Golden Age, nearly wiping out the entire lonar population and plunging the Krinar society into panic and bloody turmoil.

Korum smiled. "You're making good progress on our history then. What do you think so far?"

"I think it's very interesting," Mia answered honestly. It was also a little scary, how savage they had been in the past, but she didn't want to tell him that. She tried to picture Korum as one of the Krinar primitives, hunting down his prey, and it was a surprisingly easy feat, requiring very little imagination on her part. She could see many of the predatory characteristics still present in his species, from the sinuous way they moved to the territorial traits she'd seen Korum display in regard to her.

"You can continue later," he said, absentmindedly stroking her thigh. As usual, his touch sent a shiver of pleasure through her body. "We shouldn't be late to dinner—it's considered highly insulting to the host."

"Of course," Mia said, getting up immediately. The last thing she wanted was to offend someone. "Should I dress up somehow?" She was lounging in the jeans and T-shirt that she'd been wearing when she arrived in Lenkarda yesterday. Somehow, the house had already managed to clean them because she'd found them fresh and folded on the dresser in the bedroom.

Korum was apparently two steps ahead of her because he was already opening the door to the walk-in closet. "I created a wardrobe for you," he explained, "so you don't have to rely on me for every outfit. Here, let me show you."

Curious, Mia walked over to take a look, and her jaw nearly dropped. The closet was filled with beautiful light-colored dresses, shoes ranging from barely-there sandals to soft-looking boots, and various accessories. "You made all of this?"

Korum nodded. "I had Leeta send me all of her fashion designs. Aside from working in my company, she dabbles with clothing creation."

Leeta was Korum's distant cousin, and Mia had briefly met her a few times back in New York. She wasn't the warmest and friendliest individual, in Mia's opinion, but her clothing designs seemed quite nice.

"You mean you're not a fashion expert?" Mia pretended to be shocked, comically widening her eyes. He'd certainly been eager to get rid of her entire former wardrobe back in New York.

He laughed. "Far from it. I do know when clothes are being used as a shield, though," he said pointedly, referring to her tendency to wear ugly but comfortable clothes when left to her own devices.

Mia fought a childish urge to stick out her tongue at him. "Yeah, whatever," she muttered.

"For tonight, you can wear this," Korum said, pulling out a delicate-looking light-pink dress.

Mia put it on, secretly pleased by the heat in Korum's eyes as she changed in front of him, and walked over to look in the mirror. Like all Krinar clothes so far, the dress fit her perfectly, ending just above her knees, and didn't require any kind of bra underneath. There were no sleeves, and her back was left entirely exposed. However, her shoulders were covered with wide ruffled straps, and the square neckline at the front was surprisingly modest. The color was beautiful, giving her pale cheeks the illusion of a rosy glow.

"I've noticed you don't wear any kind of bright or dark clothing," Mia commented, wondering about that peculiar fact. "In general, you seem to favor light colors in everything. Is there a particular reason for that?"

Korum smiled, looking at her with a warm glow in his eyes. "There is. Bright or dark colors have historically been associated with violence and vengeance in our culture, and we prefer not to have them around in the normal course of daily life. Of course, when we leave our Centers and interact with humans, we usually wear human clothes—and we don't care about the colors as much for that. In fact, some of us enjoy clothing that we'd never normally wear here or on Krina—like the bright red dress you saw Leeta wear in New York. If she were to dress like that among the Krinar, everyone would think she'd gone crazy and was planning a vendetta of some kind."

Something clicked for Mia. "Is that why the Protector was wearing black at the trial? Because he's on a warpath?"

"Exactly," Korum said. "He's making a statement that he believes he's been wronged and that he intends to seek revenge."

"Seek revenge how?" Mia wondered, and Korum shrugged, apparently not in the mood to discuss politics right now. Since they didn't have much time, Mia decided to let it go for now and focus instead on the upcoming dinner.

"Here, you can wear these shoes," Korum said, handing her a pair of soft ivory booties. Like all K footwear, these seemed to have a flat sole. Apparently, the concept of high-heeled shoes was not as popular among Krinar females as it was among human women.

Mia pulled on the boots—which immediately conformed to her feet and became comfortable—and tried to tame her hair a bit with her fingers. After lounging for hours, she had a serious bedhead look going on, with her long curls tangled and sticking out in all directions. After a couple of minutes, she gave up on the hopeless cause. Even with the regular use of Korum's wonder shampoo, her hair would never be as straight and sleek as she'd like.

"It looks beautiful, Mia. Leave it," Korum said, observing her efforts with quiet amusement.

Mia couldn't help smiling at him. It was one of the things she found peculiar about him: he actually seemed to have a thing for her hair, often touching it and playing with the curls. Since she'd never seen a curly-haired K, she assumed he simply liked it because of the novelty factor.

"Okay, then I'm ready, I guess . . ."

"One more thing," Korum said, coming up behind her and fastening an unusual iridescent necklace around her neck, his warm fingers brushing against her throat. It was a deceptively simple design, just a tear-shaped pendant on a thin chain, but the shimmery material made it indescribably beautiful. It was as if all colors of the rainbow were gathered around her neck, competing with each other for attention.

"Wow," Mia breathed, touching the pendant with reverence. "What is it?"

"It's a genuine shimmer-stone necklace," Korum explained. "Shimmer-stone occurs naturally only in my region of Krina, and this one has been passed down through generations in my family. It's just shy of a million years old."

Mia turned around to stare at him in shock. "And you're putting it on me? What if I lose or damage it?"

"You won't," Korum reassured her, smiling faintly. And offering her his arm, he asked, "Shall we go?"

Speechless, Mia looped her arm through the crook of his elbow and followed him out—with a million-year-old Krinar family heirloom sparkling merrily around her throat.

* * *

Five minutes later, they stood before a cream-colored house that looked a lot like Korum's. The ride to the other end of the colony took less than a minute in the small aircraft Korum had created explicitly for that purpose.

As they approached, the wall of the house disintegrated in front of them, and they walked in.

A tall, lean Krinar male stood in the middle of the room, dressed in the usual light-colored garb. His hair was the lightest shade of brown Mia had ever seen on a K, almost sandy-colored, and his hazel eyes had a greenish undertone that looked particularly exotic with his golden skin. The smile on his narrow, ascetic-looking face was broad and welcoming.

Walking up to Korum, he touched his shoulder with his open palm. "Korum, it's such an honor to have you here," he said. His manner was somewhat deferential, and Mia realized that it was probably a big deal for him—having a member of the Council in his house.

Korum smiled back and reciprocated the gesture. "I'm glad to see you too, Arman. Thank you for the invitation."

While the two Ks were greeting each other, Mia examined her surroundings with a great deal of curiosity. This was the first fully Krinar dwelling she had been to—with the exception of the arena—and she was fascinated by its almost Zen-like aesthetic. There was absolutely no clutter anywhere; in fact, there didn't seem to be any furniture with the exception of two large floating planks. Mia guessed those were meant to serve as places for the guests to sit. The outside walls were fully transparent, while the rest of the interior was a beautiful shade of cream.

"And you must be Mia," Arman said, turning and addressing her directly.

Mia smiled at him. "Yes, hi. It's nice to meet you."

To her surprise, Mia realized that she liked this K. There was a kind look in his eyes, and something almost gentle in the way he spoke that made her feel very much at ease in his presence.

"Oh, it's very nice to meet you as well," Arman said, his smile getting wider. "Maria has been looking forward to meeting you ever since we learned about you yesterday."

At that moment, a human girl walked into the room. Dressed in a beautiful halter-style white dress that showed off her slim, curvy figure to perfection, she was strikingly pretty and bore a strong resemblance to a young Jennifer Lopez.

Smiling hugely, she swiftly came up to Mia and warmly embraced her, brushing her lips against Mia's left cheek. Some kind of exotic perfume tickled Mia's nose. Slightly startled, Mia awkwardly hugged her back.

"Oh my dear, how are you?" she exclaimed in Spanish, pulling back to look at Mia. "I'm Maria, and I'm so glad to see you! What a lovely necklace! How are your first couple of days here? Did Korum show you around already? You poor thing, you must be so overwhelmed with everything right now! I remember I didn't even know how to use the toilet at first!"

Mia blinked, overwhelmed only by the girl's enthusiasm. She was like a pretty tornado, sweeping along everything in her path. "I'm good, thanks," Mia answered in Spanish, inwardly still marveling at her new language abilities. "I haven't really seen much of the Center yet—I only arrived yesterday."

"Oh, you haven't gone to the beach yet? It's so nice, you really should!" Turning to Korum, she frowned at him, her smooth brow furrowing slightly.

Korum laughed. "Hint taken. I'll show Mia the beach tomorrow."

"Maria!" their host exclaimed. "Please be nice to our guests!"

"I'm always nice," Maria retorted, grinning. "That's why you love me." Coming up on tiptoes, she kissed Arman on the cheek, and Mia could almost see him melting on the spot, unable to withstand the potent force of the girl's charm.

With a big grin on his own face, Arman turned his attention back to Mia and Korum. "She's incorrigible," he said, and there was such happiness in his voice that Mia could only gape at him in open-mouthed amazement. "Please ignore her and follow me. The dinner is all ready."

They followed Arman into another room. In the middle of the room was another large floating plank, oval in shape, surrounded by four floating seats. Why all K furniture seemed to float, Mia had no idea. On the large plank—which Mia assumed functioned as a table—there were about twenty different dishes, ranging from familiar tropical fruits and vegetables to some exotic-looking salads, dips, and stew-like concoctions.

Sitting down on one of the chairs, Mia felt it adjusting to her body and smiled. All K inventions seemed to be designed with a focus on maximum comfort and convenience.

The dinner flew by, dominated by light conversation and amusing stories about the Costa Rican flora and fauna. Mia learned that Arman was an artist, and that he came to Earth to study human culture and the arts. He had met Maria shortly after his arrival. Her family used to own land in the area where the Ks had built their Center, and Arman had been one of the Krinar responsible for making sure that the displaced humans were appropriately compensated. Theirs seemed to be a love at first sight.

"From the moment I saw him, I knew I wanted him," Maria confided, her dark eyes sparkling. "I didn't care that he wasn't human, or that everybody was scared of them. I knew he couldn't be as bad as they said—he was far too nice for that." And reaching out, she squeezed his hand, beaming at Arman with a megawatt smile.

Observing the two lovers, Mia felt a strange pressure in her chest that was very much like jealousy. They seemed to be genuinely in love, despite the obstacles Mia had always viewed as insurmountable. And Maria was far too happy for someone who had so few rights in the Krinar society. Clearly, her formal status as a charl had very little bearing on her relationship with Arman. If anything, it seemed that her K lover was quite content to let her take the lead in many things, his own laid-back personality complemented by her outgoing nature.

By the time the dinner ended, Mia found herself forgetting many of her concerns and simply enjoying the company of this likable couple.

They were sweet and tender with each other, and Maria didn't seem intimidated by either of the two Ks. She even reprimanded Korum again for not giving Mia a proper tour of the Center, for which Korum laughingly apologized. It could've been a regular double-date, except that two of the participants were from a different galaxy.

Finally, Mia reluctantly said goodbye to them and headed home with Korum, mulling over the strangeness of what she'd just seen, her heart filling with hope for things she rationally knew had to be impossible.

* * *

The Krinar replayed the results of his latest experiment, watching the recording over and over again.

Everything seemed to be working as he'd hoped. Soon, he would be able to implement the next part of his plan. It was unfortunate that the Keiths had failed, but it was ultimately just a minor setback.

Now he wanted to look at his enemy again . . . and that little charl of his.

For some reason, he found those recordings to be particularly fascinating.

CHAPTER EIGHT

On the short ride back, Mia couldn't help thinking about the other couple. A human and a K, so happy together—it seemed to go against everything Mia had been told by the Resistance and everything she'd learned about the role of charl in Krinar society. How did they manage such a feat? And wasn't Maria worried that she would ultimately lose Arman when her beauty faded and he remained the same?

Of course, Arman was as different from Korum as anyone she'd ever met. It was difficult to believe that he was a member of the same predatory species. He seemed far too kind and gentle to be a K, and Mia couldn't imagine him holding Maria here against her will. Indeed, it seemed like Maria had been the one to initiate their relationship. Clearly, there were just as many varieties of personalities among Ks as there were among humans.

And Mia had managed to meet one who wouldn't have been out of place in the primeval Krinar forests of billions of years ago.

Korum would've been a very successful hunter, Mia decided, with his blend of ruthlessness and sheer smarts. His ambition had propelled him to the top of the modern Krinar society, and she had no doubt he would've been successful in any type of environment—it was just the way he was. He knew exactly what he wanted, and he didn't hesitate to go after it.

And for now, he wanted her.

Sighing, Mia looked at the floor as they landed in the clearing right next to Korum's house. The ship touched the ground softly, and one of its walls immediately disintegrated, creating an opening for them.

Getting up, she exited the aircraft and followed Korum to the house. "Are we far from the beach?" she asked, remembering Maria mentioning it earlier.

"No, it's actually walking distance," Korum said as they entered the house. "I'll show you the way tomorrow, if you'd like, so you don't have to be cooped up in the house when I'm not around. Just don't go into the ocean without me—the surf can be very strong here, and the currents are unpredictable."

"I'm a good swimmer," Mia told him. "You don't have to worry about me."

"It doesn't matter." Korum stopped and gave her a strict look. "You either promise me you won't go into the water alone, or you don't go to the beach without me at all."

Mia mentally rolled her eyes. The dictator was back. "Fine. I won't go into the water by myself." Having grown up in Florida, she knew exactly what to watch out for in terms of rip currents and rogue waves, and the ocean didn't scare her. Still, she didn't want Korum preventing her from going to the beach, so she decided against arguing with him further.

"Good." He sounded satisfied. "Then I'll take you there tomorrow morning."

"What about the trial?"

"It doesn't start until eleven in the morning. If you wake up before then, we can take a walk to the beach, and I'll show you some of the nearby sites. Later on, I'll give you a more thorough tour."

"That would be nice, thanks," Mia said. "Can I observe the trial again tomorrow? It was really fascinating . . ."

He smiled at her. "Of course. It will be Loris's turn to present—that should be particularly interesting to see."

"Why does he hate you so much?" Mia asked, curious to learn more about Krinar politics. "Did you have some kind of differences before his son was accused?"

Korum's lips twisted slightly. "Differences is one way of putting it. He had a company that competed with mine a few hundred years ago. His designs were far inferior, though, and he ultimately ended up having to close it down. His son—Rafor—worked with him at the time as one of his lead designers, and he lost a lot of his standing in society when the company went out of business. Loris had other ventures at the time, and he was deeply involved in politics, so his standing took a much smaller hit and recovered quickly. His son's, however, never did."

So Rafor was the Keith with the design background, the one who had provided the Resistance with K gadgets. It all made sense now. His designs had never been as good as Korum's; it was no wonder that the Resistance had failed.

"And Loris hates you for that? For Rafor losing his standing?" Mia wasn't sure she fully understood the standing concept, but it seemed to be quite important for the Krinar.

"He does," Korum said. "He hates it that his son wasn't good enough as a designer, and he blames me for Rafor never doing anything else productive with his life. And now that Rafor has also proven to be a pathetic traitor . . ."

"He blames you for that as well?" Mia guessed, staring up at Korum with a slight frown. "Is that why he intends to seek revenge?"

Korum nodded, his eyes glittering with something that looked like anticipation. "Indeed."

"It doesn't bother you?" Mia asked, trying to understand her lover better. He looked almost as if he were relishing the other K's hatred. "That someone hates you so much, I mean?"

"Why should it bother me?" He looked amused at the thought. "He's hardly the first, and he won't be the last."

Mia stared at him. "You don't care if people like you? If they are your friends or your enemies?"

Korum laughed. "No, my sweet, why would I? If someone wants to be my enemy, it's their choice—one that they will ultimately regret."

"I see," Mia said, another piece of the Korum puzzle clicking into place for her. She knew that there were people like that, individuals so confident in themselves—or arrogant, depending on how one looked at it—that they seemed to lack the usual drive to please others. And her lover appeared to be one of them. If anything, it looked like he thrived on conflict. She wondered if it was a K-specific trait or simply a part of Korum's personality.

Before Mia could finish fully analyzing that thought, Korum stepped closer and lifted his hand to brush her hair back from her face. "That's enough talk about politics," he said, cupping her cheek with one large warm hand, his eyes beginning to gleam with familiar golden undertones. "I can think of far more pleasant things we could be doing right now."

Mia's heartbeat immediately quickened, and the muscles deep within her belly tightened, reacting to his touch and the unmistakable sexual intent in his voice. Such a Pavlovian response, the psychology student in her noted wryly—her body was now fully conditioned to respond to him this way, to crave the pleasure that only he could provide. The lack of control over her own flesh bothered Mia on many levels, making her feel even less in charge of her own life, her own decisions.

Bending down, he wrapped one arm around her back and placed the other under her knees, effortlessly lifting her up into his arms. Mia closed her eyes, burying her face against his shoulder as he swiftly carried her toward the bedroom.

As he'd said earlier, the labels placed on their relationship didn't matter—at least not when it came to this.

* * *

When they got to the bedroom, he placed her down on the bed and straightened for a minute. Bemused, she watched as he placed a small white dot on his right temple.

"What is it?" she asked him warily when he leaned over her again.

"You'll see," he said mysteriously, with a wicked gleam in those amber eyes. And then he touched her temple as well. Startled, Mia raised her hand and felt a small protrusion. He had placed a dot on her also.

Feeling nervous, Mia opened her mouth to ask him again, but he kissed her in that moment and all rational thought left her head. His hand closed over her right breast, kneading the small globe, his thumb flicking lightly over her nipple, and Mia felt a surge of heat go through her. His other hand buried itself in her hair, holding her head still as his tongue invaded her mouth. She could taste the hunger in his kiss, and she wondered vaguely what had provoked him.

All of a sudden, she could no longer feel the softness of the bed beneath her and her ears were ringing from loud music, the pulsing beat reverberating through her bones. Gasping in shock, she pushed at Korum, and he let her go, watching with an unsettling mixture of amusement and burning lust as she sat up, gaping at the scene in panic and disbelief.

They were on the floor inside what looked like a large metal cage. All around them, Mia could see gyrating bodies, grinding and pushing against each other. Stunned, she realized they were dancing. The flickering lights above them cast everything in shades of blue and purple, adding to the surreal feel of the situation.

"Where are we?" she yelled, jumping to her feet and staring at Korum in frightened astonishment. Did he teleport them somewhere, or was this some strange and new virtual world?

He laughed, rising from the floor smoothly. "Come here," he said, pulling her toward him.

Angry and confused, Mia tried to resist, but it was useless, of course. Within seconds, he had her pressed against his body, and she could feel his erection pushing at her stomach.

"So I learned something interesting today," Korum said softly, his voice somehow carrying above the music. His eyes were nearly yellow in the strange flashing lights of the dance floor. "My sweet little charl seems to have a thing for touching me in public places—when she thinks no one is watching, of course. When she thinks I can't feel it."

Mia swallowed, remembering her actions earlier, before the trial began. She'd played with Korum, secure in the knowledge that no one would ever find out . . . yet somehow he knew. Was he mad at her? Did he intend to punish her somehow?

"Where are we?" she asked, staring up at him warily. "Why did you bring me here?"

"We're in the most exclusive nightclub in Beverly Hills," Korum told her. "And I'm going to give you exactly what you want."

Mia's stomach twisted with a strange mixture of fear and excitement. "Korum, please, I don't think—"

Before she could finish the sentence, he grasped her butt and lifted her up, pressing her back against the wall of the cage, her thighs spread wide and his pelvis flush against her own. Mia gasped again, feeling his cock prodding at her sex through the thin barrier of their clothing. Then his mouth was over hers again, his kiss so deep and penetrating that she could barely breathe.

He intended to fuck her in public, Mia realized with some semi-functioning part of her brain, horrified and yet unbearably aroused at the thought. Surely this couldn't be real, she thought desperately, surely he wouldn't do that to her . . . or would he?

She tried to twist away from his mouth, her nails digging into his shoulders, but he wouldn't let her, biting her lower lip in warning until she had no choice but to give in. The roar of her own heartbeat was almost louder than the blaring music around them as she fought to maintain some semblance of sanity in what seemed like an utterly insane situation.

Holding her up with one arm, Korum used his other hand to grasp the skirt of her dress and lift it higher, leaving the front portion of her lower body naked. Mia whimpered in panic, frantically raking her nails down his bare shoulders as he freed his cock too. She could feel the blunt force of it pressing against her delicate opening, and then he began to push inside, ignoring the way her muscles tightened in an attempt to deny him entry.

It was all happening so fast that Mia could barely process the situation, the flashing lights and the pounding music adding to her sense of disorientation. She felt unbearably hot, her body burning with a strange combination of searing shame and feverish desire as his cock continued to push deeper inside her, her narrow sheath reluctantly stretching around its thick girth. With her full weight supported only by his arm, she couldn't limit the depth of his penetration in any way, and he felt too large inside her, the head of his shaft almost bumping up against her cervix. For a few moments, pain threatened, but then her body adjusted, softening and melting around him, and the discomfort receded, leaving only a scorching need in its place. At the same time, his mouth continued to plunder her own, the invasion of his tongue mimicking the relentless push of his cock.

Her senses completely overwhelmed, Mia couldn't string together a single thought, could only feel as he began to move his hips, the force of his thrusts pressing her into the cage wall. The metal links dug into the soft skin of her exposed back, and the pulsing beat of the music seemed to echo inside her, the noise from the dancing crowd a dizzying buzz in her ears. Her vision darkened for a second, his kisses draining her of oxygen, but then his mouth lifted, letting her catch her breath, and the fainting sensation receded, bringing her back to semi-awareness of the situation.

Frantically sucking in air, Mia shut her eyes tightly and tried to pretend that this wasn't happening, that he wasn't truly fucking her in a cage in the middle of a nightclub. It couldn't be real, any of it; surely, she couldn't really feel the hard metal pressing into her back, couldn't hear the crowd screaming and whooping in tune to the blasting music. Yet the relentless thrust and drag of his cock inside her couldn't be mistaken for anything else, nor could the moist heat of his mouth as it traveled down the side of her neck.

A wave of hot shame rolled through her again, somehow adding to the powerful tension gathering inside her. His pace picked up, his hips hammering at her, and every muscle in her body seemed to tighten simultaneously, the pleasure so sharp it was almost intolerable . . . and then she could only scream as the climax crashed over her with the force of a tidal wave, her inner muscles squeezing and releasing his cock several times.

As the orgasmic sensation faded, Mia slumped in Korum's arms, burying her face in the crook of his neck. She could feel him shuddering as well, could hear his hoarse groan as his shaft throbbed and jerked inside her, releasing his seed in warm bursts.

Now that it was over, all she could feel was scalding embarrassment, and angry tears filled her eyes, leaking out through the corners. She didn't want to look around, didn't want to face the people who were sure to be avidly watching them.

More tears fell, moistening his neck. Mia wanted to disappear, to pretend this was all some horrible dream, but there was no escaping the stark sensations. His softening shaft was still buried inside her, and she could feel the cage digging into her back. And just when she thought she couldn't bear it any longer, he murmured in her ear, "We're not really here, darling. You know that, right?"

"What?" Mia jerked back, staring at him in shock and disbelief. She could hear the hypnotic beat of the latest dance-hop single, could feel him inside her, and he was telling her it was all happening inside her head?

His lips curled into a small smile. "Did you think it was real?"

"Let me down," she said quietly, hot fury rushing through her. "Let me down right now."

He actually listened to her this time and lowered her to the ground, slowly withdrawing from her. Her trembling legs refused to support her weight for a second, and he held her carefully, looking down at her with a slightly amused expression on his face. The dress fell back into place, covering her lower half again.

As soon as she could stand on her own, Mia pushed at Korum's chest, and he took a step back, giving her some breathing room. Just to confirm what he'd told her, Mia slowly turned in a circle, staring at the dancers outside their cage.

No one was looking at them. Not a single person. The music kept blaring, the dancers kept grinding against each other, and nobody was paying them any attention. *This wasn't real after all.* It was all happening virtually, just like at the trial. Or was it?

Turning back toward Korum, she asked evenly, "Did we just have sex, or did you simply mind-fuck me?"

Instead of replying to her question, Korum lifted his hand to his right temple and pressed on it lightly. The club dissolved around them, reality shifting and adjusting, and Mia found herself standing on the floor next to one of the bedroom walls. He was standing there too, less than a foot away from her, his shorts unfastened and his now-flaccid sex partially visible.

Blinking to clear the slight blurriness in her vision, Mia took stock of her current state. Her sex felt swollen and a little sore, like it usually did after intercourse, and she could feel the wetness of his sperm sliding down her leg.

So the sex part had definitely been real.

Mia couldn't decide if that made her feel better or worse about the situation. Now that the adrenaline rush was over, she found herself shaking slightly, feeling cold despite the warmth in the room.

"I need a shower," she told him, refusing to look at him.

"Mia," he said softly, his hand wrapping around her upper arm when she tried to walk past him, "you're not going to tell me you didn't like it, are you?"

"Of course I didn't!" Tears welled up in her eyes again as she relived the sharp feelings of burning humiliation and unwilling arousal, and she tried to yank her arm away from him. A useless effort, of course; he didn't even seem to feel her struggle.

"Liar," Korum said, and she could hear the amusement in his voice. "I could feel exactly how much you didn't like it when you came, your little pussy squeezing me for all its worth."

Mia felt her cheeks turning a bright red. "I'm going into the shower right now," she repeated, wanting nothing more than to get away.

"All right," he said. "I will go with you." And before she could object, he picked her up again and carried her into the bathroom, placing her on her feet next to the jacuzzi.

"I wanted to go alone," she told him mutinously as he pulled down her dress, leaving her standing there naked with the exception of the necklace around her neck and the soft booties on her feet. She touched the necklace lightly, finding the place where it apparently locked in place, and carefully took it off, placing it on the side of the jacuzzi. She had no intention of showering with a million-year-old piece of alien jewelry around her neck.

He smiled at her, taking off his own clothes. "Why would you want that?"

"Because I don't like you right now," she told him bluntly. Actually, that was a huge understatement. It was more that she felt like doing something violent to him—such as slapping that smile right off his beautiful face.

"Because I gave you what you wanted but would've been too scared to ask for?" he asked, cocking his head to the side.

"I didn't want that," Mia told him vehemently. "And the fact that I came has nothing to do with anything. I'm more than just the sum of my physical responses—"

"Of course you are," Korum said, coming up to her and crouching down to remove the boots from her feet. Mia stared down at him resentfully, fighting a ridiculous urge to stroke the dark, lustrous-looking hair on his head. Fluidly rising to his feet and looking down at her with a half-smile, he added, "If you had been truly uncomfortable or scared, I would've stopped immediately and brought us back here. I could feel your excitement, your pleasure at doing something forbidden. That's why you played with me in the virtual world today—because underneath that shy exterior, you secretly love the thought of being just a little bit bad . . ."

Mia didn't have a good answer to that, so she lowered her gaze and padded toward the shower. He came in with her as well, adjusting the settings so that the water cascaded over both of them. Pouring the pleasantly scented shampoo in his hand, he applied it to her hair, his strong fingers massaging away the tension in her scalp.

After her hair was clean and soft, he turned his attention to her body, tenderly washing each part until she forgot all about her anger in the sheer bliss of his skilled caresses. And just when she thought he was done, he knelt down and brought her to another peak with his mouth, his lips and tongue soft and gentle on her sensitive flesh.

Utterly relaxed and incredibly sleepy, Mia barely felt him toweling her off and carrying her to bed. As soon as her head touched the pillow, she passed out, not even cognizant of lying in his warm embrace.

CHAPTER NINE

The next morning, Mia woke up with the memory of their virtual sex session fresh in her mind.

She still couldn't believe that Korum had done that to her—that he had made her believe he was fucking her in public, of all things—and she couldn't believe she had responded like that, despite her feelings of embarrassment and humiliation. Even now, she could feel herself getting wet at the thought, and she cursed her own susceptibility to him. He seemed to know her sexual needs far better than she did, and had no hesitation about pushing her boundaries. She wanted to stay mad at him, she really did. But, if she were to be honest with herself, she had to admit that she had enjoyed the experience on some level. It had been terribly exciting, having sex in public like that—particularly since she now knew that there was no need for shame, as no one had actually seen them.

Stretching, she yawned and then remembered the promised beach outing. Jumping out of bed and putting on her robe, she went to brush her teeth and splash some water on her face before going to look for Korum.

To her surprise, he was nowhere to be found. Before she could wonder about his whereabouts, she heard something in the living room and left the kitchen to investigate. Sure enough, Korum was just walking in through the opening in one of the walls.

And Mia gasped in horrified shock at the sight.

Far from his usual immaculate self, her lover looked like he had just rolled in the mud, his clothes dirty and torn. And were those . . . *traces of blood* on his arms and face?

Seeing her standing there, Korum flashed her a quick grin, his teeth startlingly white in his dirt-streaked face. "You woke up early. I was hoping you'd still be asleep and I'd have a chance to shower before you saw me like this."

Mia finally found her tongue. "What happened? Are you all right?"

He laughed, his eyes glittering with excitement. "I'm fine. I was just out playing *defrebs*—it's a type of sport I enjoy."

"Oh . . ." Mia exhaled in relief. "So it's like a ball game or something?"

"More like a type of martial arts," he explained, walking toward the bathroom.

Curious, Mia followed him there, watching as he stripped off his dirty clothes, dropping them on the floor and revealing the magnificent body underneath. He smelled deliciously sweaty, and his golden skin gleamed with perspiration. He looked like a warrior fresh from battle, and she could now see that those were definitely scratches and bloody streaks on his arms and legs.

"Is that what you do for exercise? Martial arts?" she asked, perching on the edge of the jacuzzi as he turned on the shower, adjusting the controls. The dirty clothes had already disappeared, having been absorbed into one of the walls, and the floor was again spotless. Another useful function of the house, Mia guessed.

"Pretty much," he admitted, stepping under the water. His voice sounded a little muffled by the water spray, so she came closer to hear him better. "We rarely exercise the way many modern humans do, in a gym environment or doing only one type of physical activity. Instead, we usually engage in some type of sports. Defrebs is particularly popular because it's the closest we get to fighting outside of the Arena—"

"Arena?"

"Ah, you haven't gotten to that part of your reading yet . . ." He paused for a few seconds, lathering his hair and rinsing out the shampoo before continuing. "The Arena is a place where our citizens get to resolve certain irreconcilable differences. If, let's say, I believe that someone has done me irreparable harm, I can challenge him to the Arena—and he would have to accept my challenge or lose much of his standing."

Mia looked at the foggy shower glass with surprise. "So what would you do in the Arena? Fight?"

"Exactly. No weapons are allowed, but everything else goes. The goal is to win, to subdue your enemy completely while everyone watches . . ."

Mia laughed incredulously. "What, like gladiators in ancient Rome?"

"Where do you think the Romans got the idea?"

"What? Seriously?"

Korum shut off the water and opened the door, grabbing a towel from a nearby rack. "Absolutely. The same group of scientists I told you about earlier—the ones who had been the source of many of your Greek and Roman myths—they're responsible for that as well. A couple of them missed that aspect of life on Krina, so they gradually introduced the tradition into Roman culture and then it took on a life of its own. We were quite surprised, actually, how long the games persisted and how popular they became."

Mia could hardly believe her ears. "And you still have these games? In the modern era?"

"Sure," he said, his eyes bright with golden undertones. "It's a way for us to satisfy certain . . . urges . . . that would otherwise get in the way of a peaceful and prosperous society."

Urges? She blinked, watching him warily as he finished drying himself off. So the Krinar did still have the violent tendencies she'd just finished reading about. No wonder there had been so many rumors about their brutality during the days of the Great Panic—

Before she could analyze that thought any further, he came up to her and lifted her up by the waist. Startled, Mia grabbed his shoulders as he slanted his mouth over hers, kissing her with tightly leashed aggression. Playing the sport had clearly excited him, and she could feel his cock hardening against her leg even through the thick fabric of her robe. Her own response was instantaneous, her sex clenching with desire and her nipples pinching into tight buds.

Sensing her arousal, he growled low in his throat and backed her up against the wall, his hands tearing at the tie holding her robe together. Bending his right knee, he set her astride it, causing her naked sex to grind against his leg, and Mia moaned into his mouth, the pressure on her clitoris turning her on even more. His hands migrated lower, grabbing her thighs and opening them wide, and then he was inside her, impaling her with no further preliminaries.

Mia cried out at the hard force of his entry; as aroused as she was, he was still too large for her to accommodate easily, and her delicate inner channel felt stretched to the point of pain. He paused for a second, letting her adjust, and then he slowly began thrusting, still holding her legs open, preventing her from controlling the sexual act in any way. The thick head of his cock nudged her G-spot with each stroke, and the wide-open position allowed his pelvis to press against her clitoris each time he bottomed inside her, causing the pressure to build further and further.

Finally, she climaxed with a scream, her entire body spasming in his arms. Unable to resist the rhythmic pulsations of her inner muscles, he came too, groaning harshly against her ear.

Panting, Mia hung in his grasp until he carefully lowered her to the ground, slowly withdrawing from her and handing her a tissue.

Her knees wobbled a little, and he held her up, staring down at her with a slightly perplexed look on his beautiful face. "Believe it or not, I didn't really mean for this to happen," Korum said, a self-deprecating smile curving his lips. "I honestly don't know why I don't seem to have any control around you. It's like I have to get inside you every chance I get . . ."

Her pussy still throbbing with the remnants of her orgasm, Mia moistened her lips and shrugged slightly, absurdly flattered by his admission. "It's okay . . . It's not like I don't enjoy it . . ."

"Oh really?" he teased, a big grin breaking out on his face. "You enjoy it? I would've never guessed—"

Mia frowned at him, cleaning herself up with the tissue. "You did promise me a trip to the beach, though," she reminded him, wanting to change the topic. The strength of her own sexual response to him—of her feelings for him in general—still made her uncomfortable. Why couldn't she have fallen for someone less complicated? Why did it have to be this hard, uncompromising man with his domineering nature? Even Arman would've been an easier person to have a relationship with; at least with someone like him, she would've felt a little more in control, instead of constantly feeling off-balance.

"We should still be able to make it," Korum said, creating an outfit for himself with the aid of the nanomachines and putting it on. "I'll make you breakfast and we'll go."

"Okay," Mia said. "I'll grab a quick shower and be right there."

* * *

Seven minutes later, Mia entered the kitchen and saw that Korum was making something green in a regular human blender.

"What is that?" she asked him, curiously observing the strange concoction.

Korum smiled, his features lighting up at the sight of her. "Ah, I was hoping you'd be quick." Taking two steps toward her, he dropped a light kiss on her forehead and then returned to his task. "This is a blend of mango, banana, spinach, and bowit—that's a type of sweet nut from Krina. Are you hungry?"

"Always," Mia admitted with a sheepish smile. The smoothie sounded very promising. "Do we have enough time to swim before the trial begins?"

"Absolutely," he said, and then started up the blender. Mia put her hands over her ears at the noise, which thankfully lasted only about ten seconds. Once the room was quiet again, he added, "We have about two hours, so I should be able to show you some interesting places around here and then we could go for a quick swim."

"That would be great," Mia said, eager to get out and explore the area. "I was feeling pretty cooped up yesterday—"

"Of course," he said, pouring the green shake into a tall, clear cup and handing it to her. "I don't want you to feel that way. Try this—it should be quite good."

Mia took a sip of the thick concoction, and her tastebuds nearly exploded with the sweet, rich taste. It was unlike anything she'd ever tasted before, with hints of chocolate, cream, and a completely indescribable something underneath the more familiar fruity flavors. "Wow." She swallowed and licked her lips. "Whatever that bo-thing is, it's absolutely amazing."

Pleased at her reaction, Korum smiled. "Yes, it's my favorite as well. It takes the bowit plant five years to reach full maturity, so this is the first time we've been able to harvest these nuts here, on Earth. They're quite tasty and go with a lot of different dishes."

"Can I take this with me?" Mia asked, wanting to get a head start on the day. "That way, I can just dress quickly and we could go . . ."

"Sure, why not?" Korum poured a cup for himself as well. "Let me show you our swimwear."

Leaving the kitchen, he walked toward the bedroom, sipping his shake. Mia followed him, curious to see what a K version of a bathing suit was like.

Entering the room, he placed his cup on the commode and headed toward the closet. Pulling out what looked like a tiny scrap of white fabric, he laid it on the bed and said, "This is what our women typically wear."

Mia stared. "Uh . . . I don't see how that would fit me." Her parents' Chihuahua, maybe, but definitely no one bigger than that.

He laughed. "The material is stretchy. Try it on."

Still dubious, Mia put down her own shake and approached the bed.

Picking up the material, she carefully examined it.

"It goes on over your head," Korum said. "Here, take off your robe, and I'll show you how to put it on."

"Okay," Mia said, untying the robe and dropping it on the bed. She was completely naked underneath, and she could feel the heat of his gaze as it traveled down her body. When his eyes came back up to her face, they were almost purely gold in color. Mia's breathing quickened, and she could feel her nipples tightening, her body responding to his need.

She heard him take a deep breath, as though inhaling her scent, and then he said huskily, "Here, this goes on like this." Stretching the bandana-like piece in his hands, he lowered it over her head, letting go when it was securely sitting around her hips. His fingers brushed against her stomach in the process, causing her to feel all warm inside again.

Her lips slightly parted, Mia stared at him, unable to believe she could want him again so soon.

"Don't look at me like that," he said, his voice sounding rough. "I promised you an outing this morning, and that's what we're going to do."

Mia flushed. "Of course." This was ridiculous; he was turning her into a nymphomaniac. Surely, it couldn't be normal, to want someone like that all the time.

Trying to distract herself, she looked down at the bandanna-like piece of cloth. To her surprise, it had stretched to cover her torso, turning into an unusual one-piece swimsuit. The fabric looped between her legs, concealing her pubic region and the center of her butt, then ran up the sides of her ribcage and lightly cupped her breasts, hiding the nipples from view. Like all K clothing, the material adhered to her shape perfectly and seemed to be sitting on her quite securely despite the fact that there were no ties of any kind to hold it up.

The overall effect was incredibly sexy, Mia realized, and her cheeks turned pink at the thought of leaving the house like that. "Is that all I'm going to wear?" she asked, looking up at Korum.

He shook his head. "No, you would also wear this on top," he said, handing her what looked like a basic white sheath. "You can take it off when we get to the beach."

Mia wriggled into the sheath and walked over to the mirror to take a look. It seemed like a simple tube-top dress, just made of some thin and clingy fabric. Not all that different from a coverup one might wear on a Florida beach.

"You can put on these boots," Korum said, handing her a pair of grey knee-highs. "Since we're going on foot and you don't like insects, these might be the best option for you."

Willing to wear anything to minimize exposure to Costa Rican creepy-crawlies, Mia pulled on the boots. Casting one last look at her reflection in the mirror, she picked up her smoothie from the commode. "I'm ready."

"Let's go then." Grabbing his own cup, Korum led her out of the house and into the green jungle outside.

The first place Korum showed her was a beautiful grotto with two mid-sized waterfalls. The water fell from a distance of about twenty feet into a small, shallow pool and then drained into a small river. On the side of the river, there were a number of large rocks, and the grass looked soft and green. A very inviting place to just relax and read, Mia decided, noting the grotto's location.

After the waterfalls, they walked over to another, larger river—an estuary draining into the ocean. According to Korum, it was an excellent place to view the local wildlife, including various species of birds and howler monkeys. "That sounds fun," Mia told him, and he promised to take her on a boat tour one of these mornings.

Following the estuary west, they finally arrived at the beach. As Korum had warned her, the surf was quite healthy, with reasonably sized breakers pounding against the shore. In the distance, Mia could see some people—likely Krinar—enjoying the ocean as well, but the area around them was completely deserted.

"We only have about thirty minutes at this point," Korum told her. "After that, I have to get to the trial."

"Of course," Mia said, grinning. "How about a quick swim then?" And without waiting for his response, she pulled off her boots, wriggled out of her sheath, and ran toward the ocean.

He caught up with her immediately, swinging her up into his arms before she could get so much as a toe into the water. "Gotcha," he said, his eyes filled with warm amusement.

Mia laughed, the feeling in her chest lighter than anything she'd experienced in recent weeks. Looping her arms around his neck, she told him, "Okay, but now you have to go in with me. And if the water is too cold for you, I don't want to hear any complaints."

"Oh, a challenge?" he said, raising one eyebrow at her. "We'll see who complains first . . ." And holding her in his arms, he strode decisively into the waves.

Shrieking with laughter at the sudden immersion into cool water, Mia held her breath as a big wave covered their heads. She could feel the strong pull of the current and realized that Korum was likely right about the potential dangers of swimming by herself. With him, however, she felt completely safe; he could obviously resist the drag of the water with ease, his Krinar strength more than a match for the surf.

The wave receded, and Mia rubbed her eyes with one hand, trying to get the salt water out. When she finally opened them, Korum was looking down at her with a strange smile.

"What?" she asked, feeling a bit self-conscious.

"Nothing," he murmured, still smiling. "You just look very cute like this, with your eyelashes and hair all wet. Reminds me of that day when you were caught in the rain."

"You mean the second time I saw you, when I sneezed all over you?" Mia asked wryly, still somewhat embarrassed at the memory.

He nodded. "You were the cutest thing I'd seen in a long time, all dripping curls and big blue eyes . . . and I could barely stop myself from kissing you right then and there."

Mia gave him a disbelieving look. "Really? I thought I looked terrible, like a drowned rat."

He laughed. "More like a drowned kitten, if you want to use animal analogies. Or a wet fregu—that's a cute, fluffy mammal we have on Krina."

"Do you have any of them here?" Mia asked, suddenly excited at the prospect of seeing some alien fauna. "In Lenkarda, I mean—"

Korum shook his head. "No, the fregu are not domesticated in any way, and we don't take wild animals out of their habitats. We don't domesticate animals in general."

"So no pets of any kind?" Mia asked, surprised.

Another wave approached at that moment, and Korum lifted her higher, enabling her to keep her head above water this time. "No pets," he confirmed once the wave passed. "That's a uniquely human institution."

"Really? I would've never thought that. My parents have a dog," Mia confided. "A little Chihuahua. She's very cute."

"I know," Korum said. "I've seen recordings."

Somehow Mia wasn't shocked. "Of course you have," she said, sighing. She knew she should be upset at this invasion of her family's privacy, but she felt oddly resigned instead. Her lover clearly had no sense of proper boundaries, and Mia was too content right now to spoil it with another argument. Still, she couldn't resist asking, "Is there anything you don't know about me or my family?"

"Probably not much at this point," he admitted casually. "Your family is fascinating to me."

Her family? "Why?" Mia asked, puzzled. "We're just a regular American family—"

"Because *you* are fascinating to me," Korum said, looking at her with an inscrutable amber gaze. "And I want to better understand who you are and where you're coming from."

Mia stared at him. "I see," she murmured, but she didn't see, not really. Why someone like him—a brilliant K with such a high standing in their society—would be interested in a regular human girl was beyond her comprehension.

Suddenly, he grinned at her, and the strange tension dissolved. "So how about you show me just how good of a swimmer you are?" he suggested playfully, letting go of her.

Mia grinned back, feeling almost unbearably happy. "Watch and learn," she told him cockily, and headed for the ocean depths with a strong, even stroke, secure in the knowledge that she was far safer with Korum in deep water than she would be in a kiddie pool with a lifeguard.

* * *

The Krinar watched his enemy frolicking in the water with his charl.

Initially, he hadn't really understood the girl's appeal; she'd seemed like a typical human to him. A pretty little human, but nothing truly special. However, as he kept observing her, he'd slowly begun to notice the fine delicacy of her facial features, the creaminess of her pale skin. Her body was small and fragile, but it was perfectly curved in just the right places, and there was an innocent sensuality in the way she moved, in the angle at which she held her head when she spoke.

To his shock, the K realized that he wanted to bury his fingers in her thick, curly hair and inhale her scent, to lick her neck and feel the warm rush of blood in her veins through that soft skin. That was the best part about sex with human women—the knowledge that just a tiny bite away, paradise awaited.

The craving caught him by surprise. It wasn't part of his plan. He'd thought himself above such nonsense, such primitive urges. He rarely indulged these days; he couldn't afford the distraction. There was too much at stake to throw everything away for the sake of fleeting physical pleasure.

With a heroic effort, he pushed away the fantasy and focused on the task at hand.

CHAPTER TEN

After their swim, Korum brought her back home, jumped into the shower, and left within two minutes, moving like a whirlwind. Bemused, Mia could only watch as he paused to brush a quick kiss on her forehead and then practically flew out the door.

Following his departure, Mia also took a shower and fortified herself with a snack of mango and walnuts, preparing for another potentially lengthy presentation. Then, putting on the bracelet Korum had given her yesterday, she settled comfortably on the couch and immersed herself in the show.

The second day of the trial started with the now-familiar chime.

As before, Mia found her way through the crowd toward Korum's podium and perched on top of it. This time, she refused to touch his virtual self in any way, her cheeks heating up at the memory of what he'd done to her last night as a result of her actions yesterday.

Today there were fewer greetings and preliminaries. After the accused and the Protector appeared in the arena, the audience went completely silent, watching with tremendous interest as the proceedings unfolded.

Like the last time, Loris was dressed in all black. The expression on his face was pinched and strained, and the look he threw in Korum's direction was filled with so much rage and bitterness that Mia involuntarily shivered. After a few seconds, he seemed to get himself under control, and his features smoothed out, his face becoming expressionless.

Stepping forward, he addressed the spectators in a loud, ringing voice. "Dear Earth inhabitants and fellow citizens of Krina! You have been shown evidence of a terrible crime—a crime so horrifying that it is almost beyond belief. And if you were to believe the recordings shown to you yesterday, you would obviously judge these people—and my son among them—to be guilty.

"But you have to ask yourself, is this plausible? How can seven young people with no history of social deviancy all of a sudden conspire to forcibly deport fifty thousand Krinar from Earth, endangering all of our lives in the process? Endangering *my* life in the process? How can they hatch this elaborate plot, arming humans with Krinar weapons and technology? And for what? A chance to help the humans? Does that make sense to any of you?"

The crowd was deathly silent. Mia held her breath, unable to tear her eyes away from the black-clad figure standing so imposingly in the arena.

"Well, it didn't make sense to me. I know my son, and he has his faults—but would-be mass murderer is not among them. And that's why I had to step forward and take on the role of the Protector—because this trial is a farce. It's a very real attack on these young people, and I have no choice but to defend them—"

Turning around for a quick second, Mia peeked at Korum, trying to see his reaction to all of this. There was a look of calm amusement on his face, and he seemed to be watching the proceedings with polite attentiveness.

"I have spoken with Rafor and each of his friends extensively, and none of their stories match," Loris continued. "In fact, they are downright confused. So confused that they don't recall doing anything along the lines of what they have been accused of—so confused that they can barely remember many of the key events of the past year . . .

"Now I know what many of you are thinking. Obviously, if they were guilty, pretending not to remember would be a good way to stall the proceedings, to cast some doubt on the validity of these accusations. And that was my initial thought as well . . . which is why I commissioned a memory scan to be done by the leading mind experts based here on Earth. Four different mind laboratories have performed their examinations—laboratories based in Arizona, Thailand, Fiji, and Hawaii—and the results are indisputable.

"All seven of the accused have had their memories tampered with."

A shocked murmur ran through the crowd, and Mia could see the surprised looks on the Councilors' faces. Sneaking another look behind her, she could see that there was now a very slight, almost imperceptible frown on Korum's face. He seemed puzzled.

"Now many of you know that there aren't many people capable of doing something like that. In fact, I believe that there are fewer than thirty individuals on this planet who have anything to do with mind manipulation. However, one esteemed member of the Council does comes to mind—"

Another murmur ran through the crowd at the last sentence, and Saret slowly rose from behind the podium. "Are you accusing *me* of something?" he asked in a tone of utter disbelief.

"Yes, Saret," Loris said, and Mia could hear the barely suppressed rage in his voice again. "I am accusing you and your friend Korum of tampering with the memories of my son and the others. I am accusing you of violating their minds with the goal of advancing your own political agenda. I am accusing Korum of staging the whole sequence of events, right down to the attack on the colonies, with the sole purpose of destroying me and upsetting the balance of power on this Council to satisfy his own insatiable ambition. And I am accusing you of helping him cover his tracks by mind-raping my son and the other young people standing in front of you here today!"

The crowd broke out into a cacophony of arguments and shocked exclamations, and Mia turned around again to look at Korum. She had no idea how to react to Loris's words. Could there be any truth to them?

Korum was sitting there outwardly calm, his expression completely unreadable. Only the faint yellow striations around his pupils gave away any hint of the emotion inside. Getting up slowly, he approached the center of the arena where the Protector was standing.

"Very nicely done, Loris," Korum said, his tone light and mocking. "That was quite creative. I have to say, I wouldn't have expected you to go in this direction at all—though I can see why you would. Kill two birds with one stone and all that . . . Of course, there are still all the recordings, not to mention all the witnesses, that clearly show your son and his cohorts acting quite rationally, with no trace of mental confusion whatsoever—"

"Those recordings are worthless," interrupted Loris, his face taut with barely controlled anger. "As we all know, someone of your technological prowess can fake anything along those lines—"

"I will gladly submit the recordings for examination by the experts," Korum said, shrugging nonchalantly. "You can even choose some of these experts—as long as they stake their reputation on the veracity of the results. And of course, other Councilors have already interrogated the witnesses. Councilors, was there anything in anyone's story to contradict the recordings?"

Arus rose in response. Swallowing nervously, Mia watched as yet another one of Korum's opponents walked toward the center of the arena. What if he sided with Loris? Would Korum be in trouble then? She couldn't bear the thought of anything happening to him as a result of these accusations.

"I will speak on behalf of the Council," Arus said in a deep, calm voice. Once again, there was something about the open, straightforward look on his face that made Mia want to trust him, to like him. A very useful trait for a politician to have, she realized—especially for an ambassador.

"As much as I'd like to support Loris's quest to protect his son," he said, "there is no doubt that all the witnesses interviewed thus far—from human Resistance members to the guardians involved in the operation— told a very similar story. And unfortunately, Loris, the story substantiates the recordings." There seemed to be genuine regret in Arus's voice as he was saying this.

"Witnesses can be bribed—"

Arus shook his head. "Not so many. We have gathered over fifty testimonies from completely different individuals, both human and Krinar. I'm sorry, Loris, but there are simply too many of them."

"Then how do you explain the memory loss?" Loris asked bitterly, staring at Arus with resentment.

"I can't explain that," Arus admitted. "The Council will have to investigate the matter—"

"I can perhaps venture a guess," Korum said, and Mia could practically feel the buzz of anticipation in the crowd. "There is a human trial defense strategy that's frequently utilized in developed countries. It involves trying to prove that the accused is insane, mentally incapable of standing trial. Because, you see, if they are judged to be mentally ill, then they can't be held responsible for their actions—and instead of getting punished, they are sent for treatment.

"Now the Protector is fully aware that the evidence points to the guilt of the accused. Of course, he can't claim that his son is insane and therefore didn't know what he was doing. No, he can't claim that at all— but he *can* say that his son's mind has been tampered with, that he's had his memories forcibly erased. Of course, the fact of the matter is there is only one person who would benefit from Rafor and the other traitors losing their memories—and that's neither me nor Saret."

"Are you accusing me of violating my own son's mind?" Loris asked incredulously, and Mia could see his hands clenching into fists.

"Unlike you, I don't accuse without evidence," Korum said, giving him a cold smile. "I am merely venturing a guess."

The noise from the crowd grew in volume. Curious to see how Saret was reacting to all of this, Mia turned her attention to his podium. He was watching the proceedings with a slightly bemused look on his face, as if he couldn't quite believe he'd gotten dragged into this. Mia felt bad for him. Not that she knew much about Krinar politics, but Korum's friend seemed like someone who didn't enjoy getting caught in the crossfire.

Her lover, on the other hand, was clearly in his element. Korum was enjoying his enemy's helpless rage.

"All the guesses and accusations are useless at this point," said Arus, and the crowd fell silent again. "The Council will have to examine the results from the laboratories before we can proceed in that direction. In the meantime, we'll show the testimonies from all available witnesses to shed further light on this case." And with a small gesture, he called up a three-dimensional image, just as Korum had done yesterday.

More recordings, Mia realized, sighing at the thought that today's proceedings were likely to last even longer. If they were showing testimonies from fifty witnesses, then the trial could last well into the night.

Settling even more comfortably on Korum's podium, Mia prepared for a lengthy and potentially boring viewing session.

* * *

The Krinar watched the recordings with satisfaction.

It had all worked out so perfectly, just as he'd hoped. No one would know the truth, not until it was too late for them to do anything.

He was glad he'd had the foresight to erase the Keiths' memories. Now they would never be able to explain, to point to him as the leader behind their little rebellion.

He was safe, and he should be able to implement his plan in peace.

Particularly if he could manage to keep his mind off a certain human girl.

CHAPTER ELEVEN

After about five hours of watching the recordings, Mia had finally had enough. Exiting the virtual trial, she got up from the couch and went into the kitchen to get something to eat. It was truly exhausting, paying attention for so long, and she had no idea how Korum and the other Ks sat there so attentively this whole time.

As before, the house gladly provided her with a delicious meal. Feeling daring, Mia asked for the most popular traditional Krinar dish— provided that it was suitable for human consumption. When the dish arrived a few minutes later, she nearly moaned with hunger, her mouth salivating at the appetizing scent. It appeared to be a stew again, with a rich, salty flavor that was vaguely reminiscent of lamb or veal. Of course, she hadn't had those delicacies in over five years, so that could be simply her imagination. Like all K food she'd tried so far, this stew was also entirely plant-based.

It was still light out when Mia got done with her meal, so she decided to venture outside for a bit. Putting on a pair of boots and a simple ivory dress, she told the house to let her out and smiled with satisfaction when the wall dissolved for her, just as it usually did for Korum. Grabbing the tablet-like device Korum had given her yesterday and a towel from the bathroom, Mia headed to the waterfalls, looking forward to spending a couple of hours reading and learning more about the early history of the Krinar.

Arriving at her destination, Mia located a nice patch of grass that didn't seem to be near any ant hills. Spreading out her towel there, she lay down on her stomach and immersed herself in the drama of the end of the first Krinar Golden Age.

"Hello? Mia?" The sound of an unfamiliar voice calling her name jolted Mia out of her absorption with the story.

Startled, Mia looked up and saw a young human woman standing a few feet away. Dressed in Krinar clothing, she had a vaguely Middle Eastern look to her, with large brown eyes, wavy black hair, and a smooth olive-toned complexion.

"Yes, hi," Mia said, getting up and staring at the newcomer. At first glance, the woman—more of a girl, really—seemed to be in her late teens or early twenties, but there was something regal in the way she held herself that made Mia think she might be older. Although she lacked Maria's vivid looks, there was a quiet, almost luminous beauty in her heart-shaped face and tall, slender figure. Another charl, Mia realized.

"I'm Delia," the girl said, giving her a gentle smile. She spoke in Krinar. "Maria told me she'd met you yesterday, and I wanted to stop by and welcome you to Lenkarda."

"It's nice to meet you, Delia," Mia said, giving her an answering smile. "How did you know where to find me?"

"I stopped by Korum's place, but no one seemed to be home," Delia explained. "So I was actually taking the scenic route home and saw you reading here. I hope you don't mind—I didn't mean to interrupt . . ."

"Oh, no, not at all!" Mia reassured her. "I'm very glad you came by! Please have a seat." Gesturing toward the other end of the towel, Mia sat down on one end of it. Delia smiled and joined her, gracefully lowering herself onto the fabric.

"Have you been living in Lenkarda long?" Mia inquired, studying the other girl with curiosity.

"I've been here since the Center was built," Delia said. "You could say I'm one of the original residents, in fact."

Mia's eyes widened. This girl had been a charl for almost five years? She had to have met her Krinar right after K-Day. "That's amazing," she told Delia earnestly. "How do you like living here?"

Delia shrugged. "It's a little different from what I'm used to. I prefer our old home, to be honest, but Arus needed to be here—"

"Arus?" Could this be the same Arus she'd just seen virtually?

"Yes," Delia confirmed. "Have you already heard the name?"

"I have," Mia told her carefully, not sure how much she should say to someone who was apparently with Korum's opponent. "He's on the

Council, right?"

Delia nodded. "Yes, and he's also in charge of relations with the human governments."

"Oh, yeah, that's right," Mia said, trying to figure out how much the girl knew about the apparent tension between their lovers.

As though reading her mind, Delia gave her a reassuring look. "You don't have to worry, Mia," she told her. "Even though our *cheren* have had their share of political differences, I'm not here as Arus's representative or anything like that. I just thought you might be feeling a little overwhelmed with everything and could use someone to talk to—"

Mia gave her a sheepish smile. "I'm sorry, I didn't mean to imply—"

Delia smiled back. "You didn't. Don't worry about it. I just wanted to clear up any misunderstanding and set your mind at ease."

"So how long have you and Arus been together?" Mia asked, eager to change the subject. "And is that what you would call Arus, your cheren?"

"Yes," Delia said. "Cheren is what a charl would call his or her lover."

"I see." Now she had a Krinar term for what Korum was to her. "So when did you meet Arus? Was it when they first arrived?"

"I met him a long time ago." Delia gave her a calm smile. "What about you? Have you been with Korum long?"

Mia shook her head. "Not at all. I only met him about a month ago in New York, in Central Park."

"When you were part of the Resistance?" Delia asked, staring at her with those large, liquid brown eyes.

Mia flushed slightly. Everyone in Lenkarda seemed to know her involvement with the attempted attack on the colonies. "No," she said. "I only met the Resistance fighters later."

"So you became Korum's charl first and *then* joined the Resistance?" Delia seemed perplexed by that sequence of events.

Mia sighed. "They approached me soon after I met him, and I agreed to help. I thought I was doing the right thing at the time."

"I see," Delia said, studying her carefully. "I guess Korum is not the easiest cheren, is he?"

The color in Mia's cheeks intensified. "I'm not sure what you mean," she said, staring at Delia with a slight frown on her face.

"I'm sorry." Delia looked apologetic. "I didn't mean to pry into your relationship. It's just that you seem so young and vulnerable . . ."

"I can't be that much younger than you," Mia said, somewhat offended by the girl's assumption.

Delia laughed, shaking her head ruefully. "I'm sorry, Mia. I put my foot in it again, didn't I? Look, I didn't mean to insult you in any way . . . All I wanted to say is that I know how difficult it can be in the beginning, being involved with one of them. Your cheren also has a certain reputation for ruthlessness, and I guess I just wanted to make sure that you're okay—"

"I'm fine," Mia said, frowning at Delia again. She didn't need to hear about Korum's reputation from this girl; she knew better than anyone just how ruthless her lover could be.

"Of course," Delia said gently. "I can see that you are."

"How did you meet Arus anyway?" Mia asked, wanting to shift the conversation in a different direction.

Delia smiled. "It's a long story. If you'd like, I can tell you sometime." Getting to her feet, she said, "Arus just told me that the trial is over and he's on his way home. I should be getting back. It was really nice to meet you, Mia. I hope we get to see each other again soon."

Mia nodded and got up also. "Thanks, it was really nice to meet you, too. I should probably head back as well."

"That's not a bad idea," Delia said, still smiling. "I'm sure Korum will be wondering where you are."

Mia waved her hand dismissively. "Oh, he knows, with the shining and all."

"Of course," Delia said, and for a second, there was something resembling pity on her beautifully serene face. Before Mia could analyze it further, the girl added, "Listen, Maria is organizing a little get-together on the beach in about three weeks—a picnic of sorts, if you will. It's her birthday, and she mentioned that she wanted me to invite you if I saw you today. Most of the charl from Lenkarda will be there, and it might be a good way for you to meet some more of us and make some friends . . ."

A charl beach party? Mia grinned, excited at the idea. "Oh, I'll definitely be there," she promised.

"That's great," Delia said, the smile returning to her face. "We'll see you there then." And raising her hand, she lightly brushed her knuckles down Mia's cheek in a gesture that almost seemed like a caress. Surprised, Mia lifted her hand to her cheek, but Delia was already walking away, her graceful figure disappearing into the trees.

* * *

Entering the house, Mia heard rhythmic thumping sounds coming from the kitchen. Curious, she went to investigate and saw that Korum was already there, chopping up some vegetables for dinner. Mia's stomach grumbled, and she realized that she was quite hungry.

Seeing her walking in, Korum looked up from his task and gave her a slow smile that made her feel warm inside. "Well, hello there. I was just beginning to wonder if I'll have to go searching through the woods for you. You didn't get lost, did you?"

"No," Mia told him, grinning. "I just met another charl, actually. A girl named Delia . . . and she invited me to a beach party!"

"Delia? Arus's charl?"

Mia nodded enthusiastically. "Do you know her?"

"Not well," Korum said. "I've met her a few times throughout the years." He didn't seem particularly happy at this turn of events, his expression cooling significantly.

"You don't like her?" Mia asked, some of her earlier excitement fading. "Or is it just because she's with Arus?"

Korum shrugged. "I don't have anything against her," he said. "What did you talk to her about? And what beach party is this?"

"It's Maria's birthday, and she's organizing a get-together for the charl living here in Lenkarda," Mia told him. "And we really didn't have a chance to talk much. Delia said she's been with Arus for a long time—I think she must've met him shortly after you guys arrived. Mostly she was just being friendly, though. Oh, and she told me a new term I've never heard before: cheren."

Korum smiled, and Mia thought he almost looked relieved. "Yes, that's what you would call me."

"What does it mean, exactly? Is there a comparable human word for it?"

"No, there isn't," Korum said. "Just as there isn't one for charl. It's unique to the Krinar language."

"I see," Mia said, walking over to the table and sitting down. "Well, the beach party will be in three weeks. It's all right if I go, right?"

"Of course," he said, looking up to give her a warm smile. "You should definitely go if you want, make some friends. I think Maria is very nice, and she seemed to like you quite a bit yesterday."

"I liked her, too," Mia admitted, smiling at the thought of seeing Arman's charl again. "She's exactly how Latino women are often portrayed in the American media—really pretty and outgoing. By the way, I forgot to ask Delia today . . . Do you know where she's from? Delia, I mean . . ."

"Greece, I think," Korum replied, placing cut vegetables into a big bowl and sprinkling them with some brownish powder. Swiftly mixing everything, he brought the salad to the table and ladled it onto each of their plates.

Mia quickly consumed her portion and leaned back against the chair, feeling replete. Like everything Korum made, the meal had been delicious, with the familiar flavors of tomatoes and cucumbers mixing well with the more exotic plants from Krina. It was also surprisingly filling, considering that it was only vegetables. "Thank you," Mia told him. "That was great."

"Of course. I'm glad you enjoyed it."

"So I read some more of your history today," Mia told him, watching as he fluidly rose from the table and carried the dishes to the wall, where they promptly disappeared.

"And what did you think?" He came back to the table carrying a plate of strawberries.

"I was pretty shocked," Mia told him honestly. "I can't believe your society survived the plague that almost wiped out those primates. I'm not sure if humans could've gone on if eighty percent of our food died out in a span of a few months."

"We almost didn't survive it," Korum said, biting into a strawberry, and licking the red juice off his lower lip. Mia suppressed a sudden urge to lick the juice off him herself. "More than half of our population was killed in fights and battles during that time, and many others died from the lack of the necessary hemoglobin. If the synthetic blood substitute hadn't come through in time, we would've all perished. As it was, it took millions of years for us to recover, to get back to where we were before the plague almost wiped out the lonar."

Mia nodded. She'd read about that. The aftermath of the plague had been horrible. At the core, the Krinar were a violent species, and that violence had been unleashed when their survival was threatened. Regions fought other regions, centers attacked other centers within their region, and everyone tried to hoard the few remaining lonar for themselves and their families. Even after the synthetic substitute became available, bloody conflicts had continued, as tremendous losses suffered during the post-plague days had left deep scars on K psyche. Almost every family had lost someone—a child, a parent, a cousin, or a friend—and the quest for vengeance became a feature of everyday life.

"How were you able to move past that? All the wars and the vendettas? To get to where you are today?" The brief glimpse she'd had of Krinar life in Lenkarda seemed greatly at odds with the history she'd

322

just learned.

"It wasn't easy," Korum said. "It took a long time for the memories of that time to fade. Eventually, we implemented laws curbing violent behavior and outlawed vendettas. Now, Arena challenges are the only socially and legally acceptable way to seek revenge and settle disputes that cannot otherwise be resolved."

Mia studied him curiously. "Have you ever fought in the Arena?"

"A few times." He didn't seem inclined to elaborate further. Instead, he rose from the table and asked, "How do you feel about a post-dinner walk on the beach?"

Mia blinked, surprised. "Um, sure. You don't think it'll get too dark soon?"

"I can see pretty well in the dark, plus there is some moonlight. You have nothing to be afraid of."

"Okay, then sure." If she didn't get eaten by mosquitoes, then this could be really nice.

Taking her hand, Korum led her outside. The sun had just set, and there was still an orange glow behind the trees, which appeared like dark silhouettes against the bright sky. The temperature was getting a little cooler, the day's heat starting to dissipate, and Mia could hear the chirping of some insects and the rustling of leaves in the warm, tropical-scented breeze. A few feet away, a large iguana scooted off a rock and into the shrubs, apparently seeking to avoid them.

"How did the rest of the trial go?" Mia asked. "I stopped watching all the witness testimonies after about five hours."

"It was fairly uneventful," Korum said, smiling down at her. "You didn't miss much."

"Do you think anyone believed Loris when he made those accusations against you?"

"I'm sure some did." He didn't sound overly concerned about that. "But he has no evidence to substantiate his claims."

"Arus seemed to be on your side," Mia said, carefully stepping around a fallen log. It was getting darker by the minute, and they were still a good distance away from the beach.

"He has no other choice," Korum explained. "He has to side with the evidence."

"Why don't you like him?" Mia asked, looking up to him. "He doesn't seem like a bad person . . ."

"He's not," Korum admitted. "Just misguided in some ways. He doesn't always see the big picture."

"And you do?"

Korum's smile widened. "For the most part."

For the next couple of minutes, they walked in companionable silence, with Mia concentrating on where she was stepping and Korum seemingly absorbed in thought. There was something very peaceful about this moment, from the soft glow of the twilight to the quiet roar of the ocean in the distance.

For the first time, Mia fully realized just how tumultuous her relationship with Korum had been thus far. In many ways, it was like a roller coaster ride, with plenty of passion, drama, and excitement, but very few moments like this, where she got to spend time with him without her pulse racing a mile a minute from either sexual arousal or some strong emotion. When she'd imagined herself having a boyfriend, this was always how she'd pictured it—long, pleasant walks together, quiet time spent simply enjoying the other person's presence. And in this moment, she could pretend that's exactly what Korum was to her—a boyfriend, a regular human lover whom she could take to meet her parents without worry, someone with whom she could have a future . . .

Suddenly, her foot hit a rock, and Mia stumbled. Before she could do more than gasp, Korum caught her and lifted her up into his arms.

"Are you all right?" he asked, looking down at her with concern.

In response, Mia wrapped her arms around his neck and lay her head on his shoulder, feeling unusually needy. "I'm fine. Just being a klutz."

"You're not a klutz," Korum denied. "You just don't see well when it gets dark."

"True," Mia said, inhaling the warm scent of his skin near the throat area. She felt strangely content like this, being held so gently in his powerful arms. It occurred to her that she no longer feared him, at least on a physical level. It was hard to believe that just a few days ago, she thought he might kill her for helping the Resistance.

He walked for a few more minutes, carrying Mia, until they reached the beach. Setting her down carefully, he kept his hands on her waist. "Do you feel up for a swim?" he asked, and Mia could make out the sensuous curve of his lips in the faint light of the almost-full moon.

"I'm not wearing a bathing suit," Mia said, looking up at him. The night air was also getting a little cooler—perfect for a walk, but likely less pleasant on wet skin.

"There's no one around," he told her. "Except me. And I've seen you naked."

For some reason, that simple statement jolted Mia out of her calm contentment. Her lower belly tightened with arousal, and her nipples hardened. She felt much warmer all of a sudden, as though the hot sun was still beaming down on them. Staring up at him, she asked, "What if someone comes by?"

"They won't," Korum promised. "I reserved this portion of the beach just for us tonight."

He had reserved the beach just for them? She hadn't realized someone could do that. But it made sense, of course, that if anyone could, it would be Korum; as a Council member, he likely enjoyed special privileges in Lenkarda.

Apparently getting impatient with her lack of response, Korum decided to take matters into his own hands. Taking a couple of steps back, he stripped off his own clothes and removed his sandals, dropping everything carelessly on the sand. Mia's breathing quickened. His tall, powerfully muscled body was now completely naked, and the moonlight revealed the hard erection between his legs.

"Take off your clothes," he ordered softly. "I want you naked right now."

Staring at him, Mia licked her suddenly dry lips. She could feel the soft material of her dress rubbing against her hard nipples and the moisture starting to gather between her thighs. Her whole body felt sensitized, her heart beating harder and blood rushing faster through her veins. Memories of last night's disturbing—yet incredibly erotic—experience were suddenly at the front of her mind, and she swallowed nervously, wondering if he intended to teach her another lesson or fulfill some other fantasy she didn't know she had.

He didn't say anything else, just stood there waiting, watching her expectantly. Mia wondered just how good his night vision was. She couldn't see the expression on his face in the dim light and had no idea what he was thinking right now.

Her hands trembling a little, she slowly pulled off her boots. The sand felt cool under her bare feet, no longer retaining the warmth of the sun.

"Now the dress," Korum prompted, and there was a roughness in his voice that made her think his patience was near the end.

Mia obeyed, pulling the dress over her head and dropping it on the sand. She was now completely naked, and she could feel herself shivering slightly in the evening ocean breeze.

He stepped toward her then and reached out to cup her shoulders, pulling her closer to him. "You're so beautiful," he whispered, leaning down to kiss her. His hands left her shoulders and curved around her butt cheeks instead, lifting her up against him until the hardness of his cock pressed into her belly.

His mouth slanted over hers, and she could feel the smooth warmth of his lips and the insistent push of his tongue penetrating her mouth. Everything inside her softened, melted, and she moaned quietly, wrapping her arms around his neck. His hands tightened on her butt, squeezing the small round globes, and then he was lowering her to the ground, putting her down on top of their clothes. His right hand found its way down her body, forced apart her legs, his fingers exploring her tender folds with a maddeningly gentle touch. Mia squirmed, her hips lifting toward him, wanting more, and he obliged, one long finger penetrating her opening and finding the sensitive spot inside. The familiar tension began to gather in her belly, and she twisted her hips, needing just a tiny bit more . . . and then she was hurtling over the brink with a small cry, her inner muscles pulsing in orgasmic relief.

Lying there bonelessly in the aftermath, she felt his hands pulling her legs wider apart. His arousal brushed against her thighs, the tip of his cock impossibly smooth and hot. He was pressed against her opening, and Mia's breath caught in anticipation of his entry, her body instantly craving more of the pleasure she had just experienced.

"Tell me you want me," he whispered, and there was something strange in his voice, some dark note she'd never heard before.

"You know I do," she told him softly, feeling like she would die if she didn't have him right now. Her skin felt too tight, too sensitive, as though it couldn't contain the need that was burning her from the inside.

"How much?" he demanded roughly. "How much do you want me?"

"A lot," Mia admitted, staring up at him, her pelvic muscles clenching with desire and her clitoris throbbing. What did he want from her? Couldn't he tell how much her body yearned for his?

He lowered his head then, kissing her again, even as his cock pressed forward and entered her in one powerful thrust. Mia cried out against his lips, suddenly filled to the brim. Before she could fully adjust to the sensation, he began to move, his hips thrusting and recoiling, the hard rhythm reverberating through her insides in a way that made her forget all about his strange behavior. She heard her own cries, though she wasn't conscious of making them, his roughness somehow adding to the coiling tension inside her—

And then he stopped, just as she was seconds away from finding release. Frustrated, Mia moaned, writhing underneath him, unable to control the convulsive movements of her body. "Korum, please . . ."

"Please what?" he murmured, withdrawing from her. His hand found its way between their bodies, and he pressed his fingers lightly against her clitoris, keeping her balanced on the exquisite edge of pleasure-pain. "Please what?"

"Please fuck me," she whispered, nearly incoherent with need. He pressed harder against her folds, and Mia cried out, the knot of tension inside her growing even tighter.

"Tell me you love me," he ordered, and Mia froze, the unfamiliar words reaching through her daze, startling her for a second out of her sensual fog.

"Tell me, Mia," he said sharply, and his finger slipped inside her, finding the spot that always drove her insane and pressing on it rhythmically until she was almost crying with frustration, her body writhing and twisting in his arms.

Nearly incoherent, she screamed, "I do! Please, Korum . . . I do!"

"You do what?" He was relentless, completely unyielding in his demand.

"I love you," she sobbed, knowing that she would regret it later but unable to help herself. "Korum, please . . . I love you!"

His fingers left her then, and she could feel his cock again, pushing into her, and she shuddered with relief as he resumed his thrusting, reaching deeply inside her, filling the pulsing emptiness within. At the same time, his hand buried itself in her hair, arching her throat toward him, and Mia felt the heat of his mouth on her neck and the familiar slicing pain signifying his bite. Almost instantly, her world dissolved into a blur of sensations, the long-awaited climax rushing through her with so much force that she blanked out for a few seconds, barely cognizant of his harsh cry as he found his own release a minute later.

The rest of the night passed in a haze, with him taking her again and again in blood-induced frenzy until she could come no longer, her throat hoarse from screaming and her body wrung dry from unending orgasms. It didn't seem real, any of it, with her senses unbearably heightened from the chemical in his saliva and her mind empty of all thought, her entire being caught up in the extreme ecstasy of his touch.

Finally, at some point before dawn, Mia passed out in his arms, with the ocean waves pounding against the shore a few feet away and the moon shining down on their entwined bodies.

CHAPTER TWELVE

Opening her eyes the next morning, Mia stared at the ceiling as the memories of last night flooded her brain.

She'd told him she loved him, she remembered with a twisting sensation in her stomach. Like an idiot, she'd let him rip away her one remaining shred of protection, baring her heart and soul. Now he could toy with her feelings, just as he played with her body. And why? Why had he done this to her? Wasn't it enough for him that he fully controlled her life? Did he have to possess her on an emotional level as well, stripping away her last bit of privacy?

She could deny it today. She could say that he had tortured the words out of her—and that much would be true. But he would know that she was lying if she tried to go back on her reluctant confession.

Groaning, Mia buried her face in the pillow, wishing she could sleep longer. The last thing she wanted was to face him today.

After about a minute, she talked herself into getting up and going into the shower. To her surprise, there was no trace of sand anywhere on her body. Korum must've brought her home and washed her last night—or at some point this morning. She didn't remember that part at all. She was also surprised that she didn't have any soreness after last night's sexual marathon; in New York, Korum would often have to use his healing device on her after a night like this. He had probably done it when she was sleeping, Mia decided.

Stepping under the hot spray of the shower, she closed her eyes and tried to think about something else besides seeing Korum today.

It turned out to be an impossible task. Her mind kept dwelling on what she would say to him when she saw him next, how he might act, whether he would be his usual mocking self ... She desperately wished she could get away for a couple of days, just go home to her own apartment—but that was obviously not a possibility.

Exiting the shower, Mia toweled off and put on the robe. Steeling herself for a potential encounter, she ventured into the living room. To her relief, Korum wasn't there. He must be at the trial, Mia realized. Checking the time, she was shocked to see that it was already three in the afternoon.

Padding into the kitchen, she requested a plate of fruit for breakfast and brought it with her into the living room. It was probably too late to go into the virtual world of the trial; if it started at the same time as yesterday, the presentations would be wrapping up in another couple of hours. So instead, Mia curled up on the couch and tried to distract herself by reading the latest Dan Brown thriller.

Looking up from the book, Mia checked the time. It was almost five o'clock. Her stomach rumbled, reminding her that she had barely eaten today. She was also still wearing her bathrobe and house slippers.

Getting up, Mia went into the bedroom and put on a pretty white-and-pink dress and a pair of flat, strappy sandals. She had no idea when Korum would be done with the trial, but yesterday he was home by early evening and already making dinner when she got back from her conversation with Delia. For some reason, she didn't want to look like a slob when he got home tonight, although she had no idea why she cared about that. For a brief second, she thought about leaving to take a walk in the hopes of avoiding him for a while longer, but then she decided not to be a coward. It's not like she could go far, or even someplace where he wouldn't immediately find her. The tracking devices embedded in her palms broadcast her whereabouts to him at all times. It was best to just face him and get it over with.

He came home an hour later.

Hearing Korum enter, Mia looked up from her book, and her heart skipped a beat at the sight. Dressed in the more formal trial clothes, he looked simply gorgeous, his bronze skin contrasting beautifully with the white color of his shirt and his powerful physique emphasized by the tight fit of his outfit. The look in his amber eyes was surprisingly warm, as if he hadn't spent last night torturing her with the goal of exposing her silly feelings.

As Mia watched warily, he approached and picked her up from the couch, lifting her up for a brief kiss.

"I have a surprise for you," he said, carefully placing her back on her feet and keeping his hands still on her waist.

"A surprise?" Mia asked, startled.

Korum nodded, smiling down at her. "We're going out for dinner with Saret and one of his assistants."

"Okay . . ." Mia said, frowning at him slightly. "That sounds good, but what's the surprise?"

His smile widened. "The reason why we're meeting with them is because they want to find out more about your psychology knowledge and experience, to better figure out how and where you could be of most use in Saret's lab."

"What do you mean?" Mia could hardly believe her ears. "What does Saret's lab have to do with anything?"

"Well, since school and career are so important to you," said Korum, "I wanted to make sure I'm not depriving you of anything by bringing you here. You seemed interested in Saret's specialty earlier, and, from what I understand, your field of study is similar to his. One of his assistants recently left, creating an opening at his lab. Of course, there are already about ten applicants for the position, but I convinced him to take you on for a couple of months, just to try things out. Obviously, this will be a great learning opportunity for you, but you might also provide him with some unique insights, given your background—"

"And he agreed to take me on? A human?" Mia asked incredulously, her heart jumping in her chest.

"He did," Korum answered. "He owes me a couple of favors, plus he said he likes you."

"You're telling me that I can work in a K laboratory alongside your top mind expert?" Mia said slowly, needing to hear him confirm it just in case. She was nearly hyperventilating with excitement. This was an unbelievable, impossible opportunity. How many humans had a chance like this, to study Krinar minds from their own perspective? Scientists would sell their soul to the devil to be in her shoes right now. Mia wanted to jump up and down and laugh out loud, and she knew there was a huge grin on her face.

"If you're interested," he said casually, but there was a gleam in his eyes that told her he knew exactly how much this meant to her.

"*If* I'm interested? Oh, Korum, I don't even know how to thank you," Mia told him earnestly. "Obviously, this is a phenomenal opportunity for me! Thank you so, so much!"

He smiled, looking pleased with himself. "Of course. I'm happy you like the idea. As to how you can thank me . . ." His eyes took on a familiar golden tint, and he sat down on the couch, pulling her down next to him. "A kiss would be nice," he told her softly.

Mia's grin faded and she tensed, remembering last night. For a moment, she'd forgotten what he'd done, what he'd forced her to say, too distracted by the amazing opportunity he was presenting her with. But now it was at the forefront of her mind again. Was he going to act like it hadn't happened? If so, she would be more than happy to play along.

Staring him in the face, Mia buried her fingers in his hair and brought his head toward her. His hair felt thick and soft in her hands, and his lips were smooth and warm underneath hers. He tasted delicious, like some exotic fruit and himself, and she kissed him with all the passion and excitement she was feeling. When she finally stopped, his breathing was a little faster, and Mia could feel her own nipples pinching into tight buds underneath her dress.

"Mmm, that was quite a thank-you," he murmured, looking at her with a soft smile. "Maybe I should find internships for you every day."

"I might expire from excitement if you do," Mia told him honestly. "Seriously, this is more than I could've ever expected or imagined. Thank you again."

"You're welcome," he said, obviously enjoying her reaction. "Now, are you ready to go? The dinner is in fifteen minutes, and we shouldn't be late."

Mia got up and twirled in front of him. "Can I wear this, or should I change?"

"This is perfect. Just add some jewelry, and you're good to go."

* * *

They left the house a few minutes later, after Mia put on her million-year-old shimmer-stone necklace. Korum had already created the small aircraft that would take them to dinner, and Mia climbed in through the dissolving wall, sitting down on one of the floating planks and making herself comfortable. She was already starting to get used to this mode of transportation.

"Are we meeting them at a restaurant?" she asked, curious if such a thing existed in Lenkarda. Thus far, the only meal she'd had outside of

Korum's home was at Arman's.

Korum nodded. "Something like that. It's called the Food Hall, and we get a private booth there. The idea is similar to a human restaurant, but there are no waiters of any kind. The food tends to be much fancier than what you'd get at home, with more exotic ingredients than something my house or I would typically go for."

"So do Ks meet at this Food Hall, just as we would go to a restaurant to socialize?"

"Exactly," Korum confirmed. "It's a popular place for business meetings and other such occasions. Dates, also, but most prefer a bit more privacy for that."

"Why?" Mia asked as the little aircraft took off soundlessly.

"Sex in public is considered rude," Korum explained, looking at her with a wicked smile. "And dates frequently result in sex."

Mia felt her face getting warm. "I see. More frequently than in human society?"

"Probably—though I haven't seen any hard data to substantiate that assumption. Our society tends to be much more liberal about such matters. With the exception of mated couples, everyone's on birth control, so we don't have to worry about unwanted pregnancies. Also, there is no such thing as a sexually transmitted disease among the Krinar. There's really no reason for us not to enjoy ourselves."

Mia suddenly felt extremely and irrationally jealous, imagining Korum "enjoying himself" with some unknown Krinar female. He'd told her she was the only woman in his life and had been ever since they met, and she believed him—there had been no reason for him to lie. Still, she couldn't get the images of Korum entwined with some beautiful K woman out of her mind.

Before she could ask him any more questions, the aircraft landed softly in front of a large white building. Shaped similarly to Korum's house, it was also an elongated cube with rounded corners, only much bigger in size.

Korum exited first and then held his hand out to her. Mia accepted it, gripping his palm tightly. This was her first public outing in Lenkarda, and she felt both excited and nervous about encountering other Krinar. Mostly, though, she hoped she wouldn't seem like an idiot to Saret and his assistant. She wished she'd had a chance to review notes from some of her classes, just in case they decided to quiz her on what she'd learned thus far in her psychology studies.

Holding her hand, Korum led her toward the building. As they approached, the wall dissolved to let them in, and they entered a large hallway with opaque walls and a transparent ceiling. Nobody came out to greet them, but there were a number of Ks milling about, both males and females, dressed in a mix of formal and casual clothing.

At their entrance, several dozen heads turned their way, and Mia gripped Korum's hand tighter, startled to be the center of attention. Korum, however, didn't acknowledge the stares in any way, walking at a leisurely pace down the hallway. Mia did her best to imitate his composure, looking straight ahead and concentrating on not gawking at the gorgeous creatures who were openly—and rudely, in her opinion—studying her and her lover.

Just before it seemed like they would reach the end of the hallway, the walls to their right parted, and Korum led her into the opening. It turned out to be a small, private room where Saret and another male Krinar were already waiting for them.

As they entered, Saret rose from his floating seat and stepped toward Korum, greeting him with the palm on his shoulder. Her lover reciprocated the gesture with a small smile.

"I'm glad you could come out tonight," Saret said, looking at them both. "Mia, is this your first time visiting the Food Hall?"

Mia nodded, feeling a little nervous. If all went according to plan, this K would soon be her boss. "Yes, I haven't been out too much yet."

"Of course," Saret said. "Your cheren has been occupied with the trial, like many of us. Now, Korum, have you met Adam?"

"I haven't had the pleasure," Korum said, turning to the other Krinar. "But I've heard quite a bit about this young man."

Adam got up and, to Mia's surprise, held his hand out in a very human gesture. "I've heard quite a bit about you as well," he said. His voice was deep and smooth, and the way he pronounced certain words in Krinar made him seem almost like a foreigner.

Smiling slightly, Korum reached out and shook Adam's hand. "I see you haven't quite gotten the hang of our greetings."

The other K shrugged. "I'm familiar with the customs by now, but they still don't come naturally to me. Since you've lived in New York for quite some time, I figured you wouldn't mind." Then, turning to Mia, he smiled at her warmly and said, "I'm Adam Moore. And you must be Mia Stalis, the girl I've heard so much about."

Mia blinked, not sure if she'd just imagined hearing a K introduce himself with what seemed like a human first and last name. "Yes, hi," she said, giving him a smile in return. Korum had called him a young man, and she wondered how old he really was. Physically, he seemed to be about the same age as Korum and Saret.

"Adam has a very unusual background," Saret said, apparently sensing her confusion. "Come, have a seat, and we can chat more over dinner."

"That sounds like a good idea," Korum said, pulling a pair of floating seats toward them. Mia perched on one of them, letting it adjust to her body shape, and Korum did the same. The seats floated closer toward the other two Krinar, who had also sat down by that time. Now the four of them were arranged in a circle around what looked to be a tiny floating table. Upon closer inspection, Mia could see that the table was actually more like a tablet of some kind, filled with Krinar writing and images of various appetizing platters. A menu, she realized.

"We've already requested our meal," Saret told them. "You can go ahead and choose."

"Do you want me to order for you?" Korum asked Mia, his lips curving into a dimpled smile.

"Sure," Mia told him, happy to delegate that task. Even though her embedded translator made it possible to read Krinar writing, she had no idea what most of the dishes were.

Korum waved his palm over the table. "Okay, I just ordered for both of us. The food should get here in a few minutes."

Mia thanked him and turned her attention back to the other Ks, giving them a smile.

Saret smiled back at her, his brown eyes twinkling. "How are you enjoying your first few days in Lenkarda?"

"It's a beautiful place," she told him honestly. "The beach is very nice. I grew up in Florida, so I really miss it in New York. I mean, we have the ocean and everything there, but it's just not the same."

"Too dirty and polluted, right?" Saret said.

"It's pretty dirty," Mia admitted. "And crowded. Even in the summer, the beaches right around the city are not the greatest. And, of course, the weather is not optimal for beach-going most times of the year—"

"Do you ever go out to Jersey Shore or the Hamptons?" asked Adam. "Those beaches are much nicer."

"No, I haven't had a chance," Mia answered. "I don't have a car, and I'm not usually in New York during the summer, anyway. During the school year, the weather is nice enough for a beach outing only in September, and I'm typically too busy to take the bus somewhere for an entire weekend. Why, have you been there?"

"I actually grew up in Manhattan," Adam said. "So I've gone out to both Jersey Shore and the Hamptons quite a bit with my family."

Mia's eyes widened in shock. "Your family?"

Adam nodded. "I was adopted by a human family when I was a baby. They had no idea what I was, of course, and neither did I, at least until K-Day."

"Really?" Mia stared at him in fascination. To her, he looked very much like a K, with his dark brown hair, golden skin, and hazel eyes. He also had their way of moving, an almost cat-like grace common to many predators. Of course, prior to K-Day, nobody knew that the Krinar existed, so it was feasible that he could've been mistaken for a human. "So you only recently discovered that you're a K?"

"I knew that I was different, of course," Adam said with a shrug. "But I had no idea I was actually from another planet."

"But how did no one find out? I mean, you must've been much stronger and faster than the other kids . . . And what about blood tests and immunizations?"

"It wasn't easy," Adam admitted readily. "My parents are amazing people. They realized early on that I was not a regular kid from Romania and did everything in their power to protect me."

"But how did this even happen?" Mia was still trying to wrap her brain around such an improbable situation. "How did you end up on Earth as a baby—and before K-Day, no less?"

"It's a long story," Adam replied, suddenly looking colder and much more dangerous. Watching him now, Mia could easily imagine him filling Korum's shoes in another couple of hundred years. "And probably not a good fit for dinner conversation."

"Of course," Mia apologized swiftly. Clearly, she'd hit a sensitive spot. "I didn't mean to pry—"

"No worries," Adam said, smiling at her again. "I know the whole thing is very strange, and I don't blame you for being curious."

The food appeared in that moment, with dishes emerging from the wall to Mia's left and floating to land on the table—which immediately expanded into a fairly sizable surface. Mia's plate seemed to be a mixture of some strange purplish grain and a bunch of green and orange bits of unfamiliar-looking plants. Everything was arranged in elaborate flower-like shapes and swirls, resembling a work of art more than actual food.

Korum appeared to have ordered the same thing for himself. Taking a bite of the concoction, Mia almost moaned in pleasure, her tastebuds in heaven from the incredible fusion of sweet, salty, and tangy flavors. For a couple of minutes, there was only silence as all four of them concentrated on their meal.

Saret finished his food first and pushed away the plate, which immediately floated away. Coming back to the earlier topic of conversation, he told Mia, "As you can imagine, Adam is still trying to figure out our way of life. In some ways, you two actually have a lot in common, which is why I brought Adam with me today. Despite his youth, he's one of my most promising assistants—and that's partially because of the unique perspective he brings as a result of his background. I would not normally take on someone in their twenties—an adolescent in our society—but Adam is much more mature than a typical Krinar of that age."

Mia nodded, her palms beginning to sweat. Now they were getting to the reason behind this dinner. She pushed away the rest of her food to better concentrate on Saret.

"Korum tells me that you have a strong interest in all matters of the mind—that, in fact, it's your chosen field of study. Is that right?" he asked, looking at her expectantly.

"I'm a psychology major at NYU," Mia confirmed. "From what I understand, psychology is much narrower in scope than your specialty . . . but I would love to learn about anything having to do with the mind."

"And how much do you know already? What did they teach you at NYU so far?"

Mia felt herself shifting into her "interview mode," her nervousness somehow translating into a greater clarity of thought and speech. Drawing on everything she remembered, she told Saret about her basic psychology classes, as well as the more advanced, specialized courses she'd begun to take recently. She spoke about the paper she'd just finished writing for Child Psychology and about the internship she had last year at a Daytona Beach hospital counseling victims of domestic abuse. She also explained her plan to get a Master's degree and work as a guidance counselor, so she could positively influence young people at an important time in their lives.

Saret and Adam both listened attentively, with Saret occasionally nodding as she mentioned some of the key concepts she'd learned in her classes. Korum observed everything quietly, seemingly content to just watch her as she spoke animatedly about her education.

Finally, Saret stopped her after about a half hour. "Thank you, Mia. This is exactly what I wanted to know. You do seem quite passionate about your chosen . . . major . . . and I think you could be a useful addition to my team. Would you be able to start tomorrow?"

Mia almost jumped from excitement, but controlled herself in the last moment and simply gave Saret a huge grin. "Absolutely! What time do you want me there?" Then, remembering that she should probably consult the K who ran her life, she quickly looked at Korum. He nodded, smiling, and Mia's grin got impossibly wider.

"Can you be there by nine in the morning?" Saret asked. "I know you need more sleep than us, but I believe that's a standard business start time among humans . . ."

"Of course," Mia said eagerly. "I can also come earlier, whatever the regular time is for you—"

Out of the corner of her eye, she saw Korum shaking his head at Saret.

"No, there's no need," Saret said. "There's absolutely no urgency, and you'll be of greater use to us if you're not sleep-deprived. Just come at nine, okay?"

Mia nodded, feeling like she was floating on air. "Sure, I can't wait!"

Adam smiled at her enthusiasm. "It's a very steep learning curve," he warned. "I've been working in this lab for the last two years, and I can tell you that I'm still learning fifty new things a day."

Mia grinned again, too hyper to feel properly intimidated. "That's fine—I love to learn." Turning to Saret, she told him earnestly, "Thank you for this opportunity. I will do my best to make myself useful."

"Of course," Saret said with a smile. "I look forward to seeing you tomorrow." And getting up, he repeated the earlier greeting, touching Korum's shoulder before walking out.

Adam followed his boss's example, rising to his feet and shaking Korum's hand again before departing. Mia noticed that he didn't offer his hand to her for some reason, even though he had to know that it was somewhat rude to ignore her like that. She guessed there was a taboo of some kind about touching women—or maybe just other Ks' charl—likely having to do with the Ks' territorial nature. Since even Adam was following this particular custom, there had to be a fairly compelling reason.

Finally, Korum and Mia were left alone.

Getting up, her lover smiled at her warmly. "You did great—I could tell that Saret was impressed. I'm very proud of you."

Mia gave him a big smile and got up also, his words filling her with a happy glow. "Thank you. And thanks again for making this possible."

"Of course," Korum said, pulling her closer to him and burying his hand in her hair. Holding her pressed against his body and her face tilted up toward him, he said softly, "Now tell me again that you love me."

Staring up at him, Mia froze, her euphoria fading and a terrible sense of vulnerability taking its place. He *wasn't* planning to ignore what happened last night.

She moistened her lips. "Korum, I . . ." She tried to lower her gaze, to look away, but it was impossible with the way he was holding her.

"Tell me, Mia." His eyes were turning a deeper shade of gold. "I want to hear you say it again."

She desperately wanted to deny him, to tell him that she'd been out of her mind last night, but the words simply wouldn't form on her tongue.

Because she did love him, so much that it hurt, so much that she could barely think past the powerful emotions filling her chest. At some point in the last few weeks, he'd gone from being an aloof and dangerous stranger to someone she couldn't imagine her life without. And as much as she hated her loss of freedom, she also loved the numerous little kindnesses he showed her on a daily basis, the way he made her feel so alive . . .

He was right: she had been merely content with her life before she met him. She'd had a comfortable, mostly happy existence. But she hadn't truly lived.

"Tell me, my darling," he urged softly, his hand slipping out of her hair to gently cup her cheek. "Tell me . . ."

"I do. I love you," she whispered, staring up at him, wondering what he would say now, whether he would somehow use her admission against her.

But he just smiled and leaned down to kiss her, his beautiful lips touching hers so tenderly that she felt her heart squeezing in her chest. "Does it make you happy, being able to have an internship here?" he murmured, lifting his head and regarding her with a warm glow in his golden eyes.

Mia nodded. "Of course," she said quietly. "You know it does."

"Good. I want you to be happy here," he said softly, stepping back and releasing her from his embrace. And then, taking her hand, he led her out of their private room and into the hallway.

* * *

They arrived at the house a couple of minutes later.

During the short ride, Mia kept her gaze trained on the transparent floor, though she could hardly see the scenery below with her mind occupied by the evening's events. In some strange way, it was almost liberating to open herself up to Korum like this, to tell him how she really felt. Now she didn't have to constantly be on her guard, worried that he would guess that she'd fallen in love with him. She didn't have to fear that he would mock her for being a silly young girl and confusing sex with emotions.

No, he hadn't mocked her at all. Contrary to her expectations, he seemed to welcome the emotional aspect; in fact, he'd practically forced her to admit she loved him. He hadn't reciprocated with his own words of love, but then she hadn't really expected him to. He'd said in the past that he cared for her, and she believed him. But love? Could someone like Korum truly fall in love with a human? Arman seemed to love Maria, but their relationship was so different from what Mia had with her cheren.

No, she didn't know if Korum could ever love her, and she didn't want to drive herself insane wondering—not right now, not when she felt so happy and was so eagerly looking forward to starting her internship tomorrow.

They exited the aircraft, and Korum swiftly disassembled it, activating the nanomachines with a small gesture. Mia watched him, her heart feeling like it would burst from her chest, unable to contain the feelings within. Every movement of his tall, muscular body was imbued with barely leashed strength, his Krinar hunter heritage evident in the predatory grace with which he held himself. He was so far from someone she could've ever imagined herself with—and so wrong for her in many ways—yet he was the only man who had ever made her feel this way.

After the ship was gone, turned back into its individual atoms, Korum lifted her into his arms and carried her into the house, heading straight for the bedroom. Mia clung to him, desperately craving physical contact, wanting the incredible pleasure only he could give her.

They entered the bedroom, and he gently placed her on the bed. Lying there, Mia watched as he removed his shirt, revealing his powerfully built chest and muscular stomach. His shorts were next, and then he was fully naked, his large cock already hard and his balls swinging heavily between his legs. His body was the epitome of masculine beauty, Mia thought hazily, her own body reacting to the sight with almost instant arousal.

Before she had a chance to fully admire him, he climbed on top of her and pulled up her dress, exposing her nether regions to his burning gaze.

Without any preliminaries, he spread her legs and paused for a few seconds, seemingly fascinated by her sex.

Her entire body flushing, Mia tried to close her legs, feeling far too exposed like that, but he wouldn't let her, not until he'd had a chance to look his fill. Finally, raising his head, Korum murmured, "You have the prettiest little pussy I've ever seen. Did I ever tell you that?"

Mia shook her head, flushing even hotter.

"You do," he said softly. "All delicate pink folds and tiny clit—like the prettiest little flower." And before Mia could say anything, he bent his head toward the object of his admiration, carefully separating the said folds with his fingers, his tongue unerringly finding the sensitive area around her clitoris.

Startled by the sudden lash of pleasure, Mia cried out and arched against his mouth, her entire body tensing from a sensation so intense that it was almost intolerable. Her hands somehow found their way into his hair, tightening there, trying to force him into a harder rhythm that would give her immediate release. But Korum refused to be rushed, and his tongue continued its maddeningly light strokes around her nub, keeping her hovering right on the edge. And just when Mia thought she would go out of her mind, he finally pressed the flat side of his tongue against her clit, moving it back and forth with just enough force for her to reach her peak with a loud scream, her whole body quaking from the strength of her climax.

Panting and weak, she lay there as he watched her sex pulsating from the orgasm, his interest apparently still not fully satisfied. Once she had recovered a bit, he started to climb on top of her again, but Mia whispered, "Wait."

To her surprise, he listened, pausing for a second.

Still trembling slightly in the aftermath of what she'd just experienced, she sat up and gave Korum a challenging smile, her left hand reaching out to stroke his balls. "Turnabout is fair play," she said softly. "Why don't you lie down now?"

His eyes turned a deeper shade of gold, and Mia could feel his balls tightening within her hand. It excited him, she realized, when she took the initiative like that.

"How about I stand?" he suggested instead, and Mia nodded, liking the idea even more. Getting on her knees on the tall bed, she reached out and ran her hands down his chest, reveling in the feel of hard muscle covered by soft skin. His flesh was hot and firm to the touch, and she could almost believe he was a statue of some Greek or Roman god come to life.

Her right hand traveled lower, down the taut muscles of his stomach and followed the faint trail of hair down to his sex. Wrapping her fingers around his shaft, Mia felt it growing even harder in her grasp. She stroked it gently, enjoying the velvety texture of his skin there, and he groaned, closing his eyes, the expression on his face almost bordering on pain.

Encouraged, Mia pressed her lips against his chest and kissed her way down his body, slowly kneeling until her mouth was hovering just above his cock. His breath caught in anticipation, and Mia smiled and licked him, her tongue flicking lightly over the sensitive tip. He hissed, his hips thrusting at her. His hands buried themselves on her hair, bringing her face closer to his sex, until Mia had no choice but to open her mouth and let him in.

At the feel of her lips closing around his cock, he shuddered, and she could taste the faint saltiness of pre-cum. Her inner muscles tightened as a tremor of arousal ran through her.

His pleasure turned her on, Mia realized, reveling in the effect she had on him. She rarely got a chance to do this, to take him in her mouth and make him come, because he was always so focused on driving *her* crazy, making *her* scream with ecstasy in his arms.

Cupping his balls with her left hand, she wrapped the right one lower around the base of his shaft and began a slow rhythmic movement, taking him deeper into her mouth every time. She couldn't accept his full length, of course, but he didn't seem to care, his fingers tightening in her hair almost to the point of pain.

Then she could feel him swelling up even further, getting impossibly long and thick, and a warm, salty liquid spurted into her mouth as he came with a harsh cry, his head thrown back in ecstasy.

After a minute, Korum's fingers slowly unclenched in her hair as he withdrew his softening shaft from her mouth. Looking down at her, he smiled. "That was amazing," he told her and Mia stared up at him, slowly licking her lips and tasting the remnants of his seed there. She didn't know why she found it so exciting, giving him pleasure, but she did. She was fully aroused again, as though the powerful orgasm she'd just had was days in the past, instead of just minutes.

Climbing onto the bed, he brought her toward him and pulled her dress off over her head. At the sight of her naked body, his sex stirred again, and Mia's stomach clenched with anticipation as he drew her toward him, covering her mouth with his in an all-consuming kiss.

And then he took her, possessing her with his body even as he now owned her heart and soul..

CHAPTER THIRTEEN

Over the next ten days, Mia fell into a routine. Her days were almost entirely consumed with her apprenticeship at Saret's lab, while Korum occupied her evenings and—quite frequently—nights.

Interning at the lab proved to be a grueling and mentally exhausting job, yet Mia learned more in a few days there than she had during her entire three years of college. Saret made no allowances for her ignorance or for the fact that, as a human, she was slower at certain tasks than his other assistants. On the very first day, he paired her up with Adam and assigned them three projects, the most interesting of which was to figure out how to improve the process of knowledge transfer for Krinar children. Knowledge transfer, Mia had learned, was the way in which Ks educated their young—essentially imprinting the necessary information on their maturing brains, thus eliminating the need for rote learning of such basics as reading, writing, math, and history.

After giving her a whirlwind tour of the highly advanced technology used in the lab, Saret told Adam to explain to Mia the research they'd done thus far and to show her the necessary recordings and readings. By the time Mia left the lab on her first day, it had already been ten in the evening, and she had been completely exhausted. Korum had been furious with Saret, but her new boss proved surprisingly inflexible: Mia was either working as hard as the other apprentices, or he had no room for her in his lab. After a major argument between the two Ks, which included several thinly veiled threats from Korum, Saret had reluctantly agreed that Mia would go home at seven on most nights—except when they were running critical simulations. On those days, she would have to stay until midnight, same as the rest of the lab crew. Mia had protested that she didn't mind, that she loved to learn and would stay as late as necessary, but Korum refused to hear it. "You're human, and you're my charl. I'm not letting you wear yourself out like this," he told her flatly.

And her routine was thus set.

In an effort to keep up with the tremendous amount of information coming her way on a daily basis, Mia placed a number of work-related recordings on the paper-thin tablet Korum had given her earlier. The tablet turned out to be waterproof, and Mia multitasked by watching some videos during her showers. Korum had been less than pleased when he'd found out, muttering that she was even more obsessed with this internship than she'd been with her schoolwork, but he didn't stand in her way. In fact, he even set up a comfortable place for her in his office, where she could study next to him in the evenings while he worked on his designs.

Adam proved to be indispensable as a lab partner, and Mia quickly realized that Saret had done her a huge favor by putting them together on the projects. The young K—he was only twenty-eight, she'd learned— was razor-sharp and extremely comfortable working with a human. As a teenager, he had apparently already made a fortune in the stock market and set up his adopted human family with a sizable trust fund, ensuring that they would always have a comfortable life. He also held a number of microchip patents that Intel and Apple were bidding for and was hoping to do an apprenticeship with Korum's company in a few years. To her surprise, she learned that he actually had a human girlfriend (he refused to call her his charl). When Mia tried to pry further, sensing a fascinating story, he refused to divulge any other details. He did promise to have Mia meet her one day, and she had to be content with that.

In the first few days, Mia felt so overwhelmed that she wanted to cry, her brain hurting from the sheer amount of learning that she was trying to accomplish each day. To help her, Adam suggested that they try imprinting her with some of the necessary information, just like they would a Krinar child. Mia initially resisted the idea, but after struggling with basic data collection using some of the more complex lab equipment, she grudgingly agreed. Saret had been delighted to have a live subject to experiment on, even if she didn't qualify as either a child or a Krinar, and requested Korum's permission to try the new imprinting procedure on Mia. After grilling both Saret and Adam about the process's safety and potential side effects, her cheren gave his consent, telling Mia that he hoped it would help her with the difficulty of the initial adjustment period. As a result, Mia spent the majority of the weekend inside the imprinting chamber, her brain rapidly absorbing all the information that Saret had deemed to be useful to his assistant.

By the time Mia left the chamber on Sunday evening, she felt dizzy and nauseated, but she knew enough neurobiology to qualify for an honorary doctorate in the subject. She could also potentially perform brain surgery, particularly on a Krinar subject—although she didn't think she'd enjoy the physical aspects of that specific task. At the same time, she had—at least theoretically—mastered all the equipment in Saret's lab and now felt infinitely more comfortable with Krinar technology overall.

After the imprinting, a whole new world opened up to Mia, and her second week in Saret's lab was significantly less stressful than the first. Instead of feeling like a bumbling idiot all the time, she actually knew how to do all of the simple—and many of the more advanced—tasks that Saret required from his assistants. The three other apprentices in the lab—who had initially looked amused at her presence there—began to treat her as more of an equal, letting her share some of their tools and equipment. They were still reserved around her, as if uncertain about a human in their midst, but Mia didn't let it bother her. There had been plenty of Krinar applicants for her position, and she was only there because of Korum. It was understandable that the other apprentices thought she didn't really deserve this opportunity. Mia was determined to prove them wrong.

Now that she had a solid foundation with the imprinting, she became much faster at learning and was even able to offer some suggestions to Adam about potential improvements in the imprinting process. He had already thought of most of them, of course, but he nonetheless told Saret about Mia's progress, and her boss said that she appeared to have a natural aptitude for his field—words of praise she would've never expected to hear from a Krinar.

She loved working at the lab so much that she wondered why the previous assistant had left.

"I'm not sure," Adam told her. "Saur just up and left one day. He told Saret he was quitting, and the next day he was gone. He was always a little strange, kind of a loner—none of us knew him that well. But he was really smart. He did a lot of work with mind manipulation, which is the most complex part of what we do. Nobody has seen him since he left. I don't think he's in Lenkarda anymore."

On the home front, her relationship with Korum had undergone a significant change. After her first, rather unwilling confession of love, she felt like she had nothing left to hide, and the words now came quickly and easily to her tongue. Korum seemed to revel in the new situation, frequently demanding that she tell him how much she loved him, and there was a constant warm glow in his eyes when he looked at her. At times, she thought that he had to love her back, at least a little bit, but she didn't want to ask for fear of spoiling the fragile truce that now seemed to reign between them. Instead, for the first time in her life, she chose to live in the moment and not dwell on the past or worry about the future.

Korum's own days were occupied with the trial and all the associated politics, and he would often tell her about it over dinner. The Council had commissioned an investigation into the supposed memory loss of the Keiths, and various mind experts—including Saret—had to testify as to the validity of these findings. It was beginning to seem that the memory loss was indeed real, and the final verdict was put off until the Council could find out what exactly had happened and who was behind these strange events. Korum still suspected that Loris was the culprit, but he didn't have enough evidence to sway the rest of the Council. As a result, the Keiths enjoyed a temporary reprieve while the investigation was ongoing.

Every night, Korum made dinner for them, constantly introducing her to new and exotic foods from Krina. Afterwards, they would either go for a walk on the beach or sit in his office, quietly working side by side. Whenever Mia allowed herself to think about her life in Lenkarda, she was struck by just how different—and amazing—it was compared to her initial expectations. Far from feeling like Korum's human pet, she woke up every morning with a sense of purpose, excited to face the day ahead and learn everything her new job could teach her. Her evenings were spent enjoying the company of her lover, while her nights were consumed with passionate sex.

In bed, Korum was insatiable, and Mia realized that he had been holding back in New York. His hunger for her seemed to know no bounds, and he would often fuck her until she was completely worn out and literally passing out in his arms. Surprisingly, her body appeared to have acclimated to his lovemaking, and Mia no longer had to worry about internal soreness or achy muscles in the morning. Even on those occasions when he took her blood, she recovered with unusual ease.

He also began to introduce virtual reality into their sex life. Now, at least a couple of times a week, they had sex in a variety of public and private settings, ranging from the stage at a Beyonce concert to the top of

Mount Everest (which had been far too cold for Mia's taste). After that first time in the virtual club environment, he didn't push her too far beyond her comfort zone, although she had no doubt that he'd just begun to scratch the surface of everything he ultimately planned to do with her in bed.

On some days, she marveled at her own seemingly inexhaustible energy. While she definitely tired more easily than her Krinar counterparts in Saret's lab, she managed to work ten-plus hours a day and then spend several hours more with Korum, of which at least a couple were in bed—or wherever they happened to be when the mood struck him. She should've been exhausted and dragging all the time, but she felt great instead. She chalked it up to the fresh Costa Rican air and the general excitement of her new job.

She called Jessie after a week and told her how happy she was.

"Really, Mia? You're happy there?" Jessie asked disbelievingly. "After everything he's done to you?"

"It's different now," Mia explained to her roommate. "I was wrong to be so frightened of him in the beginning. I think he truly does care for me—"

"A blood-drinking alien who pretty much kidnapped you? Are you suffering from some weird version of Stockholm's Syndrome?"

Mia laughed. "Hey, I'm the psych major here. And no, I don't think so . . ." She didn't go into all the details about her improved relationship with Korum—it still felt too fragile and precious—but she did tell Jessie about her internship and described some of the cool new things she was learning.

"Oh my God, Mia, you're going to be an expert on the Ks when you come back," Jessie said jealously. "Okay, I can see that he's not exactly mistreating you—"

"No, far from it," Mia told her earnestly. "I actually think I'm happier than I've ever been in my life."

"But you *are* coming back to New York, right?" Jessie asked worriedly. "You're not just going to decide to stay there, are you?"

"No, of course not," Mia reassured her. "I have to finish college and everything . . ." Even if the thought of returning was not nearly as compelling as it had been just a few days ago.

She called her parents a couple of times as well, telling them that all was well and that she would be arriving home on Friday, almost exactly two weeks after she was initially scheduled to be there. Korum had cleared her vacation with Saret, telling him that Mia needed to see her family. Her boss had been less than pleased that Mia would be gone for an entire week, but he accepted it, particularly after she promised to stay in touch with Adam and keep up with the latest developments on her projects.

"What flight will you be on?" her mom asked eagerly. "We need to know so we can pick you up."

Mia winced, glad that her mom couldn't see her. She had no idea how she was going to get to Florida, and she'd been so busy at work that she'd forgotten to ask Korum about the specifics of their trip.

"I'm currently on a waitlist for an early morning flight," Mia lied, cringing internally at yet another falsehood she had to tell her parents. "But it might end up being in the afternoon, so I really don't know at this point. But don't worry—the professor arranged a rental car for me, so I don't need to be picked up at the airport."

"Okay, honey," her mom said, sounding surprised. "If you're sure . . . We truly don't mind. Are you flying into Orlando or Jacksonville?"

"Orlando," Mia told her. It sounded plausible enough.

* * *

On Thursday evening, right before their departure for Florida, they were scheduled to attend a celebration. Korum's cousin Leeta had apparently been with her mate for forty-seven years—a major milestone in Krinar culture. In Earth time, it was actually closer to fifty years, as Krina traveled around its sun at a slightly slower pace than Earth.

It was Mia's first public event in Lenkarda.

"We don't have marriage and weddings in the human sense," Korum explained, watching her get dressed in a beautiful dress that he had created for her. "Instead, when a couple wants to make a permanent commitment, they come to a verbal agreement and then document that with a recording. At that point, it's really no one's business. They don't have a party or anything like that, and their union is not considered permanent until they are together for at least forty-seven years—"

"Why forty-seven?" Mia asked curiously, sliding her feet into a pair of sparkly sandals that went with the white shimmery material of her dress. The dress itself was form-fitting, showing off every curve of her body. It was also incredibly sexy, with her back entirely exposed. Around her neck, she was wearing Korum's beautiful necklace, and her hair was decorated with a fine silvery mesh that had somehow worked its way into her hair, carefully defining and separating each curl. She looked as good as she could possibly look, and she was grateful that Leeta had taken the time to send her recorded instructions on what to wear. Korum had apparently insisted on it, wanting to make sure that Mia didn't feel uncomfortable at her first big party in Lenkarda.

"Because it's a number that we consider special. It's a fairly large prime number, and several important historical events on Krina happened in years that ended with forty-seven. Plus, it's considered to be a sufficient length of time for a couple to know if they are compatible for the long term or not. Before the Celebration of Forty-Seven, it's very easy to walk away from the union; however, the event we're about to attend tonight makes the union binding. After that point, a couple whose union falls apart loses some of their standing in society. Of course, if one person cheated or did something else to cause the union to end, his or her standing suffers the most, while the innocent party is less impacted."

"So divorces are rare among the Krinar?"

Korum nodded, smoothly rising off the bed where he had been lounging. He himself was wearing a pair of fitted white pants tucked into knee-length grey boots and a sleeveless white shirt that was made of some kind of stiff, structured material. It was apparently the traditional Krinar attire for such celebrations, and he looked simply stunning in it.

"Yes, divorces—or union dissolutions—are uncommon. However, permanent unions are also unusual. Many Krinar don't find the person they want to be with for centuries or even thousands of years, and some never enter into a traditional union for a variety of reasons. So, you see, the Celebration of Forty-Seven is a major event for us, and it will be widely attended. We can't be late."

"Of course," Mia said, following him toward the bedroom door.

Leaving the house through the usual dissolving wall, they climbed into the aircraft that Korum had sitting next to the house in preparation for their journey. The celebration was here in Lenkarda, but not within walking distance. Over the past two weeks, Mia had learned that the Krinar traveled in two ways—on foot or via small flying pods. There were no cars or ground transportation of any kind.

Sitting down on the intelligent seat, Mia enjoyed the sensation of being completely comfortable. Although it was already 10 p.m. and she'd had a long day at the lab, she was feeling quite hyper at the thought of attending this celebration. Tapping her foot on the floor, she watched as the ship took off, swiftly carrying them toward the center of the colony.

A minute later, they landed in front of a large building Mia had never seen before. Instead of being planted on the ground, it floated in the air a few feet above the tree tops. A long pathway connected one wall to the ground, serving as a bridge of sorts.

"It's the Celebration Hall," Korum explained as they exited the aircraft and walked up the pathway toward the imposing structure. The building looked to be about twenty stories high and the size of a city block. Mia was surprised she hadn't seen it on the virtual map of Lenkarda earlier.

"Is this building always here?" she asked, seeing other ships landing all around them and hundreds of Krinar stepping out.

"No," Korum answered, leading her toward the building and ignoring all the stares in their direction. "It was constructed specifically for this purpose, and it will be unmade after today. There is a much larger Celebration Hall on Krina, and that one is permanent, but there are too few of us here on Earth to justify having such a large building around all the time. The Celebration of Forty-Seven is one of the very few events that brings together the entire Krinar population of Earth. Many from Krina will also be watching virtually."

The entire Krinar population of Earth? All fifty thousand? Mia hadn't realized the full scope of this event. Nervous and excited, she clutched at Korum's arm as they entered the building.

The noise inside was nearly deafening. It appeared that thousands had already gathered, and Mia couldn't help gawking at the gorgeous creatures all around her. The females were dressed in shimmering, light-colored dresses similar to Mia's, while the male outfits resembled Korum's. Even the shortest Krinar women were several inches taller than Mia, making her wish she were wearing high heels. The building itself was beautifully decorated, with flowers and glittering surfaces everywhere. The walls were not transparent, as was usual for Krinar structures; instead, they seemed to be reflective, making the already enormous hall seem even larger.

Like at the Food Hall, the Krinar around them stared at Mia and Korum. Mia wondered if that was because they hadn't seen a lot of humans—unlikely, given the fact that they all lived on Earth—or because they were surprised to see Korum with a charl. She decided that it was the latter. Probably it was just the novelty factor of seeing a Council member accompanied by a human girl.

As they made their way through the crowd, Korum put a possessive hand around her back, pressing her closer to him. Mia had learned over the past two weeks that it was considered a serious offense for a Krinar male to touch another man's female, whether she was his mate or his charl. It was a strange throwback to their territorial beginnings. The Krinar were very liberal when it came to sex, and Krinar women had all the same rights and freedoms as Krinar men. However, once they entered into a committed relationship, no other men were allowed to touch the women without explicit consent from their cheren or their mate. In some cases, violating that rule could even lead to an Arena challenge.

Korum was particularly bad in this regard. When he picked her up at the lab on her second day there and saw Adam leaning over her to help her with one particular testing device, he had nearly flipped out. Mia had been impressed with Adam's composure in that situation; instead of cowering at Korum's rage, the young Krinar had calmly explained that he was helping Mia do her job and hadn't laid a finger on her. Thankfully, Korum hadn't done more than glower at him—Mia would've hated to see those two come to blows. Still, after that incident, Adam was particularly careful around her, always maintaining at least two feet of space between them. The last thing he needed was a jealous cheren after him, he'd explained with a laugh.

So now Korum kept her close as they walked toward the center of the giant hall. God forbid another male brush against her, Mia thought with exasperation.

As they approached the center, Mia saw a floating platform with a couple standing on it. She recognized the dark red hair of Korum's cousin, whose union celebration they were attending. It was an unusual hue for a Krinar, and Mia wondered if it was natural or dyed. Leeta's mate was as gorgeous as she was—tall, muscular, and with the typical dark Krinar coloring. They were each dressed in unusual robe-like outfits, pale mint-green in color, and stood completely still, just facing each other.

Hundreds of floating planks were arranged in circular rows all around the platform, and Korum led her to the front row. As a relative and a Council member, he apparently got the best seats in the house.

Looking around, Mia spotted a familiar figure a couple of rows behind them. Raising her arm, she waved to Delia and smiled when Arus's charl waved back at her. Turning his head to see what Mia was looking at, Korum saw Arus and gave him a cool nod of acknowledgement. The other Councilor responded in kind. Clearly, the political tensions between the two had not improved since Mia had observed their interactions at the trial.

"So what's going to happen?" Mia asked, watching as more and more Krinar piled into the building. Maybe it wasn't quite fifty thousand yet, but it certainly looked like a huge number.

"In another few minutes, they will join together and then everyone will celebrate by dancing all night," Korum said, and there was a wicked gleam in his eyes.

That gleam usually meant he was up to something. "What do you mean, join together?" Mia asked warily. Her mind was beginning to wander in a strange and inappropriate direction.

His lips parted in a smile, exposing the dimple in his left cheek. "Exactly what you think it means, my sweet. They will mate publicly, thus binding their union in the way of our ancestors."

"They will have sex in front of everyone?"

She must've turned red because Korum burst out laughing. "Yes, my darling. But don't worry, the robes they're wearing are specifically designed to give them privacy. Your delicate sensibilities won't be too offended."

"My sensibilities aren't delicate," Mia hissed at him, knowing that all the Krinar around them could probably hear their conversation. Like the vampires of legend, Ks had sharper senses than most humans, with better hearing, eyesight, and sense of smell—all courtesy of their hunter heritage.

"No?" he teased, raising his hand to stroke her cheek. "You're used to public orgies?"

Mia swatted his hand away and determinedly turned her attention to the couple on the platform. Sometimes Korum liked to play with her, telling her all kinds of naughty things just to watch her blush. Mia was not a prude, but she couldn't help her skin's involuntary reaction—and he seemed to enjoy that fact quite a bit.

In that moment, the hall darkened and the noise of the crowd abruptly subsided. A soft light came on, spotlighting the platform only. It was like a stage, Mia realized, her cheeks heating up again at the thought of what was to come. In general, she found the Krinar culture to be quite paradoxical; while their science and technology were incredibly advanced, some of their customs—like the Arena fights and now this bonding ritual—were almost barbaric.

A strange music, unlike anything Mia had heard before, began to play. The melody was haunting and powerful, and the underlying beat was both rhythmic and irregular at the same time, making Mia want to squirm in her seat. It was not dancing music, but there was something oddly sensual in it, with a few tones almost caressing her skin. She had no idea what musical instruments were used, but she had to admit that the overall result was beautiful. Korum had let her listen to some Krinar music before, and she'd found it to be quite unusual—but nothing like what she was hearing right now.

"This is the traditional bonding song," Korum whispered to her. "It's one of our oldest melodies—it dates back more than a billion years."

"It's incredible," Mia whispered back, feeling the fine hairs on the back of her neck rising as the tempo picked up.

The couple—who had been standing on the stage this whole time without movement—took a step toward each other. Their arms came up, their palms joining together, and the robes that they were wearing seemed to expand and curve around their bodies, creating a tent of sorts. Only their heads were visible now, and the expressions on their faces were calm, as though they were not about to do something very intimate in front of fifty thousand spectators.

As the music continued to play, Leeta's mate started speaking, his voice echoing throughout the hall. "For the past forty-seven years, you have been my companion, my love, my life. Without you, my future has no meaning. You are the air that I breathe, the water that I drink, the food that I consume. You are a part of me, and you will always be a part of me."

He stopped, and Mia blinked to get rid of the sudden moisture in her eyes. While simple, the words seemed truly heartfelt, and she couldn't help envying Leeta for having someone who loved her so deeply.

Leeta spoke next. "You are my mate, my love, my life," she said solemnly. "Without you, my future has no meaning. You are the air that I breathe, the water that I drink, the food that I consume. You are a part of me, and you will always be a part of me. I will be with you for forty-seven more years to come, and forty-seven years after that, and every forty-seven years into infinity."

She fell silent, and then they spoke together. "We are united," they said, and their vow reverberated throughout the building.

The music quieted for a second, and then it picked up again, only this time the beat was deeper, more sexual. To her surprise, Mia felt herself beginning to get turned on, her pulse speeding up and her belly muscles tightening at the unusual, but melodious tones. She'd never imagined that music could do something like that to her.

And apparently, she wasn't the only one. The mood of the audience seemed to shift, and Mia could sense the sudden tension in the atmosphere. A warm male hand landed on her thigh, caressing it lightly, and Mia turned her head to see Korum looking at her with a familiar glow in his amber eyes. "Now the fun part begins," he mouthed to her, and Mia's cheeks got warm again.

Surreptitiously glancing around, she saw that the other spectators were staring at the stage with a rapt expression on their faces.

In the meanwhile, the couple on the stage came even closer to each other. Even though Mia couldn't see their bodies, she could tell that they had to be touching at this point. Leeta's eyes were now closed, and she looked flushed underneath her light golden skin, while her mate seemed to be breathing harder as he gazed at her beautiful face. They didn't kiss, and there was no visible physical contact of any kind, but Mia's heart still pounded at the knowledge of what they were doing. The scene playing out on the platform was unbelievably erotic, made even more so by the fact that so much was left to the viewers' imagination.

Enthralled, Mia stared at the stage, unable to tear her eyes away.

* * *

A couple of rows away, the Krinar watched Korum's charl observing the bonding ceremony.

Her little face was pink with color, and her lips were slightly parted. He could see her small chest rising and falling with every breath, and his fingers itched to pull down her dress and expose those perfectly round, pink-tipped breasts to his gaze.

In the past two weeks, his craving had turned into an almost unbearable obsession. When he tried to analyze it logically, he knew it had something to do with the fact that she belonged to his enemy. He'd hated Korum for a long time, and the thought of taking away something he loved was exceedingly appealing.

But it went deeper than that. He found himself thinking about her constantly, fantasizing about touching her, tasting her . . . Fucking her, as he'd seen Korum do on the beach. To this day, he hadn't been able to watch that incident fully, rage and bitter jealousy coursing through his veins at the sight of his nemesis enjoying something he so desperately wanted himself.

It was incredibly dangerous, this obsession of his. He was starting to have trouble controlling himself, and he couldn't afford to let his true feelings show. There was too much at stake to throw everything away for the sake of one human girl, no matter how much he hungered for her delicate little body.

Besides, if he succeeded in his plan, she would be his.

Everything would be his.

CHAPTER FOURTEEN

After the bonding ritual was over, an opaque wall rose up around the edges of the platform, hiding the couple from view, and the music quieted down.

Her cheeks flaming, Mia rose from her seat, following Korum's example. What she had just witnessed had been far from pornographic, yet she couldn't get the rapturous expressions on the couple's faces out of her mind. Their sexual act had been hidden from view, but their feelings and emotions during the ritual had been on display for everyone to see. At the end, the music had reached a crescendo, and Mia realized that it was both imitating and facilitating their lovemaking.

Now everyone was standing. Glancing up at Korum, she saw that he was looking straight ahead. All of a sudden, he stomped his foot, once and then again and again. His actions appeared to serve as a signal of some kind because the hall was suddenly filled with loud stomping noises, as every person in the audience followed Korum's lead. Uncertain at first, Mia did it too, deciding that it was probably the K version of clapping. Korum turned his head and gave her an approving smile.

The spotlight on the stage faded, and the hall gradually became lighter. All the seats rose into the air and floated away, leaving a large empty area where the spectators had been sitting.

A different song began to play, this one more along the lines of what Mia had listened to before in Korum's house. It sounded like a mix of some kind of synthesizer, with weeping undertones and a pulsing beat. Krinar party music, Mia guessed, watching as everyone started milling about and gathering into small groups.

"What did you think?" Korum asked, putting his hand on her shoulder and looking down at her with a smile.

"I thought it was beautiful," Mia told him sincerely, and his smile widened.

"Do you want to stay for the dancing or are you too tired?" he asked.

"Oh, no, I'd love to stay!" What kind of an idiot would she be to miss out on her first Krinar dancing party?

"Well, then, let's go dance."

He led her away from the platform toward one of the corner areas that apparently functioned as dance floors. As they walked through the crowd, other Krinar stepped to the side, letting them pass. Korum nodded to a few people in acknowledgment, pausing to briefly say hello and introduce Mia to a few Ks here and there. Everyone they met seemed to treat Korum with some mixture of deference and respect, and Mia realized yet again just how powerful her lover was in the K society.

When they reached one of the corner dance floors, Mia stopped and simply stared. There was no way she would be able to dance like that. Simply no way.

The athletic grace displayed by the dancers was unbelievable—and inhuman. They didn't move—they simply *flowed* from one dance step into another. It was a spectacle unlike any other Mia had ever seen, and she tried to imagine what K athletes or professional dancers would be like—if such a thing existed.

Looking up at Korum, she said wryly, "I think I'll watch from the sidelines. This might be just a tad too advanced for me."

"Don't worry about it," Korum said, grinning down at her. "You can just follow my lead."

And before she could protest, he swept her onto the dance floor, his hands firmly holding her waist. Startled, Mia grabbed his shoulders, clinging to him as he launched into an unfamiliar series of moves.

Dancing with Korum was an experience unlike any other. She wasn't sure one could even call it dancing—it was more like being picked up and carried by a tornado. For the next hour, her feet barely touched the floor as he whirled her around in a complex routine. Laughing and gasping at some of the more extreme moves, Mia could only hold on as the room spun around her. Finally, thirsty and out-of-breath, Mia had to beg him to stop.

"That was amazing!" She couldn't help the huge grin on her face as they stopped by one of the floating tables that held a variety of interesting-looking liquids.

Korum grinned back at her. "See? You can dance." Filling a rounded cup with a pink liquid, he handed it to her.

"More like I can hang on to you as you spin me around," Mia said, laughing at the image they must've presented. She'd felt like she was flying, and it had been an incredible sensation. Taking the cup from him, she took a sip and immediately downed the whole glass.

"That was yummy," she said. "What is it?" It tasted like juice, but had a cool, refreshing aftertaste.

"It's a type of fruit cocktail. Very common at parties and other events."

"You don't drink alcohol?"

"We do." Korum pointed at the other drinks on the table. "But it's nothing that you can have. Those are designed to give *us* a buzz, so they'll probably knock you on your sweet little rear end. So stick to this cocktail, okay?"

Mia pretended to pout. After the club incident in New York, Korum seemed to go out of his way to limit her alcohol intake. She didn't actually want anything strong enough to get a K drunk, but she found it funny that Korum felt the need to warn her away.

"Don't give me that look," he said softly, his eyes glued to her mouth. "It makes me want to bite that delicious lower lip of yours."

Surprised by the sudden shift in Korum's mood, Mia reflexively moistened her lips—and realized her mistake when she heard him inhale sharply.

"That's it," he said quietly, and his voice sounded a little hoarse. "We're going home."

And before she could say anything, he ushered her quickly through the crowd, heading decisively for the exit.

When they arrived home, he stripped off her clothes as soon as they entered the house. Bemused, Mia stood there naked, watching as he disrobed as well. He was already fully aroused, and a familiar heat burned in her belly at the hungry look in his eyes.

"You're driving me crazy, you know that?" he said roughly, stepping toward her and lifting her up to stand on the couch. From this vantage point, she was a little taller than him, and she enjoyed the novelty of looking down at him.

"I'm not doing anything," Mia protested, then moaned as he pressed his hot mouth to her neck, nibbling on the sensitive spot in the area.

Tremors of pleasure ran down her body, and her eyes closed as he pulled her closer to him, his large hands stroking her naked back. His lips traveled down her neck to her collarbone, then lower, until his tongue was slowly swirling around her right nipple. Her insides clenched at the sensation.

He lifted his head, looking up at her with a burning amber gaze. "You exist. You make me want you just by breathing. Everything about you appeals to me—your taste, your scent, the look on your face when I am deep inside you. I can't go a single fucking day without touching you, without feeling you in my arms. I can't even go a few hours. And it's not enough, Mia . . . I want more. I want everything."

Mia's breath caught in her throat as she stared at him. His intensity was almost frightening.

"You have everything," she whispered, clutching his powerful shoulders. "I love you. You know that—"

"Do I?" His hands slid down her back, cupped her butt cheeks. He pulled her closer to him until her lower body was pressed against his, the tip of his hard cock prodding between her thighs.

"Of course . . ." Mia gasped as she felt him beginning to push inside.

"Tell me you're mine," he ordered, and she wondered at the dark need she saw on his face. His face was flushed and his eyes glittered with some strange emotion.

Mia licked her lips. Only the head of his cock was inside her for now, and she was desperate for more. "I'm yours," she told him softly, and then immediately cried out, her head falling back, as he entered her fully with one thrust.

"That's right," he whispered savagely, "you're mine. You will always be mine."

And for the next several hours, Mia didn't doubt him for even a second.

* * *

"How are we getting to Florida? And can you please make some more human clothes for me? I don't think I have enough here . . . And shoes . . . Maybe we should get some of my new clothes from New York?"

Feeling like a bundle of nerves the next morning, Mia paced up and down the kitchen, too wired to sleep past 7 a.m. despite getting less than four hours of sleep last night.

"I don't think I've seen you this nervous even when you were spying on me," Korum observed with amusement, slicing up a papaya for her breakfast smoothie. He was back to his normal self, having apparently gotten over whatever weird mood he was in last night.

Mia took a deep breath and plopped down on one of the chairs. "No, but seriously, I have nothing to wear. All I have are those jeans and the T-shirt that I was wearing earlier—"

"Do I ever not take care of that for you?"

It was true, he did. He always handled all the logistics, and everything came out perfectly fine.

"Okay, I am nervous," Mia confessed, bringing her thumb toward her mouth to bite at the nail before she remembered that she'd gotten rid of that nasty habit in high school.

"Why? You should be happy. You're going to see your family. Isn't that what you wanted?"

"They're going to find out I lied to them," Mia impatiently explained, giving Korum a don't-you-get-it look. "And then they're going to flip out when they meet you—"

He sighed with exasperation. "They're not going to flip out. We've discussed it already. You're going to first tell them about me, and then I'll do my best to reassure them of your safety and wellbeing."

Mia jumped up, unable to sit still. "I know, but I don't see how they would *not* flip out. I've never brought home a boyfriend before, and here I show up with a K. They've never even seen one of you except on TV."

"Well then, they'll have a new experience."

Korum was completely inflexible on this topic. As far as he was concerned, her parents would just have to get used to the fact that their daughter was now his charl. Whenever Mia tried to bring up the idea of her going to Florida by herself, he would immediately shoot it down. Far too dangerous, he'd told her, and, besides, he had no intention of not seeing her for a week. When Mia had argued that they could still see each other at night—since his super-fast aircraft could get anywhere within the globe in a matter of minutes—he reminded her of the first part of his statement. Not all the Resistance fighters had been caught yet, he explained, and thus it was not safe for her to go anywhere outside of Lenkarda by herself.

Mia blew out a frustrated breath. "Okay, fine. So are we going there by the same ship that brought us here to Costa Rica?" At Korum's nod, she continued, "And where are you planning to land? In my parents' backyard?"

He laughed. "No, my sweet. That might frighten them too much, not to mention bring a lot of unwanted attention to your family. We're going to land at a special section of the Daytona Beach International Airport, and I will make us a car there. Then we'll drive to your parents' house. Your arrival is going to be very human and straightforward."

"And you'll what? Sit in the car while I explain the whole thing to them?"

"I'll drop you off and go for a drive to explore the area. You'll call me when you're ready for me to come by. Here, drink your smoothie and stop stressing. It's going to be fine," Korum said soothingly, handing her the shake.

"Thank you," Mia told him after a few sips of the flavorful concoction. She was starting to feel marginally better. Maybe she *was* over-thinking it. "So when are we flying out?"

He shrugged. "Whenever you're ready. We can go now if you want."

"What? Like right this second?" Her nerves were back in full force.

Korum looked exasperated. "I said whenever you're ready. Finish your shake, do whatever you need to do, and then we'll go."

"Shouldn't I also get dressed?" Mia asked, giving him an anxious look. She was currently wearing her bathrobe and house slippers.

"Yes, you should. And if you'll look in the closet, you'll find an outfit I prepared specifically for today," Korum told her patiently. "Now stop panicking and get ready. Your family is waiting."

Almost vibrating with tension, Mia ran into the bedroom and opened the closet. Sure enough, Korum had prepared a pretty blue sundress for her and a pair of silvery flip-flops. There were no labels on either the dress or the shoes; her lover had obviously created them himself. He'd gotten the style right, however; the dress had the wide scooped neckline that had been featured in all the fashion magazines, and the flip-flops had just the right amount of sparkle to make them "casual daytime glam"—or whatever the magazines had labeled that look most recently. There was also a set of underwear for her: a sexy pair of lacy boy-cut panties and a matching strapless bra. Korum had clearly thought of everything.

Putting on her new human-style clothing, Mia studied herself critically in the mirror, trying to figure out how her parents would perceive her. In her own not-overly-modest opinion, she looked unusually well. Her skin was clear of all imperfections—even the freckles had somehow faded despite the hot sun—and her dark brown curls were smooth and glossy. The color of the dress complemented her eyes, turning them a deeper blue. Overall, she looked exactly as she felt—happy and healthy. Hopefully, that would help mitigate her parents' concern about the situation.

Exiting the bedroom, Mia found Korum sitting in his office, apparently tweaking a design. He had changed as well, into a pair of jeans and a white polo shirt that hugged his powerfully muscled body to perfection. On his feet, he wore a pair of brown loafers that managed to look both casual and elegant.

"I'm ready," Mia told him bravely, feeling like she was going to face the guillotine instead of her loving parents.

At the sight of her, Korum slowly smiled and golden flecks appeared in his expressive eyes. "Come here," he said softly, pulling her onto his lap before she had a chance to protest.

Leaning down, he kissed her deeply, his tongue delving into her mouth even as his hand found its way under her skirt, pressing against her lace-covered pussy. Her body reacted with swift arousal, her nipples pinching into tight buds and her sheath moistening in preparation for him.

Coming up for air, Mia moaned, "What are you doing?" His wicked fingers were now inside her panties, and she could feel them starting to stroke the area directly around her clitoris. Unable to sit still, she squirmed on his lap, feeling the tension starting to build. She couldn't believe he was doing this to her right now, so soon after last night's sexual marathon.

"I'm making sure you're less stressed when you see your parents," he murmured, and she heard the sound of a zipper being lowered. Before she could say anything else, he pulled down her underwear, leaving it hanging around her ankles, and raised her skirt. Now her naked bottom was on his lap, and his hard cock was pressing against her butt cheeks.

"Korum, please . . . I'm not sure that's a good idea . . . Oh!" she gasped as he entered her suddenly, pushing into her without any preliminaries. With her feet bound by her panties, she couldn't spread her legs wider for a more comfortable fit and he felt huge inside her, his shaft like a heated baton burning her from within.

"Shh," he whispered, his fingers finding her clitoris again. "Just relax. There's a good girl . . ."

Mia whimpered, feeling both uncomfortably full and unbearably turned on as he began to move inside her, his cock nudging at her G-spot. At the same time, he started rubbing her clit, keeping the pressure firm and steady.

Without any warning, a powerful orgasm ripped through her body, and Mia cried out, her sheath spasming around the large intruder. Korum groaned as well, his cock jerking inside her, releasing his seed in warm spurts as the rhythmic squeezing of her inner muscles sent him over the edge.

Feeling like a rag doll, Mia slumped against him. Her entire body was still trembling with small aftershocks, and she could hear his breathing slowly beginning to return to normal.

After about a minute, he rose and gently set her on her feet, handing her a soft tissue to wipe away the remnants of their lovemaking. "Feeling better now?" he asked, smiling at her.

Mia certainly felt less tense, but she was now worried about showing up at her parents' house looking and smelling like a nymphomaniac. She gave him a reproachful look as she cleaned the traces of his sperm on her inner thigh. "Now I need a shower before going anywhere . . ."

"All right." Korum grinned. "Let's take a quick rinse and then we go. Five minutes should do it." And picking her up, he quickly carried her into the bathroom, moving with inhuman speed.

True to his word, they were done and heading out within a few minutes. The pod that had brought Mia to Costa Rica was already assembled and sitting next to the house. Korum had apparently widened the clearing around his home to accommodate the ship instead of having them walk a few minutes to the spot where they had landed two weeks ago.

Entering through a dissolving wall, Mia studied the now-familiar-seeming transparent ivory walls and floating seats. The ship still didn't look like the complex piece of technology that it was, with no visible electronics or controls. Nonetheless, she knew it was capable of carrying them thousands of miles in a matter of minutes, with no ill effects from traveling so fast.

Perching on one of the seats, Mia sighed as she felt it adjusting around her, conforming to the shape of her body. It was one of the things she would miss the most in Florida—all the intelligent technology that seemed designed solely for the purpose of making their lives easier and more comfortable. She resolved to ask Korum to remake his home back into what it was before he "humanized" it for her sake; now that she had mostly acclimated to Krinar technology, she was very curious to see what his house normally looked like.

And then they were on the way, the ship rising silently and carrying them toward Florida, where Mia's parents were still blissfully ignorant of the surprise their youngest daughter had in store for them.

* * *

The Krinar watched as the ship took off.

They were gone. *She* was gone.

Watching her dance with his enemy last night had been almost intolerable. *He* wanted to be the one to have her light body pressed against him, to take her home for the night. He'd spent the next several hours imagining her in Korum's bed, and quiet rage had burned in the pit of his stomach. Maybe it was for the best that she was leaving. It would minimize the distractions in the next week.

She had looked happy, laughing as Korum twirled her around. Foolish girl. If only she knew the truth.

She would be sympathetic to his cause once he explained everything to her. She would understand—the K was certain of that.

She would want Earth to be saved.

CHAPTER FIFTEEN

"Can you please drop me off here?" Mia asked Korum as they turned onto her parents' street. "They might see the car if you pull into their driveway."

"Sure," he said, and the unimaginably expensive Ferrari Spider convertible came to a smooth stop a few houses away from Mia's childhood home.

Why Korum had chosen to make this particular car, Mia had no idea. She vaguely remembered Jessie's brother raving about it a few months ago; supposedly, it cost more than three average houses put together. When Mia had protested that a Toyota would get them around just as well, her lover had simply raised his eyebrows. "It's one of the nicer cars," he told her, "and I would like to enjoy the experience of operating one of these human vehicles. Not to mention that this is the only car design I bothered to adjust to make it reproducible by our nanotechnology."

And that was that. The little sportscar had zoomed down I-95 at over a hundred miles per hour, getting them to their destination in Ormond Beach in record time. It seemed that one of the perks of traveling with a K was not having to worry about speeding tickets; any state trooper unfortunate enough to stop them would have immediately backed off when he saw the driver.

"All right, just call me when you want me to come by. And stop worrying," Korum told her, leaning over to open the door for her and giving her a quick kiss on the lips.

"Okay, sure."

Mia climbed out of the car and shut the door, watching as he drove away. Then, taking a deep breath, she headed toward her parents' house.

The street on which Mia grew up was in a slightly older part of the city. The majority of houses there were built in the eighties and nineties, before the big real estate boom of the mid-2000s. As a result, some of their neighbors' roofs looked a little dated, with few of them covered by the solar panels that were all the rage these days. In general, the houses didn't have that glossy, brand-new look and feel that characterized some of the wealthier and more expensive parts of the area. However, the landscaping here was much nicer, with large trees providing solid shade and cutting down on energy bills.

Walking down the street, Mia absorbed the familiar atmosphere, with each house, each shrub triggering some childhood memory. There was her friend Lauren's house, where she had spent many hot summers swimming in their pool. And there were the tall oaks that they used to climb, as careless with their safety as only children could be. Lauren had ultimately gone to college in Michigan, and Mia rarely saw her these days, though they would usually catch up on the phone or Skype every couple of months.

Like many others, Mia's parents had moved to Florida from Brooklyn, lured by warm weather and affordable housing. It was a decision they'd never regretted, quickly adjusting to the slower pace of life there. Marisa had been three years old at the time, and New York had been too expensive for the young couple to purchase anything bigger than a studio there. So instead, they scraped and saved for two years—no eating out in restaurants for that entire time, her mom had proudly told her—and made a downpayment on a nice four-bedroom home in a pretty middle-class neighborhood of Ormond Beach.

Approaching the house, Mia hesitated for a second, trying to control her nervousness. Not wanting to tell any more lies, she had decided against calling her parents to let them know what time she would be arriving. Simply showing up and then explaining the whole story seemed easier. Checking her phone, she saw that it was only nine in the morning, so her parents were most likely home.

Raising her hand, she rang the doorbell. Immediately, a loud barking noise pierced the silence as Mocha, her parents' Chihuahua, did her duty by announcing the visitors. Her parents had gotten the dog when Mia left for college—as a replacement for her, her dad had always said jokingly.

Twenty seconds later, her mom opened the door. "Oh my God, Mia!"

Before Mia had a chance to say anything, she was pulled into a warm, familiar embrace. As usual, Ella Stalis smelled like lemons and some Chanel perfume.

Grinning, Mia hugged her back before pulling away. "Hi, mom. Surprise!"

"Oh sweetie, we had no idea you were arriving so early! Why didn't you call us? And where is your car?" Her mom was looking over Mia's shoulder and seeing an empty driveway. "And all your luggage?"

"It's a long story, mom. Is dad home? There's something I have to tell you."

A look of immediate concern appeared on her mom's softly rounded face. "Mia, honey, are you okay? What happened? Here, come inside—"

"Nothing happened, mom," Mia reassured her, walking into the hallway leading to the spacious living room. Mocha immediately ran away. Her parent's dog was shy with strangers and persisted in thinking of Mia as such, despite the fact that she'd seen her dozens of times. "Everything is fine. I just have an interesting story to tell you, that's all. Is dad home?"

"He's in his office," her mom said, then yelled, "Dan! Come and see who's home!"

Daniel Stalis came into the living room, still wearing his pajama pants and a robe. At the sight of Mia, his face brightened. "Mia, hon! What are you doing home so early? When did you fly in?"

Smiling, Mia stepped toward him and gave him a big hug, inhaling the familiar scent of aftershave and minty toothpaste. "Hi, dad. Oh, I missed you guys so much!"

Her dad grinned, hugging her back. "Oh, I always forget how tiny you are after not seeing you for a while. Seriously, honey, you should eat more."

"I eat like a horse and you know it," Mia told him, grinning.

"Mia has something she wants to tell us," her mom said, and Mia could hear the worried note in her voice.

Her dad frowned. "Is everything okay? Does it have something to do with that professor?"

"Yes and no." Mia was not even sure where to start. "Why don't we all sit down and get some tea? It's kind of a long story."

Her mom slowly nodded. "Of course. Let me make some tea right now. Are you hungry? Have you had breakfast? I can make some potato pancakes . . ."

"I already ate, mom, thanks. But definitely another time." Sitting down at the table, Mia twisted her hands nervously, watching as her mom put water to boil. Her dad sat down too, studying his daughter silently while the tea was getting prepared. When the water had boiled, Mia got up to help her mom carry the cups over to the table. Finally, the three of them were sitting around the table, with hot green tea steaming in front of them.

"All right, honey. Now tell us," her mom said, visibly bracing herself for the worst.

"Okay," Mia said slowly. "So I haven't been entirely honest with you guys about what's been going on in my life for the past few weeks. There was no professor, and I didn't stay in New York for this volunteer project . . ."

Seeing the surprised looks on her parents' faces, Mia plunged ahead. "You see, I actually met someone . . ."

"See, Ella, didn't I tell you Mia was acting strangely?" Her dad looked smug for a second, but her mom continued to stare at her worriedly.

Taking a deep breath, Mia continued. "The reason why I didn't tell you this is because he's not someone you would normally be comfortable with, and I didn't want you to worry—"

"Who is he, Mia?" her mom asked sharply. "A drug dealer? Someone with a criminal record?"

"No, nothing like that!" Although it might've been easier for her parents to accept if he had been. "Korum is a K."

For a moment, there was dead silence around the table. Her parents looked shellshocked, stunned speechless.

Her dad cleared his throat. "A K? As in, the aliens?"

Mia nodded, taking a sip of her tea. "I met him in a park in Manhattan a few weeks ago. We've been involved ever since."

Her mom's chin quivered. "What do you mean, involved? Involved how?"

"Ella, don't be silly," her dad said, his tone surprisingly calm. "Clearly, Mia is trying to tell us that she has a boyfriend who's a K. Isn't that right?"

Her dad was very good under stressful circumstances. "Exactly," Mia told them, her stomach twisting into knots as her mom's face crumpled and fat tears rolled down her cheeks. Feeling like the worst daughter in the world, Mia tried to reassure her. "Look, you can see that I'm perfectly fine. I know how they are portrayed in the media, and the reality is not the same at all. He's actually very caring, and he makes me happy—"

"Caring? How can those monsters be caring? Mia, they say that they drink blood!" Her mom was beside herself, her normally pale face turning red and splotchy.

"Do they drink blood?" her dad inquired, looking mildly curious.

"Only recreationally and in small quantities," Mia admitted honestly. "It's just a pleasant thing for them—they don't actually need it anymore."

Her mom buried her face in her hands. "Oh my God, I feel sick!"

"Ella, stop it," her dad said, his voice unusually firm. "Your reaction is exactly what Mia was afraid of and why she didn't tell us earlier."

Mia smiled, the knot in her stomach unraveling a bit. "Thanks, dad. Look, I know how it sounds, but believe me when I tell you that he treats me really well and makes me very happy—"

"Is he the reason you couldn't come home on time?" her dad asked, while her mom raised her head to stare at Mia with eyes that were still swimming with tears.

"Yes. We actually went to Costa Rica after my finals were over," Mia said. "I have an internship there, at a neuroscience lab, and I'm working on some really interesting projects—"

"In Costa Rica?" Her dad looked puzzled for a second, and then his eyes widened. "The K Center in Costa Rica?"

Mia gave him a big grin. "Yep. Korum got me an internship there. I'm working alongside one of their top mind experts, and you can't even imagine how much I'm learning—"

"You're working in a K Center in Costa Rica?" Her mom looked absolutely floored. "With Ks?"

"I know, I can hardly believe it myself," Mia told them, grinning hugely. "And I can now speak so many languages . . ."

"What? What do you mean?" Her dad rubbed his temples. "What languages?"

"All languages," Mia told him in Polish, knowing that he would understand her. "All human languages, plus Krinar. It's a really cool translator that Korum got me." She decided against telling them about the brain implant part of things.

Her dad's jaw dropped. "You speak Polish without an accent! Mia, how did you . . . ?"

"Krinar technology," she explained with a smile. "You can't even imagine some of the things they can do—"

"But, Mia, he's not *human* . . ." Her mom seemed to be in shock. "How can you even . . ."

"Mom, they're very similar to humans in many ways. You do know that they made us in their image, right?"

Her mom shook her head, apparently unable to believe her ears. "And that makes it okay? How did you even manage to get involved with him? You met him in the park and then what, you went on a date?"

Mia hesitated for a second. "Yes, pretty much. He actually sent me flowers, and we went to a really nice restaurant. And we've been seeing each other ever since . . ."

"Just like that?" Her mom was incredulous. "You meet one of these creatures in a park, and you go on a date with him? What were you thinking?"

She was thinking that she didn't want to die or get kidnapped. But her parents didn't need to know that. "He's very good-looking," she told them honestly. "And it was the first time I was attracted to someone so strongly."

"So you completely ignored the fact that he wasn't human? Mia, that doesn't sound like you at all . . ." Her mom was looking at her like she'd grown two heads.

"How did you get here from Costa Rica?" her dad asked quietly, watching her with an unreadable expression on his face. As usual, he was the only one who could think clearly under difficult circumstances.

Mia looked at him. "Korum brought me. We flew to Daytona on one of their ships, and then he dropped me off in a car, so I could talk to you."

"And how long are you staying?"

"What do you mean, Dan, how long is she staying? For the rest of the summer, right?" her mom asked, sounding panicked.

Mia shook her head. "I'm here for a week, mom. Unfortunately, I can't be away from the lab that long—"

Her mom burst into tears. "Oh my God, we are seeing you for the last time . . ."

"What? No! Of course not! I just have to finish out my internship, that's all. I'll come back here soon, and you can come see me in New York during the school year—"

"Where is he now?" her dad asked coolly. "If he brought you here, then where is he?"

Mia took a deep breath. "I have to call him. I wanted to have a chance to talk to you first, to explain a little bit before you meet him. But he would like to meet you himself, to reassure you that everything is fine and I'm safe with him."

"We're going to meet a K?" Her mom seemed stupefied by this turn of events.

"Yes," Mia told her. "And you'll see that there's really nothing to be afraid of." She crossed her fingers that Korum would be on his best behavior.

"All right, Mia," her dad said. "Why don't you call him? We'd like to meet this K of yours."

* * *

Half an hour later, the doorbell rang.

Mia had managed to explain a little more to her parents about Korum and their relationship, emphasizing solely the good parts. She told them how he took care of her and about his cooking hobby (her mom's face brightened a little at this), how he was genius-level smart and ran his own company, and about the incredible opportunity he'd given her by getting her this internship. As a result, by the time Korum showed up, Mia was reasonably certain that her parents were calm enough to be somewhat civil. Still, she couldn't help her anxiety as she opened the door and saw her lover standing there, looking far too gorgeous to be human.

"Hello," he said softly, leaning down to give Mia a kiss on the forehead.

"Hi. Come on in." Mia grabbed his hand and led him into the house. Pausing in the hallway for a second, she gave him an imploring look and squeezed his hand, hoping that he understood her wordless plea.

Korum smiled and whispered, "Trust me."

Mia had no other choice. Bracing herself for the worst, she led Korum into the living room.

At their entrance, her parents stood up from the couch and simply stared. Mia couldn't blame them: Korum was a striking sight. Dressed in a white polo shirt and blue jeans, her lover was the epitome of casual elegance. With his glossy black hair and golden skin, he could have been a model or a movie star, except that no human had eyes of that unusual amber hue—or moved with such animal grace. And even standing still, he projected an unmistakable aura of power, his presence dominating the room.

Taking a step toward her parents, he smiled widely, revealing the dimple on his left cheek. "You must be Ella and Dan. I'm very pleased to meet you. Mia has told me so much about her family."

Mia noticed that he didn't offer to shake their hand or make any other move to touch them. It was probably the right thing to do. Her parents were already tense enough at having a K in their house.

Her dad nodded curtly. "That's funny, because we just heard about you today."

"Dan!" her mom whispered fiercely, clearly afraid of their extraterrestrial guest's reaction. She seemed unable to take her eyes off Korum, staring at him with a dazed look on her face. Mia knew exactly how she felt.

Korum didn't seem offended at all, giving her dad a warm smile instead. "Of course," he said softly. "I understand that this is all a huge shock for you. I know how much you love your daughter and worry about her, and I would like to set your mind at ease about our relationship."

Mia's mom finally remembered her manners as a hostess. "Can I offer you anything to eat or drink?" she asked uncertainly, still staring at Korum like she wasn't sure whether she wanted to run away screaming or reach out and touch him.

"Sure," he said easily. "Some tea and fruit would be great, especially if you join me."

Mia blinked in surprise. She hadn't known that Korum drank tea. And then she realized just how extensive his file on her family had to be: he had unerringly picked the one thing guaranteed to make her mom more comfortable—her parents' daily ritual of making and drinking tea.

"Of course." Her mom looked relieved to have something to do. "Please have a seat in the dining room, and I'll bring some tea. We have some really nice local oranges . . . You do eat oranges, right?"

Korum grinned at her. "Definitely. I love oranges, especially the ones from Florida."

Ella Stalis smiled at him tentatively. "That's great. We have really good ones this week—juicy and sweet. I'll bring them right out." And blushing a little, she hurried away, looking unusually flustered.

Mia mentally rolled her eyes. Apparently, even older women were not immune to his charm.

"The dining room is this way," her dad said, looking slightly uncomfortable at being left alone with Mia and her K.

Mia walked over to Korum and took his hand, determined to show her dad that there was nothing to worry about. Smiling, she led him toward the table.

The three of them sat down.

At that moment, Mocha appeared, her little tail wagging. To Mia's huge surprise, she came directly to Korum and sniffed at his legs. He smiled and bent down to pet the dog, who seemed to revel in his attention. Mia watched the scene with disbelief; the Chihuahua was normally very reserved around strangers.

After a minute, Korum straightened and turned his attention back to the human inhabitants of the house.

"So Mia tells us she has an internship in your colony," Dan Stalis said, looking at Korum as though studying a new and exotic species—which, actually, he was. "How exactly does that work? I assume she can't really understand a lot of your science and doesn't know your technology . . ."

"On the contrary," Korum told him, "Mia is a very fast learner. She's made tremendous progress in the last couple of weeks. Saret—her boss at the lab—tells me that she's already making herself quite useful."

Mia smiled, tickled pink by his praise. "Like I told you, dad, Saret is one of their top mind experts. He's at the cutting edge of Krinar neuroscience and psychology. And I get to work with him. Can you imagine?"

Her dad rubbed his temples again, and Mia saw him wince slightly. "I can't, to be honest. The whole thing has been rather overwhelming. You'll excuse us if we're not exactly jumping for joy right now—"

"Of course," Korum said gently. "I wouldn't be either if it were my daughter."

"Do you have children?" Dan asked bluntly.

"No, I don't."

"Why not?"

"Dad!" Mia was mortified by this line of questions.

Korum shrugged, apparently not minding the prying. "Because I don't have a mate, and I wouldn't want to raise a child without one."

Her dad's eyes narrowed. "How old are you?"

"In your Earth years, I'm about two thousand years of age."

The look on her dad's face was priceless. "T-two thousand?"

In that moment, her mom walked in, carrying a bowl of oranges and a tray with tea cups.

Mia got up and rushed toward her. "Here, let me help you with that," she said, grabbing the bowl from her.

"Thanks, sweetie," her mom told her, and Mia breathed a sigh of relief that at least one parent seemed to have recovered her composure.

Setting the cups filled with hot tea around the table, Ella asked Korum, "Would you like some cream or sugar? We have coconut cream, almond cream, soy cream . . ."

"No, thank you," Korum replied politely, giving her a dazzling smile. "I prefer my tea plain."

"So do we," her mom admitted, blushing again. Mia barely stopped herself from snickering—her parent appeared to have developed a little crush on her lover.

"Ella," Mia's dad said slowly, "Korum here is apparently much older than we thought . . ."

"Oh?" her mom inquired, sitting down and reaching for an orange. Methodically peeling the fruit, she gave her husband a questioning look.

"He's two thousand years old . . ." Her dad seemed awed by that fact.

"What?" The orange dropped on the table, landing with a soft plop.

"Mom, you knew the Ks are long-lived," Mia said, getting exasperated with their reactions. "You and I watched that program together a couple of years ago, remember? It was one of those Nova documentaries about the invasion."

"I remember," her mom said, still looking like she'd been hit with a hammer. "But I didn't realize that meant thousands of years . . ."

"How exactly does something like that work if you're in a relationship with a human?" Her dad was back to being his blunt self. "Because Mia can't possibly live that long—"

"That's between me and your daughter, Dan," Korum said gently, but there was a steely note in his voice that warned against pushing in this direction. "We'll figure everything out in due time." And picking up an orange, he calmly peeled it, his fingers moving faster and more efficiently than her mom's had been.

"By the way," he added, biting into the orange, "Mia mentioned that you tend to get frequent headaches, and I couldn't help but notice that you've been rubbing your temples. Are you suffering from one now?"

Caught off-guard, her dad nodded.

At the affirmative gesture, Korum reached into his jeans pocket and pulled out a tiny capsule. Handing it to Mia's dad, he said, "This is something that should take care of the issue. One of our top human biology experts developed it specifically for cases such as yours."

"What is it? A painkiller?" Her dad studied the little capsule with no small measure of distrust.

"Yes, it works immediately as such. But it should also prevent any future occurrences."

"A migraine cure?" her mom asked, and there was a desperate look of hope in her eyes.

"Exactly," Korum confirmed, and Ella Stalis's eyes lit up.

Her dad frowned. "Are there side effects? How do I know it's safe?"

"Dad, their medicine is wonderful," Mia told him sincerely. "Truly, you have nothing to be afraid of."

"Mia is right. There are no side effects when it comes to our medications. And, Dan, the last thing I would want is to hurt the people Mia loves the most. I know you have very little reason to trust me yet, and I hope that changes in the future. If you don't want to take the medicine, it's entirely up to you. I just wanted you to have it in case you are in pain."

"Just take it, Dan. Right now," Ella ordered, giving her husband a determined look. "I don't think Mia's boyfriend would give you something bad for you. If there's even a small chance that it can really cure you, then you owe it to yourself and to your family to try it—particularly if Korum says there are no side effects."

Her dad hesitated, studying Korum's face for a few seconds. Whatever he saw there seemed to reassure him. "Do I just swallow it?"

"Squeeze it into a cup of water, and then drink it," Korum said. "It works quicker that way."

Mia's mom was already on her feet and pouring her dad a cup of water from a pitcher sitting on the table. "Here," she said, thrusting it at him.

Dan Stalis took the cup slowly and pinched the capsule between his fingers, squeezing out two drops of liquid into the water. "Is this it?" he asked, looking up at Korum.

Her lover gave him an encouraging smile. "Yes."

Cautiously sniffing it, Mia's dad took a sip. "This actually tastes good." He sounded surprised.

"Most of our medicines do."

Bringing the cup to his mouth, her dad drank the rest of the water. Almost immediately, Mia could see the tense muscles around his jawline relaxing. Smiling at him, she said, "It's working, right? You can feel it right away."

Her dad looked pleasantly surprised, and her mom's face was shining with happiness. "Yes. It seems to be instant." Turning to Korum, he said, "Thank you. That was very nice of you."

"Of course," Korum said softly. "I would do anything for Mia and the people she loves."

CHAPTER SIXTEEN

"I have to talk to my sister too," Mia said as she got into the car and waved goodbye to her parents. Her mom was holding Mocha, who very nearly followed them out, having developed an inexplicable doggy crush on Korum. "I know mom is calling her right now, but I'd like her to hear it from me as well. I told her something earlier, and I would really like a chance to explain, so she doesn't get the wrong idea about our relationship."

"What did you tell her?" Korum asked, smoothly pulling out of the driveway. He drove like he did everything else—with skill and efficiency.

"I told her I had a lover who was from Dubai," Mia admitted, blushing a little. "And I said that things wouldn't work out between us because he had to leave soon."

"I see," Korum said, and there was a noticeable chill in his voice. "And when did you tell her this?"

Crap. She really shouldn't have brought this up—but it was too late now. "When I thought you might be leaving for Krina," she confessed. "Before, you know . . ."

"Before your betrayal?"

Mia sucked in her breath. "Are you still mad at me? You said you'd let it go . . ."

"I let it go as far as I'm not going to punish you for it. But I can't quite forget it, my sweet. Not yet."

Mia bit her lip, feeling upset. "I don't understand you sometimes," she said quietly. "One minute you're so nice to me and my family, and the next you're talking about punishing me for a situation that wasn't exactly my fault—a situation that you manipulated to your advantage. What did you expect me to do? Just calmly accept the fact that I might end up as a sex slave?"

"You could've talked to me at any point and asked me whether it's true." He kept his eyes on the road, but Mia could see a tiny twitch in his tightly clenched jaw muscle.

"And if it were? What would I have done then? I would've endangered John and everyone in the Resistance and lost my only chance to help them and myself."

"At what point did I ever treat you as a sex slave?" Korum asked, and his even tone made her shiver a little. He was still not looking at her. "I gave you everything, Mia, and you kept acting like I was a villain."

Mia swallowed. "You knew I was afraid in the beginning, and you didn't give me any choice," she said, feeling old resentment rising up. "And besides, what is a charl, really? What rights do I have in your society? I know you don't treat me poorly, but you could, right? If you wanted to keep me locked up in your house, would anyone stop you?"

He didn't answer, and she could see his jaw tighten further.

They turned off Granada Boulevard onto A1A, and he drove for another few minutes before pulling into the winding driveway of a large beachfront mansion. At their approach, the wrought-iron gates swung open, letting them through.

"Where are we?" asked Mia, breaking the tense silence. She felt sick in her stomach. She hated arguing with Korum, and the last few days had been so nice, so peaceful. Why had she stupidly reminded him of what happened before?

The car came to a stop, and he put the clutch in "park" mode before turning to look at her. "Come here," he said roughly, burying his hand in her hair and leaning over to give her a deep, penetrating kiss. By the time he let her come up for air, Mia was melting bonelessly into him, almost trembling with need.

Letting her go, he climbed out of the car and came around to open the passenger door. Mia climbed out on somewhat unsteady legs as he watched her with hungry gold-tinted eyes.

She looked up at him.

"We're in a house I rented for the week," he told her. "Let's go inside." And taking her hand, he led her up the steps and into the stately white building.

The interior of their "rental house" could've easily been featured in *Architectural Digest* magazine, with its sharply designed white furniture and open layout with gleaming hardwood floors. One wall—the one facing the ocean—was made entirely of glass and provided a breathtaking view.

Turning Mia toward him, Korum bent down and kissed her again, lightly. "Why don't you go call your sister now?" he suggested, and his voice sounded a little hoarse. "When you come back, I have some plans for you."

* * *

Trying to calm her elevated heartbeat, Mia walked upstairs and into a room where she spotted an old-fashioned landline phone. When she was sure she had herself sufficiently under control and could think of something besides Korum's plans, she called her sister, dialing her cell phone number from memory.

Marisa picked up on the fifth ring. "Hello?"

"Hey, Marisa, it's me . . ."

"Mia? I was just on the phone with mom! Holy shit! You're dating a K?!?"

Mia sighed. "Yep. Listen, remember that thing I told you?"

"About your supposed wealthy executive lover?" Her sister's tone sounded caustic. "Yes, I remember perfectly."

Mia winced. "Well, I was not fully honest with you—"

"No shit!"

"I'm sorry," Mia said sincerely. "I really thought he might leave for Krina at that point and I would never see him again. I needed to talk to someone, but I just didn't feel like I could tell the whole story . . ."

For a second, there was silence. "Mia," Marisa said, sounding upset, "you can always tell me the whole story, even if it's worthy of being on the cover of *National Geographic*. I'm your sister, and if anyone can understand, it would be me."

Mia squeezed her eyes shut, feeling ashamed. "I know. I'm sorry. There was just a lot going on and I wasn't thinking clearly at the time—"

"What *was* going on? And what changed? How did it go from 'this can never work out' to meeting the parents and spending the summer in Costa Rica?"

"We worked out our differences," Mia said, not wanting to go into the particulars. "And he's staying here, on Earth."

There was again silence for a second. Then her sister said, "Seriously, Mia? A K? You couldn't choose someone of the same species?"

Mia smiled, relieved. The worst seemed to be over. "I know, it's insane—"

"Insane is putting it mildly," Marisa said seriously. "Freaking awesome is how I would phrase it."

Mia laughed, startled. "What?"

"My baby sis is dating a super-hot, wealthy alien genius who just cured dad's migraines? Hell yeah, it's fucking amazing!"

Mia couldn't believe her ears. "You're not going to read me a lecture and tell me how foolish I am to get involved with someone so dangerous and not human, and blah, blah, blah?"

"Oh please, I'm sure the parents already did that. What can I say that'll be in any way additive? No, baby sis, I'm happy for you. You've walked the straight and narrow for way too long. A little danger and spice in your life is exactly what you need. And besides, from what mom tells me, he's unbelievably gorgeous and has been around since the dawn of time. It really doesn't get any cooler than that . . . I can't wait to meet him!"

Mia grinned hugely. Her sister always managed to surprise her. "You're the best sister ever," she told Marisa. "So when am I seeing you and Connor?"

"Tonight at six. Apparently, your extraterrestrial lover invited the whole family for dinner."

"He did? When?" Mia couldn't remember him doing anything of the sort.

"I don't know. I wasn't there. Shouldn't *you* be the one to know? I thought he did it at your request . . ."

"Um . . . he takes initiative a lot when it comes to these things." Too much, considering that Mia didn't even know about the invitation. He must've talked to her parents when she visited the restroom. "So are we meeting at a restaurant somewhere?"

"It's kind of crazy that I'm the one telling you this, Mia." Marisa sounded like she was laughing. "We're coming over to your rental house. He's cooking. Still doesn't ring a bell?"

"That does sound like something Korum would do." Mia smiled, even though Marisa couldn't see her. "You're in for a treat—he's an amazing cook."

"And does the laundry, right? Unless you made up that part too?"

"Nope," Mia said, grinning. "He definitely did the laundry when we were in New York. He has this weird thing for human appliances. I think it mostly has to do with his cooking hobby, which is strange in and of itself. They have these intelligent houses that *cook* for them, Marisa. He doesn't need to lift a finger to have gourmet meals, and yet he does—"

"Oh my God, where can I find a K for myself? I'm already in love and I haven't even met the guy yet!"

Mia burst out laughing. "Hey, this one's taken! And besides, wouldn't Connor have something to say about his pregnant wife hooking up with an alien?"

"Connor would gladly give his pregnant wife to an alien right about now," Marisa said, and Mia could hear the serious undertone in her voice. "I'm so moody these days that he's slinking around the house like I might bite him. Which I might, at any moment. My emotions are beyond wacky. Don't get pregnant, sis—it's so not fun . . ."

Mia immediately sobered up. "Oh, Marisa, I'm so selfish. I haven't even asked you how you're feeling!"

"Well, I didn't exactly give you a chance, did I? But yeah, I'm still feeling crappy. The nausea is just not going away. I lost another pound in the last week. The doctor doesn't know what to do. I've been resting a lot, I tried yoga and meditation—none of it seems to work."

"Oh Marisa . . ."

"Think your boyfriend could help with that?" her sister joked.

"I don't know," Mia said seriously. "Maybe. I'll ask him. He's not a doctor, but he might have access to one of their wonder drugs."

"Oh, no, you don't have to do that . . . I was just kidding—"

"Well, I'm not. I'll ask him right now."

"Mia, please, that'll be embarrassing. I'm sure I'll get over it in another few weeks . . ."

"Uh-huh," Mia said. "By then you'll be skin and bones, if you aren't already. You don't exactly have a ton of fat to spare."

She could hear Marisa sighing with what sounded like exasperation. "Fine, you can ask, I guess. I just don't want him to feel like we're taking advantage of him—"

"Oh please, Korum *offered* the migraine cure to dad. I didn't even know there was such a thing, much less that he brought it with him. Stop worrying, please—it's not good for you right now."

"Fine, fine . . ." Her sister sounded distracted all of a sudden. "Hold on, babe, I'm talking to Mia!"

"You have to go?" Mia guessed.

"Oh, it's just Connor . . . We were supposed to go grocery shopping when mom called and then you . . ."

"Oh, well, go then. We'll see each other tonight. I can't wait!"

"Me too. Love you, baby sis! See you soon!"

"Love you too!" And hanging up the phone, Mia went to look for Korum.

She found him outside, swimming in the Olympic-sized infinity pool that apparently came with the property. He was gliding through the water like a shark, moving with unbelievable speed.

"Hi," Mia called out, and then remembered the mysterious plans he had for her. Was it something sexual? Her breathing quickened at the thought. Telling herself to focus on Marisa, she decided to ask Korum about the medication right away, before he had a chance to implement whatever those plans were.

Swimming up to the edge of the pool, Korum lifted himself out effortlessly, using only his arms. His black hair was wet and slicked back against his skull, and water droplets glittered like tiny diamonds on his golden skin. He looked mouthwateringly sexy, and Mia swallowed, realizing yet again just how gorgeous her lover truly was. Walking toward the edge of the pool, she sat down on one of the lounge chairs conveniently placed there.

"Hi yourself," he said, smiling at her warmly and sitting down on the chair next to her. He seemed to have forgotten about their earlier disagreement, and Mia smiled back at him, relieved.

It seemed like as good of a time as any to ask about Marisa. "Do you know anything about pregnant women?" she blurted out, and then flushed for some reason.

Korum's eyebrows rose, and he looked amused. "I assume you're talking about your sister?"

Mia nodded. "She's having a difficult pregnancy. Really bad nausea and all. I was wondering if maybe you might have some anti-nausea medication or something that might settle her stomach . . ."

Korum considered it, looking thoughtful for a second. "I don't have it with me, but I can probably get someone to bring it here. However, it would only be a temporary fix . . . If there's something wrong that's causing your sister to feel this way, the medicine wouldn't do anything except mask the symptoms."

"Oh, I see . . ."

"The best thing for your sister would probably be Ellet. I'll ask her to swing by this week and examine Marisa—"

"Ellet?" The name sounded oddly familiar, even though she couldn't remember where she'd heard it.

Korum smiled. "She's our human biology expert in Lenkarda. Her lab designs many of the drugs I've given you in the past, as well as the one I just gave your dad. She's excellent at what she does and knows more about human health than all of your doctors put together."

Something nagged at Mia, some elusive memory that she couldn't place. After trying to remember for a second, she gave up and returned to the issue at hand. "Oh, I see . . . Yeah, if she could take a look at Marisa, that would be phenomenal. Would she seriously do that? Come all the way out here for this?"

He shrugged. "She owes me a few favors."

"Is there anyone in Lenkarda who doesn't owe you a few favors?" Mia asked wryly, staring at him. Her lover always seemed to have something up his sleeve.

"Not many," Korum admitted, smiling at her. "I believe in having leverage—comes in handy in situations like this. Of course, Ellet would probably come out here regardless. She has a soft spot for pregnant humans."

Mia grinned, wanting to hug and kiss him in gratitude. She didn't want to fight with him; she loved him too much. Giving in to the urge, she got up and sat down on his lounge chair, ignoring his wet shorts pressing against her dress. Taking his head between her hands, she pulled his face closer and gave him a tender kiss on the lips. "Thank you, Korum," she said softly, looking him in the eyes. "I really appreciate everything you've done for me and my family."

He smiled, and his eyes held a warm amber glow. "Of course, my darling . . ."

"I love you," Mia told him sincerely. "I love you so much, and I'm sorry about everything that happened before. You're right—I should've trusted you more. Do you think you'll be able to forgive me some day?"

It was the first time she had apologized for spying on him, and she could see that she'd pleasantly surprised him. Raising his hand, he lightly stroked her cheek. "Of course," he said softly. "Rationally, I know why you did what you did, but I have a difficult time being rational when it comes to you. When you first agreed to work with the Resistance, I let anger at your betrayal cloud my thinking instead of giving you more time to adjust to our relationship. I'm sorry for that, and for the stress and worry I caused you as a result. But I'm happy you're here now, with me . . ."

"I'm happy too," Mia said, and she knew he could see the full depth of her feelings on her face. "I really am . . ."

His eyes flaring brighter, Korum leaned toward her and kissed her hungrily, as though he wanted to consume her. His hands curled around her shoulders, and he pulled her closer, dragging her onto his lap, his erection pressing into her through the wet material of his swimming trunks.

Feeling buffeted by his passion, Mia could only cling to him as he greedily devoured her mouth, his hands roaming over her body, ripping off the clothing that prevented him from touching her naked skin. His hot mouth moved to her neck, nipped the skin lightly, and she cried out, her head falling back as if it were too heavy for her neck to support. She felt unbelievably hot, like she was burning inside from a liquid flame, every inch of her sensitized and craving his touch. He seemed to feel the same, his erection throbbing against her leg and his hands moving over her almost roughly.

Her fingers curved into claws, dug into the back of his shoulders. "Please, Korum . . ." She wanted him inside her with a desperation that didn't fully make sense. "Please . . ."

He rose, still holding her in his arms, and flipped her over, putting her down on the lounge chair on all fours. And then he was bent over her, driving into her with one powerful thrust, his hard cock penetrating her without restraint.

Mia gasped, shocked at the sudden entry, her inner muscles straining with the effort to adjust to his thickness, but he didn't give her any time. Grasping her hips, he fucked her relentlessly, his hips hammering at her with such force that she couldn't catch her breath, utterly overwhelmed by the sensations. She could hear his harsh breathing and her own screams, and then her whole world consisted of nothing more than the physical, the pleasure and the pain intermingling until there was no way to tell them apart and one could not exist without the other . . . until she was nothing more than an animal, besieged by the most basic need.

It seemed to go on forever, and then he came with a guttural groan, grinding into her as though trying to merge them together. The pulsations of his cock inside her sent her over the edge, and the orgasm tore through her body, leaving her weak and shaking in its wake. Only his hands on her hips kept her from collapsing onto the lounge chair, her arms and legs trembling too much to support her weight.

After about a minute, his breathing had calmed and he withdrew from her, separating their bodies. Mia felt too worn out to move, so she was glad when he picked her up and carried her into the house.

Wrapping her arms around his neck, she mumbled into his shoulder, "Was this what you had in mind when you said you had plans?"

"Pretty much," Korum admitted, walking up to the second floor. "I did envision something more civilized, but I don't seem to have any control over myself when it comes to you. I didn't hurt you, did I?"

He had, a little, but it had only enhanced the pleasure. And besides, she felt perfectly fine now, with all traces of soreness seemingly gone. "No," Mia reassured him. "I loved it."

He walked into a large, luxuriously appointed bathroom and placed her on her feet next to a large, claw-footed tub. "That's good," he said, turning on the water and smiling at her. "Still, I think you could use a nice bath, and so could I."

And, as Mia watched, his cock began to harden again.

CHAPTER SEVENTEEN

Marisa and Connor arrived first, their 2012 Toyota pulling into the driveway five minutes before six o'clock. Korum was finishing setting the table, so Mia came out to greet them by herself.

"Oh my God, Mia! Baby sis, it's so good to see you! You look phenomenal! What has he been feeding you?" Marisa burst out as soon as she exited the car. "And holy cow, look at this place! He must be a gazillionnaire!"

Laughing, Mia gave her sister a big hug, sobering a bit when she felt the unusual fragility of her frame. "Marisa! Oh, it's so good to see you too! And Connor!"

Smiling, her brother-in-law bent down to hug her too. "There's my favorite sister-in-law. How are you?"

"Oh, I'm doing great! Here, let's go inside! Korum is just putting the finishing touches on the dinner—which should be amazing, by the way."

"Any meat?" Connor asked with a hopeful look on his face as they followed Mia toward the house. A former college quarterback, Marisa's husband was still having trouble adjusting to the post-K-Day diet.

"No, sorry, they're mostly plant-eaters. But it's really yummy stuff, anyway."

"I still find it hard to believe that vampires are vegetarians . . ." Connor muttered, and Mia laughed again.

"They're not really vampires—they're past that now," Mia explained. "And some of the plants on Krina are very rich-tasting and dense in calories. I think if we had them here, we might not have been eating meat either."

"Ooh, you've tried plants from Krina?" Marisa sounded envious. Her sister was normally an adventurous eater, and the two of them would frequently try unusual restaurants when Marisa came to visit Mia in New York.

"Yep," Mia confirmed, grinning. "And they're really tasty. But that's only in Lenkarda. Tonight, we're eating much more local."

"Ugh, I hope I can eat something. I was sick again on the way here," Marisa confided. She did look pale and rather ill. "We had to stop by a rest area. I'm surprised we got here before the parents—"

"Oh, I was just about to tell you," Mia said, pausing for a second before entering the house. "I spoke to Korum, and he's going to have one of their doctors look at you to determine what's causing the problem."

"A K doctor?" Connor looked surprised.

"Actually, she's more of a human doctor—a Krinar specializing in human biology. Korum said she's really good."

"Wow, Mia, I don't even know what to say . . ." Marisa's eyes were suddenly swimming with tears.

"Oh no, don't worry about it! It's really not a big deal—"

"Hormones," Connor explained, pulling his wife closer to him for a hug.

"Ah, I see." Mia gave Marisa a few seconds to get her emotions under control. Then, smiling at them, she asked, "Ready to go in?"

Marisa nodded, looking much sunnier, and Mia led them into the house.

Korum must've just finished what he was doing because he came into the living room at the same time. As always, he looked stunning, with the golden hue of his skin contrasting with the white color of the simple button-up shirt he was wearing. And even though they had spent most of the afternoon in bed, Mia couldn't help the twinge of arousal she felt at the sight.

Spotting her sister, he gave her a big smile and walked up to them. "You must be Marisa," he said warmly. "I can definitely see the resemblance . . ."

Marisa nodded, looking uncharacteristically shy and flustered. "Yes, hi . . ." She seemed incapable of saying anything more profound.

Recalling her first meeting with Korum, Mia knew just how her sister felt. Apparently, even marriage and pregnancy could not shield a woman fully from the impact of her lover's magnetic appeal.

Turning to Connor, Korum said, "And you're Marisa's husband, right? Connor?"

Her brother-in-law politely held his hand out. "Yes, it's nice to meet you. Korum, right?" He looked far less star-struck than his wife.

Her lover accepted his hand, shaking it briefly. "Indeed. The pleasure is all mine. Can I offer you a drink while we wait for Mia's parents?"

"A beer would be great," Connor said easily. Mia had to give him kudos for his composure. Outwardly, he didn't seem intimidated at all.

Korum smiled and disappeared into the kitchen. In that moment, Marisa caught Mia's gaze. "Wow," her sister mouthed. "Just wow."

Mia grinned. She had always been jealous of her popular older sister who'd managed to have it all—good grades, great friends, and a ton of cute boys chasing after her. And now Marisa was envious of her?

Korum reappeared, carrying a tray with a beer, a glass of champagne, and a cup filled with some milky liquid. Handing the champagne to Mia and the beer to Connor, he held the cup out to her sister. "This is something that should settle your stomach," he said kindly. "At least for the rest of the evening."

Marisa gratefully accepted the cup and drank its contents, not even bothering to question the safety of the liquid. Clearly, their dad's experience had given her the confidence to trust K medicines. "Thank you," she said, and then her eyes widened. "Oh, wow, I'm already feeling much better . . ."

At that moment, the doorbell rang. Mia's parents had arrived.

After greeting them, Mia and Korum led them into the dining room, where Korum had prepared a meal that was more like a feast. Mia felt a little bad that she hadn't helped him at all, but Korum had shooed her away from the kitchen when she'd offered, explaining that she would simply be in the way. Not the least bit offended, Mia had gone to sit by the pool and catch up on the latest developments in Saret's lab, chatting with Adam via a Skype-like device that projected his image like a three-dimensional holograph.

In the meanwhile, Korum had prepared a gourmet feast consisting of five different varieties of salads, exotic sushi-like vegetable concoctions, various types of noodle dishes with delicious-smelling sauces, and fresh fruit for dessert. A bottle of Cristal was chilling in a bucket of ice, and the table was decorated with a large centerpiece of gorgeous flowers. He had really gone all out, and Mia's heart tightened at the realization that he was actually trying to impress her family.

And impressed they were.

Her mom kept asking Korum for recipes of all the dishes they were eating, and even her dad seemed to be in a much better mood, his earlier headache gone without a trace. The atmosphere at the table was surprisingly relaxed, with her family questioning Korum about life on Krina and her lover telling amusing stories about his parents and the pranks Saret used to pull on him when they were children. Watching him, Mia realized he had deliberately steered the conversation toward those topics that would be most likely to put her family at ease . . . that would humanize him in their eyes. And even though Mia knew that he was putting on a show, she couldn't help the little melting sensation she got inside when she thought of Korum as a little boy, playing in the forests of Krina and getting in trouble with his friends.

The dinner lasted until ten. Finally, replete and happy, everyone departed. On their way out, Mia's mom kissed Korum on the cheek, and her dad shook his hand. Marisa blushed and stammered a little, thanking Korum again for the anti-nausea medication, while her husband gave him a huge smile and told him they would be coming over for dinner every night, given the awesome meal they'd just had.

As soon as her family drove away, Mia wrapped her arms around Korum's waist and hugged him tightly. Still holding him, she looked up and found him regarding her with a tender look on his beautiful face. "Thank you," she told him sincerely. "This really meant a lot to me."

He stroked her cheek gently. "I would do anything to make you happy, darling," he said softly. "You know that, right?"

Mia nodded and buried her face in his chest, feeling like she couldn't contain all the emotions filling her chest right now. She loved him so much it hurt. And in that moment, she was almost certain that he loved her too.

* * *

The next morning, Mia woke up to the sound of Krinar language being spoken. A soft female voice, oddly familiar, could be heard, interspersed with Korum's deeper tones. The doctor, Mia realized. She must've already arrived to inspect Marisa.

Getting out of bed, Mia quickly dressed and washed up, checking the time. Sure enough, her sister was supposed to get there in a few minutes.

Entering the living room, Mia saw a beautiful Krinar woman sitting there, chatting with Korum about the local beaches. Tall and slim, she reminded Mia of a Brazilian supermodel, with her bronzed skin, dark brown hair streaked with golden highlights, and sparkling hazel eyes. Again, something nagged at the back on Mia's mind, some elusive memory that she couldn't quite place.

She approached them, and the K female rose and extended her hand to Mia. "Hi," she said warmly. "I'm Ellet."

Smiling, Mia shook her hand briefly, surprised at the human greeting. Other than Korum's cousin Leeta, Mia hadn't spoken to a lot of K females. All four of the other assistants in Saret's lab happened to be male, and Mia hadn't really socialized with anyone else yet.

"Thanks for coming all the way here," Mia told her. "I can't even begin to tell you how much I appreciate your help with this."

"Oh, it's my pleasure," Ellet said, beaming with a megawatt smile and causing Mia to like her immediately. "This is my first time in Florida, and I'm loving it so far. So much like Costa Rica, yet so much more developed and with so many humans!"

Mia raised her eyebrows in surprise. Developed and teeming with humans were usually negative factors for most Krinar, but Ellet seemed to be saying just the opposite.

"Ellet loves humans," Korum said dryly. "You're her specialty. I don't know why she's even bothering to stay in Lenkarda—New York would be a much better place for her."

"It's a little too cold and dirty for my taste," Ellet said, smiling. "But Florida seems much more promising . . ."

"Really?" Mia asked, staring at her. "You would move here and do what? Open a clinic?"

Ellet smiled. "I would like to, but I probably won't be able to get permission. It goes against the mandate."

"The mandate?"

"The non-interference mandate—one of the conditions under which the Elders have agreed to let us live here, on Earth," Ellet explained, shooting Korum a quick and unreadable look.

"Oh, I see," Mia said, though she didn't really. She knew that the Ks hadn't shared any of their technology and science, and she presumed it was because they wanted to see how their grand evolutionary experiment would turn out. However, she hadn't realized there was an actual mandate in place.

Before she could ask any more questions, the doorbell rang. Marisa had arrived.

Mia went to open the door.

Once again, her sister looked wan and pale, the dark color of her hair only emphasizing the unhealthy pallor of her face. The medication Korum had given her yesterday was obviously no longer working.

"Ellet is already here," Mia told her. "She's very nice—you'll like her."

Marisa nodded, looking a little green. "Mia," she whispered, "what if they find something really wrong with me or the baby? Something that our doctors haven't been able to diagnose? What if it's something bad—like truly bad?"

"What? No! I'm sure you're perfectly fine. It's probably just some weird hormonal imbalance . . . You can't start stressing about crazy what-ifs before the doctor even looks at you! Here, come here . . ." Mia pulled her in for a hug and felt her slim body shaking in her arms.

In that moment, Ellet and Korum entered the hallway, having apparently overheard something with their sharp Krinar hearing.

"You must be Marisa," Ellet said warmly, coming up to her sister and studying her with an inquisitive look on her perfect face.

Marisa pulled away from Mia, looking a little stunned to be confronted with such a gorgeous creature.

The Krinar woman gave her a wide smile. "I'm Ellet," she said gently, "and I'm an expert in human biology. Please, don't worry, you have nothing to be afraid of. Come, let's go into the living room and I'll take a look to see if there's anything wrong. And even if there is, I'm sure that we can fix it. The human body holds few mysteries for us at this point."

Marisa nodded, looking somewhat reassured, and they all walked into the living room.

"Please, can you stand still for just one minute?" Ellet requested, reaching for a small white device that was sitting on the coffee table next to the couch. Picking it up, she directed it toward Mia's sister, running it slowly over her body from head to toe, focusing especially on her stomach area.

Then, putting down the device, she said, "Did your doctor tell you that you have borderline hyperemesis gravidarum?"

Marisa blinked. "Uh, he did mention something along those lines, but I thought that was just a name for severe nausea and vomiting . . ."

"It is. It's a condition that happens when you have excessive levels of beta hCG hormone. It could be dangerous if you get severely dehydrated, and I don't think human doctors know how to treat it other than assigning you IV fluids in the more extreme cases and making sure you rest. However, I should be able to fix it for you, so the rest of your pregnancy proceeds smoothly."

Marisa gave her a desperately hopeful look. "Really? You can make it go away?"

"I can normalize the hormone levels for you. Since you're only in your first trimester, you may still experience mild nausea every now and then, so I'll give you a little something that you can take for that. But you'll be able to eat and function normally again—and start gaining weight like you're supposed to."

"And the baby? Is everything okay with the baby?" Marisa asked tremulously.

Ellet smiled. "Yes. She's going to be a beautiful girl."

"Oh my God, a girl!" Tears of happiness filled Marisa's eyes. For as long as Mia could remember, Marisa had talked about wanting a daughter, and now it seemed like her dream would be coming true. Mia grinned at her and squeezed her hand.

"All right, ready? We'll need privacy for the next step," Ellet said.

"You can go into one of the bedrooms upstairs," Korum told her. "We'll be waiting down here."

Marisa looked a little nervous. "What are you going to do?" she asked Ellet. "Is it like an operation?"

"I won't have to cut you or anything," the K reassured her. "It's just a small device that needs to go inside you. It will take about five minutes, and then you'll be able to go home."

"Go ahead," Mia encouraged her. "It'll be okay . . ."

Marisa and Ellet went upstairs, and Mia sat down next to Korum. "Thanks again for getting Ellet to come out here," she told him. "She's wonderful."

"Yes, she's one of the nicest individuals I know," Korum admitted. "She's still relatively young, only about four hundred years old, but she's very passionate about what she does and she's made a lot of contributions to her field." He sounded admiring.

A sudden unpleasant thought occurred to Mia. "Did you and her ever . . . ?" Ellet was one of the most beautiful women Mia had ever seen, even in Lenkarda.

Korum shrugged. "It was nothing serious—just a casual fling a few years ago. It's nothing that you need to be concerned with."

Mia swallowed, the pit of her stomach suddenly burning with jealousy. "You were lovers?" A wave of nausea rolled through her as she pictured them together in bed, the K's pouty lips on Korum's body, her slender hands touching him in intimate places.

"Only briefly. You have to understand something, my sweet—sex is a fun, recreational activity for us. Unless it takes place in the context of a serious relationship, we don't assign any meaning to it."

Mia stared at him, trying to digest that for a second and to push away the unpleasant, pornographic images still lingering in her mind. "So what determines whether you're in a serious relationship or not?"

"Whether we care about the other person and to what degree."

"And you didn't care about Ellet?"

He shook his head. "No. We were too similar in some ways. It quickly became obvious that we didn't have much beyond the initial attraction—which faded within a few weeks."

"But she's so incredibly beautiful . . . How can you possibly not be attracted to her anymore? And she to you?" Mia asked quietly, feeling irrationally upset. What could Korum want with a regular human who couldn't hold a candle to one of his former lovers? If his attraction to Ellet had faded so quickly, what chance did Mia have of holding his attention longer? They had been together just over six weeks at this point. Would he get bored of her within another month?

Korum reached out and cupped her cheek in his large, warm palm. "Mia," he said softly, "what are you worrying about? I've known thousands of beautiful women, but I've never wanted one of them as much as I want you . . ."

Mia looked at him, the knot in her stomach easing.

"And you are far more appealing to me, physically, than she ever was," he continued, his eyes turning a brighter shade of gold. "How can you even have doubts about that at this point? Is it not enough that I all but keep you chained to my bed? If you were any more attractive to me, I would stay buried inside your sweet little body day and night . . . and then where would we be?"

A hot blush spread over Mia's face, and she could feel herself reacting physically to his words. At the same time, she realized that her sister and Ellet would be coming down any minute. "Korum, please," she whispered, "what if they overhear us?"

He gave her a wicked grin. "Then they'll learn something shocking—the fact that we have sex . . ."

As if on cue, Mia heard footsteps on the stairs, and Marisa entered the room, followed closely by Ellet.

Quickly pulling away from Korum, Mia jumped up and ran to her sister. "Marisa! How did it go?"

Marisa shook her head, looking like she was in a mild state of shock. "I barely felt anything when Ellet touched me, but now I'm already starting to feel less sick . . ."

"You'll feel even better in a couple of hours as the nanos gradually normalize your hormonal production," Ellet said, looking pleased. "Also, if you still have any residual traces of nausea, just take that powder I gave you and you should be fine for the rest of your pregnancy. And like I told you, I would be more than happy to come out here when it's time for you to deliver . . ."

Marisa sniffed, looking all teary-eyed, and then gave Ellet a hug, obviously surprising the K. "Thank you, Ellet, so, so much! I wish everyone knew how nice your kind can be—"

Ellet hugged her back a little awkwardly. "Thank you, Marisa, but remember what I told you. You can't go around telling people about this—or I could get in trouble. We're not supposed to interfere with humans too much—"

"Why not?" Mia asked. "What's the big deal if you help one pregnant woman?"

Korum came up to her and wrapped his arm around her shoulders, pressing her against him. "I'll explain it to you later, my sweet," he said, and there was a warning note in his tone. "For now, why don't you and Marisa hang out for a while? I have to catch up with Ellet about a few things back in Lenkarda."

He wanted to be left alone with his former lover? The sick feeling of jealousy she thought she had under control returned in full force. Nevertheless, she nodded stiffly and asked, "Marisa, would you want to go for a walk on the beach?"

Her sister smiled. "Sure. That sounds lovely," she said, and Mia knew that the signs of tension had not escaped Marisa's sharp eye.

Korum bent down to kiss her forehead and then released her from his embrace. "Go ahead," he said. "Your morning shake is in the kitchen. I made one for Marisa as well. You can take it with you if you want."

Mia thanked him, and the two sisters left, grabbing their shakes on the way.

CHAPTER EIGHTEEN

"All right, baby sis, spill. What was up with your reaction back there?" Marisa took a sip of her shake and looked at Mia expectantly as they strolled along the water, the ocean surf pounding against the sand only a few feet away.

Mia kicked a small shell out of the way, getting sand into her flip-flop in the process. "I just learned he had a thing with Ellet in the past," she told Marisa glumly. "And now he wants to be alone with her in the house. How am I supposed to react to that?"

"Ouch."

"Yeah."

Marisa was silent for a few seconds, apparently mulling that over. "I don't think he has anything going on with her anymore . . ." she said thoughtfully. "In fact, I'm pretty sure of it. He has eyes only for you—it's almost scary, actually, how intensely he watches you all the time. Still, that wasn't a very nice thing to do. But maybe he had some business to discuss with her?"

"Probably," Mia agreed, shrugging. "He said it's been over between them for a few years and it was never serious in the first place. Still, I just can't help imagining the two of them together, you know?"

For about a minute, they walked in comfortable silence, slowly drinking their smoothies and looking out over the water.

Then Marisa spoke again. "You really love him, don't you?" she asked, sounding worried for the first time.

Mia sighed and looked down at the sand. "More than I can say," she admitted. "More than I could've ever imagined."

"Oh Mia . . ."

"I know, I know. I don't need a lecture on this. It can't possibly end well, believe me, I know."

Her sister reached out and squeezed her hand. "Well, for what it's worth, he seems crazy about you. Absolutely crazy. I've never seen anything like that. He looks at you like he wants to devour you—and like he would do anything for you at the same time. He seems obsessed with you, baby sis . . ."

Mia laughed, Marisa's words startling her out of her gloomy mood. "Oh, please, I'm sure you're exaggerating. We just have good chemistry, that's all—"

"No, Mia," Marisa shook her head, looking serious. "What you guys have is way more than that. I don't even know how to describe it. He watches your every move. It's kind of uncanny, actually. And he can't seem to go more than a couple of minutes without touching you . . ."

Mia flushed a little, wondering if her sister had overheard their earlier conversation. If so, then Ellet definitively did; the Krinar tended to have a sharper sense of hearing than most humans.

"How did you end up getting involved with him, anyway?" Marisa asked with unconcealed curiosity. "You never really told me the full story, just that BS about your lover from Dubai . . . You've always been so cautious and by the rules—I can't quite picture you jumping into an affair with a K."

Mia hesitated. She didn't want to lie to her sister anymore, but she also wasn't up to telling her family the full story. "It wasn't easy for me," she admitted. "I was pretty scared in the beginning, and Korum can be . . . intimidating at times. But I was very attracted to him, obviously, and he was very persistent . . . and, well, you know the rest of the story."

Marisa regarded her intently. "I see. I'm sure there's more to it, but you can tell me when you're ready."

"Thanks, Marisa. You're the best sister a girl can ask for," Mia told her sincerely.

"I know—and very modest, too." Her sister grinned as she said this, and Mia smiled back at her.

They walked some more, each occupied with her own thoughts, until Marisa spoke again. "Is there any way things could work out for you guys?" she asked, her face serious again. "Any way at all?"

Mia shook her head. "No, I don't see how. We are literally different species—with very different lifespans. He will ultimately leave me . . . and I don't know how I will survive that at this point."

"Oh Mia . . . Baby, I don't even know what to say . . ." There was a look of intense pity on Marisa's pretty face.

"You don't have to say anything," Mia told her calmly. "It's my own fault for falling in love with him. I could've found myself a nice, normal guy—someone like Connor—but no, I had to get involved with an alien. I'm sure I will ultimately recover . . . and maybe even meet a human man that I will grow to care about."

"Have you talked to him about any of this?"

"Not, I haven't," Mia told her honestly. "I'm too happy right now to bring this up quite yet. For once, I'm trying to seize the moment—to enjoy something without worrying about the consequences . . ."

Marisa smiled, but there was still a shadow of worry on her face. "You go, baby girl. Carpe diem and all that."

* * *

The Krinar watched the two girls walking slowly along the beach. They were both pretty, but only one held his interest.

There was no point in observing her now, rationally he knew that. He should be concentrating on his enemy, not some little human who couldn't possibly be a threat to his plans.

Yet he couldn't look away.

She laughed, turning her face up toward the sun, and he zoomed in, pausing the recording for a second. Her lips were parted, showing even white teeth, and her pale skin appeared luminous, almost glowing.

She looked happy, and he almost regretted what he had to do. If it worked tomorrow, she would be upset for a while.

At least until he had a chance to take her pain away.

* * *

That evening, Korum took the whole family out to dinner, bringing them to a gourmet restaurant that had recently opened in Hammock Beach, an exclusive private community not too far from Ormond.

To Connor's happy surprise, there was actual seafood on the menu, as well as steak and caviar. The prices for animal products were astronomical, of course, with some of the dishes costing close to what some teachers made in a week. Her parents gaped at the menu, stunned, until Korum told them firmly that the dinner was his treat and that he would not hear any protests in that regard. Initially hesitant, her family ultimately gave in, with Connor ordering himself a prime rib and her parents sharing a shrimp cocktail as an appetizer and lobster as the main course. Mia got noodles made from real egg, while Marisa had some Russian-style blinis with caviar. Korum, as usual, stuck to mostly plant-based fare, although he did allow a little butter in his hibachi vegetables. "One of the tastier human inventions," he explained wryly.

The first part of the dinner passed uneventfully, with Korum politely asking her parents about their jobs and how they came to this country as children. He seemed particularly interested in the immigrant experience and the acclimation process for humans. Her parents were more than happy to talk about that, and the conversation flowed smoothly and easily.

A few glasses of wine later, however, her brother-in-law began to venture into some less comfortable territory. "So why did you guys come to Earth, anyway?" Connor asked, looking at Korum with unconcealed curiosity.

Mia froze, remembering her lover's rather low opinion of the human race and its treatment of Earth—the planet the Ks regarded as their future home.

But she needn't have worried. Korum's parent-pleasing façade was firmly in place. "Our solar system is much older than yours," he explained casually. "And our star will begin to die long before your sun. So it made sense for us to begin preparing for that eventuality. Also, it's good to be diversified in terms of locations: if some kind of a cosmic disaster were to befall Krina or our home galaxy, at least some of the Krinar would survive."

"Oh, wow, you guys really think ahead, huh?"

Connor sounded impressed, and Korum gave him a small smile before steering the conversation to Mia's childhood and what she had been like in kindergarten.

The rest of the dinner flew by, with her family competing for a chance to tell the most amusing and embarrassing story about Mia as a baby—everything from her odd preference for purple clothes when she was three to Marisa bribing her with candy to get her to do her math homework in first grade.

"I find it hard to believe that Mia ever had to be forced to do her homework," Korum said, smiling at her warmly. "I can't get her to stop doing it now. Her work ethic is incredible—even Saret is impressed, and he's had a lot of talented and dedicated assistants over the years."

Her parents grinned, looking proud and pleased, and Mia realized yet again what a skilled manipulator Korum was. He had her family eating out of the palm of his hand, despite the fact that they should've been madly worried about their youngest daughter being in a relationship with an extraterrestrial predator. Not that she minded, of course. Her lover was doing exactly what Mia wanted—setting her parents' mind at ease—and she was grateful for that.

Finally, the dinner wrapped up around ten. Saying good-bye to her family, Mia climbed into Korum's Ferrari and they drove home, with Mia feeling happy and full from the delicious meal.

* * *

Waking up the next morning, Mia bounced out of bed full of energy. Quickly brushing her teeth, she put on the two-piece bathing suit that Korum had thoughtfully left for her and went to look for him.

She found him lounging by the pool, sunning himself like a big golden cat. Unlike a human, Korum never burned, his skin always the same lightly bronzed shade. Come to think of it, Mia had somehow managed to avoid sunburn herself thus far, despite not using any sunblock. For a second, she wondered if Korum had given her something to protect her skin without her knowing and then forgot about it, too excited to start the day.

Seeing her enter the pool area, Korum gave her a slow, sensuous smile that reminded Mia of the wicked things he'd done to her last night. Her lower belly tightened with remembered pleasure. He couldn't seem to get enough of her—and she of him—to the point that Mia was beginning to wonder whether they were addicted to each other after all. Of course, Korum had warned her of blood addiction, not sexual addiction, but she couldn't imagine craving him more than she did already.

Tall shrubs and a solid white fence surrounded the pool area, blocking it from the view of anyone passing by on the beach and providing privacy for the mansion's residents. Encouraged by that, Mia came up to him and ran her hand down his chest, reveling in the feel of his smooth, sun-warmed skin.

He grinned and caught her hand, bringing it to his mouth for a kiss. "Ah, my lady awakes," he teased, his soft lips nibbling lightly at the back of her hand.

A shiver of pleasure ran through her at his touch, and she suddenly felt much warmer. Fighting a blush, she asked, "Do you want to go to the beach this morning?"

They were supposed to meet her parents for lunch today and then drive to St. Augustine to visit the Alligator Farm, one of Mia's favorite attractions in the area. However, it was only 9 a.m. right now, so they had plenty of time to kill.

"What about breakfast?" he asked her. "You're not hungry?"

"I can eat a banana on the way," Mia told him, itching to go for a swim in the ocean. "I'm still sort of full from yesterday's dinner."

"Then let's go."

The beach in front of their house was beautiful and almost completely deserted. Although it was not a private beach, there were no hotels nearby and no easy parking for the potential beach-goers. As a result, only the wealthy residents of the beachfront houses and a few hardy souls practicing long-distance beach walking were likely to be found there.

Exiting through the gated pool area, they walked on a narrow wooden bridge that led from the house to the sand, bypassing the dunes.

As soon as they stepped off the bridge, Mia kicked off her flip-flops and ran toward the water, eager to test its temperature. At this time of year, the Atlantic was not as warm as it would be later in the summer, but she didn't care. Despite the relatively early hour, it was already hot outside, and she was looking forward to the coolness of the ocean.

They swam for a solid hour until Mia felt pleasantly tired, her muscles aching from the unusual exertion. She was surprised at her own endurance; other than swimming a little in Costa Rica in the evenings, she really hadn't done much cardio in recent months. Perhaps she was still in shape from a year ago, when Jessie had signed both of them up for a 5K charity race and Mia had gone on a mad exercise spree to prepare for it. Or maybe all that nutritious food Korum was feeding her was actually that good for her body.

When they finally came out of the water, Mia stretched out on a big towel they had brought from the house, and Korum lay down beside her. Closing her eyes, she relaxed, the hot rays of the sun beaming down on her skin. She vaguely wondered if she should put on sunblock, but she felt far too lazy to move. Just a few minutes, she promised herself, just enough to produce some vitamin D . . .

A pleasant tickling sensation woke her up from her nap some time later.

Opening her eyes, she turned her head to the side, squinting a little from the bright light. Korum was lying there beside her, propped up on one elbow. Looking down at her with a smile, he was gently stroking the side of her ribcage with one long finger. His dark hair gleamed in the sunlight, and there was a warm glow in his thickly lashed amber eyes.

"What?" Mia murmured, feeling a bit self-conscious. The bikini she was wearing left very little to the imagination, and the way he was staring at her right now made her feel absurdly shy.

"Nothing," he said softly. "Your skin just looks so delectable in this light. I never realized before how pretty such pale skin could be."

"Um, thank you . . ."

"And it blushes so prettily too," he teased, brushing his fingers against her suddenly too-warm cheeks.

Mia gave him a slightly embarrassed smile. It was still so new to her, being in a relationship, having someone touching and admiring her body like that. And to have that someone be the gorgeous creature lying beside her—that was beyond anything Mia could've ever imagined.

"How long was I out for?" she asked, remembering her impromptu nap. "I really didn't mean to drift off . . ."

"Not all that long. About twenty minutes or so."

Mia yawned delicately, covering her mouth with the back of her hand. "Sorry about that . . . You must've been so bored—"

"I'm never bored with you," he said, still studying her. "I like watching you sleep. You always look so sweet and peaceful . . . like a dark-haired angel. I find it very relaxing, seeing you like that."

Mia grinned at him. Korum could be very strange sometimes. "That's good, I guess, considering how much I sleep."

He just smiled in response, tucking one of the curls behind her ear. "Are you getting hungry now? Or still full from last night's dinner?"

Mia considered it. "I could eat. But don't we have lunch with my parents soon?"

"In another two hours. You're probably going to starve by then."

"Hmm, okay. I want to go for another swim first, though."

"Sure. Want to go in now?"

"I actually have to run to the restroom first," Mia admitted. "Will you wait for me? I'll be back in a few minutes."

"Go ahead," Korum told her, grinning. "I'll wait."

Jumping up, Mia ran back toward the house. Entering the fenced pool area, she used one of the bathrooms on the first floor. Then she headed back to the beach, eagerly anticipating the pleasant coolness of the water on her overheated skin.

Approaching the tall fence, Mia pushed open the gate . . . and froze.

Right outside the fence, with the landscaping blocking her from the view of anyone on the beach, was Leslie—one of the Resistance fighters Mia had worked with.

And in her slim, muscular arms was a gun pointed directly at Mia's chest.

CHAPTER NINETEEN

For a few seconds, icy terror held Mia completely immobile, unable to think or react in any way. Just like a deer in the headlights, some part of her brain noted with morbid amusement. Her legs felt weak and heavy, as through she were caught in quicksand, and her vision had narrowed so that all she could see was the deadly weapon pointed at her.

And then a surge of adrenaline kicked in, clearing her head and sending her heart rate through the roof. If she didn't do something, she would die, Mia realized with utter clarity. Korum was too far away to help her if she screamed; the bullet would get her long before he got anywhere near the house.

"Hands up, bitch," Leslie ordered harshly, her delicate features so twisted with hatred that they were barely recognizable. "You fucking traitor, you're going to get exactly what you deserve—"

"What are you doing here, Leslie?" Mia interrupted, trying to keep the tremor out of her voice and slowly raising her hands. *Don't show your fear to a rabid dog. Never show your fear. Keep her talking. Buy yourself time.*

"Did you honestly think you could get away with it?" Leslie spit out, her arms shaking and her finger nervously tapping on the trigger. "Did you really think you could betray your entire race and live happily ever after, fucking that monster?"

Her clothes were ripped and dirty, Mia noted with some semi-functional part of her brain. The girl must've been on the run for quite some time.

"Leslie, listen to me," Mia said desperately, knowing that she probably only had seconds left. "If you shoot me, Korum will kill you. You won't be able to get away fast enough. He'll hear the shot, and he'll be on you—"

A mad, triumphant smile lit Leslie's face. For a second, she looked positively gleeful. "Oh, you think I'm risking my life to kill you?" she said contemptuously. "You think I'm that stupid? No, bitch, as much as I'd love to put an end to your worthless existence, my orders are to keep you alive—alive and out of the way while he deals with your lover . . ."

Horrified, Mia stared at her, sickening fear spreading through her veins. "What do you mean?" she whispered, her brain barely able to process the implications. "While who deals with him?"

Leslie laughed, clearly enjoying Mia's reaction. "I knew it. I knew you had fallen for that monster. I told John not to trust you, but he was stupidly convinced you were on our side. But I knew better. I knew you were just the type to fall for that pretty façade. Did he get you addicted too? Do you walk around now begging Ks to bite you every hour, like my brother did before they killed him?"

Mia's thoughts whirled in panic, her heart pounding so hard she felt like it would break through her ribcage. At the same time, a fury slowly began to build deep in the pit of her stomach. "While who deals with him?" she repeated through clenched teeth, her voice low and mean.

Leslie's lips twisted into a parody of a smile. "You think the Keiths were alone?" she said mockingly. "You think they got caught and that's the end of it?"

Stunned, Mia could only stare at her in shock.

"Oh yes, there are more Ks involved," Leslie confided, and there was cruel pleasure on her face. "Your lover's being turned into particles as we speak . . ."

Mia sucked in her breath, her lungs unable to get enough air. Her vision darkened for a second, and then rage unlike anything she had ever experienced swept through her, leaving no room for fear.

And suddenly, she knew exactly what she needed to do.

For a brief moment, her gaze drifted to a point just beyond Leslie's shoulder, and she let an expression of wild joy light up her face.

Startled, Leslie turned to look behind her for a second, and Mia sprang at her, her hands closing around the gun even as the girl realized she'd been tricked.

The force of Mia's jump brought them both tumbling down on the ground, with Mia landing on top, her desperation giving her strength she didn't know she had. However, Leslie managed to maintain her grip on the weapon, her training and larger size giving her an immeasurable advantage, and they rolled, each trying to gain possession of the gun.

The heavier girl ended up on top, her weight pressing Mia into the ground. Her knee hit Mia in the stomach, and she gasped, air temporarily knocked out of her. At the same time, Leslie wrenched at the gun with both hands, nearly tearing Mia's arm out of her socket. The pain barely registered, dulled by the adrenaline coursing through her veins and the murderous fury filling her mind.

For the first time in her life, Mia knew what it felt like to truly want to kill someone, to tear them to shreds and watch them bleed. A reddish haze taking over her vision, she fought with no regard for her own safety or anything resembling fairness. Her face ended up near Leslie's shoulder, and she bit, her teeth sinking savagely into the fleshy part of her upper arm. The fighter screamed, and Mia delighted in her pain, in the metallic taste of blood filling her mouth. Her knee came up hard, smashing into Leslie's pubic bone with all the force that Mia could muster, and the girl gasped, her grip on the weapon loosening slightly.

That was all the opportunity Mia needed.

Instead of pulling at the gun, she pushed down, twisting at the same time. Leslie's index finger caught in the trigger guard, twisted with it, and the girl screamed as the digit snapped, bending unnaturally backwards.

Taking advantage of her distraction, Mia yanked at the weapon, wrenching it away from Leslie's hand.

And then, hardly cognizant of her own actions, she brought it down with savage force on top of Leslie's skull.

The girl's body went slack, blood seeping out from where the hard metal object made contact with her head. Gasping and shuddering, Mia pushed her away, her mind filled with only one thought: getting to Korum before it was too late.

Jumping up, she grabbed the gun and ran, ignoring the unconscious girl left lying on the ground.

Mia ran faster than she'd ever run in her life, her lungs burning and the rough wooden bridge floor cutting into her bare feet. The gun felt heavy in her hand, unfamiliar.

On the other end of the bridge, she could see a male Krinar standing with his back turned toward her, his right arm outstretched and pointed at Korum—who stood utterly still, his gaze glued to the object in the other K's hand.

Leslie hadn't lied. In another minute, it might be too late. Slowing slightly, Mia lifted her hand, aimed at the broad back of the K ahead of her, and squeezed the trigger.

Nothing happened except a soft snick. *Not loaded, the damn thing was not loaded.*

Throwing the weapon aside, she ran faster again. Dark spots danced in front of her eyes, interfering with her vision as her brain fought to get sufficient oxygen. Everything around her blurred, greyed out, as she sprinted toward the scene with every ounce of strength still left in her body. All she could see, all she could focus on, was the deadly scene ahead.

And then she was there, seeing the K looming in front of her, his large body shaking and sweat glistening on the back of his neck. Through the roaring of her heartbeat in her ears, Mia vaguely heard the soothing tone of Korum's voice as he tried to convince the K to put the weapon away, to just listen—and glimpsed the horror on her lover's face as he saw her running and realized her intention.

With no further thought, Mia leapt on top of the K, heedless of the futility of her attack, her fingers grabbing his hair and viciously yanking on it. Startled and screaming in sudden pain, the K flung her away from him with one powerful blow, sending her flying into the dunes nearly twelve feet away.

Her left side slamming heavily into the ground, Mia lay there for a moment, stunned, the wind completely knocked out of her. And then her lungs expanded and she drew in a gasping breath, sucking in some much needed air. Dizzy and disoriented, she tried to get up, rolling over onto her stomach and then attempting to rise up onto all fours.

As she moved, an agonizing pain shot up her left arm.

Whimpering, she glanced at her side, and her head spun at the sight of white bone sticking out through a bloody tear in her skin. Sudden hot nausea boiled up in her throat, and she retched uncontrollably, the contents of her stomach emptying onto the dry grass of the dune.

Falling onto her right side, she tried to crawl away, her limbs weak and shaking, when strong arms lifted her, cradling her against a familiar chest.

His entire body trembling, Korum knelt in the sand, holding her in his arms and rocking back and forth. His breathing was harsh and ragged, and Mia could hear his heart beating like a drum in his chest.

405

"Mia . . . Oh my sweet, I thought I lost you . . ." The terror in his voice was a mirror image of the fear she'd felt at the sight of him in danger. He seemed incapable of saying anything else, just holding her pressed against him as he fought to regain control of himself. Even in his panic, he seemed mindful of her injured arm, taking care not to cause her any more pain.

"Th-the K . . ." she managed to croak out. "D-did he . . . ?"

"Don't worry about it," Korum said rawly. "He's no longer a threat. You're alive and that's all that matters."

Still holding her, he got to his feet. "Don't look," he said roughly, carrying her toward the bridge.

Mia closed her eyes for a second, but it made her feel even more sick and nauseated, so she opened them right away.

And saw immediately why Korum had warned her not to look.

Lying on the sand, just a few feet away from them, was what used to be his attacker. The body was hardly recognizable as such now, with the right arm missing and a bloody hole where the head and neck used to be. Blood was everywhere, all over the place, covering the disfigured corpse, soaking into the sandy ground.

For a brief second, she thought it couldn't be real, but the metallic odor was undeniable, as was the underlying stench of something much more foul, like sewage. The scent of death, she realized with some still-rational part of her brain. She'd never smelled it before, but something primitive inside her knew and recoiled from it.

A horrified moan escaped her throat before she could suppress it.

Korum cursed, and his pace picked up until he was almost running toward the house, still taking care not to jostle her injured arm.

Closing her eyes, Mia tried to take deep breaths, to convince herself that she'd just seen a scene from a movie, that there wasn't really what used to be an intelligent being lying there dead and mangled in the sand of Ormond Beach. But the images before her eyes were too vivid and undeniable, and her stomach twisted. If she hadn't emptied it just a minute ago, she would have vomited again.

The K who held her in his arms had just literally torn apart his opponent.

CHAPTER TWENTY

Her stomach churning, she instinctively pushed against Korum's chest with her right hand, but he ignored her feeble attempt to free herself.

"Shh, my darling, it'll be all right," he whispered to her fiercely, entering the pool area and carrying her toward the house.

As they went through the gate, Mia opened her eyes again and saw that Leslie's body was still lying there, right outside the pool gate. With a strange detachment, she wondered if the Resistance fighter was dead too. She knew she should be horrified at the thought, but she simply felt numb right now—numb and cold inside.

Korum carried her up the stairs and into the large bathroom on the second floor. Placing her gently on her feet, he turned on the shower and adjusted the water settings while Mia stood there, weaving slightly and listlessly observing his actions. A kind of merciful haze had descended on her mind, partially shielding her from the brutal reality of the situation. She knew what she was seeing, but it didn't seem to touch her in any way, as though it were happening to someone else.

Korum's entire body was covered with blood and sand, his hair encrusted with it. He looked like he had been through a battle—which, actually, he had been. If she had understood that gruesome scene correctly, he had killed the other K with his bare hands.

Hot bile rose in her throat again, and she held it back with effort. Even though she knew it was self-defense, she was still horrified that her lover was capable of that level of violence.

But what frightened her even more was the fact that she was too.

Because underneath it all, she was ferociously glad that the other K was dead—that it was his body, not Korum's, lying there in pieces. If he had succeeded in his attack . . . If he had managed to kill Korum, Mia would have gladly killed him herself—either that, or died trying.

Her eyes drifted to the left, and she saw her own reflection in the large mirror hanging on the wall. Streaks of dried blood were all over her face, all around her mouth area—from when she'd bitten Leslie, she realized. Dirt, sand, and dried bits of grass covered her mostly naked body, and small twigs were stuck in her hair, adding to the overall murderous madwoman impression.

"Here, let's get you in there," Korum said softly, carefully picking her up and bringing her into the shower stall where he'd gotten the water to perfect temperature.

The hot spray felt amazing on her skin, and Mia realized that she felt chilled, frozen inside despite the hot weather. She was also trembling. Her body must've gone into shock, she thought with almost clinical objectivity. She didn't dare look at her arm for fear of embarrassing herself again; for now, the pain was somehow tolerable, as though she'd received an anesthetic of some kind. Unlike most people, Mia had never broken anything before, and she wondered if this is what it always felt like. If so, then it was truly not all that bad, definitely survivable.

"Stay here," Korum told her. "I'll be right back with something for your arm."

Mia obediently nodded, and he disappeared for a minute, returning with a small pill in his hand. Stepping into the shower, he gave it to her and told her to swallow it.

She did so, and the dull throbbing pain eased almost immediately.

"Close your eyes and don't look," he said. "I mean it, Mia. Keep them shut."

Taking a deep breath, she squeezed her lids tightly. She could feel his hands on her injured arm, manipulating it gently—and somehow, it didn't hurt at all when he straightened it, popping the bone into place.

"It's done," he told her hoarsely. "You can open your eyes now."

Mia looked at him, and the frozen shell encasing her suddenly cracked.

Harsh sobs broke out of her throat, and she sank to the floor, shaking uncontrollably. All the terror and the violence she'd just experienced came rushing to the front of her mind, completely overwhelming her. She could've lost him, they could've both died, he had brutally slaughtered another Krinar, and she might've killed Leslie . . . It was too much, all of it, and Mia brought her knees to her chest, her body shuddering with the force of her gasping sobs.

"Mia, shhh, darling, it's over. It's over, I promise you . . ." he murmured, kneeling and gathering her closer to him. Reaching up, he directed the shower head so the water cascaded over them and simply let her cry, knowing that was exactly what she needed right now.

After a few minutes, her sobs began to quiet, and he lifted her, placing her carefully on her feet and removing her swimsuit. Then, pouring soap into his palm, he washed every inch of her and shampooed her hair, removing all traces of blood and dirt from her body. Afterwards, he did the same to himself, until they were both completely clean.

Turning off the water, he stepped out of the shower stall and came back with a big fluffy towel, which he wrapped around her. Too traumatized to do anything else, Mia just stood there, accepting his ministrations.

"Is she dead?" she asked dully, thinking of the girl she'd left bleeding and unconscious by the pool gate.

Korum shook his head, toweling himself off as well. "I don't think so—I saw her breathing as we passed by. I called the guardians who were in the area watching your family. They're almost here. They'll take her into custody and clean up the rest—"

"Who was he? Did you know him?"

For a second, rage flashed in his eyes, and then Korum controlled himself with visible effort. "I did," he said, and she could hear the barely suppressed anger in his voice. "I had no idea he was involved with the Keiths, none at all. I can't believe he fooled all of us like that."

Mia continued to look at him, and he took a deep breath, trying to calm himself.

"His name was Saur," Korum explained evenly. "He worked in your lab—in Saret's lab—ever since we first came to Earth. He was the one who left a few weeks ago, creating the opening that you filled. Saret had always spoken very highly of him. Saur was his youngest and most brilliant assistant—at least until Adam had arrived. I don't know what motivated him to get involved with the Keiths; he had so much to offer our society . . . And why he came out here to kill us, I have no idea . . ."

"To kill *you*," Mia corrected him, feeling cold again at the thought. "Leslie told me her orders were to keep me alive and out of the way while he dealt with you . . ."

His eyebrows rose. "I see," he said thoughtfully, leading her out of the bathroom and into the bedroom.

He had already prepared clothes for her to wear to lunch with her parents—a pretty peach-colored sundress and a silky white thong—and he dressed her carefully, as though she were a small child, his hands particularly gentle around her broken arm.

Which didn't hurt at all now, Mia realized.

Mildly curious, she glanced down at her left side and blinked, hardly able to believe her eyes. Where there had been a bloody gash with bone sticking out just a few minutes ago, there was now perfectly smooth skin, without even a trace of any injury.

Surprised, Mia moved her arm, and it worked quite well. She lifted it, flexing her bicep, and everything appeared to be functioning normally. How did a little pill do this?

In general, she felt much better now. The shower and the medicine he'd given her had done wonders for her physical state, even if her mind was still trying to come to terms with everything they'd just been through.

"It should be all right now," Korum said, watching her testing out the arm.

He had already dressed himself as well, putting on a white T-shirt and a pair of jeans. He looked so gorgeous—and so *alive*—that Mia almost started crying again at the thought of what had almost happened.

"Now," he said softly, coming up to her and tilting her chin up with his fingers, "tell me . . . What the fuck you were thinking, risking your life like that?"

Mia blinked at him, startled by the quiet fury in his voice. "Leslie said he was going to kill you. Sh-she said you were b-being turned into p-particles . . ." Her voice trembling with remembered horror, she could barely hold back the tears that filled her eyes again.

"So you what? Jumped an experienced fighter who held a gun on you? Tackled a Krinar who could kill you with one blow?" Korum was almost shaking with rage now, his eyes completely taken over by those dangerous yellow flecks. "Don't you realize how fragile, how delicate you are? How easily something can hurt you, snuff out your life completely?"

Mia swallowed. "I couldn't bear it if something had happened to you—"

"To me? How do you think I would've felt if something had happened to *you*?" He was almost beside himself, his teeth tightly clenched and a muscle pulsing in his jaw. She had never seen him in this state, and Mia vaguely wondered if she should be afraid. After all, he had just brutally killed an intelligent being. Yet, for some reason, she couldn't muster up even an ounce of fear. Somehow, in the last couple of weeks, she had gone from thinking he would kill her for spying on him to feeling completely safe with him. Even angry, he wouldn't hurt her; she now knew it with bone-deep certainty.

"I don't know," she told him, and watched his eyes turn even brighter. Faster than she could blink, he picked her up and sat down on the bed, cradling her on his lap. Holding her so tightly that she could barely breathe, he buried his face in her hair, and Mia could feel the fine tremors shaking his big, muscular frame.

"You don't know?" he whispered harshly. "You truly don't know that you mean everything to me?"

Hardly daring to believe her ears, Mia pushed at his chest to put a little distance between them so she could look up at his face. "I do?"

"Of course, you do." His gaze burned into her with an intensity she had never seen before. "How could you doubt it?"

"Are . . . are you saying you love me?" she asked tremulously, afraid to even voice such a possibility. What if he said no? What if she'd misunderstood him, and he would now laugh at her silliness? Her chest tightened in anxious anticipation.

"Mia, I love you more than life itself," he said, his voice rough with emotion. "If anything happened to you . . . If you were gone, I would not want to go on living. Do you understand me?"

Mia nodded, too overcome by her own feelings to say anything. He loved her? This beautiful, amazing man loved her?

His eyes narrowed. "And if you ever, ever put your life in danger like that—"

Mia didn't let him finish. Instead, she reached up and buried her hands in his hair, bringing his head down toward her. And then she kissed him, expressing the full depth of her emotions in the way in which they had always communicated best.

At first, he froze, as if wary of hurting her, but then he groaned low in his throat and kissed her back, his hands tightening around her again and his mouth hungry and desperate on hers.

Mia clung to him with equal desperation, her earlier fear and adrenaline morphing into a frenzy of arousal. He was alive—they were both alive—and her body wanted, needed to reaffirm that fact in the most primitive, instinctual way possible.

She ended up on her back on the bed, pinned underneath his hard, muscled weight, her hands frantically tearing at his T-shirt. She felt like she was starving, like she would die without his touch, her body crying out to be filled by him. His kiss consumed her, his tongue stabbing deep into her mouth, and Mia sucked on it, craving his taste, wanting all of him. She felt unbearably hot, her skin too tight, too sensitive to contain the desire burning within her, and she arched toward him, frantically trying to get even closer.

He groaned again, her frenzied response provoking an equally passionate reaction from him. His left hand twisted in her hair, holding her head still for his mouth's ravishment, while his right hand bunched up the skirt of her dress, exposing her lower body. Now only her tiny thong and his jeans stood between them, and he made short work of that too, tearing off her underwear and unzipping his pants. And then he was inside her with one powerful thrust, his cock penetrating her in one smooth slide.

Gasping at the shock of his sudden entry, Mia dug her nails into his shoulders, both stunned and immeasurably relieved to have him inside her. He was unbelievably hot and thick, and the blunt, heavy force of him was exactly what she needed right now. Her muscles quivered, stretching around his large shaft, even as her inner core melted, liquefied at the feel of him filling her so perfectly, quenching the emptiness inside.

He began to move, each stroke pressing her deeper into the mattress, and she was screaming, the tension inside her peaking until her entire body seemed to explode with the force of her orgasm, her sheath uncontrollably pulsing and clenching around his cock.

Panting, he rose up on his elbows, staring down at her with eyes that were almost pure gold. Droplets of sweat were visible on his forehead, and his face was flushed underneath the bronzed hue of his skin. He looked magnificent and savage, and Mia couldn't look away from the blazing intensity in his gaze. He hadn't climaxed yet, and his cock was still hard inside her.

"You're mine," he told her hoarsely, and Mia couldn't dispute the truth of that, not with him lodged so deeply inside her body, inside her heart. She felt incredibly vulnerable like this, but she now knew that he was vulnerable too—that she also held power over him.

"And you're mine," she whispered back, her hands tightening on his shoulders, and felt his shaft jerk inside her as his body reacted physically to her words.

He began thrusting heavily into her again, his hips hammering and recoiling, imprinting himself on her flesh with a ferocity that she almost matched. She felt each thrust deep within her belly, the head of his cock pushing against her cervix, the pleasure so sharp it was verging on pain . . . and then she could feel him swelling up further inside her and her body tightened as another violent orgasm ripped through her. At the same time, he bucked in her arms, achieving his own climax with a hoarse cry, his semen releasing inside her in a few short, warm bursts.

For about a minute, they stayed like that, their bodies joined together as their breathing returned to normal and their heartbeats slowed. Mia had never felt so connected to another person in her life. It was as though they had ceased to be separate individuals, as though the sexual act had linked them together in some way that went beyond the physical. She could feel his heart beating in tune with her own, the heat and scent of his body surrounding her, cocooning her as he held her in his embrace, his weight pleasantly heavy on top of her.

After a while, he rolled off her and gathered her toward him, letting her lie on top of his chest. She knew that she should get up and clean herself, that they had to leave soon for the lunch with her parents, that there was still a lot they needed to discuss—but in this particular moment, she just wanted to lie there with him, shutting out the rest of the world.

She loved him, and he loved her, and that was all that mattered right now.

* * *

The guardians arrived a few minutes later, their ship landing soundlessly on the beach near the house. Zipping his still-intact jeans and dropping a kiss on her forehead, Korum went to greet them, leaving Mia to freshen up before their lunch.

Getting up, Mia noted wryly that her legs were still trembling a bit and her sex throbbing subtly in the aftermath of their passionate encounter. She had no idea what sex would be like with another man, with a human man, but she strongly suspected that what she experienced every night—and frequently during the day—was far from typical. Maybe in the future, when they'd been together longer, their insatiable desire for each other would ease a little, but for now, no amount of sex seemed enough. Was this what Korum had meant by their unusual chemistry? Had he known it would be like this from the very beginning?

Going to the bathroom, she splashed some water on her face and tried to smooth her curls into a more presentable state. Underneath the paleness of her skin, her face glowed with subtle color, and her lips were fuller, swollen a little from his kisses. She looked happy and satisfied, a far cry from the traumatized mess she'd been earlier in the day. She also looked and smelled like she'd just had sex. Another quick shower was clearly in order.

Ten minutes later, she was clean and dressed in a different outfit. It was almost time for them to drive to St. Augustine, so she went to look for Korum.

She found him in the pool area, talking to three Krinar males who were dressed in what looked like light grey uniforms. She remembered seeing similar uniforms on the Ks who had apprehended the Keiths two weeks ago.

These had to be the guardians Korum had mentioned.

One of the guardians held Leslie, who was now conscious and looked like she had a bad headache, or maybe a concussion. Mia felt hugely relieved. She hadn't killed her after all, nor did it seem like she'd caused any permanent damage. However, Leslie did look terrified to have been captured by the creatures she regarded as real-life monsters, and Mia almost felt bad for her, remembering how scared she'd been of Korum in the beginning. Almost—because she couldn't forget the fact that the girl had held her at the gun point and conspired to kill Korum.

Now that she could think again, Mia wondered why Saur wanted Leslie to keep her—Mia—alive and out of the way. Did he think she would somehow be of use to the Resistance? Or did he want something else from her? And why was Korum his target? None of it made any sense.

Suddenly, something occurred to her. The memory loss of the Keiths! If Saur had access to some of the lab's technology and enough knowledge, he might've been the one to erase their memories. In fact, Adam once mentioned that Saur had worked on mind manipulation.

Excited, Mia approached Korum and the guardians. Giving him a huge smile, she said, "I just realized something . . . If Saur worked in Saret's lab—"

Korum nodded approvingly. He had obviously figured it out already. "Exactly. This would explain quite a bit—though I still don't really understand his motivations."

Leslie observed their exchange with a bitter expression on her pain-twisted face. "Xeno bitch," she muttered, shooting Mia a hate-filled look.

"Keep your mouth shut," Korum said coldly, staring at the girl with a contemptuous look on his face. "You should thank whatever pathetic deity you pray to that Mia didn't get hurt today—and that the gun was not loaded. If anything had happened to her, you and all your Resistance buddies would have learned the true meaning of suffering. Do you understand me?"

The fighter visibly gulped, but refused to look away. Mia reluctantly admired her courage; had Korum said that to *her*, she would've been scared out of her wits. Maybe Leslie was too, but she had a pretty good poker face.

Mia wondered what was going to happen to the girl. Did the Ks intend to let her go after embedding surveillance devices in her, as they'd done to the Resistance fighters who had attacked them? She determined to ask Korum about that later, when they were alone. Despite everything, she still hoped that Leslie wouldn't be punished too severely for her actions; the fighter didn't seem like a bad person—just very misguided in her hatred for the Ks.

Two more guardians came in through the gate. "It's done," one of them said in Krinar. "All the evidence has been recorded and removed."

"Good," Korum told them. "Thank you for coming out here so quickly."

The guardian who had just spoken nodded. "Of course. If you think of anything else relating to this attack, just contact us."

Korum promised to do so and the guardians left, taking Leslie with them.

"What are they going to do to her?" Mia asked, observing the look of panic on the girl's face as a guardian carried her away in the direction of the beach.

"She'll undergo some rehabilitation," Korum said. "She's caused too much trouble at this point, and we'll give her the same treatment that we gave the other Resistance leaders we've captured thus far."

"A rehabilitation?"

Now that Mia had spent some time in Saret's lab, she knew that influencing someone's mind to that degree was a very complex and delicate process. It was easy to cause irreparable damage, and every brain was highly unique—what worked for one person might not work for another. Mind-tampering was the most advanced branch of Krinar neuroscience—and even Saret admitted that it was still very imperfect.

"Not the same kind of rehabilitation as for the Keiths," Korum said. "A much milder version. It doesn't take as much effort with humans; she might simply walk away with a small memory loss."

Mia had thought of something else in the meanwhile. "Korum," she asked slowly, "you're not going to be in trouble, are you? Because of what happened on the beach?" Because of the Krinar he'd torn apart—but she couldn't quite bring herself to say that.

He gave her a reassuring smile. "No. It was a very clear case of self-defense, and I have recordings to prove it."

"Recordings?"

He lifted his hand, showing her his palm. "Having embedded technology is very handy. Also, if we need to go even further, we can get some images from the satellites we have in Earth's orbit. What happens on a public beach like that is never a secret. There might be an investigation, just to follow protocol, but there won't be a trial."

Mia exhaled a sigh of relief. "I'm so glad." Stepping toward him, she wrapped her arms around his waist and hugged him tightly, inhaling his warm, familiar scent. He hugged her back, pressing her against him with one hand and stroking her hair with another. They stood like that for a minute, simply enjoying each other's nearness, letting the horror of the day dissipate in the warmth of their embrace.

CHAPTER TWENTY-ONE

Mia's parents met them for lunch in St. Augustine at a small, quaint restaurant called The Present Moment Cafe. Before K-Day, it was one of the few vegan restaurants in the area, showcasing various exotic ingredients and unusual raw dishes. These days, such places were much more common—diners and steakhouses were now the rarity—but the cafe still enjoyed the reputation of being one of the best at gourmet plant-based food.

Korum again insisted on paying for the meal, and her parents acquiesced after a few half-hearted protests. During the lunch, he entertained them with some stories about his initial visit to Earth seven hundred years ago and how different Europe was at that time. Mia could see that her parents were absolutely fascinated—and so was she, to be honest—and time passed by very quickly.

Looking at him interacting so easily with her family, Mia marveled at Korum's incredible composure—or maybe it was simply good acting skills. He laughed and joked with her parents as though nothing had happened, as though he hadn't just killed a fellow K with his bare hands. She tried not to think about that, to move past this morning's events, but she couldn't help the disturbing images that kept flashing into her mind.

Although Mia knew that violence had been a big part of Krinar history and culture, it didn't seem like it was anymore. At least, Mia hadn't run into anything of the sort during her two-week sojourn in Lenkarda. She knew that Korum's favorite sport consisted of fighting—and she knew about the Arena challenges. But that was a far cry from killing someone on the beach. Was Korum bothered by his actions at all, or did he not care? Was the man she loved—and who apparently loved her back—a remorseless killer? And if he was, did *she* care?

After a couple of hours, they said goodbye to her parents and drove to the Alligator Farm, one of St. Augustine's most popular attractions. Korum seemed very interested in seeing the cold-blooded creatures, explaining that they were quite different from anything they had on Krina.

As they wandered through the paths, studying the various species of alligators and crocodiles, Mia decided to bring up something that had been on her mind since this morning.

"Have you killed before?" she asked, trying to sound nonchalant about the whole thing.

Korum stopped and looked at her. "I was wondering when you'd get around to that," he said softly, and there was an unreadable expression on his face. "What would you like me to tell you, my sweet? That I've never been in any other situation where I've had to defend myself and others? That I've managed to live for two thousand years without ever having to take a life?"

Mia swallowed, staring up at him. "I see."

"Do you?" His mouth twisted slightly. "Do you really? I know you've lived a very sheltered life, my darling, and I'm glad for you. If I could've spared you what you saw this morning, believe me, I would have."

"How many?" Mia knew she should stop, but she couldn't help herself. "How many people—Krinar or human—have you killed in your life?"

He sighed. "Not as many as you're probably thinking right now. When I was young, I was very hot-headed and got into a few fights over matters that now seem quite trivial. Several of my opponents challenged me to the Arena, and I accepted their challenge. And once we were in the Arena . . . Well, you might not understand this, but it's very hard for us to stop once the first blood gets spilled. In the heat of battle, we operate purely on instinct—and our instinct is to destroy the enemy at all costs. That's why the Arena fights are so dangerous and so rare these days, because the outcome is often quite deadly—"

"Why hasn't your government outlawed it, then?" Mia interrupted, trying to understand this peculiar quirk of Krinar culture. "Why not get rid of such a barbaric custom? Your society is so advanced in every other way . . . ."

"Because the violence is more contained this way—better controlled, if you will," he explained calmly, watching her with those amber eyes. "If someone has a problem with me, they can just challenge me in the Arena instead of going after my family. Vendettas still happen occasionally, but they're much more rare than in the past—and our society is much more peaceful as a result. Technically, it's illegal to kill someone in the Arena, but nobody has ever been prosecuted for getting carried away in a fair fight."

"Is that what happened today? You got carried away during the fight?"

He nodded, his mouth tightening. "I did . . . but my only regret is that I didn't get a chance to question him, to find out why he did what he did. He hurt you—he could've easily killed you—and he deserved exactly what he got."

Mia looked away, not really knowing what to say. He had killed to protect her—and she probably would've done the same for him—but she still found it frightening, knowing that he was capable of taking someone's life with so little compunction.

"What about humans?" she asked as they walked further, thinking of all the rumors she'd heard about K brutality during the Great Panic months. "Have you killed many humans?"

He didn't answer for a few moments. "Why are you doing this, Mia?" he said quietly as they stopped in front of a large alligator pen. "Why do you ask questions to which you don't want to know the answer?"

"I don't know," Mia told him honestly. "In some ways, you're still such a mystery to me. I love you, yet I feel like I barely know you . . ."

He gazed down into the water with seeming fascination, watching the alligators gliding smoothly through the water. The tourists gave the spot where they were standing a wide berth; like most humans, they had correctly deduced that the K among them was by far the most dangerous creature in the vicinity. Mia was now so used to this that she barely paid attention. Whenever they went somewhere in public, Korum's presence inevitably attracted frightened stares and whispers among the human population.

After a while, he turned to look at her. "Yes, Mia," he said wearily. "I've killed humans. Some in self-defense, some for other reasons. I've had many interactions with your kind over the centuries, and not all of them have been good. Is there anything else you would like to know?"

Mia moistened her lips, staring at him. "Would you have killed Peter that night? In the club? If I hadn't stopped you?"

"You didn't stop me, Mia," Korum said coolly. "I had already made up my mind to let him go with a warning. His offense was not grave enough to warrant anything more."

A breath she hadn't realized she'd been holding escaped her lips in relief. "I see."

"Of course," he added, his eyes glittering, "if he had touched you more—if he had slept with you—the outcome would've been different."

Mia's heart skipped a beat. "You would've killed him for that?" she whispered, a shiver running down her spine.

Korum didn't answer, just looked at her evenly . . . and she knew that what she had always sensed about him was true.

He *was* dangerous—not to her, but to everyone else. As civilized as he appeared on the outside, as advanced as the Ks were with their science and technology, at the core, he was a predator. A predator with a violent nature and a deeply ingrained territorial instinct.

A predator who apparently loved her as much as she loved him.

* * *

That evening, Marisa and Connor came over for dinner again, and Korum prepared a smaller version of the feast he'd made the previous day. Her sister was positively glowing, her skin flushed with healthy color and her eyes sparkling. Her appetite was back to normal, and she was again eating all her favorite foods. Whatever procedure Ellet had performed on her seemed to be having the promised effect.

Connor was beyond grateful. "I finally have my wife back," he confided to them when Marisa went to use the restroom. "The last few weeks have been hell—I was so afraid she would need to be hospitalized for the rest of the pregnancy. The horror stories we'd heard about women with her type of condition . . ."

Korum smiled at him. "I'm glad everything worked out. Ellet is quite skilled—"

Mia felt a pang of jealousy at his praise of the woman who had been his lover, but she did her best to ignore it.

"—and she was more than happy to help in this situation."

After the dinner was over, the four of them decided to go see a movie—the latest James Bond thriller featuring a K villain. Korum was highly amused by the premise, particularly the parts where the human agent managed to outwit the evil K and use the Krinar's own technology to thwart his plan of exterminating all humans. The villain was played by a human actor who actually did a fairly decent job of imitating a K with the aid of computer graphics, but Mia still found his performance inadequate. Marisa and Connor really enjoyed it, however, and peppered Korum with tons of questions on their way back to the house.

As Mia observed their interactions, she realized that her family was completely enthralled with her lover. They'd never seen his truly intimidating side, and they'd never had a reason to fear him—the way Mia did in the beginning. Instead, to them, he was a fascinating foreigner who could entertain them with endless interesting facts and stories, a generous benefactor who had already given them the priceless gift of improved health, and a kind boyfriend who treated Mia like a princess.

And Mia loved it. Never in her wildest dreams would she have expected her family to get on so well with her alien lover. She'd thought they would be frightened and worried sick about her—and they probably would've been if Korum hadn't put in the effort to win them over. That, more than anything, showed her how deeply he cared. He'd known that her family was important to her, and he'd made sure that they would be comfortable with their relationship—or at least as comfortable as they could be knowing that their daughter's boyfriend was not human.

Her thoughts turned to the future again, and she felt a familiar ache in her chest—the same sensation she always got when she thought about the inevitable end of their relationship. He loved her, but surely that couldn't last forever. How long would she remain young and pretty? Ten years, twenty if she was lucky? Granted, some of the actresses these days looked amazing even into their late forties and fifties. Maybe Mia would as well, particularly if Krinar medical prowess extended to cosmetic procedures as well. She pictured Ellet giving her a facelift and almost shuddered at the thought of the beautiful K seeing her when she was old and wrinkled.

Finally, they arrived back at the house and said goodbye to Marisa and Connor, who picked up their car and drove away.

Smiling, Mia waved to them and came into the house, where Korum was already sitting on the couch, studying something in his palm.

Hearing Mia come in, he looked up and gave her a smile. "You were very quiet on the way back," he said, regarding her inquisitively. "You didn't like the movie?"

She approached and sat down next to him. "It was entertaining," she answered, shrugging.

"Then what's the matter? Are you still upset about what happened earlier today?" He reached out and took her hand, lightly massaging her palm in a way that made her melt a little inside.

"No." Mia stared at the large hand cradling hers so tenderly. Her fingers appeared tiny and delicate in his grasp, the pale color of her skin contrasting erotically with his darker hue. "Well, maybe. I don't know. I'm trying not to think about it too much. The movie was a good distraction, actually . . ."

"So then what?" He clearly had no intention of letting it go.

Mia raised her eyes to meet his gaze. "I was just wondering about the future, that's all. I know I should focus on the present and enjoy what we have right now, but I just can't help it sometimes—"

He leaned toward her and kissed her lightly, his lips stopping her next words. "We'll talk about this when we're back in Lenkarda," he murmured, pulling back and looking at her with a rather enigmatic expression on his face. "Don't worry about anything right now. It will all work out, I promise."

Surprised, Mia blinked at him, and then she remembered that he'd mentioned something similar a few weeks ago, when they were still in New York. Unbearably curious, she opened her mouth to ask him another question, but Korum kissed her again and all rational thought left her head.

Picking her up, he carried her upstairs to their bed, and Mia didn't have a chance to think for the rest of the night.

CHAPTER TWENTY-TWO

The next morning, Mia woke up in Korum's arms. It was such an unusual occurrence that her eyes flew open as soon as she realized what was happening.

She was lying on her side, cradled against his body. They were both naked, and she could feel his semi-hard erection prodding at the curve of her buttocks. Startled, Mia turned around to look at his face and saw that he was wide awake.

At her sudden movements, he smiled and brushed his lips against her forehead. "You're awake, I see."

She nodded, blinking at him sleepily. "What are you doing here? You're usually up much earlier . . ."

"I didn't want to leave you alone," Korum explained softly, caressing her cheek. "You seemed to be sleeping restlessly, crying out every couple of hours, and I wanted to make sure you were okay."

Touched, Mia burrowed against him, holding him tightly. "Thank you," she mumbled into his shoulder. "I think I must've had nightmares after yesterday." She vaguely remembered some dreams involving guns and blood, and she was surprised that she'd actually been able to sleep through the night. Undoubtedly, Korum's presence beside her had helped in that regard.

He slowly stroked her hair. "Of course, my darling. It's entirely understandable."

"Do you ever have nightmares?" she asked, pulling back, the psychology student in her suddenly curious about the topic.

"Not typically," Korum admitted, his hand now playing with her long curls. "I usually sleep very deeply for a couple of hours, and then I wake up. I can't remember the last time I had a dream of any kind. It can happen for us, but it's rarer than for humans. Our sleep cycle is somewhat different."

"Oh, I see."

"What do you want to do today?" he asked. "We don't have any plans right now."

"I was thinking we could have dinner with my parents again tonight, but I don't know about the day . . . No beach, though—I don't think I'm ready to go back there yet."

"Of course." His body tensed for a moment. "Why don't we do something else entirely? How about a trip to Orlando? We could visit one of those theme parks with roller coasters and all—"

"What, like Disney World?" Mia gave him an incredulous look.

"Sure," he said seriously. "Or maybe Universal. That's the more adult one, right?"

Unable to help herself, Mia burst out laughing. "Really? You want to go to Universal Studios?" She pictured the two of them standing in line for the Incredible Hulk, and all the tourists freaking out at the sight of a K near their children.

"Yeah, why not?"

Why not indeed. Still giggling, Mia said, "Okay, I'm game. We can go to Islands of Adventure—that's the part of Universal that has more roller coasters. How are we getting to Orlando? Driving?"

"Might as well. I don't mind driving—it gives me a chance to see more of the area." He grinned at her, looking so charming and carefree that she couldn't help but kiss the dimple on his left cheek.

When her lips touched his face, however, she could feel his mood shifting. By now, she was so attuned to him that she realized immediately what he wanted. Sure enough, when she pulled back, he was regarding her with a heavy-lidded golden gaze. "This is why I don't normally stay in bed with you," he muttered before his lips descended on hers and his hand ventured lower between her thighs.

And for the next hour, they forgot all about Orlando, caught up in their own wild ride.

* * *

Two hours later, they were whizzing down the highway at over a hundred miles per hour. With anyone else at the wheel, Mia would've been scared out of her mind, but Korum's reflexes were better than any race car driver's and she felt utterly safe with him. For the first twenty minutes of the ride, he drove with the top down, but Mia's hair kept blowing into her face, and they had to pull over to put the top up.

"I should really cut this mess," Mia grumbled as they got back on the highway, trying to smooth down the curly explosion on her head. It was futile. Wind and her hair didn't mix.

"Don't even think about it," Korum said seriously. "I love your hair long."

Mia sighed. "Fine. Maybe I'll just get it straightened . . ."

"Why? Your curls are beautiful. Leave them just as they are."

"You're weird," Mia told him. "Most men like straight, silky hair, not this rat's nest I've got going on here—"

"I don't care what most men like. Leave the hair as it is." His tone was utterly uncompromising.

Mia smiled to herself, mentally shaking her head. Even in this small matter, he had to be in control. It was strange that she didn't mind it quite as much anymore, though nothing had really changed. She was still his charl, and he still had way too much power over her life. The difference was that now she knew that he loved her, that she wasn't just a human toy to him.

A little tidbit from her encounter with Leslie nagged at the back of her mind. "Korum," she said tentatively, "what exactly is this blood addiction you've warned me about before? Leslie said something about it yesterday . . ."

Keeping his eyes on the road, Korum asked, "What did she say?"

Mia struggled to remember the girl's exact words. "It was something like her brother was addicted and he was walking around begging Ks to bite him every hour until they killed him . . ."

For a few seconds, Korum remained silent. "That sounds like a particularly unfortunate case," he said after some time. "It must've happened not long after we first arrived here."

"What do you mean?"

"Do you remember how I told you that we no longer require blood to survive? That it's now basically a pleasure drug for us?"

"Yes, of course."

"Well, it turns out that there's a side effect to getting too much of this drug. The pleasure is so intense that it's addictive for us—and for the humans we're drinking from. However, for a Krinar to become physically addicted, he or she has to drink from the same human more frequently than a couple of times a week. Essentially, the Krinar gets addicted to the specific DNA signature in that human's blood. It's a peculiar side effect of the genetic fix that allows us to survive without blood. Some of our best scientists are currently studying this phenomenon and trying to figure out why it's happening and how it can be stopped."

Mia stared at him in fascination. "So what happens when you get addicted? Is it physically painful?"

"When the Krinar is separated from their human for whatever reason, yes. They can't go longer than a few hours without getting their fix—and that's a problem both for the human and the Krinar."

"So is that what happened to Leslie's brother? I'm not sure I fully get it . . ."

"No, it works differently for humans. Your species gets addicted to the substance in our saliva, but any Krinar's saliva would work. I don't exactly know what happened to Leslie's brother, but I can venture a guess. It sounds like he might've been involved in some of the early x-clubs—"

"X-clubs?"

"X-clubs, xeno-clubs—that's your slang term for nightclubs where humans go to interact with our kind."

Mia blinked. "I've never heard of this before. Is it like the websites where humans advertise to have sex with Ks?"

He looked vaguely amused. "Pretty much. The websites are usually for those who are just curious. Very few people posting there would consider actually going through with their fantasy. The ones who are serious about it go to x-clubs."

"Really?" Mia was amazed that she'd never come across this before. "Where are these clubs located? Are there some in New York City?"

"No, they're actually close to our Centers—we generally don't like going to major cities. That's probably why you don't know about them. There are a few in Costa Rica, some in New Mexico and Arizona, some in Thailand and the Philippines . . ."

"And Ks actually go to these places?"

Korum nodded. "Some do, especially those who are otherwise reluctant to venture outside of the Centers. I've never gone myself, because I don't have a problem spending time in human cities and towns. Many Krinar do, though; they can't stand the crowds or the pollution, so the clubs are a convenient way for them to enter into sexual relations with humans."

"So you think Leslie's brother might've gone to an x-club?"

"It's a likely possibility. In the last couple of years, these places have become more strictly regulated. Now a particular human is only allowed in twice a week, and the Krinar who go there are warned against sharing that human for the night. However, in the early days, everything was much more disorganized, and some humans got carried away. They would hook up with one or more Krinar per night and have their blood taken much too frequently."

Mia wrinkled her nose, disturbed at the thought. When Korum took her blood, it was such a transcendent experience that she couldn't imagine sharing it with anyone else. Of course, she couldn't imagine having sex with anyone else either, so it probably wasn't a fair comparison. "I see."

"My guess is that Leslie's brother became seriously addicted. Why he died, I have no idea. Perhaps he became violent and tried to force one of the Krinar women—that's been known to happen and could be one reason why he would've been killed—"

"A human forcing a Krinar?"

"I didn't say he would've succeeded. Our women are much weaker than Krinar men, but they are still stronger than humans. However, an attempt would've been sufficient to earn him a death sentence. No sane human would try such a thing, of course, but some of these addicts are not rational, particularly when they've been deprived for a while."

Mia shuddered. The whole thing sounded awful. "Is there a cure?" she asked, trying to imagine how desperate those poor people must be.

"Not yet. As far as I know, it's still in the experimental stages."

"When did you learn about this? The addiction, I mean? Was it before or after you came here?"

"We've known about it for a few thousand years, but it wasn't regarded as a real problem until we came here. It mostly happened with charl and their cheren, and it was considered to be part of the bond between the couple. And since those relationships were exceedingly rare, nobody really thought anything of it. Of course, now that we're living among humans, it's very different."

"I see . . ." Mia looked out the window, trying to understand the implications. Something didn't quite make sense to her, but she couldn't place her finger on it right now.

And then it hit her.

Turning back to look at him, she frowned in puzzlement. "Korum, what would happen when the charl passed away? To the Krinar, I mean?

If they were addicted to that specific human, how did they go on?"

For a second, Korum didn't answer. Then he said softly, "The charl wouldn't pass away, Mia."

Stunned, Mia stared at him. "What do you mean?" she whispered, unsure if she had heard him right.

He was silent again, and she could see the tightening of the muscles in his jaw. All of a sudden, he swerved into the right lane and headed for the exit, disregarding the sound of screeching brakes and the outraged honking from the drivers he cut off. Startled, Mia gripped the door handle with her right hand, trying to hang on. A minute later, he pulled into the parking lot of Comfort Inn and put the car into "park" mode.

Turning to her, he said quietly, "We don't let the humans we love die, my sweet. You, Maria, Delia—you're all as close to immortal as a biological being can get. You won't age, you won't get sick, and any injuries you get—as long as they're not beyond repair—will heal quickly, as they do for me."

CHAPTER TWENTY-THREE

For a few seconds, Mia could only gape at him in shock. Was this a joke? "B-but h-how?" she stammered. "I'm not Krinar—"

"No, you're definitely not Krinar," Korum agreed. "You're human, just as you've always been."

"So then how?" Mia could barely process what he was telling her. "How is this possible?"

"Have you noticed that you've been healing quicker? Maybe feeling better, more energetic?"

Mia nodded, her heart galloping in her chest.

"And you've never wondered how that's possible? How your arm healed so quickly yesterday?"

"I thought you gave me something," Mia whispered. "That pill yesterday . . ."

"The pill was a painkiller; it didn't have the ability to heal you like that. For that, I would've needed specialized equipment similar to the devices I've used on you before. No, my darling, your arm mended so well because there are now millions of highly advanced and complex nanocytes in your body, and their sole function is to keep you healthy by repairing any damage—whether it's on a cellular or DNA level."

"What?" Dark spots swam in front of her vision, and she inhaled deeply, realizing that she'd stopped breathing for a second. "What do you mean? How would they have gotten into my body?"

"Ellet implanted them at my request the first night after you arrived in Lenkarda," he explained, studying her with a watchful amber gaze. "I brought you to her lab, and she performed the procedure."

Mia's head was spinning, and she couldn't seem to wrap her brain around what he'd just told her. "Y-you brought me to Ellet's lab? While I was sleeping? You did this to me over t-two weeks ago?"

"Yes," he said, his eyes slowly turning more golden. "I didn't want to chance something happening to you by delaying it any further."

She stared at him, utterly bewildered. "Why didn't you tell me? Why didn't you ask me before you did it?"

"I couldn't take a chance that you'd refuse," he said simply. "You were still too angry, too resentful when I had first brought you there. And frankly, my darling, I was too angry with you—too hurt and angry to offer this to you at the time and have an entire discussion on this topic. Your betrayal wounded me, Mia. Logically, I understood why you did it, but it still hurt me more than anything anyone had ever done . . ."

Mia swallowed, tears welling up in her eyes. "I'm sorry . . . I really am so sorry about that—"

"And later on," Korum continued, his gaze holding hers, "after the procedure was done, I delayed telling you because I wanted to see how our relationship would develop, whether you would grow to feel as strongly about me as I felt about you . . ."

"You were testing me?"

He nodded. "In a way. I know how much immortality would mean to most humans. I wanted you to love *me*—and not just the long life I could give you. I was going to tell you when we came back to Lenkarda, but the topic kept coming up, and I didn't want to lie to you."

Her thoughts racing a mile a minute, Mia reached for the door, her hand scrambling to find the handle in the unfamiliar vehicle.

"What are you doing?" he asked sharply, his eyes narrowing.

"I . . . I need a minute," she said tremulously, her arm shaking as she pushed open the door. She felt violated and invaded, and the realization that the man she loved had done that to her was making her sick. "I just need a minute—"

Before she could get out of the car, he was already there, looming over the passenger side. "Stop it, Mia. You're not going anywhere."

Feeling like she was hyperventilating, Mia scrambled out of the car, ignoring his order. She needed some distance between them right now, needed to find a way to come to terms with everything she'd just learned.

He grabbed her arm as she tried to slide past him. "Stop acting like this. You said you loved me—you even risked your life yesterday to save me—and you're upset about the fact that we can be together long term?"

Mia frantically shook her head, trying to yank her arm away—a futile attempt, of course. "No, of course not!" She could hear the edge of hysteria in her own voice. "But you didn't even ask me! How could you do something this big without asking me?"

"Do what?" His tone was ice-cold, and his expression hard. "Give you perfect health? A long life?"

Mia felt like her head would explode. "Implant something into my body! Perform a medical procedure on me without my knowledge or consent!"

"I gave you a gift, Mia." His eyes were almost purely yellow at this point. "It's not like I stole your kidney—"

"You stole my free will!" Mia was vaguely aware that she was yelling, but she didn't care right now. Her vision was hazy with rage, and she could feel herself trembling with the force of her emotions. All the frustration of the past few weeks boiled to the surface. "You stole my ability to make any decisions in my life! Yes, I love you, but that doesn't give you the right to treat me like a possession. Don't you understand, Korum? Don't you realize how that makes me feel, knowing that you can do something like that to me?"

He stared at her, and she could see the muscle pulsing in his tightly clenched jaw. "I did what was best for you. I gave you immortality, Mia. Wasn't that what you were worrying about? Our future together?"

"The future where I'm treated like a slave for centuries to come? The future where I don't have any say over my own body, my own life? That kind of future?" Mia asked bitterly, too furious to think about what she was saying.

She heard him inhale sharply. "Get in the car, Mia," he ordered, his voice low and cold. "You're being irrational."

"Or what?" she said defiantly. "You're going to force me in? You're going to make me?"

"If I have to. Now get in."

Shaking with helpless anger, Mia got in and watched as he shut the passenger door and walked over to the driver's side.

"We're going back to the house," he said, pulling out of the parking lot with the sound of squealing tires. "I don't think a theme park is the best idea right now."

* * *

The ride home passed in tense silence, with Mia looking out the window and Korum concentrating on driving. It took less than thirty minutes to make the drive back, with the speedometer pushing a hundred-and-thirty. Thankfully, they weren't stopped by the police. Mia had a strong suspicion that any state trooper unfortunate enough to confront Korum in this mood wouldn't have fared well.

As much as she'd wanted to have some time to herself, the silent drive accomplished nearly the same thing, giving her time to think. With her temper slowly cooling, the full implications of what he'd just told her dawned on her. He'd made her immortal—or at least as close to immortal as a biological being could get, she mentally corrected herself. She could still die if her body was damaged beyond repair, just as Korum could—but not from aging or disease, like the rest of humanity.

Did that mean that she would now live for thousands of years? She couldn't begin to comprehend that length of time. She was only twenty-one now, and even thirty seemed far away. A thousand years? It was like something out of a fairy tale. Never aging, never getting sick . . . He was right; it was every human's dream come true. It was *her* dream come true.

But the way he'd done it . . . Mia stared at her palms, where she still had tracking devices implanted from the time he'd shined her. Why had she been so surprised that he would do something else to her? He obviously regarded her as "his"—his charl, his to do with as he pleased. Yes, he'd given her an impossible, priceless gift, but he had also taken from her any semblance of an illusion about the true nature of their relationship. He wasn't her boyfriend or her lover; he was her master. She didn't have any say when it came to her own body, her own life, and he clearly saw nothing wrong with doing whatever he wanted to her.

For the past couple of weeks, she'd lived in a dream world, reveling in being with him, in the phenomenal opportunity he'd given her, in the way he'd interacted so well with her family . . . And all this time, she hadn't known that he had fundamentally changed her, that she was no longer the same Mia she had always been.

Immortality. It seemed so crazy, so impossible . . . For millennia, people had searched for that elusive fountain of youth, and yet the Ks had had it all along. A shiver ran through her as she fully understood what that meant: the Krinar had the power to indefinitely extend human lifespan, and they chose not to.

The non-interference mandate.

That had to be the only explanation. The Krinar had created her kind, and they continued playing God with them. Humans were nothing more than an experiment to them, and Mia realized how foolish she'd been to hope that Korum would ever see her as an equal. He might love her in his own way, but he didn't see her as a person, as someone who had the same basic rights as he did. How could he when his species regarded humans as nothing more than their creations, the result of their grand evolutionary design?

The car pulled into the driveway, and Mia got out as soon as it stopped, rushing into the house. She couldn't look at Korum right now, couldn't talk about this rationally. Not yet, not until she'd had a chance to digest this further.

To her relief, he didn't follow her, giving her some much needed space.

She ran upstairs and locked herself in one of the guest bedrooms. The lock was beyond flimsy, of course; it probably wouldn't deter a human man, much less a Krinar. But it still made her feel a tiny bit better, having that barrier between them.

Sitting down on the bed, Mia looked down at her hands, clenched so tightly on her lap. On her right thumb, there had always been a tiny scar; she'd cut herself with a kitchen knife when she was seven, trying to peel an apple. The scar was now gone. Why hadn't she noticed that before?

Getting up, she walked over to the large mirror hanging on the wall near the entrance. The image reflecting back at her looked remarkably normal. Same pale face, same unruly dark curls. Yet upon closer inspection, she could see the subtle differences. Her skin, usually lightly freckled, was completely smooth and white, without even a hint of any blemish. The minor sun damage she'd accumulated in her twenty-one years seemed to have disappeared. Her hair looked healthier as well, without any split ends—yet she hadn't seen the inside of a salon in over six months.

Lifting her arm, she flexed it slightly, watching the small muscle moving beneath her skin. Even her body had changed slightly; she'd always been thin, but now she looked a little more toned, as though she'd been exercising regularly. She remembered how she'd been able to swim for an hour, how she'd fought Leslie and won . . . It appeared that improved fitness was one of the benefits of this procedure.

No wonder Ellet had seemed so familiar to her. Mia recalled the dream she'd had when she first arrived in Lenkarda—a dream where a beautiful woman was touching her with her elegant fingers. Ellet. It had been Ellet. Korum had brought Mia to her lab for the procedure, and Mia must've been semi-awake for at least part of it.

Walking back to the bed, Mia lay down and curled up into a little ball, bringing her knees to her chest. She felt nauseous, and she knew that it was all in her head. She couldn't get sick now; it was a physical impossibility. But the unpleasant sensation in her stomach lingered, her insides twisting as she imagined Korum drugging her and bringing her to his former lover. She pictured Ellet performing the procedure on her unconscious body and shuddered.

How could he have done this to her? How could he have given her something so precious, something she hadn't even dared to hope for, while at the same time destroying her trust? And how could she be with someone who could do something like that, who could completely disregard her will?

Yet how could she not?

Mia tried to imagine a future without Korum, and the years stretched in front of her, grey and empty. If she'd never met him—if she'd never experienced his passion, his caring—she would've been content, but now . . . Now he was as necessary to her as air. Even though they'd only been separated for a few minutes, she felt his absence so acutely it was as if a part of her was missing. If he ever left her, she wouldn't be just devastated; she would simply cease to exist, to function as a person. She would be nothing more than a broken empty shell, a mere shadow of her former self.

Was that how he felt about her too?

Tears burned in her eyes at the thought. Was that why he'd done this, because he couldn't wait, couldn't bear the possibility of any harm befalling her if he delayed the procedure by even a couple of weeks? Had he taken away her freedom of choice because of the strength of his feelings for her?

She tried to imagine how she would've felt if someone she loved was weak and fragile, prone to illness and injury. Korum had always been so strong, so invulnerable; other than that time on the beach—and before, when she'd been working with the Resistance—she'd never really had to worry about his health and wellbeing.

But he worried about her constantly. She knew that.

He went out of his way to take care of her, to make sure she was warm and well-fed, to heal all her injuries, no matter how minor. Knowing how important school and career were to her, he hadn't tried to limit her in that regard. Instead, he'd provided her with an incredible opportunity, giving her a chance to feel happy and fulfilled in that part of her life. He'd even made sure that her family was comfortable with their relationship. He'd given her everything—except the ability to make her own decisions.

No, she couldn't imagine a life without him—and now she didn't need to. For better or for worse, they could be together forever, and her foolish heart filled with joy at the thought. She didn't know if she could forgive him for doing the procedure without her consent—not quite yet, at least—but she could try. She would have to try. She loved him too much not to.

After all, they now had centuries to figure it all out.

CHAPTER TWENTY-FOUR

Ten minutes later, Mia headed downstairs, ready to talk. She had a million questions for Korum, and she couldn't wait to get the answers.

To her surprise, she found him standing in the living room, staring out the window at the ocean beyond. Hearing her footsteps, he turned around to face her, and Mia froze on the stairs, shocked by the remote look on his face.

His eyes seemed empty, as though he was looking straight through her, and the expression on his face was hard and shuttered, giving nothing away.

"Korum?" Mia was aware that her voice trembled slightly, but she couldn't help herself. She'd seen him cold and mocking, she'd seen him angry and passionate, but she'd never seen him like this before. It was as though a stranger was looking at her right now, a stranger with the familiar features of the man she loved.

"The car keys are over there," he said, gesturing at the coffee table. His voice was flat and unemotional. "I'll make sure that Roger sends all your things to your parents' house. For now, I transferred money into your bank account, so you can buy some basic necessities until your luggage arrives."

"What?" Mia whispered inaudibly, feeling like all air had left the room. Her chest felt like it was getting squeezed in a giant vise, and she couldn't seem to get her lungs to work.

"The guardians will continue to watch over you and your family for now, until we're sure that Saur was acting alone. You should be safe enough now that he and Leslie have been caught."

Her brain couldn't seem to process what he was telling her. "K-Korum? What are you talking about?"

He turned away then, looking out the window again. "That's all, Mia. You can go."

Hardly aware of her actions, Mia slowly walked down the stairs, a cold sensation spreading throughout her body. "Go where?" she asked, unable, unwilling to understand. Pausing a few feet away from him, she stood there trembling, desperately needing him to turn around, to look at her with that warm smile of his.

But he didn't. He was like a statue, completely still and unmoving. "I assume to your parents' house," he finally said. "Isn't that where you usually spend your summers?"

"You want m-me to leave?" Mia could barely choke out the words through the constriction in her throat. A black pit of despair seemed to yawn underneath her, ready to engulf her at any moment. Surely he couldn't mean that, surely he didn't really want her to go . . .

"Take the car," he said, still looking out the window. "You know how to drive, right?"

"I don't have my driver's license with me," she said numbly, staring at his back.

"If any cops stop you, I'll take care of your ticket. Your license and the rest of your things will be delivered to you this week."

Her throat closing up, Mia wrapped her arms around herself, trying to contain the agony within. "Why?" she whispered hoarsely. "Why do you want me to leave?"

"Isn't that what you wanted?" he asked coldly, turning around to look at her. His face was completely expressionless; only the faint yellow flecks in his irises gave away any hint of emotion. "Isn't that what you've been fighting for all these weeks? Your freedom? Well, you have it." He turned away again, effectively dismissing her.

Feeling like she was suffocating, Mia desperately sucked in air. "Korum, please, I don't understand—"

"Is my English not clear enough for you?" His words lashed at her like a whip. "You're free to go. Leave, get out of here."

Almost choking on the sob rising in her throat, Mia backed away, the pain of his rejection nearly unbearable. The back of her knees touched the coffee table, and her hand automatically closed around the car keys lying there. Grabbing them, Mia turned and ran out of the house, her vision blurred by tears streaming down her face.

She got as far as the car before sinking down to the ground. Her entire body was shaking, and she could barely draw in enough air through the compression in her chest. For some reason, Korum didn't want her anymore. He wanted her to leave. After everything, he was letting her go.

It didn't make sense; none of it made sense. Leaning against the car, Mia sat on the hard ground, hugging her knees and rocking back and forth. After a couple of minutes, when the initial shock of agony had subsided, she tried to gather her thoughts, to attempt to understand what had just happened. Surely, there had to be a logical explanation for this. Why would he bother making her immortal if he was planning to walk away from her all along? Why would he have gone so far as to make her family like him if he didn't care about her? Why would he have told her that he loved her? Had it all been a lie? Had he been toying with her all along? The thought was so excruciating that Mia had to push it away for the sake of her sanity.

Or was it all her fault? Did her reaction to his revelation make him change his mind about their relationship? Perhaps he was beginning to tire of her already, and this had been the last straw for him. Mia raised her fist to her mouth, biting down hard to contain a moan of pain. She couldn't imagine her life without him, and he didn't want her anymore. She'd lost him; for whatever reason, she'd lost him . . .

She should get in the car and leave, try to salvage some pride instead of crying in his driveway, but she couldn't make herself move. If she left now, she might never see him again. He had no reason to be in New York anymore, and there was no guarantee she would ever be allowed in Lenkarda again. If she drove away, the person she loved more than anything would be gone from her life.

She couldn't allow that to happen.

Her face wet with tears, Mia resolutely got up, brushing the dust and gravel off her dress. If Korum truly didn't want her, she needed to hear him say so. He would have to explain himself because she wasn't leaving without a fight. He had forced his way into her life, into her heart, and now he thought he could walk away without an explanation? She might have been too afraid to question him in the beginning, but she wasn't anymore. If he wanted to get rid of her, he would have to physically remove her from the premises. She wasn't leaving until they talked about everything.

And wiping her cheeks with the back of her wrist, Mia headed back into the house to confront the only man she'd ever loved.

* * *

Korum was standing in the same spot, still looking out the window. Hearing her approach, he turned around. For a second, a flash of something appeared on his face before it smoothed into its expressionless mask again.

"You didn't leave," he said quietly, studying her dispassionately. She knew his sharp gaze didn't miss the remnants of tears on her face or traces of dirt on her legs.

"No," she said, her voice rougher than usual. "I didn't leave."

"Why not?" He inquired, looking mildly curious, as though they were talking about nothing more important than a movie she didn't enjoy.

Mia's eyes narrowed. "Why do you want me to go?" she countered, her chin lifting. "Yesterday, you said you loved me, and now you don't want to be with me?"

His expression darkened, and his eyes turned that dangerous shade of gold again. "Mia, if you don't walk away right now, you won't be able to. Ever. Do you understand me?"

Her heart hammering in her chest, Mia stared defiantly at him. "No, I don't. I don't understand you at all." And instead of walking away, she took a step in his direction.

In the blink of an eye, he was next to her, moving so fast that she jumped in surprise. His hand flashed toward her and closed around the front of her dress, holding her in place as he loomed over her. "What don't you understand?" he said softly, and she heard the barely controlled rage in the velvety smoothness of his voice. "You want me to beg you to stay? To tell you how much I love you again?"

Her chest rapidly rising and falling with every breath, Mia swallowed to get rid of the obstruction in her throat. She'd never seen him in this kind of mood before, and she was almost frightened. Almost—because she now knew that he would never hurt her. Not physically, at least.

"Why didn't you leave when I gave you a chance, Mia?" he whispered harshly, jerking her toward him until she was pressed against his body, feeling the heat radiating from him and the hard bulge growing in his jeans. "Don't you know how much it cost me to let you go?"

He wasn't trying to get rid of her. He was giving her freedom because he thought that's what she wanted.

The truth dawned on her, and Mia almost burst into tears again. Korum loved her; he loved her enough to let her walk away, to overcome his own need to keep her with him.

For the first time, he was giving her a choice.

Her heart filling with incandescent joy, Mia stared up at him, seeing the signs of strain on his beautiful face. He loved her, and he was letting her walk away. The magnitude of his gesture didn't escape her. This gorgeous, powerful man had never been denied anything he truly wanted before—and she now knew beyond a shadow of doubt that he wanted her. His intellect and ambition had propelled Korum to the top of Krinar society, and he was used to having an extraordinary amount of influence and control. Here on Earth, his power was even greater; as a member of the race that conquered her planet, he could do almost anything without consequences. Among humans, he was like a god.

What would it be like, to wield that kind of power? Would she have been able to restrain herself if she knew that she could take anything she wanted? Have anyone she wanted? Mia had never asked herself that question before, and she wondered if she would like her own answer.

The fact that he was giving her a choice now . . . She knew how difficult it was for him, how much it went against his nature. He considered her his, and by Krinar law, she belonged to him. For Korum to relinquish that power, to let her leave him—that, more than anything, showed her how much she now meant to him.

So instead of flinching away in fear of his temper, she slid her hands up his chest, gripping his face between her palms. Holding his gaze with her own, she whispered, "I don't want to go. I don't ever want to go . . ."

His eyes flared brighter, and she could see his pupils expanding even as his mouth descended on hers, his lips hard and almost bruising. His tongue invaded her mouth, his kiss all-consuming, and she met him eagerly, reveling in the frantic hunger she could taste in his kiss. His hands migrated to her back, tightened until she could barely breathe, and she could feel his large body trembling with the intensity of his emotions.

Pulling back for a second, he growled, "You're staying," and Mia nodded, even though it wasn't a question. Standing up on tiptoes, she kissed him again, and felt the room tilt as he swung her up into his arms, carrying her to the couch.

The control he exerted over himself earlier was completely gone, and she could feel the primitive need driving him now. He wasn't gentle, and she didn't want him to be, not right now, not when she so desperately craved his passion. His hands ripped off her dress, her underwear, and then he was plunging into her, wild with the urge to get inside, to claim her in the most basic way possible.

At the force of his entry, Mia cried out and arched toward him, her fingers curving into claws, digging into the back of his neck. He felt impossibly hard and thick, stretching her, filling her until she forgot all about the agony of nearly losing him, lost in the driving power of his thrusts.

His right hand fisted in her hair, pulled her head to the side, exposing her neck, and then he bit her, the sharp edges of his teeth slicing across her skin. Mia gasped at the sudden pain, and then his mouth latched onto the wound and the world around her dissolved as ecstasy rushed through her veins.

For the next several hours, all she knew was the dark rapture of his embrace.

ANNA ZAIRES

CHAPTER TWENTY-FIVE

"So tell me more about this immortality thing," Mia said lazily, watching as he lifted one long curl and traced a circle with it on his own shoulder.

They were lying in bed side by side, having sated themselves yet again this morning.

Mia could hardly remember the rest of the day yesterday. After he'd bitten her, she didn't regain her senses until late in the evening, when he'd woken her up from exhausted sleep in order to feed her dinner. Then he brought her back to bed, and she passed out again, opening her eyes this morning only to find him watching her with a hungry look on his face. "Finally," he'd muttered before stripping away the blanket and crawling down her body, his skilled mouth bringing her to orgasm before she was even fully awake. Afterwards, he'd taken her again, as though he couldn't bear to be physically separated from her for even a few hours.

Now he turned his head to look at her, a warm glow in his eyes. "What do you want to know?" he asked, smiling.

"Everything," Mia told him. "Have you always known how to do that—to make humans immortal? And how does it work, exactly? Am I still human, or am I some weird hybrid? Do I also have enhanced speed and strength? And will I ever change physically, or is this how I'm going to look for the rest of my life?"

He laughed, rising up on his elbow. "That's quite a few questions. Let me start with the easy ones. Yes, you're still human. No, you're not really that much stronger or quicker than you were, although you're in somewhat better shape. However, you do heal very fast. If you wanted to get stronger, it would be easy for you; all you'd need to do is start lifting weights and doing exercise. Your body regenerates so rapidly now that you won't need any downtime, and you could become as fit as any of your top athletes in a matter of weeks.

"You have more endurance now too, again because of your body's rapid healing properties. And no, you're definitely not a hybrid of any kind. The nanocytes mimic the natural functions of your body and repair all damage; that's really all they do. They restore your body to its optimal state, so yes, you won't really change physically going forward. You're going to remain young and beautiful for years and centuries to come."

Mia listened to his explanation, her pulse beginning to pound with excitement. "Wow," she whispered in amazement. "I don't even know what to say. Just . . . wow."

Korum grinned at her, and then his expression became more serious. "As to the first part of your question, this is a relatively new technology for us. We've only had it for the last few thousand years."

"A few thousand years? That's a really long time . . ." They could've given humans immortality at any point in the last few thousand years?

He sighed. "If you say so."

"Korum," Mia said tentatively, "what exactly is this non-interference mandate? Is that the reason why you haven't shared any of your technology with us?"

He nodded. "Yes. The non-interference mandate was set by the Elders, and it supersedes any laws that the Council can pass—"

"The Elders?"

"The oldest Krinar in existence. There are nine who are known as the Elders; they're the ones who have been around for millions of years. Lahur is the oldest among them, and it's said that he's been alive for over ten million years."

Stupefied, Mia stared at him. "Ten million years?" Ten million years ago, humans didn't even exist as a species. And there were Krinar around who were that old?

"It's unimaginable for me as well," Korum said, understanding her awe. "They had to have seen so much, learned so much throughout their lives. There's nothing that can compare to the wisdom of the Elders."

"Where are they?" Mia asked, goosebumps springing up all over her body as she tried to picture someone that ancient. "Did any of them come to Earth?"

"No, they're on Krina. For the most part, they're very reclusive; few Krinar have ever met them, and that's how they like it. I've seen Lahur from a distance, but I'm one of the few who has."

Mia frowned, perplexed. "So how did they set the mandate? How do they enforce it?"

"They don't have to enforce it, Mia. The Elders are revered in our society; to go against them is an offense punishable by death."

"But why did they do it? Why set that mandate in the first place?"

"I don't know their exact motivations," Korum admitted. "But I do know that two of them were part of the team of scientists that guided human evolution. They were the original creators of your species. If I had to venture a guess, I would say that they are still overseeing that project."

Mia's frown deepened. "So why did they let you come to Earth in the first place?"

"Because the Council—specifically, myself, Saret, and a few others—was able to convince them that it was necessary for the ultimate survival of the Krinar. Your weapons, your technology were evolving so rapidly and in such a destructive direction that you were endangering your planet. And since we will ultimately need to call Earth home—when our star dies in a hundred million years or so—we couldn't allow you to make this planet uninhabitable."

Mia digested that quietly. She still didn't fully understand this Elder situation. "So how is it that you were able to make me immortal despite this mandate?"

"By claiming you as my charl." His eyes glittered at her. "We're allowed to make exceptions for our charl."

"I see." Mia looked at him, remembering his assertion that being a charl was an honor. Now she could understand why he thought so. Yes, the charl may have few rights in the K society, but they had something no other humans could achieve—perfect health and an incredibly long lifespan. Even in modern-day United States, there were probably many who would gladly trade whatever rights and freedoms they enjoyed for a chance to live even a few extra decades, much less hundreds or even thousands of years.

"What about my parents and my sister?" Mia asked, holding her breath. "Does the mandate make exceptions for them?"

A look of genuine regret appeared on Korum's handsome face. "No, Mia, I'm sorry. It doesn't. I'll do everything I can to keep them healthy and maximize their natural lifespan, but I can't give them what I gave you."

Painfully biting her lip, Mia looked away. She'd suspected that might be the case, but it still hurt to hear him confirm it. She would remain young and healthy, while everyone around her would age and pass away.

The thought was unbearably depressing.

"My darling, come here," he murmured, pulling her into his arms. "I'm sorry, I really am. For what it's worth, I will petition the Elders on your behalf. I just don't know if it will do anything."

"Thank you," Mia whispered, staring him in the eyes. "Thank you for that, for everything."

"I love you," he said softly, his hand stroking her back. "And I'll do anything for you. You know that, right?"

Mia smiled, her heart overflowing with emotion. "I love you more . . ."

"That would be impossible," he told her, and the intensity in his voice startled her. "I love you so much it hurts. If you had left me yesterday . . ."

Swallowing against a sudden surge of tears, Mia hugged him tighter. "I wouldn't have," she said thickly. "I don't ever want to leave you. I thought you didn't want me anymore . . ."

"I'll always want you." He sounded utterly convinced of that fact.

"How do you know that?" Mia asked curiously. "We've known each other less than two months. How do you know how you'll feel in a few years?"

His lips curved into a tender smile. "That's where experience comes in handy, my sweet. I know how I feel—I've known almost from the very beginning. The first time I held you in my arms, the first time we made love, I knew this was unlike anything I've ever felt before. I couldn't think of anything but you—the way you tasted, the way you smelled, the stubborn tilt to your chin . . . I thought I was losing my mind because I was becoming so obsessed with a human girl—a girl who didn't want to be with me, no less. I wanted to fuck you, yes, but I also wanted to keep you safe, to take you with me and never let you go . . ."

"Why didn't you tell me?" Mia asked, her heart skipping a beat at his words. "Why didn't you tell me how you felt earlier?"

The smile left his face, his expression turning serious. "Because I was frightened," he admitted darkly. "Because I had never felt like that before, and I didn't know how to cope with it. For the first time in centuries, I was driven by emotion, instead of reason, and I didn't always make the wisest choices when it came to you. I wanted to have you, and I couldn't think of anything beyond that need, that craving. I wasn't sufficiently patient, and I ended up scaring you . . . and then you got involved with the Resistance as a result. I loved you, and all you seemed to want is to have me permanently out of your life. Even later, when you told me you loved me, I wasn't sure if you truly felt that way, or if you were just playing along, giving me what I wanted—"

Mia shook her head, unable to believe her ears. He'd always seemed so invulnerable, and the realization that she'd had the power to hurt him all along was truly humbling. "No, Korum," she murmured, raising her hand to stroke his face. "I fell in love with you back in New York. Even though I thought you wanted to harm my kind, even though I was afraid of ending up as your sex slave, I still fell for you . . . And I can't live without you now—"

He drew in a deep breath and pressed her tighter against him, burying his face in her hair. "And I can't live without you, my darling," he whispered, "I don't think I can ever let you go, not anymore . . ."

"Then why did you? Why did you try to let me go yesterday?"

He pulled back, looking at her again. "Because I realized I couldn't force you to love me, to want to be with me." A bitter smile appeared on his lips. "I could keep you with me until the end of time, but I couldn't make you love me. It was no longer enough, you see, just to have you. I wanted more—I wanted you to love me freely. I thought you would rejoice at being made immortal, but you were upset instead . . . And I knew then that I couldn't do that to you, couldn't make you stay with me against your will—"

"Oh Korum," Mia whispered, "it's not against my will. It hasn't been against my will for a long time . . ."

His expression softened again. "I'm glad," he said quietly, brushing some hair off her face. "I want you to be happy with me. I never meant to make you feel like a slave. I just couldn't bear the thought of anything happening to you if I put off the procedure until you'd had a chance to acclimate to Lenkarda and get used to being with me. I thought I was giving you something you would want . . ."

"I do. I do want it," Mia told him sincerely. "How could you even doubt it? You've given me a priceless gift, and I didn't mean to imply otherwise . . . But, Korum, can you please promise me one thing?"

He studied her with a watchful gaze. "What?"

"Can you please never do anything to me without my consent again? Even if you think it's for the best, even if you're not sure I'll agree to it?"

He hesitated for a second, and then nodded reluctantly. She could see how much it cost him to make that concession, the extent to which it went against his nature. But he had now given her his word, and she knew that he would keep it.

"Thank you," she told him, caressing his shoulder. "This means a lot to me."

He smiled and leaned toward her, giving her a gentle kiss.

When he pulled away, Mia made a serious face and asked him, "Do you know what else would mean a lot to me right now?"

He looked a little wary. "What?"

"Some yummy breakfast," she told him, and watched his face light up with a dazzling smile.

* * *

On Friday morning, they left to go back to Lenkarda.

The rest of their visit to Florida had been uneventful, and her family had been sad to see them leave. Korum promised to bring Mia back for a couple of days before the end of summer, which earned him a tearful hug from her mom and a sincere thank-you from her dad. Marisa had been particularly emotional, thanking Korum again for everything he'd done for them and then blushing fiercely when he gave her a kiss on the cheek as goodbye.

"I'm going to miss them," Mia told him as they drove toward the airport where he was planning to create their ship. "I really wish I could see them more often."

"You'll be able to," Korum said, keeping his eyes on the road. "Once I'm sure that it's completely safe, there's no reason why you can't drop in every couple of weeks or so. It doesn't take that long to get here from Lenkarda—"

"From Lenkarda?" Mia inquired delicately. "I thought we were going back to New York in the fall . . ."

Korum sighed. "If you still want that, then yes."

"Why wouldn't I?"

He shrugged. "You don't really need the degree if you're going to continue working at Saret's lab. It's not like you'll learn anything more in school than you would staying in Lenkarda—"

"Is that what you're hoping?" Mia asked. "That I would decide not to go back to school?"

"I prefer Lenkarda to New York," he admitted, "but I don't mind if you decide to finish college. I know it's still important to you, and I promised that I would bring you back for the school year. Nine months— that's nothing in the grand scheme of things, and if it gives you peace of mind . . ."

For the first time, Mia thought seriously about the possibility of not finishing school. Korum was right: what she was learning at her apprenticeship was head and shoulders above anything the university had to teach her. And if Lenkarda were to be her home, a college degree was meaningless. Would Saret allow her to return to the lab after such a long absence? She would hate to lose this opportunity in order to write a few more papers and study for a few more exams. She needed to discuss this with her boss and soon, Mia decided.

They arrived at the Daytona Beach International Airport, and Korum assembled the ship in a far-off section there, out of sight of any other humans. As the aircraft quietly took off, Mia remembered how frightened she'd been when she'd left New York, flying to Lenkarda for the very first time. Was it only three weeks ago? It seemed like a lifetime had passed between now and then.

The girl who had left New York had been frightened and traumatized, uncertain about her fate and unsure whether she could trust the man she loved—the one she had regarded as an enemy, the one she had betrayed.

She was no longer that girl.

This Mia felt utterly secure in Korum's love.

Over the past few days, their relationship had undergone yet another subtle shift. There was an openness to it now that had been missing before. Until they'd had that discussion—until he'd given her a choice— Mia had still had doubts about their relationship. It had been an uncomfortable feeling, knowing that he held all the power and had no qualms about using it—and she now realized that she'd held a part of herself back as a result, that she had still subconsciously resisted him.

Now, however, it was different—it felt different. Yes, she was still his charl, but she no longer felt like he owned her. He loved her enough to let her walk away, to relinquish his control over her, and that knowledge was like a balm to her soul, soothing the scars left by the tumultuous beginning of their affair.

Every evening, after dinner with her family, they had gone for a long walk on the beach and just talked. She'd learned about some of Korum's past relationships (there had been many) and about the fact that he had never been in love before. He'd actually thought himself incapable of it. "It really caught me by surprise, the depth of my feelings for you," he'd confessed, and she realized yet again how difficult it had been for him to let her go. The fact that he'd done it proved to her that his feelings were real—that their sexual liaison could ultimately become the genuine partnership she'd always hoped it would be.

And now, as their ship flew to Costa Rica, Mia reached over and squeezed Korum's hand. "I love you," she said, and watched as a warm smile appeared on his beautiful face.

Her life couldn't possibly get any better.

EPILOGUE

They were returning.

Saur had failed, but the Krinar had suspected he would. Korum was too good of a fighter to be killed so easily. Of course, he hadn't counted on Mia getting hurt. That part had been unacceptable. If his enemy hadn't killed Saur, the K would've done so himself.

Soon she would be near him again. The Krinar raised his hand and stared at it, imagining himself touching her delicate flesh, stroking that silky skin. She would be so small, so fragile in his arms. So vulnerable. He could do anything he wanted to her, and she wouldn't be able to resist.

His cock stirred at that thought, and he cursed his apparent inability to control himself. In anticipation of her arrival, he'd ventured out to a nearby x-club and gorged himself on human girls. All three of them had been pretty, with ambitions of a career in Hollywood. One had even had curly hair, though it was more of a dirty blond shade that hadn't appealed to him nearly as much. He'd fucked them for hours, yet he'd left the place still unsatisfied.

He wanted *her*.

And soon he would be able to have her—and anything else he wanted. His week had been quite productive.

Another few days, and he'd be all set.

Close Remembrance

The Krinar Chronicles: Volume 3

Part I

PROLOGUE

The Krinar walked down the street in Moscow, quietly observing the teeming human masses all around him. As he passed, he could see the fear and curiosity on their faces, feel the hatred emanating from some of the passersby.

Russia was one of the countries that had resisted the most—and where the toll of the Great Panic had been the heaviest. With a largely corrupt government and a population distrustful of all authority, many Russians had taken the Krinar invasion as an excuse to loot at will and hoard whatever supplies they could. Even now, more than five years later, some of the storefronts in Moscow were still bare, their taped-over windows a testament to the tumultuous months that had followed their arrival.

Thankfully, the air in the city was better now, less polluted than the Krinar remembered it being a few years ago. Back then, a heavy smog hung over the city, irritating him to no end. Not that it could hurt him in any way, but still, the K far preferred breathing air that didn't contain too many hydrocarbon particles.

Approaching the Kremlin, the K pulled the hood of his jacket up over his head and tried to look as human as he could, paying careful attention to his movements to make them slower and less graceful. He didn't delude himself that the K satellites weren't watching him at this very moment, but no one in the Centers had any reason to suspect him. He'd made it a point in recent years to travel as much as he could, frequently appearing in major human cities for one reason or another. This way, if anyone cared to profile his behavior, his latest expeditions would not

453

cause any alarm.

Not that anyone would bother profiling him. As far as everyone was concerned, those Krinar who'd helped the Resistance—the Keiths, as they'd been called—were safely in custody, and poor Saur had been blamed for erasing their memories. It couldn't have worked out better if the K had planned it that way himself.

No, he didn't need to conceal his identity from the Krinar eyes in the sky. His goal was to fool the human cameras stationed all around the Kremlin walls—just in case the Russian leaders became alarmed before he had a chance to visit the other major cities.

Smiling, the K pretended to be nothing more than a human tourist as he did a leisurely lap around Red Square, the soles of his shoes grinding into the pavement and releasing tiny capsules that contained the seeds of a new era in human history.

Once he was done, he headed back to the ship he'd left in one of the nearby alleys.

Tomorrow, he would see Mia again.

Saret could hardly wait.

CHAPTER ONE

"Oh my God, Korum, when did you have a chance to do this?"

Mia stared at her surroundings in shock. All the familiar furniture was gone, and Korum's house in Lenkarda—the place she had begun to think of as her home—looked very much like a Krinar dwelling now, complete with floating planks and clutter-free spaces. The only thing that remained from before were the transparent walls and ceiling—a Krinar feature that Korum had allowed from the very beginning.

Her lover grinned, showing the familiar dimple in his left cheek. "I might've snuck away for an hour or so while you were sleeping."

"You went all the way from Florida to here just to change the furnishings?"

He laughed, shaking his head. "No, my sweet, even I'm not that dedicated. I had to take care of a couple of business matters, and I decided to surprise you."

"Well, color me surprised," Mia said, slowly turning in a circle and studying the strange sight that had greeted her upon their arrival back in Lenkarda.

Instead of the ivory couch, there was now a long white board floating a couple of feet off the floor. From what Korum had explained to her once, the Krinar were able to make their furniture float by using a derivation of the same force-field technology that protected their colonies. Mia knew that if she sat down on the board, it would immediately adapt to her body, becoming as comfortable as it could possibly be. A few other floating planks were visible near the walls, with a couple of them occupied by some type of indoor plants with bright pink flowers.

The floor was also different—and unlike anything Mia had seen in any other Krinar houses. She tried to remember what those other floors had been like, but all she could recall was that they were hard and pale, like some type of stone. She hadn't paid them too much attention at the time because Krinar flooring materials didn't seem all that different from something one would find in a human house. However, what was under her feet right now had a very unusual texture and an almost sponge-like consistency. It made Mia feel like she was standing on air.

"What is that?" she asked Korum, pointing down at the strange substance.

"Take off your shoes and see," he suggested, kicking off his own sandals. "It's something new that one of my employees came up with recently—a variation on the intelligent bed technology."

Curious, Mia followed his example, letting her bare feet sink into the cushy flooring. The material seemed to flow around her feet, enveloping them, and then it was as though a thousand tiny fingers were gently rubbing her toes, heels, and arches, releasing all tension. A foot massage . . . only a thousand times better. "Oh, wow," Mia breathed, a huge blissful smile appearing on her face. "Korum, this is amazing!"

"Uh-huh." He was walking around, seemingly enjoying the sensations himself. "I figured this would appeal to you."

Her feet in paradise, Mia watched as he made a slow circle around the room, his tall, muscular body moving with the cat-like grace common to his species. Sometimes she could hardly believe that this gorgeous, complicated man was hers—that he loved her as much as she loved him.

Her happiness was so absolute these days it was almost scary.

"Do you want to see the rest of the house?" He stopped next to her and gave her a warm smile.

"Yes, please!" Mia grinned, as eager as a kid in a candy store.

Three days ago, during one of their evening walks in Florida, she'd mentioned to Korum that it would be nice to see his house as it was before he 'humanized' it for her sake. As thoughtful as the gesture had been at the time, Mia was now used to the Krinar lifestyle and no longer needed the reassurance of familiar surroundings. Instead, she wanted to see how her alien lover had lived before they met. He'd smiled and promised to change the house back promptly—and he'd obviously taken that promise seriously.

"Okay," he said, staring down at her with a slightly mischievous look on his beautiful face. "There's one room that you haven't seen at all yet, and I've been dying to show you . . ."

"Oh?" Mia raised her eyebrows, her heart starting to beat faster and her lower belly tightening in anticipation. His eyes now had a golden undertone, and she guessed that whatever it was he wanted to show her would soon have her screaming in ecstasy in his arms. If there was one thing she could always count on, it was his insatiable desire for her. No matter how often they had sex, it seemed like he always wanted more . . . and so did she.

"Come," he said, taking her hand and leading her toward the wall to their left.

As they approached, the wall did not dissolve as it usually did. Instead, Mia felt herself sinking deeper into the spongy material beneath her feet. Her feet were absorbed first, then her ankles and knees. It was like quicksand, except it was happening right in the house. Giving Korum a startled look, she clutched at his hand. "What—?"

"It's okay." He gave her palm a reassuring squeeze. "Don't worry." The same thing was happening to him too; she could see the floor practically sucking him in.

"Um, Korum, I don't know about this . . ." Mia was now buried up to her waist, and her lower body was feeling decidedly strange—almost weightless.

"Just a few more seconds," he promised, giving her a grin.

"A few more seconds?" Mia was now chest-deep inside the weird material. "Before what?"

"Before this," he said as their descent suddenly accelerated and they fell completely through the floor.

Mia let out a short scream, her grip tightening on Korum's hand. At first there was only darkness and the frightening sensation of nothingness beneath her feet, and then they were suddenly floating in a softly lit circular room with solid peach-tinted walls and ceiling.

As in, literally floating in mid-air.

Gasping, Mia stared at her lover, unable to believe what was happening. "Korum, is this—?"

"A zero-gravity chamber?" He was grinning like a little boy about to show off a new toy. "Yes, indeed."

"You have a zero-gravity chamber in your house?"

"I do," he admitted, obviously pleased with her reaction. Letting go of Mia's hand, he did a slow somersault in the air. "As you can see, it's a lot of fun."

Mia laughed incredulously, then tried to follow his example—but there was no good way for her to control her movements. She had no idea how Korum had managed to somersault so easily. She was moving her arms and legs, but it didn't seem to do much for her. It was like she was floating in water, only without any sensation of wetness.

She couldn't tell which way was up or down; the chamber was windowless, and there was no clear distinction between the walls, floor, and ceiling. It was as though they were in a giant bubble—which probably wasn't all that far from the truth. Mia was no expert on the subject, but she imagined it wasn't easy to create a zero-gravity environment on Earth. There had to be a lot of complex technology surrounding them and negating the gravitational pull of the planet.

"Wow," she said softly, drifting in the air. "Korum, this is amazing . . . Is this something other Krinar have too?"

He had managed to get to one of the walls, and he used it to push off, propelling himself back in her direction. "No—" he reached out to grab her arm as he floated past her, "—it's not something many of us have."

Mia grinned as he pulled her toward him. "Oh yeah? Only you?"

"Perhaps," he murmured, wrapping one arm around her waist and holding her tightly against him. His eyes were turning more golden by the second, and the hardness pressing against her belly left no doubt of his intentions.

Mia's eyes widened. "Here?" she asked, her pulse speeding up from excitement.

"Hmm-mm . . ." He was already bringing her up (or was it down?) to nibble at the sensitive area behind her earlobe.

As always, his touch made her entire body hum in anticipation. Arching her head back, she moaned softly, liquid heat moving through her veins.

"I love you," he whispered in her ear, his large hands stroking down her body, pulling down her dress. It drifted away, but Mia hardly noticed, her eyes glued to the man she loved more than life itself.

She would never tire of hearing those words from him, Mia thought, watching as he pulled away for a second to take off his own clothes. His shirt came off first, then his shorts, and then he was fully naked, revealing a body that was striking in its masculine perfection. The fact that they were floating in the air added an element of surrealism to the entire scene, making Mia feel like she was having an unusual sexy dream.

Reaching out, she ran her hands down his chest, marveling at the smooth texture of his skin and the rock-solid muscle underneath. "I love you too," she murmured, and watched his eyes flare brighter with need.

Bringing her toward him, he turned her so that she was floating perpendicular to him, her lower body at his eye level. Before she could say anything, he was opening her thighs, exposing her delicate folds to his hungry gaze. "So beautiful," he whispered, "so warm and wet . . . I can't wait to taste you—" he followed his words with a slow lick of her most private area, "—to make you come . . ."

Moaning, Mia closed her eyes, the familiar tension starting to coil deep in her belly. Drifting in mid-air seemed to be sharpening all sensations. Without a surface to lie on or anything else touching her body, all she could feel—all she could concentrate on—was the incredible pleasure of his mouth licking and nibbling around her clitoris, and his strong hands stroking up and down her thighs.

Without any warning, a powerful orgasm ripped through her body, originating at her core and spreading outward. Mia cried out, her toes curling from the intensity of the release, and then he was flipping her so that she faced him. Before her pulsations even stopped, his thick cock was already at her opening, entering her in one smooth thrust.

Gasping, Mia opened her eyes and grabbed his shoulders, the shock of his possession reverberating through her body. He paused for a second, then began to move slowly, giving her time to adjust to the fullness inside her. With each careful thrust, the tip of his shaft pressed against the sensitive spot deep within, making her gasp from the sensation.

It seemed to go on forever, those gentle and measured thrusts, each one bringing her closer to the edge but not quite sending her over. Moaning in frustration, Mia dug her nails into his shoulders, needing him to move faster. "Please, Korum . . ." she whispered, knowing that he wanted this sometimes—that he liked to hear her beg for the ultimate pleasure.

"Oh, I will," he murmured, his eyes almost pure gold. "I will definitely please you, my sweet." And holding her tightly with one arm, he reached behind her and rubbed the area where they were joined, gathering the moisture from there. Then, to her surprise, his finger ventured higher, between the smooth globes of her cheeks, and pressed gently against the tiny opening there.

Her breath catching in her throat, Mia stared up at him with a mixture of fear and excitement.

"Shhh, relax . . ." he soothed, his voice like rough velvet. And before she could say anything, he bent his head, taking her mouth in a deep, seductive kiss even as his finger began to push inside.

At first, it seemed to hurt and burn, the unfamiliar intrusion making her squirm against him in a futile effort to ease the discomfort. With his shaft buried all the way inside her, the additional invasion of her body was too much, the sensations strange and unnerving. Once he stopped, however, with his finger only partially inside her, the burning began to recede, leaving an unusual feeling of fullness in its wake.

Lifting his head, Korum stared down at her with a heavy-lidded gaze. "All right?" he asked softly, and Mia nodded uncertainly, unable to decide if she liked the peculiar sensation or not.

"Good," he whispered, beginning to move his hips again while keeping his finger steady. "Just relax . . . Yes, there's a good girl . . ."

Closing her eyes, Mia concentrated on not tensing up, although it was becoming increasingly difficult. The unfamiliar discomfort was somehow adding to the pressure building inside her, each thrust of his cock causing his finger to move ever so slightly, overwhelming her senses. His pace gradually picked up, his hips moving faster and faster . . . and then she was suddenly flying apart, her entire body convulsing from an orgasm so intense it left her weak and panting in its wake.

Korum groaned, grinding against her as her inner muscles rhythmically squeezed his cock, triggering his own climax. She could feel the warm spurts of his seed inside her belly, hear his harsh breathing in her ears as his arm tightened around her waist, holding her securely in place.

When it was all over, he slowly withdrew his finger and kissed her, his lips sweet and tender on hers.

And then they drifted together for a few more minutes, their bodies slick with sweat and wrapped intimately around each other.

* * *

The next morning, Mia woke up and stretched, a big grin breaking out on her face as she remembered what took place yesterday. It seemed that Korum had just begun to introduce her to the various erotic pleasures he had in store for her . . . and she could barely wait to experience it all. Rightly or wrongly, she was now completely addicted to him, to the pleasure she experienced in his arms, and she couldn't imagine ever being with anyone else—especially not with a regular human man.

It was funny: she'd always heard that relationships tended to lose their initial intensity over time, but it seemed like their passion was only getting stronger with each day that passed. Partially, it was the fact that Korum was a phenomenal lover; during his two thousand years, he'd had plenty of time to learn all the erogenous zones on a woman's body. But it was also something more, something indefinable—that unique chemistry between them that had been obvious from the very beginning.

Sometimes it scared her, the extent to which she needed him now. The craving went beyond the physical, although she couldn't imagine going even a single day without the mind-blowing pleasure she experienced in his arms. It was as if they were attuned to each other on a cellular level—two halves of a complete whole.

Still smiling, Mia rolled out of bed. Picking up her wristwatch computer, she glanced at it to check the time. To her surprise, it was already eight a.m., which meant that she had only an hour to eat breakfast and get to the lab. Although it was Saturday, it was a workday in Lenkarda, since the Krinar didn't follow the human calendar when it came to weekdays and weekends. Their 'week' was only four days in duration, instead of seven—three days of work, followed by a day of rest. Mia still thought about time in human calendar terms, however, since that's what she was used to.

Korum was already gone, so Mia asked the house to prepare her a smoothie and ran to take a quick shower. Even that was different now after Korum's remodeling efforts. Instead of the shower/jacuzzi combo that she'd gotten used to, the bathroom now had a giant circular stall with the same intelligent technology as everything else in the house. The water came out of everywhere and nowhere, washing and massaging every part of her body, with the water pressure and temperature adjusting to her needs automatically. She didn't have to apply any effort to wash herself, either; instead, lightly scented soaps, shampoos, and some kind of unusual oils were applied to her hair and skin while she simply stood there, letting Krinar technology do all the work.

After the shower was over, Mia stepped out and warm jets of air dried off her body. Her hair was automatically blow-dried too, resulting in smooth, glossy curls that could've been the result of a session at a fancy hair salon. At the same time, her mouth was filled with the taste of something refreshingly clean, as though she had just brushed her teeth.

By the time she was dressed and done with the shower, a strawberry-almond smoothie was already sitting on the kitchen table. Grabbing it on her way out, Mia left the house and headed to work.

Although she had only been gone a week, Mia found that she missed the lab environment. She loved to learn, and the challenge of mastering a difficult subject had never daunted her. Part of her initial reluctance in getting involved with Korum had been due to her fear of losing herself, of becoming nothing more than a glorified pleasure slave. But instead, she seemed to have discovered a way to become a useful part of the Krinar society, to contribute in some small way. By finding her the internship, Korum had done more than simply pad her resume; he'd also demonstrated that he regarded her as a smart and capable person—someone he could not only desire, but respect.

Arriving at the lab, Mia spent most of the day catching up on what she'd missed during her week in Florida. Despite her almost-daily chats with Adam, her project partner, she still felt like she had fallen behind on some of the latest developments. She didn't have a lot of time to get up to speed either, as Adam was planning to leave to visit his own adopted human family that afternoon.

"How did Saret let you do that?" Mia teased. "Leave for an entire week? Korum practically had to strong-arm him to let me go for that length of time, and you're much more useful . . ."

Adam shrugged. "He didn't have much choice in the matter. I told him I'm going, and that's that."

Mia grinned at him, again impressed by the young Krinar. Despite his human upbringing—or maybe because of it—he could more than hold his own with the best of them.

Finally, around four in the afternoon, Adam gave her a bunch of readings and headed out to start his vacation, leaving her alone in the lab. The other apprentices were working on a joint project with the mind lab in Thailand, and they had gone there for a few days to conclude some experiment.

Mia spent the next two hours reading and then went to check on the data that was being generated by the virtual simulation of a young Krinar brain. It appeared that the latest method she and Adam had figured out was indeed a step in the right direction. The knowledge transfer was happening at a faster pace and with fewer unpleasant side effects. Hopefully, they would be able to improve it further by the end of summer—

"How was your vacation in Florida?" a familiar voice behind her asked, and Mia jumped, startled.

Turning around, she took a deep breath, trying to calm her racing pulse. "You scared me," she told Saret, giving him a smile. "I didn't know anyone else was here in the lab."

Her boss ran his fingers through his dark hair. "I'm just finishing up a few things." He looked unusually tense, and Mia thought he seemed tired—a rarity for a Krinar.

"Is everything all right?" she asked tentatively, not wanting to overstep any boundaries. Although she had been working for Saret for a couple of weeks, she felt like she still didn't really know him. He didn't spend a lot of time in the lab, since whatever project he was working on took him all over the world. When he was in the lab, he was usually in his office—although she'd caught him watching her a few times, apparently keeping an eye on the only human he'd ever allowed into his lab.

"Of course," Saret said, his features relaxing into a smile. "Why wouldn't it be? One of my favorite assistants is back."

Feeling slightly awkward, Mia smiled back at him. "Thanks," she said. "It's good to be back. I was just looking at the data, and there's definitely progress—"

"That's good," Saret interrupted. "I look forward to your report soon."

"Of course. I will prepare it tonight—"

"No, no need for that. You can go home early today. It's your first day back, and I know your cheren will be unhappy if I keep you here late."

Surprised, Mia nodded. "Okay, if you're sure . . ." Normally, Saret disliked it when his apprentices didn't put in a full day. He'd even gotten into an argument about that with Korum when Mia had first started the internship. And now it seemed like he actually wanted her to leave . . . Still, she wasn't about to quibble; she had been planning to go home in another hour anyway.

"I'm sure." Saret smiled at her. There was something about that smile that made her uncomfortable, but she couldn't figure out what.

"Okay then, thanks. I'll see you tomorrow," Mia said, walking past him. And as she did, she could've sworn he leaned closer, breathing in—almost as if he was inhaling her scent.

Telling herself that she had an overactive imagination, Mia exited the lab and entered a small aircraft that was sitting next to the lab building. Korum had made it for her for the express purpose of traveling around Lenkarda. Like the wristwatch he'd given her, it was programmed to respond to her verbal commands. Feeling tired after a full day at work, Mia sat down on one of the intelligent seats and ordered the ship to take her home.

* * *

Saret watched Mia leave, his hands nearly shaking with the urge to reach out and touch her.

Having her so close after her long absence had been torturous. The faint sweetness of her scent permeated the lab, and he hadn't been able to stop himself from coming closer, from breathing it in. If she hadn't left then, he would've done something stupid—like bring her toward him for a taste. And he wouldn't have been able to stop with just a taste.

When he tried to analyze his own mind—like every mind expert should—he could come up with a dozen reasons for why he'd become so obsessed with her. First and foremost, she belonged to Korum. Even when they'd been children, Saret had always wanted Korum's toys. His enemy had been inventive even then, altering the designs for popular games and creating something that was better than what anyone else had. Saret had hated Korum for it then, and he hated him now. Of course, he had never let it show. Korum's enemies never fared well. It was far better to be his friend—or, at least, to act like one.

And Mia was the ultimate toy. So small, so delicate, so perfectly human. For the first time, Saret understood why her species kept pets. Having a cute creature to call your own, to stroke and touch at your whim—there was something incredibly appealing in that. Especially when that creature loved you, depended on you . . . She would make a very good pet, Saret thought wryly, with that thick mass of hair that looked so soft and touchable.

He was surprised Korum let her spend so much time away from him. Saret had tested him in the beginning, insisting that Mia put in a full day, just to see if that would convince Korum of the ridiculousness of having a human in a Krinar work environment. His nemesis was the last person he would've expected to treat a human girl as an equal. Sure, she was smart—for a human, at least—but she was also young and malleable. It wouldn't take much effort to mold her into whatever he wanted her to be. Whatever she thought she wanted now—none of that really mattered. If she had been *his* charl, he could've easily convinced her to be happy with her role in his life, in his bed. There were so many amusements for a human girl to enjoy: all kinds of virtual and real-life spa treatments, pretty clothes, interesting recordings, fun books . . . And instead, Korum had her working nonstop. No wonder she still objected to being a charl. Her cheren simply didn't know how to treat her properly.

Sighing, Saret went back into his office. All the mind analysis in the world didn't change the fact that he wanted her. And soon he would be able to have her. He just needed to be patient for a while longer.

Turning his attention back to his task, Saret brought up a three-dimensional map of Shanghai.

China was next on his list.

CHAPTER TWO

"There's nothing to worry about," Korum said soothingly, placing a white dot on Mia's temple. "They will love you, just like I do."

Mia nervously twisted a strand of hair between her fingers before tucking it behind her ear. "They won't mind that I'm human?"

"They won't," he reassured her. "They know all about you already, and they're very happy that I found someone I care so much about."

After she'd arrived home from work, Korum had surprised her with the news that he wanted her to meet *his* family as well. So now he was about to take her into a virtual reality setting where she would meet his parents. Supposedly, the environment was very lifelike, and she would be able to interact with his parents there as though they were meeting in person.

It was also on Krina.

"Are you sure I shouldn't change?" Mia knew she was stalling, but she felt ridiculously anxious. "And won't your mom mind that I'm wearing your family necklace?"

"You look beautiful, and the necklace is perfect on you," he said firmly. "My mother will be quite pleased to see it around your neck; she gave it to me explicitly for that purpose—to gift it to the woman I ultimately fall in love with."

Mia took a deep breath, trying to control her rapid heartbeat. "Okay, then I'm ready." At least as ready as she would ever be to meet her extraterrestrial lover's parents—who resided thousands of light years away.

Korum smiled, and the world around her blurred for a second.

Feeling dizzy, Mia closed her eyes, and when she opened them, she was standing inside a large, airy building that vaguely resembled Korum's house in Lenkarda. From the inside, it was fully transparent, and she could see unusual plants outside. Most of the flora was a familiar shade of green, but red, orange, and yellow hues also proliferated. It was strikingly beautiful. The inside of the building had the same 'Zen' feel to it as Arman's house. Everything was a beautiful off-white shade, and the sunlight streaming through the clear ceiling reflected off a gorgeous flower arrangement right in the middle of the room—the only touch of color in an otherwise pristine environment. The flowers seemed to grow right out of an opening in the floor. Along the walls, there were a few familiar-looking floating planks that served as multi-purpose furniture.

"It's lovely," Mia whispered, glancing around the room. "Is this your parents' house?"

Korum nodded, smiling. He looked quite pleased. "It's my childhood home," he explained, reaching out to take her hand and squeezing it lightly.

As usual, his touch made her feel warm inside, and she marveled again at how authentic this virtual reality felt. Somehow, this was even more convincing than the club where he'd taken her once to satisfy her fantasy. All her senses were fully engaged, as though she was physically present here, on a planet in a different galaxy.

Inhaling deeply, Mia realized that the air was a little thinner than what she was used to, as if they were at a high altitude. She actually felt a bit light-headed, and she hoped she would adjust to it soon. The temperature was pleasantly warm, and there seemed to be a faint breeze coming from somewhere, even though they were inside the building. There was also an exotic, but appealing scent in the air. Likely from the flowers, Mia decided. The aroma was almost ... fruity. She'd never smelled anything like it before.

As Mia studied their surroundings, one of the walls dissolved, and a Krinar woman walked in. She was tall and slim, with a supermodel's leggy build and shiny dark hair. Her eyes were the same warm amber color as Korum's. It could only be Korum's mother; their resemblance was unmistakable.

At the sight of them standing there, a huge smile lit her face. "My child," she said softly, her eyes shining with love as she looked at her son, "I'm so glad to see you." Like all Ks, her age was impossible to determine; she didn't look a day older than twenty-five.

Letting go of Mia's hand, Korum crossed the room and enveloped his mother in a gentle hug. "Me too, Riani, me too . . ."

Mia watched their reunion, feeling like she was intruding on a private family moment. She couldn't imagine what it must be like for his parents, with their son living so far away. Yes, they could meet in this virtual way, but they still probably missed seeing him in person.

Turning toward Mia, Korum smiled and said, "Come here, darling. Let me introduce you to my mother."

Curving her lips in an answering smile, Mia approached them, noticing the way the K's eyes examined her from head to toe. Her palms began to sweat. What was this gorgeous woman thinking? Was she wondering how her son had ended up with a human?

Pausing a couple of feet away, Mia smiled wider. "Hello," she said, uncertain if she should reach out and brush the K's cheek with her knuckles. She'd learned in the past couple of weeks that it was the customary greeting among Krinar females.

Korum's mother had no such reservations. Raising her hand, she gently touched Mia's cheek and smiled in return. "Hello, my dear. I'm so glad to finally meet you."

"Riani, this is Mia, my charl," Korum said. "Mia, this is Riani, my mother."

"It's such a pleasure to meet you, Riani." Mia was starting to feel more at ease. Despite the woman's luminous beauty and youthful looks, there was something in her manner that was very soothing. Almost motherly, Mia thought with an inner smile.

"Where's Chiaren?" Korum asked, addressing his mother.

"Oh, he'll be here soon," she said, waving her hand. "He was delayed at work. Don't worry—he knows you're here."

Chiaren had to be Korum's father, Mia decided. It was interesting that he called his parents by name, although it made sense too. As long-lived as the Ks were, the lines between generations were probably much less defined than for humans. Although Korum had mentioned once that his parents were much older than he was, she guessed that the difference between two thousand years and a few thousand years was not all that dramatic.

A quiet whoosh interrupted Mia's musings. Turning her head to the side, she saw the wall opening again. A darkly handsome Krinar man walked in, dressed in typical K clothing. Swiftly crossing the room, he raised his hand and touched his palm to Korum's shoulder, greeting his son.

Korum reciprocated the gesture, but he seemed much more reserved than he had been with his mother. "Chiaren," he said quietly. "I'm glad you could make it."

Something in the tone of his voice startled Mia. Was there some tension between father and son?

His father inclined his head. "Of course. I wouldn't miss your visit." Then, turning his attention to Mia, he cocked his head to the side and studied her with an inscrutable expression on his face.

Mia swallowed, needing to moisten her suddenly dry throat. Chiaren's posture, the slightly mocking curl to his lips—it was all very familiar to her. Korum might've gotten his mother's looks, but he'd definitely inherited some personality traits from his father as well. She found the K to be intimidating, with his cool dark gaze and lack of visible emotion. He reminded her of Korum when they'd first met.

"Chiaren, this is Mia," Korum said, stepping toward her and putting a proprietary arm around her back. "She's my charl. Mia, this is my father, Chiaren."

The K smiled, suddenly seeming much more approachable. "How lovely," he said gently. "Such a pretty human girl you've got there. How old are you, Mia? You seem younger than I'd imagined."

"I'm twenty-one," Mia told him, aware that she probably looked like she was in her late teens. It was a common problem for someone of her petite build—a problem that would now never go away.

Chiaren's smile widened. "Twenty-one . . ."

Mia flushed, realizing that he thought her little more than a child. And compared to him, she was. Still, she would've preferred if he hadn't looked quite so amused at her age.

"Mia, dear, tell us a bit about yourself," Riani said, smiling at her with warm encouragement. "Korum mentioned that you're studying the mind. Is that right?"

Mia nodded, turning her attention to Korum's mother. She wasn't certain how she felt about his father yet, but she was definitely growing to like Riani. "I am," she confirmed. "I started working with Saret this summer. Before that, I majored in psychology at one of our universities."

"How are you finding it so far? Your apprenticeship?" asked Chiaren. "I imagine it must be quite different from anything you've done before." He seemed genuinely curious.

"Yes, it is," said Mia. "I'm learning a great deal." Feeling much more in her element, she told them all about her work at the lab, her eyes lighting up as she explained about the imprinting project.

Afterwards, Riani asked about her family, seeming particularly interested in the fact that Mia had a sibling. Marisa's pregnancy appeared to fascinate her, and she listened attentively as Mia detailed the difficulties her sister had gone through before Ellet's arrival. After that, Chiaren wanted to know about Mia's parents and their occupations, and how human contributions to society were typically measured, so Mia spoke for a while about the role of teachers and professors in the American educational system.

Before long, she found herself engaged in an animated discussion with Korum's parents. She learned that they had been together for close to three millennia, and that Riani was almost five hundred years older than her mate. Unlike Korum, who had discovered his passion for technological design early on, both Riani and Chiaren were 'dabblers.' Most Krinar were, in fact. Instead of specializing in a specific subject, they frequently changed their careers and areas of focus, never fully reaching the 'expert' level in any particular field. As a result, while their standing in society was quite respectable, neither one of Korum's parents had come even close to being involved with the Council.

"I'm not sure how we managed to produce such an intelligent and ambitious child," Riani confided, grinning. "It certainly wasn't intentional."

Seeing the puzzled look on Mia's face, Chiaren explained, "When a couple decides to have a child, they usually do so under very controlled conditions. They choose the optimal combination of physical traits and potential intellectual abilities, consulting the top medical experts—"

"Most Krinar are designer babies?" Mia's eyes widened in realization. This explained why all the Krinar she'd met were so good-looking. They had taken control of their own evolution by practicing a form of genetic selection for their children. It made a tremendous amount of sense. Any culture advanced enough to manipulate their own genetic code—as the Krinar had done to get rid of their need for blood—could easily specify which genes they wanted in their offspring. Mia was surprised it hadn't occurred to her earlier.

Chiaren hesitated. "I'm not familiar with that term . . ."

"Yes, exactly," Korum said, giving Mia a smile. "Few parents are willing to play genetic roulette, not when there is a better way."

"But we did," Riani said, looking a bit sheepish. "I got pregnant by accident—one of the few accidents of this kind to occur in the last ten thousand years. We discussed having a child, and we both went off birth control, planning to go to a lab like every other couple we knew. Statistically, the odds of getting pregnant naturally in the first fertile year are something like one in a million. Of course, this was during my musical mastery period, and I got very caught up in vocal expression, to the point that we put off our visit to the lab for a few months. And by the time the medical expert saw me, I was already three weeks pregnant with Korum."

"I'm a throwback, you see," Korum said, laughing. "They had no control over which ancestor's genetic traits I inherited."

Mia grinned at him. "Well, I think it's pretty obvious where you get your coloring from." He could've been Riani's twin brother, instead of her son.

"It's the ambition that puzzles us," Chiaren said, shooting his son an indecipherable look. "It's really come out of nowhere . . ."

Korum's eyes narrowed a bit, and Mia sensed that this was likely the point of contention between father and son. She determined to ask Korum about it later. For now, she was curious about this new tidbit she'd learned about her lover. "So you're not a designer baby, huh?" she teased, smiling at him.

"Nope." Korum grinned. "I'm as natural as they come."

"Well, you came out perfect anyway," Mia said, studying his beautifully masculine features. She couldn't imagine how he could look any better.

To her surprise, Korum shook his head. "No, actually, I didn't. I have a small deformity."

"What?" Mia stared at him in shock. This gorgeous man had a deformity? Where had he hidden it this whole time?

He smiled and pointed at the dimple in his left cheek. "Yeah, right there. See?"

Mia gave him a disbelieving look. "Your dimple? Really?"

He nodded, his eyes sparkling with amusement. "It's considered a deformity among my kind. But I've learned to live with it. Apparently, some women even like it."

Like it? Mia loved it, and she told him so, making him and his parents laugh.

"We should probably get going," Korum said after a while. "It's dinner time, and Mia needs to get some sleep before getting up early for work tomorrow."

"Of course." Riani gave her a warm look of understanding. "I know humans tire more easily . . ."

Mia opened her mouth to protest, but then she changed her mind. It was the truth, even if she wasn't particularly tired right now. Instead she said, "It was very nice to meet you, Riani—and Chiaren. I really enjoyed talking to both of you."

"Same here, dear, same here." Riani gently touched her cheek again. "We hope to see you soon."

Mia smiled and nodded. "Definitely. I look forward to it."

"It was a pleasure meeting you, Mia," Korum's father said, giving her a smile. Then, turning to Korum, he added, "And it was good to see you, my son."

Korum inclined his head. "Until the next time."

And the world blurred around them again, causing Mia to close her eyes. When she opened them, they were standing back in Korum's house in Lenkarda.

* * *

"I like your parents," Mia told Korum over dinner. "They seem very nice."

"Oh, they are," Korum said, biting into a piece of pomegranate-flavored jicama. "Riani is great. Chiaren too, although we don't always see eye to eye on certain things."

"Why not?"

He shrugged. "I'm not sure. It's always been that way. In some ways, we're too alike, but in others, we're completely different. He's never understood why I spent all my time building up my company instead of just enjoying life and finding myself a mate, the way he did. And he hasn't really forgiven me for leaving Krina and depriving Riani of their only son, even though I frequently visit them in the virtual world."

Mia smiled, seeing shades of her own family in that dynamic. It had been difficult enough for her parents when she'd gone to college in New York; she couldn't imagine how they would've coped if she'd disappeared to another galaxy. She couldn't really blame Korum's father for being upset, particularly if he didn't understand or appreciate his son's ambition.

Still thinking about Korum's family, Mia slowly ate her stew, enjoying the satisfying combination of richly flavored roots and vegetables from Krina. Suddenly, a disturbing thought occurred to her, causing her to put down her utensil and look up at Korum.

"Would you ever want to go back to Krina?" she asked, frowning a little. "You must miss your parents, and it seems so nice there . . ."

He hesitated for a couple of seconds. "Perhaps one day," he finally said, watching her with an unreadable golden gaze. "But probably not for a long while."

Mia felt her chest tighten a little. "What about me?"

"You'll come with me, of course," he said casually, taking a sip of water. "What else?"

She took a deep breath, trying to remain calm. "To another planet? Leaving everything and everybody behind?"

His eyes narrowed slightly. "I didn't say we'd go soon, Mia. Maybe not even within your family's lifetime. But someday, yes, I may need to visit Krina and I would want you with me."

Mia blinked and looked away, her heart squeezing at the reminder of the disparity that now existed between her and the rest of humanity. Thanks to the nanocytes circulating through her body, she would never grow old and die—but she would also far outlive her loved ones. The fact that the Krinar had the means to indefinitely extend human lifespan but chose not to do so bothered her a great deal, making her feel guilty whenever she thought about the issue.

"Mia . . ." Korum reached across the table and took her hand. "Listen to me. I told you I would petition the Elders on your family's behalf, and I have begun the process. But I can't promise you anything. I've never heard of an exception being made for anyone who's not considered a charl."

"But why?" Mia asked in frustration. "Why not share your knowledge, your technology with us? Why do your Elders care so much about this issue?"

Korum sighed, his thumb stroking her palm. "None of us know exactly, but it has something to do with the fact that you're still very imperfect as a species, and the Elders want you to have more time to evolve . . ."

"We're imperfect?" Mia stared at him in disbelief. "What's that supposed to mean? What, you're saying we're defective? Like a part in a car that doesn't function properly?"

"No, not like a part in a car," he explained patiently, his fingers tightening when she tried to jerk her hand away. "Your species is very young, that's all. Your society and your culture are evolving at a rapid pace, and your high birthrate and short lifespan probably have something to do with that. If we were to give you our technology now, if every human could live thousands of years, your planet could become overpopulated very quickly . . . unless we also did something about your birthrate. You see, Mia, it's all or none: we either control everything, or we let you be mostly as you are. There's no good middle ground here, my sweet."

Mia felt her teeth snapping together. "So why not give people that choice?" she asked, angered by the whole thing. "Why not let them choose if they want to live for a long time, or if they'd rather have children? I'm sure many would go for the first option rather than face death and disease—"

"It's not that simple, Mia," Korum said, regarding her evenly. "Overpopulation is not the Elders' only concern, you see. Every generation brings something new to your society, changing it for the better. It was less than two hundred years ago that humans in your country thought nothing of keeping slaves. And now the thought of that is abhorrent to them—because generations have passed and values have changed. Do you think you could've eradicated slavery if the same people who had once owned slaves were still around today? Your society's progress would slow tremendously if we uniformly extended your lifespan—and that's not something the Elders want at this point."

"So we *are* just an experiment," Mia said, unable to keep the bitterness out of her voice. "You just want to see what happens to us, and never mind how many humans suffer in the process—"

"Humans wouldn't be around to suffer if it weren't for the Krinar, my sweet," he interrupted, looking faintly amused at her outburst. "You very conveniently forget that fact."

"Right, you made us, and now you can play God." She could feel the old resentment rising up, making her want to lash out at the unfairness of it all. As much as she loved Korum, sometimes his arrogance made her want to scream.

He grinned, not the least bit fazed by her anger. His fingers eased their grip on her palm, his touch turning soft and caressing again. "I can think of other things I'd rather play," he murmured, his eyes beginning to fill with golden heat.

And as Mia watched in disbelief, he sent the floating table away, removing the barrier between them. Still holding her hand, he pulled her toward him until she had no choice but to straddle his lap.

"You think sex will make it all better?" she asked, annoyed at her body's unavoidable response to his nearness. No matter how mad she was, all he had to do was look at her in a certain way and she was completely lost, turning into a puddle of need.

"Hmm-mm . . ." He was already leaning forward to kiss her neck, his mouth hot and moist on her bare skin. "Sex always makes everything better," he whispered, nibbling on the sensitive junction between her neck and shoulder.

And for the next several hours, Mia found no reason to disagree with that statement.

* * *

After the noise and crowds in Shanghai, the stark landscape of the Siberian tundra was almost soothing. If it hadn't been for the cold, Saret would've probably enjoyed visiting this remote northern region of Russia.

But it was cold. The temperature here, just above the Arctic Circle, was never warm enough for a Krinar, not even on the hottest summer day. Today, though, it was actually below freezing, and Saret made sure every part of his body was covered with thermal clothing before he stepped out of his ship.

The large grey building in front of him was one of the ugliest examples of Soviet-era architecture. Barbed wire and guard towers on every corner marked it as exactly what it was—a maximum security prison for the worst violent offenders in all of Russia. Few people knew this place existed, which is why Saret had chosen it for his experiment.

He openly approached the gate, not worrying about being seen by any cameras or satellites. For this outing, he was wearing a disguise, one of a couple he had developed over the years. It changed not only his appearance, but even the outer layer of his DNA, making it nearly impossible to divine his true identity. The humans knew he was a Krinar, of course, but they didn't know anything else about him.

At his approach, the gate swung open, letting him in. Saret walked briskly to the building, where he was greeted by the warden—a pot-bellied, middle-aged human who stank of alcohol and cigarettes.

Without saying a word, the warden led him to his office and closed the door.

"Well?" Saret asked in Russian as soon as they had privacy. "Do you have the data I requested?"

"Yes," the warden said slowly. "The results are quite . . . unusual."

"Unusual how?"

"It's been six weeks since your last visit," the human said, his hands nervously playing with a pen. "In the past month, we haven't had a single homicide. In the past three weeks, there have been no fights. I've been running this place for twenty years, and I've never seen anything like it."

Saret smiled. "No, I'm sure you haven't. What was the homicide rate before?"

The man opened a folder and took out a sheet of paper, handing it to Saret. "Take a look. There are usually two or three murders a month and about a fight a day. We can't figure it out. It's like all of them had a personality transplant."

Saret's smile widened. If only the human knew the truth. Satisfied, he folded the sheet and put it in the pocket of his thermal pants. "You can expect the final payment by tomorrow," he told the warden and walked out of the room.

He couldn't wait to get back on his ship and out of the cold.

CHAPTER THREE

The following two days passed uneventfully. Mia spent her time working in the lab and enjoying evenings with Korum, deliriously happy despite their occasional arguments. She had no doubt that he loved her—and it made all the difference in the world. One day, she hoped to convince him to see her kind in a different light, to appreciate the fact that humans were more than just an experiment of the Krinar Elders. For now, though, she had to be content with the possibility of an exception being made for her family—something she knew Korum was fighting hard to obtain.

At the lab, the other apprentices were still away, so Mia found herself frequently working alone, surrounded by all the equipment. Saret was in and out, and she would occasionally catch him watching her with an enigmatic expression on his face. Shrugging it off as some weird distrust for his human apprentice, she finished her report and sent it to Saret, hoping that he would give her feedback soon. While waiting, she continued to play around with the simulation, trying different variations of the process and carefully recording the results.

Tuesday was a day off in Lenkarda, and it was also Maria's birthday. The vivacious girl had sent her a holographic message over the weekend, formally inviting her to the party on the beach at two in the afternoon. Mia had gladly accepted.

"So I don't get to come?" Korum was lounging on the bed and watching her get ready for the party. His golden eyes gleamed with amusement, and she knew that he was teasing her.

"Sorry, sweetie," she told him mockingly, twirling in front of the mirror. "No cheren allowed. Charl only."

He grinned. "Such discrimination."

She wore the necklace he'd given her and a light floaty dress with a swimsuit underneath—just in case the party involved any swimming in the ocean.

"Yes, well, you know how that goes," she said, grinning back. "We're too cool for all you Ks."

She loved that she could banter with him now. Somehow, almost imperceptibly, their relationship had assumed a more equal footing. He still liked to be in control—and he could still be incredibly domineering on occasion—but she was beginning to feel like she could stand up to him. The knowledge that he loved her, that her thoughts and opinions mattered to him, was very liberating.

"All right," she said, bending down to give him a chaste kiss on the cheek, "I have to run."

Before she could pull away, however, his arm snaked around her waist, and she found herself flat on her back on the bed, pinned down by his large muscular body.

"Korum!" She wriggled, trying to get away. "I'm running late! You told me yourself it's an insult to be late—"

"One kiss," he cajoled, holding her effortlessly. She could see the familiar signs of arousal on his face and feel his cock hardening against her leg. Her body reacted in predictable fashion, her insides clenching in anticipation and her breathing picking up.

She shook her head. "No, we can't . . ."

"Just one kiss," he promised, lowering his head. His mouth was hot and skillful on hers, his tongue caressing the inside of her lips, and Mia could feel herself melting on the spot, a pleasurable fog engulfing her mind. Before she could completely forget herself, however, he stopped, lifting his head and carefully rolling off her.

"Go," he said, and there was a wicked smile on his face. "I don't want you to be late."

Frustrated, Mia got up and threw a pillow at him. "You're evil," she told him. Now she was extremely turned on, and she wouldn't get a chance to see him for the next few hours. The only thing that made her feel better was the fact that he would suffer equally.

"Just wanted you to hurry back, that's all," he said, grinning, and Mia threw another pillow at him before grabbing Maria's gift and heading out the door.

She managed not to be late, although all twelve of the other charl were already there when she arrived. Maria's invitation message had told her there would be thirteen girls total, including Mia herself.

An unusual musical mix was playing somewhere in the background. The sounds were beautiful, and Mia recognized the melody that Korum sometimes played in the house. However, interspersed with the popular Krinar tune, she could hear the more familiar flute and violin undertones.

The girls were sitting on floating chairs arranged in a circle around a large hovering plank that apparently served as a picnic table. The table was piled high with all manner of delicious-looking fruit and various exotic dishes.

Spotting Mia, Maria gave her an enthusiastic wave. "Hi there, come join us!"

Mia approached, smiling at her. "Happy birthday!" she said, handing Maria a small box wrapped in pretty paper.

"A gift! Oh my dear, you really shouldn't have!" But Maria's face glowed with excitement, and Mia knew she'd done the right thing in asking Korum to help her come up with a present.

As eager as a child, Maria tore apart the wrapper and opened the box, taking out a small oval object. "Oh my God, is that what I think it is?!?"

"Korum made it," Mia explained, pleased by her reaction. Maria obviously knew enough about Krinar technology to understand that she'd just received a fabricator—a device that would enable her to use nanomachines to create all manner of objects from individual atoms. Of course, the computer that Korum had embedded in his palm enabled him to do the same thing without any other devices—and on a much bigger, more complex scale. However, he was one of the very few who could create an entire ship from scratch. Rapid fabrication was a relatively new technology and still fairly expensive, so not all Krinar could afford even a basic fabricator—like the one he had designed for Maria. It was a highly coveted object, Korum had explained.

"Oh my God, a fabricator! Thank you so much!" Maria was almost beside herself with excitement. "This is so great—I can now make whatever clothes I want!"

"And other things too," Mia said, grinning. The little fabricator wasn't advanced enough to make complex technology, but it could conjure up all manner of simpler objects.

"Clothes," Maria said firmly. "I mainly want clothes."

Everyone around the table laughed at the determined expression on her face, and a red-headed girl yelled out, "And shoes for me!"

"Oh, what am I thinking!" Maria exclaimed amidst all the laughter. "I haven't even introduced you to everyone yet. Everyone—this is Mia, our newest arrival. As you can see, she's unbelievably awesome. Mia, you know Delia already. The lovely lady to her right is Sandra, then Jenny, Jeannette, Rosa, Yun, Lisa, Danielle, Ana, Moira, and Cat."

"Hi," Mia said, smiling and waving to all the girls. The flood of names was a little overwhelming; there was no way she'd remember all of them right away. Normally, she was shy in social situations where she didn't know most of the people, but today she felt comfortable for some reason. Perhaps it was because she already had so much in common with these girls. Few others outside of this little group could even begin to understand what it was like to be in a relationship with someone literally out of this world.

Taking a seat on the empty floating chair, Mia stared around the table with unabashed curiosity. Like her, all these girls were immortal. Did that mean that some of them were older than they looked? For the most part, they appeared young and strikingly beautiful, of various races and nationalities. However, a couple of them were merely pretty, and Mia wondered again why the godlike Krinar were attracted to humans in the first place. Was it the ability to drink their blood? If taking blood was as pleasurable as having it taken, then she could see the appeal.

Turning her attention to Delia, Mia thanked her for letting her know about the party in the first place.

"Of course," Delia said. "I'm glad you could make it. We heard you weren't in Lenkarda for the past week; otherwise, Maria would've sent you the formal invitation earlier."

"Yes, I was in Florida, visiting my family," Mia explained and saw Delia's eyebrows rise in question.

"Korum let you go there?" she asked, and there was a note of disbelief in her voice.

"We went together," said Mia, popping a strawberry into her mouth. The berry was sweet and juicy; the Krinar definitely knew how to get the best fruit.

"Oh," said Delia, "I see . . ." She seemed slightly confused by this turn of events.

"Do you ever go visit your family?" Mia inquired without thinking. "Are they still in Greece?"

Delia smiled, looking unaccountably amused. "No, they're no longer around."

"Oh, I'm so sorry . . ." Mia felt terrible. She'd had no idea this girl was an orphan.

"It's okay," Delia said calmly. "They passed away a long time ago. I now only have bits and pieces of memories about them. We didn't have photographs back then."

Mia began to get an inkling of the situation. "How long ago is a long time?" she asked, unable to contain her curiosity. No photographs? Just how old was Arus's charl?

"Oh, you don't know Delia's story?" said a brown-haired charl sitting to the right of Delia. "Delia, you should tell Mia—"

"I didn't get a chance, Sandra," Delia said, addressing the girl. "I only met Mia once before."

"Our Delia here is a bit older than she seems," Sandra said, an anticipatory grin on her face. "I just love the newbies' reactions when they hear her true age . . ."

Intrigued, Mia stared at the Greek girl. "What *is* your true age, Delia?"

"To the best of my knowledge, I will be two thousand three hundred and twelve this year."

Mia choked on a piece of strawberry she'd been eating. Coughing, she managed to clear her throat enough to wheeze out, "What?"

"Yep, you heard her right," Sandra said, laughing. "Delia is only a bit younger than some of the pyramids—"

And older than Korum. "You've been a charl this whole time?" Mia asked incredulously.

"Ever since I was nineteen," Delia said, looking at her with large brown eyes. "I met Arus on the coast of the Mediterranean, near my village. He was much younger then, barely two hundred years old, but to me, he was the epitome of wisdom and knowledge. I thought he was a god, especially when he showed me some of their miraculous technology. The day he took me to their ship I was convinced he brought me to Mount Olympus . . ."

"Where did you live this whole time? On Krina?" Mia was utterly fascinated. For some reason, she'd thought that Krinar-human liaisons were a fairly recent development. Although now that she thought about it, the existence of the charl/cheren terminology in Krinar language implied that these types of relationships had to have been around for a while.

"Yes," Delia said. "Arus took me to Krina when he left Earth. We lived there until the Krinar came here a few years ago."

Mia looked at her, imagining how shocking and overwhelming it must have been for someone from ancient Greece to end up on another planet. Even for Mia, who knew that the Krinar were not in any way supernatural, a lot of what they could do seemed like magic. What would it be like for someone who had never used a cell phone or a TV, who had no idea what a computer or a plane was?

"How did you cope with that?" Mia wondered. "I can't even picture what it must've been like for you."

Delia lifted her shoulders in a graceful shrug. "I'm not sure, to be honest. I can barely recall those early days at this point—everything is one big blur of images and impressions in my mind. I didn't handle the trip to Krina well, I remember that much. Your cheren—who wasn't even born at the time—has done a lot to make intergalactic travel safer and more comfortable. But back then, it was much more difficult. I was horribly sick during the entire trip because the ship wasn't optimized for humans, and it took me a few days to recover when I got to Krina, even with their medicine."

"Did you want to go?" Mia couldn't help feeling intense pity for a nineteen-year-old who had been taken away from everything she knew and brought to a strange and unfamiliar place.

Delia shrugged again. "I wanted to be with Arus, but I don't think I fully realized what that entailed. Obviously, I don't have any regrets now."

"Are there any charl who are older than you?"

"Yes," Delia said. "There are two of them. One is the charl of the biology expert who developed the process of extending human lifespan. He's almost five thousand years old. And another one is only about five hundred years older than me. She's originally from Africa."

"Wait, did you say he?" This was the first time Mia had heard about a male charl.

"Yes," Sandra said, joining their conversation. "I was surprised too. But some Krinar women—and men—take human men as their charl. It's much rarer, but it does happen. Sumuel—the original charl, as he's known—is actually with a mated couple."

Mia blinked. "Like a threesome?"

"Pretty much," Sandra said with a naughty grin on her face. "It's a somewhat unusual arrangement, but it works for them. The couple's daughter thinks of Sumuel as her third parent."

"The Krinar couple's daughter?"

"Yes, of course," said Delia. "We can't have children with the Krinar.

We're not sufficiently compatible, genetically."

Even though Mia had known that, hearing Delia say the words gave her an odd little ache in her stomach. Over the past few days, Mia had been so happy that she hadn't had a chance to dwell on the negative aspects of always being with someone not of her own species. Korum had told her in the very beginning that he couldn't make her pregnant, and she'd had no reason to question that. Besides, she'd had other things on her mind. However, now that Mia was certain of a future with Korum, she realized what that future held—or, rather, what it didn't hold: children.

Mia didn't feel a burning urge to be a mother, at least not right now. Having a child was something she'd always pictured as part of a pleasant, nebulous future. She'd always assumed she would finish college, attend graduate school, and meet a nice man somewhere along the way. They would date for a couple of years, get engaged, have a small family wedding, and start thinking about children after they were married for some time. And instead, she had become an extraterrestrial's charl within a week of meeting him, gained immortality, and lost any chance of a normal human life.

Not that she minded, of course. Being with Korum, loving him, was so much more than she could've ever hoped for. And if somewhere deep inside, a small part of her felt hollow at the loss of her nonexistent son or daughter . . . Well, she could live with that. Perhaps, one day, she could even convince Korum to adopt.

So Mia pasted a smile on her face and turned her attention back to Delia, asking her about her experiences on Krina and what it was like to live for so long.

Over the next hour, Mia got to know both Delia and Sandra, learning about their stories and what the life of a charl was truly like. Unlike Delia, Sandra had only been in Lenkarda for three years. Originally from Italy, she'd met her cheren by accident on the Amalfi coast. For the most part, both Delia and Sandra seemed quite happy with their lives, although Mia got the sense that Arus treated Delia as a real partner, while Sandra's cheren spoiled her rotten, but didn't take her too seriously.

After most of the food at the table was gone, Maria challenged all the girls to a drinking game that seemed similar to truth-or-dare. For the 'dare' portion, they had to drink a full shot of tequila.

"Don't worry," Sandra whispered to Mia, "you won't have a chance to get too drunk—not even if you drink five shots an hour. Our bodies metabolize alcohol really quickly now."

Mia grinned, remembering the last time she'd gotten wasted. It would've been nice to have all those nanocytes back at that club; it would've saved her quite a bit of embarrassment.

They played for an hour and Mia drank at least six shots, choosing the 'dare' option over answering some very probing questions about her sex life. Other girls had no such compunction, however, and Mia learned all about Moira's preference for black leather pants, Jenny's passion for foot massages, and the fact that Sandra had once had sex in a lifeboat.

Finally, the party came to an end. Feeling mildly buzzed, Mia headed home, eagerly anticipating seeing Korum and finishing what they had started earlier today.

* * *

Saret walked through the slums of Mexico City, dispassionately observing the dregs of humanity all around him. He had already planted the devices in the center of the city, so this excursion served no particular purpose except to satisfy his curiosity—and to reinforce in his mind the rightness of what he was doing.

On the corner, a pair of thugs were threatening a prostitute with a knife. She was reluctantly pulling money out of her bra and simultaneously swearing at them in very colorful Spanish. Saret walked in their direction, purposefully making noise, and the thugs scattered at his approach, leaving the whore alone. She took one look at Saret and ran away too, apparently realizing what he was.

Saret grinned to himself. *Fucking cowards.*

It was already after midnight, and the area was crawling with every kind of lowlife. Drug-related violence in Mexico hadn't gotten any better in recent years, and the country's government actually went so far as to appeal to the Krinar for help with this issue. After some debate, the Council decided against it, not wanting to get involved in human affairs. Saret had privately disagreed with that decision, but he voted the same way as Korum: against the involvement. It was never a good idea to openly oppose his so-called friend. Besides, it made no sense to help humans on such a limited scale. What Saret was doing would be far more effective.

He was heading back to where he left the transport pod when a dozen gang members made the fatal error of crossing his path. Armed with machine guns and high on coke, they apparently felt invincible enough to attack a K—a mistake for which they paid immediately.

The first few bullets managed to hit Saret, but none of the other ones did. Consumed by rage, he was hardly cognizant of his actions, operating solely on instinct—and his instinct was to rip apart and destroy anything that threatened him. By the time Saret regained control of himself, there were body parts all over the alley and the entire street stank of blood and death.

Disgusted with himself—and with the idiots who provoked him—Saret made his way back to the ship.

He was more convinced than ever that his path was a righteous one.

CHAPTER FOUR

The next day, Mia finished running the simulation for the third time and sent the digital results to Saret, hoping that he would get a chance to look at them soon. Without his feedback—or Adam's input—there was really nothing else she could do to move the project forward at this time.

It was only eleven a.m. on Wednesday, and she was already done with what she had set out to do in the lab for the day. Of course, she could always do some mind-related reading or watch some recordings, but that was something she tended to do in her spare time outside of the lab. Lab hours were for doing actual work, and Mia hoped she could find something to occupy herself with until she got the necessary feedback on her current project.

As usual, Saret was gone somewhere, and the other apprentices were in Thailand again. They'd left her alone in the lab—which Mia thought was probably a sign of trust. She doubted Saret would leave just anyone around all the complex lab equipment.

Getting up, she walked over to the common data storage facility—a Krinar device that was light years ahead of any human computer. Mia was just beginning to learn all of its capabilities, so she decided to use the downtime to explore it a little and brush up on some of the other apprentices' projects. The data unit responded to voice commands, which made it easy for Mia to operate it.

The next six hours seemed to fly by. Absorbed in her task, Mia hardly felt the passage of time as she read about the regenerative properties of Krinar brain tissue and the complexity of infant mind development. She took a short break for lunch—requesting a sandwich from the intelligent lab building—and then continued, fascinated by what she was learning. It seemed like the project that took the other apprentices away from the lab was even more interesting than what Mia and Adam were working on. Feeling slightly jealous, Mia decided to ask Saret if she could somehow get involved.

Finally, it was five o'clock. Although Mia typically stayed later in the lab, she decided to make an exception today, since nothing much was going on. Leaving the lab, she headed home.

Arriving at the house, she wasn't surprised to find that Korum wasn't there yet. His schedule was far more grueling than hers, although it helped that he didn't need to sleep more than a couple of hours a night. He actually got a lot of work done at night or early in the morning when Mia was sound asleep.

Making herself comfortable on the long floating plank in the living room, Mia decided to use the time to call Jessie. They hadn't spoken since before Mia's trip to Florida, and she really missed hearing her friend's bubbly voice.

"Call Jessie," Mia told her wristwatch-bracelet device, and heard the familiar dial tones as the call connected.

"Mia?" Jessie's voice sounded cautious.

"Yep, it's me," Mia said, grinning. She knew that the call would show up on Jessie's phone as coming from an unknown number. "How's it going? I haven't talked to you in over a week!"

"Oh, I'm good," Jessie said, sounding a little distracted. "How's your family? Did they already meet Korum?"

"They sure did," Mia said. "Believe it or not, they loved him. But hey, listen, are you busy right now? I can call back another time—"

"What? Oh, no, hold on, let me just go into another room . . ." A short silence, then, "Okay, I'm good now. Sorry about that. I was just hanging out with Edgar and Peter. Do you remember Peter?"

"Of course," Mia said. Peter was the guy she'd met at the club—the one Korum had almost killed for dancing with her. Mia still shuddered when she remembered that terrifying night, when she'd thought Korum had found out about her deception and was going to kill her. In hindsight, she'd been an idiot; she should've known even then that he would never harm her. But at the time, Korum had still been a stranger to her, a member of the mysterious and dangerous Krinar race that had invaded Earth five years ago.

"He still asks about you," Jessie said—a bit wistfully, Mia thought. "Edgar tells me he's really worried—"

"That's nice of him, but there's really no reason to worry," Mia interrupted, uncomfortable with the direction the conversation was taking. "Seriously, I'm happier than I've ever been in my life . . ."

Jessie fell silent for a second, and then Mia heard her sigh. "So that's it, huh?" she said softly. "You're in love with the K?"

"I am," Mia said, a big smile breaking out on her face. "And he loves me too. Oh, Jessie, you don't even know how happy he makes me. I could've never imagined it could be like this. It's like a dream come true—"

"Mia . . ." She could hear Jessie sighing again. "I'm happy for you, I really am . . . But, tell me, do you think you'll come back to New York?"

Mia hesitated for a moment. "I think so . . ." She was far less certain now than before. With each day that passed, college and all that it implied seemed less and less important. What use was a degree from a human university if she were to continue living and working in Lenkarda? She learned more in a day at the lab than she could in a month at NYU. Did it really make sense to spend another nine months writing papers and taking tests just for the sake of saying she got her diploma? And, more importantly, would Saret let her return to the lab after such a long absence? Given the rapid pace of research there, coming back after nine months would be almost like starting over.

"You don't sound sure," Jessie said, and there was a sad note in her voice.

"Yeah, I guess I'm not sure," Mia admitted. "Korum is fine with it, but I just don't know if I'll be able to return to my internship if I leave for so long . . ."

"So you like it there? At the K Center, I mean?"

"I do," Mia said. "Jessie, it's so nice here . . . I can't even begin to tell you how awesome some of their inventions are. Korum has a zero-gravity chamber in his house. Can you imagine that? And he's got a floor that massages your feet as you walk on it." Not to mention the fact that Mia was now pretty much immortal—but that was something she was not allowed to talk about outside of Lenkarda.

"Really? A floor that massages your feet?" Jessie sounded jealous now.

"Yep, and a bed that does the same thing to your whole body. All their technology is amazing, Jessie. Believe me when I tell you this: it's not a hardship to be here at all."

"Yeah, sounds like it," Jessie said, and Mia heard the resignation in her voice. "I guess I just miss you, that's all."

"I miss you too," Mia said. "Maybe I'll swing by for a visit in a couple of weeks. Let me talk to Korum about that, and we'll figure something out."

"Oh, that would be so nice!" Jessie sounded much more excited now.

"We'll make it happen," Mia promised, smiling. "I'll let you know when we're coming over. But, anyways, enough about that . . . Tell me about you and Edgar. How are things going on that front?"

And for the next ten minutes, Mia learned all about Jessie's new boyfriend, his latest acting gig, and the stuffed panda he'd won for Jessie at an amusement park. It seemed like the two of them were becoming increasingly close, and Mia was glad he made Jessie so happy. If anyone deserved to have a cute, caring guy, it was her former roommate.

Finally, Jessie had to go to dinner, so Mia said goodbye and went to change before Korum got home. He'd mentioned taking a post-dinner walk on the beach, and Mia wanted to make sure she had her swimsuit ready.

* * *

"So when do you think the Council will finally decide about the Keiths?" Mia asked, taking a bite of sweet pepper stuffed with mushroom-flavored rice. "Are they still doing the investigation?"

Korum nodded, picking up a piece of mushroom with the tong-like utensil the Krinar used in place of forks. "Loris is being difficult, as you'd expect. He's got a couple of Councilors on his side, and he's claiming there's no way Saur could've erased the Keiths' memories. Supposedly, someone from the Fiji lab told him that apprentices don't have access to that kind of equipment."

"Really? So, what, he's still saying that you and Saret are responsible for this?"

"I think he gave up on the idea of framing Saret," Korum said, a mocking smile appearing on his lips. "He's now seeking evidence to come after me."

Mia stared at him, concerned about this development. The black-garbed Krinar she'd seen at the trial didn't seem like someone who could be trifled with—and he truly hated Korum. "Do you think there's any chance he could cause trouble for you?"

"No, don't worry, my sweet," Korum said reassuringly, though his eyes glittered with something that looked like anticipation. "He's just trying to delay the inevitable. He failed as the Protector, and he knows it. Once his son and the rest of those traitors are sentenced, he'll lose all of his standing—and his position on the Council along with it."

"And you don't mind that in the least, right?" Mia asked, regarding him with a wry smile. For better or for worse, her lover tended to be quite ruthless with his opponents—a personality trait that made her glad she was now on his good side.

Korum shrugged. "It was Loris's choice to risk everything for his son. Now he'll pay the price. And if I have fewer people who stand in my way as a result, then all the better."

Mia nodded and concentrated on finishing the rest of her stuffed pepper dish. Despite everything, she couldn't help feeling just a tiny bit sympathetic toward the Protector. After all, the K was only defending his son. She imagined she'd do the same for her child—not that she had to worry about that anymore, she reminded herself. Pushing away the unpleasant thought, Mia looked at Korum instead, studying him covertly as he finished his meal.

Sometimes it was still difficult for her to believe they were so happy together. By Krinar law, she belonged to Korum—a fact that still made her very uncomfortable. As a charl, her legal standing in K society was murky, to say the least. If she didn't love him so much—and if he didn't treat her as well as he did—her life could've easily been miserable.

But she did love him. And he loved her back, with all the intensity in his nature. As a result, he seemed to be trying to suppress his inborn arrogance, knowing that it was important for her to be regarded as an equal. There was still a long way to go, of course—the gap of age and experience was too wide to be bridged easily—but he was definitely making an effort in that direction.

After they were both done with the meal, Korum stood up and offered her his hand. "Up for a walk, my sweet?" he asked, giving her a warm smile.

Mia grinned. "Sure." She loved these after-dinner walks on the beach. They'd done them almost every night when they were in Florida, and she'd learned a great deal about Korum during those quiet times.

Taking his hand, she let him lead her outside.

They walked for a couple of minutes in silence, enjoying the soft evening breeze. The sun was just setting behind the trees, and an orange glow lit the sky, reflecting off the water shimmering in the distance.

"You know," Mia said, thinking about their first meeting in New York, "I still don't know your full name. You said I wouldn't be able to pronounce it if you told me, but I've never heard anyone call you anything but Korum."

He grinned. "Our full names are generally only used at birth and at death. Do you still want to hear it?"

"Of course." She imagined something totally unpronounceable. "What is it?"

"Nathrandokorum."

"Oh, that sounds kind of nice," Mia said, surprised. "Why don't you use it more?"

He shrugged. "I don't know. That's just the way it's been with us for a long time. Full names have become nothing more than a formality. I doubt that anyone besides my parents knows that I'm called Nathrandokorum."

Mia smiled, shaking her head. Some parts of the Krinar culture were strange indeed.

They walked some more, and then Mia remembered her recent conversation with her former roommate. "Do you think we might have a chance to visit New York soon?" she asked. "I was talking to Jessie, and it would be really nice to see her . . ."

Korum smiled, looking down at her. "Of course. If you want, we can go the next time you have a day off. Unless you want to go for longer?"

"No, a day would be perfect. I guess sometimes I still forget that we can just pop on over there whenever we want."

His smile widened. "We definitely can—especially now that most of the Resistance has been captured."

"Where's Leslie?" Mia asked, remembering the girl who had attacked her in Florida. "Is she here, in Lenkarda?"

Korum shook his head. "No, she's in our Arizona Center."

"Is she . . . all right?" Mia was almost afraid to know the answer. The Resistance fighter had teamed up with Saur—the former apprentice from Saret's lab—to try to kill Korum in Florida. Now she was in K custody, about to be 'rehabilitated.' From what Mia understood about the process, the end goal was to change that part of Leslie's personality that made her a danger to society (or to the Krinar, as the matter may be). Rehabilitation—or mind tampering—was the most advanced branch of Krinar neuroscience, and Mia was just starting to learn about it at the lab.

"I assume so," Korum said, his expression cooling. He obviously hadn't forgotten the fact that the girl had pointed a gun at Mia and almost gotten her killed by Saur.

"Could you find out for me, please?" For some reason, Mia felt responsible for what happened to Leslie, even though the girl had attacked *her*. Still, she couldn't help remembering the terror on Leslie's face as she was led away by the K guardians. However misguided the fighter's intentions were, she didn't deserve to be mistreated, and Mia sincerely hoped she didn't get hurt during her rehabilitation.

Korum hesitated, then nodded curtly. "All right, I will." His jaw tightened, however, and Mia could see that he was thinking about the beach incident again.

To distract him, she squeezed his hand and gave him a big smile. "Thank you," she said. "I really appreciate it."

"Of course, my darling," he said, his expression visibly softening. "Anything to make you happy—you know that." And bending down, he brushed his lips against her mouth in a brief kiss.

"So what are the guardians, anyway?" Mia asked when they started walking again. "Are they like your police?"

"Something like that," Korum said. "They're a cross between soldiers, police, and one of your intelligence agencies. They enforce our laws, catch criminals, and deal with any kind of threat from humans. Our society is so homogenized at this point that we no longer have war on Krina, the way you do here on Earth. There are still some regional rivalries, of course, and there are always a few crazies who disagree with the way things are done by the government, but we don't have the kind of conflict that would require a standing army."

"So you guys managed to invade our planet without an army?"

Korum laughed. "If you want to think about it that way. Most Krinar males who came to Earth received military-style training because we were expecting some resistance. But no, we didn't need a big army to control Earth; all we needed was our technology."

"Of course." Mia tried to keep the bitterness out of her voice. Loving Korum the way she did made it easy to forget that she was doing the equivalent of sleeping with the enemy—even if the enemy didn't actually intend her planet any harm. It was only during these types of conversations that Mia was unpleasantly reminded of the fact that the Krinar forcefully took over her planet . . . and that the man who loved her did not necessarily have humankind's best interests at heart.

"Trust me, Mia, it was better this way," Korum said, as though reading her mind. "Your government had no choice but to accept the inevitable, and that helped minimize the bloodshed. It would've been far worse if there had been a full-out war between our people."

Mia's mouth tightened, but she nodded, knowing he was right. There was no point in resenting the Krinar's technological superiority; in a way, it did make their invasion as painless as possible. The fact that they invaded at all was a different matter, of course—but Mia didn't have the energy or the inclination to fight that particular battle. Working with the Resistance once was enough.

"Can I ask you something?" Mia said, thinking back to those crazy days when she was spying on Korum. "I don't get one thing about the Keiths' plans. Even if they were successful in getting all the Krinar to leave Earth, wouldn't your people have come back with reinforcements? I know you said they were going to kill *you*, but what about all the others? Are you the only one with the means to go back and forth between Earth and Krina?"

Korum shot her an amused glance. "No, of course not. My company has the most advanced ship designs, but the Krinar have traveled to and from Earth long before I was even born. I think the Keiths were hoping to control the protective field."

"The protective field?"

He nodded. "Up until a dozen years ago, space travel was largely unregulated. Anyone could go anywhere, as long as they had a ship to take them there. Now, however, we have a shield in place to protect Earth from unauthorized travel—the same kind of shield we recently put around Krina."

"There is a shield around Earth?" Mia looked up at him in surprise.

"It's actually a shield around the solar system," Korum explained. "Not like a barrier, but more of a disruptor field. When activated, it messes with our ships' faster-than-light capabilities."

"Why would you want something that can mess with your ships?"

"For security purposes, we want to make sure the Council is informed of—and authorizes—any travel between Earth and Krina. Also, if there happen to be any other intelligent life forms out there, and they use technology comparable to ours, the shields will afford us some protection from them."

Mia gave him an ironic look. "So they can't do to you what you did to us?"

"Exactly." He grinned at her, looking so unrepentant that Mia couldn't help but laugh.

"Okay," she said, returning to her original question, "so what were the Keiths going to do? Use the protective field to keep the rest of the

Krinar out?"

"Probably," Korum said, still smiling. "That's what I would've done in their place."

They walked for a few more minutes before they reached the ocean. As usual, this section of the beach was completely deserted. With only five thousand Ks in the Costa Rican settlement, there was plenty of space for everyone and most Krinar tended to keep out of each other's 'territories'—as informal as those were in modern times. Since Korum liked to take evening walks on this particular stretch of sand, the other Ks respectfully stayed clear of it.

"Do you want to go for a swim?" Mia asked, letting go of his hand and kicking off her shoes to test the water temperature with her toe. It was perfect—just cool enough to be refreshing.

Instead of answering, Korum pulled off his shirt, revealing a bronzed, muscular torso. "Absolutely," he said, his eyes turning more golden by the second.

Smiling, Mia took a few steps back and slowly took off her dress, loving the way his gaze was glued to her every move. She could see the erection growing in his shorts, and her nipples hardened in response, her body affected by his desire. The fact that she could do this to him by simply stripping down to her swimsuit was exhilarating—and incredibly flattering.

"Are you teasing me?" he asked, his voice low and dangerously soft.

Her heart pounding with excitement, Mia nodded, watching his eyes narrow at her answer.

"I see," he said thoughtfully. And before she could blink, he was already on her, sweeping her up into his arms and carrying her into the water.

Held securely in his embrace, Mia laughed, reveling in the coolness of the water as they went deeper and deeper. "Is this to be my punishment?" she joked as he paused, waiting for a large wave to pass them by before going further.

"Oh, you want to be punished?" he murmured, looking down at her with a heated gleam in his eyes.

Grinning, Mia shook her head. "No . . ."

"I think you do . . ." he said softly, shifting her in his arms so that he was holding her with only one hand. Before Mia could say anything, his other hand slipped inside her swimming suit and pressed against her sex, unerringly finding her clit and pinching it between his fingers.

She bucked against him, startled by the strong sensation, and he did it again, watching her face closely. "Does it hurt?" he asked, his voice like rough velvet. "Or does it feel good?"

Mia gasped as his fingers increased the pressure. "I don't know . . ."

"Oh, I think you do," he whispered. "I think you know very well . . ." His fingers slipped inside, stretching her open.

"Korum, please . . ." She could feel him curving one of the fingers inside her, rubbing against her G-spot.

"You're wet," he murmured, "so slick I can feel it even in the ocean. It makes me want to fuck you right here and now."

"So do it," Mia breathed, staring up at him. "Fuck me." She was already on the verge of orgasm—all she needed was a tiny push to bring her over the edge.

His eyes flared brighter. "Oh, I will . . ." Within seconds, she was fully naked, the torn remnants of her swimsuit floating around them. His shorts met the same fate, and then he was lowering her to her feet, letting her slide down his body. Looping her arms around his neck, Mia pressed against him. Her breasts felt tender, her nipples sensitized, and she rubbed them against his chest to assuage the ache deep within. His erection nudged at her belly, thick and hot, and her sex pulsed with the need to take him inside.

Leaning forward, she kissed his lips, tasting the salt from the ocean spray and the uniquely delicious essence that was Korum. He groaned, deepening the kiss, and Mia sucked on his tongue, stroking it with her own. At the same time, she reached under the water, wrapping her fingers around his hard shaft. It jumped at her touch, swelling up further, and Korum inhaled sharply, lifting her up and opening her thighs wide. A wave hit them, the water droplets spraying Mia's face, and she closed her eyes, grabbing onto Korum's shoulders with both hands. For a brief second, the tip of his cock brushed against her entrance, and then he pushed inside her in one powerful stroke.

Mia gasped at the invasion, her inner muscles tightening at the feel of him so deep within. Wrapping her legs around his waist, she held him there, reveling in the amazing sensation.

"Fuck," he groaned. "You feel so . . . fucking . . . good . . ." He punctuated each word with a small, shallow thrust, his pelvis grinding against her clitoris, and Mia cried out as a sudden climax ripped through her, causing her sex to spasm around his thickness. He groaned again, and continued thrusting into her, lifting her up and down on his cock with a relentless rhythm that sent her over the edge again, just a few minutes later. This time, he joined her, and she felt the warmth of his release deep inside her belly.

And then they simply floated there, letting the waves rock them back and forth.

CHAPTER FIVE

The next morning, Mia again found herself alone in the lab. Saret was still traveling and hadn't sent her his feedback, so she continued learning about the other projects until her stomach rumbled, reminding her that it was time to eat.

Getting up, she stretched and requested a popular Krinar stew for lunch. The intelligent lab building provided it five minutes later, and Mia sat down to eat at one of the floating table-planks.

For some reason, her thoughts kept turning to the conversation she'd had with Korum yesterday and the Resistance fighter she'd helped capture. Leslie was going to undergo mind manipulation, and Mia couldn't help wondering how much the girl would be changed in the process. She couldn't imagine someone tampering with *her* thoughts, feelings, and memories, and she felt bad that another person would be subjected to something so invasive. Surely there had to be a better way to dissuade Leslie from her futile fight against the Krinar. Perhaps someone could talk to her, explain that the Krinar didn't have any sinister intentions toward Earth . . . Of course, it was possible that the girl's hatred of the invaders went too deep to allow for rational thinking.

Sighing, Mia finished her meal and went back to the data storage unit. As she was about to pull up the infant mind development project, she paused, remembering a tidbit Adam had mentioned to her at some point. Saur—the K who'd tried to kill Korum—had once been an apprentice in this very lab, and he was supposedly quite good at mind manipulation. If some of his old projects were still stored here, they might help her gain a better understanding of what was going to be done to Leslie.

Suddenly excited, Mia ordered the unit to locate all the data that Saur had added. There was a lot, but she had plenty of time to kill.

Making herself comfortable, Mia dove into the intricacies of the tampered mind.

Five hours later, she got up again, deeply puzzled. She'd just begun to scratch the surface of everything Saur had worked on, but none of it was directly related to memory erasure. There were plenty of notes and recordings on behavioral conditioning and memory implantation—but only brief mentions of intentional memory removal.

If Mia understood it correctly, Saur had never even done memory wipe simulations, much less had any practice with live subjects.

Frowning, Mia stared at the data unit, oddly disturbed by what she'd just learned. Something didn't quite make sense to her. If Saur didn't know how to erase memories, shouldn't Saret have said something about that to the Council? Her boss always knew who was working on which project; he was the one who gave everyone their assignments.

Maybe she was wrong. Maybe there was some other data storage place that she didn't know about where other projects were kept. It was possible: Mia was still new and learning her way around.

It was also possible that Saur simply hadn't bothered inputting some of his projects into the common database. Adam had mentioned once that the dead apprentice was a bit strange—a loner who didn't get along with anyone else. He could've easily had trouble following the lab's protocol.

Still, Mia couldn't shake an uneasy feeling in her stomach, a nagging sense that something wasn't quite right with this picture. She needed to talk to Korum and soon.

Pausing to send Korum a brief holographic message telling him that she'd be home in a few minutes, Mia headed toward one of the exit walls.

And as she was about to walk out, the wall in front of her dissolved, and her boss came into the lab.

"Well, hello there," Saret said, looking down at her with a smile. "You didn't go home yet? I was hoping you'd get a chance to take it easy, with all of us out and about these past couple of days."

Mia smiled back, trying to hide her nervousness. "No, I was just brushing up on some of the other projects here," she said, staying as close to the truth as possible. "The one Aners is working on is really interesting. You know, with the infant mind development?"

"Sure." Saret's smile changed—becoming almost indulgent, Mia thought. "That's a great project for you to get involved with. We can talk about it later, once you and Adam are done with your current task."

"Great!" Mia injected the appropriate amount of enthusiasm into her voice and tried to ignore the way her palms had begun to sweat. "I'm really looking forward to it. Thanks again for giving me this opportunity."

"Of course." Saret's brown eyes gleamed as he took a couple of steps toward her. Pausing less than two feet away, he said, "I'm glad you're having a good time here."

Mia nodded, still maintaining a big smile on her face. Maybe she was being an idiot, but the vibes she was getting from her boss today made her decidedly uncomfortable. All she wanted was to go home and talk to Korum about what she'd learned. Most likely, there was a good explanation for everything, but on the slight chance there wasn't, she didn't want to linger in the lab any longer than necessary. And it was the second time Saret had acted almost . . . weird.

"Okay, then," she said brightly, looking up at his darkly bronzed face. "Please take a look at the report when you get a chance, and I'll head on out for now. Unless you need me?"

Saret smiled again. "I always need you," he said, and there was an unusually soft note in his voice. "But you must have your rest, I understand . . ." And Mia's heartbeat spiked as he leaned even closer, his eyes seemingly glued to her exposed shoulder.

"All right then—" she backed away, "—I'll see you soon." And turning around, she took a step toward the wall leading to the outside.

"Is anything wrong, Mia?" Saret was suddenly in front of her, blocking the way. "You seem worried."

Every hair on Mia's body was standing on end. "Sorry," she said insincerely, forcing a quick laugh. Even to her own ears, it sounded fake. "I'm just thinking about going to New York to see my roommate, that's all."

"Oh, is that right?" Saret cocked his head to the side. "And when are you planning to go?"

"Oh, it won't be for long." Mia cursed herself for blurting out that tidbit and prolonging the conversation. "We'll go on one of the rest days—"

"So why are you so anxious?" Saret asked, a strange look in his eyes. "Is it because you found something you shouldn't have?"

Mia swallowed, a cold chill snaking down her spine. "I'm not sure what you're talking about . . ."

Saret smiled—the same friendly smile that had made Mia like him before. Now she found it frightening instead. "What made you look at Saur's files today?" he inquired casually. "Don't you know it's against the lab protocol to access other apprentices' projects?"

Mia shook her head. She hadn't known, in fact. Staring at Saret, she felt like she was seeing him for the first time. He was Korum's friend. Why was he doing this? Why had he misled everyone about Saur's abilities? And, more importantly, what did he intend to do to keep Mia from telling everyone?

Thinking furiously, she realized that denial would be useless at this point. Somehow Saret knew about Mia's discovery. "Why?" she asked him instead, keeping her voice steady despite the fact that her hands were beginning to shake. "Why didn't you tell the Council Saur couldn't have done it?"

Saret's smile widened. "Because it was convenient to have them think he did," he explained, and there was something triumphant in his gaze. "It wasn't what I originally intended, but it worked out regardless."

Her fear growing by the minute, Mia took a step back. Her every instinct was screaming for her to get out, *now*. Maybe there was still a good explanation for Saret's actions, but she couldn't take that chance. Casting aside all remnants of politeness, Mia swiftly lifted her wristwatch-bracelet to her face. "Call Kor—"

But she didn't get a chance to complete her request. His hand was suddenly around her wrist, holding it in a steely grip. Strong fingers ripped away the device, crushing it in the process.

"Oh, no," Saret said softly, dragging her toward him until she was pressed flat against his muscular body. "You don't get to call him anymore, you understand?"

Stunned and terrified, Mia stared at the K who'd been her boss and mentor for the past month. His hand was wrapped around her wrist, twisting it in such a way that she couldn't move at all. To her horror, Mia realized that he was hard, his erection pressing threateningly into the softness of her belly.

"What are you doing?" she whispered, hot bile rising in her throat. "Korum will kill you for this, you know that . . ."

Saret's eyes glittered. "Oh, will he, now? He's more than welcome to come find you here. The lab is set up quite nicely for his arrival."

"What?" Surely he wasn't saying—

"I mean, when your cheren arrives, I'll have a little surprise for him,"

Saret said, giving her a gentle smile. "You see, Mia dear, it's about time you knew the truth about your lover. Come, let's go into my office and we'll talk."

And without giving her a choice in the matter, he pulled her toward the back of the room, his fingers wrapped firmly around her wrist. Upon their approach, one of the walls dissolved, creating an entrance into the space Saret used for private projects.

Her knees weak with fear, Mia stumbled as he tugged her into the opening, the wall sealing shut behind her. Before she could fall, however, Saret caught her, lifting her up in his arms.

"There," he said soothingly, sitting down on one of the floating planks with her held tightly in his lap. "I've got you . . . No need to worry— you'll be all right," he added, apparently feeling the tremors shaking her frame.

"Let go," Mia whispered, pushing at his chest with all her strength. She could feel a hard bulge pressing against her thighs, and her stomach twisted with nausea. Her voice rose hysterically. "Let me go, right now!"

He didn't reply, his eyes darkening as he stared at her. The expression on his face was almost . . . enraptured, Mia realized with horror. For some reason, he wanted her, and there was nothing she could do to stop him if he decided to act on that inclination.

"You said you were going to tell me something about Korum," she said in desperation, her voice shrill with panic. "What don't I know about him?"

Saret blinked, his gaze clearing a little. "Oh, yes," he said, a self-deprecating smile appearing on his lips. "We were going to talk, weren't we? Here, you better have a seat . . ." And lifting her off his lap, he placed her next to him, keeping one hand wrapped firmly around her arm.

Mia immediately tried to scoot back further, but his grip tightened, preventing her from moving from the spot.

"Listen to me, Mia," Saret said, a small frown creasing his forehead, "I know you don't understand why I'm doing this right now and it all seems crazy to you. But, believe me, it's for your own good—for the good of all humanity. What your cheren intends for your people is not pretty, and he needs to be stopped. Do you know what he's trying to get the Elders to agree to?"

Mia shook her head, her stomach churning as his grip softened on her arm, his thumb gently massaging her skin.

"He wants to take your planet from you. Did he tell you that?"

"No," Mia managed to say, her heart pounding so hard she could barely think. Saret was lying to her, of course. He had to be.

"My so-called friend is a power-hungry monster," Saret said, his gaze hardening. "It wasn't enough for him to achieve the highest standing on Krina. Oh no, Mia dear, he had to extend his reign to another planet—to your planet. If it hadn't been for him, we would've never come to Earth. He was the one who convinced the Elders it was necessary to control your planet, to save it for the future generations of Krinar. And now he plans to take it from you completely. Do you understand what I'm saying?"

Mia nodded, wanting to keep him talking. She would listen to his lies for as long as necessary if it would only buy her time. In another few minutes, Korum would realize that she didn't come home as promised. Would he come looking for her then? Walk into whatever trap Saret seemed to be setting? *Please don't let anything happen to him. Please don't let anything happen to him.*

"You see, Mia," Saret continued, "all I want is what's good for your people—what's good for the greatest number of intelligent beings. I want to liberate Earth, free it from the tyranny of Korum and the Council. I want you to have your planet back."

"Why? What does it matter to you?" Was Saret one of the Keiths? And if so, how had he managed to escape detection for so long?

"Why? Because I've always wanted to do something great." Saret's voice was filled with barely suppressed excitement. "All our contributions to society, all this—" he waved a hand toward the lab, "—pales in comparison with liberating billions of intelligent beings, with giving them a better life . . . a peaceful life free from terror. I don't want to be remembered for coming up with yet another way to enhance memories, Mia. I want to be the one to bring peace to Earth."

"Peace to Earth?" That sounded insane to her. "But we're not at war with the Krinar—"

"Oh no, getting rid of the Krinar is just the beginning." Saret laughed. "You see, Mia, I can also give your people a better life. I can make it so you don't have to spend your few short decades fearing war, drive-by shootings, terrorist attacks . . . I can give you what humans have been dreaming about since the beginning of time: a life free of fear and violence. Wouldn't you want that, Mia? Wouldn't you like that for your people?"

"What are you talking about?" Was there such a thing as mental illness among the Ks? Was she stuck here with a madman?

"I know you don't understand now, but you will—I promise you that." Saret's face was almost glowing with fervor. "When your murder rates drop to zero and war is a thing of the past, your world will know that a new era in human history has arrived—and they will thank me for it."

Mia stared at him, unable to comprehend what he was saying for a minute. Then a horrifying and implausible idea occurred to her. "Saret," she said slowly, looking at the K known to be one of the greatest mind experts, "are you talking about some kind of mind manipulation for humans?" *Please let him laugh and tell me it's not true. Please don't let it be true.*

Saret gave her a pleased smile, his hand now caressing her arm, making her skin crawl. "Yes, Mia dear, that's exactly what I'm talking about. I always knew you were bright for your species. You see, over the past few years, I developed and perfected a new technique, a way to monitor certain neural impulses while simultaneously stimulating the pain and pleasure centers of the brain—"

Mia sucked in her breath. "Are you saying—" Her voice broke for a second, and she had to start again. "Are you saying you developed some kind of mind control?"

Now Saret laughed, his brown eyes crinkling with amusement. "No, of course not. Hopefully you've learned enough by now to know that true mind control is impossible. No, my technique allows me to direct certain behaviors—to condition the brain, if you will. Every time someone has a violent thought, for instance, I can make them experience pain. Every time they obey me—pleasure. Imagine: an entire planet full of peaceful humans . . . Wouldn't you want that, Mia?"

What Mia wanted was to throw up. "But how? How can you do something like that on a mass scale?"

Saret grinned, obviously enjoying her reaction. "Well," he said, "that's where Rafor and the rest of the Keiths come in. As you probably know, Rafor was nowhere near as good as your cheren at technological design, but he was decent enough to occupy a high position in his father's company. After Korum put them out of business, poor Rafor was left at loose ends. You see, since he lost his standing, no one else would hire him as a designer, and he was forced to dabble in a variety of subjects that didn't interest him nearly as much as his original chosen field. He even came to me a couple of years ago, asking if he could do an apprenticeship at the lab.

"I declined, of course. He was nowhere near qualified enough to be here. You weren't either, being a human and all, but at least you had the passion for the subject. He didn't even have that." Saret let out a chuckle. "But, in any case, I did offer him a chance to help me out on a private project, to design the nanocytes I needed to implement the plan. He understood immediately what I was trying to do—it aligned well with his own sympathetic views toward humans—and he did an excellent job creating both the nano design and the dispersion mechanism."

Mia listened to him intently, hardly daring to breathe. What he was telling her now was so incredible—and so terrifying—that she could barely process what she was hearing.

"Of course, Rafor failed miserably at the first part of the plan," Saret continued. "He was supposed to get rid of Korum and the rest with the help of the Resistance, but he got caught instead."

Mia swallowed to get rid of the dryness in her throat. "So you erased their memories," she guessed, and Saret nodded, smiling.

"I did. I had no choice. It was the only way to protect myself and the rest of the plan. Plus, it did give the Keiths a chance at the trial."

"So the Protector was right: you were the one all along—"

"He was partially right." Saret's smile was bright and happy. "He thought I erased their memories to help Korum, but nothing could be further from the truth. It hindered your cheren's agenda quite a bit—a nice, if not entirely intentional, side effect of the whole thing."

"Why do you hate him so much? He thinks of you as a friend—"

The dark-haired K laughed, throwing his head back. "Of course he does—I made sure of that. Only an idiot would want Korum for an enemy. I've seen him destroy those who stand in his way, and I've never made that mistake."

"You're making that mistake now," Mia cautiously pointed out, glancing at where his fingers were still wrapped around her arm. If Korum were here, Saret would already be dead. If there was one thing she'd learned over the past few weeks, it was just how territorial Krinar males tended to be.

"Oh, because I'm touching his precious charl?" Saret said, his eyes gleaming with a mixture of excitement and some other unidentifiable emotion. "Don't worry, Mia dear, you won't be his for long. You'll be free of him soon. Just as soon as he gets here . . ."

Mia's blood turned to ice. "Are you—" She had to stop for a second because she couldn't force the words past the constriction in her throat. "Are you planning to kill him?" she finally managed to say.

"Most likely." Saret smiled at her again—that same friendly smile that made Mia want to scream. "It would probably be easiest. Of course, I could always try to capture him and put him through the same process as Saur. That would be the ultimate prize: having Korum himself in my control—"

"Saur? You mind-controlled Saur?" Mia stared at him in horrified disbelief. Had Saret actually made his former apprentice attack them in Ormond Beach?

"No." Saret looked disappointed at her lack of understanding. "Not mind control. I told you that. Mind conditioning. My technique works very subtly. It doesn't turn people into mindless zombies or whatever it is you're imagining—"

"But you mind-conditioned Saur to want to kill Korum?"

"I did," Saret admitted with a look of pride on his face. "It wasn't easy, believe me. All Krinar have immune system shields that repel nanocytes; it's something that was developed thousands of years ago after someone tried to use medical nanotechnology in warfare. I was only able to penetrate Saur's defenses after dozens of physical injections—and even then, the mind-conditioning only worked because Saur was weaker than most. That's why I wanted the Krinar to leave Earth: because I can't control them effectively. With humans, it's much easier. You're completely unshielded; all I need to do is release the nanocytes into the air in the most populated areas and they'll find their intended targets."

Mia's head was spinning. "So let me get this straight . . . You're trying to get rid of your own kind so that you can mind-control—or, rather, mind-condition—all the humans on Earth?"

"When you say it that way, it does sound crazy, doesn't it?" Saret smiled wryly. "But yes, that is indeed what I'm trying to do. I want to bring peace to your people, Mia. Is that such a bad thing? Think about it for a minute. Wouldn't you want to live in a world where you can walk down the street at night without worrying about getting killed or raped? Where serial killers are the stuff of horror movies, instead of existing in real life? No more school shootings, no more terrorism or war . . . Doesn't that sound like something you'd want?"

Mia stared at him. For a moment, the picture he painted did seem strangely appealing. "Of course," she said. "But what you're talking about is an invasion of our minds. You want to take away our free will—"

"Free will?" Saret raised his eyebrows. "How do you define free will? Your people will be free to live as they please, to be with whomever they want, to do whatever they want . . . They just won't be able to kill or hurt others when the urge strikes them."

"And they will worship you, right?" Mia said, her eyes narrowing. "That's what you ultimately want, isn't it? An entire planet full of puppets who will obey your every command?"

Saret laughed, shaking his head. "Put like that, it does sound awful, doesn't it? But no, Mia dear, that's not how I see it. Your people will worship me, true—but that's because I will be their savior. I will be the one to bring an end to their suffering, to liberate their planet and bring them peace."

"And what are you planning to do with the rest of the Krinar here?" Mia asked, the thought just occurring to her. "Korum foiled your plan with the Resistance, and all your people are still here. Don't you think they would notice if all the humans suddenly became peaceful? If murder rates went to zero overnight?"

"It wouldn't happen overnight," Saret said. "Complete mind conditioning takes many days, if not weeks. But yes, they would ultimately notice, of course—which is why I'll have to get rid of everyone in the Centers and make sure the protective field prevents anyone else from coming here any time soon."

Mia took a deep breath, fighting the urge to throw up. Surely he didn't mean— "Get rid of everyone how?"

He sighed. "By killing them, of course."

All color faded from Mia's face. "Killing all fifty thousand Krinar?" she whispered, unable to comprehend the evil required to do murder on that scale.

Saret shrugged. "The majority of them, yes. Some might survive, of course, but most will perish."

"Perish how?" Mia could hear the hysterical edge in her own voice. "How can you possibly kill so many?"

"By utilizing that same nano weapon Rafor and the Resistance planned to use as a threat," Saret explained, looking at her calmly. "The design Korum gave us through you was faulty, of course, but it had enough of the right elements that I've been able to hire someone to perfect it. It's almost ready now; my designer is just putting the final touches on it."

"So let me get this clear," Mia said, staring at the psychopath sitting next to her, "you want to murder fifty thousand of your own kind in your quest to bring peace to Earth? And you don't see anything wrong with that?"

"Of course I do." Saret frowned. "Do you think I'll enjoy that part of the plan? I would've gladly sent them back to Krina or tried to control them if I could. But I can't. All I can do is try to make them disappear in as painless of a way as possible. I know it's not exactly consistent with my pacifist agenda. But you see, Mia, the good of the many far outweighs the needs of the few. We should've never come to your planet; it was your cheren's endless ambition that brought us here in the first place. Now we must atone for what we did; we must pay for our sins against your kind—"

"Are you going to kill me, too?" Mia felt her fear fading as a strange numbness started to set in. What he was intending was so horrific she simply couldn't process it fully. "Or are you planning to make me into a puppet? That's why you're telling me this, isn't it? Because you're not worried that I'll tell anyone?"

Saret grinned, releasing her arm and covering her hand with his palm instead. His touch felt scalding on her skin, making her realize how icy her hands had become. "The thought of you as a puppet is rather appealing, I must say," he said, his eyes darkening again. "And maybe I'll do that eventually . . . But I'd rather not tamper with your mind too much at first. I quite like you as you are right now."

"So what are you going to do with me then?" Mia's tone was almost disinterested. "If you're not going to kill me, that is—"

"I won't kill you," Saret reassured her. "I'm simply going to make sure you don't remember this conversation—or anything else that happened in the past few months. It'll be for the best, you'll see . . . I know you got attached to that monster, and you'd probably miss him if he was gone. But this way, you'll be free from his influence forever. It will be as though he had never been in your life."

Mia stared at him, acidic rage starting to burn in the pit of her stomach. "You're going to kill Korum and erase my memory to make me forget him?"

"No, Mia dear," Saret said, smiling. "I wouldn't be that cruel to you. I will erase your memory first. That way, you won't feel anything when he dies. I don't want to put you through that kind of trauma, you see. Painful memories like that are the hardest to get rid of, and the last thing I'd want is to give you nightmares that linger in your subconscious—"

"You're insane," Mia said, her anger growing by the second. She welcomed the feeling because it helped clear the fog of terror from her brain. "You really think that's a mercy, invading my brain like that? And why do you care about me, anyway? You're about to murder fifty thousand Krinar without a second thought, and I'm just Korum's charl—"

"You know, I've asked myself that same question." Saret's forehead creased in an introspective frown. "You're just a human girl—a pretty one, to be sure—but nothing all that special, to be honest. I didn't understand at first why Korum was so obsessed with you. But then a funny thing happened, Mia—" he leaned forward, his eyes gleaming darkly, "—I started wanting you myself."

He paused for a second, and then continued, ignoring the look of horrified disgust on her face. "Believe me, it's been hell, seeing you all the time and knowing that I don't have the right to touch you, that *he's* the one taking you to bed every night. But now things will be different. When you wake up, it will be as if he never existed . . . and you will be mine, the way you should've been from the very beginning."

Sickened to her very core, Mia tried to yank her hand away, hot nausea boiling up in her throat. He held her for a second, then let go, watching with a smile as she jumped back like a scalded cat.

"Never," she hissed, backing away toward the wall. "Do you hear me? I don't know what you're imagining here, but I'll never be with you willingly. You might be able to force me, but that's all it will ever be between us, memories or not—"

"Why?" Saret asked, still smiling. "Because you think you're in love with him? What does a twenty-year-old know about love? He seduced you, Mia, that's all. When he's gone from your life, I'll do the same—and you'll love me just as much as you thought you loved him."

Mia laughed, her desperation making her reckless. The thought of forgetting Korum and being forced to share the bed of a would-be mass murderer was so repugnant she thought she'd rather die. Maybe she could goad him into killing her. "Oh, really?" she said contemptuously. "I'm not even the least bit attracted to you, Saret. You're like dog food to me. I wanted Korum from the beginning—from the first moment I saw him. But not you. Never you. Do you understand me?"

As she spoke, she could see the smile fading from Saret's face, his expression hardening. "We'll see about that," he said, getting up and stalking toward her. "Once your memories are gone, you'll be singing a very different tune, believe me."

"No!" Mia screamed as he reached for her. Her nails curved into claws, raked down his arms as he grabbed her. "Get away from me, you sick fuck! No!!!"

Ignoring her yells and struggles, Saret lifted her and carried her out of his office, his arms like iron bands around her body. Walking to the far side of the lab, he placed her on one of the floating planks by the wall.

The intelligent surface immediately wrapped itself around her arms and legs, holding her completely immobile while Saret reached into the wall and took out a small white device.

"No!" Mia tried to twist her head as he approached her again. "No! Don't!"

Saret paused for a second, looking down at her. "I'm sorry, Mia," he said softly. "I wish it weren't necessary. If I had only met you first . . . But this won't hurt, I promise . . ." And pressing the device to her forehead, he gave her a gentle smile.

That smile was the last thing Mia saw before her world faded into darkness.

Part II

CHAPTER SIX

Korum checked the time again.

Mia should've been home already. Her message had reached him twenty minutes ago, and he'd immediately cut short the testing session with his designers, unable to resist the urge to see her as soon as possible.

While waiting for her, he'd quickly prepared dinner, making her favorite *shari* salad and a mushroom-potato dish from a recipe given to him by Mia's mother. He'd asked Ella Stalis for it before they left Florida, wanting to surprise Mia with it someday. He loved seeing her small face light up with pleasure and excitement when he did things like that. Her happiness meant the world to him these days.

Where was she?

Mildly annoyed, Korum queried his computer to determine her location. The complex device embedded in his palm was completely synced with his neural pathways—so much so that using it was the equivalent of thinking in a certain way. Not all Krinar liked the idea of being so integrated with technology, with many choosing to stick to old-fashioned voice commands and stand-alone devices instead. Korum thought it was idiotic to be so mistrustful, but then again, he had designed the computer himself and understood its limits and capabilities. Many of his kind had no idea how even simple human electronics worked, nor did they have a desire to learn—something he would never understand.

As soon as he sent the mental query, her location came to him with crystal clarity: the lab. She was still at the lab. The tracking devices he'd once embedded in her hands were proving to be quite useful, even now that she was no longer involved with the Resistance.

His lips quirking in a smile, Korum thought about her reaction whenever the topic of his shining her came up. She was like an angry kitten then, all tiny claws and ruffled fur. It made him want to cuddle her and fuck her at the same time—a confusing mix of desires she always evoked in him.

He supposed he should feel bad for shining her. And sometimes, he almost did. She resented the fact that he would now always know her location, not understanding that it gave him a tremendous peace of mind. She was so fragile, so human . . . If he had his way, she would never leave his side; he'd always keep her next to him where he could protect her.

But he knew she wouldn't want that. It was important to her to have her independence, to excel in her chosen field and contribute to society. He understood and respected that, but it still didn't make it any easier on him. When they'd been in New York—before he'd given her the nanocytes that made her less vulnerable—it had been all he could do to let her venture out on her own, especially in a human city where something as stupid as a car accident could easily claim her life. That's why he'd always had a guardian following her then, staying no more than a hundred yards away at any given time. She'd never suspected, of course, nor was Korum ever planning to tell her. But it had been for her own protection; even back then, he hadn't been able to bear the thought of anything happening to her.

Checking the time again, Korum saw that twenty-five minutes had passed. Why was she still at the lab? Had something happened to delay her? If Saret was making her work late again, he'd have a serious talk with him. By now, Mia had proven herself quite useful, and Korum was certain his friend wouldn't terminate her apprenticeship even if she had to work fewer hours.

Sending another mental query, Korum reached out to the communication device he'd made for her—what she called her wristwatch-bracelet. To his surprise and growing disquiet, he couldn't connect to it at all; it was as if there was only emptiness where digital signals should've been.

Something was wrong.

Korum knew it with sudden certainty. Raising his hand, he stared down at his palm, his eyes following the tiny pulses of light playing underneath his skin. It was a way for him to concentrate, to utilize specific mental pathways that were more complex than those required for basic daily tasks.

This particular path was not something he'd used in recent weeks, not since the Resistance was defeated. Mia didn't know about this either, and Korum wasn't planning to tell her. There was no need; he'd stopped using the device to monitor her activities. The only reason why it was still on her is because the process for removing it was fairly complicated—and because he liked the idea of having it there for emergencies.

Keeping his eyes glued to his palm, Korum sent a deep probe, activating the tiny recording device hidden underneath Mia's left earlobe. It would allow him to hear everything in her vicinity and, more importantly, to check on her vital signs.

As soon as the device came on, some of the tension left his muscles. She was okay, her heartbeat strong and her breathing steady.

And yet . . . Korum frowned, listening carefully. Everything was quiet—too quiet. If she was still working, she should've been moving around, talking to whomever had delayed her. Instead, it was as if she was asleep right now.

Asleep . . . or unconscious.

As soon as he thought of the second possibility, he knew he was on the right track. But why would she be unconscious? This didn't make any sense. And was that . . . ? He listened again. Were those someone else's movements he was hearing around her?

His unease morphed into full-blown worry.

Getting up, Korum strode swiftly to the wall and exited the house. Pausing for a few seconds, he sent a mental command to have a transport pod created with all possible speed. While the nanomachines did their job, he reached deep into the recording device's archives. All the recorders he designed worked like that; even when they weren't activated to broadcast in real time, they were still collecting data and storing it internally.

It took a second, and then he was accessing the recorder's memories, scanning through them to find the right spot. He started with the exact moment when Mia sent him her message. Instead of listening to the recording at normal speed, he had his computer create an instant transcript, which he then read in a few seconds.

And as Korum understood what he was reading, every cell in his body filled with volcanic fury.

He couldn't even begin to process the magnitude of the betrayal—nor the sheer evil that was about to be unleashed by a man he'd considered a friend for the past two thousand years. And Mia . . . No, he couldn't think about it. Not now, at least. If they were all to survive, he needed to focus, to control his rage and pain.

Utilizing every ounce of willpower he possessed, Korum reached for the coolly rational side of himself and began to analyze the best way to handle the situation.

* * *

Saret watched impatiently as Korum finally left the house and created the transport pod. Now his nemesis would come looking for Mia, hopefully with minimal—if any—suspicions.

Of course, it would never do to underestimate him. The bastard always had some nasty surprises for those who did. Still, Korum had no reason to think anything sinister was going on, and he would certainly never expect Saret to try to kill him.

It was unfortunate that Mia had come across those files today. Saret had always known that someone could snoop around and figure out that Saur hadn't been quite as knowledgeable about memory erasure as he'd been portrayed to be. Saret should've moved the files, but everyone in the lab knew better than to access other people's work without Saret's explicit permission.

Everyone, except one human girl, as it turned out.

Then again, maybe on some level, Saret had wanted her to find out. He'd enjoyed explaining his plan to her and watching the emotions on her expressive little face. She hadn't understood fully, of course, still too caught up in Korum's web to think clearly.

It had made him angry, what she'd said about not being attracted to him. She'd been lying, of course, trying to goad him into doing something stupid. He was a Krinar male in his prime; he knew full well that human women desired him. And she would want him too; he had made sure of that.

He would be gentle with her at first, not like Korum had been when they met. Saret had seen some of the recordings from the beginning of their relationship at the trial, and it had made him angry, the way his nemesis had handled her then. Saret would make a better cheren, he was certain of that.

Now where was Korum?

Frowning, Saret looked at the image again. It appeared his enemy was in no hurry. Instead of flying to the lab, Korum was standing next to the ship and leisurely chatting with some Krinar woman Saret had never seen before. He was almost . . . flirting with her? *Fucking bastard, already cheating on Mia.*

Well, no matter, Korum would get here soon enough. And when he did, he would be in for a nice little surprise.

Unbeknownst to all, Saret had spent the past several years building a high-tech fortress within the lab. All Krinar buildings were durable, meant to withstand anything from a nuclear blast to a volcanic eruption. His lab, however, went a step further: the walls were weaponized—designed to kill anyone who tried to enter once Saret activated the protection mode. They were also impenetrable by any form of nanotechnology because Saret had installed the same shields that served as the Centers' defenses.

It hadn't been easy, doing this. Weapons were not something that the general population had easy access to, especially specialized nano-weapons like those embedded in his walls. Saret had been forced to call in a lot of favors and spend a sizable chunk of his personal fortune to get everything set up exactly as he wanted it. It had cost him even more to keep everything a secret.

Now, however, it would all pay off. In another couple of days, the nano-weapon that he planned to use in the Centers would be ready. The dispersion devices with the nanocytes had already been planted in all the key human cities.

All he needed now was patience.

Another ten minutes, and Saret was losing what remained of that patience. What the hell was taking Korum so long? Had Saret underestimated his enemy's attachment to the girl? It looked like the bastard was still flirting with that woman. There he was now, laughing and touching her arm. *What the fuck?* Whatever happened to his obsession with Mia? Had she been just a toy for him all along?

As soon as the thought occurred to Saret, he dismissed it. No, something was up. He was suddenly certain of it.

Was his enemy playing him for a fool? Was he even now being fed a false image? There was no way to tell; the figures Saret was watching looked completely real. But, as Saret knew full well, looks could be deceiving.

He had to face the possibility that Korum had figured out something was going on.

Moving swiftly, Saret armed himself and put on a protective shield that wrapped around his entire body. The lab walls were still his best defense, and he had every intention of confronting his nemesis here, where Saret had the home advantage. He felt no fear, though his pulse spiked in anticipation of the upcoming fight.

Glancing at Mia, Saret made sure that she was still unconscious, lying restrained on the medical float. She might wake up soon, and he was hoping to have all the unpleasantness over with before that happened.

Ignoring the adrenaline rushing through his veins, Saret sat down next to her and stroked her arm, marveling at the smoothness of her pale skin. She looked so pretty, with her dark lashes fanning across her cheeks and that soft mouth slightly parted. What was that human children's story? Sleeping Beauty? Actually, she looked more like Snow White, Saret decided, with her milky complexion and dark hair.

Leaning down, he kissed her lips, brushing them lightly with his tongue. As he'd suspected, she was delicious; just that tiny taste was enough to make him hard. If he had more time, he would've taken her right then and there, unconscious or not.

But he didn't have more time. He needed to stay focused. One way or another, Korum would be here soon.

Getting up, Saret walked over to the image again. By now, he was almost certain it was fake.

Where was Korum?

Saret began to pace, too agitated to sit down again.

When it all began two minutes later, he didn't even notice at first.

A low humming sound was his first warning that something was wrong. The noise seemed to fill the air, gradually increasing in volume until it was almost a roar to his sensitive Krinar hearing.

Then the walls began to melt. Saret had never seen anything like it before: the material designed to withstand a nuclear blast seemed to liquefy from the top down, as if the building was made of wax.

Now Saret tasted fear. Sharp and acidic, it pooled low in his stomach. This wasn't supposed to happen. He was supposed to be safe here, in his carefully constructed fortress . . . but he wasn't. Saret didn't know of any weapon that could do this—that could penetrate the same shields that protected the colonies—but his eyes didn't lie. The walls were literally melting around him.

There was only one thing left to do: retreat and live to fight another day. For a second, Saret considered taking Mia with him, but she would slow him down and he couldn't take that risk. He would have to come back for her.

Casting one last look at the unconscious girl on the float, Saret activated the emergency escape chute and disappeared through the building floor.

CHAPTER SEVEN

"I want him found. By any means necessary. Do you understand me?" Korum was aware that his voice sounded sharp, but he could no longer contain the icy rage coursing through his veins.

Alir, the leader of the guardians, nodded. "We'll bring him to you," he promised, his black eyes cold and expressionless.

"Good," Korum said curtly.

Turning around, he stalked toward the back of the room, where Ellet was sitting beside Mia and running diagnostic tests.

At his approach, the Krinar woman looked up, signs of strain evident on her beautiful face. "She should regain consciousness soon," she said softly. "But, Korum, I'm afraid the damage has been done."

"What are you saying?" He didn't want to believe it, couldn't accept that possibility.

"I'm afraid the scan is showing signs of trauma consistent with a memory loss. I'm so sorry—"

"No. You must be wrong." His fists clenched so hard his nails entered his skin, drawing blood. "There must be something we can do—"

"I'll look into it," Ellet said, rising from her sitting position. "But this type of erasure tends to be irreversible, I'm afraid."

Korum took a step forward. "I don't want you to look into this, Ellet," he said evenly. "I fucking want you to drop whatever else you're doing and bring her memory back."

Ellet frowned. "You know I'll do my best—"

"Do better than that." Korum knew he wasn't being rational, but he didn't care. He had never felt this way before—so savagely murderous.

He wanted to tear Saret apart, to rip him up piece by piece and hear him scream in agony. He wanted to eviscerate the man he'd once regarded as a friend and bathe in his blood, like the ancients used to do with their enemies.

Underneath the swirling rage and bitterness at the betrayal, guilt—heavy and terrible—sat uncomfortably on Korum's shoulders. Mia had been hurt—hurt because of him. Because he'd failed to protect her from the monster in their midst. Because he'd been far too trusting. If it hadn't been for him, she would've never had that internship, would've never been exposed to Saret's sick cravings.

If he hadn't brought her to Lenkarda, she would've never been in harm's way.

How could Korum not have seen it earlier? How could he not have sensed that kind of hatred? His greatest enemy had turned out to be one of his closest friends—and he hadn't known until it was too late.

And now he could see pity on Ellet's face. She knew how he felt about Mia and could probably guess at his mental state right now. "I will, Korum," she said soothingly. "I promise you, I'll do everything possible to help."

Korum took a deep, calming breath. It wasn't Ellet's fault his friend had turned out to be the worst psychopath in modern Krinar history. "Thanks," he said quietly.

Ellet smiled, looking relieved. "You can take her home now, if you'd like. She'll wake up naturally in a few hours, and it might as well be at your house. The fewer of us she has to deal with at first, the better."

Korum nodded. "Of course." Bending down over Mia's float, he carefully picked her up, cradling her gently against his chest. She was so light, so fragile in his arms. The realization that she could've been killed today was like poison in his veins, burning him from the inside.

Saret would pay for what he did to her—for what he planned to do to them all. Korum would make sure of that.

* * *

Mia let out a small huffing sound and wrinkled her nose, one slim hand coming up to brush a dark curl off her cheek. Her eyes were still closed for now, although it was obvious she was starting to regain consciousness.

Sitting on the edge of the bed, Korum watched her slowly wake up, unable to tear his eyes away. Logically, he knew she wasn't the most beautiful woman he'd ever seen, but it didn't matter. To him, she was perfect. He loved everything about her; each and every part of her delicate little body turned him on. Even now, as she lay there in her pale pink dress, he had to fight the urge to touch her, to bring her closer to him and bury himself deep inside her.

The unsettling mixture of lust and tenderness she evoked in him was unlike anything he'd ever felt before. Like many Krinar, Korum had always regarded sex as a fun recreational activity. Most of his prior relationships had been casual affairs, similar to the fling he'd had with Ellet a few years ago. He liked women and he enjoyed their company outside of the bedroom as well, but he had never wanted to be with one on a permanent basis—had never felt the urge to claim one as his own.

Until Mia.

For some reason, this human girl appealed to his darkest, most primitive instincts. The way he felt about her went beyond sexual desire, beyond a craving for her tender flesh. What he really wanted was to possess her completely, to have her be his in every possible way.

It was not an unknown phenomenon among the Krinar. In ancient times, Krinar males needed to hunt and to protect their territory—and they were far more likely to do an effective job if they were strongly attached to their mates. It had been a simple evolutionary adaptation at the time—a male's obsessive fixation on one specific female. Deeper than lust, stronger than love, it was a powerful combination of the two that ensured a man would give up his life to protect his woman and their offspring.

Over the years, as Krinar society became more civilized, that kind of attachment became less important to the species' survival, and the genetic tendency toward it weakened over time. It still happened, of course, but it was a fairly rare occurrence in modern times—which was why Korum hadn't realized what was going on when he first met Mia.

He hadn't understood at first why he was feeling that way. All he'd known was that he wanted her—and that he had to have her. Even her initial reluctance hadn't been enough to deter him; if anything, her wariness had intrigued him, triggering the predatory instincts he normally managed to suppress.

He had never pursued someone like that before, had never been less than considerate of a woman's wishes, but with Mia, he had been ruthless. He'd gone after her with all the intensity in his nature, disregarding all notions of right and wrong. In less than a week, he'd gotten what he wanted: Mia in his bed, in his apartment—his to take whenever he wanted.

It had taken him far longer to earn her love.

To this day, he couldn't help the anger that stirred in his stomach when he thought about her involvement with the Resistance. Rationally, he knew he couldn't blame her for fighting back, for not trusting him in the beginning. She was a mere child in comparison to him; he should've been more cognizant of her fears, should've patiently seduced her instead of forcing her into the relationship. Perhaps then she wouldn't have believed the fighters' lies, wouldn't have betrayed him the way she did.

But he hadn't been patient. The strength of his emotions had caught him off-guard, blinding him to everything but the need to have her. What had begun as a sexual obsession had quickly become something much deeper, and Korum hadn't known how to cope with that. He'd acted out of hurt and anger, using her against the Resistance as punishment for spying on him, when he should've simply explained everything to her, made her understand his intentions.

The fact that she loved him now was a miracle—one that he was grateful for every day. And if she didn't remember him when she woke up, then he would use that as an opportunity for a new beginning, as a way to make amends for what happened before.

One way or another, Mia would love him again.

The alternative was unthinkable.

Finally, her eyelids fluttered open. She blinked, looking confused, then stared at him in open-mouthed shock.

Gently stroking her arm, Korum smiled. "Hello, my darling," he said, purposefully injecting a soothing note into his voice. What he really wanted was to hug her to him, but that would frighten her if she had indeed lost her memory and he was now a stranger to her.

As it was, he could hear her heartbeat speeding up, feel the sudden tension in her muscles as she realized what he was. Her small pink tongue came out, licking her bottom lip in that unconsciously provocative gesture that always drove him insane. He could see the fear in her eyes . . . and it was like a knife to his heart, the pain sharp and slicing.

Yanking her arm away, she scrambled back, toward the other side of the bed. "What am I doing here? Who are you?"

Korum could hear the panic in her voice, and he forced himself to remain still, to not make any movements in her direction.

"I'm Korum," he said instead, looking for any sign of recognition on her face. But there was none. Pushing away his disappointment, he asked, "What's the last thing you remember, my sweet?"

She visibly swallowed, scooting back even further. "I'm in class," she whispered. "I'm taking a test . . ."

"What test, my darling? What class are you in?" *Just how much memory had Saret erased?*

"My . . . my Child Psychology class," she answered, her voice shaking slightly.

Korum exhaled in relief. "So it's your Spring Semester." She'd only lost a couple of months, not years as he'd initially feared.

She nodded, still looking terrified. "What do you want from me? Why did you bring me here?" He could hear the rising hysteria in her voice.

Korum sighed. This was going to be difficult. "It's complicated, Mia," he said softly. "Would you like me to explain?"

She nodded again, her blue eyes wide and fearful.

"Then come here, and we'll talk," he said, watching as she tensed further. "I promise you, I won't hurt you in any way . . . Just sit here, beside me." He patted the bed, needing to have her closer.

She hesitated, and he saw the emotions flitting across her fine-featured face. He could tell the exact moment when she decided she had nothing to lose by accommodating his request. After all, he was a Krinar and thus equally dangerous up close or ten feet away.

Her slim body shaking, she slowly moved back in his direction, watching him warily. When she was close enough, Korum reached out and took her hand, warming her chilled skin between his palms.

She jerked initially, then stilled, her gaze trained on his face.

Korum smiled, some of the tension inside him easing because she allowed his touch. "We're lovers, Mia," he said gently, watching her reaction. "You don't remember me because you lost some of your memory. It's June now, and we're in Lenkarda, our Center in Costa Rica."

CHAPTER EIGHT

Mia stared at the gorgeous Krinar male who was now softly rubbing her hand. What he'd just told her was pure insanity. They were lovers? She'd lost her memory? Out of all the crazy scenarios running through Mia's mind, this hadn't even been on the list of possibilities.

Was he toying with her? If so, why, and what was the real story? Mia tried to control her panic long enough to think, but it was like a part of her brain was filled with fog. Even recent events—spring break, the exams—seemed blurry in her mind, as if they'd happened long ago instead of in the last couple of weeks.

"You don't believe me, do you?" the K asked, his amber-colored eyes watching her with unsettling warmth.

"No, of course not." Her voice was surprisingly calm. All things considered, Mia felt like she was handling this reasonably well. She wasn't crying or screaming, and she was actually carrying on a conversation with an alien who had most likely kidnapped her. An alien who might or might not drink human blood—and who was now stroking her wrist in a way that made her belly tighten with strange excitement.

Why wasn't she more afraid of him? Everything she knew about his kind suggested she should be terrified for her life.

But she wasn't.

She was freaking out because she didn't know where she was or how she'd gotten there—or why she was with a K who claimed to be her lover—but she wasn't truly afraid. If anything, she found his presence oddly comforting, his touch both soothing and electrifying. Had he done something to make her react this way?

"Of course not," he repeated, giving her an understanding smile. "How could you believe something so crazy without proof, right?"

Mia nodded, unable to tear her eyes away from that smile. The dimple in his left cheek fascinated her; it was so boyish, so incongruous with the rest of his appearance.

"All right, my darling." His voice was disconcertingly tender. "Let me show you proof." And still holding her hand, he gestured to the side, where a three-dimensional holographic image suddenly appeared in mid-air.

Mia gasped, startled, and then she saw that the image was of herself and the K beside her. They appeared to be walking on the beach, talking and laughing. The K reached down and picked up the girl in the image, lifting her as effortlessly as if she was made of air. She laughed again, then wound her arms around his neck, kissing him with such passion that Mia's cheeks heated up.

"What is that? Where did you get this video from?" Mia felt herself furiously blushing as the K kissed the girl back, holding her up with one arm and using the other to reach underneath her dress.

"It's just a recording from one of our satellites," the K named Korum explained, watching her with an unusual golden gleam in his eyes. For some reason, Mia could feel herself getting turned on by that look, her heart starting to beat faster and her nipples hardening underneath the thin fabric of her dress. She desperately hoped the K didn't notice; it would be embarrassing—and potentially dangerous—if he knew how much he affected her.

And then she realized what he just said. "Wait, your satellites were spying on us?"

"Our satellites are always recording everything," he explained, those sensuous lips curving into a smile. "But don't worry, my sweet, only our computers get to see it, unless someone places a specific request—the way I did."

Mia's pulse quickened, this time from anxiety. "Are you saying we never have any privacy from you?"

"Of course not," the K said casually. "You don't have much of it from your own government either. You know that, right?"

Mia blinked. She did know that. GPS and cell phones had made it practically impossible for a person to hide, and she knew that various government agencies used all the means at their disposal to track down terrorists and other criminals. As a law-abiding citizen, she'd never thought much about the fact that all her activities—from browsing the

Internet to placing a phone call—could be monitored if necessary. She'd just accepted it as a part of life in the twenty-first century. But, for some reason, the idea of Krinar satellites watching her every move was more than a little disturbing.

Frowning, Mia realized she was acting as if the image being shown to her was real. There was absolutely no assurance of that; as advanced as the Krinar were, surely it would be child's play for them to conjure up whatever video they wanted, three-dimensional or not.

"How do I know you didn't make this up?" she said, gesturing toward the image where the couple were now engaged in a full-blown make-out session. Her blush deepening, Mia looked away again.

"You don't, of course," the Krinar said. "I could make this up if I wanted to. I have hundreds of other recordings I could show you, and you'd be smart not to trust any of them."

Mia laughed nervously, surprised by his frankness. "Okay then, how can you prove any of this to me?" She couldn't believe she was even entertaining the idea that this could be real. How could any rational person believe this? Surely she would remember if she'd had sex with a gorgeous alien . . . or even just had sex in general.

The K smiled again. "There are a number of ways," he said. "Let's start with the fact that you understand me right now, even though I'm speaking to you in Krinar."

Mia gaped at him in shock. She had definitely understood what he was saying, even though he'd said the last sentence in a language she was sure she'd never heard before. "Wait, what?" Her words came out in that same language. "You're talking to me in Krinar?"

"Yes, and you're answering me in Krinar too," he said, his smile widening. "And now I'm talking to you in Italian. You still understand me, right?"

Mia nodded, her head spinning from the impossibility of it all.

"That's because you have a tiny implant that acts as a translator," the K explained, this time in English. "I gave it to you as soon as we came here, to Lenkarda. It allows you to speak and understand any known language, both human and Krinar."

"But—" Mia didn't even know where to begin. "How do I know you didn't just give it to me now? And wait, did I hear you say before that it's June? The last thing I remember is in March. How would I have lost a chunk of my memory? This makes no sense—"

The K sighed and raised his hand, gently tucking a stray curl behind her ear. "I know, Mia," he said softly. "I know this is going to be difficult for you to accept. Let me tell you a little story, and then I'll demonstrate to you that I'm not lying. Okay?"

"Okay," Mia agreed, mesmerized by the warm look on his beautiful face. How could someone that gorgeous be her lover? Maybe this was all just an unusually realistic dream. Could she even now be sound asleep, with her unconscious creating this stunning creature? If he was indeed her lover, then she was the luckiest girl in the world—though she still didn't see how such a thing was possible.

"Good," he said, his golden eyes gleaming. "Then let me tell you about us starting from the beginning . . ."

And for the next twenty minutes, Mia listened in shock as he went through their initial meeting in April and detailed the tumultuous affair that followed as a result. When he began to explain about her involvement with the Resistance, Mia's jaw simply dropped.

"I was spying on you?" Where on Earth had she gotten the courage to do that? Although he was being gentle with her now, Mia had a feeling this particular K could be quite dangerous if provoked. In general, his kind weren't known for their forgiving nature, their violent streak amply demonstrated during the fights of the Great Panic.

"You were," the K confirmed, his jaw tightening a little. "But I was at fault too, because I knew you were doing it and fed you false information."

Mia gave him an incredulous look. "And you're saying we're lovers? After all that?"

"We're more than lovers, Mia. You're my charl."

"Charl?"

He nodded. "It's our word for what you are to me. The best approximation would be something like human mate."

"Like a wife?" Mia could hear her own voice rising in disbelief.

He smiled. "Not exactly, but you could think of it that way, yes."

Mia stared at him. "But you said I met you in April and it's only June now. When did we have a chance to get married?"

He hesitated for a second. "It doesn't work like that, my darling. There is no formal ceremony in a charl-cheren relationship."

"So then how *does* it work? How is this different from just being boyfriend and girlfriend?" Not that she could even picture this beautiful creature as her boyfriend. But a husband? Her mind boggled at the thought.

"It's different, Mia, because I couldn't give a mere girlfriend what I gave you," he said quietly. "Because by claiming you as my charl, I have brought you fully into our world, with all that it entails."

Mia's heart started beating faster again. "And what does it entail?"

"A much longer lifespan," he said softly. "Freedom from aging and disease. Immortality, as you like to call it."

* * *

Korum could see her eyes widening, skepticism warring with excitement on her face. The curl that he'd just tucked away behind her ear came loose again, refusing to be contained. He loved that rebellious curl; it always lured his fingers to her hair, making him want to touch its soft, thick mass.

In general, he was both surprised and pleased by her reaction thus far. She was naturally cautious, so some wariness was to be expected, but she was far less frightened than he would've expected her to be. She didn't cringe away from his touch, nor did she seem to object to his nearness. Somehow, despite her lack of conscious memories, she must still recognize him on some level, must still trust him not to hurt her.

"You have the ability to make humans immortal?" she asked, a small frown creasing her smooth forehead.

Korum sighed, not wanting to go down that path again. "We do," he said patiently. "But not all humans—only those that become a part of our society. I'm currently trying to get an exception for your parents and sister, though—"

"You know them?" she interrupted. "You've met my family?"

"I do, and I have," Korum confirmed, glad that it was the case. It would've been much worse if she'd lost her memory before their Florida trip. "And that's how you're going to know I'm telling you the truth, my sweet. You're going to speak to Marisa and your parents."

Mia looked startled at the idea, and then her face lit up. By now Korum knew her well enough to understand that he'd just managed to dispel whatever fears she harbored over being separated from her loved ones.

Her strong attachment to her family was one of Mia's main vulnerabilities, and Korum had not hesitated to exploit it in the past—to use it to bind her even closer to him. It had been surprisingly easy to win over both her parents and her sister. He had carefully researched everything about them before their meeting, and they had reacted exactly as he'd hoped, their initial distrust fading as they saw that Mia was happy and loved.

And that made Mia even happier and more attached to *him*.

Rightly or wrongly, Korum knew that he would do anything to keep her that way. She might not remember it now, but she had loved him once—and she would again. For now, though, he needed to prove to her that he was neither crazy nor playing a trick on her.

"Here, use this," he said, giving her a new wrist computer he'd made a couple of hours ago. This time, he'd added visual capabilities to it, to make it even easier for her to stay in touch with her family. Showing Mia how to operate the device took another minute, and then she was connecting to her parents' Skype account, her mother's voice and image appearing in the room.

Smiling, Korum walked across the room and sat down in the corner, giving the two women some privacy. He could still hear everything they were discussing, however, and he listened with a great deal of curiosity.

As usual, his little charl seemed very concerned with not causing her parents any worry. Instead of letting on that she lost her memory, Mia kept the conversation light and generic, inquiring about her parents' health and asking how Marisa was doing. Grinning, Korum listened as Ella Stalis blithely chatted about the latest developments in Marisa's pregnancy (three pounds gained!) and how much they'd enjoyed having Mia and Korum in the area.

Though her sister's pregnancy had to have come as a shock to Mia, she gamely oohed-and-aahed at the right moments, acting as if everything was normal. She even managed to laugh and promise to come for a visit again soon, as though she remembered the last trip perfectly. Korum couldn't help admiring her for this; he knew how lost and anxious she must be feeling right now, and he was more than a little impressed with her composure.

Finally, Mia finished her conversation and looked at him. "Do you want this back?" she asked uncertainly, indicating the wrist device he'd given her.

"No, that's yours to keep." Korum got up and walked toward her. "Did this help? Do you believe me now?"

"I don't know," she whispered, and he saw the pain and confusion on her face. "If this is all true, then what happened? How did I manage to lose such an important part of my life? Did I hit my head or something?"

"Or something." Korum tried to push away enraging thoughts about Saret's betrayal. The last thing he wanted was to frighten her right now. Raising his hand, he gave in to the urge to stroke her cheek instead, reveling in the familiar feel of her soft skin underneath his fingers.

She blinked at him, her thick lashes sweeping up and down like dark fans. To his immense satisfaction, she didn't flinch away from his touch. If anything, she seemed to lean toward him, as though she was also craving physical closeness.

Unable to resist any longer, Korum bent his head and kissed her, holding her face gently with his hands. Just a kiss, he promised himself, just one small kiss . . .

At first she was stiff, her mouth closed against the intrusion of his tongue. He could feel her heart beating frantically in her chest, sense her momentary panic, and then her lips softened, parted a bit. Her hands came up, pressing lightly against his chest, as if uncertain whether to push him away or hold him close.

Her response, when it came, was much more tentative than usual, but it was enough to drive him insane. The taste of her, the smell of her, was intoxicating, like a drug surging through his veins. He deepened the kiss without realizing it, one hand slipping down her back to press her closer to him, his cock so hard he felt like he was about to explode.

It was only her quiet whimper that brought him back to his senses. Lifting his head, Korum looked at Mia, his breathing hard and uneven.

Her pale cheeks were flushed, her lips swollen. He could smell her desire, feel the heat rising from her skin, and he knew that if he reached between her legs now, he would find her wet and slick, her body ready for him. But her mind was a different matter, Korum realized, and the look in her eyes now was that of fear and confusion.

His own body raging with unfulfilled need, Korum fought for control, knowing that he needed it now more than ever. "I'm sorry," he said, forcing himself to let her go. "I wasn't going to do this so soon . . ."

She took a couple of steps back and stared at him, her small chest moving up and down, drawing his attention to the hardness of her nipples underneath her dress. Korum swallowed, remembering their pale pink hue, the way they tasted in his mouth, how they pebbled under his tongue.

No, don't fucking go there now. Lifting his eyes back to her face, Korum said, "I know you're not ready for this yet, my sweet. I won't hurt you, I promise . . ." And he meant it. He would sooner lose a limb than do anything to traumatize her while she was so vulnerable.

She bit her lip, then nodded, crossing her arms around her chest in a defensive gesture that sent a pang of regret through Korum. He hated it sometimes, the all-consuming lust he always experienced in her vicinity. She was so tiny, so delicate, her body unsuited for the hard demands he often placed on it. No matter how careful he tried to be, he knew he wasn't always the most gentle lover, his overwhelming need for her constantly testing his self-control.

"So what happened?" she asked again, still watching him warily. "Why don't I remember you, or my sister getting pregnant, or any of this? How did I lose two months of my life?"

Korum took a deep breath, trying to control the anger still boiling in his veins at the thought of Saret. "Someone I knew and trusted—a man who pretended to be my friend for a long time—did this," he said evenly. "This person wiped out a portion of your memory as a way to get at me . . . and because he also wanted you."

"Really?" Her eyes widened. "Another K?"

"Yes, another Krinar," Korum confirmed before explaining the whole story, starting from Mia's internship and ending with Saret's betrayal. Not wanting to overwhelm her, he downplayed the part about Saret's ultimate intentions for her people, as well as some of the complexities of Council politics. She didn't need to know everything all at once; as it was, he could see that it was already almost too much for her. He wanted to wrap his arms around her and hold her, soothe her distress, but he knew she wouldn't welcome it now—not after the way he'd almost attacked her earlier.

The best thing to do right now was to give her time, he decided. Time and space to think about everything she'd learned.

"I have to go now," Korum said, his heart squeezing painfully at the look of relief on her face. "There are a few things I have to take care of. Why don't you relax, take it easy for now? I'll be back in a couple of hours and we can have lunch. If you get hungry in the meantime, just say what you want out loud and it will be given to you. Unless you're hungry now?"

She shook her head, her dark curls moving around her shoulders. "No, I'm fine, thanks."

"Good. Feel free to explore the house if you wish. I know everything's going to look strange to you now, but it's all fairly intuitive, so it shouldn't be too bad." He smiled, remembering how much Mia enjoyed that aspect of life in Lenkarda. "All the furniture is intelligent, so don't be startled if it conforms to your shape. The house is intelligent too, so feel free to ask it for food or anything you need."

"Okay," she said, giving him a small smile in response. "Thanks."

Pausing for a moment longer, Korum drank in that smile. Then he walked out, leaving her alone to process everything she'd just learned.

CHAPTER NINE

Exiting the house, Korum quickly created a transport pod and headed toward a small round building in the heart of the Center—the gathering place for routine Council meetings.

Walking in, he greeted the other Councilors, nodding coolly toward Loris and a couple of his other opponents. While all of them could participate in the meeting virtually, everyone living on Earth had chosen to attend in person today, given the important topic at hand.

Taking a seat on one of the floats, Korum carefully watched the Councilors' faces, seeking to gauge their collective mood. What he'd done to Saret's lab building was bound to have frightened them, shaking their belief in the impenetrability of the Centers' defenses. Some of the Council members failed to comprehend the necessity for technological progress, clinging to what was known and familiar instead of advancing with the times.

"Welcome, Korum," Arus said, turning toward him. "I'm glad you're able to join us today. Is your Mia all right?"

"She is, thanks," Korum said, appreciating the concern. If anyone understood his feelings for Mia, it was probably Arus, whose devotion to his own charl was widely known. Although they didn't always see eye-to-eye on every issue, Korum respected the ambassador and even liked him to some extent.

Arus inclined his head in response. "Good. I'm glad to hear it. Delia was worried when she heard about what happened."

"Please tell Delia she's more than welcome to stop by," Korum said quietly, aware that the whole Council was watching their exchange. "I'm sure Mia could use a friend right now."

Out of the corner of his eye, Korum could see a smirk on Loris's face. His long-time enemy was clearly enjoying the situation, both the fact that Korum had fallen for a human girl and the entire debacle with Saret. Toxic rage crawled through Korum's veins again, but he didn't let anything show on his face, keeping his expression mildly amused. Let Loris enjoy his discomfort for now; the so-called Protector wasn't going to be on the Council much longer, given his son's now-almost-proven guilt.

"All right then. We have a lot to discuss today." It was Voret, one of the oldest members of the Council. "The guardians reported to us that all of Saret's dispersion devices have been located and neutralized, thanks to Korum warning us about them in time. Apparently, they had been scheduled to go off simultaneously in approximately thirty-two hours from now. We also found the designer who had the nano-weapon. He was in Thailand and has now been arrested. The weapon was already fully functional, and Alir thinks that Saret planned to use it shortly after he succeeded in unleashing the mind-control devices among the human population. Arus, you spoke with the United Nations?"

"Yes. I glossed over the situation when I explained it to them," the ambassador answered. "They already have their hands full dealing with the military leaders who had aided the Resistance, and there is no need to scare them at this point. They just need to be aware that Saret is on the loose, so that their intelligence agencies can keep an eye out for him. I didn't go into any detail beyond informing them that he's a dangerous individual who needs to be apprehended promptly."

"Good," Voret said. "You did the right thing. They already don't trust us, and if they knew about the mind-control devices, they would probably panic again."

"And with good reason this time," Korum said, thinking about Saret's insane plan. "If he managed to get Saur to attack me, imagine what he could've done with human minds."

"Indeed," Voret said, and Korum could see him preparing to approach the topic that was likely of most interest to the Council today. "Now as far as the other events that took place yesterday . . ."

"Yes?" Korum prompted when the other Councilor trailed off. He knew exactly where Voret was headed, but he wanted to hear what he had to say.

Voret gave him an uncomfortable look. "Now, Korum, we all watched the recordings of the events, and some of the things we saw were . . .

disturbing, to say the least."

Korum smiled, not the least bit surprised. "Which part disturbed you the most, Voret?" he asked. "Was it the fact that Saret planned to annihilate us all in his quest to mind-fuck the humans? Or that none of us had a clue?"

Voret frowned. "You know I'm referring to the way you were able to breach the lab's shields. We'll address the Saret situation in greater detail once we have more information from the guardians, but first we need to know if we're safe here, inside our Centers. Did you develop a weapon that can penetrate our force-shields?"

"I did," Korum said, enjoying the expressions of shock and fear on some of the Councilors' faces. "But don't worry—I've also developed better shields. Both are still in experimental mode, which is why no one has heard about this before."

"And you used this weapon yesterday?" Arus asked, raising his eyebrows.

"Yes. I had no choice once I learned how Saret had set up the lab."

"How did you learn that?" It was Voret again.

"By scanning the lab building. Once I knew what Saret intended, it wasn't difficult to figure out that he would have some pretty strong defenses in place. Which he did. I distracted him by feeding him an image of myself from three years ago and used the time to build the weapon based on my experimental designs."

Voret's frown deepened. "And when were you going to tell us about these new designs of yours?"

"When they were ready to be used," Korum said evenly. Voret and the others forgot sometimes that Korum was under no obligation to share anything with the Council. He chose to do so for the good of all Krinar, but he had no intention of seeking the Council's permission and approval on every project.

"Could anyone else gain access to this weapon?" Arus asked, focusing on the more important part of the issue. "Korum, are you certain no one else has these designs?"

"I'm the only one," Korum said, understanding the ambassador's concern. "None of my designers have been involved in this project yet, and no one has access to these files."

"Not even your charl?" It was Loris this time, his voice practically dripping with sarcasm. "Are you sure she can't steal the data and run to her friends in the Resistance?"

Korum gave him a sardonic look. "No, Loris. She can't. Besides, what would the Resistance do with this information without your son? We all know now how useful he was to them . . . and to Saret."

Loris got up slowly, his face darkening with anger. "Those were lies! Nobody would believe them for a minute—"

"Oh really?" Korum said coldly, looking at the black-haired Krinar with contempt. "We all saw the recording—and heard Saret explain Rafor's role in his plans. Your son is as guilty as Saret himself, and he'll be punished accordingly."

Loris's hands clenched into fists, his knuckles turning white. "Saret was *your* friend," he hissed, apparently no longer able to contain himself. "For all we know, you're the one behind it all and are now just waiting for the right moment to use your new weapon on us—"

"Loris, that's enough!" Arus's voice cracked through the air like a whip. At the resulting silence, the ambassador continued in a calmer tone, "We understand your need to protect your son, but, unfortunately, the evidence against him continues to build. Given this new information, we'll need to have another trial session tomorrow. It may be the final session—"

Loris's entire body shook with rage now. "Fuck you, Arus. And fuck all of you. Rafor is not a traitor. That—" he pointed in Korum's direction, "—is the only traitor here, and you are all too fucking blind to see!"

"The only blind person here is you, Loris," Korum said calmly, watching his enemy unraveling right in front of his eyes. "And tomorrow, when the Council judges the Keiths to be guilty, the entire world will know about your failure."

That appeared to be the last straw. With an enraged roar, Loris launched himself at Korum, leaping across the room with full Krinar speed.

Acting on instinct, Korum turned and twisted his body, reflexively shielding his head and throat. As Loris slammed into him, he met the brunt of the attack with his shoulder, jabbing his elbow into Loris's side as they fell to the floor and rolled toward the middle of the chamber.

With the hard floor scraping his skin, Korum felt his own rage spiking, every cell in his body filling with bloodlust. His fingers curled into claws and raked across Loris's arm, taking out a chunk of muscle and sinew. At the same time, his arm hooked around Loris's neck in one of the more complex *defrebs* moves, baring his throat to Korum's teeth—

"Enough! That's enough!" Strong hands were pulling them apart, dragging them to separate sides of the room. Still rational enough to comprehend what was happening, Korum didn't struggle as Arus and another Krinar held his arms, preventing him from continuing the fight. Loris, however, was completely out of control, twisting and yelling as two other Councilors held him pinned against the wall. Finally, he seemed to run out of steam, panting and glaring at Korum in hatred. His arm was a bloody mess that was just beginning to heal.

"You can unhand me now," Korum said, his own breathing slowly calming as he glanced at the two men still holding him in an iron grip.

"Sorry, Korum," Arus said, his lips curving into a faint smile as he released Korum's arm and took a step back. "Couldn't let you kill him here."

Voret followed Arus's example, letting go of Korum's other arm.

"That's fine," Korum said, wiping his bloody hand on his shirt. "We'll continue this in the Arena. That's what that was, wasn't it, Loris? A challenge?"

The black-haired Protector stared at him, his chest heaving with fury. "Yes," he ground out between tightly clenched teeth. "You could call it a challenge."

"Good," Korum said, giving him a wide, predatory smile. "A challenge it is, then." He hadn't had a good Arena fight in a while, and he could feel his blood heating up with anticipation.

"Loris, that's not a good idea," Arus said, taking a few steps in the Krinar's direction. Korum was unsurprised by his concern; Loris and the ambassador were usually on good terms, frequently teaming up against Korum and Saret. Korum imagined it must be difficult for Arus now, taking the side of his former opponent against a man he'd considered his ally.

Loris laughed bitterly. "Oh really, Arus? Not a good idea?"

Arus gave him an even look. "He excels at *defrebs*. When was the last time you fought?"

Loris's upper lip curled with derision. "Yeah, fuck you too, Arus. You think I've gone soft? I've had more kills in the Arena than this fucker has had fights."

"Then the challenge has been issued." Voret stepped forward, his voice taking on a formal cadence. "Since the trial is tomorrow, the Arena fight will take place the day after at noon."

And with that, the Council meeting was adjourned.

* * *

Mia sat on the bed, staring blankly at the green forest outside the transparent wall. She was immortal, and she had a K lover—who was something like her husband, but not really.

It was so incredible she could hardly fathom it, her mind twisting and turning in a million different directions.

After the K left, she'd called both Marisa and Jessie, needing additional confirmation of the impossible claims he was making. Both her sister and her friend had been quite happy to hear from her—and both had mentioned Korum in the course of Mia's conversation with them. Marisa had gone on and on about her pregnancy and how much better she was feeling thanks to Korum's involvement of someone called Ellet, and Jessie had asked whether Mia had decided when she and Korum were coming by for a visit.

Still in a state of shock, Mia had managed to give Jessie a vague answer—something along the lines of still needing to talk to Korum—and listened politely as her sister gushed about her newest ultrasound results. To her relief, neither one of them seemed to suspect that anything was wrong, that the Mia they'd spoken to today was far from normal.

She didn't know why she was so hesitant to reveal the truth about her condition to anyone, but she was. She didn't want to make her family and friends worry, yes, but she was also almost . . . embarrassed.

How could this have happened to her? How could her entire family know her alien lover, while he seemed like a stranger to her? How could she have forgotten *making love* to someone so extraordinary? When he'd kissed her, her body had responded in a way Mia had never experienced before—or at least didn't remember experiencing before. It had been almost frightening, the degree to which she'd lost control in his arms. If he had continued kissing her instead of stopping when he did, she could've easily fallen into bed with him—she, who didn't remember going beyond a few kisses with guys before.

The strangeness of her reaction to everything kept throwing her off-balance. He was an extraterrestrial—someone from a different species—yet she was barely freaking out at being told that he was her lover. She even believed him now, after just a few conversations with her family and Jessie. Theoretically, he could still be lying to her; her family could've been threatened or brainwashed to say what they did. Hell, he could've even had them replaced by some kind of robots that looked and sounded like them. It wasn't as if Mia knew what the Ks were truly capable of.

And yet . . . she believed him. Something inside her seemed to recognize him on some level, even if she couldn't consciously remember him. She had been glad when he left her alone, giving her time to digest everything, but now she found herself missing him, craving the comfort of his presence. It made no logical sense, but it was true: a stranger felt more necessary to her than people she'd known her whole life.

Everything he'd told her thus far was one big jumble in her mind. The Resistance, human sympathizers among the Ks, her spying on him—it all sounded more like a movie than anything that could've actually happened to her. Why would she have done something so crazy? How could she have wanted something other than to be with this gorgeous man—alien or not?

Blowing out a frustrated breath, Mia looked down at her hands, trying to make sense of this insane situation. Why would she have helped the Resistance? She'd never thought there was any point to fighting against the Ks, not after they'd taken control of her planet and basically left humans alone.

Yet she had supposedly fought against the Ks—or at least had tried to help those who did. According to Korum, it hadn't been a very successful effort.

Then again, maybe she was wrong to trust him now. Sure, he'd been kind to her thus far, and her family seemed to like him, but she had no idea what he was really like. What if she was trusting someone who shouldn't be trusted? It's not like she knew what the Ks ultimately wanted from humans. There *were* those rumors about them drinking blood. For all she knew, Korum could've been the one to wipe her memory, making her forget something terrible about him.

Her head was beginning to hurt from all the speculation, so Mia got up and started pacing around the room. Her surroundings were strange and foreign, yet she didn't feel uncomfortable here. She had already explored the rest of the house, marveling at the intelligent floating objects that served as tables, chairs, and couches. They were definitely a major improvement over human furnishings. She also liked the overall house aesthetic, with the transparent walls and ceiling and a clean, Zen-like feel to the entire space.

Could an evil villain live in such a beautiful, peaceful place?

As soon as the thought crossed her mind, Mia laughed out loud, unable to help herself. She was being ridiculous, and she knew it. There was absolutely no reason to build some crazy conspiracy in her mind. So far, Korum had been nothing but nice to her.

In fact, she was very much looking forward to spending more time with him and re-learning everything she had forgotten.

Finally, after what seemed like forever, Mia heard something in the living room. Coming out of the bedroom, she saw that the K—or Korum, as she thought of him now—had just walked in through what appeared to be an opening in one of the walls. As Mia watched, the opening narrowed and solidified, leaving a transparent wall where an entrance used to be.

At the sight of her, his face lit up with what looked like genuine pleasure. "Hello, my sweet." He gave her a wide smile that exposed the dimple in his left cheek. Mia wanted to kiss that dimple. In general, she wanted to kiss and lick him all over, just to see if his smooth golden skin was as delicious as it looked.

Wow, I'm in lust. Mentally shaking her head at the strangeness of it all, she gave him an answering smile. "Hi."

"Sorry it took me so long," he said, walking across the room toward the kitchen area. "The Council meeting was more eventful than I expected. You must be starving by now—"

"I'm all right—" Mia followed him into the kitchen, "—but I could definitely eat. Are you going to order something?" She was beyond curious about how the Krinar fed themselves. It was also encouraging that he was planning to eat, as opposed to doing something scary—like drinking human blood. She really needed to ask him about that at some point; hopefully, the whole thing was nothing more than a weird rumor.

"I was going to cook something," he said, "but ordering will probably be faster. Here, have a seat for now while the house preps our meal."

Mia gingerly perched on one of the floating planks, making herself comfortable. "You cook?" she asked, studying him in fascination as he sat down across from her.

He smiled. "I do. It's a hobby of mine."

She smiled back, both intrigued and relieved. Her earlier suspicions seemed even sillier now. So far her K lover was about as close to a dream man as one could get, and she couldn't wait to learn more about him. There were so many questions running through her mind she didn't even know where to start.

"Did you get a chance to talk to the rest of your family?" he asked, watching her with a knowing half-smile.

"I spoke to Marisa and Jessie," Mia admitted.

"And? Do you believe me now?"

She shrugged. "I suppose you could've faked those interactions somehow, but I don't know why you would go to those lengths. The most logical conclusion is that you are indeed telling me the truth—even though that still seems crazy to me."

He grinned. "I know, my sweet. Believe me, I realize that."

"So what do we do now?" she asked, unable to look away from that dazzling smile. "Where do we go from here?"

"We get to know each other again," he said, his expression becoming more serious. "And in the meantime, I'll be looking into a way to potentially reverse your memory loss."

Mia's heart jumped with excitement. "Is there a way?"

"Not that I currently know of," he admitted. "But that doesn't mean it doesn't exist—or that we won't come up with it over time."

"Oh, I see." Mia fought to suppress her disappointment. "In that case, can you please tell me a little bit about yourself? I would really like to know more . . ."

"Of course, my darling, I would be happy to," he said softly.

And throughout their delicious meal, Mia learned all about her lover's role on the Krinar Council, his passion for technological design, and the fact that he was much older than she could've ever imagined. As they talked, Mia could feel herself falling deeper and deeper under his spell, wanting to give in to the temptation of his smile, his touch, the warmth in his gaze as he looked at her. He was a beautiful and fascinating man, and she couldn't help envying that girl who had been her—the one who'd known him from the beginning, the one he seemed to love.

Memory or not, she could see why she had fallen for him—and she could easily envision history repeating itself.

CHAPTER TEN

Korum watched her animated face over lunch, loving the shy, yet admiring glances she directed his way during their conversation. The attraction between them was as strong as ever, and he had no doubt he would be able to seduce her again. Perhaps even tonight—though she might not be ready for that.

For once, Korum was determined not to pressure Mia into his bed. When they'd first met, the strength of his desire for her had caught him off-guard, causing him to act in ways he would've normally condemned. He didn't want to repeat the same mistakes, no matter how much his cock insisted that she was *his*—that she belonged to him and he had the right to take her, to pleasure her, whenever he chose. Graphic sexual images danced in his head as he watched her enjoying her meal, imagining her soft little mouth nibbling on his flesh instead of the piece of fruit she was consuming.

It didn't help that he was still on an adrenaline high after Loris's attack. Fighting often boosted his already strong libido, the increased aggression translating into a primitive urge to fuck. It was always that way with Krinar men—and human ones too, as far as he knew. Violence and sex had been intertwined since the beginning of time, both appealing to the same male drive to dominate and conquer.

But no matter how much his body demanded it, Korum didn't want to push her. She seemed to be responding so well to the entire situation, looking at him with curiosity and desire instead of fear. If he could just be patient, she would come to him herself, lured by the same need that crawled under his skin.

So, as the lunch went on, Korum kept a tight leash on himself, not even touching Mia in case his good intentions flew out the window. He told her more about the nanocytes in her body and showed her some of the capabilities of Krinar technology, creating a silver cup using nanos and then dissolving it the same way. He also explained about her internship and how she had already begun to contribute to the Krinar society, enjoying the way her eyes lit up with excitement at the thought.

Toward the end, as they were finishing dessert—a platter of freshly cut mango with pistachio sauce—Korum noticed that Mia seemed a little nervous, as though there was something on her mind. Unable to resist any longer, he reached across the table and took her hand, massaging her palm lightly with his thumb.

"Is there something you'd like to ask me, my sweet?" he said, smiling, watching as a pretty blush crept across her cheeks.

"Um, maybe . . ." The color on her face intensified. "Okay, you're probably going to laugh at me, but I just have to know . . ." She swallowed. "Is there any truth to the rumors that you guys drink blood?"

At her innocently provocative question, Korum almost groaned, his cock instantly hardening to the point of pain. She didn't know, of course, that human blood and sexual pleasure were inseparable in the mind of a modern Krinar—and that bringing up the topic like that was the equivalent of asking a Krinar to fuck you. Even the most amazing sex paled in comparison to the ecstasy of the combined act of blood-drinking and intercourse.

"There is some truth to them," Korum said carefully, glad that she couldn't see his raging hard-on. "It was once necessary for our survival, but it's not any longer." And trying to suppress his overwhelming need to take her, he went through the complicated story of Krinar evolution and the seeding of the human race.

"So now you drink blood for pleasure?" Mia asked, staring at him with a shocked, yet intrigued expression on her face.

"Yes." Korum hoped she would drop the topic before he completely lost it.

She didn't. Instead, she looked at him, her cheeks flushed and her eyes bright with curiosity and something more. "Did you—" she stopped to moisten her lips, "—did you ever take my blood?"

Korum thought he might literally explode. Something of what he was feeling must've shown on his face because she gulped nervously and pulled her hand out of his grasp. *Smart girl.*

There was a moment of awkward silence, and then she asked

hesitantly, "Why do your eyes do that? Turn more golden, I mean . . . Is that a Krinar thing?"

Korum took a deep, calming breath. When he was reasonably certain he wasn't going to pounce on her, he replied, "No, it's just a weird genetic quirk. It's most common among people from my region of Krina. My mother has it too, and so did my grandfather."

"Your grandfather?"

Korum nodded. "He was killed in a fight when my mother was about my age."

"What about your grandmother and your other grandparents?"

"My grandmother from my mother's side died in a freak accident when she was exploring one of the asteroids in a neighboring solar system. Some even thought it was a suicide, since my grandfather was killed only a few years before that. As for my father's parents, they dissolved their union shortly after my father's birth—one of the very few couples to do so after having children. Apparently my grandmother wanted out, but my grandfather didn't—and he ended up getting into an Arena challenge with the man she took as her lover. My grandfather didn't survive, and my grandmother took her own life shortly after that, apparently too sick with guilt to go on living. It was not a happy story."

Her eyes filled with sympathy. "Oh, I'm sorry—"

"It's all right, my sweet. It happened before I was even born. It's unfortunate, but death is a tragedy that happens to everyone at one point or another. Humans might view us as immortal because we don't age, but we are still living beings—and we can still be killed, no matter how advanced our technology is or how fast we heal. That's why the Elders are so revered in our society: because it's nearly impossible to live that long without meeting with one deadly accident or another."

"You've mentioned these Elders before." Mia was clearly fascinated. "Who are they? Do they rule Krina?"

"No." Korum shook his head. "They don't rule in the sense of being involved in politics or anything like that. That's what the Council is for: to deal with ongoing matters. The Elders provide guidance and set direction for our species as a whole."

"Oh, I see." She looked thoughtful for a second. "So how old are they?"

"I believe the youngest is just over a million Earth years," Korum said, smiling at the look of wonder on her face. "And the oldest is somewhere around ten million."

She stared at him. "Wow . . ."

"Wow indeed," Korum agreed, enjoying her reaction.

When the lunch was finally over, they took a long walk on the beach and talked some more. Korum held her hand as they leisurely strolled on the sand, reveling in the feel of her small fingers squeezing his palm so trustingly.

He had been worried initially that her memory loss would set them back months, that she would be frightened of him again. But instead, it seemed as if a part of her still knew him—maybe even still loved him. Her calm acceptance of the situation was both surprising and encouraging, particularly since there was no guarantee they would ever be able to reverse the damage Saret had caused.

After the Council meeting, Korum had visited Ellet, hoping that the human biology expert had made some progress toward finding a fix. While the human brain was not her specialty, Korum had hoped she might've been able to learn of some research being done in that direction. To his tremendous disappointment, Ellet hadn't come across anything, despite reaching out to dozens of Krinar scientists on both planets. She had also spoken to all the mind experts at the other Centers. As far as she knew, there was no way to undo a memory wipe of the kind that Saret had used.

"So what made you decide to come to Earth?" Mia asked as they stopped to sit down on a pair of large rocks. In front of them, a small estuary flowed into the ocean, serving as an obstacle to further passage but creating a very scenic view. "I know you told me how you planted life here and basically created humans, but why come here and live alongside us? From what you've said, Krina sounds like a very nice place to live. Why bother leaving it?"

"Our sun is an older star," Korum explained, repeating what he'd once told her. "It will die in about a hundred million years. At that point, we'll need another place to live—and Earth appeals to us for obvious reasons."

She frowned, wrinkling her forehead in a way he found very endearing. "But that's so far away . . . Why would you come now? Why not wait another ninety million years or so?"

Korum sighed, recalling their last discussion on this topic. "Because your species was becoming very destructive to the environment, my sweet. We wanted to make sure that we had a habitable planet for when we needed it." That was the official story, at least. The full explanation was more complicated and not something he was ready to share with Mia quite yet.

Her frown deepened. She obviously didn't like hearing that—but then his charl tended to get defensive when he criticized her kind. He couldn't really blame her for that; she was as loyal to her people as he was to his.

"So when your star begins to die, all the Krinar will come to Earth?" she asked, her eyes narrowing slightly.

"Most likely," Korum said. He actually hoped that wouldn't be the case, but he couldn't tell her that yet.

"Then what would happen to us? To the humans, I mean? Do you really intend to live with us side by side? Wouldn't the planet be too crowded then?"

Korum hesitated for a moment. She was asking all the right questions, and he didn't want to lie to her—but he couldn't tell her the truth yet either. The last thing they needed was for some rumors to spread and cause the humans to panic again.

"Not necessarily," he hedged. "Besides, that's not something we'll have to worry about for a very long time."

She looked at him, obviously trying to decide how much he could be trusted. Korum could practically see the wheels turning in her head. He loved that about her: her unabashed curiosity about everything, the logical way her mind processed information. She was young and naive, but she was also very intelligent, and he had no doubt that one day she would leave her own mark on society.

For now, though, Korum needed to distract her from this particular line of questions. Smiling, he reached over and brushed her hair away from her face. "So what do you think of Lenkarda so far? Are you starting to feel more comfortable, or is it still very strange to you?"

She gave him a small smile. "I don't know, honestly. It's not as strange as it should be. I don't *remember* anything here, but it's like I know it on some level. And it's the same thing with you—"

"I'm as familiar to you as the furniture?" Korum teased, watching as her smile widened into a full-blown grin.

"You are . . ." She laughed ruefully. "I don't understand how any of this works, but you're not nearly as scary as you should be. None of this is, for some reason."

Korum felt his chest expanding to fill with something very much like happiness. "That's good, my sweet," he said, stroking the softness of her cheek. "You shouldn't be scared of me. I would never hurt you. You're my everything; you're my entire world. I would sooner die than hurt you.

Believe me, there's no reason to be afraid . . ."

As he spoke, he could see her smile fading and a strangely vulnerable expression appearing on her face instead. "Do you—" she swallowed, her slim throat moving, "—do you love me?"

"I do," Korum answered without hesitation. "More than anyone I've ever loved in my life."

"But why?" She seemed genuinely confused. "I'm just an ordinary human, and you're—" She stopped, her cheeks turning pink again.

"I'm what?" Korum prompted, wanting to see more of that pretty blush. He wasn't sure why he found it so appealing, but it never failed to arouse him. Then again, she turned him on simply by breathing, so it wasn't all that surprising he found her flushed cheeks irresistible.

The color in her face deepened. "You're a gorgeous K who's been around since the dawn of time," she said quietly. "What could you possibly see in me?"

Korum smiled, shaking his head. His little darling had never understood her appeal, never realized how tempting she was to the male of both species. Everything about her, from the soft, thick curls on her head to the creaminess of her skin, seemed to be made for a man's touch. She might not be classically beautiful, but in her own delicate way, she was quite striking, with those large blue eyes and dark hair.

In hindsight, Korum should've known better than to let her work in such close proximity with another unattached male. He couldn't really blame Saret for wanting her, for craving something that he himself was so obsessed with. He wanted to tear his former friend apart for what he'd done, but he understood—at least partially—why Saret had done it. If the roles had been reversed, and Mia had been someone else's charl, Korum didn't know how far he would've gone to get her for his own, how many taboos he would've broken in his quest to possess her.

Of course, her physical appeal was only a part of it now. Reaching over, Korum took her hand again. "I see in you the woman I love," he said, not even trying to hide the depth of his emotions. "I see a beautiful, smart girl who's sweet and brave and has the courage of her convictions. I see someone who'll do anything for those she loves, who'll go to any lengths to protect those dear to her. I see someone I can't live without, someone who brightens every moment of my existence and makes me happier than I've ever been in my life."

Mia inhaled, her eyes filling with moisture. "Oh Korum . . ." Her slender fingers twitched in his grasp. "Korum, I don't even know what to say—"

"You don't have to say anything," he interrupted, ignoring the pain of her inadvertent rejection. "I know I'm still a stranger to you. I don't expect you to feel the same way about me now as you did before. Not yet, at least . . ."

She nodded, and a single tear rolled down her face. "I hate this," she confessed, her voice breaking for a second. "I hate that such a big part of my life disappeared, that I lost everything that brought us to this point. I need you, but I don't know you, and it's driving me crazy. I loved you too, didn't I? Even though all that stuff happened between us, we were still in love, right?"

"Yes," Korum said, his hand tightening around her palm. "Yes, we were very much in love, my darling." And unable to resist any longer, he gently wrapped one arm around her back, bringing her closer to him. She buried her face against his shoulder, and he could feel the wetness from her tears on his bare skin. The sweet scent of her hair teased his nostrils, her nearness making his cock harden again.

Don't be such an animal. She needs comfort now, Korum told himself. And ignoring the lust raging through his body, he let Mia cry, knowing she needed this emotional release.

After a minute, she pulled away, looking up at him through tear-spiked lashes. "I'm sorry," she whispered, "I didn't mean to cry all over you . . ."

Korum smiled, wiping away the wetness on her cheeks with his knuckles. "You can cry all over me any time you want." Her tears were as precious to him as her smiles. He hated to see her sad, but liked the feel of her slender body in his arms, enjoyed being the one to soothe her, to make her pain go away.

Even if, more often than not, he had been the cause of that pain.

* * *

They spent the rest of the day together on the beach, with Korum patiently explaining everything Mia had once known and forgotten about the Krinar. He told her about blood addiction and xenos, the Celebration of Forty-Seven and the importance of 'standing' in Krinar society. She listened attentively, asking questions, and Korum gladly answered them, knowing how much she needed to catch up on.

"So do you have the concept of money? How does your economy work?" Her eyes were bright and curious as they continued their discussion over dinner.

"Yes, we definitely have the concept of money." Korum paused to take a bite of his peanut-flavored soba noodles. "We work and get paid for the contributions we make to our society. The greater the contribution, the greater the pay, regardless of the field. However, wealth is not as important to us as it is to humans. Our economy is neither purely capitalist nor government-run; it's kind of a blend of the two. For the most part, everyone has their basic needs met. There's no such thing as homelessness or hunger on Krina. Even the laziest Krinar lives quite well by human standards. But, to have anything beyond food, shelter, and daily necessities, you have to do something productive with your life— you have to contribute to society in some way."

She was looking very interested, so Korum continued his explanation. "Financial rewards are only a part of the reason why people work, though. The main motivation is the need to be respected, to be recognized for our achievements. Few Krinar want to go through life having others look down upon them. You see, for us, having a low standing is almost like being an outcast. Someone who's never done anything useful in his life will ultimately find himself treated with contempt by others. Having a high standing is much more important than being wealthy—although the two usually go hand-in-hand."

"So wealthy Krinar have a high standing, and vice versa?" Mia asked.

"No, not necessarily. One could be wealthy through inheritance or family, but that doesn't mean that person will have a high standing. Rafor, Loris's son, is a prime example of that. His father gave him all the wealth he could possibly need, but he couldn't give him a good standing. That can only be earned—or lost—through one's own efforts."

Mia looked puzzled. "Wait, how do you lose standing through your own efforts?"

"There are a number of ways," Korum said. "Committing a crime is an obvious one. So is doing something dishonorable, like cheating on your mate. It's also possible to lose standing by failing at something important. For instance, Loris took that risk by assuming the role of the Protector for his son and the Keiths. Once they are judged guilty, his standing will be much lower and he'll no longer be on the Council. That's why he challenged me to the Arena today—because he has very little to lose at this point."

Her eyes widened with surprise. "What do you mean, he challenged you?"

Korum hesitated. Perhaps he shouldn't have mentioned it to Mia just yet, but it was too late now. "Remember I told you about the Arena earlier today?" he asked.

"You said it was a way to resolve irreconcilable differences . . ." A small frown appeared on her face.

"Yes," Korum confirmed, "it is. And that's what Loris and I have: an irreconcilable difference of opinion. I think his son is a traitorous lowlife, and he disagrees."

"So he challenged you to a fight? But I thought you said those were dangerous—"

"They are." Korum smiled in anticipation, familiar excitement zinging through his veins. He needed this sometimes: the danger, the adrenaline, the raw physical challenge of subduing an opponent. As much as he enjoyed fighting during defrebs matches, he was always aware that it was just a game, that everyone would walk away with nothing more than a few scrapes and bruises. There was no such guarantee in the Arena, which is what made it so thrilling.

"So you could be killed?" Mia's eyes were beginning to glisten with moisture, and Korum realized that she found the idea more than a little disturbing. He definitely shouldn't have brought this up yet.

"There is a small chance," he said carefully, not wanting to upset her further. "Although killing is technically illegal, it's usually forgiven if it happens in the heat of an Arena battle. But you don't need to worry, my sweet. I can take care of myself."

She didn't seem convinced. "You said he hates you." Her voice quivered a little. "Wouldn't he *try* to kill you?"

"He can certainly try," Korum said, "but I'm not going to let him. You have nothing to worry about—"

"He's not a good fighter?"

"He is," Korum admitted. "Or at least he used to be. I don't know his skill level these days."

"Don't do it," she said, reaching over to grab his hand. "Please, Korum, don't do this fight—"

"Mia . . ." He sighed, covering her hand with his own. "Listen to me, darling, once a challenge has been issued, it cannot be undone. I can't walk away from this fight, and neither can Loris. We're both committed, do you understand that?"

"No," she said stubbornly, "I don't. I don't want you to risk your life like that—"

"It's not as big of a risk as you think," Korum said. "When he attacked me today, it took me all of ten seconds to get to his throat. If that had been an Arena fight, he would've been declared a loser at that point."

It was equally likely that Loris would've been dead, but Korum didn't want to tell Mia that. Human women and violence generally didn't mix well—especially when the woman in question was a sheltered young girl.

"So when is the fight supposed to be?" She still looked upset.

Korum sighed. He really should've kept quiet about this. "The day after tomorrow," he said. "At noon."

CHAPTER ELEVEN

Mia stood in the circular room that functioned as a shower stall, letting water jets pummel every inch of her body. Under normal circumstances, she would've loved the novelty of showering in an alien dwelling. Like everything else in the house, the shower was intelligent, adjusting automatically to her needs. All Mia had to do was stand there and let the amazing technology wash, scrub, condition, and massage her. It was wonderfully relaxing—or would've been, if she could just turn her brain off and not think about what Korum had told her at dinner.

He'd been dismissive of the danger of the upcoming fight, but Mia couldn't be so blasé. When he'd mentioned Loris's challenge, her blood had run cold, gruesome images of dismembered bodies flooding her mind. What if something happened to Korum? He wasn't truly immortal; he could be killed, just like his grandfather.

The thought of Korum dying was unbearable, unimaginable. It didn't matter that Mia had only known him—or remembered knowing him—for a day.

This day had been the best one of her conscious life.

Spending time with Korum had been incredible. She had never had that kind of connection with anyone else before, had never felt so magically alive in another man's presence. It went beyond sexual desire, beyond simple physical need. It was as though every part of her longed to be with him, to soak in his essence. She wanted him with a desperation that made no sense, with a passion that was almost frightening in its intensity.

Somewhere in the back of her mind, Mia knew she was acting

irrationally, completely unlike herself. A normal person in this type of situation would ask Korum to take her home, back to New York or Florida, where she could come to terms with the memory loss and gradually re-enter her normal life—such as it was these days. She shouldn't want to cling to an extraterrestrial, shouldn't be so calm about living in his house, separated from everyone and everything she could recall.

And yet she didn't want to ask him, didn't want to think about leaving him even for a moment. Mia had no doubt her psychology classmates would've had a field day analyzing her strange reactions, from the ease with which she'd accepted the impossible to her unhealthy dependence on a man she'd known for only a short period of time. But she didn't care; all she knew was that she needed Korum—and that he seemed to need her too.

Had her former boss—Saret—known it would be like this? Had he realized that erasing a part of her memory didn't destroy whatever it was that bound her and Korum together? Somehow Mia doubted it. If what Korum had told her about Saret's intentions was true, the mind expert would've been unpleasantly surprised by her continued attachment to Korum and lack of interest toward him.

After the shower was over, Mia stepped out of the circular stall, letting the water drip off her onto the strange sponge-like substance on the floor that kept massaging her feet. Korum had explained that all she needed to do was stand there and let the technology take care of her bathroom routine, so Mia was taking him at his word.

Sure enough, warm jets of air quickly dried off her body, while a small tornado seemed to engulf the area around her head, blowing around each strand of her hair and filling her mouth with a taste of something refreshingly clean. By the time it was done, Mia was dry from head to toe, her curls defined and shaped to perfection, as if she'd just emerged from a fancy hair salon. Her mouth also felt like she'd just brushed her teeth.

Nice.

All that was left was to put on some clothes. Pulling on a thick, fluffy robe that Korum had thoughtfully given her earlier, Mia looked at the mirror that made up one of the walls, noting the sparkle in her eyes and the flush that colored her cheeks. Her heart pounded in anticipation, and her stomach felt like it was hosting an entire colony of butterflies.

If there was even a small chance that she might lose Korum in two days, then every moment they had together was precious. And as nervous as the idea made her, Mia wanted to know her lover fully—to experience again that which she had forgotten.

She wanted Korum to take her to bed.

* * *

Korum sat on the edge of the bed, waiting for Mia to finish her shower. He'd showered already, using his fist to take the edge off the lust that had ridden him hard all day.

Spending so much time with her, touching her, smelling her—it had almost driven him insane. Under normal circumstances, they would've had sex a couple of times on the beach, or when they'd gotten home before dinner. And instead, he'd had to content himself with a few light touches and caresses that had only added to his hunger, making his skin prickle and his cock swell with need. If he hadn't masturbated in the shower, she would've been in serious danger of getting jumped this evening. As it was, Korum was still feeling quite edgy, and he was hoping to work off some of his excess energy by going for a defrebs session early in the morning—or at night, as humans thought of the hours between three and four a.m.

It was already past eleven in the evening, which was Mia's normal bed time. Korum wasn't the least bit tired himself, but he wanted to tuck her in and hold her until she fell asleep—even if doing so would torture him further. It was important to start getting her accustomed to him, to get her to feel comfortable with his touch ... because Korum didn't know how much longer he could go without having her.

To distract himself, he looked down at his palm, sending out a mental query to check on the progress of the search for Saret. The guardians had found traces of Saret's presence in Germany, but then his trail had gone cold again. However he was moving around, he was managing to do so out of sight of Krinar satellites and other spying devices—a feat that Korum reluctantly admired, even though the thought of Saret on the loose made him see red.

"What are you doing?" Mia's softly spoken question jerked him out of his absorption with the search.

Looking up, Korum smiled at the sight of her standing there, her small feet bare and the robe wrapped all over her slender body. Her hands were twisting together in a gesture that betrayed her nervousness. "I'm just checking up on a couple of things," he replied. "How was your shower? Did you like it?"

She moistened her lips, drawing his attention to her mouth. "It was awesome," she said. "Like everything else here."

"Good," Korum said, watching her closely. Was she afraid to be near a bed with him? Gentling his tone, he said, "Come, let's go to sleep, my sweet. You've had a long day. You must be so tired."

She nodded uncertainly and approached him, her movements imbued with an unconscious sensuality that was as much a part of her as those beautiful curls. Korum shifted and raised his knee slightly, seeking to hide the erection tenting his pants again.

When she was a foot away, she stopped, and he could hear her rapid heartbeat. A warm, feminine scent reached his nostrils, sending more blood rushing toward his groin.

She was not afraid, Korum realized. She was turned on.

Hardly daring to breathe, he reached out and took her hand, bringing her closer until she was sitting on the bed next to him. At his action, he could hear her heartbeat spiking, a mixture of apprehension and excitement written on her face.

"Mia," he asked softly, "are you sure?"

She nodded, her soft mouth trembling. "Yes," she whispered. "I'm sure . . ."

His body reacted to her words with painful intensity, his cock hardening further and his balls drawing up against his body. But when he leaned over to kiss her, he kept his lips gentle, tender—as her first time should be.

She'd come to him that other first time too, but she'd done it as a challenge, as a way to assert her independence and spite him in some small way. He hadn't cared then, glad to just have her there, in his apartment, in his bed. And in his rush to take her, he'd hurt her, tearing through her virginity with all the care of a rutting animal.

This was his chance to make up for it. She was a virgin again—in mind, if not in body. And Korum was determined to make sure that there would be no pain for her this night, only pleasure.

He kissed her softly, with just his lips at first, stroking her hair and back with soothing motions. She tasted fresh and sweet, her scent familiar and enticing. Her small hands came up, curved around the back of his neck, her fingers reaching into his hair, sending shivers of pleasure down his spine. Not wanting to deepen the kiss, Korum moved his lips to her cheek, then the underside of her jaw, tasting the sensitive skin there.

She moaned, arching her head back, exposing more of her pale throat to his mouth, and Korum kissed her there too, fighting the urge to take her blood at the same time. He would do it, but not today, not for this first time.

Carefully, so as not to startle her, he pulled at her robe, opening it as he continued kissing her, his mouth moving to her collarbone and then below.

Her body was beautiful, slim and curved in all the right places, her skin smooth and inviting to the touch. Korum slowly ran his hand over her breasts and her flat belly, marveling at the delicacy of her frame. His palm could almost cover her entire ribcage, his skin strikingly dark against the pale perfection of hers.

He could see the pulse beating rapidly in the side of her neck, hear her elevated breathing, and he knew she was as anxious as she was aroused. Raising his head, Korum caught her staring at him, her face flushed and her lips slightly parted.

"I love you, Mia," he murmured, reaching up to move that stray curl off her face. "You know that, right?"

She nodded shyly, still watching him with her huge blue eyes. Those eyes made him want to slay dragons for her, rip apart anyone who dared try to hurt her.

"Don't be afraid, my darling," he said, sliding one arm under her knees and another around her back. Lifting her up, he placed her carefully in the middle of the bed. "I'll make it good for you, I promise..." And moving back for a second, Korum removed his shirt and shorts, letting his erection spring free.

Before she had a chance to do more than give him one apprehensive glance, Korum climbed on top of her, nuzzling her neck and shoulder again until she let out a quiet moan. Then he slowly began to make his way down her body, ignoring his cock's insistent throbbing. There would be times when he would take her hard and fast, but this wasn't going to be one of them. Tonight was all about her.

Cupping the round globe of her breast, he delighted in its firmness, in the way her nipple hardened against his palm. Her breasts weren't large, but they were perfectly shaped, just right for her slight frame. Bending his head, he tasted her nipple, laving it with his tongue, then sucking on it with a firm pull.

She moaned again, arching toward him, and he repeated the treatment on the other breast, enjoying the way her nipples looked afterwards: all pink and shiny.

Her stomach was next, and he kissed the soft skin there, tonguing her belly button and feeling her abdominal muscles tensing as his mouth continued moving lower. Her legs were closed, so Korum pulled her thighs apart, ignoring the hitch in her breathing as he gazed upon her moist folds and the dark triangle of curls above. Like the rest of Mia, her pussy was small and delicate, sweeter than anything he'd ever tasted.

Lowering his head, Korum breathed in her intoxicating scent and then gently licked the area around her clitoris, teasing her, letting her arousal slowly build. As he continued, he could hear her gasping every time his tongue approached her sensitive nub, feel the way her hips kept rising off the bed toward his mouth. He knew she was very close to the edge, but he wasn't ready to let her go over. Not yet at least.

Moving his hand, he used his index finger to slowly penetrate her, sliding it inside her slick channel, carefully stretching her, readying her for him. She was so tiny inside she even felt tight around his finger, and Korum suppressed a tortured groan as his cock twitched against the sheets in painful arousal.

She cried out as his finger slid deeper, rubbing against that spot that always drove her insane, and then Korum could feel her convulsing, her inner walls pulsing around his finger as she found her release.

Unable to wait any longer, he crawled back up her body, keeping her thighs open with his knee. Holding himself up with one elbow, he used his other hand to direct himself to her small opening, letting the head of his cock slide inside, and then pausing to let her adjust to his size.

At his entry, she inhaled sharply and grasped his shoulders, gazing up at him. His entire body straining from the rigid control he was exerting over himself, Korum began to push in further, keeping the penetration gradual and slow to avoid hurting her. As his cock went deeper, sweat beaded up all over his body and his breathing became harsher, more erratic. She was warm, wet, and tight—and Korum thought he might literally explode on the spot.

Using all his willpower, he paused when he was all the way in, letting her get used to the feel of him deep inside her body. "Are you okay?" he managed to ask in a rough whisper, looking down at her.

She licked her lips. "Yes."

"Good," Korum breathed. He wasn't sure he could've stopped if she'd said otherwise. He was seconds away from orgasm, his balls drawn tightly against his body and his spine prickling with the familiar pre-release tension.

But he didn't want to come yet, not until he'd had a chance to pleasure her one more time. Using his right hand, Korum reached between their bodies, finding the place where they joined and lightly stimulating her clitoris with his fingers. At the same time, he began to move inside her, partially withdrawing and then pushing back in.

She moaned again, her fingers tightening around his shoulders and her sharp nails digging into his skin. He could feel the heat rising off her body, hear her breathing changing, and he knew she was almost there. Finally letting go of his restraint, he began to thrust with increasing speed, climbing the peak higher and higher, every muscle in his body shaking from the intensity of the sensations. Suddenly, she cried out, her inner muscles clamping down on his cock, and he exploded with a roar, his seed shooting out in several powerful spurts.

When it was over, Korum rolled off Mia onto his back and pulled her on top of him, so that she lay partially draped over his chest. They were both breathing hard, their bodies limp and covered with sweat.

Korum knew he should say something, but he couldn't seem to gather his thoughts. There was sex—and then there was what he experienced with Mia. He'd never imagined that he could want a woman so much, that he could get so much pleasure out of the simple act of fucking.

It wasn't as if he was inexperienced. Far from it. In his centuries of existence, he'd engaged in sexual acts of every type and every flavor. There was no stigma associated with promiscuous behavior in Krinar society, and unattached individuals were encouraged to experiment to their hearts' content.

Yet Korum could not remember ever feeling the kind of bone-deep satisfaction he experienced with Mia. He'd always wondered how mated individuals—or those who had a charl—remained faithful throughout their lives. The idea of not having variety had seemed strange and unnatural to him. Since meeting Mia, however, he couldn't imagine wanting to be with another woman. She was all he wanted, all the time, every time.

His breathing finally calming, Korum looked down at the curly head lying on his chest. Feeling content, he stroked her hair, grinning when he heard a quiet yawn.

"Want to take a quick rinse and then go to sleep?" he murmured, still smiling as she looked up.

She gave him a deliciously sleepy look, then yawned again. "Sure, that would be nice . . ."

Laughing softly, Korum wrapped his arms around her and got up, carrying her toward the shower. Still holding her, he stepped inside and sent a quick mental command to the water controls. Two minutes later they were clean and dry, and Korum carried her back to bed, enjoying the trusting way she clung to him the entire time.

Placing her back on the bed, he lay down beside her and pulled her into his embrace, curving his body around her from the back. Utterly relaxed, he closed his eyes and let her even breathing lull him into sleep as well.

CHAPTER TWELVE

Slowly waking up the next morning, Mia stretched and smiled, remembering last night. The entire experience had been amazing, like something she could've only dreamed of. Was sex always like this? Or was it just sex with Korum?

After that first time, he'd taken her again at some point in the night, waking her up by sliding into her. Somehow she had already been wet, and she'd orgasmed within minutes—something she would've expected to be difficult, given how satisfied she'd felt after the previous time.

But she was apparently as insatiable as her alien lover.

Grinning like a Cheshire Cat, Mia got up, put on a peach-colored sundress, and did her morning bathroom routine. Korum was already gone, so she asked the house for some yummy breakfast and then curled up on one of the floating planks that functioned as a couch. "Some reading material, please," she requested, and laughed as a razor-thin tablet-like device floated toward her from one of the walls.

Yesterday, when Korum told her about her role at the mind lab, he'd mentioned that she used to keep work-related documents and recordings on this tablet. Mia was intensely curious about it, trying to imagine how she'd functioned in a Krinar work environment given her unfamiliarity about their technology and science. From what Korum had explained, a lot of the knowledge had been transferred to her via the same process that was used to teach Krinar children, and she was secretly hoping that she'd retained some of it despite the memory wipe. She certainly felt more comfortable in Lenkarda than could be expected, and she was pretty sure she knew things about the brain that were far beyond what she'd learned in college.

Using a verbal command to open one of the files, Mia made herself comfortable and began the process of re-learning everything she had partially or completely forgotten.

* * *

"The Council has reached a decision."

Arus's words carried throughout the large arena-like room where the public portion of the trial took place. Almost every Krinar on Earth—and many residents of Krina—were there virtually or in person.

Korum leaned forward, waiting to hear the words that would seal the fate of the traitors. In front of him, he could see Loris standing straight, garbed all in black. The Protector's fists were tightly clenched, knuckles almost white, as he braced himself to hear his son's sentence.

"Rafor, Kian, Leris, Poren, Saod, Kula, and Reana," Arus said clearly, "the Council finds you guilty of conspiring with the human Resistance movement to attack the Centers and endanger the lives of fifty thousand of your fellow citizens. You are also found guilty of breaking the non-interference mandate by sharing Krinar technology with the said Resistance movement. Additionally, Rafor, the Council judges you guilty of aiding and abetting the dangerous individual known as Saret in his plan to commit mass murder and illegally manipulate human minds."

The Protector visibly paled, and the Keiths looked like they were punched in the stomach. A murmur ran through the crowd, then died down as the spectators fell silent to hear the rest.

"The sentence for the above crimes is complete rehabilitation."

Korum leaned back, listening to the uproar in the audience. In that moment, he felt uncharacteristic pity for Loris, who had just lost his only son. Whatever their differences had been in the past, it wasn't Loris's fault Rafor had turned out to be a failure and a criminal. Korum couldn't blame Loris for wanting to defend his child, no matter how undeserving that child was.

However, Korum had no regrets about the role he'd played in their conviction. Rafor and his friends got exactly what they deserved: an almost complete erasure of their personalities. They were too dangerous to be subjected to partial rehabilitation, their actions too heinous to be forgiven. If there was one thing Korum despised, it was someone who tried to hurt his own people for the sake of greed and power—the way these traitors had.

The brief flicker of sympathy he felt for Loris died down as the Protector turned and gave Korum a hate-filled glare. Loris's face was colorless underneath the bronzed tone of his skin, and his eyes glittered with something resembling madness. It was the look of someone who had nothing left to lose, and Korum recognized that his opponent would do everything in his power to leave him lying in pieces tomorrow. Of course, Korum had no intention of letting that happen. He didn't want to kill Loris, but he would do what was necessary to defend himself.

After the uproar in the crowd died down, the Keiths were taken away, and Korum got up, heading toward the exit. What he wanted now was Mia, but he couldn't go home yet.

He needed to reach out to the Elders again to move the project forward—and to check on his petition about Mia's parents.

* * *

"You have a visitor, Mia."

Startled by the unfamiliar female voice, Mia looked up from her reading material. Through the transparent wall, she could see a young human woman standing outside. Blowing out a relieved breath, Mia realized that the voice she'd just heard had to be Korum's intelligent house letting her know about the guest.

"Of course," Mia said, as though she talked to alien technology all the time. "Can you please let her inside?"

"Yes, Mia." And the wall in front of the visitor dissolved, creating an entrance.

Getting up from the floating plank, Mia smiled at the dark-haired girl who gracefully stepped through the opening.

"Hi," Mia said, knowing she was probably greeting someone she'd already met before.

"Hello, Mia," the girl said, giving her a gentle smile. "I know you don't remember me, but I'm Delia. We've met a couple of times before. I'm also a charl here in Lenkarda."

"It's nice to meet you again, Delia." Mia was glad that her guest seemed to know about her condition. "I apologize in advance about my lack of recognition—"

"It's not your fault," Delia interrupted, her large brown eyes soft with concern. "How can you even apologize for something like that? I came by to see if you were all right after what happened. It must be so devastating, to wake up not knowing where you are or how you got there . . ."

Mia studied the girl, noting her quiet, yet luminous beauty and the maturity that belied her apparent youth. "Thanks, Delia," she said. "I'm actually surprisingly okay. I don't know why, but I seem to be dealing with everything quite well."

"And Korum?"

Mia gave her a questioning look. "What about Korum?"

"Is he—" Delia hesitated a little. "Is he being kind to you?"

"Of course." Mia frowned. "Why wouldn't he be? He's my . . . cheren, right?"

Delia gave her a radiant smile. "Of course. I was just heading to the waterfalls, where you and I first met. Would you be interested in coming with me? It's a really beautiful spot. I don't know if Korum showed it to you yet—"

"He hasn't," Mia admitted. "And I would love to join you." She was curious about this girl—this other charl—and she was hoping to find out more about Lenkarda and her former life there.

"Great," Delia said, still smiling. "Then let's go."

The walk to the waterfalls took a little over twenty minutes. As they made their way through the forest, Mia asked Delia about her story, wanting to find out how she'd become a charl. Then she listened in shock and fascination as the Greek girl told her about meeting Arus on the shores of the Mediterranean almost twenty-three centuries ago and how her life had unfolded since.

"When I first arrived on Krina, humans were treated very differently than they are today," Delia explained. "Two thousand years ago, many Krinar thought we were little better than primates, with our lack of technology and primitive social mores. A few, like Arus, recognized that we were not all that different from them, but most refused to think of us as an equally intelligent species. That attitude still persists today to a certain extent, although the rapid pace of progress here in the past couple of centuries has impressed many on Krina."

"They thought we were like monkeys?" Mia frowned, not liking that at all.

Delia nodded. "Something like that. I can't really blame them; after all, they were the ones to create us and make us into what we are today."

"How did they do that?" Mia asked, having wondered about that for a while. "I mean, a Krinar can almost pass for a human, and vice versa. Appearance-wise, it's like they're a different human race, rather than a separate species. I know they guided our evolution, but it's still kind of crazy . . ."

"It's actually not all that crazy," Delia said. "They tinkered with our genes for millions of years, suppressing those traits that would've made us look different from them. They allowed certain subtle variations—like eye, skin, and hair color—but they ensured we would be very similar to them otherwise. It was something their Elders wanted, I believe."

Mia looked away, pondering that for a while as they continued walking through the forest. "So what do you think they want with us now?" she asked once they reached their destination.

"The Krinar?" Delia sat down on a grassy patch near the water and turned toward Mia.

"Their Elders," Mia clarified, sitting down next to her.

"Who knows?" Delia shrugged. "Even the Council doesn't fully know the motivations of the Elders. They're something like gods to them, although the Krinar don't have religion in the traditional sense."

"I see." Mia considered everything she'd learned so far. "So how do the Krinar think of us now? Korum said I worked in one of their labs. Surely they wouldn't let me do that if they thought that I was just an unusually smart monkey. Not to mention, they marry us . . ."

"Marry us?" Delia looked surprised. "What do you mean?"

"Isn't that what being a charl is? Like being married to one of them, only without the official ceremony?" That was the impression Mia had gotten yesterday from her conversation with Korum.

Delia regarded her with a thoughtful brown gaze. "I guess you could think of it that way," she said slowly. "Particularly if you apply the definition of marriage as it used to be in the past."

"In the past?"

"Yes," Delia said. "Before your time. When a wife lawfully belonged to her husband."

"What do you mean, belonged?"

"By Krinar law, a charl belongs to her cheren, Mia. We don't really have any rights here. Korum didn't tell you that?"

Mia shook her head, feeling an unpleasant tightness in her chest. "Are you saying we're their . . . slaves?"

Delia smiled. "No. The Krinar don't believe in slavery, especially not as it was practiced during my time. Most charl are very well treated and loved by their cheren. They truly do regard them as their human mates. But it's not exactly the type of equal relationship a modern girl like you would be accustomed to."

Mia stared at her. "How so?"

"Well, for instance, a Krinar doesn't need your permission to make you his charl. Arus asked me, but many cheren don't."

"Did Korum ask *me*?" Mia waited for the answer with bated breath.

"I don't know," Delia said regretfully. "I've never been privy to the particulars of your relationship. However, from what I know about Korum—and from the fact that you helped the Resistance before—I would guess that he wasn't quite as considerate of your feelings as he should've been."

Mia frowned. "What do you mean, what you know about Korum?"

Delia looked at her, as though weighing whether to proceed further. "Your cheren is a very powerful, very ambitious man," she finally said. "Many on the Council think he has the ear of the Elders. He's also known to be quite autocratic and ruthless with his opponents. That's why I was initially worried about you—because I didn't think Korum would be a particularly caring cheren. But I think I was wrong. From what I could tell, you seemed happy with him before. The last time we met, at Maria's birthday, you were practically glowing. And even now, when most women would be feeling lost and intimidated, it looks like you're doing well—and Korum has to be the one responsible for that."

Mia studied the other girl, wondering if there was something else Delia was not telling her. "You don't like my cheren, do you?"

"I don't know him personally," Delia said carefully. "I just know that Arus and he have clashed in the past over a number of different issues. But I'm glad he's good to you. When I first saw you, you seemed so young and vulnerable . . . and I couldn't help but worry about you. Now I see that you're stronger than I originally thought. You might even be a good influence on Korum. Arus thinks your cheren truly loves you—which is something we would've never expected from him."

"I see." Mia drew in a deep breath and looked away, trying to process what she'd just learned. Perhaps her silly thought about Korum as a villain wasn't as far-fetched as it seemed. Not for the first time, she wished she could remember the past couple of months, so she could better understand this complex relationship she was in. What exactly was Korum to her? What did it mean to be his charl? And which was the real Korum? The tender lover of last night, or the ruthless Councilor Delia had described?

Perhaps he was both. Mia considered that for a minute. Yes, she could definitely see how that could be the case. After all, Korum himself had told her about how he had used her in the past to crush the Resistance.

Yet he seemed to truly love her now—and Mia couldn't help the warm feeling that spread through her at the thought.

Turning back toward the Greek girl, Mia looked at her. "Delia," she said quietly, bringing up a topic that had been worrying her since yesterday, "do you know what happens in an Arena fight?"

"Yes." Delia gave her a sympathetic look. "You know about Loris's challenge?"

"Korum told me about it yesterday," Mia said. "Have you ever seen one of these fights? Are they common?"

"They're not as common as they used to be a long time ago, but they still happen with some regularity. There are usually a couple of fights a year, sometimes more."

"And how dangerous are they?"

Delia hesitated for a second. "Arena fighting is the number one cause of death for the Krinar," she finally said. "Followed by various accidents."

Mia felt like she'd been punched in the stomach. "Does someone always die during a fight?"

"No, not always. Sometimes the winner can control himself enough to stop in time. Generally, though, Krinar men don't have the best control over their instincts during the heat of battle." The Greek charl didn't seem particularly bothered by that.

Mia swallowed. "I see."

"But to answer your earlier question, I do think Krinar attitudes toward humans are changing," Delia said, coming back to their previous discussion. "Two thousand years ago, the idea of a human working in a Krinar lab would've been unthinkable. They've come a long way since then, and I see things improving more and more every day. The fact that they're living here on Earth, among us, is a game changer in many ways. They see now that we truly *are* their sister species, that we have the potential to achieve as much as they did."

"They no longer think we're just smart monkeys?" Mia said, only half-jokingly.

Delia smiled. "Some still do, I'm sure. But it's no longer the consensus view. And the more relationships like yours and mine there are, the more accepted humans will become in the Krinar society." She paused for a second. "So you see, Mia, you don't have to be fighting the Krinar to help your people. You just have to get one of them to fall in love with you."

* * *

Five thousand miles away, Saret got up and smiled at the human girl lying curled in a little naked ball in his bed. She was petite, no more than five feet tall, and her dark brown hair fell in soft waves around her narrow face. Other than her brown eyes, she looked very much like Mia. He'd found her in Paris yesterday.

She stared at him, and he could see the fear and hatred on her small face. It was unfortunate that she'd been engaged when he met her, with her wedding planned for next month. She had been understandably resistant to his attentions, and he didn't have the time to seduce her properly.

It had been wrong to take her, of course. Saret knew that. At this point, however, it didn't matter. Everyone already thought him a monster, and stealing one human was a harmless prank in the grand scheme of things. He had bitten her during sex, so he knew she'd found pleasure with him too. She wasn't Mia, but he had still enjoyed fucking her, pretending that the slim body in his arms was the one he truly wanted.

Saret knew he had no hope of eluding the guardians for much longer; it was only a matter of time before he would be captured. Now that he had gotten a chance to think, he realized how Korum had known what to expect. It was very simple, really. His enemy must've been monitoring his charl even more thoroughly than he had admitted to Saret. In hindsight, Saret should've expected something like that; it was his own fault he'd underestimated Korum's obsession with Mia.

No, Saret knew he wouldn't be able to hide for much longer. He'd been utilizing various disguises, but he could sense the guardians getting closer. Yesterday, he had taken a risk and connected to the Krinar network. He'd tried to hide his identity, but he was sure Korum would eventually find his traces in cyberspace. Still, Saret had needed to know what was happening in Lenkarda and whether the Council had found out about his plan.

What he'd learned had made him both angry and excited at the same time. Angry—because his carefully planted nano dispersion devices had already been discovered and neutralized. And excited—because he finally knew how to get rid of Korum once and for all.

His enemy's upcoming fight would be his last.

Saret would make sure of that.

CHAPTER THIRTEEN

The first thing Korum saw when he entered the house was Mia, curled up on the long float and absorbed in whatever she was reading on her tablet.

At his entry, she looked up and smiled, her face bright with excitement. "Hi," she said. "How was your day?"

Korum felt a surge of tenderness, even as his body reacted predictably to her nearness. "Hello, my sweet," he said, stepping toward her and bending down to give her a brief kiss. He had been thinking about her all day today, reliving every moment of the previous night in his mind. He couldn't wait to re-introduce her to the pleasures of lovemaking, to taste her delicious body over and over again.

He wanted to take it slow again, but the second his lips touched hers, her slender arms came up, looping around his neck, and all his good intentions evaporated in an instant. Her mouth was soft and sweet as he deepened the kiss, her scent warm and feminine. He could hear her breathing speeding up, smell her desire, feel her body arching up toward him . . . and his blood almost boiled in his veins.

Without a conscious thought, his hands went to her dress, and the fragile fabric ripped underneath his fingers, exposing the delicate flesh underneath. She gasped, and he could feel her nails digging into the back of his neck as he sucked at the tender spot near her shoulder. Her heart rate spiked, and she moaned as his hand went to her thighs, pushing between them to get to her tight opening.

She was hot and slick around his fingers, and Korum used the last vestiges of his self-control to bring her to orgasm by rhythmically pressing his thumb against her clit. As soon as she convulsed with a soft cry, he knew he could not hold out any longer. Tearing off his own clothes, he grabbed her legs and pulled her toward him until only her upper body was lying on the float. Then he pushed inside her in one powerful thrust.

She cried out, her body tensing, and Korum groaned as her inner muscles squeezed his shaft, preventing him from going deeper. Her eyes snapped open, focusing on him, and Korum held her gaze, knowing that she could see the dark craving written on his face. His cock throbbed inside her snug channel, and it wasn't enough. The animal inside him needed to possess her on a level that went beyond the sexual, to imprint himself on her mind as well as body.

"You're all mine," he whispered harshly, hardly realizing what he was saying. "Do you understand me?"

She just stared at him, her face flushed and her lips slightly parted, and Korum could feel his temperature rising. A wave of pure possessiveness swept through his body. His buttocks tightened as he pushed deeper into her, holding her thighs wide open to aid in his penetration. She gasped, her face contorting with a mix of pain and pleasure, and he could hear her breath catching in her throat.

Leaning forward, he let go of her legs and slid one arm under her upper back, bringing her closer. His other hand found its way to her hair, holding her head partially arched back, her slender neck exposed. "Say it, Mia," he commanded, driven by a primitive need to claim her. "Say you're mine."

"I'm . . ." She seemed to have trouble saying the words, her blue eyes clouded with some unknown emotion, and the urge to dominate her grew stronger. Bending his head, he took her mouth in a savage kiss, his hand slipping down to her folds and his thumb pressing hard on her clitoris. Her inner walls tightened around his cock like a fist, and she moaned into his mouth.

"You're mine," he repeated, drawing back for a second, and she nodded, staring up at him, her lips swollen and shiny.

"Say it."

"I'm yours." Her whisper was barely audible, but it satisfied his craving for now.

Leaning down, he kissed her again, more gently this time, even as he began thrusting with a smooth, steady tempo. His balls drew up against his body as pure, unadulterated pleasure coursed through his veins, all courtesy of the small girl in his arms. Closing his eyes, Korum let the sensations wash over him, reveling in her taste, in the feel of her soft skin under his fingers . . . in the tight clasp of her body around his cock.

And just when the pleasure became too intense, he felt her convulse around him with a soft cry, sending him over the edge.

* * *

A few hours later, Korum woke up to the familiar feel of Mia lying pressed against his side. Her breathing was quiet and even, and he knew she was deeply asleep, worn out by his sexual demands. He'd managed to abstain from drinking her blood this time, since he'd indulged fairly recently, but he hadn't been able to stop himself from taking her a couple more times throughout the night.

Sometimes he wondered if it was normal, the way he craved her all the time. He'd always had a strong sexual drive, but he'd never felt the urge to have one woman over and over again. With Mia, he simply couldn't get enough, and he wasn't sure he liked being so dependent on one tiny human girl.

In general, his obsession with her bothered him on multiple levels. As happy as she made him, the depth of his feelings for her was unsettling. If he ever lost her . . . Korum couldn't bear to even think of that possibility, his chest squeezing in agony at the idea.

Slowly disengaging from her, Korum got up, trying to be as quiet as possible to avoid waking her up. She needed far more sleep than a Krinar, and he always made sure she got enough rest. Even with the nanocytes in her body, she was still far too fragile and vulnerable for his peace of mind. If he had his way, she would never go anywhere alone, always staying safely by his side.

But Korum knew she would hate it if he restricted her independence too much. As it was, she resented the few safety measures he'd implemented. She viewed the tracking devices as a way to control her, as an invasion of her privacy, not understanding how important her safety and well-being were to him.

It was already five in the morning—a late start to the day for Korum. Normally, he would already be working at this time, but he hadn't gone to sleep until three hours ago, staying up late to satisfy his hunger for Mia. He needed her even more than usual, feeling edgy and restless in anticipation of the upcoming fight.

He wasn't afraid. In fact, the prospect of danger excited him. It had always been this way; in his youth, he'd even provoked a couple of fights just to feel that rush of adrenaline. As he got older, however, he'd learned to suppress that part of his nature, to use sports as an outlet for excess energy. As a result, he hadn't been in a real fight—with the exception of Saur's attack in Florida—for a solid eighty years.

He did worry about having Mia at the Arena, though. The venue would be crowded, with almost every Krinar on Earth attending the event in person. Those on Krina would watch virtually. The idea of having her out in public after everything that happened made him uneasy, even though he knew there was little real danger. The fight was to be in Lenkarda, while Saret was somewhere out in the human world.

Still, Korum would've kept her away if it weren't for the fact that doing so would be the equivalent of insulting her in public. Arena fights were considered to be one of the most important and interesting parts of Krinar life, and everyone—charl included—was expected to be there. Deliberately excluding Mia would make it seem like Korum was punishing her for something—which couldn't be further from the truth.

Thinking about it further, Korum decided to have two guardians watching Mia at all times. He would also arrange to have her sitting next to Delia, just in case his charl needed reassurance from an older, more experienced friend. That way, he wouldn't have to worry about her during the fight—and thus be able to fully concentrate on his opponent. Even a moment of inattention in the Arena could be deadly.

In the meantime, he had a few hours before the main event. The best thing to do at this point was to catch up with his designers and make sure that they were working on the prototype of the shielding technology he'd recently developed. Voret and the rest of the Council were understandably worried about utilizing the old shields now, so that project had to take priority.

Casting one last look at his sleeping charl, Korum left the house.

CHAPTER FOURTEEN

Mia waited for Delia to pick her up, her foot tapping nervously on the floor. She was almost sick with anxiety in anticipation of the fight, and she was glad the other charl was going to be with her during the event.

To distract herself, Mia took a deep breath and looked down at the gleaming material of her white dress. Korum had left it for her this morning, and she'd figured she was supposed to wear it to the event. Unlike the usual light and flowing Krinar clothing, her outfit today was made of some stiff, relatively thick cloth and fit her body closely. It had a subtle shine to it, as did her sandals today. Korum had also given her a beautiful necklace to put around her neck. If Mia didn't know better, she would've thought she was getting dressed up for her own wedding.

She hadn't seen Korum this morning, although he'd called and promised to meet her in the Arena before the fight officially began. When they'd spoken, she could hear a note of barely suppressed excitement in his voice, and she knew he was looking forward to this barbaric ritual.

It still struck her as odd that she felt so attuned to him after just a couple of days. She could sense his moods, discern his emotions. She could even predict some of his reactions. When he'd come home last night, she'd known exactly what would happen when she wrapped her arms around his neck and transformed an innocent kiss into something more. As much as she had enjoyed their first night together, it had been obvious to her that Korum was holding himself back, that he was trying to make allowances for her 'inexperience.' And, while she had appreciated his restraint, it somehow wasn't enough. Last night, she hadn't wanted sweet and gentle; she'd wanted him wild and out-of-control, his true nature fully revealed.

His possessiveness both scared and thrilled her. If she didn't want him so much, she would've been frightened by his passion, by his insistence on her giving him every part of herself. It made her wonder what would happen if she ever tried to leave him. Would he let her go, or would he stop her from going home? Could he stop her? If Delia were to be believed, humans had very few rights inside Krinar settlements—an idea that bothered Mia quite a bit.

Of course, none of that mattered right now, in light of the upcoming fight. Looking impatiently at her wristwatch-bracelet device, Mia saw that it was already twenty minutes before noon. *Where was Delia?* The wait was heightening Mia's anxiety.

Two minutes later, she finally saw a small transport pod landing outside, next to the house. Delia came out of the aircraft and waved to her. Relieved, Mia smiled, glad to see the other girl. Arus's charl was wearing a dress that was similar to Mia's, and she looked stunning, her dark hair smooth and threaded with some strange-looking jewelry.

Quickly exiting the house, Mia approached the Greek girl. "Thanks for picking me up," she said as she got closer.

"Of course," Delia said. "I would've done it even if Korum hadn't asked. You must be so frightened right now."

"I'm beyond frightened," Mia admitted. "I feel like I could puke when I think about it."

Delia smiled. "I can see that. Here, come inside, and we'll head over there."

"Has Arus ever been in one of these fights?" Mia asked, following her into the aircraft and taking a seat on one of the floating chairs inside.

"A few times," Delia replied, giving her an understanding look. "And every time I thought I'd have a heart attack. Believe me, I know exactly what you're going through."

"It was probably worse for you," Mia said. "At least I've only known Korum for a couple of days." Although it might as well have been a couple of years, given the nearly paralyzing fear she was feeling at the thought of losing him.

Taking a deep breath, Mia tried to calm herself by studying her surroundings. After all, she had never been in an alien aircraft before— or, at least, didn't remember the experience. To her surprise, she could see that the inside of the pod resembled the interior of Korum's house to a large degree, with light colors, transparent walls, and floating seats. There was no obvious 'technology,' as she was used to seeing it in the human world. Instead, everything seemed to work effortlessly, almost like magic.

As the aircraft took off, Mia could see the green forest through the transparent floor. In the distance, the blue waters of the Pacific Ocean sparkled in the bright sun. It was a beautiful day, and, under any other circumstances, Mia would've greatly enjoyed the ride. As it was, she couldn't stop thinking about what was to come.

Another question occurred to her, and she looked up, meeting Delia's gaze. "How long do these fights tend to last?" Mia asked, her imagination conjuring up a horrifying day-long bloody ordeal.

"Anywhere from a few minutes to a couple of hours," the Greek girl said. "It really depends on how evenly the opponents are matched. There's also a short ceremony before, and a longer one after, during which the winner celebrates."

"Celebrates how?"

Delia smiled, and there was a mischievous twinkle in her brown eyes. "Well, an unattached male will often choose one or more unattached females, and they will couple in a *shatela*—a tent-like structure in the middle of the Arena. Attached men will usually do the same with their mate."

Sex in public? Was Delia serious? Mia could feel furious color flooding her face. "And those with charl?"

Delia laughed. "That depends. Arus is very considerate when it comes to my human sensibilities, and he would usually just kiss me in the Arena and wait until we got home to celebrate properly. Others have been known to treat their charl just like Krinar women in this situation."

"So you're saying that if Korum wins, he might want to have sex in front of everyone?"

"Perhaps," Delia said, grinning. "Nobody will really see you, though, since you'll be inside the shatela. They might only hear you."

"Oh great. That makes it so much better," Mia muttered. She remembered what Korum had told her about the Celebration of Forty-Seven, and how she had been glad that, as a human, she wouldn't be expected to participate in the exhibitionist spectacle. But now it seemed like there was no getting away from it—unless Korum 'respected her human sensibilities.' Just one more thing for her to worry about during the fight.

Before she had a chance to think about this further, the transport pod landed quietly in a wooded area.

"We're here," Delia said, getting up.

Mia got up as well and followed her out of the aircraft. It looked like they were in the middle of the forest. "Where is here?"

Delia turned toward her, and Mia was shocked to see an excited gleam in her eyes. "The Arena," she said and gestured toward a tree-covered hill in front of them.

Mia raised her eyebrows but didn't say anything as they walked toward the elevation. She could hear a dull roar in the distance, like a massive waterfall of some kind. Was the Arena near a river? Carefully stepping forward, she concentrated on avoiding bugs or whatever else could be crawling in a Costa Rican jungle. Her thin-soled sandals were not exactly hiking-friendly, and Mia sincerely hoped she wouldn't get stung or bitten before they got to the fight. If she recalled correctly, tarantulas were one of the hazards of this part of the world—although she was now supposedly immune to such dangers, with the nanocytes circulating throughout her body and quickly repairing any cellular damage.

As they got further up the hill, Mia realized that the sound she was hearing was the muted buzz of a crowd. Somewhere nearby, thousands of Ks were gathered to watch the fight. Apparently eager to join them, Delia ran up the rest of the hill, moving with almost Krinar-like grace herself. "Here it is," she said, turning toward Mia and pointing straight ahead.

Her heart pounding and her palms sweating, Mia hurried to catch up with the other charl. When she reached the top of the hill, she stopped dead in her tracks.

The green valley below was a spectacle unlike any other she had ever seen in her life. Thousands—no, tens of thousands—of Krinar were gathered below. Tall and golden-skinned, the aliens were dressed in blindingly white clothing that shimmered in the sunlight. While the majority mingled on the ground, a number of them occupied floating seats that were arranged in circles around a large clearing. It was like a round football field, only with the spectators floating in the air instead of sitting in the bleachers—or like a high-tech version of an ancient Roman amphitheater. The latter was probably a better comparison, Mia thought, given what was about to take place.

"Mia! There you are!"

Turning to her right, Mia saw Korum approaching them. Unlike everybody else, he was dressed in his usual clothes—a light-colored shirt and pair of shorts. Coming closer, he pulled her to him for a quick hug and kissed her forehead. "How are you, my sweet?" he asked, looking down at her with a warm smile.

Mia could feel her heart beating faster at his nearness. "I'm good. Are you ready for the fight?"

"Of course." He stroked her cheek with his fingers, then turned toward Delia. "Thanks for bringing Mia here," he said, giving the other girl a smile. His left arm was still wrapped around Mia, holding her pressed tightly against his side.

"It was my pleasure," Delia said, giving Korum a regal nod. "I'll let you two catch up. Mia, when you're done, please come join me. We're sitting over there." She pointed toward a row of floating seats that were closest to the clearing.

"I'll bring her there in a minute," Korum promised, looking faintly amused at the other girl's imperious manner.

As soon as Delia disappeared into the crowd, he bent his head and brought Mia up for a more thorough kiss, one of his large hands cupping her skull and the other holding her lower body pressed against his. She could feel the hardness of his erection pushing against her belly, the strength of his arms surrounding her, and heat flooded her body, culminating in the sensitive area between her legs. His lips and tongue teased and caressed her mouth, pleasuring her, consuming her, until she forgot all about the crowds around them, caught up in a sensual daze.

When he finally let her come up for air, she was desperately clinging to him, heedless of their public location.

"Fuck," he cursed in a rough whisper, lifting his head and staring down at her with bright golden eyes, "I can't wait for this fight to be over. You drive me insane sometimes, you know that?"

Mia licked her lips, tasting him there. She was so aroused she could barely stand it, her hips moving involuntarily, trying to rub against him. Yet something nagged at the back of her mind, breaking through the fog of desire clouding her brain.

She pushed at his chest, trying to put some distance between them so she could think. "Delia said . . ." Mia hesitated, not knowing how to phrase it. "Delia said the victor celebrates by, um . . ."

"By fucking?" Korum asked, his eyes still filled with a golden glow. "Is that what she told you?"

Mia nodded, her cheeks burning.

Korum took a small step back, but still held her close. "It's true," he said, his voice low and husky. "If I win, I would be expected to celebrate that way. Would it be a problem?"

Mia stared up at him. "You mean . . . You'd want to do it in public?"

"It's not exactly public, my sweet," he said, one corner of his mouth tilting up. "We'd be in a shatela—a structure specifically designed for that purpose. But yes, I would very much like to fuck you after the fight. Your sweet body would be my reward."

* * *

Korum could see her pupils expanding, making her blue eyes look darker. Her breathing was uneven, and her cheeks were a pretty pink color. She was turned on, almost as much as he was right now. If this was already after the fight, he was sure she wouldn't protest if he brought her to a shatela, stripped off that tight dress, and plunged his cock between her thighs. He liked the idea of claiming her in front of everyone; it appealed to something primeval deep within him.

"Korum, I—"

"Shhh," he said, lifting his finger to her lips in a gesture he'd seen humans make. "Don't worry about it now. I won't force you to do anything you don't want to do."

And Korum meant it. He had not set out to prove anything when he kissed Mia, but her reaction clearly demonstrated her susceptibility to him. Despite the memory loss, she was as strongly attracted to him as before—a realization that filled him with bone-deep masculine satisfaction. He would never force her, but he also likely wouldn't have to. He suspected his little charl was more adventurous than she thought herself to be.

She was still watching him warily, so he bent his head and kissed her delicious mouth again. Just a brief kiss this time, no more than a brush of his lips against her own. His body screamed for him to do more, to take her now, but there was no time. He had to go get ready for the fight.

But even a small kiss was enough to distract her right now. Her eyes looked soft again, hazy with desire. Korum had to force himself to look away in order to regain control.

"Come," he said hoarsely, "let's get you to your seat. I have to go now, but I want to make sure you're settled with Delia before I leave."

"Of course." She seemed anxious again, some of the color leaving her face. "Is it starting at noon sharp?"

"Yes," Korum said, taking her hand and starting to lead her through the crowd. "We tend to be punctual, so we have exactly ten minutes before the ceremony begins."

They walked toward the front row, where Delia and Arus were already in place. Only one float next to Delia remained empty, and Korum led

Mia there. As they approached, the crowd parted, letting them through. His acquaintances gave him polite nods as they passed, while others stared at him and his charl with unabashed curiosity. This didn't bother Korum one bit. As a Council member with a certain reputation, he was used to this type of attention. Mia was a figure of interest as well, given rumors of her involvement with the Resistance. The Krinar did not consider staring rude; on the contrary, it was a sign of respect to look at someone directly.

"Oh, good," Delia said as they got to her seat. "I was worried you wouldn't make it before the start of the fight."

"No worries, we're here," Mia said, blushing a little. Korum suppressed a smile, knowing she was embarrassed about their public make-out session. His little darling was still such an innocent; he enjoyed her shyness almost as much as he liked curing her of it.

Arus gave Korum a level look. "We'll take good care of Mia, I promise. You don't need to worry about her right now."

"Thanks," Korum said, glad that the other Councilor understood his unspoken concern. Even knowing that it was safe, he still felt uncomfortable leaving Mia alone in public. What happened with Saret had left an indelible impression in his mind, and he knew he would have to work hard to overcome his fear of losing her.

All around them, other Krinar settled in their floats, clearing out of the aisles and emptying the Arena field. Less than five minutes remained before the start of the ceremony, and Korum still had to prepare, mentally and physically, for what was to come.

"I have to go," he said reluctantly, watching Mia's eyes fill with moisture at his words.

"Be careful," she whispered, looking up at him. "Please, Korum, be careful." And wrapping her arms around his waist, she gave him a fierce hug, holding him for several long seconds.

Touched, Korum hugged her back and then gently stepped out of her embrace. "I love you," he said, giving her one last smile.

"And I love you," Mia whispered as he started to walk away.

Korum stopped in his tracks, hardly daring to believe his ears. Turning his head, he saw that her eyes were glistening with unshed tears. He wanted to grab her, to ask her if she really meant it, but there was no time. Instead, he gave her the biggest smile he could and continued on toward a small structure on the far side of the Arena.

The ceremony was about to begin.

* * *

Mia sat down on her floating seat, feeling like a vise was squeezing her heart. Despite all of Korum's reassurances, she knew there was a very real chance that she was seeing him for the last time.

The thought was so agonizing that Mia couldn't breathe for a moment.

"Mia? Listen to me, Mia. He's going to be fine, okay?" It was Delia, her voice calm and soothing.

Mia blinked, focusing on the other charl with effort. "I know," she said with a confidence she didn't feel. "Of course, I know that."

The Krinar male who was with Delia gave her a reassuring smile too. "She's right, Mia," he said in a deep, quiet voice. "Your cheren is very good at this. He's never lost a fight yet. I'm Arus, by the way. We've never met in person before."

"Oh, hi," Mia said, automatically offering her hand for a handshake. "It's nice to meet you."

Arus's smile got wider. "No handshake allowed, I'm afraid," he said gently. "I wouldn't want to end up on that field facing Korum next."

"Oh, right." Mia withdrew her hand, mildly embarrassed. "I'm sorry; I forgot. Korum did tell me a little bit about your customs yesterday."

"You have nothing to be sorry about," Delia said. "I'm very impressed by how quickly you're re-learning everything. It took me a long time to get as comfortable as you seem to be right now."

"Yeah, I don't know why that is," Mia admitted. "Maybe I'm remembering things on a subconscious level."

"You also seem to have strong feelings for Korum already," Arus observed, his dark eyes filled with speculation as he looked at Mia. "More than could be expected in this situation. I wonder why. I'm not a mind expert, but this seems fairly unusual."

"Really?" Mia frowned in puzzlement. "I thought maybe a memory erasure procedure doesn't get rid of memories completely—"

"It's supposed to," Arus said. "If it's a standard memory wipe, then you should be as you were a few months ago: with zero knowledge of our world or Korum. The fact that you're adjusting so quickly is . . . interesting, to say the least."

Mia looked at him, wondering what it all meant. Ever since she woke up in Lenkarda, her feelings and reactions have been strange. Was it possible that Saret had screwed up and didn't succeed in erasing her memories fully after all?

A loud chime-like sound startled Mia out of her speculations.

The pre-fight ceremony was beginning.

A tall Krinar male dressed in an unusual blue outfit stepped out of one of the small structures on the edges of the Arena and walked toward the middle of the field.

"That's Voret," Delia whispered, leaning toward Mia for a second. "He's one of the oldest Council members."

Mia nodded, her eyes glued to what was happening below.

"Residents of Earth and those watching us on Krina right now," Voret said, his deep voice filling the entire amphitheater, "welcome to the ancient rite of the Arena Challenge. As all of you know, the fight today is between two of our esteemed Council members: Loris and Korum. The cause of this Challenge, like all others, is a disagreement that can only be settled in blood."

Voret raised his arm and blue light seemed to flow from his fingertips, becoming a giant three-dimensional image floating in mid-air. It showed a strange forest, with green, yellow, red, and orange plants. "For generations, we have gathered in the Arena to witness the resolution of such a disagreement. It all began after the Great War, when we nearly tore each other apart after the demise of the *lonar*—our source of life-giving blood. Violence was a way of life then—and it would still be today if not for the Arena Challenge."

The floating image began to change, as though a camera was zooming in on a particular portion of that alien forest. Mia stared in fascination as the image showed a Krinar male, dressed in some brown-colored scraps of material, leaping through the trees with a speed that would make Tarzan jealous. Below him, small humanoid creatures were scurrying on the ground, their bodies covered with light blond hair and nothing else. These had to be the lonar, Mia realized, seeing the predatory look on the Krinar male's face as he stalked them from above. He wasn't as beautiful as the modern Ks; his features were rougher, less symmetric, though he still had the typical K coloring of dark hair and golden skin.

"We have evolved as hunters. Predators." Voret's voice echoed throughout the Arena. "We need violence. We crave it. For a peaceful society to function, we need an outlet—a way to resolve disagreements that would otherwise lead to conflict and war. The Arena is that outlet."

The Krinar in the image leapt from the trees above, jumping down on the ground in front of the hapless lonar. They screamed in fear, their cries oddly monkey-like, and turned to run, but it was too late. One of them—a female—was already caught in the K's steely embrace, and he was slicing his sharp teeth over her neck. Bright red blood trickled down her neck and chest, its color startling against the primate's light-colored fur.

"The extinction of the lonar nearly destroyed us. The fact that we survived is a testament to the heroic efforts of those scientists who came up with a blood substitute in the middle of war and chaos."

The image changed now, no longer showing the forest or the Krinar feeding on the helpless female. Instead, three strong-featured male Ks were displayed, their harsh faces more similar to the ancient hunter's than to the gorgeous Krinar surrounding Mia.

"In the Arena, we honor all those who came before us—and all those who will come after. With this rite of violence, we honor peace—and the laws that make it possible."

Now the floating image was showing the same colorful forest as before—only this time it was populated by the pale oblong structures that served as modern Krinar dwellings. A couple was strolling through the woods, a K male and female, wearing the light-colored clothing Mia was used to seeing. They looked beautiful and happy, walking together while holding hands. The image lingered for a few seconds, then winked out of existence, leaving only Voret standing in the middle of the Arena.

He remained quiet for a second, and then his voice boomed again. "Now it is time for the fighters to join me. Loris and Korum, please enter the Arena."

Mia held her breath as the two Ks emerged, Korum from a structure to the right of Mia and Loris from a structure to the left. Instead of the usual Krinar attire—or the formal white clothing of the spectators—they each wore a pair of calf-length pants that were the color of fresh blood. Their feet and chests were bare, except for swirls of red paint that decorated their arms and torsos.

Swallowing to moisten her dry throat, Mia stared at her lover in fascination. He looked gorgeous—and utterly savage. Sitting in the front row, she could see the yellow-gold color of his eyes, light and striking against the bronze hue of his skin. His semi-nakedness only accentuated the power of his body; his muscles flexed and rippled as he walked, his posture graceful and threatening at the same time.

The other Krinar was an inch or two taller, with a slightly bulkier build. The expression on his hawk-like features was dark and full of hatred.

The two fighters approached the blue-clad figure in the middle of the Arena, pausing respectfully a couple of feet away. Voret turned toward Loris and addressed him, "Loris, you have chosen to challenge Korum today. Is that true?"

"Yes," the Krinar said, his eyes glittering with the same dark anticipation Mia could see on Korum's face.

Voret nodded, apparently satisfied. Turning to Korum, he asked, "Do you accept Loris's challenge?"

"I do," Korum replied.

"Then let the fight begin."

CHAPTER FIFTEEN

Korum watched as Voret lifted his arms—a signal to begin. At the same time, the float that was underneath Voret's feet activated, lifting the Councilor into the air high above the Arena. It was the only way the Mediator—a role filled by Voret today—could stay safe during the fight.

His eyes glued to his opponent, Korum slowly began circling Loris, looking for the best opportunity to strike. He could feel his heart beating harder, the blood circulating faster through his veins. His mind was clear and razor-sharp, focused entirely on his enemy. It was always that way for him in the Arena; the adrenaline boosted Korum's concentration, enhanced his reflexes. Somewhere in the back of his mind, he was aware that Mia was watching him right now. He could feel her gaze on his skin, and it gave him even more of a rush than the upcoming fight itself.

Loris responded by moving in a slow circle as well, his dark eyes burning with hatred. Korum gave him a taunting smile, wanting to enrage him further. It was one of the most basic principles of defrebs: the fighter who keeps a cool head wins. When Loris had attacked him in the Council meeting chamber, it had been laughably easy for Korum to subdue him—partially because the Protector had been completely out of control.

A smile: such a simple thing, but it worked. Loris's jaw tightened, the muscle near his ear twitching. And then he struck, his right arm lashing out, his fingers hooked into a deadly weapon.

Korum avoided Loris's strike with ease, his body twisting at the last moment. At the same time, his foot kicked out, hitting Loris's knee with so much force that Korum could hear the other man's joint snapping in half.

Loris screamed in pain, stumbling back, and Korum leapt on top of him, using the momentum from his jump to bring the Protector to the ground. Up-close combat was dangerous, but less so now that his opponent was partially—albeit temporarily—crippled. His fist smashed into Loris face, once, then again and again, each movement lightning-fast. At the same time, Korum's knee slammed into Loris's side, bruising his internal organs.

This was not going to be a long fight.

In fact, subduing the Protector was so easy that Korum should be able to avoid killing him altogether.

* * *

Two rows away from Mia, Saret waited for the perfect moment to strike, all of his attention focused on the combatants. It was risky to be so close to the stage, but it maximized his odds of success—and put him within grabbing distance of Mia, if the opportunity presented itself.

Of course, when he'd chosen this location, he didn't know Korum's charl would be so heavily guarded. Not only was she sitting next to Arus, but there were also at least two guardians watching her. Saret had spotted them earlier. They tried to blend with the crowd, but their sharp gazes betrayed their true purpose: they were there to protect Mia.

Saret wondered if Korum suspected anything, or if he was just being paranoid about his charl's safety. Either way, it looked like Mia was out of Saret's reach for now—at least while Korum was alive. Once his enemy was out of the way, however, it would be a different matter. Unless another influential Krinar took Mia as his charl, she would be brought to Krina, where Saret would be able to claim her under his other identity.

Saret's interest in different identities had started several centuries ago, long before he had begun developing his plans for humans. He had been put in charge of rehabilitating a criminal who was a master of disguises, pretending to be three people at once, complete with different physical appearances, legal documents, and established lives. Saret had been so fascinated that he'd spent countless hours learning all about the man's craft. The criminal had been more than happy to tell him everything he knew in exchange for a milder version of rehabilitation than the one he'd been sentenced to.

Saret's second identity had started off as a joke, as a way to see if he could get away with something like that in their technologically advanced society. And, to his surprise, he'd discovered that he could; all it took was the right tools, knowledge of several government databases, and a couple of centuries to create a convincing new persona.

Saret—the mind expert—was now considered a criminal. Juron, however, was a law-abiding citizen of Krina who was currently doing some individual space exploration in the Krinar solar system. It would be Juron who claimed Mia as his charl next.

All Saret needed was to kill Korum right now, and at least that part of his plan would be successful. Then he could try to bring peace to Earth again.

His current disguise was yet another identity he had started to develop here on Earth. It was not as airtight as that of Juron, but it was good enough to get him past all the security and into Lenkarda for the fight. No one suspected right now that the man sitting so close to the stage was the most wanted Krinar in the universe.

Saret glanced at Mia again, then looked away. It wouldn't do to stare at her openly, even though many others were doing the same thing. She was oblivious to everything, all of her attention focused on the fight. Saret cursed under his breath. It seemed like his little experiment had backfired in a major way, and she was growing attached to that bastard again.

That was really unfortunate. Now she would be more than a little upset when he died.

Slowly raising his hand, Saret aimed at the stage and waited for the perfect moment. When Korum jumped at Loris, Saret knew the time had come.

Taking a deep breath, he activated the weapon.

* * *

Korum raised his fist to deliver another blow, and in that moment his arm froze.

A wave of pain traveled down his body, starting at the back of his neck. His limbs felt uncontrollably heavy, his muscles shaking with the effort of holding himself up.

A basic stun weapon. Korum knew it with sudden certainty. The guardians' scanners were designed to catch anything dangerous, but this kind of stunner used an older, simpler technology—one that was much more difficult to detect from a distance.

Reflexively clutching the back of his neck, Korum felt himself sliding off Loris's body. His back hit the ground, leaving him lying there helpless, unable to move for a few precious seconds. To the spectators, it would look like Loris had delivered him a hidden blow of some kind; the stunner possibility would not occur to anyone right away.

Despite the danger—or maybe because of it—Korum's mind operated with crystal clarity, analyzing the situation in an instant. There was only one person motivated enough to risk doing something like that.

Saret. He was here at the fight.

The hit had been to the back of Korum's neck. He knew what a basic stunner felt like, had experienced its sting before. Just like a human gun, it was a weapon that had to be aimed from a specific location.

A location that could be triangulated.

Ignoring the pain and weakness racking his body, Korum sent a mental query to his internal computer . . . and then he knew.

His enemy was only steps away from Mia.

Fear, sharp and gut-wrenching, slithered through Korum's veins, followed by a rage so intense his entire body shook with it.

He couldn't save himself right now, but he'd be damned if he failed to protect Mia again.

Closing his eyes, Korum focused on connecting to the guardians' private communication network.

* * *

Mia stifled a scream as she saw Korum jerk convulsively and then slide off Loris's body. Up until now, he had seemed invincible, utterly in control of the situation. She had even begun to relax, some of her fear ebbing as she'd witnessed her lover's effortless display of skill in the Arena.

Until everything changed in an instant.

What happened? She could see Korum clutching the back of his neck as if something bit him there. He seemed dazed, weakened by something.

What the fuck happened?

She could see Loris rising to his feet. He was already moving better, his Krinar body recovering from the injuries Korum had inflicted on him.

And Korum was still lying there, like he couldn't move. Even his eyes were closed, preventing him from seeing his opponent.

"No!" Mia heard her own scream echoing through the Arena. Delia grabbed her arm, keeping her from jumping from her seat as Loris attacked Korum's prone body.

She could see the glee on the other K's face as he struck again and again, could smell the metallic odor of blood that turned their painted bodies a brighter red.

It was Korum's blood.

"No!" Another agonized scream tore from her throat. Now there was a sickening sound of fist connecting with flesh, over and over again. "No, stop!" Mia wrenched her arm out of Delia's hold and jumped to her feet.

"Mia, don't! You can't interfere—" The Greek girl tried to grab her again, but Mia shook her off like a fly, desperate to get into the arena.

She managed to take two steps before a steely arm went around her waist, pressing her against a hard male body. Mia clawed at that imprisoning arm, heedless of all but the slaughter happening in front of her eyes. "Stop the fight! It's a setup! Can't you see? He can't fight! It's a setup!" The arm only tightened further. "Let me go! Let me fucking go!"

Mia was vaguely aware that she was screaming like a banshee, yelling out anything that came to mind, but it didn't matter. Arus was holding her now, and she was furiously fighting him, trying to twist out of his grasp. It was impossible to win against a Krinar, but it didn't matter.

Mia was past any semblance of rationality.

* * *

Korum could feel the blows from Loris's fist, his body shuddering in agony as the Protector's claw-like fingers gouged out chunks of his flesh.

Emboldened by Korum's apparent weakness, his enemy was taking his time torturing him before inflicting the killing blow. The pain was shocking, nauseating, but Korum fought the darkness that threatened to pull him under, knowing that all would then be lost. He was vaguely aware that his kidneys and spleen were damaged, that his ribs were crushed and his left collarbone broken, but it didn't matter because he could feel the effect of the stun shot starting to wear off.

In the background, he could hear Mia screaming and crying, the pain in her voice ripping at his heart. With each second that passed, the debilitating weakness that rendered him so helpless was dissipating, his body beginning to function with a semblance of normality.

He needed to survive a little longer. Just a little more, and he might stand a chance, instead of lying there like a piece of meat.

For now, though, he was still far too weak. To fight back at this point would be deadly. Loris was playing with him, putting on a show, trying to regain his standing through this display of his fighting prowess—but at any sign of renewed resistance from Korum, he would go straight for Korum's throat.

So Korum let the blows rain down on him, not even groaning when Loris kicked him over and over again. He ignored the pain of bones breaking and tendons ripping apart, concentrating only on remaining conscious.

And when Loris finally reached for his throat, Korum gathered every bit of strength in his damaged and torn body . . . and let his rage boil over.

His left arm—the only limb that remained semi-functional—hooked around Loris's throat with a deadly grip, pulling the Protector close. And before his opponent could react, Korum's teeth were sinking deep into his flesh, biting through his spinal column and severing the connection to the brain.

Blood spurted everywhere: in Korum's eyes, his hair, his mouth . . . He was covered with blood, the taste and smell of it consuming him, adding to the black fury surging through his veins. He was no longer thinking or reasoning; he was bloodlust incarnate, craving more and more. His teeth sank into Loris's throat again, ripping at it, tearing it apart, until there was nothing left.

CHAPTER SIXTEEN

Saret watched in shock and furious disbelief as Loris's severed head rolled down the field. The Councilor's dark eyes were open and unseeing, his mouth slack and covered with blood.

All around him, the crowd was going wild. People were on their floats, in the aisles, screaming and stomping their feet. Korum's name was being chanted over and over again, making Saret feel sick to his stomach.

He had to get out of there. Now, before it was too late. He could analyze his failure later; all that mattered at this point was getting away.

Rising from his seat, he joined the screaming spectators in the aisle. Out of the corner of his eye, he could see Mia struggling against Arus, trying to get to her lover. Saret desperately wished he could grab her and take her with him, but she was too well-protected here. He would have to come back for her again.

Pushing through the crowds, Saret slowly made his way toward the exit, doing his best not to draw undue attention to himself. He was almost there when he felt a sudden zapping sensation through his entire body.

Stunned and helpless, he collapsed on the floor, barely cognizant of the guardians surrounding him.

* * *

Korum didn't know how long he remained in that mindless state of rage. It could've been minutes or hours. By the time he came back to his senses, Loris's head was lying several meters away from his body, his eyes vacant and his neck looking like it had been savaged by a wild animal.

Dead. His opponent was dead.

Korum's own body was in agony, and he could feel the darkness trying to overtake him again. Only the knowledge that there was still something he needed to do kept him from the sweetness of oblivion.

His greatest enemy was not the one lying on the field; he was the one hiding among the spectators—and Mia was still in danger.

Groaning in pain, Korum managed to get up on his hands and knees, his muscles shaking from the effort. He was dimly aware that the crowd was cheering for him, that Voret was formally announcing him as the winner.

None of that mattered to him now. All he cared about was Mia, and getting to her before Saret did. Korum's body was healing, but not fast enough, and he cursed himself as his shattered femur refused to hold his weight, his leg collapsing beneath him as he tried to get to his feet.

"We got him. It's all right; she's safe." Strong hands were suddenly holding him up, helping him get to his feet. It was Alir—the leader of the guardians.

Korum's head spun, and his stomach churned with nausea as his damaged body protested the new vertical position. "Where is he?" he managed to say, his voice hoarse and ragged.

"There." Alir pointed near the exit with his left hand while providing support for Korum with his right.

Korum squinted in that direction, the sun blinding him for a moment. When his vision cleared, he saw an unfamiliar Krinar being collared by three guardians. The man's features were completely different from Saret's, his eyes larger and his chin more prominent.

"He's got a very good disguise," Alir said, understanding Korum's unspoken question. "Even the outer layer of DNA is different, which is how we didn't detect his presence before. But the shooter's coordinates you sent us matched this man's location perfectly, and an internal DNA sample showed that it is indeed Saret."

Intense relief mixed with bitter regret, leaving Korum conflicted about this turn of events. He had wanted to be the one to catch Saret, to punish him for what he'd done to Mia. But instead, his former friend was now in the hands of the Krinar law keepers. No matter how badly Korum wanted to kill him, Saret would now live to stand trial.

"Korum!" Mia's voice reached his ears, jerking him out of his dark thoughts. Looking up, he saw her slight figure running down the field, her dark hair flying behind her. The happiness that filled him at the sight was so acute that he forgot all about Saret and his betrayal, focusing only on the girl he loved.

Then she was next to him, and he could see that she was pale and shaking, her dress torn in one spot. Her beautiful face was wet with tears. One pale arm lifted toward him, her hand trembling as though she wasn't certain if she could touch him. "You're alive," she whispered, and he could hear the disbelieving note in her voice. "Oh my God, Korum, you're alive . . ."

And Korum realized exactly what she was seeing. He was covered with blood, both his own and that of Loris. He could taste its metallic tang on his tongue, smell it surrounding him, and he knew it was all over his hair, his face, his mouth.

Fuck. He must look like something out of a nightmare, especially with the rapidly healing parts of his body where Loris had torn out chunks of his flesh.

Remembering her reaction to Saur's remains on the beach, Korum mentally cursed himself for letting Mia see him like this. He had been hoping to avoid killing Loris partially for this reason—because he didn't want his little human traumatized by seeing her lover brutally kill someone. This should've been an easy fight, one during which Korum could've restrained himself, kept from giving in to the primitive instincts of his species. If it hadn't been for Saret's interference, Korum could've easily subdued his opponent, defeating him but graciously letting him live. And instead, he had been utterly savage, like a cornered animal.

His legs were already feeling better, so Korum shrugged off Alir's support and carefully reached for Mia, bringing her toward him. He knew there was a chance he might repulse her now, but he needed her. Needed to feel her softness, to inhale her clean, sweet scent.

To his surprise, she wrapped her arms around him, holding him so tightly that it hurt his half-healed ribs. She was shaking, her slender body trembling in his embrace.

"It's all right, my sweet," he murmured, some of his tension draining as he realized she was not afraid to touch him. "It's going to be all right . . ."

"I thought—" With her face buried against his shoulder, Mia's voice was barely audible. Her hands were icy on the bare skin of his back. "I thought he killed you . . . Oh God, Korum, I thought you were dead—"

"No," he soothed, reveling in her apparent concern for him. "No, my darling, he didn't. It's over now—"

A sob broke out of her throat. "He hurt you. I saw him hurting you, again and again. Korum, he was killing you—"

"It's okay, I'm all right," Korum whispered, his heart aching at the horror in her voice. "Everything's going to be fine. I'm sorry you had to see that. It wasn't supposed to be like that, believe me . . ."

She drew in a shuddering breath and pulled back to look up at him. Her eyes were reddened, her lashes dark and spiky from tears. "What happened? I saw you fall and then it was like you couldn't fight anymore. Did Loris cheat somehow? Did he do something to you?"

"It wasn't Loris," Korum explained, trying to keep the fury out of his voice. "It was Saret. He was in the audience, just a few seats away from you. He shot me with a stunner—a weapon similar to a stun gun—so I couldn't move for a bit."

She gasped. "He tried to kill you? Is that what the commotion over there was about? I wasn't paying attention—"

"Yes," Korum said. "I sent the guardians after him as soon as I realized what was happening."

"You sent the guardians? How?"

"Remember I told you I have an embedded computer?" Korum asked.

Mia nodded, staring at him. She still looked pale, even though the tremors wracking her frame were beginning to subside.

"I was able to use it to contact the guardians."

She blinked, and he could see that she wasn't absorbing what he was saying, her mind still consumed by what had just happened.

Alir stepped in front of him, making Korum aware of his presence again. "The victory ceremony is about to start," the guardian said quietly. "Are you able to participate?"

Korum considered it for a moment, holding Mia against his side, then gave Alir a short nod. "I should be fine." He was still in pain, but it was a healing kind of pain. His body was repairing itself from the inside, the cells regenerating themselves. In another few minutes, he would be almost back to normal.

Of course, given everything that happened, a regular ceremony with a public claiming of his charl was out of the question. Even though his recovering body was beginning to stir at her nearness, Korum was fully cognizant of his current appearance. He was dirty, sweaty, and covered in blood—not exactly appealing to a human girl. She had also just been through a major shock, and the last thing she needed was to deal with unwanted sexual advances from a man she probably now saw as a savage killer.

Alir inclined his head in a gesture of respect and walked off the field, his tall, broad frame moving with a warrior's gait. Korum had played defrebs with the man several times in the last couple of years, and he'd lost more than once. The guardians were excellent fighters, their profession requiring them to stay in top shape, and Korum was glad that he'd never had to face one of them in the Arena.

"All you have to do is stay with me right now," Korum told Mia when Alir was further away. "Under the circumstances, the post-fight ceremony will be brief."

"Because you're hurt?" she asked, and he could hear the strain in her voice.

"No, I'll be fine. But you're not ready for anything like a victory celebration right now," Korum said softly. "What we need is to go home."

* * *

As the ceremony began, Mia tried to focus on the event, but her mind kept flashing back to the gruesome images of the fight.

Flash. Korum lying on the ground, unable to move.

Flash. Blood spraying everywhere. That terrible gloating expression on Loris's face.

Flash. Korum striking back with the speed of a cobra. The sudden terror on the other Krinar's face.

Flash. More blood.

Flash. Loris's head torn off his body.

No, stop it! Mia wanted to scream, but they were in public, and she couldn't do it, couldn't embarrass Korum like that. He was holding her hand now, and they were on a large float in the middle of the Arena. The same Krinar who had led the beginning of the ceremony was speaking again, saying something else about the history of Arena fighting, but his words were sliding past Mia's ears. There was a sense of unreality to the proceedings; Mia kept feeling like she was inside a dream—or, more aptly, a nightmare.

Only Korum's touch felt real. She wanted to crawl into his embrace and never come out. When he had held her earlier, she'd felt some of her terror ebbing away, but now she felt cold again, her teeth chattering despite the heat of the bright Costa Rican sun.

He was alive. Mia still couldn't believe it. It had to be a miracle of some kind. How could anybody survive those kinds of injuries? She had known the Krinar healed quickly, but Korum had been almost literally torn apart. There had been so much blood. *Oh God, the blood.*

Mia swallowed hard, trying to contain her nausea. If she never saw the color red again, it would be too soon. No wonder the Krinar preferred light colors in their daily lives; they probably needed the contrast after the violent spectacle of the Arena.

Korum had almost died today. Her alien lover—so strong, so seemingly invincible—had been nearly brought down by treachery. For a few dark moments, Mia had been sure that he *was* dead—and she had wanted to die too. It had felt like her heart was being torn open, each blow to Korum's body smashing something deep within her soul. She had never experienced such agony before, and she never wanted to feel it again.

She was dimly aware that Voret had stopped speaking, that he was addressing Korum now, asking him about a celebration. She saw Korum starting to shake his head, and something came over her. Acting purely on instinct, she leaned closer to Korum and whispered in his ear, "I want you. Please, Korum, I want you."

He turned his head to look at her, his expression incredulous, and she squeezed his hand, wordlessly telling him that it was okay, that he could celebrate in the way of his people.

Rightly or wrongly, she needed him now, and she didn't care about anything else.

Mia could see his pupils expanding, his irises turning a brighter shade of gold. With the blood and dirt covering him, he looked like a savage, like one of those ancient hunters Voret had shown at the beginning of the ceremony. She wanted him so much she ached with it, her body needing to affirm life in the most basic way possible.

He hesitated for a second, staring at her, and then he raised his hand, curving his large palm around her right cheek. "Mia . . ."

"Please, Korum." She held his gaze, knowing that he could see the sincerity of her intentions on her face. She needed to feel his touch on her skin, needed him to make her forget the horror of the past hour.

His eyes glittering, he leaned forward and said softly, "You don't know what you're asking, my sweet. I can't be . . . gentle right now."

Mia swallowed, her inner muscles clenching at his words. "I don't want you to be."

He looked at her for another few seconds, and she could see the pulse beating in the side of his muscular neck. Then, as though unable to help himself, he bent his head and kissed her, his arms wrapping around her and pulling her onto his lap.

In the background, Mia could hear the crowd roaring, the spectators cheering and stomping their feet, but it didn't bother her. All she could concentrate on was the heat of his mouth consuming hers, the pressure of his erection against her buttocks, the feel of his strong hands rubbing up and down her back. There was a faint metallic taste that should've repelled her, but instead it turned her on even more. The man kissing her right now was a predator, a killer—and she wanted him exactly as he was, no holds barred.

Lifting his head, he stared down at her for a second, his breathing heavy and his skin flushed underneath the streaks of grime and blood. All around them, the crowd was going wild, chanting their names. Mia had a sudden thought that that's what rock stars must feel like, surrounded by their screaming fans.

As though in response to that, a strange music began to play, with notes so deep that Mia could feel the vibrations deep in her bones. The rhythm was uneven, almost jerky. It should've sounded discordant, unpleasant, but instead, it added to the pulsing heat between her legs, making her skin feel tighter and her heart beat faster.

Korum was reacting to it too, his cock hardening even more, pushing into the softness of her bottom. Still holding her, he stood up and began walking toward a tent-like structure in the center of the Arena, carrying her like a prize of war.

Mia clung to him, feeling almost intoxicated. Her head was spinning, and everything seemed surreal, as though it was happening in a dream. The psychology student in her recognized that it was her brain's response to trauma, that she wasn't thinking clearly, but it didn't matter. She was dying with need, and Korum was the cure for what ailed her.

They got to the tent, and he placed her on her feet, keeping her pressed against his body. Instead of them going inside, the tent appeared to move and flow around them, mostly covering them from the view of the crowd. Mia was vaguely aware of the thinness of the walls, of the fact that thousands of curious Krinar eyes were watching the structure right now, but she wasn't fully processing that information. They had some kind of privacy, and that was good enough for her.

As soon as the tent walls stopped moving, Korum took a step back, releasing her from his embrace. "Take off the dress." His voice was unusually rough, and she could see the tension in his powerful shoulders.

With his eyes a bright yellow, he looked wild, more animal than man. "Take it off, Mia."

She obeyed, shimmying out of the dress, her excitement mixed with a tiny dollop of fear. He hadn't even touched her, and she could see that he was already close to losing control.

Before her dress even hit the ground, he was already on her, one of his hands delving between her thighs and another grabbing her hair. His mouth descended on hers even as his finger pushed inside, into her small opening. He was rough, almost frantic, and Mia realized that he hadn't been lying before, about not being able to be gentle. She was wet, but her muscles still tensed involuntarily, her body resisting the aggressive penetration.

Suddenly, he withdrew his finger and used the hand holding her hair to push her down, onto her knees. Tiny rocks and gravel dug into the soft skin of her kneecaps. "Suck it," he said harshly, tearing open the front of his pants. "I want your mouth right now."

His erection sprang free, brushing against her cheek. Mia opened her mouth, letting him inside, and he groaned as her lips closed around the head of his cock. He tasted salty, the tip already coated with pre-cum. She swirled her tongue around his shaft, mimicking what she'd once seen done in porn. He let out a sound that sounded like a growl, and his hands fisted tighter in her hair, holding her head steady as he began to move his hips, fucking her mouth with his cock.

Mia focused on taking small breaths, trying not to choke as most of his length pushed into her mouth, pressing against the back of her throat. He thrust again and again, and then he was coming with a harsh groan, his seed shooting out in warm, salty spurts. When he was done, he slowly withdrew from her, his cock still semi-hard.

Swallowing, Mia licked her lips and stared up at him, strangely aroused by what had just occurred. Pleasuring him like this turned her on, almost as if he had been touching her too.

He held her gaze, and she could see that his eyes remained bright, his hunger as strong as ever. His sex was stirring again, hardening in front of her face. One orgasm had just taken the edge off, she realized as he pulled her up onto her feet.

When he touched her again, he was gentler, his desire more controlled. His hands and mouth traveled down her body, caressing and worshipping every inch of her skin. Mia closed her eyes, quiet moans escaping her throat as pleasurable tension began to gather low in her belly. Then he was kneeling in front of her, his face at the level of her hips, his hands cupping the smooth curves of her buttocks. Bringing her toward him with one hand, he used the other to penetrate her with one finger, being much more careful this time. At the same time, his mouth delved into the soft curls at the apex of her thighs, his tongue reaching between her folds to stroke her clit.

Mia jerked from the startling lash of sensations, her entire body tensing as his finger rubbed against the sensitive spot deep inside. She could feel the growing pressure, and her knees began shaking, her legs suddenly too weak to support her weight. If it hadn't been for his finger inside her and his hand on her ass, she would've collapsed, falling down on the ground beside him.

"Come for me," he whispered, his hot breath washing over her sex, and she did, his words sending her over the edge, providing that elusive something she didn't even know she needed. Everything inside her tightened and released, the pleasure so sharp it felt like an explosion along her nerve endings.

When the pulsations stopped, he withdrew his finger and tugged her down again. This time, they were both kneeling on the hard ground. Looking at her, he lifted his hand and slowly licked his finger—the one that had just been inside her. "I love your taste," he murmured, his eyes filled with such hunger that her mouth went dry. "It makes me want to fuck you again and again, just to have it on my tongue."

Mia drew in a shaky breath, her sex clenching with need.

Before she could say anything, he lay down on the ground, lifting her up and placing her astride his thighs. His cock was completely hard again, standing up straight from his body. "Ride me, Mia," he said, watching her with a half-lidded gaze.

"Yes," she whispered, "I will." And grasping his thick length with her right hand, Mia guided him to her opening, her eyes closing as the broad head began to push inside. She lowered herself slowly, teasing them both, and was rewarded with a low groan that escaped from his throat.

When he was all the way inside, she opened her eyes, meeting his burning gaze. With his face streaked with grime and blood, he looked dangerous—cruel even. She was almost literally riding a tiger—a predator who could tear her apart in the blink of an eye. Instead of scaring her, the thrill of it only added to the desire coursing through her veins.

As she began to move, she kept her eyes trained on him, watching as tiny beads of sweat appeared on his forehead and a muscle pulsed in his jaw from his apparent effort to restrain himself. His hands tightened on her hips, his fingers digging into her soft flesh, and then he was lifting her up and down on his cock, going deeper and deeper with every stroke.

The tension inside her spiraled again, and Mia threw back her head, her mouth open in a soundless scream. A powerful orgasm rippled through her body even as Korum kept thrusting faster and faster, seeking his own release. When he came, the grinding motions of his pelvis intensified her aftershocks, leaving her completely wrung out. Breathing hard, Mia collapsed against his chest, her muscles like limp noodles and her mind emptied of any thoughts.

She was so relaxed she didn't even react when he pulled her higher, bringing her neck closer to his mouth. It was only when she felt a strange slicing pain that Mia realized what was happening ... and her world dissolved into an ecstatic frenzy of blood and sex.

Part III

CHAPTER SEVENTEEN

Korum woke up to the unfamiliar feel of hard ground underneath his back. Before he even opened his eyes, he remembered everything that had occurred earlier—including Mia's voluntary participation in the celebration.

He could feel her slight weight on his arm, hear her quiet breathing, and he knew she was deeply asleep, worn out from the double ordeal of the fight and the celebration. Moving carefully, Korum freed his arm, gently lowering her head to the ground. Then he stood up and created fresh clothes for both of them. A pair of shorts for himself and a robe for Mia—just enough to afford them some coverage in case any spectators remained in the Arena.

He was thirsty and hungry, but otherwise he felt great, his body practically thrumming with energy. The scientists said there was no physiological need for lonar or human blood, given the genetic fix, but many on Krina thought that some kind of a psychological need remained. Korum wasn't certain if he believed that, but he did know that he rarely felt as satisfied as those times when he indulged himself with Mia.

Holding the robe, he crouched next to her and studied her for a few seconds, enjoying the sight of her naked body. He rarely got a chance to watch her like this; usually his need for her was so intense he couldn't look at her bare flesh without fucking her immediately afterwards. Even now, after last night's sexual marathon, he could feel the warm stirrings of desire—although it was nothing compared to his usual craving.

She was lying on her back, one slim arm extended over her head and the other bent across her ribcage. Fascinated by her breasts, Korum reached out and stroked one pale mound, smiling when the nipple hardened at his touch. Her skin was as soft as anything he had ever felt, its silky texture a constant lure for his fingers.

Wrapping her in a fluffy robe, he lifted her up. She didn't even stir, her sleep so deep it bordered on unconsciousness. It was always like that after he took her blood: her human body needed to recuperate from the excess of sensations.

And so did his, albeit to a lesser extent. Korum could see how others had gotten addicted to their charl; Mia's blood was a powerful temptation for him, its effect more potent than that of any drug. He used to think blood addicts were weak, but now Korum wondered if there was really that much difference between physical and emotional addiction. He certainly couldn't imagine needing Mia more than he already did.

Carrying her out of the shatela, Korum walked toward the grassy area where he'd left his transport pod. He hadn't bothered disassembling it earlier, so it was now waiting for them.

Looking around, he saw that the Arena was completely empty. It was also early morning, the sun just beginning to come up. Grinning, Korum realized that he must've been in the shatela much longer than usual. It was his first time celebrating with a human, and it was by far the best experience he'd had.

They reached the transport pod, and Korum sent a quick mental command to have them taken home. A minute later, they were walking into his house, with Mia still asleep in his arms.

As soon as they were inside, Korum headed straight for the cleansing room—the bathroom, in human terms. He was still covered in dirt, dried blood, and sweat, and some of the grime had rubbed off on Mia, leaving her pale skin marred with dark streaks.

Another mental command from him, and the water came on, warm jets softly massaging their bodies and rinsing away all traces of yesterday's activities. Korum enjoyed the sensation; it was both energizing and soothing at the same time. A few minutes later, both he and Mia were clean and dry, and he carried her to bed, knowing she needed to get more sleep. She was so exhausted she hadn't even woken up during the cleansing.

Laying her on the bed, Korum let the intelligent material flow around her and then covered her with a soft sheet, knowing that she liked the feel of blankets. Kissing her forehead, he took one last look at the girl he loved and headed out to start his day.

* * *

"He refuses to talk to us," Alir told Korum as they walked toward the other side of the guardians' building. "He says he will only talk to you."

"Will he now?" Korum said, not bothering to hide the sarcasm in his voice. "And what gives him the impression he's in a position to make demands?"

Alir shrugged. "I don't know. But he seems convinced that you will be interested in hearing what he has to say. He says it has to do with Mia."

Korum's hands clenched into fists at the mention of his charl. The fact that Saret dared bring up her name—

"The report for the Elders is ready," Alir said, changing the topic. "Would you like to review it?"

"Yes," Korum said. "Send it to me. I'll run it by the Council."

Alir nodded. "Will do."

They had reached their destination, and Alir stopped before going in. "Do you want me there?"

"No." Korum was certain of that. "I want to speak to him alone."

"Then he's all yours." Turning around, Alir walked back, leaving Korum on his own.

Korum waited until the leader of the guardians was gone, and then he took a step forward, toward the wall that shielded his enemy from his view. The wall dissolved, forming an entrance, and he stepped inside.

Saret was sitting on a float, a crime-collar around his throat. Korum smiled at the sight. He remembered having an argument with Saret about the collars a few hundred years ago, with his former friend trying to convince him that the collars were demeaning and unnecessary. Korum had disagreed, believing that the shame of the crime-collar was part of the deterrent for would-be criminals.

It was good to see Saret wearing one now, particularly in light of his views about it.

"I see you're out of your disguise now," Korum observed, studying his enemy's familiar features. "Miscalculated a bit, did you?"

Saret gave him a cold smile. "Apparently. I underestimated how much Loris hated you. If I had known he would try to prolong the process of killing you, I would've shot you twice."

"Live and learn," Korum said. "Isn't that what humans say?"

"Indeed." Saret's eyes gleamed with something dark.

Korum gave him a mocking look and sat down on another float, stretching out his legs in a gesture of disrespect. "You wanted to talk to me," he said coolly. "So talk."

"All right," Saret said. "I will. How is Mia doing, by the way? She seemed a bit upset yesterday."

Korum felt a surge of anger, but kept his expression calm, amused. "She was. But she's happy now, as I'm sure you can imagine."

"Of course she is," Saret said. "And adjusting so well to life here, isn't she? It's almost as if she didn't lose her memory fully, wouldn't you say? It's like she still knows you on some level, maybe even loves you. And she's so accepting of everything. Nothing fazes her for long. Amazing, isn't it?"

Korum froze for a second, a chill running down his spine. The only way Saret could know that would be—

"Yes," Saret said. "I see you're on the right track. I miscalculated again, you see. Mia was supposed to end up with me, not you."

"What did you do to her?" Korum said quietly, the fine hair on the back of his neck rising.

Saret laughed. "Nothing too awful, believe me. I merely made sure she would be receptive. She's still herself . . . mostly."

"What did you do?" Without even realizing what he was doing, Korum found himself out of his seat, his hand wrapped around Saret's throat.

Saret made a choking sound, his hand tugging at Korum's fingers, and Korum forced himself to release him, taking a step back. He was shaking with rage, and he knew he would kill Saret if he didn't put some distance between them.

"It's called softening," Saret said, rubbing his throat. His voice was raspy from Korum partially crushing his trachea. "It's a new procedure I developed specifically for humans. A softened mind doesn't feel fear as sharply. It's also more open to new impressions, new ideas." Saret paused dramatically. "New attachments. In fact, such a mind seeks something— or, rather, someone—to attach *to*."

Korum stared at Saret, ice spreading through his veins.

"And that someone can be anyone, you see. It should've been me— but instead, it was you."

You're lying. Korum wanted to scream, to deny what he just heard, but he couldn't. It made too much sense. The girl he met in New York wouldn't have accepted everything with such ease, wouldn't have invited him into her bed after knowing him for just a day. She would've been frightened and mistrustful, and he would've had to earn her trust and affection all over again. And instead, she seemed to love him with hardly any effort on his part.

Except she didn't. Not really. Her feelings for him weren't real. None of it was real. Her behavior, her apparent attachment to him—it was all a result of Saret's procedure.

"Does she still have her memories?" Korum buried the agony deep inside, where it couldn't cloud his thinking. "Or did you erase them anyway?"

Saret grinned, visibly delighted by the question. "No, the memories are gone. It just seems like they're there because she's absorbing everything like a sponge, learning at an incredible rate. Pretty soon, she'll be more acclimated to our world than she was before—if she's not already."

"Can you undo it?" Korum knew it was futile, but he had to ask.

"What, the softening or the memory loss?"

"Both. Either."

Saret's grin widened. "I can't. And even if I could, I wouldn't. You might have her now, but you'll never truly have her. You'll never know if anything she feels for you is genuine—or if she would've felt the same about any other man who spent time with her upon her awakening."

Korum looked at the man he'd once considered a friend. Memories of their childhood, happy and carefree, flashed through his mind, leaving the bitter taste of regret in their wake. "Why?" he asked quietly.

"Why do I hate you?" Saret lifted his eyebrows. "Or why did I do all of this?"

Korum just continued looking at him.

"The answer is the same to both," Saret said, his grin fading. "I was tired of always being in your shadow. No matter how much I achieved, how high I climbed, I was always just Korum's buddy. Korum the inventor, Korum the designer, Korum who brought us here to Earth. Your ambition knew no bounds—and neither did my hatred of you."

"Yet you supported me," Korum said, the pain of the betrayal somehow distant, not fully reaching him yet. "You were always on my side on the Council. You helped me get us here, to Earth."

"I did," Saret agreed. "Because I knew it was foolish to do anything else. Even the Elders dance to your tune these days, don't they?"

Korum didn't justify that with a response. Instead, he gave Saret a look of contempt. "So all your grandiose plans for humans, your supposed desire for world peace, it was all out of petty jealousy?"

"No," Saret said, his eyes narrowing. "I saw a way to shape history, and I took a chance. What could be a greater achievement than peace for an entire planet? Do you think any of your gadgets could compare to that?"

"An achievement that would've involved the deaths of fifty thousand Krinar."

"Yes," Saret said, and he had the gall to look regretful for a moment. "That would've been unfortunate. Unavoidable, but unfortunate."

"Unfortunate?" Korum could hardly believe his ears. "What is wrong with you, Saret? How did you get to be this way?"

Now Saret was beginning to look angry. "What is wrong with *me*? You ask me that while you're standing there, with Loris's blood still fresh on your hands? You think something is wrong with me because I wanted to better the lives of billions by killing a few thousand? How many Krinar have you killed in the Arena, Korum? Twenty, thirty? And what about humans? You think I don't know that you enjoy killing, just like the rest of our fucked-up race?"

Korum stared at him, trying to understand this man he'd known his whole life. "You're wrong," he said quietly. "I don't enjoy killing. I didn't want to kill Loris yesterday—and I wouldn't have if you hadn't interfered. I like the fights themselves, not the end result of them. And that's how our fucked-up race is, as you should know, since you're the mind expert here. We love danger and violence—we crave it—but we don't have to be murderers."

"And yet we are," Saret said. "You can fool yourself all you want, but that's what we ultimately are. We came to Earth and thousands of humans died during the Great Panic as a result. And what you want to do now will result in more deaths. She won't forgive you for that, you know."

"Won't your procedure take care of that?" Korum said, his mouth curving into a bitter smile. "Isn't she going to love me now no matter what?"

Saret shook his head. "No. With enough provocation, her love will turn to hate. You just wait and see."

CHAPTER EIGHTEEN

Mia woke up with a scream, her heart racing and her skin covered with cold sweat.

In her dream, Korum's body had been a mangled, mutilated corpse, swimming in a river of blood. She had tried to save him from that river, to pull him ashore, but it had been futile. The current had been too strong, tearing him out of her hands and carrying him away, down to the waterfalls, where the water was as dark as dried blood.

Sitting up straight, Mia tried to get her breathing under control. It was just a bad dream. Korum had won the fight. He was safe.

Safe—and fully recovered, if yesterday's celebration was anything to go by.

Remembering just how recovered he had been, Mia immediately felt much better. Her lover's stamina was literally out of this world. The pleasure he had given her had been incredible, almost more than she could stand. She'd never felt such ecstasy as when he'd bitten her; she never could've imagined that such sensations even existed.

Smiling, she climbed out of bed and headed toward the shower. The fight was over, Saret had been captured, and there was nothing else to fear.

She and Korum were safe at last.

Humming to herself, Mia let the cleaning technology do its thing while she stood there thinking about her lover—and how essential he had become to her again.

When she was clean and dry, she went to the kitchen and had the house prepare some breakfast for her. According to the information on her tablet, her lab partner Adam was supposed to return from his week-long vacation today—which meant that Mia could start relearning everything she had forgotten about her apprenticeship.

The lab wouldn't be open, given the recent events, but she was hoping there would be some way for her to continue learning about the mind. The subject fascinated her now more than ever.

* * *

Korum walked aimlessly down the ocean shore, letting the roar of the pounding surf drown out the cacophony in his head. For the first time in his life, he felt lost. Lost and hopeless . . . and angry.

His anger was directed mostly at himself, though a healthy portion of it was reserved for Saret. Korum hadn't let himself think about his friend's betrayal before, too focused on Mia and her memory loss. Then the fight had consumed his attention. Now, however, there was nothing to distract him from the fact that a man he'd regarded as a friend had turned out to be his greatest enemy.

Korum knew he wasn't universally liked. It was a state of affairs that had never bothered him before. He was respected and feared, but there were only a few individuals he'd ever considered his friends. Most of them remained on Krina, busy with their lives and careers there. Saret had been the only one to accompany him to Earth.

Even as a child, Korum had always been self-sufficient. He had discovered his interest in design early on, and that passion had consumed his life—until Mia. Now he had two passions: his work and the human girl who was his charl. He wasn't a loner, but he rarely needed the company of others. Unlike most, Korum was just as happy by himself—or now spending time with Mia—as he was surrounded by people.

Saret's betrayal proved to be agonizing on multiple levels. Korum had trusted Saret; he'd confided in him for centuries, sharing his goals and dreams. They'd played together as children, discussed their sexual conquests as teenage boys, and often worked toward a common goal as members of the Council. When had Saret begun to hate him? Or had it always been that way and Korum had just been too blind to see it? Could any of his friends be trusted, or were all of them like Saret, just waiting to strike when his back was turned?

These thoughts were both painful and disturbing. Self-doubt was not in Korum's nature, but he couldn't help wondering whether he had brought this upon himself. He knew he could be harsh and arrogant at times—even ruthless when it came to achieving his goals. Had he done something to make Saret hate him to such extent? Or was it simply jealousy, as Saret himself had intimated?

Reaching the estuary where he'd sat with Mia on the rocks before, Korum stripped off his clothes and waded into the surf, letting the water cool him down. He'd always found the ocean therapeutic. The power of the waves appealed to him, and he especially liked it when the current was strong, as it was right now with high tide. It picked him up, carrying him out to deeper water, and Korum let it, floating along until the shore was a few miles away. Then he began to swim back, the tug of the current providing enough resistance to make it a challenge. The mindless exertion of swimming helped clear his mind, and he felt a tiny bit better when he finally emerged from the water.

Sitting down on the rocks, he let the sun shine down on his bare skin, warming him up again. The worst thing about Saret's betrayal wasn't what it did to Korum: it was the consequences for Mia. She had not only lost her memories, but her freedom of thought as well. Whatever she felt for Korum now was involuntary, a byproduct of this 'softening' Saret had done to her. His sweet, beautiful girl was not the same person she'd once been; her mind had been tampered with in the most unforgivable way.

She had been afraid of that, Korum remembered. When she'd first arrived in Lenkarda, she had been hesitant about the language implant, afraid of having alien technology in her brain. Korum had been amused at the time, but it turned out she'd been right to fear. Saret had been dangerous all along.

And Korum had failed to protect her. The thought gnawed at him, eating him from the inside. He, who had never failed at anything before, had been unable to protect the person who meant the most to him. Could Mia ever forgive him for that? And if she could, how would he know whether her feelings were real? If Saret were to be believed, she would now accept most things with equanimity, her reactions different from what they would've been before.

Getting up, Korum pulled on his clothes and began walking home. It would be a lengthy walk, but he was in no rush. Mia was there, and, for the first time ever, he was less than eager to see her.

He would have to tell her what he learned today. She would want to know, would want to make her own decisions about what to do next.

And if she chose to leave him, he would have to let her go.

Even if it killed him to do so.

* * *

Mia exited the house and walked to the transport pod that was waiting for her. She'd messaged Adam from her wristwatch-bracelet device, and the K had agreed to meet with her, sending his little aircraft to pick her up and take her to the lab.

Getting in, Mia settled on one of the floating seats, feeling it adjusting around her. She was getting so used to K technology that she didn't even have to think about how to use anything—it was all starting to seem perfectly natural to her.

She was curious to meet her former partner and dive back into that part of her life in Lenkarda. She had found a few recordings where Adam was explaining something, and she had been impressed with not only his intelligence, but also his ability to take complex subjects and put them in simple, easy-to-understand terms.

Two minutes later, she landed in a clearing in front of a mid-sized building that looked like it had been through something extraordinary. The walls were partially gone, as though something had melted them from the top down, but the interior looked perfectly intact.

Adam was standing there, waiting for her. As Mia emerged from the pod, he smiled—a bright and genuine smile that lit up his handsome face. He had what Mia was coming to think of as typical K coloring: dark hair and eyes and that beautifully bronzed skin.

"Well, howdy there, partner," he said, his eyes crinkling attractively at the corners. "I heard our boss turned out to be Doctor Evil and practiced some of his craft on you."

Mia grinned, immediately liking this Krinar. "Yep, you heard right. You leave for a week and that's what happens."

"So you don't remember me now?" he asked, his expression becoming more serious. "How much did he wipe out?"

"When I woke up here a couple of days ago, my latest memories were from March," Mia explained, watching as the K's jaw tightened.

"That fucking bastard," Adam said, anger seeping into his voice. "I'm sorry, Mia. I wish I'd been here—"

Mia waved her hand dismissively. "Don't be silly. Nobody suspected anything; he was too good. He even managed to sneak into the fight yesterday and almost kill Korum."

"Yeah, I heard about that too," Adam said. "I watched the recording of the fight this morning."

"Oh, right." Mia tried not to blush. If Adam had seen the fight, then he might've also watched the celebration afterwards.

"Do you want to go inside?" Adam asked, motioning toward the ruined building. "I think we can extract a lot of the files and data. I spoke with the other apprentices, and they're fine with it."

"Sure," Mia said quickly, grateful for the change of subject.

Walking up to the building, they climbed through a ragged opening in one of the walls. The usual wall-dissolving mechanism appeared to be malfunctioning—which was hardly surprising, considering the condition of the building.

"What's going to happen to the lab?" Mia asked when they were inside. "What's the normal protocol for something like this?"

Adam shrugged. "There is no normal protocol. This lab is Saret's, so technically we're now trespassing on his property. Although I think the government might own it now, given Saret's crimes. I'm not really sure how these things work. My best guess is that most of the information will be transferred to the labs in the other Centers—and maybe some other mind expert will want to open a new lab here in Lenkarda."

"What about you? Why don't they have you take over the lab?"

"Me?" Adam raised his eyebrows. "I'm too young and inexperienced as far as they're concerned."

"You are?" Mia looked at him in surprise. He looked to be a man in his prime, outwardly similar to Korum. "How old are you?"

"Oh, that's right, I almost forgot that you don't remember." Adam smiled. "I'm twenty-eight, only a few years older than you. I am also a fairly recent arrival in the Centers. I grew up in a human family, you see."

"You did?" Mia's eyes went wide. "How?"

"I was adopted as an infant," Adam said. "Now why don't we start going through some of Saret's files and see if there's anything useful there? Maybe we can shed some light on your condition."

Mia was dying to ask more questions about Adam's origins, but he didn't seem to be in a mood to talk about it, so she focused on the task at hand instead. Adam showed her how to operate some of the lab equipment, and they began digging through mountains of information, searching for anything memory-related.

Six hours later, Mia got up and rubbed her neck, her brain feeling like it would explode from everything she'd learned today. Adam was still as focused as ever, going through file after file with no trace of tiredness.

Hearing Mia's movements, he looked up from the image he was studying and gave her a warm smile. "You should go home, Mia. It's getting late. I'll work here some more, and then I'll leave as well."

Mia hesitated. "Are you sure?" She was mentally exhausted and starving, but she felt bad leaving Adam on his own.

"Of course," Adam said. "Now go. This is plenty for today."

* * *

Korum paced in the living room, too wound up to sit still. When he had gotten home an hour earlier and found the house empty, his immediate thought had been that something had happened to Mia—that Saret had found a way to get to her after all.

Of course, that wasn't the case. A quick check had revealed her location, and then it had been easy to access the satellite images and see her talking to Adam outside Saret's lab several hours earlier. Still, those few seconds before Korum had been assured of her safety had chilled him to the bone.

Now he was fighting an urge to go to the lab and bring Mia home. He wanted to hold her and feel the warmth of her body in his arms, maybe for the last time. Once he told her the truth about her condition, she would be more than justified in wanting to leave him. As terrible as her memory loss had been, the other procedure was far more invasive, altering her brain in a way that she would likely find unforgivable. Now she would never know if the way she felt about Korum—or about anything in general—was real or if it was a result of what Saret had done.

A dark temptation gnawed at Korum. What if he didn't tell her? What if she continued in blissful ignorance, happy with her life as it was? Other than Saret and Korum, no one else knew the truth. He could keep her, and she would love him—and he would be the only one to know it wasn't real love.

A couple of months earlier, Korum wouldn't have hesitated. He had wanted her, and he'd simply taken her, disregarding her wishes. If he had been faced with this dilemma then, it would've been an easy decision to make: keep her and all else be damned. But he couldn't do that anymore, couldn't treat her like a child or a pet, as she'd once accused him of doing. He wanted her to stay, but it had to be of her own free will—even if that free will had been somewhat tampered with.

No, he had to tell her, and he had to do it soon.

Finally, Korum saw a pod landing outside. Mia came out, and the aircraft took off, heading back to wherever it came from.

Despite his black mood, Korum couldn't help smiling as she entered the house. She was dressed in a cream-colored dress that left most of her back bare, and her dark hair was pinned up in a thick, messy knot. The hairstyle was surprisingly sexy, exposing her delicate nape and drawing his attention to the elegant column of her throat.

"Honey, I'm home," she said, grinning from ear to ear.

Unable to help himself, Korum laughed and picked her up, bringing her up for a thorough kiss.

When he lowered her back to her feet, her smile was almost blinding. She looked at him as though he was her entire world—and Korum's heart felt like it would shatter into a million pieces.

"How was your day, my sweet?" he asked, his hands still holding her waist.

"It was great," she said, still grinning. "I met Adam again. He's very nice. I like him a lot."

Korum felt a surge of jealousy, but he tamped down on it, refusing to give in to the emotion. Mia had always liked her partner, but, as far as Korum knew, her feelings were entirely platonic. Besides, the young K already had a human he was obsessed with; Korum had found that out during a background check he'd done on Adam shortly after Mia started working with him.

"We did a lot of digging through Saret's files," Mia continued, her eyes shining with excitement. "Adam thinks we might learn something useful about my condition this way."

At that moment, her stomach rumbled and her cheeks turned pink in response, making Korum smile. "I'm guessing someone's hungry," he teased.

"Busted," she said, laughing.

Smiling, Korum let her go and headed to the kitchen. A few minutes later, they were sitting down to a meal of grilled vegetable sandwiches with miso-avocado dip.

Mia quickly devoured everything on her plate, and so did he, his appetite strong after his swim earlier today. For dessert, Korum had the house make them a kiwi-mango pie with a crust made of ground macadamia nuts—and tea for Mia.

As they were enjoying the treat, Korum reached across the table and took her hand, stroking the middle of her palm with his thumb. "Mia," he said quietly, "there's something I have to tell you."

She froze for a second, apparently reacting to the serious note in his voice. "What is it?"

"I spoke to Saret today," Korum said, his fingers tightening around her palm. "He didn't just wipe out your recent memories. He also did something to make you . . . more accepting of things."

* * *

Mia stared at her lover, unable to believe what she was hearing. "What? What does that mean?"

"He called it 'softening'," Korum said, and the expression on his face was grim. "It was apparently a way to make you more amenable to his advances. If he didn't lie about it, you don't experience fear as strongly as you did before . . . and you're also more open to new impressions."

Mia frowned. "I don't understand. How would this have helped Saret?"

"Because you're not only more open to new impressions—which explains why you're acclimating so well—but you're also prone to new attachments." Korum's mouth was tight with anger.

"New attachments?" And then it dawned her. "He thought I would fall in love with him? That's insane!" She laughed, inviting him to share the joke.

Korum didn't respond, and her amusement faded. "Wait a second," she said slowly. "Are you saying what I think you're saying?"

"I'm sorry, Mia. I really wish it wasn't true."

Automatically shaking her head, Mia pulled her hand out of his grasp and rose to her feet. "But that's ridiculous," she said. "Are you saying that I'm not myself? That everything I think and feel is a product of some madman's procedure? That what I feel for *you* isn't real?"

Korum got up as well. "It's all my fault," he said, his voice heavy with guilt. "I should've been there. I should've protected you from him—"

"No." Mia refused to believe this. "How do you know he wasn't lying? Wouldn't it make sense for him to lie?"

"It would," Korum said. "It would make all the sense in the world. And that's why I want to have you seen by the mind lab in Arizona. We'll go there tomorrow."

"But you don't think he's lying."

"No." Korum gave her a pained look. "I don't."

"Why not?" Mia whispered, her voice starting to shake.

"Because you haven't been fully yourself, my sweet," he said gently. "The differences are subtle, but they're there. You've noticed it too, haven't you?"

Mia sucked in her breath. She had. Of course she had. She'd wondered at how well she was adjusting to her new world, to living in an alien colony with a lover she'd just met. A lover who was now as necessary to her as food and air.

"Couldn't there be a different explanation for this?" Mia knew she was clutching at straws, but the alternative was too much to process. "What if my memories aren't really gone? What if they're still there, suppressed somewhere deep inside? That would explain everything: why I feel so comfortable here, why I'm learning so fast, why I fell in love with you—"

Korum closed his eyes for a moment. When he opened them, his gaze was bleak. "You didn't, Mia. You didn't fall in love with me. You barely know me."

"But if I still remember you on some level—"

He drew in a deep breath. "You don't, my sweet. Ellet ran tests on you before you woke up, and there were signs of damage consistent with a memory loss. I really wish it were otherwise, believe me."

Mia blinked, swallowing hard to contain the growing knot in her throat. He thought she was damaged. Defective. Incapable of real emotions. "So what now?"

"It's your decision," Korum said, his voice oddly flat. "You can either stay with me or return to your old life."

"Return to my old life?" She could barely say the words. "You . . . Y-you want me to go?"

"What? No!" He looked startled at the idea. "Of course I don't want you to go. You're my entire life now, don't you understand that?"

Mia almost shuddered with relief. He still wanted her, despite the damage from the procedure.

"You are my entire life as well," she told him. "I know you think the way I feel is the result of what Saret did, but I don't believe it. I loved you before, despite everything that happened between us, and I fell in love with you again in these past couple of days. You may not think it's real, but I know my own mind. Yes, I noticed I'm not reacting to things as I would've expected, but so what? Isn't it a good thing that I'm learning so fast? That I'm becoming as comfortable in Lenkarda as I was once in New York? Even if it is a result of Saret's procedure, it doesn't change the fact that that's how I am now—that that's the way I think and feel. It doesn't make my emotions any less strong . . . or any less real."

As she spoke, the little grooves of tension bracketing his mouth began to dissipate. "Are you sure, Mia?" he asked, his eyes filling with familiar golden heat. "Is this what you really want?"

"To be with you? Yes!" Mia had never been more certain of anything in her life. The thought of leaving him, of going back home and never seeing him again, was unbearable. When she'd thought he was dead, she had wanted to die too. Life without Korum was not worth living.

"Then you will be with me." His voice was rough, his hands hurried as they reached for her and pulled her into his arms.

His mouth was ravenous, like he wanted to consume her, and Mia responded in kind, her hunger matching his. She ached for his touch, his embrace. The shocking ecstasy of their post-Arena lovemaking had left her wrung out, drained, and yet she already wanted more. More of Korum, more of the magic.

His hands were frantic on her body, ripping off the dress, leaving it lying in shreds on the floor. His clothes met the same fate. Before she could blink, she found herself pressed against the wall, her thighs spread wide as he lifted her up, rubbing his erection against her bare sex.

"Fuck," he growled. His expression was that of a man in pain, his breathing harsh and uneven. "I have to be inside you, Mia. Now."

"Yes," she whispered, holding his blazing gaze. "Yes . . . please . . ."

As though she had given him permission, he plunged into her, his shaft unbearably thick and long, stretching her, filling her to the brim. Mia cried out, the pleasure-pain of his possession as intense as it was startling. With the way he was holding her, she was completely open to him, unable to control the depth of his penetration in any way. He was in so deep she could feel him nudging against her cervix, her channel tightening in a futile effort to keep him out.

He paused for a brief second, letting her catch her breath, and then he began hammering into her, his thrusts pressing her into the wall. Mia moaned, her body overwhelmed by the sensations. There was no slow build, no gradual transition from discomfort to pleasure; instead, the orgasm hit her suddenly, her inner muscles spasming around his cock with no warning.

He groaned, his pace picking up further, and she climaxed again with a scream, unable to control her body's helpless response. Her skin was too hot, and she was panting, gasping for breath, but he was relentless, driving her toward her third peak mere minutes after her second.

And just when Mia thought she couldn't take anymore, he came with a savage roar, his head thrown back and his cock pulsing deep inside her.

* * *

The next morning, Korum waited impatiently as Haron—the mind expert in the Arizona Center—carefully examined Mia.

She was lying on a float, her eyes closed and her expression relaxed. She had been lightly sedated to allow for a more thorough examination of her brain. Haron was brushing her hair back, exposing more of her forehead to attach his equipment there.

Korum had given the other male permission to touch her in this instance, but he still felt like ripping him apart for it. He had been equally angry to learn of Arus restraining her during the fight, even though he knew it had been for Mia's own protection. The territorial instinct was primitive—and completely irrational given the circumstances—but Korum couldn't help it. When it came to Mia, he was no more evolved than an amoeba.

By the time the examination was over, Korum was in a dark mood. "Well," he demanded as soon as Haron put away his equipment.

The mind expert lifted his broad shoulders in a shrug. "I don't know," he said, giving Korum a puzzled look. "Her brain is healthy, but it does show signs of recent memory erasure. There's also something else, something that I've never seen before."

"The softening procedure," Korum said. "Do you think it could be that?" He had told Haron about Saret's claims, and the mind expert had been very intrigued.

"It could be," Haron said. "I honestly haven't come across anything like this before. If Saret says he invented the procedure, then that would make sense." He sounded admiring, making Korum want to do something violent to him again.

"Can you fix it?" Korum already knew the answer but he had to ask.

Haron shook his head. "I don't think so, not without chancing some real damage to her brain in the process. Whenever we come up with something new here, we do extensive testing in a simulated environment first, before experimenting with live subjects. I could try, of course, if you want—"

"No." Korum could never take that kind of risk with Mia. "Forget it."

As their ship headed back to Lenkarda, Korum held Mia on his lap. She was awake but a little groggy, and she seemed content to just sit there, with her head resting on his shoulder. He stroked her hair, enjoying the feel of soft curls under his fingers.

Their conversation yesterday had gone very differently than he'd feared. Mia had been shocked and disbelieving at what Saret had done, but what had upset her the most was the idea of leaving him. And Korum had been glad. He had been so fucking glad and relieved that she wanted to stay. He honestly didn't know what he would've done if she'd said she wanted to go home. He wanted to think that he would've let her . . . but, deep inside, he knew otherwise. He couldn't bear the thought of being apart from her for a day; how would he have survived a lifetime without her?

He wouldn't have. It was that simple. He would've tried if that had been what she wanted, but the odds of failure would've been high. Korum had no illusions about himself. Altruism was not in his nature. He would've suffered for a while—out of guilt for letting her get hurt, out of desire to make up for past wrongs—but he would've eventually come for her.

She stirred in his arms, interrupting his musings. Raising her head, she gave him a sleepy smile. "Where are we going now?"

"Home, my darling," Korum answered, the remainder of his black mood fading as he gazed upon her beautiful face. As much as he wanted to reverse Saret's procedure and undo any damage done to this exquisite creature, he was happy to have her no matter what. Even if she didn't truly love him now, he hoped she would develop genuine feelings for him over time.

And Korum would make sure her love didn't turn to hate when she learned the truth about his plans.

CHAPTER NINETEEN

The next month flew by. Korum found himself busier than usual, with his designers finalizing the new shields for the Centers and the Council trying to decide Saret's fate.

After several meetings, it was determined that a trial like that of the Keiths would not work in this instance. With Saret having been a long-term member of the Council, nobody was completely impartial and emotions were running high. Korum wasn't the only one who had considered Saret a friend. The mind expert had been generally liked, with his seemingly laid-back personality and friendly manner. The magnitude of his attempted crime was beyond belief, and even complete rehabilitation seemed too mild of a punishment for what he had intended. Finally, the Council reached out to the Elders for guidance—an initiative on which Korum took the lead, since he had other things to discuss with the Elders as well.

Between that and his regular work, Korum barely found time to sleep—because he also wanted to spend as much time with his charl as possible. Mia's attachment to him seemed to be growing every day, and Korum no longer doubted the strength of her feelings. As she'd said, whatever Saret had done to her, that was the way she was now—and they both had to accept it.

On the plus side, Korum kept getting surprised by how well Mia was adjusting to everything . . . and how independent she was becoming.

Prior to her memory loss, she had been hesitant to wander around Lenkarda on her own, wary of his people and intimidated by some of their technology. Other than going to the lab and to a few scenic places he'd shown her, Mia had usually stayed home with him. Her free time had also been more limited, given the rigid schedule Saret had set for his apprentices. Now, however, since she and Adam were largely learning on their own, Korum discovered that his charl appeared to have a thirst for adventure—and indulged it at every opportunity.

One day she went swimming in the ocean near the estuary, on a day when the current was relatively weak. Nonetheless, Korum—who had gotten into the habit of checking on her location every hour—felt his blood freeze in his veins when he saw that she was a good quarter-mile away from shore. He'd immediately gone straight there, only to find her swimming leisurely, clearly enjoying herself. By the time she came out of the water, he'd managed to calm himself enough to have a rational discussion about the dangers of this particular spot, and she had agreed to be more careful going forward—but Korum still felt shaken by the incident for several days after that.

Her other excursions were less dangerous. She developed a fondness for hiking and recording images of the local wildlife with her wristwatch-bracelet device. Howler monkeys, iguanas, even some large insects—she would record them all and send the images as photographs and videos to her family, to share more with them about her new home.

She also grew closer to Delia, frequently meeting her for morning walks on the beach. Korum encouraged the friendship, glad that Mia was building other relationships in Lenkarda. Maria came by sometimes as well, and Korum had made it a point to invite her and Arman to dinner a couple of times.

Their main disagreement revolved around Mia's status as a charl. "Don't you understand how that makes me feel, knowing that legally I belong to you just because I'm human and you said so?" she told him once. "Don't you see how barbaric that is?"

Korum didn't view it that way at all. Yes, she was his—his to protect, his to love and cherish. Taking a charl was a serious lifelong commitment. Under Krinar law, Korum was responsible for Mia's actions. If she ever broke the mandate, for instance, he would be the one to answer for it to the Elders. Mia would never again be a regular human, not with the nanocytes in her system; even if she left him, Korum would always have to watch over her, to make sure she didn't reveal any non-public information about the Krinar. A charl was neither a slave nor a pet, and most cheren thought of them as their human mates—something that Mia couldn't seem to grasp.

"How could I be your mate when I don't have any rights here?" she said, and her stubbornness made Korum want to bend her over his knee and spank her pretty little behind. "I never agreed to be your mate—or your charl—in the first place, did I? And besides, we can't even have children together . . ."

Korum couldn't argue with that last point, and the charl issue remained unresolved, hanging over their heads and occasionally popping up during some more heated conversations—although those were becoming increasingly rare as their relationship evolved.

Seeing that Mia was becoming comfortable with Krinar technology, Korum gave her a fabricator of her own—a more advanced version of what he had made for Maria's birthday. It was powerful enough to create anything Mia needed in the course of the day, including a transport pod.

Her happiness at this gift had been off the charts.

"Thank you! Oh my God, Korum, thank you so much! This is awesome!" She almost smothered him with kisses, her eyes shining and her entire body vibrating with excitement. For the next several hours, she played with the fabricator nonstop, creating and un-creating one thing after another, while Korum basked in her joy.

Shortly after that, Mia decided to go to New York—in an aircraft she created herself. Korum gave her the design for that; it was a more complicated machine than the transport pod that was used around the Center. She made the ship while he watched with a smile, proud of how much she had learned already.

They went to New York together, since Korum was reluctant to have her so far away on her own. He knew it was illogical; after all, she had lived in the human city for years before they met with no harm coming to her at all, and both Saret and the Resistance had been eliminated as a threat. Still, he couldn't shake his irrational fear for her safety. It was either go with her or forbid her to go at all, and Korum knew she would not take well to the latter option.

On the morning of their trip, Mia used the fabricator to make them human clothes.

"Hmm, let's see," she said, grinning wickedly. "How about a pink T-shirt for you?"

"Sure." Korum stifled a laugh at her crestfallen expression. "I'd love a pink T-shirt." His people didn't associate colors with gender, and he personally liked all pastel shades. He knew she'd been hoping he would bristle at what she viewed as a feminine outfit, but he couldn't care less—

as long as she didn't make him wear a skirt. He would draw the line at a skirt.

"Fine," she grumbled, "you're no fun." But she created a pink T-shirt anyway, which Korum put on without any hesitation. Thankfully, the jeans she handed him were of the regular dark blue variety.

"You know," she said thoughtfully, studying him after they were both dressed, "pink actually looks hot on you."

Korum laughed. "Why, thank you, my sweet. I'm flattered." She looked very sexy herself, dressed in a pair of well-fitting jeans, high-heeled ankle boots, and a silvery tank top that showed off her newly toned arms and shoulders. With the nanocytes in her body, Mia had significantly more endurance when it came to physical activity, and her recent interest in hiking and swimming had done wonders for her slim body. Korum had always found her irresistible, but now he could barely keep his eyes—and hands—off her.

"You told Jessie we'll be landing on her roof?" he asked as they entered the ship.

"Yep. She knows we're coming and even got permission from the building manager."

In order to save time, they had decided to go directly to Jessie, instead of flying to one of the designated Krinar landing areas. The idea behind these areas was to minimize disruption to the human population in the big cities. Even today, the sight of Krinar aircraft frequently resulted in car accidents. Apparently, frightened human drivers tended to be distracted drivers. As a Council member, Korum could get away with not following this landing guideline, but he still tried to be circumspect in large cities like New York.

Jessie greeted them on the roof when they landed. She was standing there with a young human male who could only be Edgar, her new boyfriend. Korum recalled seeing him once before, at the nightclub where Korum found Mia dancing with another man. That particular incident wasn't one of Korum's favorite memories.

Nevertheless, he smiled at Jessie and Edgar, determined to play nice. He knew Mia's former roommate was concerned about her. She had been a witness to the rocky start of Korum's relationship with Mia, and he still wasn't her favorite person—something Korum planned to remedy today.

Mia smiled too, and he could see that she was genuinely happy to see her friend. She was also nervous, judging by the tight clasp of her fingers around his palm. For some reason, she still hadn't told her friends or family about her memory loss. When Korum had confronted her about it, she'd given him some vague answer about not wanting to worry anyone and he'd had to be content with that.

"Mia!" Jessie flew at her as soon as they stepped out of the ship, and the two girls hugged, laughing and squealing.

Korum grinned at their exuberant reunion, then stepped forward, offering his hand to Edgar in a human greeting gesture. "Hello. I don't think we formally met."

"No, we haven't," Edgar said dryly, accepting his handshake. "The last time I saw you, your hand was wrapped around my friend Peter's throat. I'm guessing that wasn't a great time for introductions."

"Indeed," Korum said, his eyes narrowing a bit. This human dared to remind him of that day? Peter had been lucky Korum had been able to control himself as well as he had. Every time Korum thought of that boy kissing Mia, he saw red. *Play nice*, he reminded himself, and rearranged his features into a more friendly expression. "So you're an actor," he said, steering the conversation toward a topic the human would be sure to enjoy.

"I am." Edgar took the bait. "I'm on that newest show on CBS. It's called *The Vortex*. Maybe you've heard of it?"

"I've seen all the episodes," Korum said. "I'm actually a big fan. I couldn't believe what happened with Eva last week—I never would've expected her sister to turn up like that."

Edgar's eyes lit up. "Oh no way! You watch the show? Is it popular among the Ks?"

It was popular among one particular K who needed to watch it as preparation for this trip. "Sure," Korum said. "We like entertainment as much as humans."

Mia had finished hugging Jessie and came up to Edgar as well. "Hi, Edgar," she said. "It's great to see you again."

Korum concealed a smile. Little liar. She didn't remember the guy at all, but she was putting on a good show. Edgar wasn't the only actor here today.

"Hi, Korum." It was Jessie. There was a familiar look of distrust on her pretty face, and Korum inwardly sighed. Out of everybody, this particular friend of Mia's would be most difficult to win over. He could see it in the stubborn tilt of her chin as she looked at him. She resented him for taking Mia away from her—and for his initial high-handed tactics.

It was a good thing Korum was always up for a challenge. "Hello,

Jessie." He gave the human girl a warm smile.

They went inside, to the apartment Jessie had shared with Mia. Korum knew that a number of NYU students lived in the building due to its proximity to campus and reasonable (for New York) rent, but Korum had always thought the place was unfit for habitation. The paint in the hallways was peeling, and he could smell the rot in the old, musty walls. When he'd first met Mia, he couldn't wait to get her out of there and into his comfortable penthouse.

Jessie had prepared a veggie platter, beer, and some chips for them to snack on, and the four of them sat down in the living room. Later on, Korum planned to take them all out for a restaurant meal, but for now, this was as good of a spot to hang out as any.

Korum purposefully sat down next to their hostess. Mia sat on her other side, and Edgar made himself comfortable on a beanbag chair across from Korum. A couple of beers later, any hint of initial awkwardness had dissipated and conversation flowed freely. For a couple of young humans, Mia's friends were actually quite interesting, and Korum found himself unexpectedly having a good time. Jessie and Edgar had great chemistry together, joking around and teasing each other, and he could see Mia's initial tension draining away as nobody seemed to suspect anything about her lack of memory.

When everybody was sufficiently relaxed, Korum began his charm campaign against Jessie. He started off by inquiring about her summer, and then listened attentively as she told him all about her internship with a large pharmaceutical company. Korum already knew this, since he'd done his research prior to coming to New York. However, he also knew that people liked to talk about themselves, so he kept asking Jessie questions. In the meantime, Edgar was showing Mia posters of his latest show on the other side of the room.

"Is this company your first choice for full-time employment?" Korum asked Jessie, and she nodded, a hopeful look on her face.

"It's the first choice of everyone who's not going straight into medical school," she explained. "Since I want to do research first, this would be the perfect place to do it. It's super-competitive, of course. They hire ten times as many interns as they need full-time research assistants for next year, so even having an internship there doesn't guarantee an offer."

And just like that, Korum knew what he had to do. "You shouldn't worry," he said gently. "I'll put in a good word for you with the management."

"You would?" Jessie looked at him in astonishment. "You know

Biogem's management?"

"I do," Korum said. It wasn't much of a lie, since he would know them soon.

"Oh, wow. You don't have to do that, Korum," she protested faintly, but Korum could see that her heart wasn't in it. She wanted this very badly, and he was handing it to her on a silver platter.

"I want to," he said firmly. "You're obviously deserving of this opportunity, and I know Mia would want you to have it."

Jessie smiled uncertainly. "Well, in that case, thank you. I would appreciate any help in that direction."

And Operation Jessie was complete.

When the beer and snacks were no longer enough, they went out for an early dinner. Korum took them to a new French restaurant that was getting rave reviews—and that was known for serving traditional meat-based dishes at astronomical prices. He stuck to his usual plant-based diet, but Mia and her friends each ordered something from the animal kingdom. Korum didn't mind if they indulged once in a while. The Krinar had been mainly concerned with the environmental impact of human dietary habits, and occasional meat-eating wasn't nearly as disastrous for the planet as what humans in developed countries had been doing before.

After dinner, they went out for drinks. Knowing that the girls wanted some privacy, Korum unobtrusively maneuvered himself and Edgar toward the far end of the bar, letting Mia and Jessie be on their own next to the window. He still kept an eye on them, just to make sure they weren't bothered by anyone, but otherwise, he focused most of his attention on Edgar.

"Do you play any sports?" he asked Edgar when their beers arrived. It was one of the many things the Krinar had in common with humans: games that required physical ability and skill.

The actor nodded. "I played soccer in college, and I still do that occasionally for fun. I also recently took up boxing, to get in shape for my next role."

"Oh, really?" Korum said. "Do tell me about it."

* * *

Mia smiled to herself when she saw Korum and Edgar on the other end of the bar. She knew exactly what he was doing and why: her lover wanted her and Jessie to have some girl time.

"Wow, Mia," Jessie said after the bartender handed them their cocktails. "I have to say, I'm beginning to see why you fell for him. He's so much nicer than I initially thought."

Mia grinned. "Yeah, he's great." She had no idea how Korum had been when they met, but she had some suspicions based on what he'd told her—and what she'd observed from his interactions with others over the past month. The love of her life was definitely not someone she would ever want for an enemy.

"You seem different too," Jessie said. "Stronger, more confident . . . and even more beautiful. Whatever he's doing for you seems to be working."

"He makes me happy," Mia told her. "Oh, Jessie, he makes me so unbelievably happy. I never thought I could be in love like that. It's like a fairytale come true."

"Complete with an extraterrestrial Prince Charming?"

Mia laughed. "Sure." Korum was not exactly Prince Charming, but she didn't plan on telling Jessie that. She liked the new friendly dynamic between her lover and her friends, and she had no intention of upsetting it.

No, she knew that Korum was far from perfect. She loved him, but she was not blind to his flaws. He was possessive to the extreme, paranoid about her safety—and manipulative when he needed to be. She hadn't missed the way he had deliberately spent time with Jessie, softening her up. It had worked too; her former roommate seemed to have a much better opinion of him now.

"It doesn't bother you that he's so much older?" Jessie asked, her dark eyes gleaming with curiosity. "Edgar is twenty-six, and he jokes that I'm the younger woman. I can't even imagine dating someone Korum's age . . ."

"He's not that old for a Krinar, believe it or not," Mia said, smiling. "There are some who are much, much older. But, yes, sometimes the age gap is a challenge. There are definitely times when I feel like he's amused by me. He never makes me feel stupid or anything like that, but I know he thinks I'm very young."

"He doesn't treat you like a kid?"

"No." Mia shook her head. "He doesn't. He's ridiculously overprotective, but that's as far as that goes."

Jessie regarded her thoughtfully. "Do you think this is a long-term thing for you?" she asked, a small frown marring the smoothness of her forehead. "I mean, marriage and the whole enchilada? How would that even work with a K if they don't age like we do?"

Mia took a big gulp of her cocktail and coughed when it went down her windpipe. "Um, I'm not sure we're at that point yet," she said when she finally caught her breath. Korum had impressed on her that nobody outside of Lenkarda was supposed to know about her lengthened lifespan. It had something to do with a mandate set by their Elders. Mia hated the restriction, but she knew better than to break these rules. As Korum had explained, humans who knew too much would get their memories wiped—and Mia would never want to subject any of her friends or family to that process.

"But eventually?" Jessie persisted. "Have you thought about that? If you guys stay together, what happens when you get older? And what about kids?"

Mia shrugged. "We'll cross that bridge when we get to it." She didn't want to think about children right now. It was the one thing guaranteed to spoil her good mood. The DNA differences between humans and Krinar were too great to allow for biological offspring—a fact that made sense but was still agonizing to dwell on.

"Anyways," Mia said, wanting to change the subject, "how about you and Edgar? How serious are you two getting?"

Jessie's smile was as bright as the sun. "I met his parents last week," she confided. "And next week, I'm taking him to meet mine."

"Wow . . . Jessie, that is big!" As far as Mia knew, this was the first time her friend was going to have a guy meet her family. Although Jessie's parents had been in America for a long time, they still retained some of the traditional Chinese customs and attitudes. Bringing home a boyfriend was a serious matter, and the boyfriend in question had to be ready to answer some very probing questions about his career and future life plans.

"Yeah," Jessie said wryly. "I warned Edgar that he's going to get grilled, but he's cool with that."

Suddenly, Mia felt a light touch on her bare arm. "May I buy you ladies a drink?" an unfamiliar male voice asked, and Mia turned her head to see an attractive dark-haired man who looked to be in his late twenties.

"We're here with our boyfriends," Jessie said quickly, an anxious note in her voice.

"Okay, no problem," the guy said, and disappeared into the crowd.

Mia looked at Jessie, eyebrows raised. Her friend had just been uncharacteristically rude, and she couldn't figure out why. And then she saw where Jessie was looking.

Korum was staring in their direction, his jaw tightly clenched and his eyes a bright golden yellow. Mia smiled and waved to him, wanting to diffuse the tension. She knew he didn't like any man touching her, but the guy had been harmless.

"He's not going to flip out again, is he?" Jessie sounded scared.

"What? No, of course not," Mia said automatically, and then she remembered Korum telling her something about an incident at a nightclub in the early days of their relationship. He'd said that she and Jessie had gone out on their own, and some guy had kissed her. Based on Jessie's reaction, Mia guessed that Korum had downplayed his own response to that.

"Uh-huh," Jessie said doubtfully.

"He won't," Mia said with confidence, looking directly at Korum. She knew perfectly well that he could hear her.

He stared back at her. His eyes still had those dangerous golden flecks in them, but one corner of his mouth tilted up, a ghost of a smile stealing across his face. Mia continued looking at him, her own eyes narrowed, and the smile became a full-blown grin, transforming his features from merely gorgeous to out-of-this-world sexy. Then he turned away and continued speaking to Edgar, as though nothing had happened.

"Holy shit," Jessie breathed, her eyes huge. "You did it! Mia, you fucking did it . . ."

"Did what?"

"You tamed a K."

CHAPTER TWENTY

Another two weeks passed after the New York trip. Mia found herself loving her new life . . . and contemplating not going back to finish her last year of school.

Lenkarda was as close to paradise as she could imagine. Summer was the wet season in that region of Costa Rica, which meant sunny mornings and tropical rain showers in the afternoon. As a result of all that rain, everything turned lush and green, with the waterfalls and rivers full to bursting. Mia often spent her mornings exploring the woods nearby, taking pictures of the local wildlife, and the second half of the day working in the lab with Adam.

Haron, the mind expert from Arizona, had agreed to take over Saret's lab as a temporary solution to keep the place open. Too much important research had been going on there to simply shut it down. Mia had first met the K during their brief trip to Arizona and she wasn't sure she liked him that much. She got the feeling he regarded her as something of a medical curiosity, due to her condition. Nevertheless, he didn't mind if she continued working in the lab, and he mostly left her and Adam alone—which suited Mia just fine.

With each day that passed, Mia became more and more entrenched in life in Lenkarda. Her friendship with Delia continued to develop, and the two girls often went swimming and snorkeling together—something that eased the minds of both of their cheren. "At least Delia can call for help if anything happens and vice versa," Korum said one evening while they were lying in bed. "And she knows which areas to avoid."

Korum's overprotectiveness drove Mia insane. When she complained about it to Delia, the older girl laughed. "Oh, just get used to it. Arus is the exact same way, believe me. You'd think after centuries together he'd realize I'm capable of taking care of myself, but no. If he had his way, I'd never leave the house without him."

"How do you cope with that?" Mia asked, studying her hands. She knew about the tracking devices there, and she *really* hated them. When she'd found out about the shining—after questioning Korum as to how he always seemed to know her exact location—she had been furious and insisted that Korum remove the devices. He refused, explaining that he needed to know that she was safe. They ended up having a long argument that culminated in Korum taking her to bed. The devices were still there for now, but Mia had every intention of removing them at the first opportunity.

Delia shrugged her slim shoulders. "I don't know," she said. "I know that Arus loves me and that he's afraid of losing me. I'm as necessary to his existence as he is to mine—and I try to make allowances for that. Over time, both of us have learned the value of compromise, and you and Korum will too."

Having Delia for a friend was like having a mentor and a girlfriend all wrapped up in one graceful package. At times, she was as wise and mysterious as a sphinx, but, other times, she was just like any other young woman Mia's age, acting as playful as a teenager. This unusual personality mix was relatively common among the Krinar, Mia discovered. They lived for a long time, but they never felt *old*. Their bodies were as healthy at ten thousand years of age as they were at twenty, and everybody around them shared their longevity, so they rarely experienced the types of losses that an unusually long-lived human would.

"You know, you don't fit the stereotype of a brooding immortal at all," Mia told Korum once, after a particularly fun play session in their zero-gravity chamber. "Shouldn't you be all moody and hating life instead of enjoying it so much?"

Korum grinned in response, white teeth flashing. "How could I hate life when I have you?" he said, lifting her and twirling her around the room.

When he finally put her down, Mia had been breathless with laughter.

"Life is to be enjoyed, my sweet," he said, still holding on to her, the expression on his face unexpectedly serious. "That's why I love you so much. I *enjoy* you, Mia—you enhance every moment of my existence. Your smile, your laugh—even your stubbornness—make me happier than I've ever been before. Even when we're not together, the thought of you makes me feel content, because I know that you're here, that when I come home, I can hold you, feel you—" his eyes gleamed brighter, "—fuck you."

Mia stared at him, her nipples hardening as her skin prickled with arousal.

"Yes," he said, his voice low and husky, "let's not forget about that last part. I very much enjoy fucking you. I love the way you moan when I'm deep inside you, the flush on your cheeks when you're turned on . . . I love the way you smell, the way you taste. I want to eat you like dessert . . ." He reached between her legs, his fingers parting her folds, stroking her there, spreading the moisture around her opening. "Your pussy is sweeter than any fruit," he whispered, sinking to his knees and lifting the bottom of her dress, "more delicious than chocolate . . ."

And Mia nearly climaxed right then and there at the first touch of his tongue. Moaning, she buried her fingers in his hair, holding on to him as his skilled mouth brought her to a peak, pleasuring her until she shattered into a million pieces.

* * *

"Say that again," Korum demanded, staring at Ellet.

"I think I found someone who can reverse Saret's procedure and undo Mia's memory loss," Ellet repeated, crossing her long legs. They were sitting in Ellet's lab, where Korum had brought Mia after rescuing her from Saret's clutches.

"Who?"

"An up-and-coming apprentice at the Baranil lab. Apparently she has just developed a way to undo almost any mind procedure. It's all very hush-hush, which is why we didn't know about this earlier. You can imagine the implications of something like that. Everyone who's undergone any kind of rehabilitation would want this."

"The Baranil lab," Korum said, staring at Ellet. "On Krina."

"Yes."

"I see." Korum got up and started to pace.

"Do you even need it anymore?" Ellet asked, staring at him with her large dark eyes. "Mia seems quite happy as is . . . and so do you." There was a slightly wistful note in her voice.

Korum glanced at her sharply. Though they had been lovers, he'd never had any deeper feelings for Ellet—and he had been sure she didn't have any for him either.

As though to answer his unspoken question, Ellet smiled. "I'm happy for you," she said softly. "I really am. What you and I had has been over for a long time. I just never thought a human girl would be the one to make you feel this way."

Korum sighed, running his hand through his hair. "Me neither, Ellet. Believe me, it's quite a shock to me as well."

"Oh, I believe you," Ellet said, still smiling. She was beautiful—objectively, Korum recognized that—but her looks now left him cold. Every woman he saw these days was measured against Mia and found wanting—another side effect of his obsession with his charl.

"Can you please connect me with this apprentice?" Korum asked, returning to the subject at hand. "I'd like to speak to her."

Leaving Ellet, Korum headed toward his own laboratory, where his designers worked. Although they could all work remotely, meeting only in virtual environments, something about physical proximity tended to foster the creative process, resulting in improved team cohesiveness and more innovative project outcomes.

Entering the large cream-colored building, Korum greeted Rezav, one of his lead designers, and went into his office, a private space where he usually did his best work. This past week had been a quiet one, with his employees relaxing after last month's rush to finalize the designs for the new shields. Normally, this would've been the perfect time for Korum to work on his own designs—but the past couple of weeks had been far from normal.

Making sure that nobody could enter his office, Korum attached a virtual reality node to his temple and closed his eyes. When he opened them, he was standing next to a large river, surrounded by the familiar green, red, and gold tones of Krina vegetation.

The sun was bright, even hotter than at the equator on Earth. Korum could feel its rays on the bare skin of his arms, and he basked in the pleasant sensation. Drawing in a deep breath, he let his lungs fill with pure, clean air and the heady aroma of blooming plants.

"Quite different from Earth, isn't it?" a deep voice said to his right, and Korum turned his head to see Lahur standing there, less than five feet away. He hadn't heard the Elder's approach—but then no one could move quite like Lahur. The ancient Krinar was the ultimate predator, his speed and strength as legendary as the man himself.

"Yes," Korum said simply. "Quite different." If there was one thing he had learned during his recent interactions with the Elders, it was the importance of saying as little as possible. Lahur—the oldest of them all—liked silence and seemed to have contempt for those who spoke unnecessarily.

The fact that Lahur was speaking to Korum at all was incredible. Korum was no stranger to the Elders, having appealed to them numerous times for various Council matters. However, all of his prior communications had been done through the official channels, and the Elders almost never met with the Councilors in person—either virtually or in the real world. So when Korum had reached out to the Elders on Mia's behalf several weeks ago, he had never expected to have his request taken seriously, much less to be granted a virtual meeting.

A virtual meeting that had somehow turned into an entire series of interviews in the weeks to come.

Lahur stared at him, his eyes dark and unfathomable. Like Korum, he had been conceived naturally, not in a lab, and his asymmetrical features were closer to those of the ancients than to the modern Krinar.

"We have considered your request," the Elder said, his unblinking gaze trained on Korum.

Korum didn't say anything, only inclined his head slightly. Patience was the key here. Patience and respect.

"You wish your charl's family to be brought into our society. To have them share her extended lifespan."

Korum kept silent, holding Lahur's gaze with his own.

"We will not grant you your request."

Korum fought to hide his disappointment. "Why?" he asked calmly. "It's just a few humans. What harm would it do to bring them to Lenkarda and have them share fully in my charl's life?"

Lahur's eyes darkened, turning pitch black. "You argue for them?"

"No," Korum said evenly, ignoring the way his pulse had picked up. "I argue for her—for Mia."

Lahur stared at him. "Why? Why is one of these creatures so important to you?"

"Because she is," Korum said. "Because she means everything to me." He knew he had just done the equivalent of exposing his throat to Lahur, but he didn't care. It was no secret that Mia was his weakness, and trying to hide it from a ten-million-year-old Elder was as pointless as beating one's head against a wall.

To Korum's shock, a faint smile touched Lahur's lips, softening the harsh lines of his face. "Very well," the Elder said. "You have convinced me—and I'll give you one chance to convince the others. Bring the humans here and let them speak on their own behalf." He paused for a second, letting the full impact of his words hit Korum. "I would like to meet this Mia of yours."

CHAPTER TWENTY-ONE

"What's wrong?" Mia asked after the second time Korum fell silent, as though absorbed in his thoughts.

They were eating a late dinner on the beach—a romantic outing Korum had suggested the day before. Mia had expected something over the top . . . and it was. All around them, hundreds of tiny lights floated in the air, looking like a cross between stars and fireflies. The sun had already gone down, and these lights, along with the new crescent-shaped moon, were the only sources of illumination.

For their meal, Korum had prepared dozens of little dishes, mostly of the finger-food variety. They ranged from tiny sandwiches made with a delicious artichoke paste to some exotic fruits Mia had never tasted before. It was a spread fit for a king. Mia had been greatly enjoying everything—until she noticed Korum's oddly distracted manner.

"What makes you think something is wrong?" he asked, his lips curving in a sensual smile, but Mia wasn't fooled. There was definitely something on his mind.

"Don't you think I can tell by now when you're worried about something?" Mia cocked her head to the side, staring at her lover. He could still be a mystery to her at times, but she was getting to know him better with each day that passed.

He looked at her, his gaze almost . . . calculating. "You're right, my sweet," he said finally. "There is something I need to talk to you about."

Mia swallowed. The last time Korum had needed to talk to her about something, she'd found out that her mind had been tampered with. What could it be this time?

"It's nothing bad," Korum said, seemingly understanding her concern. "In fact, it's all good news."

"What is it?" Mia couldn't shake an uneasy feeling.

"We found someone on Krina who can reverse Saret's procedure," Korum said, watching her closely. "She can undo everything he's done to you—including the memory wipe."

"Oh my God . . ." Mia didn't even know what to say. "But, Korum, that's awesome!"

He smiled. "It is. And there's something else."

"What?"

"Do you remember my petition to the Elders about your family?"

Mia almost stopped breathing. "About making them immortal like me?"

"Yes."

"Of course I remember," Mia said, her heart beginning to pound in her chest with a wild mixture of hope and apprehension.

"There's a chance they might grant it."

This time, Mia couldn't contain an excited scream. Jumping to her feet and laughing, she launched herself at Korum, who got up just in time. "Thank you! Oh my God, Korum, thank you!"

"Hold on, my darling," he said, gently pulling her away. "It's not that simple. It requires something you might not want to do."

Mia stared at him, some of her excitement fading. "What?"

"We would have to go to Krina and take your family with us."

* * *

That night, Mia couldn't sleep. She kept waking up every hour, her mind buzzing with a million different questions and concerns. As Korum had explained, the trip to Krina would serve two purposes: to undo Saret's procedure and to present Mia's case in front of the Elders. "They want to meet you," he had said, shocking Mia into silence.

A large warm body pressed against her back, startling her out of her musings. "You're awake again," Korum murmured, pulling her into his arms. "Why aren't you sleeping, my darling?"

"Why do the Elders want this?" Mia couldn't stop thinking about it. "Why do they want to see us? I thought they were like your gods or something. What could they want with me and my family?"

Korum sighed, and she felt the movement of his chest. "They're not gods. They're Krinar, like me—only much, much older. As to why they want to see you, I don't know. They have taken an unusual interest in my petition, meeting with me several times and asking a lot of questions about you and your parents."

"And they didn't say they would grant your request, right?" Mia turned in his arms, so that she would be facing him.

"No," Korum said, the faint glow of moonlight from the transparent ceiling reflecting in his eyes, "they didn't. However, Lahur said he would give us one more chance—and he implied he would be on our side."

"Lahur is the oldest?"

"Yes. He's the one who's lived for over ten million years."

Mia shivered, goosebumps appearing on her arms.

"Cold?" Korum drew her closer, pulling a blanket over them.

"No, not really." His naked body was like a furnace, generating so much heat that she was never cold when she slept next to him. The temperature in Korum's house was always comfortable too—cooler at night, warmer during the day. It was tailored specifically to meet their needs. When Mia had lived in Florida, she'd always hated air-conditioning; the cold air was too startling after the heat outside, and usually cranked up too high for her taste. In Lenkarda, intelligent structures kept the inside of the buildings at a perfect temperature, creating micro-zones of climate around each person.

"We don't have to go, you know." Korum gently stroked her back. "We can stay here. You've adapted to everything so well. If the memory loss doesn't bother you, then nothing has to change—"

"No," Mia said, burrowing against his chest. "If it was only that, then we could consider staying. But my parents, my sister . . . If there's even a chance they can live a longer life, we have to do this. I could never live with myself otherwise."

"I know, my darling," Korum said softly. "I know that."

"Couldn't we meet with the Elders virtually?" Mia drew back to look at his face. "That's how you met with them, right?"

"Yes," Korum said. "But they don't consider that a real meeting. When Lahur said he wanted to meet you, he meant in person, in real life."

"Old-fashioned, is he?" Mia said wryly.

Korum laughed. "That's the understatement of the century."

Mia fell silent, thinking about the upcoming trip again. "Do you think we'll be back soon?" she asked after a few seconds.

"I don't know," Korum said. "It depends on what the Elders want."

* * *

The next day Korum watched as Mia rang the doorbell at her parents' house. He knew she was worried about this part: telling her family about Krinar life extension capabilities and convincing them to go to Krina.

She was wearing human clothes today, a pair of shorts and a T-shirt. As much as Korum liked seeing her in dresses, he had to admit that the shorts looked good on her, showing off her shapely legs. Maybe he should have her dress like this more frequently.

Mia's mother opened the door with a huge smile on her softly rounded face. "Mia! Korum! Oh, I'm so glad you two came by!" She embraced Mia first, and then Korum found himself enveloped in a perfumed hug.

Smiling, he brushed a light kiss on Ella Stalis's cheek and stepped into the house, following the two women inside. Mocha, the tiny dog Mia had called a Chihuahua, ran out of one of the rooms, barking happily and trying to jump at Korum. He bent down and petted the little animal, which immediately rolled onto its back and presented its belly— apparently to be rubbed as well.

"Wow, Korum, she loves you," Mia said wonderingly. "I can't believe she acts that way with you. She's normally so shy with strangers . . ." And to prove her point, Mia extended her hand to the dog, which instantly turned over and ran away.

Korum grinned. It seemed like small, cute creatures had a thing for him.

Mia's parents had a lovely place—the epitome of what he thought of as American human. It had a comfortable, lived-in vibe, with overstuffed couches showing minor signs of wear and family photographs everywhere. Korum particularly enjoyed seeing those of Mia as a child. She had been a pretty toddler, with her long curls and big blue eyes. For a second, those photos made him ache to hold a daughter of his own, with Mia's features—a strange and impossible urge he'd never felt before.

Mia's father walked into the living room just as they sat down on the couch. Mia jumped to her feet. "Dad!"

"Oh, Mia, honey, I'm so glad to see you!" Dan Stalis embraced his daughter, kissing her cheek.

Korum got to his feet as well and extended his hand in a human greeting. "Hello, Dan."

"Korum, it's good to see you as well," Mia's father said, shaking his hand. He was more reserved than he had been with Mia, and Korum knew her father was still partially on the fence about their relationship. Korum couldn't blame him; if he had been in the human's shoes, he wouldn't have been nearly as accepting of someone taking his daughter away.

"Where's Marisa?" Mia asked when everybody sat down again. "Is she coming?"

"Yes, she should be here in a few minutes," her mother replied, still beaming with happiness at having her daughter home. Mia was glowing as well. Watching them, Korum was more convinced than ever that he had done the right thing in reaching out to the Elders. His charl would've been miserable if she'd had to watch her parents aging and withering away, knowing all the while that Korum had it in his power to prevent that from happening.

"Can I offer you some tea? Maybe some fruit?" Ella asked, addressing Korum. "Are you two hungry? I made a delicious beet salad yesterday—"

"I'm all right, thank you," Korum said, softening his answer with a smile. "We ate just before we came here."

"I'll take some tea," Mia said. "But don't worry, mom—I'll get it myself." Getting up, she walked toward the kitchen, leaving Korum by himself with the two older humans.

Ella and Dan Stalis were watching him strangely, almost expectantly, and Korum had a sudden flash of intuition. They thought he and Mia were getting engaged—and likely expected him to ask them for permission, in the old-fashioned human way.

Korum felt an unexpected flicker of regret for letting them down. That wasn't why he and Mia had come today at all, nor had the idea ever occurred to him before. As far as he knew, no Krinar had ever married a human; it just wasn't done that way. By claiming Mia as his charl, Korum had already made a commitment to her—even if she didn't necessarily view it the same way.

To his relief, the doorbell rang again, diffusing the awkward moment. Both humans got up and hurried to the door, letting their older daughter and her husband in. Mia came out of the kitchen as well, a broad smile on her face.

Korum stood up to greet them as they walked into the door. He kissed Marisa on the cheek and shook Connor's hand, genuinely glad to see the young couple. Mia's sister was just beginning to show, her trim figure rounding out with the baby, and she looked radiantly happy.

At the light brush of his lips against her cheek, Marisa blushed, her fair skin as sensitive as Mia's. Korum suppressed a smile. He knew human women found him attractive, and he rather liked having that effect on them. It was better than having them cringe in fear, as they sometimes did because of what he was.

Connor didn't seem to mind his wife's reaction, smiling as calmly as before. Korum couldn't understand his placidity. If Mia had blushed at the touch of another man, that man's lifespan would've been numbered in minutes. Humans were definitely more laid back about such matters; some males were as possessive as the Krinar when it came to their women, but the majority were not.

Mia greeted them next, and then everybody walked back to the couch area.

"All right, baby sis," Marisa said, taking a seat on the sofa. Her husband pulled up a chair next to her. "Tell us what's going on."

Mia took a deep breath and Korum squeezed her hand for encouragement. "I'm immortal," she said baldly. "I can now live as long as Korum—and if you come with us to Krina, you might be able to also."

For a moment, there was complete silence in the room. Then everybody started speaking at once. In the cacophony of voices, it was impossible to hear any specific question. Only Dan Stalis was quiet, leaning against a table and observing the proceedings with an expression of mild curiosity on his face.

"You're not surprised," Korum said, looking at Mia's father.

"No," Dan said. "I'm not."

"Why not?" Korum asked.

"Because it makes all the sense in the world," Dan Stalis replied. "How else could you and Mia be together? She has never talked about a future with you, yet she never seems upset when we bring it up. How could that be when she loves you and wants to be with you? And besides, you cured my migraines with nothing more than a small capsule. It's not that big of a stretch to think your people could cure other things, like cancer or heart disease." He paused for a second. "Maybe even aging."

Korum smiled, involuntarily impressed by the human.

"Dan, you never said anything to me." Ella's tone was bewildered. "In all the times we discussed Mia, you never once voiced these suspicions to me!" Her voice rose at the end, her eyes narrowing as she stared at her husband.

"It was never anything more than a guess," Dan said soothingly. "Ella, sweetheart, I didn't want to get your hopes up in case I was wrong."

"So are you now a K?" Marisa was looking at her sister with a shocked expression on her face. "Do you drink blood too?"

"Wait," said Connor, "can we go back to the part where we can all be immortal if we go to Krina?"

Mia opened her mouth to reply, and Korum squeezed her hand again. "Let me try to explain, my sweet," he said, "and then we'll answer any other questions your family might have."

Everybody fell silent, staring at him, and he continued, "We do have the means of curing cancer—and aging and any other maladies that may plague humans. The way that's done is by the insertion of nanocytes— nanomachines that mimic the functions of cells in a human body. They clean up any and all ongoing cellular damage and allow for rapid healing of injuries. That's all they do; there's no transformation from one species to another.

"Mia has these nanocytes in her body. I gave them to her a couple of months ago. And you're right, Dan. That's the only way we would be able to be together longer term."

Korum paused and surveyed the room. "The reason why Mia didn't tell you about this earlier—and why you've never heard of this before—is something called the non-interference mandate. It's set by our Elders. We're not allowed to do anything that would significantly alter the course of natural human progress. That's why we don't share our technology or science with you: because doing so is forbidden. The only exceptions to that rule are humans we call charl: those like Mia, with whom we enter into serious relationships."

"But why?" Connor asked, frowning. "Why have that mandate in the first place?"

"I don't know," Korum admitted. "There are many theories, the most popular of which is that the Elders are still conducting their experiment in regard to your evolution. They were there to see the beginning of your species, and they want to see how you turn out with minimal interference from us—"

"What do you mean, in the beginning? Just how old are these Elders of yours?" Dan interrupted, looking at Korum.

"Old," Mia answered for him. "Very old. Like ten million years old."

Mia's father visibly paled. "Ten *million* years old?"

"Yes," Mia said. "When Korum said they were there for the beginning of the human race, he wasn't kidding. Two of the Elders were actually in charge of overseeing our evolution way back when. Right?" She looked up at Korum.

"Yes, exactly," he confirmed.

"So if there's this mandate in place, why are you telling us about this stuff now?" Mia's mother asked, looking confused. "And what was that you said before, about going to Krina?"

"I petitioned the Elders on your behalf," Korum explained. "To have you undergo the same procedure as Mia. They didn't exactly agree to it, but they made a very unusual request: to see Mia and your family in person."

"The Elders want to see *us*?" Ella Stalis looked like she was about to faint.

"Yes," Korum said. "They want to see you and Mia in person."

"Why?" It was Dan again.

"I don't know," Korum said honestly. "I wish I could tell you."

"So let me get this straight . . . They want us to come to Krina, but they don't guarantee that they will give us these nanocytes?" Connor asked, his frown deepening. "They're asking us to leave our lives behind on the remote chance that this might happen?"

"Yes." Korum didn't bother to sugarcoat the situation.

"What would happen if you disobeyed these Elders?" Marisa asked, her slender hands twisting together. "If you broke the non-interference mandate?"

"It depends," Korum said. "If it's just a minor infraction, it results in a loss of standing—that's something like our reputation—and there are frequently financial and other penalties. If it's something more serious, then it's treated as a criminal offense on par with murder."

"Oh," Marisa said faintly.

"So let me get this straight," Dan Stalis said. "You're giving us the possibility of having an infinitely long lifespan, but only if we go with you to another planet."

"Yes."

"And what would happen if we refuse?" Connor asked, a stubborn look on his face. "What if we don't want to uproot our entire lives to fly off into space?"

Korum shrugged. Truth be told, he wasn't certain what would happen if any of Mia's family decided against accepting the Elders' invitation. In the normal course of events, if humans found out something they shouldn't have, they would have a portion of their memories erased. But this was different, and he didn't know what guidelines applied in this case.

"No, Connor, you can't refuse," Mia said, glowering at her brother-in-law. "Don't you understand? If the Elders grant our request, you and Marisa—and your baby—would be able to live for thousands of years. How could you refuse something like that? And, mom, dad, you guys will be young again. Wouldn't that be awesome?" She cast a pleading glance around the room. "Please, don't make me watch you all die because you're scared. Korum is offering you a shot at immortality. How could you turn that down?"

CHAPTER TWENTY-TWO

The next two weeks passed in a flurry of preparations for the departure. Mia's parents, Marisa, and Connor each requested a leave of absence from their jobs and put their finances in order. Of them all, Connor seemed the most hesitant, though Marisa convinced him that they had to go—if only for their baby's sake. After many discussions, it was decided that if the Elders didn't grant them immortality, then they would come back to their regular lives—after first signing an agreement not to reveal any confidential information about the Ks. If the petition succeeded, however, then Lenkarda would be their new home, just as it was for Mia.

To alleviate any concerns about her sister traveling during pregnancy, Mia spoke to Ellet and had her examine Marisa one last time. "She's perfectly healthy," Ellet reassured them, "and routine space travel shouldn't pose any issues. Now if she went off exploring new galaxies, I would be worried, but a simple trip between Krina and Earth—that's the safest thing there is these days."

Mia called Jessie and spoke to her, explaining that she would be away for a while and won't be coming back for the school year. Jessie wasn't the least bit surprised, though she did cry when Mia said she didn't know how soon she would return. Since Mia couldn't tell Jessie the real reasons for the trip, she had to let her think it was Korum's business taking them away.

"Can Jessie come too?" Mia asked Korum after that heart-breaking conversation. "I know you said family only, but she's like family to me—"

"No, my sweet," Korum said regretfully. "The Elders even balked at

Connor coming along. I had to work very hard to convince them that a brother-in-law is the equivalent of a real sibling. If Connor's parents had been alive, I don't think it could've worked—that would've been too many humans to get an exception for."

Mia swallowed. She hadn't realized how close she'd come to losing her sister, who would've likely chosen to stay behind with her husband. It was the first time Connor's lack of family was in any way a plus. Mia had always felt sorry for her brother-in-law because his mother, a single parent, had passed away from breast cancer seven years ago . . . but now that fact may have enabled Mia's family to stay together.

Adam prepared a bunch of notes and recordings for her to take to the mind lab on Krina. "Don't forget to give it to that apprentice," he told Mia. "It's got everything I could find in Saret's files about memory loss and softening. It's not much—he must've destroyed most of the data before—but it might help them figure out your condition."

"Thanks, Adam." Mia smiled at the K. "It was awesome having you for a partner."

Adam grinned, white teeth flashing. "Right back at you, partner. Ping me when you guys land and settle in; I'd love to hear how your meeting with the Elders goes."

"Of course," Mia said. She knew Adam had a very good reason for wanting to know the outcome of Korum's petition: his entire adopted family was human—as was the mysterious girlfriend he never talked about.

* * *

"Saret is going to be on the ship with us," Korum told Mia as they walked on the beach the evening before their departure. "The Council wants him back on Krina so the Elders can try him themselves."

Mia's stomach twisted with remembered fear. She still had occasional nightmares from the Arena fight—horrifying dreams in which Korum didn't emerge as the victor. Saret had come far too close to killing her lover, and she could never forget the agony of those moments when she'd thought she lost Korum.

As though reading her mind, Korum said, "There's nothing to worry about, my sweet. He'll be locked up the entire trip."

"Which will only be a couple of weeks, right?" Mia asked.

"Yes," Korum confirmed. "Getting sufficiently far away from Earth is what's going to take the longest. This is a very crowded solar system and we have to make sure nothing interferes with our ship's warp capabilities."

Mia laughed, forgetting all about Saret for the moment. "Warp capabilities? Like the warp drive in our science fiction—the thing that lets you go faster than the speed of light?"

"Yes," Korum said. "Very similar to that. It bends space-time, allowing us to travel from one point in the universe to another almost instantaneously."

"How does it do that?" Mia asked in fascination. Physics had never been her strongest subject, but even she knew that weird things happened near the speed of light—and that faster-than-light travel had been considered impossible until the Ks arrived.

Korum smiled, apparently pleased by her interest. "I can't explain fully without going into some complicated math, but I can give you a rough idea," he said. "Essentially, our ships create a huge energy bubble that causes a contraction in the space-time in front of it and an expansion in the space-time behind it. That's what propels us from one place to another—the push-and-pull of space-time itself. We don't need to reach the speed of light at any point; we bypass it altogether."

"Wouldn't something like that require a lot of energy? What do you use for fuel?"

"Well, the energy bubble around the ship uses a combination of positive and negative energy," Korum said. "Negative energy is something that your scientists are just now beginning to explore. And yes, you're absolutely right: warping space-time requires a tremendous amount of energy. Fortunately, we have it in abundance. We also use antimatter as a fuel source; that's what powers our ship when we're not in warp mode."

Mia's eyes widened. "Antimatter?"

"It's the most powerful energy source there is," Korum explained.

Mia fell silent, thinking about the magnitude of what she was about to do. Tomorrow, she would leave Earth for an as-yet-undetermined length of time, with a lover who wasn't even human. She was entrusting the fate of her entire family into his hands.

It should've been a scary thought, but somehow it wasn't. Instead she was almost giddy with excitement. How many people got a chance like that? To see a different planet, to go to Krina—the origin of all life? And meeting the Krinar Elders . . . She still couldn't wrap her mind around that one. She, a regular human girl, would see the actual creators of mankind.

It was enough to make anybody's head spin.

* * *

The next morning they went to Florida to pick up Mia's family, flying in a larger transport pod Korum had created specifically for that purpose. Everyone was already gathered at Mia's parents' house, with their bags packed and ready. Even though Korum had explained that they didn't need most of their things, the humans insisted on bringing their own clothing and other items they saw as necessities.

This time, Korum landed the pod on the street in front of the Stalis house. Mia had explained that her parents already told all their neighbors about the upcoming trip (though not the reason for it), and nobody would be too shocked to see an alien aircraft landing in their quiet neighborhood.

Emerging from the pod, Korum and Mia walked to the door and rang the doorbell. All around them, people were slowly coming out of their houses, driven by curiosity about their neighbors' extraterrestrial connection. Korum could hear their whispers, giggles, and gasps of excitement and fear. An older couple a few houses away were on the phone with their children, complaining that the 'K evil' had come to Ormond Beach. They likely thought he couldn't hear them, not realizing how acute Krinar senses were.

None of this bothered Korum. In the past, he'd tried to be considerate, to make sure that his presence in the small town didn't draw too much attention to his charl's family. Now, however, it didn't matter. If the Elders agreed to their request, Mia's relatives would never be able to return to their regular lives.

Marisa opened the door to let them in. "Hi guys," she exclaimed brightly. "Come on in! We're almost ready."

"Awesome!" Mia had a huge grin on her face as they entered the house. "Are you excited? I know I am—"

"Oh my God, am I excited? Are you kidding me? I haven't slept for two nights . . ."

Korum smiled and followed the two sisters as they continued chattering all the way to the kitchen. Mia's parents and Connor were already gathered there, eating their breakfast.

"Korum!" Ella exclaimed, her eyes lighting up. "Will you join us? I made some potato pancakes with fresh berry jam."

"Sure," Korum said, sitting down at the table. "I'd love some pancakes." Mia and he ate about an hour ago, but he was curious to try the dish Mia had said was her mother's specialty.

In that moment, Mia came up behind his chair and kissed his cheek, her hair tickling the back of his neck. "Already hungry?" she teased, her hands gently kneading his shoulders. Her easy display of affection made him want to hug her. He hadn't known how much he needed that from her until she started touching him like that in the past few weeks. Before, he had almost always been the one to initiate physical contact, both of the sexual and more casual variety.

Of course, whenever she was this close to him, he got hard, but the discomfort was a small price to pay. Korum shifted in his seat, raising his knee slightly in case any of his human companions happened to glance under the table.

"Mia, honey, how about you?" her mother asked. "Do you want some pancakes too?"

"I'd love some, mom, thanks." Mia let go of Korum's shoulders and sat down in the chair next to him. Korum reached over and took her hand, craving more of her touch.

"Ooh, so lovey-dovey," Connor said, chewing on a pancake. "Look at those two, Marisa."

"Shut up, Connor," his wife said, walking over to put the water to boil. "It's not like they're an old married couple like us." But there was a big smile on her face as she said it, and Korum knew she was joking. From what he had seen, Marisa and her husband were very affectionate with each other.

Korum didn't mind Connor's teasing; he loved Mia and had no intention of hiding his feelings from her family. Let them see how much he cared for her. After all, they were trusting him enough to leave their entire lives behind.

He hoped the Elders wouldn't deny them the nanocytes. He hated the thought of disappointing Mia's family—and Mia herself. Somehow, almost imperceptibly, Korum had grown to care about these people. In the past two weeks, he'd had a lot of interactions with each of Mia's relatives, answering their questions about Krina and what to expect during the trip—and he'd found that he genuinely liked them. He saw shades of Mia in both her parents and her sister, and frequently found Connor's company amusing. If someone had told Korum a few months ago that he would feel this way about a bunch of humans, he would've laughed in their face. But ever since he met Mia, his predictable life had gone down the drain.

Ella Stalis brought out the pancakes and served everyone. Tasting his portion, Korum immediately complimented her cooking, loving the combination of sweet jam with the savory potato. She glowed, obviously pleased. In that moment, Korum could see the beauty she must've been in her youth—and would likely be again after the procedure.

Finally, all the food had been eaten and dishes put away. Korum helped clean up, loading everything into the dishwasher. Human appliances had always interested him for some reason; they were so primitive and graceless, yet they managed to do their job for the most part.

At that moment, the tiny dog ran out of one of the rooms, barking and jumping at Korum again. Before he had a chance to do anything, Marisa grabbed it off the floor. "Mocha!" she chastised the animal. Turning to Korum, she gave him an apologetic smile. "Sorry about that. We kept her in the bedroom so she's not in the way while we're packing, but she got out somehow—"

"That's okay; I don't mind," Korum assured her. Then a sudden thought occurred to him. "What are you going to do with the dog when you leave?"

Marisa stared at him. "She's coming with us, of course."

Korum blinked slowly. "I see."

"That's not a problem, is it?" Marisa asked anxiously. "I know my parents would die without her—"

"No, it's not a problem," Korum said. Unexpected, but not a problem. He should've known they would want to bring the furry creature; humans often had unnatural attachments to their pets. He would have to make some last-minute adjustments to the ship's layout to accommodate the dog's presence, but it wouldn't be anything major.

Twenty minutes later, everybody was ready to go. Korum brought five large suitcases outside and loaded them onto the aircraft, ignoring the curious stares from the neighbors.

"Be careful, they're heavy," Dan Stalis admonished him, and Korum suppressed a smile. Mia's father clearly didn't understand the full extent of the differences between Krinar and human bodies. The suitcases were no heavier to him than Ella's little purse was to her. Still, his concern was rather touching.

When they were all inside the aircraft, Mia made sure they were comfortably seated on floats. Her mother held the dog on her lap, clutching it with a desperation that betrayed her nervousness.

"Goodbye, Ormond Beach. Goodbye, Earth," Mia's sister whispered as the aircraft took off, carrying them upward, beyond Earth's atmosphere, where the big ship awaited them for their interplanetary journey.

CHAPTER TWENTY-THREE

As their ship ascended, Mia watched the shrinking buildings and landmarks below. The pod's transparent walls and floor allowed for an amazing 360-degree view. Within seconds, their aircraft was above the clouds and blinding sunlight streamed in, causing Mia to squint until Korum did something that minimized the glare.

"Wow," Marisa breathed, echoing Mia's own feelings. "This is so not like traveling by airplane . . ."

"We're moving much faster than your planes," Korum explained. "In another few minutes, we'll be reaching our destination right outside of Earth's atmosphere."

Mia reached over and squeezed his hand. Her heart was pounding with excitement and trepidation, and she could only imagine how the others must be feeling. Her dad was looking a little pale, and her mom was holding Mocha so tightly that the little dog was squirming. Even Connor was uncharacteristically quiet, a look of awe on his face.

"It'll be all right, my sweet," Korum said, leaning over to kiss her temple. "Everything will be fine."

"I know," Mia said quietly. "It's just incredible, that's all."

He smiled, showing that sexy dimple in his left cheek. It made him look even more gorgeous than usual, and Mia desperately wished they were alone right now, instead of surrounded by her family.

As though reading her mind, Korum whispered to her, "Later," and Mia felt her cheeks heating up. His smile changed, became more suggestive, and she pinched his arm in response.

He lifted his eyebrows questioningly, and Mia gave him a frown. "Not in front of my parents," she mouthed, and his smile turned into a full-blown grin.

Determined not to let him make her blush, Mia looked down, watching with barely controlled excitement as they got further and further away from Earth. When she was little, she had dreamed of being an astronaut, of going to the stars and exploring distant galaxies. Like most kids, she had grown out of that, eventually choosing a more suitable profession. Now, however, she was being given a chance to live that long-ago childhood dream, and it was beyond amazing.

Soon, they were so far away that she could see Earth in its entirety—a beautiful blue planet that looked far too small to be home to billions of people. Looking at it, Mia couldn't help but realize just how vulnerable the entire human race was, tied as they were to this one place that looked so defenseless in the vastness of space.

"What are you thinking about?" Korum asked, reaching over to stroke her knee.

"I was thinking I understand now why the Krinar want to diversify," Mia said, "why you don't want to bet your survival on any one planet. It looks so fragile like this . . ."

"Yes, it does, doesn't it?" Korum's hand tightened on her knee. When she looked up at him, he was looking at her with a strange expression on his face. Before she could ask him about it, though, she heard her mom gasp.

"Oh wow, Korum!" Ella Stalis exclaimed. "Is that your ship?"

Mia looked up. They were approaching something that looked like a large bullet. Dark-colored, it was surprisingly plain-looking, completely unlike any starship she had ever seen in science fiction movies.

"That's it?" she asked, trying to keep the disappointment out of her voice. Krinar transport pods looked more advanced and futuristic than this ship that could supposedly go faster than the speed of light.

"That's it." Korum smiled. "It's not quite how your people imagined it, is it?"

"No, it's not," Connor said, speaking for the first time since their transport pod took off. "How did all those thousands of Krinar fit into that? It looks kind of small . . ."

"Oh, this is not the ship that brought us here," Korum explained. "You're right; that one is much bigger. This ship is something that I made specifically for our journey. There are only about seventy of us who are going to Krina this time; there was no need to use the bigger ship for so few people."

"You can do that?" Mia's dad asked, staring at Korum in disbelief. "Just like that, you can create a ship that can go to a different galaxy?"

"Korum can do it," Mia said, understanding her dad's confusion. "Not every Krinar can. He is the one who came up with this design. Right?" She looked at Korum.

"Yes," her lover confirmed. "This particular design is mine. We had ships with faster-than-light capabilities before, of course, but these are the latest generation. They're safer and easier to operate."

"I see," Dan said, looking at Korum with a mixture of shock and respect. The same emotions were reflected on Ella's face. Apparently Mia's parents had not understood the extent of Korum's technological prowess until this moment.

As the pod approached the ship, Mia could see one of the ship's sides dissolving to let them in. Since all Krinar houses had similar entrance technology, she barely blinked at the sight. Her family, however, found it very impressive.

"How exactly does this intelligent stuff work?" Marisa asked. "Do the walls actually think for themselves?"

"No," Korum said. "This is not artificial intelligence in the true sense of the word. It's not self-aware in any way. When I say 'intelligent technology,' what I really mean is that it's an object that's able to carry out its specific function in a way that mimics the capabilities of an intelligent being. So, for instance, my house can make meals, maintain temperature that's just right for our bodies, keep out unwanted visitors, and clean itself. It performs those tasks as well as a human or a Krinar would—but you can't really carry on a conversation with it."

"That's so cool," Connor said. "Do you guys have robots that you *can* talk to?"

Korum smiled indulgently. "Yeah, those were popular a few thousand years ago and then kind of went out of style. Now they're mainly used to entertain small children, although some adults like them too."

Before Connor could ask any more questions, their pod touched the floor of the ship, landing softly. Marisa clapped. "Bravo! That had to be the smoothest ride ever."

Korum laughed, rising from his seat. "We're here," he said. "Until we reach our destination, this will be your new home."

When they disembarked, Korum gave them a tour of the ship. Despite its unassuming outer layer, the inside of the spacecraft was as beautifully decorated as any Krinar house. Light colors, floating furnishings, exotic plants—the ship had everything Mia had gotten used to in Lenkarda, and she immediately felt at home there.

Mia's parents were beyond impressed. "Korum, this is so gorgeous," her mom kept saying. "And the view! Dear God, the view!"

The view was truly stunning. The outer walls of the ship were see-through from the inside, just like in most Krinar buildings, and there were plenty of areas where one could observe space in all its glory. Without the interference from the atmosphere, everything was sharper, clearer, the stars looking brighter than anything Mia had ever seen on the ground.

Korum had prepared special quarters for Mia's family, closely replicating the interior of her parents' house. "I hope this works for you," he told them. "If not, I can change it to anything else you prefer."

"Oh, no, this is perfect," Mia's dad said, walking over to sit down on a big overstuffed couch. "All that floating stuff is a bit intimidating, to be honest with you."

"Good, I'm glad you like it." Korum smiled, and Mia wanted to kiss him for his thoughtfulness. "I'll have a special area made for Mocha as well, to make sure she can run around and use the bathroom there."

The few Ks they met during the tour were pleasant to Mia's family, having been already apprised of their presence by Korum. They all stared, of course, but Mia was already used to that. Two of the female crew members seemed particularly intrigued by the little dog that Mia's mom insisted on carrying around with her.

"That is so cute!" One of them exclaimed, reaching over to pet Mocha. "Oh, I've never seen one of these up close!"

The dog tolerated the attention, but Mia could see she wasn't happy about it. It seemed Korum was the only K Mocha truly liked.

After the tour, Mia's family decided to rest. Her sister was particularly tired, worn out by all the excitement. "It's nap time," Connor said, smiling at his wife, and she nodded, stifling a yawn.

Mia and Korum were finally on their own.

* * *

"Looks like it's just us," Mia said, smiling at Korum. They had just gotten to their own private quarters, complete with a large circular bed similar to the one in Korum's house.

"Indeed." His eyes were starting to gleam with the familiar golden light.

Holding his gaze, Mia slowly and deliberately hooked her thumbs under the straps holding up her sundress and pushed them down over her shoulders. "Oops," she whispered. "I can't seem to take this off. I might need your help . . ."

Korum's nostrils flared, and she could see the tension invading his muscles. "Come here," he growled.

Mia shook her head. "No. You come here." She knew exactly what she wanted, and it did not involve Korum taking over this time.

His eyes narrowed. He looked dangerous now, like a wild predator who couldn't be controlled, and her heart started beating faster from the thrill of what she was trying to do. "Come," she repeated, crooking her finger at him.

He came. Or, rather, he practically leapt across the room. In a second, he was next to her, his muscular body large and intimidating, pressing her against the wall. "You need help with this dress, do you?" His fingers tugged at the flimsy straps, the thin material nearly coming apart in his strong hands.

"Yes," Mia breathed, looking up at him. "I do. Be gentle, though. And after you take it off me, I want you to undress for *me*."

His eyes turned almost yellow. "Is that right?"

"That's right," Mia said. "And then I want you to lie down on the bed." Her heart was pounding so hard it felt like it was about to explode, and her body was melting with need. She wanted him badly . . . but on her own terms.

For a second, she thought he wouldn't comply, but then he took a step back. "All right," he said, his voice unusually rough. "Turn around."

Mia suppressed a triumphant smile and did as he asked. The dress she was wearing was human-style, with a zipper in the back, and his fingers felt hot on her bare skin as he unzipped it all the way. As soon as he was done, Mia stepped to the side and let the dress drop to the floor. Underneath, she was wearing a tiny blue thong—something she'd put on this morning specifically with Korum in mind.

He sucked in his breath. "Mia . . . You little tease . . ."

She lifted her brows. "You don't like?" She did a little twirl, pretending not to see the explosive heat in his gaze as he stared at her.

A muscle pulsed in his jaw. "Are you torturing me?"

"I don't know," Mia purred. "Am I?" Turning her back to him, she bent over and slowly pushed down the thong, the way she'd seen it done in movies. Then she stepped out of it. When she turned toward him again, he looked almost feral, his eyes glittering and his hands clenched into fists.

"Your turn," Mia said, watching him in fascination. Would he lose control and take her now? She loved it when she could get him into that state, completely mindless with need for her. His savage passion didn't frighten her; instead, it made her want him even more.

He took a deep breath, then another, and she saw his hands slowly unclenching. Then, still staring at her with a burning gaze, he pulled his T-shirt over his head and unzipped his jeans, pushing them down his hips. He wasn't wearing any underwear, and he was already fully aroused, his erection aggressively jutting out.

Mia's mouth went dry at the sight. Her lover was male perfection personified. Every muscle on his powerful body was clearly defined, the smoothness of his golden skin marred in only a few places by a smattering of dark hair. She wanted to jump on him and lick him all over.

"Lie down on the bed," she managed to say, her voice thick with desire.

He did as she asked, but she could see that his self-control wouldn't last long. Suddenly, an idea came to her. "My fabricator, please," she said out loud, knowing the intelligent ship would understand what she wanted. Sure enough, a few seconds later, one of the walls dissolved and Korum's gift floated out directly into Mia's hands.

"What are you doing?" Korum asked, watching her warily from the bed, and she gave him a wicked grin.

"You'll see."

Holding the fabricator in her hand, she told the gadget, "Handcuffs with a key, please," and then waited while the nanomachines did their job.

Korum sat up, staring at her with an unreadable expression on his face. "And what do you think you're doing with those?"

Mia put down the fabricator and picked up the handcuffs. "Putting them on you, of course."

"Oh really?"

"Yes, really," Mia said firmly, climbing onto the bed next to Korum. "Now give me your wrists."

He hesitated for a second, then extended his hands, the lust on his face now tempered with amusement. "You think those will hold me?"

"Probably not," Mia admitted, putting the handcuffs on him. Each of his wrists was as thick as both of hers combined, his forearms bulging with muscle. "But that's not the point, is it?"

"What *is* the point, my sweet?" he asked softly, watching her with a heavy-lidded gaze. "Are you trying to prove something?"

Instead of answering, Mia gave him a light push, getting him to lie flat on his back with his handcuffed arms raised over his head. Then she climbed on top of him, straddling his stomach until his erection was only a couple of inches from her opening. Leaning down, she braced herself on his chest and whispered in his ear, "The point is that you're mine, and I get to do whatever I want with you."

He drew in a sharp breath and his hips arched, trying to bring his cock closer to her entrance. "And does that include letting me get inside your tight little pussy?" His voice sounded hoarse, strained with need.

"Oh yes." Mia moved down until his shaft was between her nether lips, her clitoris rubbing against its side. The skin covering his cock was soft, almost delicate, and she closed her eyes, savoring the feel of it against her sex.

"Mia . . ." he groaned, bucking underneath her. "Put it in. Now."

Deciding not to torture him—or herself—any longer, Mia wrapped her hand around his length and guided him into her. Biting her lip at the stretching sensation, she slowly lowered herself until his cock was almost all the way in. She paused, getting used to his thickness, and then let him in deeper, not stopping until he was in all the way.

He groaned again, his arm muscles flexing with the effort to keep from reaching for her right then and there, and his cock jerked inside her. Mia knew he was dying to take control, to make them both come, and she wondered at his unusual restraint.

She didn't have to wonder long. Before she could move again, she found herself flipped over onto her back, his large body pressing her into the mattress. His eyes were wild, his gaze unfocused. He had managed to tear apart the metal links holding the cuffs together, and his hands were on her thighs, holding them wide open for his thrusts.

Crying out, Mia wrapped her arms around his neck, barely able to hold on as he hammered into her, driven solely by the primitive instinct to mate. Her body slid back and forth on the mattress with each movement of his powerful hips, and the intelligent bed softened around them, became more like a pillow in texture, protecting her from any injuries.

Her first orgasm hit her like a freight train, and Mia screamed, bucking in his arms, but he was merciless, utterly relentless. The second one, mere moments later, made her literally see stars, yet he continued fucking her, ferocious in his need.

It was too much. Mia felt like she would break apart, like she would shatter from the intensity of the sensations. Her body was no longer her own, her mind was no longer her own. There was only heat and sweat and his body, over her, in her, surrounding her. They were melded together, fused by the white-hot ecstasy of their joining.

By the time he shuddered over her, Mia was incoherent, her voice hoarse from her screams and her body shaking from the unending swells of pleasure. And just when she thought it was over, she felt his teeth slicing across the vein in her neck . . . and sending her spiraling even higher.

CHAPTER TWENTY-FOUR

If anyone had told Mia an intergalactic voyage would be as easy as going on a cruise, she would've laughed out loud. Yet it was indeed the case. They spent almost a week flying away from Earth at sub-light speeds—so as not to cause any disturbances with the warping of space-time—and then they activated the warp drive, landing within a few days flight to Krina. All of this was done so smoothly that Mia didn't feel anything. It wasn't until Korum told her they were in a different galaxy that she knew the ship had made the jump.

"Are we going to see the Elders right away?" Mia asked as they were lying in bed the evening before their arrival. Since they were both less busy with other matters, she and Korum had spent a lot of time with each other during the trip. Mia was taking a break from learning about the mind, and Korum didn't have any urgent Council issues to worry about. Mia slept late, hung out with her family in the mornings, and spent the majority of her day with Korum—an activity that invariably culminated in several hours of sexual bliss.

"No," Korum said. "We'll go see the mind expert first, to restore your memory." And to undo the softening—but that part went unsaid. Mia knew they were both anticipating and slightly dreading the reversal of the procedure, unsure of just how much—if anything—would change between them as a result.

Staring at the transparent wall in their bedroom, Mia could see unfamiliar stars and constellations in the sky. They were already in the Krinar solar system, a strange and beautiful place with ten planets circling a star that was roughly 1.2 times the size of Earth's sun. Krina was the fourth planet in terms of distance from its sun, and it was strikingly similar to Earth in its size, mass, and geochemical composition. "That's why Earth is so important to us," Korum explained. "It's closer to Krina than anything else we've come across in all the years we've been exploring the universe."

The main difference between the two planets lay in its moons. Earth had only one, while Krina had a grand total of three—one about the size of Earth's and two smaller ones. "We get some spectacular tides," Korum told her. "They're more like small tsunamis. Earth is better in that sense; in most places, you can live right next to the ocean and not have to worry about anything more than an occasional hurricane. On Krina, the ocean is more dangerous, and we don't have any settlements within twenty miles of the shore."

To Mia's surprise, she learned that when Korum referred to the ocean on Krina, he meant The Ocean—as in, one huge body of water. Unlike Earth, where the original supercontinent of Pangaea had broken apart into several continents, Krina had one giant landmass that served as home to all the Krinar. Tinara, Korum had called it.

That fact also explained something that had puzzled Mia before: the relative lack of variety in Krinar appearance. Her lover's people all tended to be dark-haired with bronzed skin, and, while there were variations in coloring, there were significantly fewer differences among Ks than between humans of different races. The Krinar were more homogeneous—which made sense if they had all evolved together on this supercontinent.

"So why does your cousin Leeta have red hair?" Mia asked. She'd met the beautiful Krinar woman a couple of times since her memory loss. "Is there a gene for that in the K population?"

Korum shook his head. "No, not really. Some of us have hair with a slightly auburn tint to it, but nothing like the shade Leeta is wearing now. She has altered the structure of her hair molecules since coming to Earth, probably because she likes that look."

"And there are no blond, blue-eyed Krinar?"

"No," Korum said. "No Krinar with hair as curly as yours either. With your curls and blue eyes, you'll really stand out on Krina."

"Oh great," Mia muttered. "I'll be stared at even more."

Korum smiled. "Yes, you will be. But that's not a bad thing."

Mia shrugged. She knew the Krinar didn't regard staring as rude, but she was still uncomfortable with that specific cultural difference. "So when are we meeting your family?" she asked, switching gears. "Are they going to be there to greet us when we arrive?"

"No. I told them we'll visit them right after you regain your memory. You've already met my parents once before, and you'll probably feel better if you remember that original meeting."

Mia yawned and turned over, pressing her back against Korum's chest and letting him spoon her from behind. He hugged her, pulling her closer. "Go to sleep, my sweet," he murmured in her ear, and Mia drifted off, feeling warm and safe in his embrace.

* * *

"Oh my God, is that it? Is that Krina?" Marisa rose from her seat, pointing at the planet that was growing in size before their eyes. Mia was staring at it too, her heart beating like a drum from anticipation and excitement.

"Yes," Korum confirmed, smiling at them. "That is indeed Krina."

They were all sitting around a floating table, having breakfast. It was their last meal on the ship before their arrival. Connor was unusually quiet again, and Mia could see that her parents were just picking at their food, apparently too nervous to eat normally.

They were sitting in one of the rooms that had a wall facing the outside of the ship—a wall made of the same transparent material as the Krinar houses. Korum had chosen it on purpose, to let them watch as they approached Krina for the first time.

Their ship was moving with incredible speed, and soon the planet was visible in greater detail. "We're coming from the Tinara—the supercontinent—side," Korum explained. "That's why you don't see a lot of water, the way you do on Earth."

And it was true. The sight before them was quite different from NASA images of Earth from space. Mia could see only a thin ring of blue; instead, everything was dominated by a giant brown landmass in the center—the supercontinent. As they got closer, she realized that what she had mistaken for a brown hue was actually a combination of green, red, and yellow colors.

Soon, they entered the atmosphere, and Mia noticed a faint reddish glow around the ship. "That's our force shields protecting us from heat and friction," Korum explained. "We're still moving fast, so if it weren't for our shields, we'd burn to a crisp."

Gradually, the glow faded, and the ship slowed. As they broke through the cloud cover, Mia saw a large forest spread out below them, strikingly colorful ... and unusually untouched. Where one might've expected to see cities and skyscrapers, there were only trees and more trees.

"We're going to a special landing area for intergalactic ships," Korum said, apparently anticipating their questions. "It's a good distance from any of our Centers."

"Why aren't we taking a transport pod down, the way we took it to get to the ship?" Mia's dad asked. "Why land this whole ship?"

"Good question, Dan," Korum said. "When we were on Earth, we took the transport pod up because there are no good landing areas for ships like this. That might change in the future, but for now, it's easiest to keep these types of ships in orbit around Earth. Here on Krina, we're equipped for this, so there is no reason for us not to land."

Now Mia could see a large clearing ahead, with some structures that resembled giant mushrooms. It had to be the landing field. Sure enough, their ship headed directly there and a few minutes later, they touched the ground.

They were officially on Krina.

As they exited the ship, Mia felt a blast of heat reminiscent of Florida weather at its hottest. It was also difficult to breathe, and she felt light-headed as she tried to draw in more air. Grabbing Korum's hand, she waited for a wave of dizziness to pass.

"Are you okay?" he asked, wrapping his arm around her back to support her.

"Yes," Mia said. "The air is just thinner here, I think." It was also unusually and pleasantly scented, like blooming flowers and sweet fruits.

"It is thinner," Korum confirmed. "Our atmosphere in general contains a little less oxygen than you're used to, and this particular region happens to be at a higher elevation. You should adjust soon, though, with your nanocytes."

Mia was already starting to feel better, but now she had a new worry. "What about my parents? And Marisa and Connor? How will they adjust?" Her family was just now coming out of the ship, about ten yards behind them.

"Most humans tolerate our atmosphere well, after an initial acclimation period," Korum said. "But don't worry; I know your parents aren't in the best of health, so I made sure our medicine experts were on hand." He pointed toward a small pod that had just landed next to the ship. "They will help your family with any kind of issues."

At that moment, two Krinar women exited the pod. Tall, dark-haired, and graceful, they came up to Korum and smiled. "I'm Rialit, and this is my colleague Mita," said the shorter woman to the right. "Welcome to Krina."

Korum inclined his head. "Thank you, Rialit. And Mita. I would like you to help my human companions. My charl is fine, but her relatives may require your assistance."

"Of course," Rialit said, turning toward Ella and Dan. They and Marisa seemed a little pale, and Connor looked like he was trying to gulp as much air as possible.

The medicine experts hurried over, holding some small devices, and, a minute later, everyone appeared to be back to normal. Korum thanked the two women and they left, their pod taking off a few minutes later.

"Wow," Mia's mom said, staring at the departing aircraft, "I can't believe they run those little things over us, and we can breathe again. What did they do to us?"

"I think they created a small oxygen field around you," Korum said. "This way, you will have a more gradual adjustment. The field will dissipate over the next couple of days, but it'll do it slowly, so your bodies will get used to breathing our air."

"Amazing," Dan said. "Simply amazing."

Mia smiled. "Isn't it, though?"

While they were talking, Korum had started the process of creating a transport pod to take them to their final destination: his house. Mia's sister gasped as the ship began to take shape, and Connor and her parents simply stared in shock. Mia grinned at their reactions; it wasn't that long ago that everything Korum showed her seemed like a miracle. Now she could do a lot of the same things, even if she didn't understand the technology behind it. Then again, most people didn't understand how phones and televisions worked, but they could still use them—just as Mia could use her fabricator.

Once the pod was done, everybody climbed inside and got comfortable on the floating seats. "Love these things," Marisa said, a blissful look on her face as the seat conformed to her shape. Mia guessed that her sister was already starting to feel some pregnancy-related aches and pains, and she determined to talk to the medicine experts about that. Marisa was likely too shy to say anything herself.

As their pod took off, Mia looked down at the transparent floor, her breath catching in her throat at the realization that she was actually here.

On Krina.

On the planet that was the origin of all life on Earth.

CHAPTER TWENTY-FIVE

The flight to Korum's house took a mere two minutes, the aircraft flying too fast for Mia to see anything more than a blur of exotic vegetation below. As soon as they landed, she jumped up, eager to see Krina up close.

"Hold on, honey," her dad said, catching her arm as she was about to run out of the ship. "That's an alien planet. You don't know what's out there in the woods."

"He's right, my sweet," Korum said. "I need to show all of you a few things first, to avoid any potential issues. Stick close to me for now, and don't touch anything."

Exiting the pod, he led them toward an ivory-colored structure that was visible through the trees.

As they walked, Mia marveled at the beautiful vegetation that surrounded them. While green colors predominated, there were a lot more red and yellow plants than one would find on Earth. In places she could even see bright purple leaves peeking through the wide rounded stalks of grass-like growth that covered the forest floor. Here and there, flowers of every shade of the rainbow added a festive touch to everything. These flowers seemed to be responsible for the pleasant smell Mia had noticed upon their arrival.

The tree trunks were of varying colors as well. Brown was common, but so was black and white. One tree that Mia particularly liked had white branches and bright red leaves with yellow centers. "That's gorgeous!" she exclaimed, and Korum laughed, shaking his head.

"That particular beauty is poisonous," he said. "Whatever you do, don't let any of the tree sap get on your skin—it acts like acid."

"Really?" Mia stared at her surroundings with newfound caution. Her parents looked frightened, and Connor put a protective arm around Marisa, pulling her closer to him.

"There's no need to be scared," Korum said. "You just need to know that you can't touch the *alfabra* tree. Same thing for that plant over there—" He pointed toward a pretty-looking green bush that was covered with white and pink blooms. "It likes to eat anything that lands on it, and has been known to consume larger animals."

Something flew by Mia's ear and she reflexively swatted at it, gasping when she felt a sudden light pinch. Lowering her hand, she stared at it in disbelief. "Oh my God, Korum, what is that?"

A blue-green creature was sitting in the middle of her palm, its huge eyes almost half the size of its three-inch body. It had only four legs, but there seemed to be hundreds of tiny fingers on each one, all of them digging into Mia's skin. There were also tiny wings that didn't seem big enough to propel it through the air.

"That's a *virta*," Korum said, gently lifting the creature off Mia's palm and throwing it away. "It's harmless—you just shocked it and it grabbed on to you. They eat some leaves and an occasional *mirat*."

"Mirat?" Connor asked.

"Yes, mirat," Korum said, pointing toward one of the brown tree trunks.

When Mia looked closer, she could see that what she had mistaken for solid wood was actually some type of a jelly-like substance—and that it quivered and moved, expanding and contracting in a creepy way.

"Mirat are similar to your bees, although they don't sting," Korum explained. "They're social insects, and they build these complex structures around trees. Our scientists love studying them. There's a lot of debate as to whether the collective mind of a mirat hive displays signs of higher intelligence. We never bother them, and they generally know to avoid us and our dwellings. If you touch their hive, you'll get dizzy from the fumes they emit, so it's best to stay away from them."

"That's crazy," Marisa said, looking worried. "Is there anything else like that we should know about?" She was holding her stomach in a protective gesture.

"Yes," Korum said. "That, right there—" he pointed at a small red insect-like thing on the floor, "—is also something you have to be careful of. It bites and likes to burrow inside the skin. They're not poisonous or anything, but extracting them is very unpleasant. There are also some large predatory animals, but you're unlikely to encounter them in this vicinity. They're afraid of the Krinar and generally avoid our territories."

Connor was frowning. "Korum, no offense, but that's a lot of shit we need to worry about here. I don't think we realized we'd be living in the middle of an alien jungle."

Korum didn't seem offended in the least. "Our jungle is far less dangerous than your cities, as long as you don't stumble around blindly," he said calmly. "And my house is completely safe and critter-free. In a few days, you'll know exactly what to watch out for, and you'll be able to go outside without me. Until then, I'll accompany you everywhere and you won't run into any problems."

Connor opened his mouth to say something, but Mia's mom interrupted him, exclaiming, "Oh, wow, Korum, is that your house?"

While they were talking, they had reached the ivory-colored, oblong-shaped dwelling. To Mia's eyes, it looked very similar to Korum's house in Lenkarda—a place she now thought of as her home. To the others, though, it had to look strange and foreign.

"Yes," Korum said, smiling at them. "It is indeed."

"You don't have any doors or windows?" her dad asked, examining the structure with visible curiosity.

"No, dad," Mia said. "It has intelligent walls, just like the ship that brought us here. They're probably see-through from the inside. Right, Korum?"

"That's right," her lover confirmed, and Mia grinned, feeling like she would burst from excitement. She was actually on Krina!

Korum did a quick tour of the house, showing her family how to use everything. Mia's parents seemed a bit overwhelmed, so he created a separate 'humanized' suite of rooms for them, just as he had on the ship. Her sister and brother-in-law, however, decided to stay in the main portion of the house, preferring the comfort of K technology to the more familiar human-style furniture.

"I love this thing." Marisa was sprawled out on the intelligent bed in her room, a blissful expression on her face at the massage she was receiving. "I never want to leave it."

"I know, right?" Mia sat down next to her sister. "All their stuff is unbelievably awesome like that. The first time I fell asleep on a bed like this I thought I'd died and gone to Heaven."

"No kidding." Marisa closed her eyes, moaning in pleasure. "So freaking good . . ."

"I'll leave you to it," Mia said, grinning. "Get some rest, okay?"

Marisa didn't reply, and Mia realized that her sister was already drifting off to sleep, her pregnant body requiring more rest than usual.

Connor was taking a shower, and her parents were relaxing too, so Mia went to find Korum. "I'm ready," she told him. "Now is as good a time as any."

He got up from the float in the living room where he had been sitting, his tall, muscular body as graceful as a panther's. "Are you sure?" he asked, and she could see the concern written on his beautiful face.

"Yes," Mia said, lifting her hand to stroke his thick dark hair. "I'm sure."

He caught her hand and brought it to his lips, tenderly kissing each knuckle. "Then let's do it," he said softly. "Let's get your memory and your old self back."

* * *

A slender brown-haired Krinar woman walked around Mia, attaching little white dots to her forehead, temples, and the back of her neck. Mia had fully expected to be knocked out for the reversal of Saret's procedure, but the mind apprentice—Laira—said Mia had to be conscious.

"There you are," Laira said with satisfaction. "All done. Now please have a seat. It can be on Korum's lap if you want." She winked, and Mia laughed, liking this K woman. According to Korum, Laira was young, less than two hundred years of age, and already considered a rising star in the field of mind studies.

Korum smiled and pulled Mia onto his lap. "Sure, I'm happy to hold her."

"I bet you are." Laira grinned. "That's a cute charl you've got there."

"Excuse me," Mia said, putting a possessive arm around Korum's neck. "That's a gorgeous cheren *I've* got."

"True, true," Laira said, laughing. Then her expression turned more serious. "All right, Mia, this is what you can expect now: it will feel like your mind is going blank. Then you'll feel a rush of images and impressions as your memory returns and the procedure is reversed. As the memories come, I want you to focus on them one at a time, so you absorb them slowly. That's why you have to be awake for this, even though I know it's going to be uncomfortable for you."

"Is she going to be in pain?" Korum asked, his arms tightening around Mia.

"No, just discomfort, like I said," Laira replied. "Are you ready, Mia?"

"Yes." Mia braced herself.

"Here we go then."

At first, Mia felt a pleasant lassitude stealing over her and she closed her eyes. Her mind felt like it was drifting, as though she was about to fall asleep. There was a strange sensation of nothingness, of blankness.

Suddenly, it was like a bomb going off in her brain, an explosion of colors, feelings, and shapes, all appearing at once. Mia gasped, her fingers digging into Korum's arm as she tried to cope with the onslaught. It was too much, like a 3D IMAX movie with too many special effects, only streamed directly into her brain.

Somewhere far away, she could hear Korum's voice. It was furious, demanding. "Stop it! Stop it right now! Can't you see she's in pain?"

"She'll get through this . . ." It was Laira's voice, calm and soothing. Mia latched onto it, needing something steady in the maelstrom that was engulfing her mind.

At first it was unbearable, and she screamed silently, too overwhelmed to emit any actual sound. Laira hadn't lied. There was no pain; there was just agony. It felt like Mia's brain was being filled to the brim, her skull stretching and straining to contain it all.

And just when she thought her head would literally explode, the agony started to ease, colors and shapes separating into images, those images and emotions turning into specific events. Memories began to coalesce, taking shape one by one until she could grasp them, integrate them into what she already knew and remembered.

There was the party at the end of March, shortly before she met Korum. Jessie had dragged her to it, and Mia had ended up having a good time after a few drinks. She'd danced with a few guys, even exchanged phone numbers with one of them, but nothing ever came of it. If only she'd known then the strange turn her life would take . . .

The memory of her first meeting with Korum flashed through her mind, and Mia relived the sharp feeling of fear, mixed with the first stirrings of desire. The man who held her so lovingly now had terrified her in the beginning, his arrogance and casual disregard for her wishes leading her to assume the worst about his species.

More memories . . . Her first time in Korum's bed, John explaining to her about charl, the incident at the club where Korum had nearly killed Peter . . . Korum holding her while she cried, Mia bringing him to meet her parents for the first time... The good, the bad, the ugly—she remembered it all, and it was like a void inside her was disappearing, the before and after colliding, making her feel whole for the first time since Saret's attack.

Saret! Mia remembered him too. She'd liked him, regarded him as her boss and mentor. He had been the one to give her the language implant, to let her intern in his lab at Korum's request. Mia relived the excitement she'd felt when Korum had told her of the opportunity, the thrill of learning what thousands of human scientists could only dream of.

And then her last memory from before: Saret cornering her in the lab. Mia remembered her terror, her shock at learning of his intentions for the human race... Her disgust when he admitted to wanting her, the sick feeling in her stomach when he told her of his plans for the Krinar... And that awful darkness taking over when he wiped out a major chunk of her life and altered her brain.

Now the present and the past were one again. Mia became aware of Korum stroking her hair, raining gentle kisses on her face. Still keeping her eyes closed, Mia relived the more recent events, from her awakening in Korum's bed to the trip to Krina. She tried to compare her emotions then to the way she felt now—and to the way she had always been.

Saret hadn't lied. When Mia had woken up without her memories, she hadn't been completely herself. She had indeed been more accepting, more open to new experiences. She could see that now. However, that had been a good thing. In his quest to soften Mia toward him, Saret had inadvertently created the perfect conditions for her to overcome the pain and confusion from her memory loss. Instead of agonizing, Mia had been acclimating. Instead of worrying, she had been learning.

And instead of fearing Korum again, she had been falling in love with him. Really, truly falling in love with the beautiful, tender Krinar who had greeted her upon awakening. Korum of the recent months wasn't the same person she'd met in the park that day in April; his arrogance had been tempered by caring, his indifference to her wishes turning into a desire to make her happy. He loved her, of that Mia had no doubt now. He loved her with the same intensity, the same desperation as she loved him.

As the present and the past were joined, so too were Mia's feelings and emotions. Everything she had felt before was magnified now, strengthened by the trials and tribulations of the past couple of months.

Opening her eyes, Mia smiled at her K lover.

CHAPTER TWENTY-SIX

Seeing her smile, Korum shuddered with relief. "Mia, my sweet, are you all right?" For the past ten minutes, she had been as stiff as a board, her face pale and even her lips drained of color. She hadn't reacted to anything, as though she'd been in a coma.

"She's fine. Right, Mia?" Laira stepped closer, bending down to peer at Mia's face, and Korum fought the urge to strangle the apprentice. His charl had obviously been in pain, and he knew he would never forgive Laira for that.

"I'm okay now," Mia said softly, as though understanding his feelings. Lifting her hand, she stroked his cheek, the tender gesture cooling some of his anger.

"Do you remember anything?" Laira's voice interrupted them again.

"Yes," Mia said, looking up at her. "I remember everything. Thank you for that."

She remembered. She remembered everything. Korum felt like he could breathe again, the terrible guilt inside him easing for the first time since he'd learned of Saret's betrayal.

"What about the softening procedure?" he asked Laira, his arms unconsciously tightening around the girl on his lap.

"That should be reversed too," Laira said. "Mia, do you feel any different in that regard?"

"I don't know," Mia said, a small frown appearing on her face. "I can see that my reactions were a little off before, when I woke up in Lenkarda, but I don't feel any differently now."

"You don't?" Korum asked, and Mia smiled.

"No," she said, her gaze warm and soft. "I don't."

Another weight lifted off Korum's shoulders, making him feel lighter than air. Up until that moment, he hadn't known how much he'd dreaded the answer to that question. Mia had loved him before her memory loss, he'd known that, but some part of him had still been afraid that her feelings after Saret's procedure hadn't been as real—and that undoing the procedure would destroy whatever love she thought she felt for him.

Mia made a move to get up, and he forced himself to let her go, even though he wanted to keep holding her forever.

Getting up himself, he turned toward Laira and gave her a cool nod of thanks. Although the procedure had worked, Korum still couldn't quite forget the tortured expression on Mia's face during those awful ten minutes. He'd felt helpless, unable to do anything to ease her suffering, and he wouldn't forget that any time soon.

Not the least bit disturbed by his obvious displeasure, Laira grinned at him. "Looks like you got your charl back, all safe and sound."

"Yes," Korum said, putting a supportive arm around Mia, who still looked too pale. "Looks like it indeed."

Their flight back to Korum's house took about twenty minutes, since Laira's lab was located a few thousand miles from his home region of Rolert. Korum could see that Mia was fascinated by the view outside their transport pod, and he directed the aircraft to fly at a lower altitude and with slower speed, to give her a chance to observe more.

He tried to view Krina as she would be seeing it, and he had to admit that his home planet was beautiful. The giant landmass of Tinara was home to a tremendous variety of flora and fauna, and, from the air, the vegetation looked like a colorful carpet of green, with some red and gold tones mixed in. There were large lakes and rivers, some as blue and clear as the Caribbean, and others a rich blue-green.

The Krinar settlements were sparse, mostly clustered around these bodies of water. There were no cities as such, only Centers that served as focal points of commerce and business. The majority of Krinar lived on the outskirts of these Centers, commuting in for work and other activities.

Korum's own house was next to Banir—a mid-sized Center in the Rolert region, near the middle of the supercontinent and close to the equator. When Korum had brought Mia and her family there earlier in the morning, they'd all commented on how hot the weather was—even hotter than Florida in the summer. The heat didn't bother Korum, but he knew humans were more sensitive to it, so he had made sure to get them inside quickly. This evening, when the temperature cooled, he planned to take them to the nearby lake to swim and look at some of the local wildlife.

"That's Viarad," Korum told Mia as they flew over a particularly large Center. "It's the closest thing we have to a planetary capital. A lot of research and development happens there, and it's also where the Arena fights and other major gatherings take place."

Mia looked up at him, her eyes bright and curious. "Your cities are nothing like our own," she observed. "I don't even see a lot of buildings, much less skyscrapers and the like."

"They are there," Korum assured her. "Not skyscrapers, but there are plenty of large buildings for various commercial purposes. You don't really see them from the air because of all the trees. The forest surrounding Viarad has some of the tallest trees on Krina, with many exceeding a twenty-story building in height."

Her eyes widened. "Twenty stories?"

"At least," Korum said. "Maybe more. Those trees are ancient; some of them have been there for over a hundred million years."

"That's incredible." Her voice was filled with wonder. "Korum, your planet is amazing."

He smiled, enjoying her enthusiasm. "It is, isn't it?"

Even flying at a slower speed, they reached his house just a few minutes later. Korum led Mia inside the house, where her family were relaxing from the journey. "I'll make us dinner," he told her. "You can rest for a bit if you want. You've been through a lot today."

"I'm all right," Mia said, and he could see she wasn't lying. The color in her cheeks was back, and she seemed fully recovered from her earlier ordeal. "I'll go hang out with my parents if you don't mind."

"No, of course not, go ahead," Korum said. "I'll see you soon."

* * *

The dinner Korum prepared was as unusual as it was delicious, consisting of a bunch of local seeds, fruits, and vegetables prepared in creative ways. Mia and each member of her family discovered something new that they greatly enjoyed.

One of the dishes consisted of a teardrop-shaped vegetable with purple skin that tasted like a cross between tomato and zucchini. It was stuffed with nutty-flavored grain that had a bubble-like texture. Mia's dad loved that dish, going back for seconds and thirds as soon as he finished. In the meanwhile, Mia and Marisa were both crazy about the kalfani stew, with its rich, hearty flavor, while her mom and Connor kept eating the exotic fruit that was their dessert. "All of this food is safe for human consumption," Korum told them. "Not everything on Krina is, but I made sure these specific foods would be fine for your digestive system."

After dinner, Korum took them to the lake that was near his house. The sun was setting, and Mia could see the three moons starting to appear in the sky, despite the fact that there was still plenty of light.

As they walked, he showed them various plants and insects, explaining a little bit about them. "That's a *nooki*," he said, pointing at a large yellow spider-like thing with what looked like hundreds of legs. "They extract nutrients from the soil, almost like plants do. Our children like to play with them because they do some funny stuff when you startle them." He clapped his hands next to the creature, and it puffed up, each of its legs nearly tripling in thickness and its torso turning bright red. "It's completely harmless, so you don't need to be afraid of it."

Mia smiled and reached for the creature, curious if it would let her touch it. It scurried away, looking like a clumsy bright-colored ball.

Korum grinned at her, and Mia laughed, feeling incredibly happy. Standing up on tiptoes, she placed her hands on his cheeks and brought his face toward her, giving him a quick kiss on the lips. "I love you," she said, holding his gaze, and her heart squeezed at the naked look of love she saw there.

"Hey, lovebirds, take a look at this!" Connor yelled, and Mia wanted to punch him for interrupting the moment.

Korum gave her a rueful smile, and walked over to see what Connor was talking about. Mia followed, still unhappy with her brother-in-law. As soon as she got there, however, all her displeasure was forgotten. "Oh, wow," she breathed, "what is that?"

On a tree branch just a few feet off the forest floor, partially hidden by leaves, was a tiny furry creature that looked like a cross between a lemur and a kitten. Brown-colored, it had huge blue eyes and a short fluffy tail.

"That's a baby *fregu*," Korum said softly. "They're very cute, but they bite sometimes, so don't try to pet it."

"Fregu?" The word sounded familiar for some reason. Then Mia remembered. "Hey, you said I reminded you of one of these!" she told

Korum accusingly, then burst out laughing because she herself could see the resemblance.

The fregu was only the first of their encounters with Krinar wildlife. There were birds with four wings, insects that were the size of a small bird, and plants that acted more like animals. One time, Connor almost stepped on a snake-like creature that screamed at him and rolled away, its long thin body moving like a rolling pin.

Finally, they reached the lake. It was a sizable body of water, probably a couple of miles wide and several miles long. The shore of the lake was covered with fine grey sand and small black rocks. It made the water itself look dark and mysterious.

"Is it safe to swim?" Marisa asked, kicking off her sandal and dipping a toe in to test the temperature.

"Yes," Korum told her. "There are some dangerous predators in there, but nothing that comes this close to the shore. This lake is very deep, and there are all kinds of things living there, but they generally don't go into shallow waters. Just in case, though, wear this." He handed her a thin clear bracelet that he made just a second ago. "It repels aquatic animals by emitting a sound they find very unpleasant."

Mia and the others received the same kind of bracelet, and then they all went for a swim, enjoying the refreshing escape from the heat outside.

CHAPTER TWENTY-SEVEN

Mia woke up the next morning with a nagging feeling of unease in her chest. For some reason, she kept dreaming about Saret and that day in the lab. In her dream, Saret was touching her, making her skin crawl with disgust, and there was nothing Mia could do about it other than scream silently in her head because she was paralyzed and unable to move.

Too wired to sleep more, Mia got up and went to take a shower. Korum was away somewhere, and Mia didn't know if her family was still sleeping or not. From the sun's position outside, it had to be very early in the morning.

Standing under the water spray, she yawned, feeling unusually tired. Maybe she shouldn't have gotten up yet. The stupid dream was still on her mind, and she scrubbed her skin thoroughly, trying to wash it away. In reality, Saret had barely touched her, so she didn't know why her subconscious even went there this night.

To dispel any lingering impressions from the dream, she mentally went over the actual events of that day, starting from when she ran into Saret on her way out. He had been so happy to talk to her about his plans, to tell her everything he intended to do to humans and his fellow Krinar. Mia guessed it hadn't been easy for him, never confiding in anyone else, always trying to play a role, to hide his true nature. With her, since he thought she would never remember their conversation, he had felt safe dropping the mask he normally wore.

In hindsight, it was almost funny, all of his crazy ramblings about bringing peace to Earth and acting as a savior to her people. He had even tried to convince her that Korum had some evil plans of taking over her planet. It was so ridiculous that Mia chuckled to herself. Had he really thought that she would be sympathetic to his cause? That because she had been willing to believe the worst of Korum once she would make that same mistake again?

Stepping out of the shower, Mia let the drying technology do its work. Then, feeling marginally better, she went back into the bedroom to find her fabricator and get dressed.

To her surprise, Korum was there, sitting on the bed. He was dressed in a typical Krinar outfit of light-colored shorts and a sleeveless shirt. For some reason, his hair was wet.

"You're awake," he said, looking at her naked body with a familiar sensual gleam in his eyes. "I went swimming in the lake because I figured you'd be asleep for quite some time. Why are you up so early?"

"Bad dream." Mia sat down next to him. His hands immediately went to her breasts and squeezed them lightly, as though he couldn't resist touching her.

"Why, my sweet? What dream?" There was a concerned look on his beautiful face, even as his hands continued playing with her breasts, his thumbs brushing against her nipples in a way that sent a spear of heat right down to her core.

Mia could hardly think with him doing this to her. "Um . . . just that thing with Saret . . ." Her head fell back, her neck arching as he bent down to nibble on the sensitive spot near her collarbone.

"What thing?" he murmured, one of his hands now slipping between her thighs, stroking her aching sex.

"Just that . . . conversation . . ." Mia gasped as his finger slid inside her, one thumb pressing on her clit while his other hand continued playing with her nipple.

"What about it?" he whispered, his hot breath washing over her neck, giving her goosebumps all over.

"I don't . . . I don't know," Mia managed to say, her inner muscles clenching around his finger as a wave of heat went through her body. She was so close . . . so close . . .

Korum withdrew his finger and pushed her down, so that she was lying flat on her back with her legs hanging off the side of the bed. Kneeling on the floor, he pulled her legs over his shoulders and brought her sex toward his mouth.

At the first touch of his warm, wet tongue on her clit, Mia shattered into a million pieces. The release was so powerful that she arched off the bed, her eyes squeezing shut as waves of pleasure radiated through every part of her body.

Before the waves had a chance to fade, he was already inside her, his shorts ripped open at the crotch area and his thick length buried deep within her small channel. Gasping at his abrupt entry, Mia grabbed his shoulders, holding on tightly as he began to stroke in and out, stimulating the nerve endings that were still sensitive from her orgasm. Panting, she opened her eyes and met his golden gaze.

He was staring at her with an intense look of hunger on his face. Bending his head, he took her mouth in a savage kiss, ravaging her with his tongue even as his cock continued to plunge into her from below. One of his hands held her hair, keeping her head immobile, while his other hand slid down her side and underneath her hips, touching her folds where they were joined. His finger rubbed around her entrance, gathering the moisture there, and then that same finger burrowed between her cheeks and pushed into her other opening.

Overwhelmed by the sensations, Mia moaned helplessly. With the way he was holding her, she couldn't do anything but feel. He was on top of her, inside her, all over her, and she couldn't catch her breath, her heartbeat skyrocketing as the tension within her spiraled higher and higher. His finger in her ass seemed impossibly large, invasive, yet there was a dark pleasure there too, an unusual feeling of fullness that added to the sensuality of the moment.

Without any warning, everything inside her tightened and convulsed, and Mia came, her body twisting and shuddering in his arms. He groaned, grinding against her, trying to get even deeper, and she could feel his cock pulsing within her as he found his own release.

After a couple of minutes, he slowly withdrew from her. "All right?" he asked softly, and Mia nodded, too limp and relaxed to move.

He smiled and picked her up, carrying her to the shower for another quick rinse, and then they got dressed and ready for breakfast with her family.

At breakfast, Mia found her attention wandering, her mind again turning to her dream and that conversation with Saret. After a few minutes of dwelling on it, she realized what was bothering her.

Why did Saret try to claim that Korum was the villain? Was he delusional, or did he think Mia would be so gullible as to believe his lies? And why bother lying to her at all, if he was planning to erase her memory shortly afterwards? She tried to think of his exact words, something about Korum wanting to take her planet. What the hell did that even mean? The Krinar were already there, on Earth, sharing it alongside humans—which is what Korum had said was their intention.

Still, Mia couldn't quite shake an uneasy feeling. She knew her lover had a ruthless streak—and she knew he was loyal to his people. Could that loyalty extend as far as wanting to get rid of an entire rival species to gain a precious resource? Korum had told her himself that Earth was unique, that out of all the planets out there, it came closest to mimicking Krina. And now that Mia was here, she could see that it was indeed the case; if anything ever happened to Earth, humans would be more than happy to live on Krina—and likely vice versa with the Krinar.

Putting down her tong-like utensil, Mia studied her lover as he conversed and joked with her family. It seemed impossible that there could be something sinister hidden beneath his beautiful exterior and warm smile. Could he love her and simultaneously want to destroy her people? Just how far did his ambition extend?

Taking a bite of her food, Mia tried to think about it rationally. Surely she would've known if she had fallen for a monster. Nobody could hide such darkness for so long. Korum was no angel—and he didn't necessarily hold her kind in the highest regard—but he would never go so far as to take their planet away.

Or would he?

The food she just swallowed sat heavily in Mia's stomach. Excusing herself, she got up and went to the restroom to freshen up. Splashing some water on her face, she stared in the mirror, seeing the poorly concealed look of panic in her eyes.

She needed to talk to Korum and she needed to do it now, before the old doubts and suspicions got a chance to poison their relationship again. If there was anything Mia had learned from the Resistance fiasco, it was the folly of jumping to conclusions and assuming the worst. She was no longer the girl who was too scared to talk to her K lover for fear of betraying her people. Korum now belonged to her as much as she belonged to him—and one way or another, she would know the truth.

Breakfast seemed to last forever. Mia smiled and chatted with her family, all the while squirming with impatience inside. She could see Korum giving her occasional questioning glances, and she knew he could tell that something was wrong, that her smiles had a brittle edge to them.

Finally, it was over. Marisa returned to her room to take a post-meal nap—something she'd started doing recently to combat pregnancy-related tiredness—and Connor joined her, not wanting to be separated from his wife. Mia's parents retired to their room as well, to read and watch some shows about Krina that Korum had set up for them.

"Do you want to go for a walk?" Mia asked Korum as soon as her parents were out of the earshot.

His eyebrows rose. "It's not too hot for you right now?"

"It should be fine." Mia had no idea if it would be fine or not, but she wanted to get out of the house—and out of her family's earshot.

"Okay, sure." Korum got to his feet as smoothly as only a Krinar could. "Let's go."

The blast of heat hit Mia as soon as they exited the house. It was around eleven in the morning, and the sun was incredibly bright in the cloudless sky. All around them, Mia could hear the chirping and singing of insects, birds, and other creatures—some seemingly familiar, others strange and exotic.

They walked for a few minutes toward the lake, following the same path they took yesterday. In the light of day, their surroundings were even more beautiful and striking than they had been at twilight, but Mia couldn't focus on that now. Her stomach was twisted into knots, and she felt nauseated, as though she'd eaten something that didn't agree with her.

"All right, Mia." Korum stopped in a shaded area when they reached the lake and pulled her down to sit beside him on a thick patch of grass-like plants. "What's wrong, my sweet? What's going on with you this morning?"

Mia looked at the man she loved more than life itself. "I want to know if there's any truth to what Saret said."

His gaze was steady and unblinking. "Which part?"

"The part—" Her voice broke mid-sentence. "The part about you wanting to take Earth from us."

For a moment, there was only silence, during which they stared at each other. Then he said softly, "We want to share your planet with you. I told you that."

"Then why did Saret say you want to take it from us?" Something didn't ring true. "Is he completely deluded, or is there something I should know? What are your real intentions, Korum? How exactly are you going to share our planet when your sun finally dies?"

He was again silent for a few seconds, his face hard and unreadable. "You still don't trust me, do you?" he finally said. "After everything, you still think I'm the bad guy."

Mia drew in a shaky breath, the unpleasant feeling in her stomach getting worse. "No, Korum. I don't think that. I don't want to think that. I just want to know the truth. All of it." He still looked implacable, so she added, "Please, Korum ... If you truly care for me, please tell me everything."

CHAPTER TWENTY-EIGHT

"All right." His voice was colder than anything she'd heard from him in a long time. "Keep in mind, though, my sweet, no one outside of the Council and the Elders knows what I am about to tell you. You can't share this with anyone else, do you understand me?"

Mia nodded, holding her breath.

"We're not going to take Earth from you," he said. "We'll take Mars. And then we'll give humans the option of relocating there, once we have created the proper conditions for life."

Mia stared at him in shock. "What? Mars? But ... but that's uninhabitable."

"It is uninhabitable now," Korum said. "Once we're done with it, it's going to be like paradise. The planet already has water in the form of ice. We'll warm it up, create an atmosphere, and give Mars a magnetic field to mitigate solar radiation and keep the atmosphere from escaping into space. Even the gravity differential can be fixed; our scientists have recently come up with a way to enhance surface gravity and make it similar to that of Earth and Krina."

"But—" Mia found herself at a loss for words. "Wait, so you want Mars, not Earth?"

Korum sighed. "No, Mia. We want a place for our species to continue flourishing once our sun begins to dim. It's unfortunate, but we can't keep our star from dying. Maybe one day we'll discover a way to fix that too, but for now, we have to plan for the worst. Earth would be our second choice, after Krina, and Mars would be our third."

"So you do want Earth?" Mia felt like she wasn't getting something.

"Yes." His amber gaze was cool and even. "Of course we do. At least the warmer parts of it. But we're not going to kill humans for it, or whatever it is Saret implied. We'll give your people the option of remaining on Earth or relocating to the newly transformed Mars in exchange for significant wealth and other perks."

"You'll bribe humans to leave Earth?" Mia stared at him in disbelief.

"Yes." A small smile appeared on his lips. "You could call it that. There are plenty of regions on Earth that are poor, where daily existence is a struggle. We'll offer those people the option of moving to a place that's very much like paradise, where all their basic needs would be met and they would live like kings. Don't you think that would be appealing to someone in rural India or Zimbabwe?"

Mia blinked. She could see his logic—but she could also see a big problem with what he was saying. "If Mars is going to be so great," she said slowly, "why wouldn't the Krinar want to live there themselves and leave our planet alone?"

"Some of us will probably want to live on Mars," Korum said. "It's not out of the question that you and I might move there at some point. But there will always be those who are uncomfortable with what they view as artificial nature, those who would much rather live on a planet that's gone through billions of years of natural evolution—even if that planet has been somewhat polluted and damaged by humans."

"So they will come live with us—with humans, I mean—on Earth?"

"Yes," Korum said, "exactly. We'll build more Centers on Earth, so that some Krinar can live there. And in exchange for humans ceding us that space, we'll give them a much more luxurious environment on Mars. It'll be a win-win for both species."

"And if humans would not want to cede that space?"

His eyes narrowed. "Why wouldn't they? Do you really think a subsistence farmer in Rwanda would object to never having to do back-breaking work again? To being able to feed his family every day with tasty, nutritious food? Whoever comes to Mars will have access to free healthcare, education, housing . . . whatever they need. We're not going to do to your people what Europeans did to Native Americans. That's not our way."

"You didn't really answer my question," Mia said slowly. "If people don't want to go, are they going to be forcibly transported to Mars? Are you going to take their land from them no matter what?"

"We're going to do whatever is necessary to ensure the survival—and continued prosperity—of our species, Mia," he said, his eyes cold and bright under the dark slashes of his eyebrows. "Just like your kind would."

A chill ran down Mia's spine. "I see."

"What did you expect to hear, my sweet?" His tone was softly mocking. "Did you want me to lie to you, to tell you that we would never take what we need if we couldn't get it some other way?"

"No," Mia said. "I didn't want you to lie to me. I never wanted you to lie to me." Getting to her feet, she went to stand by the water, staring at the dark blue surface with unseeing gaze. She didn't know what to think, how to even begin to approach this situation.

What Korum had just described sounded relatively harmless, even generous compared to what human conquerors had done throughout history. Yet Mia knew it wouldn't be so simple. The Krinar arrival several years ago caused a major panic that spawned the Resistance movement and resulted in thousands of deaths. It was folly to think that the same thing wouldn't happen when people learned about the Ks' intentions for Mars. Even if the Krinar relocated only those who went willingly, the general population would be deeply suspicious—and likely with good reason. Once the Krinar had a place where they could move humans with a clear conscience, what would prevent them from doing so?

Korum came up behind her and wrapped his arms around her chest, pulling her up against him so that the top of her head was nestled under his chin. "I'm sorry, Mia," he said quietly. "I didn't mean to be harsh with you. Of course you have a right to know—and I shouldn't blame you for not trusting me after the way we first met. I don't want to harm your kind. I truly don't—especially now that I've fallen for you and met your family. We'll do our best to ensure that everything goes smoothly, that all your governments are fully on board and informed about what's going on. Nobody has to get hurt. We'll make sure everybody comes out ahead in this."

Mia wanted to melt into his embrace, to let him reassure her that everything would be all right, but she couldn't be an ostrich hiding her head in the sand. "When are you going to do this?" Her voice sounded dull, empty. "When are you going to transform Mars?"

"Soon," Korum said, his arms tightening around her. "I have just received the final go-ahead from the Elders to proceed."

"But why Mars?" Mia couldn't understand that part. "Why don't the Krinar just take some planet in another solar system? If you can do this, this kind of thing—"

"Terraforming," Korum said. "It's called terraforming."

"Right," Mia said. "If you can terraform Mars, why not just do it to a planet elsewhere? Why does it have to be in such close proximity to Earth?"

"Because the proximity to Earth will make the project easier," he explained quietly. "We've never done something of this magnitude before, and we'll need a base from which our scientists and other experts can operate. Earth can serve as that base for now. This won't be an easy task. It will take years—possibly decades—to make Mars habitable, and it will be nice to have our Centers on Earth close by in case of any emergencies. Once we've worked out all the kinks in the process, then we can terraform other planets located in habitable zones throughout the different galaxies."

"Other planets besides Earth and Mars?" Mia turned in his arms, meeting his gaze. For the first time, she realized the full depth of his ambition—and it shook her to the core. "You're building an empire, aren't you?" she breathed. "A real-life intergalactic empire... Earth, Mars, these other planets in the future—the Krinar will rule them all, won't they?"

"Yes." His eyes gleamed brightly. "We will."

* * *

Korum could see the shock on her face, and he softened his tone. "Would that be such a bad thing, my sweet? Your people will benefit from this as well. If anything were to happen to Earth, humans would survive and prosper at our side."

He could feel the tension in her delicate frame, and he cursed Saret for planting doubts in her mind that day. Korum had planned to tell everything to Mia in due time, to explain his intentions in the most reassuring way possible. He'd known there was a possibility she would question him after she regained her memory, but he hadn't anticipated his own reaction to her questions. Her distrust, her propensity to think the worst about him—it was all too reminiscent of the beginning, when she had spied on him and betrayed him to the Resistance. The wounds from that time were still too fresh for him to be able to remain as calm and soothing as he'd hoped to be.

"At your side—and under your control, right?" She made a move to free herself, and Korum let his arms drop, taking a step back to give her some space. He didn't bother responding to her question; the answer to that was obvious.

An intergalactic empire . . . He didn't usually think about it in such terms, but it was not a bad description for what he hoped to accomplish in his lifetime. Ever since he could remember—ever since he had been a small child—Korum had dreamed of exploring and settling other planets. He saw it as their destiny. As beautiful as Krina was, it was also just one tiny planet among trillions—a piece of rock dependent on its star and vulnerable to various cosmic disasters.

Earth had always fascinated him, with its Krina-like characteristics and a species that was strikingly similar to the Krinar themselves. In his youth, Korum, like many others, had regarded humans as inferior, with their weak, fragile bodies and primitive way of living. It wasn't until the recent centuries that he'd begun to understand that these beings were as intelligent and resourceful as the Krinar themselves. In the past, what Mia feared would have been a legitimate concern: Korum of a thousand years ago wouldn't have hesitated to simply take Earth away from her people. Now, however, he didn't want to deprive humans of their planet; he just wanted to ensure that the Krinar had a place on it too.

He had never thought his ambition was particularly outrageous. He knew that other people did, however. Even his own father seemed intimidated by Korum's drive at times, not understanding that his son merely wanted what was best for their species. A group of planets populated and controlled by the Krinar was a logical next step in their evolution, and Korum saw nothing wrong with working toward that goal.

Now he just had to make his charl see things from his perspective. "Mia, listen to me," Korum said, watching her intently. "I know you're afraid, but I'm not lying to you. I didn't tell you any of this before because it's the equivalent of classified information—not because I was trying to conceal something evil. I just received final clearance from the Elders for Mars, and we'll reach out to your governments next, to inform them about our intentions. That way, they can adequately prepare the population and nip any potentially dangerous rumors in the bud. Nobody has to get hurt in this—and we'll do our best to ensure that it doesn't happen."

Her sexy little tongue came out to lick her lips, and he found his eyes glued to her mouth, picturing that tongue licking something else entirely. *Damn it, focus.* With effort, Korum lifted his gaze to meet hers, ignoring the stirring in his cock. Now was not the time to think about sex; he had to convince her he wasn't about to exterminate her kind or steal their planet.

"Do you swear?" Her voice was soft, tremulous, and he could see hope warring with doubt on her face. She wanted to trust him, but she needed more reassurance. "Do you swear that you don't intend my people any harm? That when you build your empire, it won't be at the cost of my species' well-being?"

"Yes, my darling," Korum said. "I swear it. Unless humans strike at us, we won't do anything to harm them. Those who wish to leave Earth will be well compensated for their choice, and we'll live alongside your people on Earth, Mars, and whatever other planets we find. It won't be so bad, my sweet. I promise you that."

And stepping toward her, he drew her into his embrace again, exhaling in relief when he felt her arms sliding around his waist as well.

CHAPTER TWENTY-NINE

Mia put on the shimmerstone necklace Korum had given her and surveyed herself critically in the three-dimensional mirror located in the bedroom. She was dressed in formal Krinar clothing, a gleaming white dress similar to the one she'd worn to the fight. Her hair was pinned up and covered with a silvery net that matched the sandals on her feet. She looked festive—and ready to face the Elders.

By all rights, she should be nervous. After all, she was about to meet the oldest Krinar in existence, whose names were legend among Ks and whose mandates determined the fate of humanity. The Krinar who were about to decide her family's lifespan. Yet she felt strangely calm, as if nothing could touch her right now.

Her mind kept dwelling on this morning's conversation with Korum, going through it over and over again. Mars, Earth, an entire intergalactic empire . . . There was really no end to her lover's ambition. Mia had no doubt that Korum would ultimately achieve his goal—and that he would be at the helm of this empire he was about to build.

And she would be at his side. Her head spun at the thought. She, who had never wanted anything more than a quiet, ordinary life, would be there to watch the Krinar empire taking shape, at the side—and in bed—of the man who was going to make it happen.

Did that make her a traitor to her people? Or was it like Delia said, that by Korum falling in love with her, she had already done more to help humanity than any efforts by the Resistance?

She believed him when he promised the Krinar wouldn't harm humans on purpose. He had always kept his promises to her. She just wasn't sure how everything would unfold when people learned of the Ks' intentions for Mars. Would there be renewed anti-K movements? Would the human population panic and try to strike at the invaders, leading to the Krinar retaliating against them? Mia would be devastated if that happened.

But the thought of leaving Korum was unbearable. She couldn't live without him; it was as simple as that. She loved him with every fiber of her being, and she knew he loved her just as fiercely. Maybe that made her a traitor . . . or maybe it made her the luckiest woman alive. Only time would tell.

For now, there were Elders to meet.

"It's best if I do most of the talking," Korum said as they approached a clearing in the middle of the forest. "They don't like unnecessary conversation."

"Of course," Mia said. "We won't say a word."

"No, you might have to," he told her. "They'll probably want to talk to you and your family directly—in which case, I strongly suggest you respond to their questions as honestly and concisely as you can."

Mia nodded in agreement. Out of the corner of her eye, she could see her parents holding hands as they walked. Her mom was pale, and her dad looked grim, like he was going to an execution. Marisa and Connor trailed behind them, looking nervous and excited at the same time.

Unlike Mia, the others were dressed in human attire. It was their choice. "What, am I going to squeeze into something like that at my age?" her mom had said, indicating Mia's form-fitting, open-backed dress. Korum hadn't objected; since none of them were charl, they weren't considered a part of Krinar society and could thus wear whatever they wanted. Her dad had put on a suit and tie, and so did Marisa's husband. Her mom and Marisa wore semi-formal dresses and high heels. Mia hoped they weren't too uncomfortable, traipsing through the forest like that in the heat.

The fact that the Elders wanted to see them out in the open—as opposed to in some building—didn't surprise Mia in the least. The Ks were remarkably attuned to nature, and Korum had told her that some of the Elders shunned artificial dwellings altogether, choosing to live as their primitive ancestors once did: in the hollow trunks of giant trees or in cave-like rock formations in the mountains. They also jealously guarded their territory, not allowing anyone to come within a dozen miles of their chosen areas. This spot in the woods was considered neutral ground, a place where the Elders would often meet to discuss various matters and socialize with each other.

"Very few Krinar have ever had the privilege of seeing the Elders in person, as you're about to do," Korum said as they paused in front of the clearing. "It's about the greatest honor there is."

Mia took a deep breath, trying to still the fine trembling in her fingers. Now that they were actually here, her previous calmness had deserted her, and her heart was beating frantically in her chest. What if she accidentally did or said something that angered the Elders? In that case, they might deny Korum's petition or worse. She had no idea what these ancient Krinar were capable of.

"Ready, my sweet?" Korum asked, and she nodded, putting her hand in his. Then they walked together into the clearing, Mia's family following in their wake.

There were nine Ks standing there, three women and six men. They were all looking at Mia and her family, their faces utterly expressionless. Physically, they seemed to be in their prime, no older than Korum or any other Krinar Mia had met. All the males were tall and powerfully built, and even the females seemed sturdier than usual. The shortest of the Elder women was probably just over six feet in height, with lean, well-defined muscles covering her frame. To Mia's surprise, they were all dressed in modern Krinar clothing, their light-colored outfits contrasting with the bronzed hue of their skin.

While the women were beautiful in a warrior-princess kind of way, the men were more mixed in appearance. One male K in particular resembled the recording of the ancients far more than he did the other Krinar. Although his harsh, craggy features held a certain attraction, he looked too rough to be considered handsome. Mia wondered if any of the Elders had a mate, or if they had survived for millions of years without forming any deep attachments.

Korum let go of Mia's hand and inclined his head respectfully, saying nothing. Mia followed his example, keeping her gaze trained on the Elders the entire time. In Krinar culture, it was considered rude to look down or away when meeting with a figure of authority; open staring was the way to go.

One of the women stepped forward, her movements smooth and flowing. Coming up to Mia, she brushed her knuckles against her cheek in the traditional greeting between females. Mia smiled and reciprocated, hoping she wasn't doing something wrong. Judging by the approving gleam in Korum's eyes, she had done exactly the right thing.

After greeting Mia, the woman circled around the other humans, studying them with visible curiosity. She didn't say a word or make any gestures toward them, but Mia could see the sweat droplets on her dad's forehead. He had to be very anxious, because he didn't normally perspire that much from the heat.

Still silent, the woman went back toward the Elders and resumed her original position near the two other females. Then nine pairs of dark eyes simply looked at them, watching them with a cool, deep intelligence that seemed distinctly inhuman.

Mia looked back at them, trying to figure out which two were involved in guiding human evolution. In a way, she was meeting real-life gods, the creators of the human race. The idea was so mind-boggling that she didn't dwell on it too much. She was less likely to collapse in a trembling heap if she thought of these Elders as nothing more than somewhat older versions of Korum. And truthfully, to a twenty-one-year-old, there wasn't a tremendous difference between someone who was two thousand years of age and someone who was two million. Both were incredibly old—or so she kept telling herself.

Finally, after what seemed like an hour, the rough-featured male stepped forward, approaching Mia and Korum. "So this is your charl," he said, his voice low and exceptionally deep. Mia thought his walk resembled that of a lion, all lean muscle and predatory intensity.

Korum inclined his head. "Yes."

"Unusual," the Elder said, cocking his head to the side as he studied Mia. "Very unusual."

Mia fought the urge to quail under that penetrating gaze. She felt like the ancient K was stripping her bare, seeing her every fear and vulnerability.

"Why do you think we should make an exception for your family, Mia?" the Elder said suddenly, addressing her directly.

Mia swallowed to get rid of the knot in her throat. She had been mentally preparing for some type of interview, but she still felt caught off-guard. Nevertheless, when she spoke, her voice was surprisingly even, betraying nothing of her inner turmoil. Adrenaline was surging through her veins, sharpening her focus, and the words that came out of her mouth were unusually crisp and clear.

"I don't think you should make an exception for my family," she said, looking up at the Elder. "I think you should share your technology with the entire human race. If you won't do that, for whatever reason, then think about this: by being with Korum, I now share his lifespan. Since that's something that you and your colleagues allowed, you must see the logic in that. Without the nanocytes in my body, I would age and pass away in a few decades, while Korum would remain the same—and that would be unbearable for both of us because we love each other." She paused, taking a deep breath. "And it would be equally unbearable for me to watch those I love—" she gestured toward her family, "—get sick and die."

The ancient K was still looking at her, and she could see a glimmer of amusement on his face. It softened his features slightly, making him appear just a tiny bit less intimidating. Mia wanted to say more, but she remembered Korum's admonition about being concise when answering questions and decided to shut up instead. She had said everything there was to say; short of repeating her points and appealing to their sense of ethics and morality, there was nothing else to add.

The Elder stared at her for a few more seconds and then turned away. Mia could sense some sort of wordless communication going on between him and the others, and then he turned back toward Mia and Korum.

"We'll make our decision soon," he said, addressing Korum this time.

Then he went back toward the rest of the Elders, and they all melted away into the forest, leaving Mia, Korum, and her family alone in the clearing.

* * *

"That was Lahur," Korum told his charl during their trip back to the house. "He's the one I told you about—the oldest Krinar alive. The woman who came up to you and your parents is Sheura; she's an evolutionary biologist, and she was involved in the human project from the very beginning."

"Oh, no wonder she seemed so curious about us! Do you think they'll do it? Do you think they'll agree to it?" Mia was perched on a float next to him, her eyes bright with excitement. Korum knew she was likely still feeling the rush from the meeting, and he smiled at her, proud of the way she had conducted herself with the Elders. He'd known she was nervous, of course, but she'd maintained her composure throughout—better than many Krinar would have in her place.

"I don't know, my sweet," he said honestly. "Nobody can predict what the Elders are going to do. I hope they saw whatever it was they wanted to see today. All we can do now is wait."

"Do we have to remain on Krina while they decide?" Mia's mother asked, and Korum could see that she looked much more calm now, relieved to have the ordeal over with.

"Yes," Korum told her, "that would probably be best. They said soon, so it shouldn't be too long. Besides, you haven't even met my parents yet. I know they are anxious to see everyone." Korum also had another reason for wanting Mia's family on Krina, but now was not the right time to discuss it.

"Oh, we'd love to meet them too!" Ella exclaimed. "Wouldn't that be great, Dan?"

"Sure," Mia's father said. "We would absolutely enjoy meeting them."

"Good," Korum said. "Then I will make the arrangements."

CHAPTER THIRTY

Humming to herself, Mia got dressed and ready to go to Korum's parents' house. She remembered liking Riani and Chiaren during their virtual meeting, and she was looking forward to seeing them again. She had a suspicion her parents would like them too, though they would likely be awestruck by their youth and beauty.

If the Elders gave their permission, Mia's parents would also regain their youth. She wanted it so badly she could taste it. She had seen pictures of her mom and dad when they were Mia's age, and they had been a cute couple, her dad tall and handsome and her mom pretty and carefree. She wanted to see them like that in real life, healthy and vigorous, without the various aches and pains that came with middle age.

Just as she was putting on her dress, Korum walked into the bedroom. He appeared even more gorgeous than usual, his face glowing with some unknown emotion. Coming up to Mia, he bent his head to brush a kiss against her lips. "You look beautiful, my sweet," he said softly, tucking one of her curls behind her ear.

"Thank you." Mia beamed at him. "So do you."

"I have a little something I'd like you to wear," he said, looking at her with a mysterious smile. "Another piece of jewelry."

"Oh sure." Mia had already put on the shimmerstone necklace for the meeting with his parents, but she didn't mind wearing something else instead—or in addition to. Accessorizing had never been her strong suit, although she had every intention of learning how to do it. She had already gotten better at dressing fashionably; jewelry was the next step.

To her complete and utter shock, Korum took a step back and

lowered himself to one knee. In his hand was a small black box. As she stared at it, the box opened, revealing the most beautiful ring she had ever seen in her life. Small and delicate, it appeared to be made of the same iridescent material as her necklace, with a larger round shimmerstone set in the middle.

"Mia," Korum said quietly, looking up at her with those incredible amber-colored eyes, "I know things between us haven't always been easy, and I can't promise you there won't be difficulties ahead. But I do know one thing. I want you, now and always, more than I've ever wanted anyone in all my years of existence. I want you in my life, in my bed, and by my side for as long as we are both alive. I want to cherish you and protect you; I want to lay the world at your feet. I want your face to be the first one I see when I wake up and the last before I go to sleep. I want to make you as happy as you make me. Mia, my sweet, I am hopelessly in love with you. Will you do me the honor of becoming my wife?"

Mia opened her mouth but no words came out. Instead, she could feel a strange burning sensation in her eyes. "You . . . you want me to marry you?" she finally managed to whisper, afraid she somehow misheard him. "But—" she swallowed, "—you're Krinar! You can't marry a human!" Her voice rose incredulously at the end.

"I can do whatever I want," Korum said, and she couldn't help smiling inside at the arrogant note in his voice. Even on his knees, he sounded like king of the world. "Just because no one else has done it doesn't mean I can't. I want you to be mine in every sense of the word— by Krinar *and* by human law. Mia, darling, will you marry me?"

The burning in her eyes increased, and a tear escaped and rolled down her face. "Yes," she said almost inaudibly, her vision blurring with moisture. Her chest felt tight, and she couldn't seem to catch her breath. "Yes, my love, I will marry you."

His answering smile was as blinding as the Krinar sun. Rising to his feet, he reached for her left hand and slid the ring onto her ring finger. It fit perfectly, shimmering with every color in the visible spectrum.

"Oh, Korum . . . It's—" Mia was openly crying now, tears of happiness running down her cheeks. "It's beautiful . . ."

"Not as beautiful as you," he said softly, drawing her into his embrace. "Nothing could ever be as beautiful as you." And cupping her face in his large hands, he kissed the tears off her cheeks, his lips tender and reverent on her skin.

* * *

They agreed to share the news with Mia's parents when both families would be gathered together, and Korum now watched with amusement as Mia did her best to hide her left hand in the folds of her dress during the trip to his parents' house. He'd told her she could take the ring off for now, but she had vehemently refused. "What if I lose it?" she said in a horrified tone, and Korum didn't argue. He liked seeing the piece of jewelry on her finger, liked knowing that there was a visible symbol of their commitment to each other.

He wasn't sure when he had become so enamored with the idea of marrying her in the human way. During that visit to her parents' house, the thought had been planted in his mind, and it had been brewing there for the past month. He'd known that Mia still felt uncomfortable being his charl; the way she saw it, he held all the power in their relationship. It was an ongoing source of contention between them, and Korum knew she would never be completely happy as long as she felt like she had no rights among his people.

The more Korum had contemplated the problem, the more it seemed like marriage could be the solution. By publicly marrying Mia on Krina, he would elevate her standing in their society. She would no longer be merely a charl, a human who belonged to him; she would be the equivalent of his mate, long before the Celebration of Forty-Seven.

She would also officially belong to him in the eyes of her people. Korum liked that quite a bit. If any human male dared to look at her, he would see the ring on her finger and know that this woman was taken. Those rings were a clever custom, Korum had recently realized. They allowed a man to mark his territory in a very civilized manner. Mia was now his fiancé, just as she would soon be his wife—and nobody would have any doubts about that fact.

Of course, their marriage would also give Mia's parents peace of mind. Although the Stalis family had accepted their relationship, Korum knew they would be far happier if they could call him something other than their daughter's boyfriend. Now he would be their son-in-law, a much stronger tie in their eyes, and they would feel more reassured about his commitment to Mia.

Their transport pod landed in front of his parents' house, and he led Mia inside, with her parents, sister, and brother-in-law trailing behind them. His human family, he thought wryly. It was so unlikely he could still hardly believe it, but these people were important to Mia—and they were becoming increasingly important to him as well.

Riani and Chiaren were waiting for them. As Korum entered the house, he saw his mother first, standing there with a huge smile on her face, and his father's more austere presence immediately behind her. They had been shocked when he'd first told them about Mia, but glad too. Korum sometimes wondered if his parents thought he would go through life without ever finding someone to love.

Stepping forward, he gave Riani a hug and greeted his father with the more formal touch to the shoulder. Then, turning to Mia's family, he introduced them to his parents.

To his surprise, the two sets of parents clicked almost immediately. Within minutes, they were chatting animatedly and trading stories of their children's youthful exploits. "Oh my God, this is embarrassing," Mia whispered in his ear, blushing when Ella laughingly revealed her infant daughter's habit of freeing herself from diapers and crawling around their backyard chasing after squirrels.

"What are squirrels?" Riani asked curiously, and Mia's father explained all about the little mammal with the bushy tail.

Marisa and Connor, who had been watching the whole thing with bemusement, came to sit next to Korum and Mia on the other side of the room. "Wow, they're really getting along, aren't they?" Marisa told her sister, and Mia laughed, her eyes sparkling with happiness.

It seemed like the perfect moment to make the announcement.

Getting up, Korum pulled Mia to her feet. All eyes immediately turned toward them. "We have something we'd like to share with you," Korum said, looking around the room. His parents seemed puzzled, while the humans stared at him with barely concealed delight. "I have asked Mia to marry me, and she has agreed."

Mia grinned and lifted her left hand, displaying the shimmerstone ring on her finger.

The room exploded. Laughter, shrieks, and congratulations filled the air. Everybody seemed to be hugging everyone else, and his parents gamely went along with the excitement, even though Chiaren kept throwing questioning looks in his direction. As Mia had said, no Krinar had ever married a human, and the very concept of marriage was foreign to his people. A mating union that was marked by the Celebration of Forty-Seven was the closest Krinar equivalent. Korum intended to explain his rationale to his parents later; for now, it was enough that they knew just how much he loved his charl.

After the initial hoopla died down, Korum said to Mia's parents, "I wasn't sure if I should request your permission first or not. From what I understand of this custom, it's rarely done in modern times. I hope you don't mind—"

"Mind?" Ella exclaimed. "Of course we don't mind!" Her eyes were gleaming with tears, and Korum wondered what it was about marriage that made human women so emotional.

The rest of their time together was spent discussing potential dates for the wedding (Korum insisted on it being no later than next week), the location (Mia liked the lake near his house), and the logistics of a human wedding ceremony on a planet so far away from Earth.

"Don't we need someone to marry you?" Connor asked. "A priest, a rabbi, a judge, someone? And if it's to be legally recognized back home, don't you need to register somewhere on Earth?"

Korum had already thought of these obstacles. "One of the charl living on Krina was actually a judge in Missouri," he told everyone. "I have already reached out to request her assistance. As far as registration goes, we'll transmit our signatures electronically to the Daytona Beach Clerk of the Circuit Court. I'm sure they will make an exception for us, given the circumstances."

* * *

For Mia, the next five days seemed to pass in the blink of an eye. As soon as news about their engagement spread, there was an endless parade of visitors to Korum's house, all wanting to meet her and her family.

Korum's friends, acquaintances, employees, business contacts, even Council members . . . Mia met so many Ks during her short engagement that she couldn't keep track of all the names and faces. To her surprise, she could sense echoes of the same respect they showed Korum in their attitude toward her. It was subtle, but it was there. Her opinion was asked more often, and they spoke to her directly, frequently bypassing Korum altogether. After wondering about it for a couple of days, Mia realized that they were now treating her more as Korum's mate and less as his charl. In their eyes, she was no longer merely a human who belonged to one of them; she was going to be a true part of their society.

Mia particularly liked Jalet and Huar, Korum's long-time friends. Like Korum's parents, Jalet was a dabbler, a jack-of-all-trades. Smart and funny, he seemed to know about everything under the sun, and Mia loved listening to his stories about life on Krina. Huar, on the other hand, was quiet and serious. He was considered to be an expert on ocean studies. Both Huar and Jalet had also been friends with Saret, and they were horrified to learn about his true nature.

"The four of us were like your Musketeers," Jalet told her, referring to the classic Dumas novel. "We got into so many adventures in our youth. I thought about accompanying Saret and Korum to Earth, but I was stuck on a project and the timing didn't work out."

"That was probably for the best." Korum grinned at his friend. "For all we know, he might've tried to kill you too."

"You know," Huar said thoughtfully, "now that I think about it, it's not all that surprising that Saret went after you, Korum. He was quite ambitious, but very secretive about it. You've always known what you wanted and pursued it openly, but Saret liked to scheme and maneuver behind the scenes, so nobody knew it was him. I suspected he might be jealous of you, but I never realized how deep that jealousy ran."

"None of us knew what he was really like," Korum said. "Saret managed to fool everyone, especially me." Mia could hear the bitter note in his voice, and it made her heart ache. He never talked about it much, but she knew he still blamed himself for putting her in harm's way.

"My love, you know he was probably a psychopath, right?" Laying a reassuring hand on Korum's knee, she gave him a serious look. "He was smart enough to hide it, but that's what he ultimately was. All charm on the surface, and a complete lack of remorse underneath. He was clever too, clever enough to wear a mask for centuries." Mia remembered reading about psychopaths in one of her college classes, and they were a truly fascinating breed. She didn't know if Saret fit the textbook definition—or if Ks could even be true psychopaths in the medical sense—but he certainly displayed some of the traits, including a grandiose sense of self-worth.

Korum smiled in response, hugging her to him, but she could see that it would be a long time before the wounds inflicted by Saret's betrayal would heal.

In addition to all the visitors, there was plenty to be done in preparation for the wedding itself. With the virtual help of Korum's cousin Leeta, Mia created herself a beautiful white dress that incorporated some elements from both cultures. She also made flattering outfits for her family that were largely Krinar in style, but took into account their personal preferences.

In the meantime, Korum fabricated an enormous ceremonial hall that floated above the lake near his house. The size of an Olympic stadium, it was designed to accommodate over a hundred thousand guests—a number that made Mia's head spin every time she thought about it.

"How big is this wedding going to be?" she gasped when she saw the giant structure.

"As big as it needs to be," Korum replied, looking at her steadily, and Mia realized that he was making a public statement. By marrying her in front of all of Krina, he was proclaiming that humans had officially arrived, that they were no longer an inferior species that could only exist on the fringes of the Krinar society.

Korum was addressing her concerns about her place in his world.

CHAPTER THIRTY-ONE

The day before the wedding was supposed to take place, the Elders finally reached a decision about Saret. As soon as Korum heard the news, he went to visit his former friend, feeling a strange need to see him one last time.

Saret was confined in Viarad, in a heavily guarded building where dangerous criminals awaited their trial. The past couple of months had not been kind to him. If Korum didn't know better, he would've thought Saret had aged somehow. His gaze looked dull and empty, and his skin appeared oddly ashen. It was like he had lost all hope, and, for a brief moment, Korum felt pity for his enemy, his thoughts turning to their childhood together.

But then he remembered what Saret had done to Mia—and what he intended to do to them all—and the feeling of pity faded. Korum had never known the real Saret; whatever good times they'd had together were as fake as Saret's friendship.

"Come to gloat, have you?" Saret's voice broke the silence. "I suppose you heard about my sentence." His lips twisted bitterly, his fingers tugging reflexively at the crime-collar around his throat.

"No," Korum said truthfully, "I didn't come to gloat."

"Then why are you here?"

"I don't know," Korum admitted. "I guess I needed some closure."

"Closure?" Saret laughed, a harsh sound that grated on Korum's ears. "What kind of closure?"

Korum shrugged, unsure of the answer to that.

"Jalet and Huar came to see me yesterday," Saret said, his eyes glued

698

to Korum's face. "They told me all about your little human bride and how your wedding is going to be the biggest event of the millennium. Congratulations. I guess you brainwashed her better than I ever could. Even after that bitch Laira undid my procedure, Mia still wants you. Did you tell her what you're planning to do to her people?"

"Yes," Korum said. "I explained everything. She understood. I never intended to harm her kind, only to make room for us on their planet."

"Yeah, right." Saret gave him a sarcastic look. "Do you think I don't remember how you regarded humans once? How you said Earth should've been ours by right?"

Korum stared at his former friend in disbelief. "You truly thought I still held those views? Saret, that was over a thousand years ago! Everything has changed since then. *I* have changed since then—"

"Oh really? And what made you change? A tight little cunt and a pair of big blue eyes?"

Korum felt a strong urge to do something violent to Saret, but restrained himself at the last moment. "No," he said, keeping his voice even. "I saw how quickly they were progressing and becoming more like us. I realized centuries ago that I had been wrong about them—that so many of us had been wrong. Surely you knew that."

"No, I didn't know," Saret said. "Or maybe I knew and didn't believe it. It doesn't matter now, does it? After today, I will be no more. That's why you came to see me now, isn't it? To watch me die?"

"You won't die," Korum said calmly. "They sentenced you to a new version of complete rehabilitation, one that Laira herself came up with recently. Unlike the old one, it can't be reversed."

Saret laughed bitterly. "Right. Like I said, after this procedure I will be no more."

"Goodbye, Saret." Korum took one final look at his former friend and walked out, putting an end to that chapter of his life.

When he got home, Mia was waiting for him, an anxious look on her face. "How did it go?" she asked, getting up from the float where she had been reading her tablet. "Did you get a chance to talk to him?"

"Yes." Korum drew her toward him for a hug. The familiar feel of her in his arms was soothing, taking away his stress and tension. As much as Korum hated to admit it to himself, seeing Saret today had been painful. Despite his betrayal, despite everything, Korum had thought of him as a friend his whole life, and he couldn't help mourning the loss of that illusion.

She wrapped her arms around his waist and held him, her small hands rubbing up and down his back. Somehow she knew he needed comfort now; she always knew what he needed these days.

After a couple of minutes, she pulled back slightly and looked up at him, her blue eyes filled with sympathy. "When are they going to do it?" she asked quietly. "When is the procedure going to take place?"

"This afternoon," Korum said, lifting his hand to brush a curl off her cheek. "In just a couple of hours."

"And then what? What happens to those who are rehabilitated like that?"

"He'll be taken to a special re-education facility, where the rehabilitated are taught how to become productive members of society again. He'll know about his old identity, of course, but he'll be given a chance to start over, to build a new life for himself."

"And he'll be completely changed? He won't want to do those things again?"

"Most likely not," Korum said. "And besides, he'll be under close surveillance for centuries to come. At the least sign of renewed criminal tendencies, he will undergo the procedure again."

She moistened her lips, and Korum found himself staring at her mouth, his thoughts suddenly taking a sexual turn. "Do you think we'll run into him at some point?" she asked. "If he's going to re-enter society after his rehabilitation, do you think we'll see him again?"

Korum tried to tear his mind away from the image of her lips wrapped around his cock. "Probably," he managed to say. "But don't worry—he'll be a very different man." Despite the seriousness of the conversation, he could feel his body hardening, reacting to her nearness as it usually did.

Undoubtedly feeling the bulge against her stomach, Mia gave him a knowing smile and pressed closer, rubbing her breasts against his chest. Korum inhaled sharply, feeling her peaked nipples through the two layers of clothing that separated them. Her eyes darkened, her pupils expanding, and there was a hint of color stealing across the paleness of her cheeks. She was getting aroused; he could see it . . . and feel it and smell it. The warm, sensual scent of her was like an aphrodisiac to him, sending blood rushing through his veins and making his cock throb with need.

Still looking up at him with that seductive smile, she licked her lips again, slowly this time. The sound that escaped his throat was closer to a growl. She knew exactly what to do nowadays, how to drive him wild in the shortest possible span of time.

Desperate for her taste, Korum bent his head and kissed her, reveling in the way her tongue curled around his, stroking and caressing the interior of his mouth. She was a skilled kisser now, a far cry from the shy virgin he'd forced into his bed back in New York. Her fingers found their way into his hair, her nails delicately scratching his scalp, and he almost groaned, rocking his hips back and forth, pushing his erection into her belly.

His skin felt hot, and suddenly their clothes were too confining, too much in the way. Korum pulled down the top of her dress, imprisoning her arms in the fabric and baring her pretty breasts to his gaze. They were white, firm, and perfectly round, and her nipples were a beautiful pink-rose color. Unable to resist the temptation, he dropped to his knees and brought those small hard nipples toward his mouth, sucking first one and then another. She moaned, arching toward him, her hands holding the back of his head, and Korum slid one hand under the skirt of her dress, feeling the softness of the curls between her thighs.

"Korum, please," she whispered, and he knew she was aching for more, just as he was. Still tonguing her nipples, he pushed one finger inside her, his balls tightening at the warm, slick feel of her interior channel. He wanted her to come, but at the same time, he wanted to keep torturing her, to make her scream with pleasure in his arms. His thumb entered between her folds, found her small clitoris, and he pressed on it lightly, keeping his touch too gentle for her to reach her peak. She bucked against him, and Korum did it again, loving the helpless little sounds that tore from her throat. His cock felt like it would explode, but he kept pushing his finger inside her, feeling a gush of moisture with every stroke.

Sweet, she was so fucking sweet to him. Ripping apart her dress, he bared her stomach and the dark triangle between her thighs, his mouth leaving her breasts to kiss every inch of the skin he exposed. There was so much he wanted to do to her, so many ways he wanted to take her, and he would do it all in time, but for now he needed to take it slow, to gradually introduce her to all the pleasures of the flesh. She was trembling in his arms, her delicate inner walls quivering around his finger, and he pushed a second finger inside her, stretching her, his thumb still playing lightly with her clit.

"Korum . . ." Her tortured moan was like music to his ears, and he smiled triumphantly, gently scraping his teeth across the delicate skin of her stomach. He didn't break the skin, but she still gasped at the sting, and he felt her pussy tighten around his fingers, coating them with more delicious moisture.

"Yes," he murmured, "yes, you can come for me now . . ." And she did, her head thrown back with a scream, the pulsations of her inner muscles adding to the blazing heat inside him.

Withdrawing his fingers, Korum licked them, savoring her taste, then tugged her down on the floor beside him. The intelligent material was soft around them, massaging their knees and calves with tiny finger-like appendages, but Korum barely noticed the pleasant feeling, focusing only on the woman in his arms.

Mia was still shaking, her breathing fast and uneven in the aftermath of her orgasm, and Korum arranged her pliant body so that she was on her hands and knees, facing away from him. The curve of her perfectly shaped ass was an unbearable temptation. He could see the wet, swollen folds of her sex and the tiny rose of her other opening, and he wanted to be in both places at once, to fuck her in every way possible.

Pushing his thumb inside her slick channel, he gathered the moisture from there and then used it as a lubricant, pressing that same finger to her ass. She cried out, her muscles resisting the intrusion, and he paused, letting her get used to the sensation before he continued slowly working it into her tight passage. When it was all the way in, he grasped her hips with his other hand and sank his cock deep into her pussy.

She arched, moaning, and Korum sucked in his breath, his thumb feeling the movement of his shaft inside her through the thin wall that separated her two orifices. *So fucking sweet.* The pleasure was unbelievable, almost intolerable. Unable to wait any longer, Korum began fucking her without restraint, feeling her inner muscles clinging to his cock, gripping him so tightly he felt like he was about to explode.

And then he did, his head thrown back with a deep roar. She screamed too, bucking against him, and Korum felt her inner muscles milking him, squeezing every drop of semen from his body.

Panting, he sank down on the floor, still buried deep inside her. After a few moments, he withdrew his thumb and pulled her naked, trembling body against him. She was breathing as hard as he was, and he kissed the delicate shell of her ear, knowing she needed tenderness after the way he just took her like a savage. "I love you," he whispered, and she turned toward him with a smile—the smile of a woman who had just been thoroughly satisfied.

"And I love you," she said softly, stroking his face with her fingers.

They lay like that for a while longer, just holding each other and enjoying the feel of skin against skin. Then Korum heard Mia's stomach rumble.

She blushed slightly, and he grinned. "Shower and lunch?"

"Yes, please," she said, then laughed as he picked her up and carried her into the bathroom.

* * *

The guardians came for Saret at two in the afternoon. Alir was among them, his black eyes cold and expressionless.

When they reached for him, Saret shrugged off their hands and walked out of the room on his own, following them toward his execution chamber.

Laira was already there, looking somber as befitting the occasion. Saret had met her once and immediately disliked her. She reminded him of Korum. Same sharp intelligence, same ruthless ambition. She applied to work in his lab a few decades ago, before she became known as a rising star in the field. After a brief interview, Saret turned down her application, enjoying the crushed look on her face when he told her she was unqualified.

There was some twisted irony in her being his executioner today.

They strapped him down on a float, making sure he was fully restrained for what was to come. Saret didn't fight them. What would be the point? The guardians were armed to the teeth, and even if they weren't, they were skilled fighters. He wouldn't stand a chance. At this point, all Saret cared about was dying with dignity.

And death is what this would be. Even though his body would remain, his mind—that which made him Saret—would be gone, thoroughly erased. He would never be himself again; his memories, his personality, his essence—it would all be wiped out.

Laira approached him, holding a small white device in her hands. Saret recognized it. He'd used a version of it on Mia just a couple of months ago.

"I am sorry," Laira said, pressing the device to his forehead. "I am truly sorry for this."

Her face was the last thing Saret saw before his world faded into darkness.

CHAPTER THIRTY-TWO

The morning of their wedding dawned crisp and clear.

"Mia, honey, you look—" Her mom wiped away tears. "You look so gorgeous . . ."

"Thank you, mom," Mia said softly. "You and Marisa look beautiful too." She wasn't lying; her sister was stunning in a cream-colored dress with gently draped folds that skillfully concealed her slight baby bump, while her mom appeared remarkably youthful in a peach-colored sheath that flattered her rounded figure. Her dad and Connor were dressed in Krinar clothing as well, looking surprisingly sharp in their fitted white pants, boots, and structured sleeveless shirts.

"I can't believe my baby sister is getting married," Marisa sniffled, her eyes filling with moisture too. That wasn't unusual, though; Mia's sister cried at the drop of a hat these days.

"And to a K, no less," Connor jumped in, a big grin on his face. "Dan, did you ever think such a thing would happen to your youngest?"

"No," her dad said dryly. "I certainly didn't."

Mia's family were sitting in a private room in the giant hall structure, watching Mia putting the final touches on her hair. As a wedding gift, Leeta had sent her a design for a beautiful hair accessory, and Mia was now placing it on her head. Made of some sparkling metals and shiny white-colored stones, it went all around her hair and through each curl, making Mia look like a fairy princess.

Her dress only added to the impression. It was long, covering her feet, with a wide skirt and a strapless sweetheart neckline that pushed up her breasts and flattered her slim torso. It would've been a classic wedding dress, if it weren't for the fact that Mia's entire back was left exposed in the style of her usual Krinar outfits. Since the dress was long, Mia decided to wear high heels, giving herself four extra inches of height—which made her almost as tall as the shortest Krinar women.

"Korum hasn't seen you yet, has he?" her mom asked anxiously, and Mia shook her head, smiling at the superstition.

"He hasn't, mom, relax."

Mia knew she should be feeling nervous herself. After all, didn't all brides freak out, at least a little bit? And Mia had more cause to freak out than most, given the size of her wedding and the fact that the entire Krinar race would be watching the unprecedented event either virtually or in person.

However, she didn't have even a hint of bridal jitters. All she could feel was a warm glow of happiness. Korum had taken care of all the logistics, handling the wedding preparations with the same calm assurance as he did everything else, so there was nothing to worry about on that front. As for their future together, she knew it wouldn't always be smooth sailing, but their love was strong enough, real enough, to survive whatever obstacles lay ahead.

Some part of her still couldn't believe that this was happening, that she was about to get married to a K she had once feared and regarded as an enemy. Although only a few short months had passed, so much had changed in her life—and in Korum's life. They had each learned the value of compromise, of seeing the other person's point of view. Mia had grown stronger, more confident, while Korum had begun tempering his natural arrogance and controlling tendencies. He was still ridiculously overprotective, of course, but Mia hoped that would ease with time, as memories of Saret's attack gradually faded. Korum's possessiveness was a different matter; she strongly suspected that part of his personality would never change.

"You know, you're going to be a celebrity back home," Marisa said thoughtfully, watching Mia. "My baby sis—the first human to marry a K! If the media gets ahold of it, you'll be all over the news . . ."

"I know." Mia mentally shuddered at the thought. She and Korum had already discussed the disturbing possibility. "When we come back to Earth, we'll likely be living in Lenkarda, so it won't be so bad for us. For you guys, though . . . You might want to consider moving to Lenkarda too, regardless of what happens with the petition." It went without saying that Mia's family would have to live in the Centers if they were granted immortality, just like charl.

Taking one last look in the mirror, Mia turned and smiled at everyone. "I'm ready."

* * *

Dressed in a white human-style tuxedo, Korum stood waiting at the altar. As the first notes of the traditional human wedding march began to play, his pulse jumped in anticipation. In a matter of minutes, Mia would be walking down that aisle, and he would finally see his human bride.

Two hours ago, her parents had pulled her away and warned him very strictly that he couldn't lay eyes on her until the ceremony began. Bad luck or something ridiculous like that. Korum hadn't been pleased, since he had wanted to help Mia dress—and maybe sneak in a quickie before the lengthy celebration—but Ella Stalis had been adamant and Korum had grudgingly given in. Arguing with his soon-to-be mother-in-law was not high on his list of priorities today.

As the music continued, he cast a quick glance around the large celebration hall. Decorated in white and silver tones, it was filled to the brim. In addition to Korum's family, friends, and various acquaintances, many members of the Krinar elite were attending in person. The rest of Krina—and the Krinar residents of Earth—were experiencing it virtually. Everyone was watching him with unbridled curiosity, and Korum knew they were wondering why he was doing it, why he was marrying his charl. Even Arus had been puzzled. "Isn't that redundant?" he'd asked Korum after a Council meeting in which Korum had participated remotely. "You and Mia are already as good as married. She's your charl."

Korum had simply smiled, not bothering to explain his reasons. Mia was indeed his charl, and now she would also be his wife.

In the distance, he could hear her footsteps. Her father was leading her in, as per the old custom of giving the bride away. Korum grinned to himself. He would gladly take her off their hands.

As she appeared at the other end of the aisle, on her father's arm, his breath caught in his chest. Mia looked radiant, more beautiful than any woman Korum could ever remember seeing. She was glowing, her blue eyes shining with happiness and her lips curved in a wide smile. The dress emphasized her tiny waist and pushed up her deliciously round breasts, drawing his attention to her cleavage. Just seeing her like that made him want to pick her up and carry her to bed—and keep her there for the next several hours.

Soon, Korum promised himself, and did his best to push all thoughts of sex out of his mind. It was impossible, however, because he simply couldn't tear his eyes away from her. As she glided down the aisle, he found himself hungrily watching her every step, drinking in the delicacy of her features, the elegant lines of her neck and shoulders. Her skin looked so soft, so touchable that Korum's fingers actually itched with the urge to stroke it, to feel it all over.

Then she was there, next to him, and the music reached a crescendo, then quieted down. Korum took Mia's hand and turned toward the blond human woman who would perform the ceremony. Once a judge in Missouri, Lana Walters was now a charl living on Krina, and she was honored to be part of such a historic occasion.

"Dear friends, family, and all who are present or watching us today," Lana said in a husky voice, "we are gathered here today to witness the marriage of Nathrandokorum and Mia Stalis, the first time such a union has ever taken place." She paused for dramatic effect. "Korum, do you take Mia to be your lawfully wedded wife, to have and to hold, to love and to cherish, in sickness and in health, until death do you part?"

"I do," Korum said, looking at Mia. At his words, her smile became impossibly bright, dazzling him with its beauty.

"And you, Mia? Do you take Korum to be your lawfully wedded husband, to have and to hold, to love and to cherish, in sickness and in health, until death do you part?"

"I do." Her voice was strong and clear, without even a hint of hesitation.

"Then I pronounce you husband and wife. You may kiss the bride."

Korum didn't need any urging. Bringing Mia toward him, he bent his head and kissed her, the delicious taste of her sending a surge of blood straight to his groin. It took all his willpower to stop after a minute. When he pulled away, she was looking up at him with her mouth slightly swollen and her blue eyes soft with desire.

As one, the crowd stood up and began stomping their feet in the Krinar version of clapping. The floor shook as a hundred thousand guests stomped in unison and cheered for them. Taking Mia's hand, Korum lifted their joined palms into the air, whipping the crowd into an even greater frenzy.

It was time to celebrate.

* * *

Mia couldn't stop laughing as her husband whirled her around the dance floor, as effortlessly as if she was a doll. All around them, other Krinar couples were dancing too, their movements so complex and fluid that Mia would never be able to replicate them on her own. Her family was watching from the sidelines, looking as awed as Mia felt at the inhuman grace and athleticism of the dancers.

Despite the traditionally human wedding ceremony, the party afterwards was decidedly alien. It reminded Mia of Leeta's union celebration in Lenkarda. Everything, from the exotic music to the corner location of the dance floors, was purely Krinar. Floating seats, reflective walls, and shiny decorations abounded.

Mia could see that her parents were overwhelmed by all the glitter and the gorgeous crowds surrounding them. Marisa and Connor, on the other hand, seemed to love it. Mia's brother-in-law even tasted one of the local alcoholic beverages. "Strong shit," he said approvingly after his eyes stopped watering. Mia and the others stuck to the refreshing pink juice cocktail, unwilling to try anything strong enough to give Ks a buzz. After a little while, Korum's parents joined Mia's family, and they all conversed while Korum stole Mia away to the dance floor.

After about an hour of vigorous dancing, Mia had to beg for mercy. "You realize I'm human, right?" she laughingly told Korum, stopping to catch her breath.

At that moment, they were approached by a tall Krinar man. "Congratulations," he said, smiling at them. "I'm Kellon, Ellet's cousin."

Korum smiled back, and they exchanged the traditional Krinar greeting, touching each other's shoulder with their palms.

"I have a wedding gift for you," Kellon said, "from Ellet."

"Oh?" Korum arched his eyebrows, and Mia looked at the K. What did the human biology expert want to give them?

"For the past several years, Ellet has been working on a very ambitious project," Kellon said, "and she finally had a big breakthrough last night. It's something that would be of particular interest to you both—which is why she asked me to approach you today, during your wedding."

"What is it?" Mia asked, unbearably curious.

"She has been trying to figure out how humans and Krinar could have biological offspring together . . . and she thinks she finally has a solution."

"A solution?" Mia whispered, hardly daring to believe her ears. "Are you talking about human-Krinar babies?" Her husband seemed to be frozen in place, staring at the other K in shock.

"Yes," Kellon confirmed. "The process is far from perfect yet, and Ellet has a lot of kinks to work out, but she's been able to figure out how to combine the DNA from both species in such a way as to produce viable offspring. A few more years and the two of you may be able to have a child—if you're so inclined, of course."

"Is she sure?" Korum's voice was calm, but his eyes were nearly yellow with strong emotion. "Is Ellet absolutely sure about this? If this is just some simulation she ran—"

"No," Kellon said, "she's sure. She's run at least a hundred simulations, and every single one of them produced the same results. For the first time ever, it's going to be possible for charl and cheren to have children together."

"Thank you, Kellon," Mia said thickly, "and please thank Ellet for us. This . . this is the best wedding gift we could've received." She felt like she would burst into tears at any moment, and she looked away, blinking furiously to hold back the moisture that filled her eyes. A child with Korum! It was beyond her wildest dreams.

"Yes," Korum said softly, "please convey our most sincere thanks to Ellet. She has our gratitude."

Kellon inclined his head respectfully and walked away, melting into the crowd.

As soon as he was gone, Mia turned to her husband. "A baby! Oh my God, Korum, a baby!" She grabbed his hand, squeezing it between her palms in excitement.

"A baby," he repeated, and there was a strange expression on his face. "Our baby."

Some of Mia's excitement waned. "You . . . You do want a child, right?" she asked uncertainly. "I mean, I know it would be partially human and everything—"

"Want one?" He stared at her like she had just grown two heads. When he spoke again, his voice was low and filled with intensity. "Mia, my sweet, I love you. A child who would be part you and part me? How could I not want that?" Covering her hands with his other palm, he drew her toward him, his eyes gleaming. "I want it very, very much."

Mia beamed at him, feeling like her heart would overflow with happiness. "If we had a daughter, we could call her Ivy. I've always loved that name. What do you think?"

"I think I like it very much," he murmured, bending his head and giving her a deep, passionate kiss.

They decided to share the news with their families after the wedding.

There were simply too many people around right now for such an important—and private—announcement. Still, Mia couldn't get her mind off Ellet's gift.

"Do you think the procedure will be perfected by the time I'm thirty?" she asked Korum as he led her back to the dance floor. "I've always wanted to have a baby before I was thirty—"

"Thirty?" Her husband laughed. "Mia, darling, your age is irrelevant now. Our child could be born when you're thirty—or when you're five hundred and thirty. It really doesn't matter—"

"It matters for my parents," Mia said quietly. "I would want them to see their grandchildren, to know them in their lifetime." It was the one thing that worried her: the fact that they still had not received an answer from the Elders.

Korum started to say something when the music suddenly stopped. All the noise died down, a deathly silence descending out of nowhere. Everyone seemed frozen in place, staring at the entrance.

"What's going on?" Mia whispered, stepping closer to Korum.

"Hush, my sweet," he said quietly, putting a protective arm around her back. "It looks like Lahur is here."

Mia barely suppressed a gasp. From what Korum had told her, the Elders never came out to socialize with the other Krinar or to attend any public events. They were essentially loners, holding themselves apart from the general population. And now Lahur, the oldest of them all, was here at their party?

The crowd slowly parted, and Mia could see a tall, powerful man making his way toward them. As he approached, she recognized the hard features of the Elder she'd spoken to in the forest. He was dressed in formal Krinar clothing, like all the other guests, but the fancy outfit did little to conceal his predatory nature. Even among other Krinar, he seemed more savage somehow, a panther roaming among house cats.

"Welcome, Lahur," Korum said calmly, inclining his head toward the newcomer. "We are pleased you could join us."

"Thank you." Lahur's deep voice held a note of amusement. "I'm not here for long. I came to give you a wedding present. That's a custom of yours, isn't it, Mia?"

Mia stared at the Elder in shock. "Yes," she managed to say. "It's a human wedding custom." She was surprised she was able to speak at all, with her heart beating as hard as it was.

"Well then," Lahur said, his dark eyes trained on her, "I would like to tell you that we have granted your petition. Your family will be given all the rights and privileges of those we call charl."

A shocked murmur ran through the crowd at his words, and Mia inhaled sharply, her eyes filling with tears of joy. "Thank you," she whispered, looking at the dark visage of the ten-million-year-old alien in front of her. "Thank you so very much . . ."

"Yes," Korum said, his arm tightening around Mia's back. "Thank you for a wonderful wedding present. My wife and I are truly grateful."

Lahur inclined his head, acknowledging their thanks. Then he turned around and walked away, the crowd parting again to let him through.

The music started up again, and the party resumed. Running up to Mia, Marisa gave her and Korum a hug, sobbing with happiness, and her parents embraced each other, tears running down their faces. Connor shook Korum's hand, and Mia could see that her brother-in-law's eyes were glistening too.

For the first time in history, an entire human family would be given immortality—a gift more precious than anything they could've ever imagined.

Looking up at her husband—her beautiful K lover—Mia smiled through her tears. "I love you," she told him softly. "I love you so very much."

"And I love you," he said, watching her with warm amber-colored gaze.

Their happiness was complete.

EPILOGUE

Lahur stood in the forest clearing, feeling the warm breeze on his face. The others were gathered around him, their faces as familiar to him as his own. These people—the ones known as the Elders—were among the few whose company Lahur could tolerate for more than ten minutes at a time.

"So what now?" Sheura asked, watching him with her calm dark gaze.

Lahur looked at her. "What do you think?"

"I think it's time," she said quietly. "I think we have to do it."

"I agree." It was Pioren, Sheura's partner in the experiment. "We can no longer stand by and observe. The project has succeeded all too well. They're like us. Our best and brightest are now mating with them."

"Yes," Lahur said, "they are." Seeing the curly-haired human girl by Korum's side had been a revelation. She wasn't the first human he'd met, but something about her had touched him, penetrating the layer of ice that encased him these days. For a moment, Lahur had been able to feel the powerful bond that existed between her and her cheren, to bask in the love they had for each other.

Out of all the young ones, Lahur found Korum to be among the most interesting, probably because he reminded Lahur of himself in his youth. Same drive, same willingness to do what's necessary to achieve his goals. Lahur had no doubt that Korum would succeed in building a Krinar empire, taking them all on an unprecedented journey.

A journey that Korum planned to undertake with a human girl by his side.

There could be no clearer sign that they needed to wrap up the experiment.

"Let's do it," Lahur said. "You're right. It's time. We need to share our technology with them, to give them all what we gave only to a select few. Their evolution is complete."

And as he looked around the clearing, seeing agreement on the other faces, Lahur had only one thought:

Nothing will ever be the same again.

SNEAK PEEKS

Thank you for reading the Krinar Chronicles series! I hope you enjoyed it. If you did, please mention it to your friends and social media connections. I would also be hugely grateful if you helped other readers discover the book by leaving a review on Amazon, Goodreads, or other sites.

While Mia & Korum's story is over (for now), there will be many more novels—and potentially other series—set in the Krinar world. Additionally, I am working on some non-Krinar books, including those in contemporary settings. Please visit my website at www.annazaires.com and sign up for my newsletter to be notified when the books become available.

Thank you for your support! I truly appreciate it!

And now please turn the page for a little taste of *Twist Me* and some of my other upcoming works . . .

EXCERPT FROM *TWIST ME*

Author's Note: This is a dark erotic novel, and it deals with topics some readers may find disturbing. Please heed the warning! It's also a bit different from my other books in that it's written in first person.

* * *

Kidnapped. Taken to a private island.

I never thought this could happen to me. I never imagined one chance meeting on the eve of my eighteenth birthday could change my life so completely.

Now I belong to him. To Julian. To a man who is as ruthless as he is beautiful—a man whose touch makes me burn. A man whose tenderness I find more devastating than his cruelty.

My captor is an enigma. I don't know who he is or why he took me. There is a darkness inside him—a darkness that scares me even as it draws me in.

My name is Nora Leston, and this is my story.

WARNING: This is NOT a traditional romance. It contains disturbing subject matter, including themes of questionable consent and Stockholm Syndrome, as well as graphic sexual content. This is a work of fiction intended for a mature, 18+ audience only. The author neither endorses nor condones this type of behavior.

* * *

It's evening now. With every minute that passes, I'm starting to get more and more anxious at the thought of seeing my captor again.

The novel that I've been reading can no longer hold my interest. I put it down and walk in circles around the room.

I am dressed in the clothes Beth had given me earlier. It's not what I would've chosen to wear, but it's better than a bathrobe. A sexy pair of white lacy panties and a matching bra for underwear. A pretty blue sundress that buttons in the front. Everything fits me suspiciously well. Has he been stalking me for a while? Learning everything about me, including my clothing size?

The thought makes me sick.

I am trying not to think about what's to come, but it's impossible. I don't know why I'm so sure he'll come to me tonight. It's possible he has an entire harem of women stashed away on this island, and he visits each one only once a week, like sultans used to do.

Yet somehow I know he'll be here soon. Last night had simply whetted his appetite. I know he's not done with me, not by a long shot.

Finally, the door opens.

He walks in like he owns the place. Which, of course, he does.

I am again struck by his masculine beauty. He could've been a model or a movie star, with a face like his. If there was any fairness in the world, he would've been short or had some other imperfection to offset that face.

But he doesn't. His body is tall and muscular, perfectly proportioned. I remember what it feels like to have him inside me, and I feel an unwelcome jolt of arousal.

He's again wearing jeans and a T-shirt. A grey one this time. He seems to favor simple clothing, and he's smart to do so. His looks don't need any enhancement.

He smiles at me. It's his fallen angel smile—dark and seductive at the same time. "Hello, Nora."

I don't know what to say to him, so I blurt out the first thing that pops into my head. "How long are you going to keep me here?"

He cocks his head slightly to the side. "Here in the room? Or on the island?"

"Both."

"Beth will show you around tomorrow, take you swimming if you'd like," he says, approaching me. "You won't be locked in, unless you do something foolish."

"Such as?" I ask, my heart pounding in my chest as he stops next to me and lifts his hand to stroke my hair.

"Trying to harm Beth or yourself." His voice is soft, his gaze hypnotic as he looks down at me. The way he's touching my hair is oddly relaxing.

I blink, trying to break his spell. "And what about on the island? How long will you keep me here?"

His hand caresses my face, curves around my cheek. I catch myself leaning into his touch, like a cat getting petted, and I immediately stiffen.

His lips curl into a knowing smile. The bastard knows the effect he has on me. "A long time, I hope," he says.

For some reason, I'm not surprised. He wouldn't have bothered bringing me all the way here if he just wanted to fuck me a few times. I'm terrified, but I'm not surprised.

I gather my courage and ask the next logical question. "Why did you kidnap me?"

The smile leaves his face. He doesn't answer, just looks at me with an inscrutable blue gaze.

I begin to shake. "Are you going to kill me?"

"No, Nora, I won't kill you."

His denial reassures me, although he could obviously be lying.

"Are you going to sell me?" I can barely get the words out. "Like to be a prostitute or something?"

"No," he says softly. "Never. You're mine and mine alone."

I feel a tiny bit calmer, but there is one more thing I have to know. "Are you going to hurt me?"

For a moment, he doesn't answer again. Something dark briefly flashes in his eyes. "Probably," he says quietly.

And then he leans down and kisses me, his warm lips soft and gentle on mine.

For a second, I stand there frozen, unresponsive. I believe him. I know he's telling the truth when he says he'll hurt me. There's something in him that scares me—that has scared me from the very beginning.

He's nothing like the boys I've gone on dates with. He's capable of anything.

And I'm completely at his mercy.

I think about trying to fight him again. That would be the normal thing to do in my situation. The brave thing to do.

And yet I don't do it.

I can feel the darkness inside him. There's something wrong with him. His outer beauty hides something monstrous underneath.

I don't want to unleash that darkness. I don't know what will happen if I do.

So I stand still in his embrace and let him kiss me. And when he picks me up again and takes me to bed, I don't try to resist in any way.

Instead, I close my eyes and give in to the sensations.

* * *

Twist Me is currently available. Please visit my website at www.annazaires.com to learn more.

EXCERPT FROM *THE KRINAR CAPTIVE*

Author's Note: This is a prequel to the Krinar Chronicles. You don't have to have read Mia & Korum's story in order to read this book. It takes place approximately five years earlier, right before and during the Krinar invasion. The excerpt and the description are unedited and subject to change.

* * *

Emily Ross never expected to survive her deadly fall in the Costa Rican jungle—and she certainly never thought she'd wake up in a strangely futuristic dwelling, held captive by the most beautiful man she had ever seen. A man who seems to be more than human . . .

Zaron is on Earth to facilitate the Krinar invasion—and to forget the terrible tragedy that ripped apart his life. Yet when he finds the broken body of a human girl, everything changes. For the first time in years, he feels something more than rage and grief . . . and Emily is the reason for that. Letting her go would compromise his mission, but keeping her could destroy him all over again.

* * *

I don't want to die. I don't want to die. Please, please, please, I don't want to die.
    The words kept repeating over and over in her mind, a hopeless

prayer that would never be heard. Her fingers slipped another inch on the rough wooden board, her nails breaking as she tried to maintain her grip.

Emily Ross was hanging by her fingernails—literally—off a broken old bridge. Hundreds of feet below, water rushed over the rocks, the mountain stream full from recent rains.

Those rains were partially responsible for her current predicament. If the wood on the bridge had been dry, she might not have slipped, twisting her foot in the process. And she certainly wouldn't have fallen onto the rail that broke under her weight.

It was only a last-minute desperate grab that prevented her from plummeting to her death below. As she was falling, her right hand had caught a small protrusion on the side of the bridge, leaving her dangling in the air hundreds of feet above hard rocks.

I don't want to die. I don't want to die. Please, please, please, I don't want to die.

It wasn't fair. It wasn't supposed to happen this way. This was her vacation, her regain-sanity time. How could she die now? She hadn't even begun living yet.

No, no!

Her legs flailed, her nails digging deeper into the wood. Her other arm reached up, stretching toward the bridge. This wouldn't happen to her. She wouldn't let it. She had worked too hard to let a stupid jungle bridge defeat her.

Blood ran down her arm as the rough wood tore the skin off her fingers, but she ignored the pain. Her only hope of survival lay in trying to grab onto the side of the bridge with her other hand, so she could pull herself back up. There was no one around to rescue her, no one to save her if she didn't save herself.

The possibility that she might die alone in the rainforest had not occurred to Emily when she embarked on this trip. She was used to hiking, used to camping. And even after the hell of the past two years, she was still in good shape, strong and fit from running and playing sports all through high school and college. Costa Rica was considered a safe destination, with a low crime rate and tourist-friendly population. It was inexpensive too—an important factor for her rapidly dwindling savings account.

She'd booked this trip Before. Before the market had fallen again, before another round of layoffs that had cost thousands of Wall Street workers their jobs. Before Emily went to work on Monday, bleary-eyed from working all weekend, only to leave the office same day with all her possessions in a small cardboard box.

Before her four-year relationship had fallen apart.

Her first vacation in two years, and she was going to die.

No, don't think that way. It won't happen.

But Emily knew she was lying to herself. She could feel her fingers slipping further, her right arm and shoulder burning from the strain of supporting the weight of her entire body. Her left hand was inches away from reaching the side of the bridge, but those inches could've easily been miles. She couldn't get a strong enough grip to lift herself up with one arm.

Do it, Emily! Don't think, just do it!

Gathering all her strength, she swung her legs in the air, using the momentum to bring her body higher for a fraction of a second. Her left hand grabbed onto the protruding board, clutched at it . . . and then the fragile piece of wood snapped, startling her into a terrified scream.

Emily's last thought before her body hit the rocks was the hope that her death would be instant.

* * *

The smell of jungle vegetation, rich and pungent, teased Zaron's nostrils. He inhaled deeply, letting the humid air fill his lungs. It was clean here, in this tiny corner of Earth, almost as unpolluted as on his home planet.

He needed this now. Needed the fresh air, the isolation. For the past six months, he'd tried to run from his thoughts, to exist only in the moment, but he'd failed. Even blood and sex were not enough for him anymore. He could distract himself while fucking, but the pain always came back afterwards, as strong as ever.

Finally, it had gotten to be too much. The dirt, the crowds, the stink of humanity. When he wasn't lost in a fog of ecstasy, he was disgusted, his senses overwhelmed from spending so much time in human cities. It was better here, where he could breathe without inhaling poison, where he could smell life instead of chemicals. In a few years, everything would be different, and he might try living in a human city again, but not now.

Not until they were fully settled here.

* * *

If you'd like to know when *The Krinar Captive* comes out, please visit my website at www.annazaires.com and sign up for my new release email list.

EXCERPT FROM *WHITE NIGHTS*

Author's Note: This is a contemporary erotic romance. The excerpt and the description are unedited and subject to change.

* * *

A Russian Oligarch
Alex Volkov always gets what he wants. Once an orphan on the streets of Saint Petersburg, he's now one of the wealthiest men in the world. But one doesn't rise that far in Russia without crossing the line . . .

An American Nurse
Kate Morrell has always been capable and independent. She neither wants nor needs a man in her life. Yet she can't help being drawn to the dangerous stranger she meets in the hospital . . .

A Deadly Game
When Alex's past threatens their present, Kate must decide how much she's willing to risk to be with him . . . and whether the man she's falling for is any different from the ruthless assassin hunting them down.

* * *

"Kate, I'm sorry, but we really need you right now."

June Wallers, the nursing supervisor, burst into the tiny room where Katherine Morrell was quickly finishing her lunch.

Sighing, Kate put down her half-eaten sandwich, took a sip of water, and followed June down the hall. This was not the first time this week her allocated lunch hour had turned into a ten-minute snack break.

The recession had taken a heavy toll on New York hospitals, with budget cuts leading to hiring freezes and staff layoffs. As a result, the Emergency Room at Coney Island Hospital was at least three nurses short of what it needed to function properly. Other departments were also short-staffed, but their patient flow was somewhat more predictable. At the ER, however, it was almost always a madhouse.

This week had been particularly horrible. It was flu season, and one of the nurses had gotten sick. It was the absolute worst time for her to be out, as flu season also brought a greater-than-usual influx of patients. This was Kate's fifth twelve-hour shift this week, and it was a night shift—something she hated to do, but couldn't always avoid. But June had begged, and Kate had given in, knowing there was no one else who could replace her.

And here she was, skipping her lunch yet again. At this pace, she would be skin-and-bones before the flu season was over. The 'flu diet,' her mom liked to call it.

"What's the emergency?" Kate asked, walking faster to keep up with June. At fifty-five years of age, the nurse supervisor was as spry as a twenty-year-old.

"We've got a gunshot wound."

"How bad?"

"We're not sure yet. Lettie's kid got sick, and she just left—"

"What? So who's with the patients?"

"Nancy."

Shit. Kate almost broke into a run. Nancy was a first-year nurse. She was trying hard, but she needed a lot of guidance. She should never be on her own without a more experienced nurse present.

"Now you see why we need you," June said wryly, and Kate nodded, her pulse speeding up.

This was why she'd gone into nursing—because she liked the idea of being needed, of helping people. A good nurse could make a difference between life and death for a patient, particularly in the ER. It was a heavy responsibility at times, but Kate didn't mind. She liked the fast pace of work in the ER, the way twelve hours would just fly by. By the end of each day, she was so exhausted she could barely walk, but she was also satisfied.

The ER was teeming with activity when Kate entered. Approaching one of the curtained-off sections, Kate pulled back the drapes and saw the gunshot victim lying on the stretcher. He was a large man, tall and broad. Caucasian, from the looks of him. She guessed his age to be somewhere in the late twenties or early thirties. He had an oxygen mask on, and was already hooked up to the cardiac monitor. There was an IV drip in his arm, and he seemed to be unconscious.

Lettie, the first-year nurse, was applying pressure to the wound to stop the bleeding. There were also two other men were standing nearby, but Kate paid them little attention, all her focus on the patient.

Quickly assessing the situation, Kate washed her hands and took charge. The patient's pulse was strong, and he appeared to be breathing with no distress. Kate checked his pupils; they were normal and responded to light stimulation properly. There was an exit wound, which was lucky. Had the bullet remained inside the body, it could've caused additional damage and required surgery. A CT scan showed that the bullet had just missed the heart and other critical organs. Another inch, and the man would be occupying a body bag instead of this stretcher. As it was, the main challenge was getting the wound clean and stopping the bleeding.

Kate didn't wonder how, why, or who had shot this man. That wasn't her job. Her job was to save his life, to stabilize him until the doctor could get there. In cases like this—true life-threatening emergencies—the doctor would see the patient quickly. All other ER patients were typically in for a longer wait.

When Dr. Stevenson appeared, she filled him in, rattling off the patient's vitals. Then she assisted him as he sutured and bandaged the wound.

Finally, the victim was stable and sedated. Barring any unforeseen complications, the man would live.

Stripping off the gloves, Kate walked over to the sink to wash her hands again. The habit was so deeply ingrained, she never had to think about it. Whenever she was in the hospital, she washed her hands compulsively every chance she got. Far too many deadly patient infections resulted from a healthcare professional's lax approach to hygiene.

Letting the warm water run over her hands, she rolled her head side to side, trying to relieve the tension in her neck. As much as she loved her job, it was both physically and mentally exhausting, particularly when someone's life was on the line. Kate had always thought full-body massages should be included as part of the benefit package for nurses. If anyone needed a rubdown at the end of a twelve-hour shift, it was surely a nurse.

Turning away from the sink, Kate looked back toward the gunshot man, automatically making sure everything was okay with him before she moved on to check on her other patients.

And as she glanced in his direction, she caught a pair of steely blue eyes looking directly at her.

It was one of the other men who had been standing near the victim—likely one of the wounded's relatives. Visitors were generally not allowed in the hospital at night, but the ER was an exception.

Instead of looking away—as most people would when caught staring—the man continued studying Kate.

So she studied him back, both intrigued and slightly annoyed.

He was tall, well over six feet in height, and broad-shouldered. He wasn't handsome in the traditional sense; that would've been too weak of a word to describe him. Instead, he was . . . magnetic.

Power. That's what she thought of when she looked at him. It was there in the arrogant tilt of his head, in the way he looked at her so calmly, utterly sure of himself and his ability to control all around him. Kate didn't know who he was or what he did, but she doubted he was a pencil pusher in some office. No, this was a man used to issuing orders and having them obeyed.

His clothes fit him well and looked expensive. Maybe even custom-made. He was wearing a grey trench coat, dark grey pants with a subtle pinstripe, and a pair of black Italian leather shoes.

His brown hair was cut short, almost military style. The simple haircut suited his face, revealing hard, symmetric features. He had high cheekbones and a blade of a nose with a slight bump, as though it had been broken once.

Kate had no idea how old he was. His face was unlined, but there was no boyishness to it. No softness whatsoever, not even in the curve of his mouth. She guessed his age to be in the early thirties, but he could've just as easily been twenty-five or forty.

He didn't fidget or look uncomfortable in any way as their staring contest continued. He just stood there quietly, completely still, his blue gaze trained on her.

To her shock, Kate could feel her heart rate picking up as a tingle of heat ran down her spine. It was as though temperature in the room had jumped ten degrees. All of a sudden, the atmosphere became intensely sexual, making Kate aware of herself as a woman in a way that she'd never experienced before. She could feel the silky material of her matched underwear set brushing between her legs, against her breasts. Her entire body seemed flushed, sensitized, her nipples pebbling underneath her layers of clothing.

Holy shit.

So that's what it felt like to be truly attracted to someone. It wasn't rational and logical. There was no meeting of minds and hearts involved. No, the urge was basic and primitive; her body had sensed his on some animal level, and it wanted to mate.

And he felt it, too. It was there in the way his blue eyes had darkened, lids partially lowering. In the way his nostrils flared, as though trying to catch her scent. His fingers twitched, curled into fists, and she somehow knew he was trying to control himself, to avoid reaching for her right then and there.

If they had been alone right now, Kate had no doubt he would be on her already.

Still staring at the stranger, Kate started to back away. The strength of her response to him was frightening, unsettling. They were in the middle of the ER, surrounded by people, and all she could think about was hot, sheet-twisting sex. She had no idea who he was, whether he was married or single. For all she knew, he could be a criminal or a total asshole.

Or he could be a cheating scumbag like Tony. If anyone had taught her to think twice before trusting a man, it was her ex-boyfriend. She didn't want that kind of complication in her life again—didn't want to get involved with a man so soon after her last disastrous relationship.

But the tall stranger clearly had other ideas.

At her cautious retreat, his eyes narrowed, his gaze becoming sharper, more focused.

And then he began walking toward her, his stride oddly graceful for such a large man. There was something panther-ish in his leisurely movements. For a second, Kate felt like a mouse getting stalked by a big cat. Instinctively, she took another step back . . . and watched his hard mouth tighten with displeasure.

Realizing she was acting like a coward, Kate stopped backing away and stood her ground instead, straightening to her full 5'7" height. She was always the calm and capable one, handling high-stress situations with ease—and here she was, behaving like a silly schoolgirl confronted with her first crush. Yes, the man made her uncomfortable, but there was nothing to be afraid of. What was the worst he could do? Ask her out on a date?

Nevertheless, her hands shook slightly as he approached, stopping less than two feet away. This close, he was even taller than she'd originally thought, probably a couple of inches over six feet. She was not a short woman, but she felt tiny standing next to him. It was not a feeling she enjoyed.

"You are very good at your job." His voice was deep and a little rough, heavy with some Eastern European accent. Just hearing it made her insides shiver in a strangely pleasurable way.

"Um, thank you," Kate said, a bit uncertainly. She knew she was a good nurse, of course, but somehow she hadn't expected this stranger to acknowledge that fact.

"You took care of Igor well. Thank you for that."

Igor had to be the gunshot patient. It was a foreign-sounding name, maybe Russian. That explained the stranger's accent. Although he spoke English fluently, it was obvious he wasn't a native speaker.

"Of course. I hope he recovers quickly. Is he your relative?" Kate was proud of the casual steadiness of her tone. Hopefully, the man wouldn't realize how he affected her.

"My bodyguard."

Kate's eyes widened. So she'd been right—this man was a big fish. Bodyguard? Did that mean— "Was he shot in the course of duty?" she asked, holding her breath.

"He took a bullet meant for me, yes." The man's tone was matter-of-fact, but Kate got a sense of tightly suppressed rage underneath those words.

Holy shit. "Did you already speak to the police?"

"I gave them a brief statement. I will talk to them in more detail once Igor is stabilized and regains consciousness."

Kate nodded, not knowing what to say to that. The man standing in front of her had been shot at today. What was he? Some Mafia boss? A political figure?

If she'd had any doubts about the wisdom of exploring this strange attraction between them, they were now gone. This stranger was bad news, and she needed to stay as far away from him as possible.

"Well, I wish your bodyguard a speedy recovery," Kate said in a falsely cheerful tone. "Barring any complications, he should be fine—"

"Thanks to you."

Kate nodded again, gave him a half-smile, and took a step to the side, hoping to walk around the man and go to her next patient.

But he shifted his stance, blocking her way. "I'm Alex Volkov," he said quietly, looking down on her. "And you are?"

Kate's pulse picked up. She could feel the male intent in his question, and it made her nervous. "Just a nurse working here," she said, hoping he would get the hint.

He didn't—or he pretended not to. "What's your name?"

Kate took a deep breath. He was certainly persistent. "I'm Katherine Morrell. If you'll excuse me—"

"Katherine," he repeated, his accent lending the familiar syllables an exotic edge. His eyes gleamed with some unknown emotion, and his hard mouth softened a bit. "Katerina. It's a beautiful name."

"Thank you. I really have to go . . ." Kate was feeling increasingly anxious to get away. He was so large, standing there in front of her. She needed some space, needed a little room to breathe. His nearness was overpowering, making her edgy and restless, leaving her craving something she knew would be bad for her.

"You have your job to do. I understand," he said, looking vaguely amused.

And he still didn't move out of her way. Instead, as she watched in shock, he raised one large hand and lightly brushed his knuckles down her left cheek.

Kate froze, even as a wave of heat moved through her body. His touch had been casual, but she felt branded by it, shaken to the core.

"I would like to see you again, Katerina," he said softly. "When does your shift end tonight?"

Kate stared at him, feeling like she was losing control of the situation. "I don't think that's a good idea—"

"Why not?" His blue eyes narrowed, and his mouth tightened again. "Are you married?"

For a second, Kate was tempted to lie and tell him that she was. But honesty won out. "No. But I'm not interested in dating right now—"

"Who said anything about dating?"

Kate blinked. She had assumed—

He lifted his hand again, stopping her mid-thought. This time, he picked up a strand of her long brown hair, rubbing it between his fingers as though enjoying its texture.

"I don't date, Katerina," he murmured, his accented voice oddly mesmerizing. "But I would like to take you to bed. And I think you would like that, too."

* * *

If you'd like to know when *White Nights* comes out, please visit my website at www.annazaires.com and sign up for my new release email list.

EXCERPT FROM *THE SORCERY CODE* BY DIMA ZALES

Author's Note: Dima Zales is a science fiction and fantasy author and my collaborator in the creation of the Krinar Chronicles. He's also my husband. His fantasy novel is called *The Sorcery Code*, and I'm *his* collaborator this time. While it's not a romance, there is a strong romantic subplot in the book (though no explicit sex scenes). The book is now available everywhere.

* * *

Once a respected member of the Sorcerer Council and now an outcast, Blaise has spent the last year of his life working on a special magical object. The goal is to allow anyone to do magic, not just the sorcerer elite. The outcome of his quest is unlike anything he could've ever imagined—because, instead of an object, he creates Her.

She is Gala, and she is anything but inanimate. Born in the Spell Realm, she is beautiful and highly intelligent—and nobody knows what she's capable of. She will do anything to experience the world . . . even leave the man she is beginning to fall for.

Augusta, a powerful sorceress and Blaise's former fiancée, sees Blaise's deed as the ultimate hubris and Gala as an abomination that must be destroyed. In her quest to save the human race, Augusta will forge new alliances, becoming tangled in a web of intrigue that stretches further than any of them suspect. She may even have to turn to her new lover Barson, a ruthless warrior who might have an agenda of his own . . .

* * *

There was a naked woman on the floor of Blaise's study.

A beautiful naked woman.

Stunned, Blaise stared at the gorgeous creature who just appeared out of thin air. She was looking around with a bewildered expression on her face, apparently as shocked to be there as he was to be seeing her. Her wavy blond hair streamed down her back, partially covering a body that appeared to be perfection itself. Blaise tried not to think about that body and to focus on the situation instead.

A woman. A *She*, not an *It*. Blaise could hardly believe it. Could it be? Could this girl be the object?

She was sitting with her legs folded underneath her, propping herself up with one slim arm. There was something awkward about that pose, as though she didn't know what to do with her own limbs. In general, despite the curves that marked her a fully grown woman, there was a child-like innocence in the way she sat there, completely unselfconscious and totally unaware of her own appeal.

Clearing his throat, Blaise tried to think of what to say. In his wildest dreams, he couldn't have imagined this kind of outcome to the project that had consumed his entire life for the past several months.

Hearing the sound, she turned her head to look at him, and Blaise found himself staring into a pair of unusually clear blue eyes.

She blinked, then cocked her head to the side, studying him with visible curiosity. Blaise wondered what she was seeing. He hadn't seen the light of day in weeks, and he wouldn't be surprised if he looked like a mad sorcerer at this point. There was probably a week's worth of stubble covering his face, and he knew his dark hair was unbrushed and sticking out in every direction. If he'd known he would be facing a beautiful woman today, he would've done a grooming spell in the morning.

"Who am I?" she asked, startling Blaise. Her voice was soft and feminine, as alluring as the rest of her. "What is this place?"

"You don't know?" Blaise was glad he finally managed to string together a semi-coherent sentence. "You don't know who you are or where you are?"

She shook her head. "No."

Blaise swallowed. "I see."

"What am I?" she asked again, staring at him with those incredible eyes.

"Well," Blaise said slowly, "if you're not some cruel prankster or a figment of my imagination, then it's somewhat difficult to explain . . ."

She was watching his mouth as he spoke, and when he stopped, she looked up again, meeting his gaze. "It's strange," she said, "hearing words this way. These are the first real words I've heard."

Blaise felt a chill go down his spine. Getting up from his chair, he began to pace, trying to keep his eyes off her nude body. He had been expecting *something* to appear. A magical object, a thing. He just hadn't known what form that thing would take. A mirror, perhaps, or a lamp. Maybe even something as unusual as the Life Capture Sphere that sat on his desk like a large round diamond.

But a person? A female person at that?

To be fair, he *had been* trying to make the object intelligent, to ensure it would have the ability to comprehend human language and convert it into the code. Maybe he shouldn't be so surprised that the intelligence he invoked took on a human shape.

A beautiful, feminine, sensual shape.

Focus, Blaise, focus.

"Why are you walking like that?" She slowly got to her feet, her movements uncertain and strangely clumsy. "Should I be walking too? Is that how people talk to each other?"

Blaise stopped in front of her, doing his best to keep his eyes above her neck. "I'm sorry. I'm not accustomed to naked women in my study."

She ran her hands down her body, as though trying to feel it for the first time. Whatever her intent, Blaise found the gesture extremely erotic.

"Is something wrong with the way I look?" she asked. It was such a typical feminine concern that Blaise had to stifle a smile.

"Quite the opposite," he assured her. "You look unimaginably good." So good, in fact, that he was having trouble concentrating on anything but her delicate curves. She was of medium height, and so perfectly proportioned that she could've been used as a sculptor's template.

"Why do I look this way?" A small frown creased her smooth forehead. "What am I?" That last part seemed to be puzzling her the most.

Blaise took a deep breath, trying to calm his racing pulse. "I think I can try to venture a guess, but before I do, I want to give you some clothing. Please wait here—I'll be right back."

And without waiting for her answer, he hurried out of the room.

* * *

The Sorcery Code is now available everywhere. If you like fantasy or sci-fi, please visit Dima Zales's website at www.dimazales.com and sign up for his new release email list. You can also connect with him on Facebook, Twitter, and Goodreads.

EXCERPT FROM *MIND AWAKENING* BY DIMA ZALES

Author's Note: *Mind Awakening* is another book Dima Zales is working on in collaboration with me. It's a science fiction novel. The excerpt and the description are unedited and subject to change.

* * *

Ethan remembers being shot in the chest. By all rights, he should be dead. Instead, he wakes up in a world that seems like futuristic paradise . . . as someone else.

Who is the real Ethan? The computer scientist he remembers being, or the world-famous genius everyone appears to think he is? And why is someone trying to kill him here, in this peaceful utopian society?

These are some of the questions he'll explore with his psychologist Matilda—a woman as beautiful as she is mysterious. What is her agenda . . . and what is the Mindverse?

* * *

Ethan woke up.

For a moment, he just lay there with his eyes closed, trying to process the fact that he was still alive. He clearly remembered the mugging . . . and being shot. The pain had been awful, like an explosion in his chest. He hadn't known one could survive that kind of agony; he'd been sure the bullet had entered his heart.

But somehow he was still alive. Taking a deep breath, Ethan cautiously moved his arm, wondering why he wasn't feeling any pain now. Surely there had to be a wound, some damage from the shooting?

Yet he felt fine. More than fine, in fact. Even the pain from his rheumatoid arthritis seemed to be gone. They must've given him a hell of a painkiller in the hospital, he thought, finally opening his eyes.

He wasn't in a hospital.

As soon as that fact registered, Ethan shot up in bed, his heartbeat skyrocketing. There wasn't a single nurse or cardiac monitor in the vicinity. Instead, he was in someone's lavish bedroom, sitting on a king-sized bed with a giant padded headboard.

The fact that he could sit up like that was yet another shock. There weren't any tubes or needles sticking out of his body—nothing hampering his movements. He was wearing a stretchy blue T-shirt instead of a hospital gown, and the black pants that he could see under the blanket seemed to be rather comfortable pajamas.

Lifting his arm, Ethan touched his chest, trying to feel where the wound might be. But there was nothing. No pain, not even a hint of sensitivity. All he could feel was smooth, healthy pectoral muscle.

Muscle? Was that his imagination, or did his chest seem more muscular? Ethan was in decent shape, but he was far from a bodybuilder. And yet, as ridiculous as it was, there appeared to be quite a bit of muscle on his chest—and on his forearm, Ethan realized, looking down at his bare arms.

In general, his forearms didn't look like they belonged to him. They were muscular and tan, covered with a light dusting of sandy hair—a far cry from his usual pale limbs.

Trying not to panic, Ethan carefully swung his legs to the side of the bed and stood up. There was no pain associated with his movements, nothing to indicate that something bad might've happened to him. He felt strong and healthy . . . and that scared him even more than waking up in an unfamiliar bedroom.

The room itself was nice, decorated in modern-looking grey and white tones. Ethan had always meant to furnish his bedroom at home to look more like this, but hadn't gotten around to it. There also seemed to be some kind of movie posters on the walls. Upon closer inspection, they were more like theatrical production ads—ads that depicted a stylized, buffer, and better-looking version of himself.

What the hell?

In one of the posters, Ethan's likeness was holding rings on a pencil very close to his face. The rings were linked like a chain, and the image was titled *Insane Illusions by Razum*. In another ad, he was wearing a tuxedo and making a woman float in mid-air.

Was this a dream? If so, it had to be the most vivid dream Ethan had ever experienced—and one from which he couldn't seem to wake up. Ethan's heart was galloping in his chest, and he could feel the beginning of a panic attack.

No, stop it, Ethan. Just breathe. Breathe through it. And utilizing a technique he'd learned long ago to manage stress, Ethan focused on taking deep, even breaths.

After a couple of minutes, he felt calmer and more able to think rationally. Could this possibly be his house? Perhaps he'd suffered some kind of brain damage after being shot and was now experiencing memory loss. Theoretically, it was possible that he'd gotten a tan and started exercising—even though his rheumatoid arthritis usually prevented him from being particularly active.

His arthritis . . . That was another weird thing. Why didn't his joints ache like they usually did? Had he been given some wonder drug that healed gunshot wounds and autoimmune disorders? And what about those posters on the walls?

Doing his best to remain calm, Ethan spotted two doors on the opposite ends of the room. Taking one at random, he found himself inside a large, luxurious bathroom. There was a large mirror in front of him, and Ethan stepped closer to it, feeling like he was suffocating from lack of air.

The man reflected there was both familiar and different. Like his arms, his face was tan and practically glowing with health. Even his teeth seemed whiter somehow. His light brown hair was longer, almost covering his ears, and his skin was perfectly clear and wrinkle-free. Only his eyes were the same grey color that Ethan was used to seeing.

Breathe, Ethan. Breathe through it. There had to be a logical explanation for this. His buff build could be explained by a new exercise program. He could've also gotten a tan on a recent vacation—even though he couldn't recall taking one. However, he also looked younger somehow, which made even less sense. Ethan was in his mid-thirties, but the man in the mirror looked like he was maybe twenty-five. Surely he wasn't vain enough to have gotten plastic surgery at such a young age?

Blinking, Ethan stared at himself, then raised his hand and brushed back his hair. Everything felt real, too real for it to be a dream. Could the doctors have done something to him that had this incredible side effect? *Yeah, right, they invented the elixir of immortality and had to use it on me in ER.*

Leaving the bathroom, Ethan approached the wall and looked at another poster. There was a definite resemblance between what he saw in the mirror and the guy on the poster. In fact, he was confident that those posters were of himself—or, at least, of himself as he was right now, in this weird dream that was unlike any other.

Taking the other door, he entered a hallway that was covered with even more posters of his likeness performing various illusions. At the end of the hallway, there was a room. Likely a living room, Ethan decided, even though it was empty aside from a piece of furniture that resembled a couch.

A couch that was somehow floating in the air, as though it was hanging by some invisible thread from the ceiling.

What the . . . ? Swallowing hard, Ethan stepped into the room, trying to see if there was someone playing a joke on him.

There wasn't anyone there. Instead, in one corner of the room, several trophies were floating on top of little pedestals. Seemingly made of gold, the trophy figures were those of men holding a sword. Approaching them carefully, Ethan tried to see how they were able to float in the air like that, but there was no visible mechanism holding them up. *Weird.*

Spotting a large window on the far wall, Ethan walked over to it, needing to look outside and reassure himself that he hadn't gone crazy, that he was still in New York City and not in some strange parallel universe.

And as he looked outside, he froze, paralyzed by shock and disbelief.

* * *

If you'd like to know when *Mind Awakening* comes out, please visit Dima Zales's website at www.dimazales.com and sign up for his new release email list. You can also connect with him on Facebook, Twitter, and Goodreads . . .

ABOUT THE AUTHOR

Anna Zaires fell in love with books at the age of five, when her grandmother taught her to read. She wrote her first story shortly thereafter. Since then, she has always lived partially in a fantasy world where the only limits were those of her imagination. Currently residing in Florida, Anna is happily married to Dima Zales (a science fiction and fantasy author) and closely collaborates with him on all their works.

To learn more, please visit www.annazaires.com.

29699703R00407

Printed in Great Britain
by Amazon